100
Hair-Raising
Little
Horror Stories

100
Hair-Raising
Little
Horror Stories

Edited by
Al Sarrantonio
& Martin H. Greenberg

BARNES
& NOBLE
BOOKS
NEW YORK

This edition published by Barnes & Noble, Inc.,
by arrangement with Martin H. Greenberg

1993 Barnes & Noble Books

ISBN 1-56619-923-9

Printed and bound in the United States of America

M 9 8 7 6 5 4 3

ACKNOWLEDGMENTS

"**Ants**" by Chet Williamson—Copyright © 1987 by TZ Publications. Reprinted by permission of the Scott Meredith Literary Agency, Inc., 845 Third Ave., New York, NY 10022. "**The Assembly of the Dead**" by Chet Williamson—Copyright © 1990 by Chet Williamson. Reprinted by permission of the Scott Meredith Literary Agency, Inc., 845 Third Ave., New York, NY 10022. First appeared in NOCTULPA #4. "**At the Bureau**" by Steve Rasnic Tem—Copyright © 1980 by Steve Rasnic Tem. Reprinted by permission of the author. First appeared in SHADOWS 3. "**Babylon: 70 M.**" by Donald A. Wollheim—Copyright © 1969 by Donald A. Wollheim. Reprinted by permission of Elsie Wollheim. "**Boxes**" by Al Sarrantonio—Copyright © 1982 by Al Sarrantonio. Reprinted by permission of the author. First appeared in SHADOWS 5. "**The Candidate**" by Henry Slesar—Copyright © 1989 by Henry Slesar. Reprinted by permission of the author. "**Cemetery Dance**" by Richard Chizmar—Copyright © 1992 by Richard T. Chizmar. Reprinted by permission of the author. First appeared in NARROW HOUSES. "**The Certificate**" by Avram Davidson—Copyright © 1959 by Mercury Press, Inc.; renewed © 1977 by Avram Davidson. Reprinted by permission of Richard Grant, Literary Agent. First appeared in F&SF. "**Cheapskate**" by G. L. Raisor—Copyright © 1987 by TZ Publications. Reprinted by permission of the author. First appeared in NIGHT CRY. "**Come to the Party**" by Frances Garfield—Copyright © 1983 by Stuart David Schiff for WHISPERS. Reprinted by permission of the author. "**Dark Wings**" by Phyllis Eisenstein—Copyright © 1982 by Phyllis Eisenstein. Reprinted by permission of the author. First appeared in SHADOWS 5. "**Dead Call**" by William F. Nolan—Copyright © 1976 by Kirby McCauley. Reprinted by permission of the author. First appeared in FRIGHTS. "**Different Kinds of Dead**" by Ed Gorman—Copyright © 1991 by Ed Gorman. Reprinted by permission of the author. "**Displaced Person**" by Eric Frank Russell—Copyright © 1948 by Weird Tales. Reprinted by permission of the Scott Meredith Literary Agency, Inc., 845 Third Ave., New York, NY 10022. "**The Disintegration of Alan**" by Melissa Mia Hall—Copyright © 1985 by Melissa Mia Hall. Reprinted by permission of the author. First appeared in GREYSTONE BAY. "**Down by the Sea near the Great Big Rock**" by Joe R. Lansdale—Copyright © 1984 by Joe R. Lansdale. Reprinted by permission of the author. "**Dragon Sunday**" by Ruth Berman—Copyright © 1979 by Charles L. Grant.

CONTENTS

INTRODUCTION

You hold in your hands a very special book.

It contains one hundred carnival rides of terror.

You must remember: horror can come from any direction. It can be as subtle as a spider web's caress, or as vicious as the drop of an ax blade. It can be grim as the reaper, or as sardonic as, well, Sardonicus. It can wear the garments of science or superstition; can be dressed in the trappings of fantasy or the fancy-free.

But always it will terrify.

And one of the bluntest of its instruments is the short-short story, one of the most difficult of literary devices to master. Not only must each word be perfect—but each comma and period. Nothing can be wasted.

In the hands of master executioners, like the authors who fill this book—it can be deadly.

So . . .

Die—and die again—one hundred times . . .

—Martin H. Greenberg
Al Sarrantonio

The Adventure of My Grandfather

By Washington Irving

My grandfather was a bold dragoon, for it's a profession, d' ye see, that has run in the family. All my forefathers have been dragoons, and died on the field of honor, except myself, and I hope my posterity may be able to say the same; however, I don't mean to be vainglorious. Well, my grandfather, as I said, was a bold dragoon, and had served in the Low Countries. In fact, he was one of that very army, which according to my uncle Toby, swore so terribly in Flanders. He could swear a good stick himself; and moreover was the very man that introduced the doctrine Corporal Trim mentions of radical heat and radical moisture, or, in other words, the mode of keeping out the damps of ditchwater by burnt brandy. Be that as it may, it's nothing to the purport of my story. I only tell it to show you that my grandfather was a man not easily to be humbugged. He had seen service, or, according to his own phrase, he had seen the devil—and that's saying everything.

Well, gentlemen, my grandfather was on his way to England, for which he intended to embark from Ostend—bad luck to the place! for one where I was kept by storms and headwinds for three long days, and the devil of a jolly companion or pretty girl to comfort me. Well, as I was saying, my grandfather was on his way to England, or rather to Ostend—no matter which, it's all the same. So one evening, towards night fall, he rode jollily into Bruges.—Very like you all know Bruges, gentlemen; a queer old-fashioned Flemish town, once, they say, a great place for trade and money-making in old times, when the Mynheers were in their glory; but almost as large and as empty as an Irishman's pocket at the present day.—Well, gentlemen, it was at the time of the annual fair. All Bruges was crowded; and the canals swarmed with Dutch boats, and the streets swarmed with Dutch merchants; and there was hardly any getting along for goods, wares, and merchandises, and peasants in big breeches, and women in half a score of petticoats.

My grandfather rode jollily along, in his easy, slashing way, for he was a saucy, sun-shiny fellow—staring about him at the motley crowd, the old houses with gable ends to the street, and storks' nests in the chimneys; winking at the yafrows who showed their faces at the windows and joking the women right and left in the street; all of whom laughed, and took it in amazing good part; for though he did not know a word of the language, yet he had always a knack of making himself understood among the women.

Well, gentlemen, it being the time of the annual fair, all the town was crowded, every inn and tavern full, and my grandfather applied in vain from one to the other for admittance. At length he rode up to an old rickety inn, that looked ready to fall to pieces, and which all the rats would have run away from, if they could have found room in any other house to put their heads. It was just such a queer building as you see in Dutch pictures, with a tall roof that reached up into the clouds, and as many garrets, one over the other, as the seven heavens of Mahomet. Nothing had saved it from tumbling down but a stork's nest on the chimney, which always brings good luck to a house in the Low Countries; and at the very time of my grandfather's arrival, there were two of these long-legged birds of grace standing like ghosts on the chimney-top. Faith, but they've kept the house on its legs to this very day, for you may see it any time you pass through Bruges, as it stands there yet, only it is turned into a brewery of strong Flemish beer,—at least it was so when I came that way after the battle of Waterloo.

My grandfather eyed the house curiously as he approached. It might not have altogether struck his fancy, had he not seen in large letters over the door,

HEER VERKOOPT MAN GOEDEN DRANK

My grandfather had learnt enough of the language to know that the sign promised good liquor. "This is the house for me," said he, stopping short before the door.

The sudden appearance of a dashing dragoon was an event in an old inn frequented only by the peaceful sons of traffic. A rich burgher of Antwerp, a stately ample man in a broad Flemish hat, and who was the great man and great patron of the establishment, sat smoking a clean long pipe on one side of the door; a fat little distiller of Geneva, from Schiedam, sat smoking on the other; and the bottle-nosed host stood in the door, and the comely hostess, in crimped cap, beside him; and the hostess's daughter, a plump Flanders lass, with long gold pendants in her ears, was at a side-window.

"Humph!" said the rich burgher of Antwerp, with a sulky glance at the stranger.

"De duyvel!" said the fat little distiller of Schiedam.

The landlord saw, with the quick glance of a publican, that the new guest was not at all to the taste of the old ones; and, to tell the truth, he did not like my grandfather's saucy eye. He shook his head. "Not a garret in the house but was full."

"Not a garret!" echoed the landlady.

"Not a garret!" echoed the daughter.

The burgher of Antwerp, and the little distiller of Schiedam, continued to smoke their pipes sullenly, eying the enemy askance from under their broad hats, but said nothing.

My grandfather was not a man to be browbeaten. He threw the reins on his horse's neck, cocked his head on one side, stuck one arm akimbo,—"Faith and troth!" said he, "but I'll sleep in this house this very night."—As he said this he gave a slap on his thigh, by way of emphasis—the slap went to the landlady's heart.

He followed up the vow by jumping off his horse, and making his way past the staring Mynheers into the public room.—Maybe you've been in the bar-room of an old Flemish inn—faith, but a handsome chamber it was as you'd wish to see; with a brick floor, and a great fireplace, with the whole Bible history in glazed tiles; and then the mantelpiece, pitching itself head foremost out of the wall, with a whole regiment of cracked tea-pots and earthen jugs paraded on it; not to mention half a dozen great Delft platters, hung about the room by way of pictures; and the little bar in one corner, and the bouncing bar-maid inside of it, with a red calico cap, and yellow ear-drops.

My grandfather snapped his fingers over his head, as he cast an eye round the room,—"Faith, this is the very house I've been looking after," said he.

There was some further show of resistance on the part of the garrison; but my grandfather was an old soldier, and an Irishman to boot, and not easily repulsed, especially after he had got into the fortress. So he blarneyed the landlord, kissed the landlord's wife, tickled the landlord's daughter, chucked the bar-maid under the chin; and it was agreed on all hands that it would be a thousand pities, and a burning shame into the bargain, to turn such a bold dragoon into the streets. So they laid their heads together, that is to say, my grandfather and the landlady, and it was at length agreed to accommodate him with an old chamber that had been for some time shut up.

"Some say it's haunted," whispered the landlord's daughter; "but you are a bold dragoon, and I dare say don't fear ghosts."

"The devil a bit!" said my grandfather, pinching her plump cheek. "But if I should be troubled by ghosts, I've been to the Red

3

Sea in my time, and have a pleasant way of laying them, my darling."

And then he whispered something to the girl which made her laugh, and give him a good-humored box on the ear. In short, there was nobody knew better how to make his way among the petticoats than my grandfather.

In a little while, as was his usual way, he took complete possession of the house, swaggering all over it; into the stable to look after his horse, into the kitchen to look after his supper. He had something to say or do with every one; smoked with the Dutchmen, drank with the Germans, slapped the landlord on the shoulder, romped with his daughter and the bar-maid;—never, since the days of Alley Croaker, had such a rattling blade been seen. The landlord stared at him with astonishment; the landlord's daughter hung her head and giggled whenever he came near; and as he swaggered along the corridor, with his sword trailing by his side, the maids looked after him, and whispered to one another, "What a proper man!"

At supper, my grandfather took command of the *table-d' hôte* as though he had been at home; helped everybody, not forgetting himself; talked with every one, whether he understood their language or not; and made his way into the intimacy of the rich burgher of Antwerp, who had never been known to be sociable with any one during his life. In fact, he revolutionized the whole establishment, and gave it such a rouse, that the very house reeled with it. He outsat every one at table, excepting the little fat distiller of Schiedam, who sat soaking a long time before he broke forth; but when he did, he was a very devil incarnate. He took a violent affection for my grandfather; so they sat drinking and smoking, and telling stories, and singing Dutch and Irish songs, without understanding a word each other said, until the little Hollander was fairly swamped with his own gin and water, and carried off to bed, whooping and hickuping, and trolling the burden of a Low Dutch love-song.

Well, gentlemen, my grandfather was shown to his quarters up a large staircase, composed of loads of hewn timber; and through long rigmarole passages, hung with blackened paintings of fish, and fruit, and game, and country frolics, and huge kitchens, and portly burgomasters, such as you see about old-fashioned Flemish inns, till at length he arrived at his room.

An old-times chamber it was, sure enough, and crowded with all kinds of trumpery. It looked like an infirmary for decayed and superannuated furniture, where everything diseased or disabled

4

was sent to nurse or to be forgotten. Or rather it might be taken for a general congress of old legitimate movables, where every kind and country had a representative. No two chairs were alike. Such high backs and low backs, and leather bottoms, and worsted bottoms, and straw bottoms, and no bottoms; and cracked marble tables with curiously carved legs, holding balls in their claws, as though they were going to play at ninepins.

My grandfather made a bow to the motley assemblage as he entered, and, having undressed himself, placed his light in the fireplace, asking pardon of the tongs, which seemed to be making love to the shovel in the chimney-corner, and whispering soft nonsense in its ear.

The rest of the guests were by this time sound asleep, for your Mynheers are huge sleepers. The housemaids, one by one, crept up yawning to their attics; and not a female head in the inn was laid on a pillow that night without dreaming of the bold dragoon.

My grandfather, for his part, got into bed, and drew over him one of those great bags of down, under which they smother a man in the Low Countries; and there he lay, melting between two feather beds, like an anchovy sandwich between two slices of toast and butter. He was a warm-complexioned man, and this smothering played the very deuce with him. So, sure enough, in a little time it seemed as if a legion of imps were twitching at him, and all the blood in his veins was in a fever-heat.

He lay still, however, until all the house was quiet excepting the snoring of the Mynheers from the different chambers; who answered one another in all kinds of tones and cadences, like so many bull-frogs in a swamp. The quieter the house became, the more unquiet became my grandfather. He waxed warmer and warmer, until at length the bed became too hot to hold him.

"Maybe the maid had warmed it too much?" said the curious gentleman, inquiringly.

"I rather think the contrary," replied the Irishman. "But, be that as it may, it grew too hot for my grandfather."

"Faith, there's no standing this any longer," says he. So he jumped out of bed, and went strolling about the house.

"What for?" said the inquisitive gentleman.

"Why, to cool himself, to be sure—or perhaps to find a more comfortable bed—or perhaps— But no matter what he went for— he never mentioned—and there's no use in taking up our time in conjecturing."

Well, my grandfather had been for some time absent from his room, and was returning, perfectly cool, when just as he reached the door, he heard a strange noise within. He paused and listened. It seemed as if some one were trying to hum a tune in defiance of the asthma. He recollected the report of the room being haunted; but he was no believer in ghosts, so he pushed the door gently open and peeped in.

Egad, gentlemen, there was a gambol carrying on within enough to have astonished St. Anthony himself. By the light of the fire he saw a pale weazen-faced fellow, in a long flannel gown and a tall white night-cap with a tassel to it, who sat by the fire with a bellows under his arm by way of bagpipe, from which he forced the asthmatical music that had bothered my grandfather. As he played, too, he kept twitching about with a thousand queer contortions, nodding his head, and bobbing about his tasselled night-cap.

My grandfather thought this very odd and mighty presumptuous, and was about to demand what business he had to play his wind-instrument in another gentleman's quarters, when a new cause of astonishment met his eye. From the opposite side of the room a long-backed, bandy-legged chair, covered with leather, and studded all over in a coxcombical fashion with little brass nails, got suddenly into motion, thrust out first a claw-foot, then a crooked arm, and at length, making a leg, slided gracefully up to an easy-chair of tarnished brocade, with a hole in its bottom, and led it gallantly out in a ghostly minuet about the floor.

The musician now played fiercer and fiercer, and bobbed his head and his night-cap about like mad. By degrees the dancing mania seemed to seize upon all the other pieces of furniture. The antique, long-bodied chairs paired off in couples and led down a country-dance; a three-legged stool danced a hornpipe, though horribly puzzled by its supernumerary limb; while the amorous tongs seized the shovel round the waist, and whirled it about the room in a German waltz. In short, all the movables got in motion; pirouetting hands across, right and left, like so many devils; all except a great clothes-press, which kept courtesying and courtesying in a corner, like a dowager, in exquisite time to the music; being rather too corpulent to dance, or perhaps at a loss for a partner.

My grandfather concluded the latter to be the reason; so being, like a true Irishman, devoted to the sex, and at all times ready for a frolic, he bounced into the room, called to the musician to strike up Paddy O'Rafferty, capered up to the clothes-press, and seized upon the two handles to lead her out: ——when-whirr! the whole revel was at an end. The chairs, tables, tongs and shovel, slunk in an instant as quietly into their places as if nothing had happened, and the musician vanished up the chimney, leaving the bellows behind him in his hurry. My grandfather found himself seated in the middle of the floor with the clothes-press sprawling before him, and the two handles jerked off, and in his hands.

"Then, after all, this was a mere dream," said the inquisitive gentlemen.

"The divil a bit of a dream!" replied the Irishman. "There never was a truer fact in this world. Faith, I should have liked to see any man tell my grandfather it was a dream."

Well, gentlemen, as the clothes-press was a mighty heavy body, and my grandfather likewise, particularly in rear, you may easily suppose that two such heavy bodies coming to the ground would make a bit of a noise. Faith, the old mansion shook as though it had mistaken it for an earthquake. The whole garrison was alarmed. The landlord, who slept below, hurried up with a candle to inquire the cause, but with all his haste his daughter had arrived at the scene of uproar before him. The landlord was followed by the landlady, who was followed by the bouncing bar-maid, who was followed by the simpering chambermaids, all holding together, as well as they could, such garments as they first laid hands on; but all in a terrible hurry to see what the deuce was to pay in the chamber of the bold dragoon.

My grandfather related the marvellous scene he had witnessed, and the broken handles of the prostrate clothes-press bore testimony to the fact. There was no contesting such evidence; particularly with a lad of my grandfather's complexion, who seemed able to make good every word either with sword or shillelah. So the landlord scratched his head and looked silly, as he was apt to do when puzzled. The landlady scratched—no, she did not scratch her head, but she knit her brow, and did not seem half pleased with the explanation. But the landlady's daughter corroborated it by recollecting that the last person who had dwelt in that chamber was a famous juggler who died of St. Vitus's dance, and had no doubt infected all the furniture.

This set all things to rights, particularly when the chambermaids declared that they had all witnessed strange carryings on in that room; and as they declared this "upon their honors," there could not remain a doubt upon this subject.

"And did your grandfather go to bed again in that room?" said the inquisitive gentleman.

"That's more than I can tell. Where he passed the rest of the night was a secret he never disclosed. In fact, though he had seen much service, he was but indifferently acquainted with geography, and apt to make blunders in his travels about inns at night, which it would have puzzled him sadly to account for in the morning."

"Was he ever apt to walk in his sleep?" said the knowing old gentleman.

"Never that I heard of."

There was a little pause after this rigmarole Irish romance, when the old gentleman with the haunted head observed, that the stories hitherto related had rather a burlesque tendency. "I recollect an adventure however," added he, "which I heard of during a residence in Paris, for the truth of which I can undertake to vouch, and which is of a very grave and singular nature."

The Adventure of My Aunt

By Washington Irving

My aunt was a lady of large frame, strong mind, and great resolution: she was what might be termed a very manly woman. My uncle was a thin, puny little man, very meek and acquiescent, and no match for my aunt. It was observed that he dwindled and dwindled gradually away, from the day of his marriage. His wife's powerful mind was too much for him; it wore him out. My aunt, however, took all possible care of him: had half the doctors in town to prescribe for him; made him take all their prescriptions, and dosed him with physic enough to cure a whole hospital. All was in vain. My uncle grew worse and worse the more dosing and nursing he underwent, until in the end he added another to the long list of matrimonial victims who have been killed with kindness.

"And was it his ghost that appeared to her?" asked the inquisitive gentleman, who had questioned the former story-teller.

"You shall hear," replied the narrator.—My aunt took on mightily for the death of her poor dear husband. Perhaps she felt some compunction at having given him so much physic, and nursed him into the grave. At any rate, she did all that a widow could do to honor his memory. She spared no expense in either the quantity or quality of her mourning weeds; wore a miniature of him about her neck as large as a little sun-dial, and had a full-length portrait of him always hanging in her bed-chamber. All the world extolled her conduct to the skies; and it was determined that a woman who behaved so well to the memory of one husband deserved soon to get another.

It was not long after this that she went to take up her residence in an old country-seat in Derbyshire, which had long been in the care of merely a steward and housekeeper. She took most of her servants with her, intending to make it her principal abode. The house stood in a lonely wild part of the country, among the gray Derbyshire hills, with a murderer hanging in chains on a bleak height in full view.

The servants from town were half frightened out of their wits at the idea of living in such a dismal, pagan-looking place; especially when they got together in the servants' hall in the evening, and compared notes on all the hobgoblin stories picked up in the course of the day. They were afraid to venture alone about the gloomy, black-looking chambers. My lady's maid, who was troubled with nerves, declared she could never sleep alone in such a "gashly rummaging old building"; and the footman, who was a kind-hearted young fellow, did all in his power to cheer her up.

My aunt was struck with the lonely appearance of the house. Before going to bed, therefore, she examined well the fastnesses of the doors and windows; locked up the plate with her own hands, and carried the keys, together with a little box of money and jewels, to her own room; for she was a notable woman, and always saw to all things herself. Having put the keys under her pillow, and dismissed her maid, she sat by her toilet arranging her hair; for being, in spite of her grief for my uncle, rather a buxom widow, she was somewhat particular about her person. She sat for a little while looking at her face in the glass, first on one side, then on the other, as ladies are apt to do when they would ascertain whether they have been in good looks; for a roistering country squire of the neighborhood, with whom she had flirted when a girl, had called that day to welcome her to the country.

All of a sudden she thought she heard something move behind her. She looked hastily round, but there was nothing to be seen. Nothing but the grimly painted portrait of her poor dear man, hanging against the wall.

She gave a heavy sigh to his memory, as she was accustomed to do whenever she spoke of him in company, and then went on adjusting her night-dress, and thinking of the squire. Her sigh was re-echoed, or answered by a long-drawn breath. She looked round again, but no one was to be seen. She ascribed these sounds to the wind oozing through the ratholes of the old mansion, and proceeded leisurely to put her hair in papers, when, all at once, she thought she perceived one of the eyes of the portrait move.

"The back of her head being towards it!" said the story-teller with the ruined head,—"good!"

"Yes, sir!" replied dryly the narrator, "her back being towards the portrait, but her eyes fixed on its reflection in the glass."—Well, as I was saying, she perceived one of the eyes of the portrait move. So strange a circumstance, as you may well suppose, gave her a sudden shock. To assure herself of the fact, she put one hand to her forehead as if rubbing it; peeped through her fingers, and moved the candle with the other hand. The light of the taper gleamed on the eye, and was reflected from it. She was sure it moved. Nay, more, it seemed to give her a wink, as she had sometimes known her husband to do when living! It struck a momentary chill to her heart; for she was a lone woman, and felt herself fearfully situated.

The chill was but transient. My aunt, who was almost as resolute a personage as your uncle, sir, (turning to the old story-teller,) became instantly calm and collected. She went on adjusting her dress. She even hummed an air, and did not make even a single false note. She casually overturned a dressing-box; took a candle and picked up the articles one by one from the floor; pursued a rolling pin-cushion that was making the best of its way under the bed; then opened the door; looked for an instant into the corridor, as if in doubt whether to go; and then walked quietly out.

She hastened down-stairs, ordered the servants to arm themselves with the weapons first at hand, placed herself at their head, and returned almost immediately.

Her hastily levied army presented a formidable force. The steward had a rusty blunder-buss, the coachman a loaded whip, the footman a pair of horse-pistols, the cook a huge chopping-knife, and the butler a bottle in each hand. My aunt led the van with a red-hot poker, and in my opinion she was the most formidable of the party. The waiting-maid, who dreaded to stay alone in the servants' hall, brought up the rear, smelling to a broken bottle of volatile salts, and expressing her terror of the ghostesses. "Ghosts!" said my aunt, resolutely. "I'll singe their whiskers for them!"

They entered the chamber. All was still and undisturbed as when she had left it. They approached the portrait of my uncle.

"Pull down that picture!" cried my aunt. A heavy groan, and a sound like the chattering of teeth, issued from the portrait. The servants shrunk back; the maid uttered a faint shriek, and clung to the footman for support.

"Instantly!" added my aunt, with a stamp of the foot.

10

The picture was pulled down, and from a recess behind it, in which had formerly stood a clock, they hauled forth a round-shouldered, black-bearded varlet, with a knife as long as my arm, but trembling all over like an aspen-leaf.

"Well, and who was he? No ghost, I suppose," said the inquisitive gentleman.

"A Knight of the Post," replied the narrator, "who had been smitten with the worth of the wealthy widow; or rather a marauding Tarquin, who had stolen into her chamber to violate her purse, and rifle her strong box, when all the house should be asleep. In plain terms," continued he, "the vagabond was a loose idle fellow of the neighborhood, who had once been a servant in the house, and had been employed to assist in arranging it for the reception of its mistress. He confessed that he had contrived this hiding-place for his nefarious purpose, and had borrowed an eye from the portrait by way of a reconnoitring-hole."

"And what did they do with him? —did they hang him?" resumed the questioner.

"Hang him!—how could they?" exclaimed a beetle-browed barrister, with a hawk's nose. "The offence was not capital. No robbery, no assault had been committed. No forcible entry or breaking into the premises——"

"My aunt," said the narrator, "was a woman of spirit, and apt to take the law in her own hands. She had her own notions of cleanliness also. She ordered the fellow to be drawn through the horse-pond, to cleanse away all offences, and then to be well rubbed down with an oaken towel."

"And what became of him afterwards?" said the inquisitive gentleman."

"I do not exactly know. I believe he was sent on a voyage of improvement to Botany Bay."

"And your aunt," said the inquisitive gentleman; "I'll warrant she took care to make her maid sleep in the room with her after that."

"No, sir, she did better; she gave her hand shortly after to the roistering squire; for she used to observe, that it was a dismal thing for a woman to sleep alone in the country."

"She was right," observed the inquisitive gentleman, nodding sagaciously; "but I am sorry they did not hang that fellow."

It was agreed on all hands that the last narrator had brought his tale to the most satisfactory conclusion, though a country clergyman present regretted that the uncle and aunt, who figured in the different stories, had not been married together; they certainly would have been well matched.

"But I don't see, after all," said the inquisitive gentleman, "that there was any ghost in this last story."

"Oh! If it's ghosts you want, honey," cried the Irish Captain of Dragoons, "if it's ghosts you want, you shall have a whole regiment of them. And since these gentlemen have given the adventures of their uncles and aunts, faith, and I'll even give you a chapter out of my own family-history."

The Adventure of the German Student
By Washington Irving

On a stormy night, in the tempestuous times of the French revolution, a young German was returning to his lodgings, at a late hour, across the old part of Paris. The lightning gleamed, and the loud claps of thunder rattled through the lofty narrow streets—but I should now tell you something about this young German.

Gottfried Wolfgang was a young man of good family. He had studied for some time at Göttingen, but being of a visionary and enthusiastic character, he had wandered into those wild and speculative doctrines which have so often bewildered German students. His secluded life, his intense application, and the singular nature of his studies, had an effect on both mind and body. His health was impaired; his imagination diseased. He had been indulging in fanciful speculations on spiritual essences, until, like Swedenborg, he had an ideal world of his own around him. He took up a notion, I do not know from what cause, that there was an evil influence hanging over him; an evil genius or spirit seeking to ensnare him and ensure his perdition. Such an idea working on his melancholy temperament, produced the most gloomy effects. He became haggard and desponding. His friends discovered the mental malady preying upon him, and determined that the best cure was a change of scene; he was sent, therefore, to finish his studies amidst the splendors and gayeties of Paris.

Wolfgang arrived at Paris at the breaking out of the revolution. The popular delirium at first caught his enthusiastic mind, and he was captivated by the political and philosophical theories of the day: but the scenes of blood which followed shocked his sensitive nature, disgusted him with society and the world, and made him more than ever a recluse. He shut himself up in a solitary apartment in the *Pays Latin*, the quarter of students. There, in a gloomy street not far from the monastic walls of the Sorbonne, he pursued his favorite speculations. Sometimes he spent hours together in the great libraries of Paris, those catacombs of departed authors, rummaging among their hordes of dusty and obsolete works in quest of food for his unhealthy appetite. He was, in a manner, a literary ghoul, feeding in the charnel-house of decayed literature.

Wolfgang, though solitary and reclusive, was of an ardent temperament, but for a time it operated merely upon his imagination. He was too shy and ignorant of the world to make any advances to the fair, but he was a passionate admirer of female beauty, and in his lonely chamber would often lose himself in reveries on forms and faces which he had seen, and his fancy would deck out images of loveliness far surpassing the reality.

While his mind was in this excited and sublimated state, a dream produced an extraordinary effect upon him. It was of a female face of transcendent beauty. So strong was the impression made, that he dreamt of it again and again. It haunted his thoughts by day, his slumbers by night; in fine, he became passionately enamoured of this shadow of a dream. This lasted so long that it became one of those fixed ideas which haunt the minds of melancholy men, and are at times mistaken for madness.

Such was Gottfried Wolfgang, and such his situation at the time I mentioned. He was returning home late one stormy night, through some of the old and gloomy streets of the *Marais*, the ancient part of Paris. The loud claps of thunder rattled among the high houses of the narrow streets. He came to the Place de Grève, the square where public executions are performed. The lightning quivered about the pinnacles of the ancient Hôtel de Ville, and shed flickering gleams over the open space in front. As Wolfgang was crossing the square, he shrank back with horror at finding himself close by the guillotine. It was the height of the reign of terror, when this dreadful instrument of death stood ever ready, and its scaffold was continually running with the blood of the virtuous and the brave. It had that very day been actively employed in the work of carnage, and there it stood in grim array, amidst a silent and sleeping city, waiting for fresh victims.

Wolfgang's heart sickened within him, and he was turning shuddering from the horrible engine, when he beheld a shadowy form, cowering as it were at the foot of the steps which led up to the scaffold. A succession of vivid flashes of lightning revealed it more distinctly. It was a female figure, dressed in black. She was seated on one of the lower steps of the scaffold, leaning forward, her face hid in her lap; and her long dishevelled tresses hanging to the ground, streaming with the rain which fell in torrents. Wolfgang paused. There was something awful in this solitary monument of woe. The female had the appearance of being above the common order. He knew the times to be full of vicissitude, and that many a fair head, which had once been pillowed on down, now wandered houseless. Perhaps this was some poor mourner whom the dreadful axe had rendered desolate, and who sat here heart-broken on the strand of existence, from which all that was dear to her had been launched into eternity.

He approached, and addressed her in the accents of sympathy. She raised her head and gazed wildly at him. What was his astonishment at beholding, by the bright glare of the lightning, the very face which had haunted him in his dreams. It was pale and disconsolate, but ravishingly beautiful.

Trembling with violent and conflicting emotions, Wolfgang again accosted her. He spoke something of her being exposed at such an hour of the night, and to the fury of such a storm, and offered to conduct her to her friends. She pointed to the guillotine with a gesture of dreadful signification.

"I have no friend on earth!" she said.

"But you have a home," said Wolfgang.

"Yes—in the grave!"

The heart of the student melted at the words.

"If a stranger dare make an offer," said he, "without danger of being misunderstood, I would offer my humble dwelling as a shelter; myself as a devoted friend. I am friendless myself in Paris, and a stranger in the land; but if my life could be of service, it is at your disposal, and should be sacrificed before harm or indignity should come to you."

There was an honest earnestness in the young man's manner that had its effect. His foreign accent, too, was in his favor; it showed him not to be a hackneyed inhabitant of Paris. Indeed, there is an eloquence in true enthusiasm that is not to be doubted. The homeless stranger confided herself implicitly to the protection of the student.

He supported her faltering steps across the Pont Neuf, and by the place where the statue of Henry the Fourth had been overthrown by the populace. The storm had abated, and the thunder

14

rumbled at a distance. All Paris was quiet; that great volcano of human passion slumbered for a while, to gather fresh strength for the next day's eruption. The student conducted his charge through the ancient streets of the *Pays Latin*, and by the dusky walls of the Sorbonne, to the great dingy hotel which he inhabited. The old portress who admitted them stared with surprise at the unusual sight of the melancholy Wolfgang with a female companion.

On entering his apartment, the student, for the first time, blushed at the scantiness and indifference of his dwelling. He had but one chamber—an old-fashioned saloon—heavily carved, and fantastically furnished with the remains of former magnificence, for it was one of those hotels in the quarter of the Luxembourg palace, which had once belonged to nobility. It was lumbered with books and papers, and all the usual apparatus of a student, and his bed stood in a recess at one end.

When lights were brought, and Wolfgang had a better opportunity of contemplating the stranger, he was more than ever intoxicated by her beauty. Her face was pale, but of a dazzling fairness, set off by a profusion of raven hair that hung clustering about it. Her eyes were large and brilliant, with a singular expression approaching almost to wildness. As far as her black dress permitted her shape to be seen, it was of perfect symmetry. Her whole appearance was highly striking, though she was dressed in the simplest style. The only thing approaching to an ornament which she wore, was a broad black band round her neck, clasped by diamonds.

The perplexity now commenced with the student how to dispose of the helpless being thus thrown upon his protection. He thought of abandoning his chamber to her, and seeking shelter for himself elsewhere. Still he was so fascinated by her charms, there seemed to be such a spell upon his thoughts and senses, that he could not tear himself from her presence. Her manner, too, was singular and unaccountable. She spoke no more of the guillotine. Her grief had abated. The attentions of the student had first won her confidence, and then, apparently, her heart. She was evidently an enthusiast like himself, and enthusiasts soon understand each other.

In the infatuation of the moment, Wolfgang avowed his passion for her. He told her the story of his mysterious dream, and how she had possessed his heart before he had even seen her. She was strangely affected by his recital, and acknowledged to have felt an impulse towards him equally unaccountable. It was the time for wild theory and wild actions. Old prejudices and superstitions were done away; everything was under the sway of the "Goddess of Reason." Among other rubbish of the old times, the forms and ceremonies of marriage began to be considered superfluous bonds for honorable minds. Social compacts were the vogue. Wolfgang was too much of a theorist not to be tainted by the liberal doctrines of the day.

"Why should we separate?" said he; "our hearts are united; in the eye of reason and honor we are as one. What need is there of sordid forms to bind high souls together?"

The stranger listened with emotion: she had evidently received illumination at the same school.

"You have no home or family," continued he, "let me be everything to you, or rather let us be everything to one another. If form is necessary, form shall be observed—there is my hand. I pledge myself to you forever."

"Forever?" said the stranger, solemnly.

"Forever!" repeated Wolfgang.

The stranger clasped the hand extended to her: "Then I am yours," murmured she, and sank upon his bosom.

The next morning the student left his bride sleeping, and sallied forth at an early hour to seek more spacious apartments suitable to the change in his situation. When he returned, he found the stranger lying with her head hanging over the bed, and one arm thrown over it. He spoke to her, but received no reply. He advanced to awaken her from her uneasy posture. On taking her hand, it was cold—there was no pulsation—her face was pallid and ghastly. In a word, she was a corpse.

Horrified and frantic, he alarmed the house. A scene of confusion ensued. The police was summoned. As the officer of police entered the room, he started back on beholding the corpse.

"Great heaven!" cried he, "how did this woman come here?"

"Do you know anything about her?" said Wolfgang eagerly.

"Do I?" exclaimed the officer: "she was guillotined yesterday."

He stepped forward; undid the black collar round the neck of the corpse, and the head rolled on the floor!

The student burst into a frenzy. "The fiend! the fiend has gained possession of me!" shrieked he; "I am lost forever."

They tried to soothe him, but in vain. He was possessed with the frightful belief that an evil spirit had reanimated the dead body to ensnare him. He went distracted, and died in a mad-house.

Here the old gentleman with the haunted head finished his narrative.

"And is this really a fact?" said the inquisitive gentleman.

16

"A fact not to be doubted," replied the other. "I had it from the best authority. The student told it me himself. I saw him in a mad-house in Paris."

Ants

By Chet Williamson

Ben Piersall first saw them at the bottom of the drive, where the asphalt had been torn away by the combination of the harsh winter and the big tires of the oil delivery truck. They had a substantial hill in progress, six inches across at the center and an inch high.

Ants. Ants he didn't need. The goddamned moles were bad enough. His lawn already had more soft spots than a week-old melon. So he drew back his foot and kicked, making the dirt fly up in a waist-high arc.

That got them. They poured from the hole like a thick black thread, running in panic at the cataclysm that had ripped off the top of their city. Ben chuckled and began to stomp. In a minute the tiny scurrying motions had ended, though a few survivors still ran for cover and a multitude of wounded writhed in the furrows made by Ben's Vibram soles.

He turned and walked smiling toward the house, the mail tucked under his arm. That was fun—but not as much fun as when he was a kid and had dripped candle wax on the ants one at a time. In a few seconds you could peel the dried wax off the sidewalk and put a petrified ant in your pocket. Ben used to take a bunch to school, where they made unheralded appearances in the urinal, Mrs. Donovan's pencil cup, and Sheila Brown's milk.

But time had passed, he'd grown up, gotten married, gotten divorced, gotten tired. Small pleasures were all he could afford now. Alimony and child support allowed little else. A case of beer a week, an occasional movie, a *very* occasional roll with Mindy, the waitress at the Anchor, and whatever else he could find to amuse himself . . . like stomping ants. At least he'd been able to keep the house.

Inside, he opened a Bud and flopped on the sofa with a copy of

17

Ms. Harriet's two-year subscription was still going strong. He frowned at the article titles and picked up *Sports Illustrated* instead.

He had barely opened the magazine when his nose started to itch. He looked down its broad length and noticed a small black dot at the point where his vision crossed. Thinking it might be a misplaced period on the page, he wiggled both his eyes and the magazine, but, instead of disappearing, the dot took a few tentative steps upward on the oily film that coated Ben's proboscis.

"An ant!" he yelled, and smashed himself lustily on the nose. When he examined what stuck to his fingers, he found that it was indeed an ant, or rather crushed bits of ant head, ant thorax, and ant legs. "Ee-yuch," he said, and snapped the debris away.

Halfway through his article on football draft choices his head started to itch, right at the thin patch he called his crown and Harriet had called his bald spot. Whatever the appellation, it itched like a bitch, so he scratched madly and came away with something beneath his nail that was too dark to be dandruff. Too dark and too wiggly.

"Another one? Jesus H!" and he crushed the interloper, flinging its corpse to join its friend in the thick and tangled jungle of ten year old shag carpet. "Where the hell did *he* come from?" mused Ben, looking about for an answer. When he glanced at the left foot he'd so dapperly propped on the coffee table, he found it. His boot was swarming with little black bodies that were quickly disappearing between pant cuff and sock.

"Gaaah!" he shouted as the hairlike legs pattered over the skin of his calf. "Heeheeyahah!" He sat up faster than when the detective Harriet had hired surprised him at the Sunrise Motel, and started to smack his legs together vigorously.

When the tickling had diminished, he examined the source of the problem, unlacing the boot and turning it over. The thick depressions of the Vibram soles still sheltered dozens of the little hangers-on. Ben, now smacking his thighs, ran outside, where he smashed the boot against the sidewalk, and kept smashing until nothing remained but a nondescript blob of formic acid.

"That'll show ya, little buggers . . . wow!" he cried, as a survivor fastened its appendage to *Ben's* appendage. Ben danced about frantically, his hand thrust between waistband and belly, until he finally snagged the ant and crushed it. Then, leaving his boots outside, he went into the house, where he immediately shed his clothes, threw them in the washing machine, and ran into the bathroom.

In the shower, he made the water as hot as he could stand it, rubbed and scrubbed his skin raw with Harriet's old loofah, and dug his fingers into his scalp until it tingled on the edge of pain. Then he rinsed thoroughly, turned off the faucet, and stepped into the mat. There, goddammit, that was better. No more ants on him now.

But as he toweled himself dry, he became aware of a slight itching in his hair. He scratched, and a small ant fell out. Then another, and another.

Gasping, he staggered back, his legs bumping against the side of the tub so that he toppled backwards into it, his bare buttocks striking the porcelain with a loud smack. He still had the towel, and now he saw that it was swarming with ants, dozens and dozens of them making an ever changing pattern on the blue cloth. Throwing it from him, he stood up in the tub, naked and trembling. They were entering the bathroom by the hundreds, so thick that they seemed like a living mass of tar rolling toward the edge of the bath.

Ben grabbed the faucet handles and wrenched them on, sending hot water streaming over his body, washing down the drain the few ants that had made it into the tub. Several more dropped over the edge and were swept straight into the plumbing. After that the others stopped, and Ben could read an angry wariness in the multitude of black specks that stood between him and the door.

A minute passed while the water roared down and the room filled with steam. Then a single ant started up the wall, and others followed until a blob of darkness two feet square moved to the ceiling, over and across the room, and stopped directly above the cowering form of Ben Piersall.

Ants lay like a sheet on the floor, clung overhead to the ceiling, flowed in a wave under the crack of the door—hundreds, thousands, *tens* of thousands of ants . . .

"Stop!" Ben Piersall cried, his voice lengthened and curved by his terror and the thunder of the shower. "Please stop! I'm sorry! I'll do whatever you want, whatever . . ." He collapsed sobbing in the bottom of the tub, each hot droplet of water stinging him like a tiny mandible.

The ants watched, and smiled a collective smile.

Later that afternoon, people at the Acme Market started to wonder about Ben Piersall. They wondered why he looked so pale and nervous, they wondered why he bought six cases of pancake syrup, and they wondered, on such a hot summer day, how Ben Piersall could wear a thick, black, shiny scarf wrapped tightly around his neck and still be shivering.

19

The Assembly of the Dead

By Chet Williamson

The man was inordinately fat. He brought to mind the more bloated of the corpses Hutchinson had seen in the morgue the day before. But the living man's smile was broader, his skin not as gray. His bow was deeper than Hutchinson thought his girth would allow. The *quayabera* the man wore was huge, and simply embroidered. Beneath its sleeve Hutchinson noticed a gold Seiko watch that crimped the flesh of the wrist.

"Mister Hutchinson?" the man said. His voice was light, and surprisingly gentle. Hutchinson nodded, and the man went on in Spanish. "May I speak with you for a moment? In private?"

Hutchinson turned to the young man from the embassy and to the younger, uniformed soldier, and motioned them ahead.

"There is something, someone you seek here," the man said to Hutchinson when they were alone.

"Yes."

"He is a relative?"

"No. The relative of a . . ." Hutchinson used the English word. ". . . a constituent."

"Please?"

"Someone in my district," he explained, and the man nodded.

"Locke," the man said.

"Thomas Locke. Yes."

"You know that he is dead."

"I had heard that."

"You wish his body?"

"His family does."

"I can get Mister Locke's body for you."

Hutchinson looked at the man for a moment before speaking again. "Are you certain?"

"Please?"

"That it's him."

The man reached into a pocket and pulled out a small parcel wrapped in brown paper and twine. It was the size of a thick paperback book. "Take this. You will see. Then come and meet me." The man gave Hutchinson the directions, and told him how much money to bring. "Come alone," the man said.

"Alone?"

"You will not be harmed."

The man turned and walked away. Hutchinson rejoined the young diplomat and the soldier, and went back to the hotel. Together, he and the diplomat went to his room, where Hutchinson unwrapped the small package. Inside was a plastic bag which contained a bloodless, nearly white piece of a human hand, the little and ring fingers still attached. The diplomat turned ashen. Hutchinson's face did not change.

From his briefcase, Hutchinson drew a sheet of shiny paper divided into ten squares. In the center of each was a single fingerprint. He manipulated the piece of hand in the plastic bag until the two fingertips were outside, past the zip-loc seal. Hutchinson lifted the hand close to his eyes, and the young diplomat looked away.

"They look the same," Hutchinson said at last.

"They'd be . . . a mirror image," the diplomat said.

"Yes. Even so . . . I don't have a pad, an ink pad. But they look the same. First two fingers left hand."

"We'll send someone with you."

"He told me to come alone."

"They don't expect you to. They just say that."

"No. I have to."

"You can't be alone here." The diplomat paused. "It isn't safe."

"It's not that far," Hutchinson said.

That night, Hutchinson and the diplomat met for dinner in the hotel restaurant. The last time Hutchinson had been there, two years before, the table at which he sat had commanded a view of the street and the courtyard beyond. Now the glass was missing, and plywood planks hid the outside from view.

The diplomat sipped a Tom Collins. "It didn't bother you much, did it?"

"What?"

"The fingers. That hand."

"I've seen as much before," Hutchinson said, draining his scotch and softly crunching a pearl of ice.

"You in Vietnam?"

Hutchinson nodded. "You?"

"No. 4-F."

"Lucky."

"I don't know. It's become a status symbol now to have been there." The diplomat sipped again.

"Maybe so. I guess it got me elected."

The diplomat shook his head. "Christ, these people. I think I've been here too long. All I can see is the sickness. Selling a body . . ."

"Capitalism," Hutchinson said. "That's what we're trying to protect. Seems to be flourishing. That's all that fat man is, a good capitalist."

"Sometimes you don't sound like a congressman."

"Goods and services? Supply and demand? I sound *just* like a congressman. I've studied. Done my homework." There was a grim humor in Hutchinson's smile. "This country," he said, "*is* undoubtedly full of shit."

"But it doesn't bother you."

"No. I told you it doesn't."

The next day Hutchinson drove to where the man had said he would meet him. It was a mile outside of the city, down a side road of dirt to a small village. Hutchinson saw women and naked children, and very few men. Some soldiers with rifles sat beneath trees, scarcely looking up as he drove past.

He stopped, as directed, outside the only brick building in the village. The man he had spoken to the day before came out of the door and walked to the car, his hand extended. Hutchinson took it. It was cool and dry. "You have brought the money?" the man asked.

Hutchinson nodded.

"Drive your car behind the building. There is a shed there. See. Where I go."

The man walked around the side of the brick building, and Hutchinson followed in his car. A one-story shed roofed with corrugated metal stood in the shade of trees at the jungle's edge. Long grass grew around it, nearly hiding it from sight. Hutchinson brought the car as close as he could without miring it in the tall fronds.

"Come," the man said, and passed through the door. Inside, a refrigeration unit throbbed hollowly, and Hutchinson saw cases of canned goods with American labels. He could see his own breath, and the larger, denser clouds from the man who led him. The man stopped by a covered form, and pulled back a canvas tarpaulin.

"This is Thomas Locke," he said.

The body had been dismembered. Hutchinson looked at the left hand first, saw the thumb and two remaining fingers, and felt certain the piece in the hotel's freezer would match. The face, empty and expressionless, resembled his photographs of Thomas Locke.

22

As for the other pieces—the torso, still joined to the upper right arm and thighs, the right forearm and hand, and the two disjointed feet and lower legs—he was not sure. But then he remembered.

"The left foot," he said, pointing to it.

"Yes?"

"It is not Thomas Locke's."

"It is not?" The man's florid face shone with innocence, and he knelt by the gray-green, broken-toed appendage.

"No. Locke walked with a limp. He had no left foot. It was artificial. He used a cane."

"Ah." The man nodded, eying the foot critically. "Well." Then he looked up and smiled. "Is death not wonderful here? We can make lame men whole. As is Mister Locke before his God." The smile faded. "You will pay me still?"

"Yes."

"That is fine then. For enough money, we can find wings, and make Mister Locke an angel." The man straightened up. "I will have my friends put the body in your car."

"Not the foot," Hutchinson said.

"No," the man agreed. "Not the foot."

After the pieces were wrapped in canvas and placed in Hutchinson's trunk, he paid the man, and they left the shed. In the doorway, Hutchinson paused and looked back to where the foot still lay on the stone floor, flanked by the brown cardboard boxes of canned goods. The soldiers did not look up as Hutchinson drove out of the village, back to the city.

That night in the hotel, Hutchinson prepared for bed. When it came time to remove his socks, he sat on the bed as always, and started to roll the left sock over his ankle. Then he stopped for a moment. When he continued, he moved more slowly, deliberately. He let the sock drop quietly onto the carpet, and looked at his bare foot, gently touching the toes, kneading the sole, as if inspecting a piece of fruit in the marketplace. Then he quickly turned off the light, and finished undressing in the dark.

As the night lengthened, his feet grew large, unwieldy, until they were thick slabs of meat, heavy stones that became no lighter when he flung back the sheet and lay naked, pooled in sweat. When morning came, they were immovable.

He waited, breathing deeply, for them to come back to life. Eventually they did, allowing him to walk unsteadily into the bathroom. By the time he breakfasted, they felt fine, though he did not forget what they had become in the night.

Two days later he was home in the Georgetown apartment he

shared with his wife. She made them an excellent dinner, and afterward they went to bed and made love. Sometime before dawn, she was awakened by the sound of his ragged breathing. "What's wrong?" she whispered, thinking of bad dreams and turning on the light to banish them.

Hutchinson lay on his back, shiny with sweat, his head pressed into the pillow, his jaw jutting ceilingward. "My foot's asleep," he said through clenched teeth.

"Does it hurt?" she asked him, wondering at the tears in his eyes, thinking how out of place they seemed there, then realizing that she had never seen him cry, not even at their daughter's funeral.

At the Bureau

By Steve Rasnic Tem

I've been the administrator of these offices for twenty-five years now. I wish my employees were as steady. Most of them last only six months or so before they start complaining of boredom. It's next to impossible to find good help. But I've always been content here.

My wife doesn't understand how I could remain with the job this long. She says it's a dead end; I'm at the top of my pay scale, there'll be no further promotions, or increase in responsibilities. I've no place to go but down, she says. Her complaints about my job always lead to complaints about the marriage itself, of course. No children. Few friends. All the magic's gone, she says. But I've always been content.

When I started in the office we handled building permits. After a few years we were switched to peddling, parade, demolition licenses. Two years ago it was dog licenses. Last year they switched us to nothing but fishing permits.

Not too many people fish these days; the streams are too polluted. Last month I sold one permit. None the two months before. They plan to change our function again, I'm told, but a final decision apparently hasn't been made. I really don't care, as long as my offices continue to run smoothly.

A photograph of my wife taken the day of our marriage has sat on my desk the full twenty-five years, watching over me. At least she doesn't visit the office. I'm grateful for that.

Last week they reopened the offices next door. About time, I thought; the space had been vacant for five years. Ours was the last office still occupied in the old City Building. I was afraid maybe we too would be moved.

But I haven't been able as yet to determine just what it is exactly they do next door. They've a small staff, just one lone man at a telephone, I think. No one comes in or out of the office all day, until five, when he goes home.

I feel it's my business to find out what he does over there, and what it is he wants from me. A few days ago I looked up from my newspaper and saw a shadow on the frosted glass of our front door. Imagine my irritation when I rushed out into the hallway only to see his door just closing. I walked over there, intending to knock, and ask him what it was he wanted, but I saw his shadow within the office, bent over his desk. For some reason this stopped me, and I returned to my own office.

The next day the same thing happened. Then the day after that. I then refused to leave my desk. I wouldn't chase a shadow; he would not use me in such a fashion. I soon discovered that when I didn't go to the door, the shadow remained in my frosted glass all day long. He was standing outside my door all day long, every day.

Once there were two shadows. That brought me to my feet immediately. But when I jerked the door open I discovered two city janitors, sent to scrape off the words "Fish Permits" from my sign, "Bureau Of Fish Permits." When I asked them what the sign was to be changed to, they told me they hadn't received those instructions yet. Typical, I thought; nor had I been told.

Of course, after the two janitors had left, the single shadow was back again. It was there until five.

The next morning I walked over to his office door. The lights were out; I was early. I had hoped that the sign painters had labeled his activity for me, but his sign had not yet been filled in. "Bureau Of . . ." There were a few black streaks where the paint had been scraped away years ago, bare fragments of the letters that I couldn't decipher.

I'm not a man given to emotion. But the next day I lost my temper. I saw the shadow before the office door and I exploded. I ordered him away from my door at the top of my voice. When three hours had passed and he still hadn't left, I began to weep. I pleaded with him. But he was still there.

The next day I moaned. I shouted obscenities. But he was always there.

Perhaps my wife is right; I'm not very decisive, I don't like to make waves. But it's been days. He is always there.

Today I discovered the key to another empty office adjacent to mine. It fits a door between the two offices. I can go from my office to this vacant office without being seen from the hallway. At last, I can catch this crazy man in the act.

I sit quietly at my desk, pretending to read the newspaper. He hasn't moved for hours, except to occasionally peer closer at the frosted glass in my door, simulating binoculars with his two hands to his eyes.

I take off my coat and put it on the back of my chair. A strategically placed flower pot will give the impression of my head. I crawl over to the door to the vacant office, open it as quietly as possible, and slip through.

Cobwebs trace the outlines of the furniture. Files are scattered everywhere, some of the papers beginning to mold. The remains of someone's lunch are drying on one desk. I have to wonder at the city's janitorial division.

Unaccountably, I worry over the grocery list my wife gave me, now lying on my desk. I wonder if I should go back after it. Why? It bothers me terribly, the list unattended, unguarded on my desk. But I must push on. I step over a scattered pile of newspapers by the main desk, and reach the doorway leading into the hall.

I leap through the doorway with one mighty swing, prepared to shout the rude man down, in the middle of his act.

The hall is empty.

I am suddenly tired. I walk slowly to the man's office door, the door to the other bureau. I stand waiting.

I can see his shadow through the office door. He sits at his desk, apparently reading a newspaper. I step closer, forming my hands into imaginary binoculars. I press against the glass, right below the phrase, "Bureau Of," lettered in bold, black characters.

He orders me away from his door. He weeps. He pleads. Now he is shouting obscenities.

I've been here for days.

Babylon: 70 M.

By Donald A. Wollheim

> "How many miles to Babylon?
> Threescore miles and ten.
> Can I get there by candlelight?
> Yes, and back again.
> If your heels are nimble and light,
> You may get there by candlelight."

Sitting in his study, by the open window, Barry Kane heard the woman in the garden of the adjoining house reading *Mother Goose* rhymes to her little girl. He hadn't been paying attention consciously; it had just been a part of the noises of everyday living. His mind had been reflecting on the small urn he had just unpacked. But the word 'Babylon' struck his ear and sparked his attention; the little jingle jerked his mind away from the black, time-encrusted relic before him, and onto the woman's clear enunciation outside.

Barry frowned a bit, still idly turning the stone jug in his hand. Now that was an odd one, he thought. It was vaguely familiar; he supposed that he had run across it himself in his own childhood— and, as children do, simply had listened to it for its rhythm and ignored its meaning. Like so many of Mother Goose's poems it seemed to make not much sense.

He tried to focus his attention again on the urn. He'd only unwrapped it a few minutes ago from its careful packings and sawdust. The expedition had shipped it to him from Baghdad, along with other interesting bits they had dug out of Babylon's ruins. An odd coincidence that that particular bit of nursery nonsense should have been overheard at just this time. He wondered idly if the mother outside would be surprised to know that so close to her was a piece that had just arrived from that very Babylon.

Only "threescore miles and ten" too, Barry thought. Why didn't he up and go then? Although he'd rated as an expert on the ancient civilizations of Asia Minor, actually he'd never been abroad. But now that he knew how close it was, why . . .

He shook his head sharply. What *was* he thinking about, he asked himself angrily. Daydreaming of all things! Babylon was perhaps ten thousand or more miles away from where he sat, not the mere seventy of the rhyme. He couldn't get there in a hundred candlelights, nor many times that number. But for a moment it had seemed so clear, so simple, that he'd actually wondered why he'd never made the trip.

He smiled bleakly to himself. *Wish it really were easy.* But back to work. He took a soft brush from his desk and began to dust the little urn gently. An interesting piece. Probably not valuable, for it looked like a fairly common votary urn, as might have been found in any Babylonian household. Well . . . he amended his thoughts, studying its engraved sides, maybe not just any . . . it didn't quite fit the standard designs.

He turned it around in interest. No, it certainly didn't fit the usual patterns after all. And—why should it? If it had, the expedition wouldn't probably have bothered to air-express it to him. It had to be something they hadn't been able to classify properly, and so had hoped that he would be able to look it up in the more detailed library and references available here at the college.

So then what was it? He turned it over and squirmed uncomfortably in his seat, feeling an irritated mood come over him. He suddenly felt restless. The urn could possibly have held a votary light. It might have been possible to put a little oil in it and fire it; but it didn't quite seem to fit that bill. He bent over, looked sharply at the hollowed-out interior, poked a finger into it and scratched the side with his nail.

He looked at his fingernail with surprise. Wax. There was a slight trace of wax inside the stone urn. Maybe it was a candle-holder . . . but that, he told himself immediately, was silly. They didn't have candles in 2500 B.C.

On the other hand there was no reason to believe that the expedition had just dug it up. They might have found it for sale in some dark shop or dingy market place booth in Baghdad. It might have been used by some Iraqi for years before it found a place in the merchant's stall. There were many instances of ancient objects that had been found on the desert by wandering Arabs, who had used them for their own living purposes when they had seemed useful. Of course nowadays the Arabs were on the lookout for such stuff, to sell to the curious Westerners. But years ago, a century or two meant little in those ancient lands . . . Yes, he supposed it might have served sometime during the past four thousand years as a candlestick.

28

Can I get there by candlelight? Well, by this candlelight, maybe Babylon had indeed been only walking distance. Barry studied the engravings.

They displayed the usual Babylonian bas-relief technique: a bearded god walking stiffly, holding an object in one hand, the other raised to shield it. On the other side of the small cylindrical urn, opposite the walking god, was a giant coiled and winged snake upon whose head rose two curving horns and from whose mouth a flame was emitted. Not unconventional, thought Barry, yet he'd never quite seen the like.

Why—the object the man was carrying was a light. Barry was astonished at this realization. The god was walking with a light in his hand. And there was something else, his expert eyes now noticed: at the back of the god's feet were tiny wings. The artist had meant to convey that the figure was moving rapidly. *If your heels are nimble and light,* Barry's mind interjected idiotically.

"Oh, stuff!" Barry said aloud, surprising himself. What *was* getting into him. He was becoming dreamy. What if the man did have winged heels? That was coincidence; you might find a hundred such examples.

What I need, Barry thought, is a little exercise. I'm getting silly sitting here on a lovely sunny day like this. My mind is falling asleep. He stood up, carefully set the little black urn down, started for the door. At the door he stopped, paused a moment with an odd feeling that there must be something better to do than walking, then finally left his study, closed the door, and went for a walk.

As he passed his neighbor still seated in her yard with her child, Barry nodded politely. She still had the big Mother Goose book open on her lap.

He walked along the sunny streets of the college town with wide strides. He liked to walk, found it good exercise to calm the nerves and steady the thoughts. He began to analyse his irritation.

Somehow that nursery rhyme had got beneath his skin. It had been coincidence of course, but still, it made you think, it did.

Barry had done some work in his own student years on Middle English literature and some of his research had crossed the Mother Goose lore. He knew that many of the apparently pointless verses had once had very definite meanings. Time had erased their references and what now remained were apparently silly jingles.

For instance there was the one about Little Jack Horner, which referred to an actual personage of that name. This person, some sort of minor official in England five hundred years ago, had won himself a "plum" in the royal Christmas honors for doing some sort of secret toadying never made public. The verse had been made up in mockery by his enemies and popularized around the taverns.

Perhaps more obvious was the one about "Hark, hark, the dogs do bark," and the beggars who came to town, having some among them in *silken gowns*. This was essentially the same deal—nobility coming to beg favors of the king at Christmas-time. The people in inns and marketplaces had a way of disguising their digs at their social betters in such a fashion as to avoid *lese majesté*.

And of course the one about Banbury Cross which referred to Lady Godiva's ride.

Barry remembered his amazement at the grim story behind what had seemed one of the silliest—that about Goosey, Goosey Gander and the old man who "would not say his prayers." This was a memorial of murder most black on a day of great evil. Yet, *How many miles to Babylon* . . .

He walked steadily through the streets, thinking about it. He worked the rhyme over, tore it apart, but still he could not fathom its possible original meaning. Finally he turned back and strode home. Once returned, he felt refreshed from the air and the exercise; he sat down again at his desk, renewed his attack on the little black urn.

He worked on it for the remainder of the afternoon, digging out his files, studying pictures of similar vessels and of Babylonian deities and demons. By nightfall he had to admit he'd not gotten near to solution. Nothing fitted the designs exactly, although several seemed superficially close.

He went in to supper, found himself drifting back in thought to the urn and to the silly rhyme alternately. He was annoyed at his failure to get his mind off the side issue. He could ask some of the Lit. faculty about the verse, he thought. Probably they could tell him its origin and meaning in a minute. But not tonight.

After eating, he read the evening paper, turned on the television, watched a comedian for an hour, found him neither funny nor relaxing, turned off the machine, decided to go to bed. He was still oddly irritated, still keyed up by the obstacle to his intellect. After all, with Babylon only threescore miles and ten away . . . "by candlelight" that is, his mind corrected himself as he entered the bedroom.

What silly thoughts! Maybe by morning he'd get that jingle out of his head and be able to look at the relic in a less clouded light. He undid his tie, hesitated. "Maybe I'd better have another glance at

30

that thing," he murmured to himself. He left the bedroom, passed through the dark hall, and entered his study.

He switched the desk light on and took the little urn in his hand, studying the figure. The man was indeed walking somewhere by candlelight. And his heels *were* nimble and light.

Yet even so, Barry's mind slipped in a new twist, what man could walk seventy miles in the time it would take a candle to burn down? Assuming even that it was a large candle, it would last at most four or five hours. That meant walking at least fifteen miles an hour. He had heard somewhere that a man could run at that rate for perhaps a few seconds, but certainly not for hours.

And then of course it wasn't really seventy miles—it was twice that, because you have to get back again, too. And by the same candlelight incidentally.

That definitely put it out of possible class.

Another idea struck Barry. Maybe if he put a candle into the black stone relic and lit it, perhaps it would put some sort of special angle on the engravings and bring out some unnoticed secret details. He'd heard of such things in Egyptian statuary. Anyway, it would be an amusing experiment.

He looked around. There was a candle sticking in an ornamental silver holder on the mantel in the study. He took it down, tried the candle into the hollowed space and found it just fit, tight and neat.

He reached into his pocket for his lighter, flicked it, and lit the candle. Then, to complete the effect, he switched off the desk light.

The candlelight flickered in the room, throwing moving shadows all about. Barry stared at the black urn but it was in darkness from the glow above.

"How many miles to Babylon?" he said under his breath. And quick as a flash his mind answered:

"Three score miles and ten."

Why, of course, he thought, *of course!* It should have been *obvious,* but he asked aloud: "Can I get there by candlelight?"

Yes, and back again. It was so certain that he arose from his seat, holding the candle in its black Babylonian container, and, shielding it with his other hand from drafts, strode confidently to the door, out the hall, opened the front door, and walked out into the street.

It was all so incredibly clear now. You could go anywhere you wished if you just saw it the right way. Why, he marveled, there are two ways of getting anywhere—the difficult, ordinary way everyone stuck to—and the *obvious* way.

"If your heels are nimble and light," he said happily to himself, and increased his pace springily. "My heels are nimble and light—I'm a naturally fast walker," he laughingly told himself. His body was tingling with excitement, his mind seemed clearer than ever before. Why hadn't he ever seen how simple it was, how fast one could go places this way, this simple clear *shortcut* way!

"You may get there by candlelight," he laughed aloud, holding the candle high before him, shielding it with outstretched hand and pacing breathlessly through the night. The flickering yellow flame cast little light about. He could see almost nothing in the blackness about him. Somehow he didn't expect to. Not by the shortcut; you won't get scenery. The idea is to get there and I shall. Only seventy miles, Barry thought, and I must be eating that up fast. I'll get there before this candle is half gone.

He walked faster, the light flickering before him, the opaque dark all about. Beneath his feet was the crunch of dirt and then the swishing resiliency of sand.

Suddenly before him loomed a wall. He stopped, almost bumping into it. His breath was fast; he had been walking hard, but he was in perfect spirits. It was a bit cold out here, he thought, not as warm as it should be.

But it gets cold quickly on the desert, he thought. He held the candle up. The wall was old, it was sandswept and time-worn. It was ancient, and it was—he saw from the faint traceries of weather-worn carvings—Babylonian. He looked up feeling suddenly faint and uneasy.

There were stars above him and in their pale glow he saw that he was standing out on a desert, in the midst of a barren desert, broken here and there by bits of projecting stone, partial walls broken by time, bits of excavated basements. A thin cold wind was blowing from somewhere and there was nothing living in sight.

The candle flickered in his hand. His hand suddenly shook as with the ague, as with terror. He stared about. The candle flickered again. Something, something was breathing on it, breathing over his shoulder from behind him.

If the candle went out, he'd never get back. And as the thought struck him, at that very moment the candle—only half burned—flickered again. A nauseating breath blew past his shoulder and the candle went out.

In a split second Barry Kane remembered the other half of the engraving on the black urn, the half turned away from the walking god with the nimble heels and the light, the thing towards which his nimble steps were surely directed. He turned his head quickly, looked over his shoulder.

Now he knew that there was another significance to the injunction, *if your heels are nimble and light.* It didn't just apply to the getting there; it also meant getting back. And he'd dallied too long in Babylon.

For the ancient Babylonian sculptor had been a good artist. The engraving was true to life.

Berenice

By Edgar Allan Poe

Dicebant mihi sodales,
si sepulchrum amicae visitarem,
curas meas aliquar tulum fore levatas.

—*Ebn Zaiat*

Misery is manifold. The wretchedness of earth is multiform. Overreaching the wide horizon as the rainbow, its hues are as various as the hues of that arch—as distinct too, yet as intimately blended. Overreaching the wide horizon as the rainbow! How is it that from beauty I have derived a type of unloveliness?—from the covenant of peace, a simile of sorrow? But, as in ethics, evil is a consequence of good, so, in fact, out of joy is sorrow born. Either the memory of past bliss is the anguish of to-day, or the agonies which *are,* have their origin in the ecstasies which *might have been.*

My baptismal name is Egaeus; that of my family I will not mention. Yet there are no towers in the land more time-honored than my gloomy, gray, hereditary halls. Our line has been called a race of visionaries; and in many striking particulars—in the character of the family mansion—in the frescos of the chief saloon—in the tapestries of the dormitories—in the chiselling of some buttresses in the armory—but more especially in the gallery of antique paintings—in the fashion of the library chamber—and, lastly, in the very peculiar nature of the library's contents—there is more than sufficient evidence to warrant the belief.

The recollections of my earliest years are connected with that chamber, and with its volumes—of which latter I will say no more. Here died my mother. Herein was I born. But it is mere idleness to say that I had not lived before—that the soul has no previous existence. You deny it? —let us not argue the matter. Convinced myself, I seek not to convince. There is, however, a remembrance of aërial forms—of spiritual and meaning eyes—of sounds, musical yet sad; a remembrance which will not be excluded; a memory like a shadow—vague, variable, indefinite, unsteady; and like a shadow, too, in the impossibility of my getting rid of it while the sunlight of my reason shall exist.

In that chamber was I born. Thus awakening from the long night of what seemed, but was not, nonentity, at once into the very regions of fairy land—into a palace of imagination—into the wild dominions of monastic thought and erudition—it is not singular that I gazed around me with a startled and ardent eye—that I loitered away my boyhood in books, and dissipated my youth in revery; but it *is* singular, that as years rolled away, and the noon of manhood found me still in the mansion of my fathers—it *is* wonderful what a stagnation there fell upon the springs of my life—wonderful how total an inversion took place in the character of my commonest thought. The realities of the world affected me as visions, and as visions only, while the wild ideas of the land of dreams became, in turn, not the material of my every-day existence, but in very deed that existence utterly and solely in itself.

Berenice and I were cousins, and we grew up together in my paternal halls. Yet differently we grew—I, ill of health, and buried in gloom—she, agile, graceful, and overflowing with energy; hers the ramble on the hillside—mine, the studies of the cloister; I, living within my own heart, and addicted, body and soul, to the most intense and painful meditation—she, roaming carelessly through life, with no thought of the shadows in her path, or the silent flight of the raven-winged hours. Berenice!—I call upon her name—Berenice!—and from the gray ruins of memory a thousand tumultuous recollections are startled at the sound! Ah, vividly is her image before me now, as in the early days of her light-heartedness and joy! Oh, gorgeous yet fantastic beauty! Oh, sylph amid the shrubberies of Arnheim! Oh, Naiad among its fountains! And then—then all is mystery and terror, and a tale which should not be told. Disease—a fatal disease, fell like the simoon upon her frame; and even, while I gazed upon her, the spirit of change swept over her, pervading her mind, her habits, and her character, and, in a manner the most subtle and terrible, disturbing even the identity of her person! Alas! the destroyer came and went!—and the victim—where is she? I knew her not—or knew her no longer as Berenice!

Among the numerous train of maladies superinduced by that fatal and primary one which effected a revolution of so horrible a kind in the moral and physical being of my cousin, may be mentioned as the most distressing and obstinate in its nature, a species of epilepsy not unfrequently terminating in *trance* itself—trance very nearly resembling positive dissolution, and from which her manner of recovery was, in most instances, startlingly abrupt. In the meantime, my own disease—for I have been told that I should call it by no other appellation—my own disease, then, grew rapidly upon me, and assumed finally a monomaniac character of a novel and extraordinary form—hourly and momently gaining vigor—and at length obtaining over me the most incomprehensible ascendency. This monomania, if I must so term it, consisted in a morbid irritability of those properties of the mind in metaphysical science termed the *attentive*. It is more than probable that I am not understood; but I fear, indeed, that it is in no manner possible to convey to the mind of the merely general reader, an adequate idea of that nervous *intensity of interest* with which, in my case, the powers of meditation (not to speak technically) busied and buried themselves, in the contemplation of even the most ordinary objects of the universe.

To muse for long unwearied hours, with my attention riveted to some frivolous device on the margin or in the typography of a book; to become absorbed, for the better part of a summer's day, in a quaint shadow falling aslant upon the tapestry or upon the floor; to lose myself, for an entire night, in watching the steady flame of a lamp, or the embers of a fire; to dream away whole days over the perfume of a flower; to repeat, monotonously, some common word, until the sound, by dint of frequent repetition, ceased to convey any idea whatever to the mind; to lose all sense of motion or physical existence, by means of absolute bodily quiescence long and obstinately persevered in: such were a few of the most common and least pernicious vagaries induced by a condition of the mental faculties, not, indeed, altogether unparalleled, but certainly bidding defiance to any thing like analysis or explanation.

Yet let me not be misapprehended. The undue, earnest, and morbid attention thus excited by objects in their own nature frivolous, must not be confounded in character with that ruminating propensity common to all mankind, and more especially indulged in by persons of ardent imagination. It was not even, as might be at first supposed, an extreme condition, or exaggeration of such propensity, but primarily and essentially distinct and different. In the one instance, the dreamer, or enthusiast, being interested by an object usually *not* frivolous, imperceptibly loses sight of this object in a wilderness of deductions and suggestions issuing therefrom, until, at the conclusion of a day-dream *often replete with luxury,* he finds the *incitamentum,* or first cause of his musings, entirely vanished and forgotten. In my case, the primary object was *invariably frivolous,* although assuming, through the medium of my distempered vision, a refracted and unreal importance. Few deductions, if any, were made; and those few pertinaciously returning in upon the original object as a centre. The meditations were *never* pleasurable; and at the termination of the revery, the first cause, so far from being out of sight, had attained that supernaturally exaggerated interest which was the prevailing feature of the disease. In a word, the powers of mind more particularly exercised were, with me, as I have said before, the *attentive,* and are, with the daydreamer, the *speculative.*

My books, at this epoch, if they did not actually serve to irritate the disorder, partook, it will be perceived, largely, in their imaginative and inconsequential nature, of the characteristic qualities of the disorder itself. I well remember, among others, the treatise of the noble Italian, Coelius Secundus Curio, "*De Amplitudine Beati Regni Dei*"; St. Austin's great work, "The City of God"; and Tertullian's "*De Carne Christi,*" in which the paradoxical sentence, "*Mortuus est Dei filius; credibile est quia ineptum est; et sepultus resurrexit; certum est quia impossible est,*" occupied my undivided time, for many weeks of laborious and fruitless investigation.

Thus it will appear that, shaken from its balance only by trivial things, my reason bore resemblance to that ocean-crag spoken of by Ptolemy Hephestion, which steadily resisting the attacks of human violence, and the fiercer fury of the waters and the winds, trembled only to the touch of the flower called Asphodel. And although, to a careless thinker, it might appear a matter beyond doubt, that the alteration produced by her unhappy malady, in the *moral* condition of Berenice, would afford me many objects for the exercise of that intense and abnormal meditation whose nature I have been at some trouble in explaining, yet such was not in any degree the case. In the lucid intervals of my infirmity, her calamity, indeed, gave me pain, and, taking deeply to heart that total wreck of her fair and gentle life, I did not fail to ponder, frequently and bitterly, upon the wonder-working means by which so strange a revolution had been so suddenly brought to pass. But these reflections partook not of the idiosyncrasy of my disease, and were such as would have occurred, under similar circumstances, to the ordinary mass of mankind. True to its own character, my disorder revelled in the less important but more startling changes wrought in the *physical* frame of Berenice—in the singular and most appalling distortion of her personal identity.

During the brightest days of her unparalleled beauty, most surely I had never loved her. In the strange anomaly of my existence, feelings with me, *had never been* of the heart, and my passions *always were* of the mind. Through the gray of the early morning—among the trellised shadows of the forest at noonday—and in the silence of my library at night—she had flitted by my eyes, and I had seen her—not as the living and breathing Berenice, but as the Berenice of a dream; not as a being of the earth, earthy, but as the abstraction of such a being; not as a thing to admire, but to analyze; not as an object of love, but as the theme of the most abstruse although desultory speculation. And *now*—now I shuddered in her presence, and grew pale at her approach; yet, bitterly lamenting her fallen and desolate condition, I called to mind that she had loved me long, and, in an evil moment, I spoke to her of marriage.

And at length the period of our nuptials was approaching, when, upon an afternoon in the winter of the year—one of those unseasonably warm, calm, and misty days which are the nurse of the beautiful Halcyon,[1]—I sat (and sat, as I thought, alone) in the inner apartment of the library. But, uplifting my eyes, I saw that Berenice stood before me.

Was it my own excited imagination—or the misty influence of the atmosphere—or the uncertain twilight of the chamber—or the gray draperies which fell around her figure—that caused in it so vacillating and indistinct an outline? I could not tell. She spoke no word; and I—not for worlds could I have uttered a syllable. An icy chill ran through my frame; a sense of insufferable anxiety oppressed me; a consuming curiosity pervaded my soul; and, sinking back upon the chair, I remained for some time breathless and motionless, with my eyes riveted upon her person. Alas! its emaciation was excessive, and not one vestige of the former being lurked in any single line of the contour. My burning glances at length fell upon the face.

The forehead was high, and very pale, and singularly placid; and the once jetty hair fell partially over it, and overshadowed the hollow temples with innumerable ringlets, now of a vivid yellow, and jarring discordantly, in their fantastic character, with the reigning

---

[1] For as Jove, during the winter season, gives twice seven days of warmth, men have called this clement and temperate time the nurse of the beautiful Halcyon.—*Simonides*.

melancholy of the countenance. The eyes were lifeless, and lustreless, and seemingly pupilless, and I shrank involuntarily from their glassy stare to the contemplation of the thin and shrunken lips. They parted; and in a smile of peculiar meaning, *the teeth* of the changed Berenice disclosed themselves slowly to my view. Would to God that I had never beheld them, or that, having done so, I had died!

The shutting of a door disturbed me, and looking up, I found that my cousin had departed from the chamber. But from the disordered chamber of my brain, had not, alas! departed, and would not be driven away, the white and ghastly *spectrum* of the teeth. Not a speck on their surface—not a shade on their enamel—not an indenture in their edges—but what that brief period of her smile had sufficed to brand in upon my memory. I saw them *now* even more unequivocally than I beheld them *then*. The teeth!—the teeth! —they were here, and there, and everywhere, and visibly and palpably before me; long, narrow, and excessively white, with the pale lips writhing about them, as in the very moment of their first terrible development. Then came the full fury of my *monomania,* and I struggled in vain against its strange and irresistible influence. In the multiplied objects of the external world I had no thoughts but for the teeth. For these I longed with a frenzied desire. All other matters and all different interests became absorbed in their single contemplation. They—they alone were present to the mental eye, and they, in their sole individuality, became the essence of my mental life. I held them in every light. I turned them in every attitude. I surveyed their characteristics. I dwelt upon their peculiarities. I pondered upon their conformation. I mused upon the alteration in their nature. I shuddered as I assigned to them, in imagination, a sensitive and sentient power, and, even when unassisted by the lips, a capability of moral expression. Of Mademoiselle Salle it has been well said: *"Que tous ses pas étaient des sentiments,"* and of Berenice I more seriously believed *que tous ses dents étaient des idées. Des idées!*—ah, here was the idiotic thought that destroyed me! *Des idées!*—ah, *therefore* it was that I coveted them so madly! I felt that their possession could alone ever restore me to peace, in giving me back to reason.

And the evening closed in upon me thus—and then the darkness came, and tarried, and went—and the day again dawned—and the mists of a second night were now gathering around—and still I sat motionless in that solitary room—and still I sat buried in meditation—and still the *phantasma* of the teeth maintained its terrible ascendancy, as, with the most vivid and hideous distinctness, it floated about amid the changing lights and shadows of the chamber. At length there broke in upon my dreams a cry as of horror and dismay; and thereunto, after a pause, succeeded the sound of troubled voices, intermingled with many low moanings of sorrow or of pain. I arose from my seat, and throwing open one of the doors of the library, saw standing out in the antechamber a servant maiden, all in tears, who told me that Berenice was—no more! She had been seized with epilepsy in the early morning, and now, at the closing in of the night, the grave was ready for its tenant, and all the preparations for the burial were completed.

I found myself sitting in the library, and again sitting there alone. It seemed to me that I had newly awakened from a confused and exciting dream. I knew that it was now midnight, and I was well aware, that since the setting of the sun, Berenice had been interred. But of that dreary period which intervened I had no positive, at least no definite, comprehension. Yet its memory was replete with horror—horror more horrible from being vague, and terror more terrible from ambiguity. It was a fearful page in the record of my existence, written all over with dim, and hideous, and unintelligible recollections. I strived to decipher them, but in vain; while ever and anon, like the spirit of a departed sound, the shrill and piercing shriek of a female voice seemed to be ringing in my ears. I had done a deed—what was it? I asked myself the question aloud, and the whispering echoes of the chamber answered me—*"What was it?"*

On the table beside me burned a lamp, and near it lay a little box. It was of no remarkable character, and I had seen it frequently before, for it was the property of the family physician; but how came it *there,* upon my table, and why did I shudder in regarding it? These things were in no manner to be accounted for, and my eyes at length dropped to the open pages of a book, and to a sentence underscored therein. The words were the singular but simple ones of the poet Ebn Zaiat:—*"Dicebant mihi sodales si sepulchrum amicae visitarem, curas meas aliquantulum fore levatas."* Why, then, as I perused them, did the hairs of my head erect themselves on end, and the blood of my body become congealed within my veins?

There came a light tap at the library door—and, pale as the tenant of a tomb, a menial entered upon tiptoe. His looks were wild with terror, and he spoke to me in a voice tremulous, husky, and very low. What said he? —some broken sentences I heard. He told of a wild cry disturbing the silence of the night—of the gathering together of the household—of a search in the direction of the sound; and then his tones grew thrillingly distinct as he whispered me of a violated grave—of a disfigured body enshrouded, yet still breathing—still palpitating—*still alive!*

He pointed to my garments; they were muddy and clotted with gore. I spoke not, and he took me gently by the hand: it was indented with the impress of human nails. He directed my attention to some object against the wall. I looked at it for some minutes: it was a spade. With a shriek I bounded to the table, and grasped the box that lay upon it. But I could not force it open; and, in my tremor, it slipped from my hands, and fell heavily, and burst into pieces; and from it, with a rattling sound, there rolled out some instruments of dental surgery, intermingled with thirty-two small, white, and ivory-looking substances that were scattered to and fro about the floor.

Beyond the Wall

By Ambrose Bierce

Many years ago, on my way from Hongkong to New York, I passed a week in San Francisco. A long time had gone by since I had been in that city, during which my ventures in the Orient had prospered beyond my hope; I was rich and could afford to revisit my own country to renew my friendship with such of the companions of my youth as still lived and remembered me with the old affection. Chief of these, I hoped, was Mohun Dampier, an old schoolmate with whom I had held a desultory correspondence which had long ceased, as is the way of correspondence between men. You may have observed that the indisposition to write a merely social letter is in the ratio of the square of the distance between you and your correspondent. It is a law.

I remembered Dampier as a handsome, strong young fellow of scholarly tastes, with an aversion to work and a marked indifference to many of the things that the world cares for, including wealth, of which, however, he had inherited enough to put him beyond the reach of want. In his family, one of the oldest and most aristocratic in the country, it was, I think, a matter of pride that no member of it had ever been in trade nor politics, nor suffered any kind of distinction. Mohun was a trifle sentimental, and had in him a singular element of superstition, which led him to the study of all manner of occult subjects, although his sane mental health safeguarded him against fantastic and perilous faiths. He made daring incursions into the realm of the unreal without renouncing his residence in the partly surveyed and charted region of what we are pleased to call certitude.

The night of my visit to him was stormy. The Californian winter was on, and the incessant rain plashed in the deserted streets, or, lifted by irregular gusts of wind, was hurled against the houses with incredible fury. With no small difficulty my cabman found the right place, away out toward the ocean beach, in a sparsely populated suburb. The dwelling, a rather ugly one, apparently, stood in the center of its grounds, which as nearly as I could make out in the gloom were destitute of either flowers or grass. Three or four trees, writhing and moaning in the torment of the tempest, appeared to be trying to escape from their dismal environment and take the chance of finding a better one out at sea. The house was a two-story brick structure with a tower, a story higher, at one corner. In a window of that was the only visible light. Something in the appearance of the place made me shudder, a performance that may have been assisted by a rill of rain-water down my back as I scuttled to cover in the doorway.

In answer to my note apprising him of my wish to call, Dampier had written, "Don't ring—open the door and come up." I did so. The staircase was dimly lighted by a single gas-jet at the top of the second flight. I managed to reach the landing without disaster and entered by an open door into the lighted square room of the tower. Dampier came forward in gown and slippers to receive me, giving me the greeting that I wished, and if I had held a thought that it might more fitly have been accorded me at the front door the first look at him dispelled any sense of his inhospitality.

He was not the same. Hardly past middle age, he had gone gray and had acquired a pronounced stoop. His figure was thin and angular, his face deeply lined, his complexion dead-white, without a touch of color. His eyes, unnaturally large, glowed with a fire that was almost uncanny.

He seated me, proffered a cigar, and with grave and obvious sincerity assured me of the pleasure that it gave him to meet. Some unimportant conversation followed, but all the while I dominated by a melancholy sense of the great change in him.

he must have perceived, for he suddenly said with a bright enough smile, "You are disappointed in me—*non sum qualis eram.*"

I hardly knew what to reply, but managed to say: "Why, really, I don't know: your Latin is about the same."

He brightened again. "No," he said, "being a dead language, it grows in appropriateness. But please have the patience to wait: where I am going there is perhaps a better tongue. Will you care to have a message in it?"

The smile faded as he spoke, and as he concluded he was looking into my eyes with a gravity that distressed me. Yet I would not surrender myself to his mood, nor permit him to see how deeply his prescience of death affected me.

"I fancy that it will be long," I said, "before human speech will cease to serve our need; and then the need, with its possibilities of service, will have passed."

He made no reply, and I too was silent, for the talk had taken a dispiriting turn, yet I knew not how to give it a more agreeable character. Suddenly, in a pause of the storm, when the dead silence was almost startling by contrast with the previous uproar, I heard a gentle tapping, which appeared to come from the wall behind my chair. The sound was such as might have been made by a human hand, not as upon a door by one asking admittance, but rather, I thought, as an agreed signal, an assurance of someone's presence in an adjoining room; most of us, I fancy, have had more experience of such communications than we should care to relate. I glanced at Dampier. If possibly there was something of amusement in the look he did not observe it. He appeared to have forgotten my presence, and was staring at the wall behind me with an expression in his eyes hat I am unable to name, although my memory of it is as vivid day as was my sense of it then. The situation was embarrassing; I

to take my leave. At this he seemed to recover himself.

lease be seated," he said; "it is nothing—no one is there."

the tapping was repeated, and with the same gentle, slow e as before.

n me," I said, "it is late. May I call tomorrow?"

ed—a little mechanically, I thought. "It is very delicate of e, "but quite needless. Really, this is the only room in d no one is there. At least——" He left the sentence e, and threw up a window, the only opening in the the sound seemed to come. "See."

wing what else to do I followed him to the win- t. A street-lamp some little distance away gave h the murk of the rain that was again falling in

41

torrents to make it entirely plain that "no one was there." In truth there was nothing but the sheer blank wall of the tower.

Dampier closed the window and signing me to my seat resumed his own.

The incident was not in itself particularly mysterious; any one of a dozen explanations was possible (though none has occurred to me), yet it impressed me strangely, the more, perhaps, from my friend's effort to reassure me, which seemed to dignify it with a certain significance and importance. He had proved that no one was there, but in that fact lay all the interest; and he proffered no explanation. His silence was irritating and made me resentful.

"My good friend," I said, somewhat ironically, I fear, "I am not disposed to question your right to harbor as many spooks as you find agreeable to your taste and consistent with your notions of companionship; that is no business of mine. But being just a plain man of affairs, mostly of this world, I find spooks needless to my peace and comfort. I am going to my hotel, where my fellow-guests are still in the flesh."

It was not a very civil speech, but he manifested no feeling about it. "Kindly remain," he said. "I am grateful for your presence here. What you have heard to-night I believe myself to have heard twice before. Now I *know* it was no illusion. That is much to me—more than you know. Have a fresh cigar and a good stock of patience while I tell you the story."

The rain was now falling more steadily, with a low, monotonous susurration, interrupted at long intervals by the sudden slashing of the boughs of the trees as the wind rose and failed. The night was well advanced, but both sympathy and curiosity held me a willing listener to my friend's monologue, which I did not interrupt by single word from beginning to end.

"Ten years ago," he said, "I occupied a ground-floor apartment in one of a row of houses, all alike, away at the other end of town, on what we call Rincon Hill. This had been the best quarter of San Francisco, but had fallen into neglect and decay, partly because the primitive character of its domestic architecture no longer suited the maturing tastes of our wealthy citizens, partly because certain public improvements had made a wreck of it. The dwellings in one of which I lived stood a little way back from street, each having a miniature garden, separated from its neighbors by low iron fences and bisected with mathematical precision a box-bordered gravel walk from gate to door.

"One morning as I was leaving my lodging I observed a girl entering the adjoining garden on the left. It was a warm

June, and she was lightly gowned in white. From her shoulders hung a broad straw hat profusely decorated with flowers and wonderfully beribboned in the fashion of the time. My attention was not long held by the exquisite simplicity of her costume, for no one could look at her face and think of anything earthly. Do not fear; I shall not profane it by description; it was beautiful exceedingly. All that I had ever seen or dreamed of loveliness was in that matchless living picture by the hand of the Divine Artist. So deeply did it move me that, without a thought of the impropriety of the act, I unconsciously bared my head, as a devout Catholic or well-bred Protestant uncovers before an image of the Blessed Virgin. The maiden showed no displeasure; she merely turned her glorious dark eyes upon me with a look that made me catch my breath, and without other recognition of my act passed into the house. For a moment I stood motionless, hat in hand, painfully conscious of my rudeness, yet so dominated by the emotion inspired by that vision of incomparable beauty that my penitence was less poignant than it should have been. Then I went my way, leaving my heart behind.

In the natural course of things I should probably have remained way until nightfall, but by the middle of the afternoon I was back the little garden, affecting an interest in the few foolish flowers I had never before observed. My hope was vain; she did not ar.

a night of unrest succeeded a day of expectation and disap- ent, but on the day after, as I wandered aimlessly about the hood, I met her. Of course I did not repeat my folly of g, nor venture by even so much as too long a look to interest in her; yet my heart was beating audibly. I consciously colored as she turned her big black eyes a look of obvious recognition entirely devoid of bold- y.

ary you with particulars; many times afterward I et never either addressed her or sought to fix her I take any action toward making her acquain- orbearance, requiring so supreme an effort of entirely clear to you. That I was heels over t who can overcome his habit of thought, or r?

sh persons are pleased to call, and others, to be called—an aristocrat; and despite graces, the girl was not of my class. I h it is needless to speak—and some- n orphan, a dependent niece of the

43

impossible elderly fat woman in whose lodging-house she lived. My income was small and I lacked the talent for marrying; it is perhaps a gift. An alliance with that family would condemn me to its manner of life, part me from my books and studies, and in a social sense reduce me to the ranks. It is easy to deprecate such considerations as these and I have not retained myself for the defense. Let judgment be entered against me, but in strict justice all my ancestors for generations should be made co-defendants and I be permitted to plead in mitigation of punishment the imperious mandate of heredity. To a mésalliance of that kind every globule of my ancestral blood spoke in opposition. In brief, my tastes, habits, instinct, with whatever of reason my love had left me—all fought against it. Moreover, I was an irreclaimable sentimentalist, and found a subtle charm in an impersonal and spiritual relation which acquaintance might vulgarize and marriage would certainly dispel. No woman, I argued, is what this lovely creature seems. Love is a delicious dream; why should I bring about my own awakening?

"The course dictated by all this sense and sentiment was obvious. Honor, pride, prudence, preservation of my ideals—all commanded me to go away, but for that I was too weak. The utmost that I could do by a mighty effort of will was to cease meeting the girl, and that I did. I even avoided the chance encounters of the garden, leaving my lodging only when I knew that she had gone to her music lessons, and returning after nightfall. Yet all the while I was as one in a trance, indulging the most fascinating fancies and ordering my entire intellectual life in accordance with my dream. Ah, my friend, as one whose actions have a traceable relation to reason, you cannot know the fool's paradise in which I lived.

"One evening the devil put it into my head to be an unspeakable idiot. By apparently careless and purposeless questioning I learned from my gossipy landlady that the young woman's bedroom ajoined my own, a party-wall between. Yielding to a sudden and coarse impulse I gently rapped on the wall. There was no response, naturally, but I was in no mood to accept a rebuke. A madness was upon me and I repeated the folly, the offense, but again ineffectually, and I had the decency to desist.

"An hour later, while absorbed in some of my infernal studies, I heard, or thought I heard, my signal answered. Flinging down my books I sprang to the wall and as steadily as my beating heart would permit gave three slow taps upon it. This time the response was distinct, unmistakable: one, two, three—an exact repetition of my signal. That was all I could elicit, but it was enough—too much.

"The next evening, and for many evenings afterward, that folly went on, I always having 'the last word.' During the whole period I was deliriously happy, but with the perversity of my nature I persevered in my resolution not to see her. Then, as I should have expected, I got no further answers. 'She is disgusted,' I said to myself, 'with what she thinks my timidity in making no more definite advances'; and I resolved to seek her and make her acquaintance and —what? I did not know, nor do I now know, what might have come of it. I know only that I passed days and days trying to meet her, and all in vain; she was invisible as well as inaudible. I haunted the streets where we had met, but she did not come. From my window I watched the garden in front of her house, but she passed neither in nor out. I fell into the deepest dejection, believing that she had gone away, yet took no steps to resolve my doubt by inquiry of my landlady, to whom, indeed, I had taken an unconquerable aversion from her having once spoken of the girl with less of reverence than I thought befitting.

"There came a fateful night. Worn out with emotion, irresolution and despondency, I had retired early and fallen into such sleep as was still possible to me. In the middle of the night something— some malign power bent upon the wrecking of my peace forever— caused me to open my eyes and sit up, wide awake and listening intently for I knew not what. Then I thought I heard a faint tapping on the wall—the mere ghost of the familiar signal. In a few moments it was repeated: one, two, three—no louder than before, but addressing a sense alert and strained to receive it. I was about to reply when the Adversary of Peace again intervened in my affairs with a rascally suggestion of retaliation. She had long and cruelly ignored me; now I would ignore her. Incredible fatuity—may God forgive it! All the rest of the night I lay awake, fortifying my obstinacy with shameless justifications and—listening.

"Late the next morning, as I was leaving the house, I met my landlady, entering.

" 'Good morning, Mr. Dampier,' she said. 'Have you heard the news?'

"I replied in words that I had heard no news; in manner, that I did not care to hear any. The manner escaped her observation.

" 'About the sick young lady next door,' she babbled on. 'What! you did not know? Why, she has been ill for weeks. And now——'

"I almost sprang upon her. 'And now,' I cried, 'now what?'

" 'She is dead.'

"That is not the whole story. In the middle of the night, as I learned later, the patient, awakening from a long stupor after a week of delirium, had asked—it was her last utterance—that her

46

bed be moved to the opposite side of the room. Those in attendance had thought the request a vagary of her delirium, but had complied. And there the poor passing soul had exerted its failing will to restore a broken connection—a golden thread of sentiment between its innocence and a monstrous baseness owning a blind, brutal allegiance to the Law of Self.

"What reparation could I make? Are there masses that can be said for the repose of souls that are abroad such nights as this—spirits 'blown about by the viewless winds'—coming in the storm and darkness with signs and portents, hints of memory and presages of doom?

"This is the third visitation. On the first occasion I was too skeptical to do more than verify by natural methods the character of the incident; on the second, I responded to the signal after it had been several times repeated, but without result. Tonight's recurrence completes the 'fatal triad' expounded by Parapelius Necromantius. There is no more to tell."

When Dampier had finished his story I could think of nothing relevant that I cared to say, and to question him would have been a hideous impertinence. I rose and bade him good night in a way to convey to him a sense of my sympathy, which he silently acknowledged by a pressure of the hand. That night, alone with his sorrow and remorse, he passed into the Unknown.

The Boarded Window

By Ambrose Bierce

In 1830, only a few miles away from what is now the great city of Cincinnati, lay an immense and almost unbroken forest. The whole region was sparsely settled by people of the frontier—restless souls who no sooner had hewn fairly habitable homes out of the wilderness and attained to that degree of prosperity which to-day we should call indigence than, impelled by some mysterious impulse of their nature, they abandoned all and pushed farther westward, to encounter new perils and privations in the effort to regain the meagre comforts which they had voluntarily renounced. Many of them had already forsaken that region for the remoter settlements, but among those remaining was one who had been of those first arriving. He lived alone in a house of logs surrounded on all sides by the great forest, of whose gloom and silence he seemed a part, for no one had ever known him to smile nor speak a needless word. His simple wants were supplied by the sale or barter of skins of wild animals in the river town, for not a thing did he grow upon the land which, if needful, he might have claimed by right of undisturbed possession. There were evidences of "improvement"—a few acres of ground immediately about the house had once been cleared of its trees, the decayed stumps of which were half concealed by the new growth that had been suffered to repair the ravage wrought by the ax. Apparently the man's zeal for agriculture had burned with a failing flame, expiring in penitential ashes.

The little log house, with its chimney of sticks, its roof of warping clapboards weighted with traversing poles and its "chinking" of clay, had a single door and, directly opposite, a window. The latter, however, was boarded up—nobody could remember a time when it was not. And none knew why it was so closed; certainly not because of the occupant's dislike of light and air, for on those rare occasions when a hunter had passed that lonely spot the recluse had commonly been seen sunning himself on his doorstep if heaven had provided sunshine for his need. I fancy there are few persons living to-day who ever knew the secret of that window, but I am one, as you shall see.

The man's name was said to be Murlock. He was apparently seventy years old, actually about fifty. Something besides years had had a hand in his aging. His hair and long, full beard were white, his gray, lustreless eyes sunken, his face singularly seamed with wrinkles which appeared to belong to two intersecting systems. In figure he was tall and spare, with a stoop of the shoulders—a burden bearer. I never saw him; these particulars I learned from my grandfather, from whom also I got the man's story when I was a lad. He had known him when living near by in that early day.

One day Murlock was found in his cabin, dead. It was not a time and place for coroners and newspapers, and I suppose it was agreed that he had died from natural causes or I should have been told, and should remember. I know only that with what was probably a sense of the fitness of things the body was buried near the cabin, alongside the grave of his wife, who had preceded him by so many years that local tradition had retained hardly a hint of her existence. That closes the final chapter of this true story—excepting, indeed, the circumstance that many years afterward, in company with an equally intrepid spirit, I penetrated to the place and ventured near enough to the ruined cabin to throw a stone against it, and ran away to avoid the ghost which every well-informed boy thereabout knew haunted the spot. But there is an earlier chapter —that supplied by my grandfather.

When Murlock built his cabin and began laying sturdily about with his ax to hew out a farm—the rifle, meanwhile, his means of support—he was young, strong and full of hope. In that eastern country whence he came he had married, as was the fashion, a young woman in all ways worthy of his honest devotion, who shared the dangers and privations of his lot with a willing spirit and light heart. There is no known record of her name; of her charms of mind and person tradition is silent and the doubter is at liberty to entertain his doubt; but God forbid that I should share it! Of their affection and happiness there is abundant assurance in every added day of the man's widowed life; for what but the magnetism of a blessed memory could have chained that venturesome spirit to a lot like that?

One day Murlock returned from gunning in a distant part of the forest to find his wife prostrate with fever, and delirious. There was no physician within miles, no neighbor; nor was she in a condition to be left, to summon help. So he set about the task of nursing her back to health, but at the end of the third day she fell into unconsciousness and so passed away, apparently, with never a gleam of returning reason.

From what we know of a nature like his we may venture to sketch in some of the details of the outline picture drawn by my grandfather. When convinced that she was dead, Murlock had sense enough to remember that the dead must be prepared for burial. In performance of this sacred duty he blundered now and again, did certain things incorrectly, and others which he did correctly were done over and over. His occasional failures to accomplish some simple and ordinary act filled him with astonishment, like that of a drunken man who wonders at the suspension of familiar natural laws. He was surprised, too, that he did not weep—surprised and a little ashamed; surely it is unkind not to weep for the dead. "Tomorrow," he said aloud, "I shall have to make the coffin and dig the grave; and then I shall miss her, when she is no longer in sight; but now—she is dead, of course, but it is all right—it *must* be all right, somehow. Things cannot be so bad as they seem."

He stood over the body in the fading light, adjusting the hair and putting the finishing touches to the simple toilet, doing all mechanically, with soulless care. And still through his consciousness ran an undersense of conviction that all was right—that he should

49

have her again as before, and everything explained. He had had no experience in grief; his capacity had not been enlarged by use. His heart could not contain it all, nor his imagination rightly conceive it. He did not know he was so hard struck; *that* knowledge would come later, and never go. Grief is an artist of powers as various as the instruments upon which he plays his dirges for the dead, evoking from some the sharpest, shrillest notes, from others the low, grave chords that throb recurrent like the slow beating of a distant drum. Some natures it startles; some it stupefies. To one it comes like the stroke of an arrow, stinging all the sensibilities to a keener life: to another as the blow of a bludgeon, which in crushing benumbs. We may conceive Murlock to have been that way affected, for (and here we are upon surer ground than that of conjecture) no sooner had he finished his pious work than, sinking into a chair by the side of the table upon which the body lay, and noting how white the profile showed in the deepening gloom, he laid his arms upon the table's edge, and dropped his face into them, tearless yet and unutterably weary. At that moment came in through the open window a long, wailing sound like the cry of a lost child in the far deeps of the darkening wood! But the man did not move. Again, and nearer than before, sounded that unearthly cry upon his failing sense. Perhaps it was a wild beast; perhaps it was a dream. For Murlock was asleep.

Some hours later, as it afterward appeared, this unfaithful watcher awoke and lifting his head from his arms intently listened —he knew not why. There in the black darkness by the side of the dead, recalling all without a shock, he strained his eyes to see—he knew not what. His senses were all alert, his breath was suspended, his blood had stilled its tides as if to assist the silence. Who—what had waked him, and where was it?

Suddenly the table shook beneath his arms, and at the same moment he heard, or fancied that he heard, a light, soft step— another—sounds as of bare feet upon the floor!

He was terrified beyond the power to cry out or move. Perforce he waited—waited there in the darkness through seeming centuries of such dread as one may know, yet live to tell. He tried vainly to speak the dead woman's name, vainly to stretch forth his hand across the table to learn if she were there. His throat was powerless, his arms and hands were like lead. Then occurred something most frightful. Some heavy body seemed hurled against the table with an impetus that pushed it against his breast so sharply as nearly to overthrow him, and at the same instant he heard and felt the fall of something upon the floor with so violent a thump that the whole house was shaken by the impact. A scuffling ensued, and a confusion of sounds impossible to describe. Murlock had risen to his feet. Fear had by excess forfeited control of his faculties. He flung his hands upon the table. Nothing was there!

There is a point at which terror may turn to madness; and madness incites to action. With no definite intent, from no motive but the wayward impulse of a madman, Murlock sprang to the wall, with a little groping seized his loaded rifle, and without aim discharged it. By the flash which lit up the room with a vivid illumination, he saw an enormous panther dragging the dead woman toward the window, its teeth fixed in her throat! Then there were darkness blacker than before, and silence; and when he returned to consciousness the sun was high and the wood vocal with songs of birds.

The body lay near the window, where the beast had left it when frightened away by the flash and report of the rifle. The clothing was deranged, the long hair in disorder, the limbs lay anyhow. From the throat, dreadfully lacerated, had issued a pool of blood not yet entirely coagulated. The ribbon with which he had bound the wrists was broken; the hands were tightly clenched. Between the teeth was a fragment of the animal's ear.

Boxes

By Al Sarrantonio

They went to see the man who collected boxes.

There were two of them, Nathan and Roger, and they went in the afternoon after lunch and armed with flashlights and code kits. They carried Boy Scout Handbooks in their ski coat pockets, and candybars and a railroad flare which Roger had stolen from his father's workbench. Nathan had a whistle ring and two sticks of gum which he hoarded to himself. They went in October, when the sun was orange-red and large as a hanging jack-o'-lantern, and they went in the afternoon when the leaves danced circles at their feet in the curt wind and when the chill of winter death was beginning to settle in on porches and doorsteps. They went with caps on their heads, and the energetic joy of the young bloomed in their cheeks and in their bright angel eyes.

Sidewalks disappeared under their running feet. Nathan leaped at the near-nude branch of a tree, missing it with an ooof. Roger leaped behind him and touched it.

The wind whistled the dark day's passing.

The man who collected boxes lived at the far end of the farthest block. His house—lonely, square, and brooding—suddenly reared up before them, and they skidded to a halt.

Roger looked at Nathan.

This was the dividing line, the place where innocent adventure stopped and the breaking of rules began. Bicycles were not even allowed to be ridden to this spot. Cats shied away. The lawn around the house of the man who collected boxes was immaculately trimmed, green even in this late time of the year. No dog did his business here.

No tree grew here.

Nathan and Roger shied away from the perfect, straight front walk, crept instead across the forbidden lawn. Breathing lightly, they drew up to the side of the house. Gingerbread brown it was, and seemed still wet to the touch it looked so freshly painted. So fresh that Roger found himself reaching to touch it. Nathan slapped at his hand and motioned for him to be quiet. Roger smiled.

Around to the back they crept, stopping underneath the one window. Shivers went through them both.

They raised their heads.

Inside, dimly lit, were the colors of Christmas morning. Red and green, gold and bronze, silver, blue.

Boxes.

There they were. Stacked one upon the other, butted up against walls, on tables and chairs, filling almost every inch of space. Boxes. Enameled and lacquered, painted in watercolor, pastel, and crayon, of wood, of cardboard, of tin and beaten brass, round, square, oval, triangle, large, little, tiny, nested, oblong, flat, high, decorated with stencils or drawings, some plain, some elaborately carved, lidded, unlidded, hinged, fitted, some with brass pulls, some with brass handles, some with moldings of party colors, others green felt-lined, red felt-lined, violet felt-lined, black felt-lined, flat-topped and dome-topped, pyramid-topped, untopped, some with secret compartments, keys, spring locks, one with a tiny steel padlock, with stained-glass insets, clear-glass insets, round peek holes, false tops, one with stubby teak legs, one with the face of a monkey tattooed to its front, one with the head of a camel carved from its lid-pull, one with trick eyes set into its side that seemed to follow you back and forth, one with a knife spring-jacked into its bottom, ready to fly up on opening, one with tactile poison along its ridged lip, one with the face of a happy clown on its cover that changed to a frown when you turned it upside down. A bright pink one with peeling paint. A chocolate-colored one with a crack in one corner. One that had never been opened—and never could be. One that had never been closed. One encrusted with precious gems: rubies, a topaz, sapphires, a thumb-sized diamond, eight-sided.

Nathan and Roger stared, fascinated, into the room and their eyes made a glue bond with these boxes. This was part of the dream of their plan. To see these boxes. To peer into this forbidden window and witness the treasures of the man who collected boxes.

To be among them.

There was no communication between Nathan and Roger. Their souls were united and separate in this decision. They had come to observe and now they must touch. Boy Scout Handbooks were fumbled out of slick ski parka pockets and paged through. How to open a stuck window? As expected, there was nothing on how to open a closed window, especially one that did not belong to the scout doing the opening. Handbooks went back into pockets, and Roger, in a sudden and triumphant flash of thought, produced a small scout knife, attached to his keychain. It pulled open into a one-inch blade. Nathan was doubtful, but Roger overrode his doubt with enthusiasm.

Eyes peered over the window ledge again.

Boxes beckoned.

With care and the special skill of an amateur, Roger slipped the knife blade under the rubber seal of the outside window and tried to pry it out. Nathan suddenly grabbed his arm, stopping him. He pointed. There was a catch on the horizontal window, and it was in the open position.

Roger pocketed his tiny knife and pulled the window to the side.

It opened with a smooth hiss.

Nathan and Roger exchanged glances.

Behind them, the wind whipped up. An early moon had risen, and shone a pale crescent at their backs. The red sun was sinking. The sky had deepened a notch on the blue color scale, toward eventual black. The air bit cold.

Nathan looked at Roger and thought suddenly of home. Of Dad at six o'clock, coming home with a quart of milk, of the paperboy, of television, of the warm couch and the sharp smell of supper and Mom moving about in the next room. Of sister upstairs, playing her records too loud. Of an apple or late-peach pie, cooling by the kitchen window; the window open a crack to cool the pie but keep the chill out. Of his schoolbooks waiting in his room, neatly stacked; the neon lamp waiting to be buzzed on. Dad reading his paper and the smell of coffee. A warm bed with a crazyquilt coverlet Mom made last winter. The ticking sound of heat coming up in the baseboard. Thoughts of Halloween coming and Thanksgiving coming and Christmas coming. Kickball at recess tomorrow. Late-peach pie and cold milk.

Nathan turned to go and Roger took his arm. A look of reproach crossed his face. Somewhere at the other end of the block a dog barked once, twice. Roger held on to Nathan's arm, pulled his gaze back to the window.

To the boxes inside.

The dog barked again but Nathan did not hear it. Roger looked at him and smiled. Nathan made a step with his hands, locking them together and cradling Roger's foot, hoisting him up and over the ledge. There was momentary silence, and then Roger's face appeared on the other side. He was still smiling. He reached down for Nathan, who now locked his hands in Roger's hands and pulled himself up, over, and in.

Nathan righted himself and heard Roger sliding the window shut behind them.

There was almost nowhere to turn or step. There were boxes to the ceiling. Nathan tried to move deeper into the room and nearly knocked over a large box with carved pull knobs and black polka dots painted on its yellow surface. It tilted and began to fall toward a pile of black lacquer boxes which were stacked upon a cardboard storage box with rope handles. Nathan grabbed at it with both hands, noting its smooth and dustless finish, and righted it.

Roger, meanwhile, had found a pathway of sorts through the boxes and was disappearing behind a bronze-cornered trunk. Nathan hurried to catch up to him.

They both found themselves in a hurricane eye in the center of the room, a tiny cleared out spot walled in on all sides by boxes. It was very dim here, since the fading outside light was cut off by a row of bloodred cubes of diminishing size, starting at the bottom at about three feet square and finishing at the top with a pyramid topper of a tiny box a half inch on a side. There was enough light to see, though, and Roger cut off Nathan's attempt to snap on his flashlight, indicating that it would ruin the effect by having their own light infringe on this treasure room.

Nathan demurred, then agreed.

They sat, Indian style, in their spot and reveled in the boxes. Roger leaned over to his right, plucking at an oval tin circled with painted swans. He opened it, gazed into its bright reflective insides, and closed it again. Nathan stared up at the skyline of boxes around them, and thought how wonderful a dream this would make. There were more colors and pleasing shapes here than anywhere on earth —there must be—and he could think of no place that was more dreamlike. Roger brushed his fingers over the mottled surface of an ebony shoebox-sized box and sighed.

Light became a little dimmer.

There was a sound, and Nathan and Roger were startled. They had forgotten that they had broken into the house of the man who collected boxes; they had forgotten altogether that there was a man connected with these boxes. That had been part of the original adventure—to see the boxes, but above all to see the man who collected them. This they would be able to tell their friends—that they had not only seen the boxes but, most of all, that they had seen the man in the perfect house who kept them.

The sound came again.

It was almost a scrabbling sound—like tiny fiddler crabs loose in a wooden boat and ticking all over its inside surface. An ancient and wheezing sound—old age with claws, moving with slow careful grace and constant, inevitable movement towards its destination.

Nathan and Roger were trapped.

The sound was all around them—slow, inexorable—and, though they were on their feet and fingering their Scout Handbooks, there was nowhere to turn. Nathan could not locate the pathway back to the window; indeed, that pathway had seemed to disappear and even the line of bloodred pyramid boxes no longer stood in quite the same line. The tin box Roger had handled was nowhere to be seen.

There was the sound of a box opening.

Somewhere behind them, or in front of them, or to their left or right. A large box with a large and ponderous lid was being opened. There was a heavy, wheezy breathing. A rattling, dry cough. Another wheezing breath, and then a whispered grunt and the closing of the box lid.

A shuffling sound, the click of a light switch, a shuffling sound once more.

The room was suffused with a dull amber glow, like that in a dusty antique shop. The colors of the boxes deepened and softened.

A dry cough and the shuffling continued.

Abruptly, from behind a box with the grey-painted form of an elephant on it, the man who collected boxes appeared.

Nathan and Roger drew back.

The man who collected boxes shuffled toward them and lifted his heavy head. There were wrinkles there, so many that his eyes were almost lost to view behind them. His hair was the color of white dandelion and looked as though it would, like dandelion, fly away if breathed upon. His hands were veined and trembling, his bones gaunt.

He lifted his head, slowly, and looked out at them through the black shadows of his eyes.

He tried to speak.

He lifted his hand, painfully, and opened his mouth, but only a rasp emerged, dry as yellowed newspaper.

His hand lowered itself to his side.

Nathan looked at Roger.

At that moment, the dog at the end of the block barked again, and Nathan heard it, muffled as it was. He looked at Roger. It was six o'clock.

Late-peach pie would be cooling.

Nathan felt Roger's hand on his arm, but he pulled away. In the pale yellow light he found the slight opening between a dull blue nest of boxes and a charcoal-colored case; he slipped sideways between them and made his way through the maze of boxes to the window, sliding it open. It showed a dark rectangle of the outside world.

He climbed quickly out, hesitating on the ledge.

The dog barked once more, sharply.

He jumped down onto perfect grass.

Behind him as he ran, he heard the shuffle of shoes, and then the clean sound of one lid closing, and then another.

The Candidate

By Henry Slesar

A man's worth can be judged by the calibre of his enemies. Burton Grunzer, encountering the phrase in a pocket-sized biography he had purchased at a newsstand, put the book in his lap and stared reflectively from the murky window of the commuter train. Darkness silvered the glass and gave him nothing to look at but his own image, but it seemed appropriate to his line of thought. How many people were enemies of that face, of the eyes narrowed by a myopic squint denied by vanity the correction of spectacles, of the nose he secretly called patrician, of the mouth that was soft in relaxation and hard when animated by speech or smiles or frowns? How many enemies? Grunzer mused. A few he could name, others he could guess. But it was their calibre that was important. Men like Whitman Hayes, for instance; there was a 24-carat opponent for you. Grunzer smiled, darting a sidelong glance at the seat-sharer beside him, not wanting to be caught indulging in a secret thought. Grunzer was thirty-four; Hayes was twice as old, his white hairs synonymous with experience, an enemy to be proud of. Hayes knew the food business, all right, knew it from every angle: he'd been a wagon jobber for six years, a broker for ten, a food company executive for twenty before the old man had brought him into the organization to sit on his right hand. Pinning Hayes to the mat wasn't easy, and that made Grunzer's small but increasing triumphs all the sweeter. He congratulated himself. He had twisted Hayes's advantages into drawbacks, had made his long years seem tantamount to senility and outlived usefulness; in meetings, he had concentrated his questions on the new supermarket and suburbia phenomena to demonstrate to the old man that times had changed, that the past was dead, that new merchandising tactics were needed, and that only a younger man could supply them. . . .

Suddenly, he was depressed. His enjoyment of remembered victories seemed tasteless. Yes, he'd won a minor battle or two in the company conference room; he'd made Hayes's ruddy face go crimson, and seen the old man's parchment skin wrinkle in a sly grin.

But what had been accomplished? Hayes seemed more self-assured than ever, and the old man more dependent upon his advice. . . .

When he arrived home, later than usual, his wife Jean didn't ask questions. After eight years of a marriage in which, childless, she knew her husband almost too well, she wisely offered nothing more than a quiet greeting, a hot meal, and the day's mail. Grunzer flipped through the bills and circulars, and found an unmarked letter. He slipped it into his hip pocket, reserving it for private perusal, and finished the meal in silence.

After dinner, Jean suggested a movie and he agreed; he had a passion for violent action movies. But first, he locked himself in the bathroom and opened the letter. Its heading was cryptic: *Society for United Action*. The return address was a post office box. It read:

Dear Mr. Grunzer:

    Your name has been suggested to us by a mutual acquaintance. Our organization has an unusual mission which cannot be described in this letter, but which you may find of exceeding interest. We would be gratified by a private discussion at your earliest convenience. If I do not hear from you to the contrary in the next few days, I will take the liberty of calling you at your office.

It was signed, *Carl Tucker, Secretary.* A thin line at the bottom of the page read: *A Nonprofit Organization.*

His first reaction was a defensive one; he suspected an oblique attack on his pocketbook. His second was curiosity: he went to the bedroom and located the telephone directory, but found no organization listed by the letterhead name. *Okay, Mr. Tucker,* he thought wryly, *I'll bite.*

When no call came in the next three days, his curiosity was increased. But when Friday arrived, he forgot the letter's promise in the crush of office affairs. The old man called a meeting with the bakery products division. Grunzer sat opposite Whitman Hayes at the conference table, poised to pounce on fallacies in his statements. He almost had him once, but Eckhardt, the bakery products manager, spoke up in defense of Hayes's views. Eckhardt had only been with the company a year, but he had evidently chosen sides already. Grunzer glared at him, and reserved a place for Eckhardt in the hate chamber of his mind.

At three o'clock, Carl Tucker called.

"Mr. Grunzer?" The voice was friendly, even cheery. "I haven't heard from you, so I assume you don't mind my calling today. Is there a chance we can get together sometime?"

"Well, if you could give me some idea, Mr. Tucker—"

The chuckle was resonant. "We're not a charity organization, Mr. Grunzer, in case you got that notion. Nor do we sell anything. We're more or less a voluntary service group: our membership is over a thousand at present."

"To tell you the truth," Grunzer frowned, "I never heard of you."

"No, you haven't, and that's one of the assets. I think you'll understand when I tell you about us. I can be over at your office in fifteen minutes, unless you want to make it another day."

Grunzer glanced at his calendar. "Okay, Mr. Tucker. Best time for me is right now."

"Fine! I'll be right over."

Tucker was prompt. When he walked into the office, Grunzer's eyes went dismayed at the officious briefcase in the man's right hand. But he felt better when Tucker, a florid man in his early sixties with small, pleasant features, began talking.

"Nice of you to take the time, Mr. Grunzer. And believe me, I'm not here to sell you insurance or razor blades. Couldn't if I tried; I'm a semi-retired broker. However, the subject I want to discuss is rather—intimate, so I'll have to ask you to bear with me on a certain point. May I close the door?"

"Sure," Grunzer said, mystified.

Tucker closed it, hitched his chair closer and said:

"The point is this. What I have to say must remain in the strictest confidence. If you betray that confidence, if you publicize our society in any way, the consequences could be most unpleasant. Is that agreeable?"

Grunzer, frowning, nodded.

"Fine!" The visitor snapped open the briefcase and produced a stapled manuscript. "Now, the society has prepared this little spiel about our basic philosophy, but I'm not going to bore you with it. I'm going to go straight to the heart of our argument. You may not agree with our first principle at all, and I'd like to know that now."

"How do you mean, first principle?"

"Well . . ." Tucker flushed slightly. "Put in the crudest form, Mr. Grunzer, the Society for United Action believes that—*some* people are just not fit to live." He looked up quickly, as if anxious to gauge the immediate reaction. "There, I've said it," he laughed, somewhat in relief. "Some of our members don't believe in my direct approach; they feel the argument has to be broached more discreetly. But frankly, I've gotten excellent results in this rather crude manner. How do you feel about what I've said, Mr. Grunzer?"

"I don't know. Guess I never thought about it much."

"Were you in the war, Mr. Grunzer?"

"Yes. Navy." Grunzer rubbed his jaw. "I suppose I didn't think the Japs were fit to live, back then. I guess maybe there are other cases. I mean, you take capital punishment, I believe in that. Murderers, rape-artists, perverts, hell, I certainly don't think *they're* fit to live."

"Ah," Tucker said. "So you really accept our first principle. It's a question of category, isn't it?"

"I guess you could say that."

"Good. So now I'll try another blunt question. Have you—personally—ever wished someone dead? Oh, I don't mean those casual, fleeting wishes everybody has. I mean a real, deep-down, uncomplicated wish for the death of someone *you* thought was unfit to live. Have you?"

"Sure," Grunzer said frankly. "I guess I have."

"There are times, in your opinion, when the removal of someone from this earth would be beneficial?"

Grunzer smiled. "Hey, what is this? You from Murder, Incorporated or something?"

Tucker grinned back. "Hardly, Mr. Grunzer, hardly. There is absolutely no criminal aspect to our aims or our methods. I'll admit we're a 'secret' society, but we're no Black Hand. You'd be amazed at the quality of our membership; it even includes members of the legal profession. But suppose I tell you how the society came into being?

"It began with two men; I can't reveal their names just now. The year was 1949, and one of these men was a lawyer attached to the district attorney's office. The other man was a state psychiatrist. Both of them were involved in a rather sensational trial, concerning a man accused of a hideous crime against two small boys. In their opinion, the man was unquestionably guilty, but an unusually persuasive defense counsel, and a highly suggestible jury, gave him his freedom. When the shocking verdict was announced, these two, who were personal friends as well as colleagues, were thunderstruck and furious. They felt a great wrong had been committed, and they were helpless to right it. . . .

"But I should explain something about this psychiatrist. For some years, he had made studies in a field which might be called anthropological psychiatry. One of these researches related to the

60

voodoo practice of certain groups, the Haitian in particular. You've probably heard a great deal about voodoo, or Obeah as they call it in Jamaica, but I won't dwell on the subject lest you think we hold tribal rites and stick pins in dolls. . . . But the chief feature of his study was the uncanny *success* of certain strange practices. Naturally, as a scientist, he rejected the supernatural explanation and sought the rational one. And of course, there was only one answer. When the *vodun* priest decreed the punishment or death of a malefactor, it was the malefactor's own convictions concerning the efficacy of the death wish, his own faith in the voodoo power, that eventually made the wish come true. Sometimes, the process was organic—his body reacted psychosomatically to the voodoo curse, and he would sicken and die. Sometimes, he would die by 'accident' —an accident prompted by the secret belief that once cursed, he *must* die. Eerie, isn't it?"

"No doubt," Grunzer said, dry-lipped.

"Anyway, our friend, the psychiatrist, began wondering aloud if *any* of us have advanced so far along the civilized path that we couldn't be subject to this same sort of 'suggested' punishment. He proposed that they experiment on this choice subject, just to see.

"How they did it was simple," he said. "They went to see this man, and they announced their intentions. They told him they were going to *wish him dead*. They explained how and why the wish would become reality, and while he laughed at their proposal, they could see the look of superstitious fear cross his face. They promised him that regularly, every day, they would be wishing for his death, until he could no longer stop the mystic juggernaut that would make the wish come true."

Grunzer shivered suddenly, and clenched his fist. "That's pretty silly," he said softly.

"The man died of a heart attack two months later."

"Of course. I knew you'd say that. But there's such a thing as coincidence."

"Naturally. And our friends, while intrigued, weren't satisfied. *So they tried it again.*"

"Again?"

"Yes, again. I won't recount who the victim was, but I will tell you that this time they enlisted the aid of four associates. This little band of pioneers was the nucleus of the society I represent today."

Grunzer shook his head. "And you mean to tell me there's a *thousand* now?"

"Yes, a thousand and more, all over the country. A society whose one function is to *wish people dead*. At first, membership was purely

61

voluntary, but now we have a system. Each new member of the Society for United Action joins on the basis of submitting one potential victim. Naturally, the society investigates to determine whether the victim is deserving of his fate. If the case is a good one, the *entire* membership then sets about to *wish him dead*. Once the task has been accomplished, naturally, the new member must take part in all future concerted action. That and a small yearly fee, is the price of membership."

Carl Tucker grinned.

"And in case you think I'm not serious, Mr. Grunzer—" He dipped into the briefcase again, this time producing a blue-bound volume of telephone directory thickness. "Here are the facts. To date, two hundred and twenty-nine victims were named by our selection committee. Of those, *one hundred and four* are no longer alive. Coincidence, Mr. Grunzer?

"As for the remaining one hundred and twenty-five—perhaps that indicates that our method is not infallible. We're the first to admit that. But new techniques are being developed all the time. I assure you, Mr. Grunzer, *we will get them all.*"

He flipped through the blue-bound book..

"Our members are listed in this book, Mr. Grunzer. I'm going to give you the option to call one, ten or a hundred of them. Call them and see if I'm not telling the truth."

He flipped the manuscript toward Grunzer's desk. It landed on the blotter with a thud. Grunzer picked it up.

"Well?" Tucker said. "Want to call them?"

"No." He licked his lips. "I'm willing to take your word for it, Mr. Tucker. It's incredible, but I can see how it works. Just *knowing* that a thousand people are wishing you dead is enough to shake hell out of you." His eyes narrowed. "But there's one question. You talked about a 'small' fee—"

"It's fifty dollars, Mr. Grunzer."

"Fifty, huh? Fifty times a thousand, that's pretty good money, isn't it?"

"I assure you, the organization is not motivated by profit. Not the kind you mean. The dues merely cover expenses, committee work, research and the like. Surely you can understand that?"

"I guess so," he grunted.

"Then you find it interesting?"

Grunzer swiveled his chair about to face the window.

God! he thought.

God! if it *really* worked!

But how could it? If wishes became deeds, he would have slaughtered dozens in his lifetime. Yet, that was different. His wishes were always secret things, hidden where no man could know them. But this method was different, more practical, more terrifying. Yes, he could see how it might work. He could visualize a thousand minds burning with the single wish of death, see the victim sneering in disbelief at first, and then slowly, gradually, surely succumbing to the tightening, constricting chain of fear that it *might* work, that so many deadly thoughts could indeed emit a mystical, malevolent ray that destroyed life.

Suddenly, ghostlike, he saw the ruddy face of Whitman Hayes before him.

He wheeled about and said:

"But the victim has to *know* all this, of course? He has to know the society exists, and has succeeded, and is wishing for *his* death? That's essential, isn't it?"

"Absolutely essential," Tucker said, replacing the manuscripts in his briefcase. "You've touched on the vital point, Mr. Grunzer. The victim must be informed, and that, precisely, is what I have done." He looked at his watch. "Your death wish began at noon today. The society has begun to work. I'm very sorry."

At the doorway, he turned and lifted both hat and briefcase in one departing salute.

"Goodbye, Mr. Grunzer," he said.

Cemetery Dance

By Richard T. Chizmar

Elliott Fosse, age thirty-three, small-town accountant. Waiting alone. Dead of winter. After midnight. The deserted gravel parking lot outside of Winchester County Cemetery.

Elliott stared out the truck window at the frozen darkness. His thoughts raced back to the handwritten note in his pants pocket. He reached down and squeezed the denim. The pants were new—bought for work not a week ago and still stiff to the touch—but Elliott could feel the reassuring crinkle of paper inside the pocket.

While the woman on the radio droned on about a snow warning for the entire eastern sector of the state, storm winds rumbled outside, buffeting the truck. Elliott's breath escaped in visible puffs and, despite the lack of heat in the truck, he wiped beads of moisture from his face. With the same hand, he snatched a clear pint bottle from the top of the dash and guzzled, tilting it upward long after it ran dry. He tossed the bottle on the seat next to him—where it clinked against two others—and reached for the door handle.

The wind grabbed him, lashing at his exposed face, and immediately the sweat on his cheeks frosted over. He quickly pulled the flashlight from his pocket and straightened his jacket collar, shielding his neck. The night sky was starless, enveloping the cemetery like a huge, black circus tent. His bare hands shook uncontrollably, the flashlight beam fluttering over the hard ground. Somewhere, almost muffled by the whine of the wind, he heard a distant clanking—a dull sound echoing across the grounds. He hesitated, tried to recognize the source, but failed.

Snow coming soon, he thought, gazing upward.

He touched a hand to the lopsided weight in his coat pocket and slowly climbed the cracked steps leading to the monument gate. During visiting hours, the gate marked the cemetery's main entrance and was always guarded by a grounds keeper; a short, roundish fellow with a bright red beard. But, at one in the morning, the grounds were long closed and abandoned.

The liquor in Elliott's system was no match for the strength of the storm. His legs ached with every step. His eyes and ears stung from the frigid blasts of wind. He longed to rest, but the contents of the note in his pocket pushed him onward. As he reached the last step, he was greeted by a rusty, fist-sized padlock banging loudly against the twin gates. It sounded like a bell tolling, warning the countryside of some unseen danger.

He rested for a moment, supporting himself against the gate, grimacing from the sudden shock of cold steel. He rubbed his hands together, then walked toward a narrow opening, partly concealed by a clump of scrubby thorn bushes, where the fence stopped just short of connecting with the gate's left corner. Easing his body through the space, Elliott felt the familiar tingle of excitement return. He had been here many times before . . . many times.

But tonight was different.

Creeping among the faded white headstones, Elliott noticed for the first time that their placement looked rather peculiar, as if they'd been dropped from the sky in some predetermined pattern. From above, he ruminated, the grounds must look like an overcrowded housing development.

64

Glancing at the sky again, thinking: *Big snow on the way, and soon.* He moved slower now, still confident, but careful not to pass the gravestone.

He had been there before, so many times, but he remembered the first time most vividly—fifteen years ago, during the day.

Everyone had been there. A grim Elliott standing far behind Kassie's parents, hidden among the mourning crowd. Her father, standing proudly, a strong hand on each son's shoulder. The mother, clad in customary black, standing next to him, choking back the tears.

Immediately following the service, the crowd had left the cemetery to gather at her parent's home, but Elliott had stayed. He had waited in the upper oak grove, hidden among the trees. When the workers had finished the burial, he had crept down the hill and sat, talking with his love on the fresh grave. And it had been magical, the first time Kassie really talked to him, shared herself with him. He'd felt her inside him that day and known that it had been right—her death, his killing, a blessing.

High above the cemetery, a rotten tree limp snapped, crashed to the ground below. Elliott's memory of Kassie's funeral vanished. He stood motionless, watching the bare trees shake and sway in the wind, dead branches scraping and rattling against each other. A hazy vision of dancing skeletons and demons surfaced in his mind. *It's called the cemetery dance,* the demons announced, glistening worms squirming from their rotten, toothless mouths. *Come dance with us, Elliott,* they invited, waving long, bony fingers. *Come.* And he wanted to go. They sounded so inviting. *Come dance the cemetery dance . . .*

He shook the thoughts away—*too much liquor, that's all it was*—and walked into a small gully, dragging his feet through the thin blanket of fallen leaves. He recognized the familiar row of stone markers ahead and slowed his pace. Finally, he stopped, steadied the bright beam on the largest slab.

The marker was clean and freshly cared for, the frozen grass around it still neatly trimmed. There were two bundles of cut flowers leaning against it. Elliott recognized the fresh bundle he'd left just yesterday during his lunch break. He crept closer, bending to his knees. Tossing the flashlight aside, he eased next to the white granite stone, touching the deep grooves of the inscription, slowly caressing each letter, stopping at her name.

"Kassie," he whispered, the word swept away with the wind. "I found it, love." He dug deep in his front pocket, pulled out a crumpled scrap of lined white paper. "I couldn't believe you came to me again after all these years. I couldn't believe it . . . but I found the note on my pillow where you left it."

Sudden tears streamed down his face. "I always believed you'd forgive me. I truly did. You know I had to do it . . . it was the only way. You wouldn't even look at me back then," he pleaded. "I *tried* to make you notice me, but you wouldn't . . ."

The cemetery came to life around him, breathing for the dead. The wind gained strength, plastering leaves against tree trunks and headstones. Elliott gripped the paper tightly in his palm, protecting it from the night's constant pull.

"I'm coming now, love," he laughed with nervous relief. "We can be together, forever." He pulled his hand from his coat pocket and looked skyward. *Snow coming, now. Anytime.* A sudden gust of wind sent another branch crashing to the ground where it shattered into hundreds of jagged splinters.

Two gravestones away from it, Elliott collapsed hard to the earth, fingers curled around the pistol's rubber handgrip, locked there now. The single gunshot echoed across the cemetery until the storm swallowed it. Bits of glistening brain tissue sprayed the air, and mixed with the wooden splinters, showering the corpse. His mangled head rocked once, then lolled to the side, spilling more shiny gray matter onto the grassy knoll.

For just one moment, an ivory sliver of moonbeam slipped through the darkness, quickly disappeared. As the crumpled scrap of paper—scrawled in Elliott's own handwriting—was lifted into the wind's possession, the towering trees, once again, found their dancing partners. And it began to snow.

The Certificate

By Avram Davidson

The winter sunrise was still two hours away when Dr. Roger Freeman came to stand in front of the great door. By good fortune—incredibly good fortune—he had not been questioned in his furtive progress from the dormitory. If he had been stopped, or if his answer had been either disbelieved or judged inadequate, he might have been sent back to the dorm for punishment. The punishment would have been over, of course, in time for him to go to work at ten in the morning, but a man could suffer through several thousand eternities of Hell in those few hours. And no more than a low muffled groaning and a subdued convulsive movement of the body to show what was going on. You were able to sleep through it—if it was happening to someone else.

The great door was set well in from the street, and the cutting edge of the wind was broken by it.

Freeman was grateful for that. It was two years ago that he'd applied for a new overcoat, and the one he still had was ragged even then. Perhaps—if this was not to be his year for escape—in another year he would get the coat. He crowded into a corner and tried not to think of the cold.

After a little while another man joined him, then another, then a woman, than a couple. By sunrise there was a long line. They were all willing to risk it, risk punishment for being out before work, or for being late to work. Some merely wanted clothes. Some wanted permission to visit relatives in another locale. You could wait years for either. Or, you could wait years and not get either. And some, like Freeman, hoped against hope for a chance at escape.

Dr. Freeman stared at the door. The design was as intricate as it was incomprehensible. No doubt it made sense to the Hedderans. If you could understand it you might gain some understanding of the nature of their distant home. If you cared. It was fifty years since they had arrived, and men still knew almost nothing about them.

They were here. They would never go away. That was enough.

The man behind Dr. Freeman collapsed. No one paid any attention to him. After a moment there was a high, brief, humming. The man twitched, opened his eyes. He got to his feet.

And then the door opened.

"Proceed in the order," the voice directed—a thick, flat Hedderan voice; harsh, yet glutinous. No one tried to push ahead, the lesson had been too well learned. Dr. Freeman got on the third escalator, rode down two levels. There had been a time when you rode *up*—but that was before the Hedderans came. They didn't like tall buildings—at least it seemed so. They'd never explained—that, or anything else. What they did not like they simply destroyed.

Dr. Freeman looked behind him as he approached the office. There must have been at least a dozen people behind him. They looked at him wolfishly. So few certificates were granted, and he was first in line. He looked away. He'd stayed awake all night in order to *be* the first. No one had the right to resent him. And the next man in line was young. What did he expect . . . ?

The door opened, the voice said, *"Proceed one at a single time."* Fifty years, and the Hedderans still hadn't mastered the language. They didn't have to, of course. Roger Freeman entered the office, took the application form from the slot in the wall-machine found in every office, sat down at the table. When was the last time he had sat in a chair? No matter.

The form was in Hedderan, of course. The voice said, *"Name."* The voice said, *"Number."*

He wrote it down, Roger Freeman . . . 655-673-60-60-2. Idly he glanced at the cluster of Hedderan characters. If one could take the application form away, with Hedderan questions and English answers, perhaps—if there was time—a key could be found for translating. But it was impossible to take it away. If you spoiled it, you were out. You could apply only once a year. And if you *did* find out how to read their language, what then? Freeman's brother Bob had talked of rebellion—but that was years ago . . . and he didn't like to think what had happened to Bob. And besides, he hadn't *time*—he had to be at work by ten.

From ten in the morning until ten at night (the Hedderans had their own ways of reckoning time) he worked at a machine, pulling hard on levers. Some he had to bend down to reach, some he had to mount steps to reach. Up and down, up and down. He didn't know what the machine did, or even how it worked. And he no longer cared. He no longer cared about anything—except a new overcoat (or, at least, a *newer* one, not worn so thin), and his chances of escape.

Age. Occupation. Previous Occupation. Previous to the arrival of the Hedderans, that was. Fifty years ago. He had been a physician. An obsolete skill. Inside of every man nowadays there was a piece of . . . something . . . presumably it communicated with a machine somewhere deep in the Hedderan quarters. If you broke a bone or bled or even if you just fainted (as the young man behind him in line had), you were set right almost in the second. No one was ill for long—even worn-out organs were regenerated. Too few men had been left alive, and the Hedderans needed those who were left too much to let them sicken or die.

At last the long form was filled out. The harsh voice said, *"Now at once to Office Ten, Level Four."*

Dr. Freeman hastily obeyed. When they said 'at once,' they meant just that. The punishment might come like a single whiplash —or it might go on and on. You never knew. Maybe the Hedderans knew. But they never told. The man next behind the outer door scuttled in as Freeman left. The others waited. Not more than three could expect to be processed before it would be time to return to work.

Office Ten, Level Four, asked him the same questions, but in a different order. He was then directed to Office Five, Level Seventeen. Here his two forms were fed into a machine, returned with markings stamped on them in Hedderan.

"Office Eight, Level Two," the voice said. There, he fed his applications into the slot. After a moment they came back—unmarked.

"Name Roger Freeman. Number 655-673-60-60-2. You have a single time application outstanding. Unpermitted two. You will cancel this one. Or you will cancel that one."

Frantically he searched his mind. What application did he have outstanding? When was this rule made? The overcoat! If he went ahead with this new application and it was refused, he'd have to wait till next year to reinstate the one for the coat. And then more years of waiting . . . It was cold, the dormitory was ill-heated, he had no blanket. His present coat was very worn. Services for humans were minimal.

But he *had* to proceed with this new application. He was first in line . . .

"Speak," the thick, flat voice directed. *"Answer. Speak. Now."*

Gobbling his words in haste, Freeman said, "I cancel the one outstanding."

"Insert forms."

He did. Waited.

"Proceed to Office Ten, Level Four."

That was the second place he'd been to. A mistake? No matter, he had to go. Once again he entered. And waited.

A grunting noise caught his eye. He looked up, started, cowered. A Hedderan, his baffle-screen turned off, was gazing at him. The blank, grey, faceted eyes in the huge head, and the body, like a deformed foetus . . . then the baffle-screen went on again. Freeman shuddered. One rarely saw them. It had been years.

A piece of paper slid from the machine. He took it up, waiting for the command to proceed—where? Unless it could be accomplished before ten, there was no chance of escape for him this year. None whatever. He stared dully at the strange characters. The cold indifferent voice said, *"Name Roger Freeman. Number 655-673-60-60-2. Declared surplus. Application for death certificate is granted. Proceed for certificate to Office One, Level Five. At once."*

Tears rolled down Dr. Freeman's cheeks. "At last," he sobbed, joyfully. "At last . . ."

And then he hastily left. He had achieved his escape after all—but only if he got there before ten o'clock.

Cheapskate

By Gary Raisor

Dad drives too fast when he's upset, and Mom says that one day he's going to cause a terrible accident. Maybe even kill somebody. Dad always says the same thing to her: Elizabeth, why don't you cut off my goddamn balls, sling them over the rear-view mirror, and just be done with it?

Boy! Dad must be pissed right now. Because his face is all purple and everything is really whizzing by.

I guess it's mostly my fault that Dad is angry. You see, yesterday, I turned eleven and I was expecting a special present. But I didn't get what I asked for—they gave me a stupid old camera instead.

Can you believe that?

All I wanted was a pair of roller skates. I mean, it wasn't like I didn't drop enough hints.

Mom tried her best to smooth things over with a talk about how this had been a tough year for Dad, what with the economy being in the toilet and all. So I tried to act thrilled about the camera, but I don't think anybody was fooled.

Everything would've been fine, except they decided to dump me with the sitter. I heard them whispering about going to some big party where Mom worked. That was when I started to get mad. If Dad had enough money to take Mom to a dumb old party, then he had money for my roller skates.

I was upstairs, working on a plan, when I heard the sitter come in. Her name is Mary Ann, and Eddie, who lives down the street, said he heard she was a nympho. But nobody pays much attention to Eddie, cause he's been brain-damaged ever since Monica Pfieffer and two of her friends mooned him at the last school picnic.

Things were so boring I lay on the bed and listened while Mom and Mary Ann talked about the new sofa in the living room. Girls sure do get excited about the goofiest stuff.

Mom thinks Mary Ann is sweet, and Dad likes her, too. But I think Dad likes her because she wears mostly jogging shorts. He watches her like our dog, Skippy, watches my plate.

Only Skippy don't drool as much.

Mom told Mary Ann to make herself comfortable while she ran out to the store and picked up a few things. Mom had been gone about two minutes when Dad came out of his study and started sucking up to Mary Ann, asking her dumb stuff like how she liked college and if she had any new boy friends. They were laughing and giggling, so I thought I'd better turn on the TV before I barfed.

I was coming downstairs for a coke when I noticed how quiet it was in the living room.

So I peeked around the corner . . .

They were both sitting on the new sofa. Only Dad had his hands under Mary Ann's top, and he was breathing harder than the last time he tried to wrestle away Mom's Master Card.

I was gonna sneak back up the stairs, but then I got an idea. It was pure genius. After all, Dad *had* bought me a camera to take pictures . . .

Today, while Mom was gone to bunco, I showed one to Dad. He took one look and his face went all pale and sweaty, like he was about to faint or throw up. He kept asking why I would do such a terrible thing. Over and over. It was real monotonous.

Finally I told him to relax, that if he came across with the new roller skates, Mom wouldn't have to see the pictures. He went kinda crazy when I said that. Started making lots of threats. I gotta admit I was scared, but, after a while, he calmed down. Except for a big vein in his forehead that kept jumping around.

Then he asked, real quiet like, if this was going to be a one-time deal or if there would be other demands.

I said I didn't know. We'd have to see how my next birthday went. He sighed, just like he does when Mom gets the upper hand, and I knew he was gonna give in. All the air oozed out of him and he sort of slumped over.

So we went out and picked up a real nifty pair of roller skates, and Dad said I could even wear them home. But I don't think we're going to make it home. Dad is driving too fast and he's not keeping his eyes on the road. Mostly, he keeps looking back through the

rear window and smiling. I guess he's checking to make sure the
rope is still tied. He's speeding up again . . . *and I don't think these
skates can go much faster!*

The China Bowl

By E. F. Benson

I had long been on the look-out for one of the small houses at the
south end of that delectable oblong called Barrett's Square, but for
many months there was never revealed to me that which I so much
desired to see—namely, a notice-board advertising that one of these
charming little abodes was to be let.

At length, however, in the autumn of the current year, in one of
my constant passages through the square, I saw what my eye had so
long starved for, and within ten minutes I was in the office of the
agent in whose hands the disposal of No. 29 had been placed.

A communicative clerk informed me that the present lessee, Sir
Arthur Bassenthwaite, was anxious to get rid of the remainder of
his lease as soon as possible, for the house had painful associations
for him, owing to the death of his wife, which had taken place there
not long before. He was a wealthy man, so I was informed, Lady
Bassenthwaite having been a considerable heiress, and was willing
to take what is professionally known as a ridiculously low price, in
order to get the house off his hand without delay. An order 'to view'
was thereupon given me, and a single visit next morning was sufficient to show that this was precisely what I had been looking for.

Why Sir Arthur should be so suddenly anxious to get rid of it, at
a price which certainly was extremely moderate, was no concern of
mine, provided the drains were in good order, and within a week
the necessary business connected with the transference of the lease
was arranged. The house was in excellent repair, and less than a
month from the time I had first seen the notice-board up, I was
ecstatically established there.

I had not been in the house more than a week or two when, one
afternoon, I was told that Sir Arthur had called, and would like to
see me if I was disengaged. He was shown up, and I found myself

72

in the presence of one of the most charming men I have ever had the good fortune to meet.

The motive of his call, it appeared, was of the politest nature, for he wished to be assured that I found the house comfortable and that it suited me. He intimated that it would be a pleasure to him to see round, and together we went over the whole house, with the exception of one room. This was the front bedroom on the third floor, the largest of the two spare rooms, and at the door, as I grasped the handle, he stopped me.

'You will excuse me,' he said, 'for not coming in here. The room, I may tell you, has the most painful associations for me.'

This was sufficiently explicit; I made no doubt that it was in this room that his wife had died.

It was a lovely October afternoon, and, having made the tour of the house, we went out into the little garden with its tiled walk that lay at the back, and was one of the most attractive features of the place. Low brick walls enclosed it, separating it on each side from my neighbours, and at the bottom from the pedestrian thorough-fare that ran past the back of the row of houses.

Sir Arthur lingered here some little while, lost, I suppose, in regretful memories of the days when perhaps he and his compan-ion planned and executed the decoration of the little plot. Indeed, he hinted as much when, shortly after, he took his leave.

'There is so much here,' he said, 'that is very intimately bound up with me. I thank you a thousand times for letting me see the little garden again.'

And once more, as he turned to go into the house, his eyes looked steadfastly and wistfully down the bright borders.

The regulations about the lighting of houses in London had some little while previously demanded a more drastic dusk, and a night or two later, as I returned home after dinner through the impenetrable obscurity of the streets, I was horrified to find a bright light streaming cheerfully from the upper windows in my house, with no blinds to obscure it.

It came from the front bedroom on the third floor, and, letting myself in, I proceeded hurriedly upstairs to quench this forbidden glow. But when I entered, I found the room in darkness, and, on turning up the lights myself, I saw that the blinds were drawn down, so that even if it had been lit, I could not have seen from outside the illumination which had made me hasten upstairs.

An explanation easily occurred to me: no doubt the light I had seen did not come from my house, but from windows of a house adjoining. I had only given one glance at it, and with this demonstration that I had been mistaken, I gave no further conscious thought to the matter. But subconsciously I felt that I knew that I had made no mistake: I had not in that hurried glance confused the windows of the house next door with my own; it was this room that had been lit.

I had moved into the house, as I have said, with extraordinary expedition, and for the next day or two I was somewhat busily engaged, after my day's work was over, in sorting out and largely destroying accumulations of old books and papers, which I had not had time to go through before my move. Among them I came across an illustrated magazine which I had kept for some forgotten reason, and turning over the pages to try to ascertain why I had preserved it, I suddenly came across a picture of my own back-garden. The title at the top of the page showed me that the article in question was an interview with Lady Bassenthwaite, and her portrait and that of her husband made a frontispiece to it.

The coincidence was a curious one, for here I read about the house which I now occupied, and saw what it had been like in the reign of its late owners. But I did not spend long over it, and added the magazine to the pile of papers destined for destruction. This grew steadily, and when I had finished turning out the cupboard which I had resolved to empty before going to bed, I found it was already an hour or more past midnight.

I had been so engrossed in my work that I had let the fire go out, and myself get hungry, and went into the dining-room, which opened into the little back-garden, to see if the fire still smouldered there, and a biscuit could be found in the cupboard. In both respects I was in luck, and whilst eating and warming myself, I suddenly thought I heard a step on the tiled walk in the garden outside.

I quickly went to the window and drew aside the thick curtain, letting all the light in the room pour out into the garden, and there, beyond doubt, was a man bending over one of the beds. Startled by this illumination, he rose, and without looking round, ran to the end of the little yard and, with surprising agility, vaulted on to the top of the wall and disappeared.

But at the last second, as he sat silhouetted there, I saw his face in the shaded light of a gas-lamp outside, and, to my indescribable astonishment, I recognized Sir Arthur Bassenthwaite. The glimpse was instantaneous, but I was sure I was not mistaken, any more than I had been mistaken about the light which came from the bedroom that looked out on to the square.

But whatever tender associations Sir Arthur had with the garden that had once been his, it was not seemly that he should adopt such means of indulging them. Moreover, where Sir Arthur might so easily come, there, too, might others whose intentions were less concerned with sentiment than with burglary.

In any case, I did not choose that my garden should have such easy access from outside, and next morning I ordered a pretty stiff barrier of iron spikes to be erected along the outer wall. If Sir Arthur wished to muse in the garden, I should be delighted to give him permission, as, indeed, he must have known from the cordiality which I was sure I showed him when he called, but this method of his seemed to me irregular. And I observed next evening, without any regret at all, that my order had been promptly executed. At the same time I felt an invincible curiosity to know for certain if it was merely for the sake of a solitary midnight vigil that he had come.

I was expecting the arrival of my friend Hugh Grainger the next week, to stay a night or two with me, and since the front spare room, which I proposed to give him, had not at present been slept in, I gave orders that a bed should be made up there the next night for me, so that I could test with my own vile body whether a guest would be comfortable there.

This can only be proved by personal experience. Though there may be a table apparently convenient to the head of the bed, though the dressing-table may apparently be properly disposed, though it seem as if the lighting was rightly placed for reading in bed, and for the quenching of it afterwards without disturbance, yet practice and not theory is the only method of settling such questions, and next night accordingly I both dressed for dinner in this front spare room, and went to bed there.

Everything seemed to work smoothly; the room itself had a pleasant and restful air about it, and the bed exceedingly comfortable, I fell asleep almost as soon as I had put out the electric light, which I had found adequate for reading small print. To the best of my knowledge, neither the thought of the last occupant of the room nor of the light that I believed I had seen burning there one night entered my head at all.

I fell asleep, as I say, at once, but instantly that theatre of the brain, on the boards of which dreams are transacted, was brightly illuminated for me, and the curtain went up on one of those appalling nightmare-pieces which we can only vaguely remember afterwards.

There was the sense of flight—clogged, impotent flight from before some hideous spiritual force—the sense of powerlessness to keep away from the terror that gained on me, the strangling desire to scream, and soon the blessed dawning consciousness that it was but with a dream that I wrestled.

I began to know that I was lying in bed, and that my terrors were imaginary, but the trouble was not over yet, for with all my efforts I could not raise my head from the pillow nor open my eyes.

Then, as I drew nearer to the boundaries of waking, I became aware that even when the spell of my dream was altogether broken I should not be free. For through my eyelids, which I knew had closed in a darkened room, there now streamed in a vivid light, and remembering for the first time what I had seen from the square outside, I knew that when I opened them they would look out on to a lit room, peopled with who knew what phantoms of the dead or living.

I lay there for a few moments after I had recovered complete consciousness, with eyes still closed, and felt the trickle of sweat on my forehead. That horror I knew was not wholly due to the self-coined nightmare of my brain; it was the horror of expectancy more than of retrospect. And then curiosity, sheer stark curiosity, to know what was happening on the other side of the curtain of my eyelids prevailed, and I sat and looked.

In the armchair just opposite the foot of my bed sat Lady Bassenthwaite, whose picture I had seen in the illustrated magazine. It simply was she; there could be no doubt whatever about it. She was dressed in a bedgown, and in her hand was a small fluted china bowl with a cover and a saucer. As I looked she took the cover off, and began to feed herself with a spoon. She took some half-dozen mouthfuls, and then replaced the cover again. As she did this she turned full face towards where I lay, looking straight at me, and already the shadow of death was fallen on her. Then she rose feebly, wearily, and took a step towards the bed. As she did this, the light in the room, from whatever source it came, suddenly faded, and I found myself looking out into impenetrable darkness.

My curiosity for the present was more than satisfied, and in a couple of minutes I had transferred myself to the room below.

Hugh Grainger, the ruling passion of whose life is crime and ghosts, arrived next day, and I poured into an eager ear the whole history of the events here narrated.

'Of course, I'll sleep in the room,' he said at the conclusion. 'Put another bed in it, can't you, and sleep there, too. A couple of simultaneous witnesses of the same phenomena are ten times more valuable than one. Or do you funk?' he added as a kind afterthought.

'I funk, but I will,' I said.

'And are you sure it wasn't all part of your dream?' he asked.

'Absolutely positive.'

Hugh's eye glowed with pleasure.

'I funk, too,' he said. 'I funk horribly. But that's part of the allurement. It's so difficult to get frightened nowadays. All but a few things are explained and accounted for. What one fears is the unknown. No one knows yet what ghosts are, or why they appear, or to whom.'

He took a turn up and down the room.

'And what do you make of Sir Arthur creeping into your garden at night?' he asked. 'Is there any possible connection?'

'Not as far as I can see. What connection could there be?'

'It isn't very obvious certainly. I really don't know why I asked. And you liked him?'

'Immensely. But not enough to let him get over my garden wall at midnight,' said I.

Hugh laughed.

'That would certainly imply a considerable degree of confidence and affection,' he said.

I had caused another bed to be moved into Hugh's room, and that night, after he had put out the light, we talked awhile and then relapsed into silence. It was cold, and I watched the fire on the hearth die down from flame into glowing coal, and from glow into clinkering ash, while nothing disturbed the peaceful atmosphere of the quiet room. Then it seemed to me as if something broke in, and instead of lying tranquilly awake, I found a certain horror of expectancy, some note of nightmare begin to hum through my waking consciousness. I heard Hugh toss and turn and turn again, and at length he spoke.

'I say, I'm feeling fairly beastly,' he said, 'and yet there's nothing to see or hear.'

'Same with me,' said I.

'Do you mind if I turn up the light a minute, and have a look round?' he asked.

'Not a bit.'

He fumbled at the switch, the room leapt into light, and he sat up in bed frowning. Everything was quite as usual, the bookcase, the chairs, on one of which he had thrown his clothes; there was nothing that differentiated this room from hundreds of others where the occupants lay quietly sleeping.

'It's queer,' he said, and switched off the light again.

There is nothing harder than to measure time in the dark, but I do not think it was long that I lay there with the sense of nightmare growing momentarily on me before he spoke again in an odd, cracked voice.

'It's coming,' he said.

Almost as soon as he spoke I saw that the thick darkness of the room was sensibly thinning. The blackness was less complete, though I could hardly say that light began to enter. Then by degrees I saw the shape of chairs, the lines of the fireplace, the end of Hugh's bed begin to outline themselves, and as I watched the darkness vanished altogether, as if a lamp had been turned up. And in the chair at the foot of Hugh's bed sat Lady Bassenthwaite, and again putting aside the cover of her dish, she sipped the contents of the bowl, and at the end rose feebly, wearily, as in mortal sickness. She looked at Hugh, and turning, she looked at me, and through the shadow of death that lay over her face, I thought that in her eyes was a demand, or at least a statement of her case. They were not angry, they did not cry for justice, but the calm inexorable gaze of justice that must be done was there . . . Then the light faded and died out.

I heard a rustle from the other bed and the springs creaked.

'Good Lord,' said Hugh, 'where's the light?'

His fingers fumbled and found it, and I saw that he was already out of bed, with streaming forehead and chattering teeth.

'I know now,' he said. 'I half guessed before. Come downstairs.'

Downstairs we went, and he turned up all the passage lights as we passed. He led the way into the dining room, picking up the poker and the shovel as he went by the fireplace, and he threw open the door into the garden. I switched up the light, which threw a bright square of illumination over the garden.

'Where did you see Sir Arthur?' he said. 'Where? Exactly where?'

Still not guessing what he sought, I pointed out to him the spot, and loosening the earth with the poker, he dug into the bed. Once again he plunged the poker down, and as he removed the earth I heard the shovel grate on something hard. And then I guessed.

Already Hugh was at work with his fingers in the earth, and slowly and carefully he drew out fragments of a broken china cover. Then, delving again, he raised from the hole a fluted china bowl. And I knew I had seen it before, once and twice.

We carried this indoors and cleaned the earth from it. All over the bottom of the bowl was a layer of some thick porridge-like substance, and a portion of this I sent next day to a chemist, asking him for his analysis of it. The basis of it proved to be oatmeal, and in it was mixed a considerable quantity of arsenic.

Hugh and I were together in my little sitting room close to the front door, where on the table stood the china bowl with the fragments of its cover and saucer, when this report was brought to us, and we read it together. The afternoon was very dark and we stood close to the window to decipher the minute handwriting, when there passed the figure of Sir Arthur Bassenthwaite. He saw me, waved his hand, and a moment afterwards the front door bell rang.

'Let him come in,' said Hugh. 'Let him see that on the table.'

Next moment my servant entered, and asked if the caller might see me.

'Let him see it,' repeated Hugh. 'The chances are that we shall know if he sees it unexpectedly.'

There was a moment's pause while in the hall, I suppose, Sir Arthur was taking off his coat. Outside, some few doors off, a traction engine, which had passed a minute before, stopped, and began slowly coming backwards again, crunching the newly-laid stones. Sir Arthur entered.

'I ventured to call,' he began, and then his glance fell on the bowl. In one second the very aspect of humanity was stripped from his face. His mouth drooped open, his eyes grew monstrous and protruding, and what had been the pleasant, neat-featured face of a man was a mask of terror, a gargoyle, a nightmare countenance. Even before the door that had been open to admit him was closed, he had turned and gone with a crouching, stumbling run from the room, and I heard him at the latch of the front door.

Whether what followed was design or accident, I shall never know, for from the window I saw him fall forward, almost as if he threw himself there, straight in front of the broad crunching wheels of the traction engine, and before the driver could stop, or even think of stopping, the iron roller had gone over his head.

The Cobweb

By Saki

The farmhouse kitchen probably stood where it did as a matter of accident or haphazard choice; yet its situation might have been planned by a master-strategist in farmhouse architecture. Dairy and poultry-yard, and herb garden, and all the busy places of the farm seemed to lead by easy access into its wide flagged haven, where there was room for everything and where muddy boots left traces that were easily swept away. And yet, for all that it stood so well in the centre of human bustle, its long, latticed window, with the wide window-seat, built into an embrasure beyond the huge fireplace, looked out on a wild spreading view of hill and heather and wooded combe. The window nook made almost a little room in itself, quite the pleasantest room in the farm as far as situation and capabilities went. Young Mrs. Ladbruk, whose husband had just come into the farm by way of inheritance, cast covetous eyes on this snug corner, and her fingers itched to make it bright and cozy with chintz curtains and bowls of flowers, and a shelf or two of old china. The musty farm parlour, looking out to a prim, cheerless garden imprisoned within high, blank walls, was not a room that lent itself readily either to comfort or decoration.

"When we are more settled I shall work wonders in the way of making the kitchen habitable," said the young woman to her occasional visitors. There was an unspoken wish in those words, a wish which was unconfessed as well as unspoken. Emma Ladbruk was the mistress of the farm; jointly with her husband she might have her say, and to a certain extent her way, in ordering its affairs. But she was not mistress of the kitchen.

On one of the shelves of an old dresser, in company with chipped sauce-boats, pewter jugs, cheese-graters, and paid bills, rested a worn and ragged Bible, on whose front page was the record, in faded ink, of a baptism dated ninety-four years ago. "Martha Crale" was the name written on that yellow page. The yellow, wrinkled old dame who hobbled and muttered about the kitchen, looking like a dead autumn leaf which the winter winds still pushed hither and thither, had once been Martha Crale; for seventy odd years she had been Martha Mountjoy. For longer than any one could remember she had pattered to and fro between oven and wash-house and dairy, and out to chicken-run and garden, grumbling and muttering and scolding, but working unceasingly. Emma Ladbruk, of whose coming she took as little notice as she would of a bee wandering in at a window on a summer's day, used at first to watch her with a kind of frightened curiosity. She was so old and so much a part of the place, it was difficult to think of her exactly as a living thing. Old Shep, the white-nozzled, stiff-limbed collie, waiting for his time to die, seemed almost more human than the withered, dried-up old woman. He had been a riotous, roystering puppy, mad with the joy of life, when she was already a tottering, hobbling dame; now he was just a blind, breathing carcase, nothing more, and she still worked with frail energy, still swept and baked and washed, fetched and carried. If there were something in these wise old dogs that did not perish utterly with death, Emma used to think to herself, what generations of ghost-dogs there must be out on those hills, that Martha had reared and fed and tended and spoken a last good-bye word to in that old kitchen. And what memories she must have of human generations that had passed away in her time. It was difficult for any one, let alone a stranger like Emma, to get her to talk of the days that had been; her shrill, quavering speech was of doors that had been left unfastened, pails that had got mislaid, calves whose feeding-time was overdue, and the various little faults and lapses that chequer a farmhouse routine. Now and again, when election time came round, she would unstore her recollections of the old names round which the fight had waged in the days gone by. There had been a Palmerston, that had been a name down Tiverton way; Tiverton was not a far journey as the crow flies, but to Martha it was almost a foreign country. Later there had been Northcotes and Aclands, and many other newer names that she had forgotten; the names changed, but it was always Libruls and Toories, Yellows and Blues. And they always quarrelled and shouted as to who was right and who was wrong. The one they quarrelled about most was a fine old gentleman with an angry face—she had seen his picture on the walls. She had seen it on the floor too, with a rotten apple squashed over it, for the farm had changed its politics from time to time. Martha had never been on one side or the other; none of "they" had ever done the farm a stroke of good. Such was her sweeping verdict, given with all a peasant's distrust of the outside world.

When the half-frightened curiosity had somewhat faded away, Emma Ladbruk was uncomfortably conscious of another feeling towards the old woman. She was a quaint old tradition, lingering about the place, she was part and parcel of the farm itself, she was something at once pathetic and picturesque—but she was dreadfully in the way. Emma had come to the farm full of plans for little reforms and improvements, in part the result of training in the newest ways and methods, in part the outcome of her own ideas and fancies. Reforms in the kitchen region, if those deaf ears could have been induced to give them even a hearing, would have met with short shrift and scornful rejection, and the kitchen region spread over the zone of dairy and market business and half the work of the household. Emma, with the latest science of dead-poultry dressing at her fingertips, sat by, an unheeded watcher, while old Martha trussed the chickens for the market-stall as she had trussed them for nearly fourscore years—all leg and no breast. And the hundred hints anent effective cleaning and labour-lightening and the things that make for wholesomeness which the young woman was ready to impart or to put into action dropped away into nothingness before that wan, muttering, unheeding presence. Above all, the coveted window corner, that was to be a dainty, cheerful oasis in the gaunt old kitchen, stood now choked and lumbered with a litter of odds and ends that Emma, for all her nominal authority, would not have dared or cared to displace; over them seemed to be spun the protection of something that was like a human cobweb. Decidedly Martha was in the way. It would have been an unworthy meanness to have wished to see the span of that brave old life shortened by a few paltry months, but as the days sped by Emma was conscious that the wish was there, disowned though it might be, lurking at the back of her mind.

She felt the meanness of the wish come over her with a qualm of self-reproach one day when she came into the kitchen and found an unaccustomed state of things in that usually busy quarter. Old Martha was not working. A basket of corn was on the floor by her side, and out in the yard the poultry were beginning to clamour a protest of overdue feeding-time. But Martha sat huddled in a shrunken bunch on the window seat, looking out with her dim old eyes as though she saw something stranger than the autumn landscape.

"Is anything the matter, Martha?" asked the young woman.

"'Tis death, 'tis death a-coming," answered the quavering voice; "I knew 'twere coming. I knew it. 'Tweren't for nothing that old Shep's been howling all morning. An' last night I heard the screech-owl give the death-cry, and there were something white as run across the yard yesterday; 'tweren't a cat nor a stoat, 'twere something. The fowls knew 'twere something; they all drew off to one side. Ay, there's been warnings. I knew it were a-coming."

The young woman's eyes clouded with pity. The old thing sitting there so white and shrunken had once been a merry, noisy child, playing about in lanes and hay-lofts and farmhouse garrets; that had been eighty odd years ago, and now she was just a frail old body cowering under the approaching chill of the death that was coming at last to take her. It was not probable that much could be done for her, but Emma hastened away to get assistance and counsel. Her husband, she knew, was down at a tree-felling some little distance off, but she might find some other intelligent soul who knew the old woman better than she did. The farm, she soon found out, had that faculty common to farmyards of swallowing up and losing its human population. The poultry followed her in interested fashion, and swine grunted interrogations at her from behind the bars of their sties, but barnyard and rickyard, orchard and stables and dairy, gave no reward to her search. Then, as she retraced her steps towards the kitchen, she came suddenly on her cousin, young Mr. Jim, as every one called him, who divided his time between amateur horse-dealing, rabbit-shooting, and flirting with the farm maids.

"I'm afraid old Martha is dying," said Emma. Jim was not the sort of person to whom one had to break news gently.

"Nonsense," he said; "Martha means to live to a hundred. She told me so, and she'll do it."

"She may be actually dying at this moment, or it may just be the beginning of the break-up," persisted Emma, with a feeling of contempt for the slowness and dulness of the young man.

A grin spread over his good-natured features.

"It don't look like it," he said, nodding towards the yard. Emma turned to catch the meaning of his remark. Old Martha stood in the middle of a mob of poultry scattering handfuls of grain around her. The turkey-cock, with the bronzed sheen of his feathers and the purple-red of his wattles, the game-cock with the glowing metallic lustre of his Eastern plumage, the hens, with their ochres and buffs and umbers and their scarlet combs, and the drakes, with their bottle-green heads, made a medley of rich colour, in the centre of which the old woman looked like a withered stalk standing amid the riotous growth of gaily-hued flowers. But she threw the grain deftly amid the wilderness of beaks, and her quavering voice carried as far as the two people who were watching her. She was still harping on the theme of death coming to the farm.

"I knew 'twere a-coming. There's been signs an' warnings."

"Who's dead, then, old Mother?" called out the young man.

"'Tis young Mister Ladbruk," she shrilled back; "they've just a-carried his body in. Run out of the way of a tree that was coming down an' ran hisself on to an iron post. Dead when they picked un up. Ay, I knew 'twere coming."

And she turned to fling a handful of barley at a belated group of guinea-fowl that came racing toward her.

The farm was a family property, and passed to the rabbit-shooting cousin as the next-of-kin. Emma Ladbruk drifted out of its history as a bee that had wandered in at an open window might flit its way out again. On a cold grey morning she stood waiting with her boxes already stowed in the farm cart, till the last of the market produce should be ready, for the train she was to catch was of less importance than the chickens and butter and eggs that were to be offered for sale. From where she stood she could see an angle of the long latticed window that was to have been cozy with curtains and gay with bowls of flowers. Into her mind came the thought that for months, perhaps for years, long after she had been utterly forgotten, a white, unheeding face would be seen peering out through those latticed panes, and a weak muttering voice would be heard quavering up and down those flagged passages. She made her way to a narrow barred casement that opened into the farm larder. Old Martha was standing at a table trussing a pair of chickens for the market stall as she had trussed them for nearly fourscore years.

Come to the Party

By Frances Garfield

Dusk was fast overcoming the autumn twilight. Nora felt no closer to Steve Thomas's country house than they'd been half an hour earlier. She snuggled closer to big Jeff in the back seat and tried to see the road ahead. The headlights bravely probed a path, but the darkness seemed to nestle nearer and gloomier to either side.

Willie, in the front seat beside Sam, bent her ginger head above a crude, penciled map, which the four had begun to fear was false.

"Steve just doesn't know how to draw maps," Willie half moaned. "And he promised to put up signals to show where to turn off onto his private road. Why ever did I pick a publisher who throws his parties on the far side of nowhere?"

"But, my dear, this publisher picked you out," reminded silver-haired Sam at the wheel. "A dozen others turned you down—"

"Please. Why bring that up?" Willie appealed. But he went on.

"Here was Steve with his little regional publishing house, pretty much on the far side of nowhere itself, a county away. Regional, and he wanted a regional novel for the Christmas trade. And he liked yours very much. And here we are, on our way to cheer you on while you autograph a thousand or so flyleaves."

Sam loved his writer wife, and showed it by his teasing. Nora knew he smiled his special smile of affectionate amusement, blue eyes slanted and twinkling.

"He said there might be about a dozen guests," protested Willie. "He said he'd invited some special friends who might like my book and buy it. And tell all their friends—so they'd buy it too. For Christmas gifts. Word-of-mouth advertising, Steve called it."

"Yes. Cheaper than published advertising," remarked Sam.

"There's that little white church again," said Jeff, big and trying to sound cheerful. "How many times have we passed it? Three? Or maybe four?"

"Four, I'm sure," put in Nora. "And there's the little gray house that keeps following us."

"Damn," said Sam. "This curve looming ahead is boringly familiar. We seem to be in orbit—"

A grotesquely painted van charged into the glare of headlights, squarely in the center of the road. Sam cursed and wrenched the wheel. The car swayed onto the grassy shoulder. The tremendous van shot past, its driver goggling out, blocky white teeth gleaming from a dark thicket of beard. Then he was gone, and Sam twisted back onto the road.

"Whew," gasped Willie. "Thank God you were driving, Sam, not me."

Nora tossed her thick, black hair out of her eyes. Her hand tingled where Jeff had gripped it so powerfully. She could still see that staring, shaggy face.

"It'll be a great party if we ever get there," she said in a feeble attempt at humor. "Look, isn't that the church again?"

"I wonder if anybody will find the place," ventured Willie.

"Pessimist," chuckled Sam. He loved everything about Willie, including her novel about a woman's passion for both her husband and her husband's brother. Nora had overheard a neighbor woman ask Sam which of the characters he was supposed to be. "A little of both," he had said, with a perfectly straight face, slant blue eyes twinkling as usual.

"There'll be people there all right," promised burly Jeff. "And Nora and I are here to give you moral support, Willie." He, too, admired the book, had helped Willie read proof on it. The four were close friends, always enjoyed each other, never bored together.

"That van looks better behind us than in front of us," said Sam. "Maybe he's lost out here, too, rolling round and round. Look, a mist is coming up."

An owl hooted in the distance, strangely loud and clear above the motor's purr. No houses showed now, only great twisted trees crowded at the sides of the road, branches laced overhead. Willie gave a sudden, happy squeak.

"Look—a bit of tinsel on a post," she cried. "That's bound to be Steve's signal."

"And a driveway just past it," said Sam, turning deftly. "A long one, too."

They followed turns, rises, and falls in the bumpy road. Dark thickets massed to right and left. They heard nothing, no sound but the motor. Nora saw a grotesquely hunched tree that reminded her of a cedar of Lebanon she remembered from Winchester Cathedral. Weird.

"Turn there," directed Willie, pointing ahead. And Sam turned.

"Geez, how well you obey Willie," laughed Nora. "One word from me and Jeff does the exact opposite."

Jeff said nothing. He stared out of the window, lips clamped; his cheek had a taut crease where there should be a dimple.

Sam bumped the car over the coarse outflung roots of a great oak, and stopped on the tall grass. Ahead of them showed a great, bleakly drab house. Wavering lights from the tall windows tinted the dim evening. A broad chimney, rosy in the dusk, climbed the side wall. Large pillars rose along a wide porch.

"Okay." Jeff touched Nora's shoulder, and she felt his great hand tremble. "Let's go on in."

Willie smoothed her cap of ginger curls and freshened her lipstick. Nora shook her long, dark hair and moved to follow Jeff. "Odd," she said. "I don't see any other cars."

"They've probably been and gone," joked Sam, coming along behind with Willie. "It took us long enough to find the place."

They mounted the steps. A dark, heavy door loomed. Sam swung the huge knocker, and the door opened.

"Come in. Come in," came a booming voice.

They went in.

The man at the door was outrageously handsome, blond and tall, dressed in a tuxedo, shirtfront all foamy with lace, self-consciously cordial. "Glad you came," he greeted them.

"We had some problems," said Nora. "Where's Steve?"

"Oh, never mind Steve for a moment. My name's Patrick. Come on in and join the crowd."

The hubbub inside was unbelievable. Nora took hold of Jeff's coat, seeking reassurance. For what reason she didn't know. They had come into a huge, swarming room, a multitude of bodies. All kinds—tall, thin, short, fat, every one of them completely strange to her. Maybe Willie knew some of them, she thought. They could be part of Steve's publishing company. She stepped back to let Willie lead the way.

"Keep straight ahead," Patrick advised from behind. He was dismayingly handsome, and Nora speculated for a moment whether his hair had been permanented. "Food and drink over there," he smiled. "You'll find some friends there, probably."

"With my sort of friends, that's just where I'll find them," said Jeff, grinning now.

The four wove in and out among packed groups. Everybody was talking to everybody else and nobody seemed to notice them. A dull red fire glowed on a broad hearth, but did not seem to send out any heat. Several extremely thin men stood there and listened to a grossly heavy man. His face was bearded, toothy. Nora remembered the driver of that killer van. High along an inner wall ran a balcony. Faces looked down, the faces, perhaps, of children. One gnawed on what might have been a chicken wing.

"It's positively unreal," Nora whispered to Jeff, and it was. They seemed to walk through people, as though people dissolved from in front of them. "My imagination's going haywire," she said, and squeezed his hand for comfort.

Willie's brilliant, curly head had led the way to a butler's pantry. It, too, thronged with people, filling trays with barbecued chicken, cold cuts, sliced cheese. Baskets of crackers and little cakes sat here and there. In the midst of everything, a gigantic glass bowl of rosy liquid.

"Pink wine," whispered Sam, crinkling his nose. "The cheapest."

For a moment, they thought they saw Steve Thomas's beautiful wife balancing an empty tray toward a rear door, perhaps the kitchen. "Hey, Florence," Willie called out. But whoever it was didn't turn. She vanished so abruptly, they couldn't be sure if they'd seen her.

Sam picked up a plate and piled it high with salad and meat. "Let's dig in," he said. "That ride would give a skeleton an appetite. I'll even try this sorry wine—it's not worthy of Steve. Or is it? I think he outdid himself this time."

"There's Em Selden, there by the fireplace," said Nora to Jeff.

"Where?"

"No, she's gone. Maybe it wasn't Em. Anyway, let's stick together. What a strange bunch of people."

As she spoke, she thought she heard singing somewhere. A radio, a record player? It died away as she wondered.

"Look," said Willie, putting down her plate. "At the end of the hall. It looks like Patrick, summoning me. I'd better go see—maybe it's time for me to autograph some books."

Briskly she headed for the long hallway, striding fast on green high-heeled sandals and swinging the skirt of her flowered green dress. There were chairs lining the hall. They seemed to be heaped with mink coats. "Hmm," Nora heard her murmur as she left. "None of Steve's authors could afford those."

Nora chewed on a strangely tasteless slice of sausage as she watched Willie out of sight. "I hope she sells enough books to make this trip worthwhile."

"You're not having fun?" worried Sam.

"That means you aren't happy either." Nora looked from platter to platter. "What happened to the chicken wings? They're my favorite food?"

"If I had a pair of chicken wings, I might just fly out of here," said Jeff. Nora laughed, but Jeff didn't join her.

The crowd had grown thicker, noisier. The air seemed damp and close; it had a smell like a roomful of old clothes. Sam frowned and brushed back his silver hair.

"Let's go somewhere quiet," he said.

"How about up on the balcony with the kids?" suggested Nora.

But the balcony seemed empty, lost in dark shadows. Maybe a hint of movement. Or maybe not.

"How much of this putrid wine did you drink, Jeff?" asked Sam.

"No more than I could help. I hope Willie's in her element, autographing books."

"I'm going to go see," said Sam.

He moved toward the hallway where Willie had vanished. The crowd let him through without seeming to make way.

"At least Steve had the sense to stay away from his own party," growled Jeff. "Look there in the corner. Isn't that Genevieve and Joe?"

Nora peered. "Let's go see."

They pressed their way through a huddle of people, who made a path for them. Nobody looked familiar. Except, against a far wall—the bearded van driver? The voices, all s's and all loud, hurt their ears. The air thickened, and was hard to breathe.

"Here we are," said Jeff, reaching the corner.

But nobody stood there. Nobody. Only a flicker from the fireplace that did not seem to give off heat.

"I'll be damned," Jeff muttered. "Do we have a single friend in this room?"

They looked around. Halfway across the room drifted a face,

wan as lemon custard, peering from under the brim of a worn, shapeless felt hat. The body seemed lost in foggy darkness—they imagined a long black caftan. Behind him, or it, there grimaced the bearded driver.

"Jeff," said Nora, "I don't like it here."

"It's just that you don't know anybody," said Jeff. But his dimples did not show. "But you're right. The whole thing's a crashing bore. Let me go check with Willie and Sam. Maybe we can sneak out if they're through."

"Yes, go look for them." Nora tried to smile.

"I'll be right back."

Away he tramped, huge among the others. She watched him enter the hallway between the piled fur coats. Watched his dark head disappear. Then she stood alone, nobody noticing her, nobody talking to her. She felt dull, sticky, as though she hung in a mass of warm jelly.

Haze crawled in the air of the crowded room. It smelled, not like tobacco, not like that other familiar-grown marijuana smell. Nora did not belong there. She knew it. She hadn't been invited, really; she and Jeff had only come with Willie and Sam. For moral support. She wished they had stayed at home. Or wished, anyway, she had gone along with Jeff to find the others.

I'll follow them, she said to herself. Follow them. Maybe they're ready to go.

The hallway seemed to narrow as she entered. Those piles of furs closed in around her. Maybe the little white rabbit in the Alice book had felt closed in like that. And the hallway was shadow-barred, with open doorways shedding light along the side.

Nora looked in at a door. Music seeped out. Something in there like a little old-fashioned organ. It seemed to be playing, all by itself, a tune like a hymn, but dissonant, repelling. Voices echoed through the next doorway. Nora went there.

"Come in," somebody called. "We've been waiting."

A man in a very dark suit put out a very white hand to her. His chalky face grinned with dark, narrow teeth. His hand was clammy as it touched hers. "Come in," he said again.

Staring past him, she saw dull paneled walls, a hanging lamp that sprouted a shaky flame, a closely drawn knot of people. They, too, wore dark clothes, tight-fitted to gaunt bodies. They seemed to have faces of pale clay. Their eyes looked little and beady. They spoke from thick red lips, unintelligibly.

But on the floor lay three others, instantly recognizable—a bit of green cloth. Jeff's great, limp body. The red curls of Willie, the silver hair of Sam. None of them moved.

"Come in," a chorus, bidding.

All hands rose toward her, beckoning.

Nora screamed thinly and whirled to run.

Run anywhere, away from that little room, anywhere. A door stood at the end of the hallway. Escape. That was all she could think of. She gasped stranglingly. At the door, she clawed for the knob. She strove hard against the panel, and the door grumbled open.

She filled her lungs with fresh air. Somehow, miraculously, she was outside. Where to go? It didn't matter. Only get away.

She ran in the dark night, stumbling over the heavy coiled roots of trees, tearing her sheer hose. A slipper came off and desperately she kicked the other away. She kept running. Stones hurt her bare feet, biting painfully at her ankles. A mockingbird sang, strangely comforting. She was escaping. Away from that house.

A broad, open lawn loomed ahead of her. A beautiful house, standing tall and proud against sentinel pines. She floundered to one knee, dragged herself up again and to the door, beating at it with her fists.

"Why, Nora!"

There stood Steve Thomas, opening to her. Steve was slim, impeccable. His curled black hair was carefully groomed, a smile was on his face.

"For heaven's sake. Where have you been? Where are the others?"

She flung herself into his arms, and he held her close to quiet her trembling. "Where are they?" he asked again.

"I don't know," she chattered. "I saw them on the floor—over there at your party—"

"What are you talking about?"

She fought her choking sobs. "Over in that big house, right over there—"

"My God, Nora, there hasn't been a house there for years." Steve held her closer. "You're imagining things. No house. It burned down, long before I came here."

"B-burned down?"

"I've heard a crazy story. A bunch of far-out people, who had a belief of some sort about human sacrifice. And one night, when they celebrated it, lightning struck and burned the place to the ground, with everybody inside."

"But—"

90

"Look, Nora. There's nothing there. Nothing whatever."

Nora made herself look.

There *was* nothing there. Nothing whatever.

A Curious Dream

By Mark Twain

Containing a Moral

Night before last I had a singular dream. I seemed to be sitting on a doorstep (in no particular city perhaps) ruminating, and the time of night appeared to be about twelve or one o'clock. The weather was balmy and delicious. There was no human sound in the air, not even a footstep. There was no sound of any kind to emphasize the dead stillness, except the occasional hollow barking of a dog in the distance and the fainter answer of a further dog. Presently up the street I heard a bony clack-clacking, and guessed it was the castanets of a serenading party. In a minute more a tall skeleton, hooded, and half clad in a tattered and moldy shroud, whose shreds were flapping about the ribby latticework of its person, swung by me with a stately stride and disappeared in the gray gloom of the starlight. It had a broken and worm-eaten coffin on its shoulder and a bundle of something in its hand. I knew what the clack-clacking was then; it was this party's joints working together, and his elbows knocking against his sides as he walked. I may say I was surprised. Before I could collect my thoughts and enter upon any speculations as to what this apparition might portend, I heard another one coming—for I recognized his clack-clack. He had two-thirds of a coffin on his shoulder, and some foot and head boards under his arm. I mightily wanted to peer under his hood and speak to him, but when he turned and smiled upon me with his cavernous sockets and his projecting grin as he went by, I thought I would not detain him. He was hardly gone when I heard the clacking again, and another one issued from the shadowy half-light. This one was bending under a heavy gravestone, and dragging a shabby coffin after him by a string. When he got to me he gave me a steady look for a moment or two, and then rounded to and backed up to me, saying:

"Ease this down for a fellow, will you?"

I eased the gravestone down till it rested on the ground, and in doing so noticed that it bore the name of "John Baxter Copmanhurst," with "May, 1839," as the date of his death. Deceased sat wearily down by me, and wiped his os frontis with his major maxillary—chiefly from former habit I judged, for I could not see that he brought away any perspiration.

"It is too bad, too bad," said he, drawing the remnant of the shroud about him and leaning his jaw pensively on his hand. Then he put his left foot up on his knee and fell to scratching his ankle-bone absently with a rusty nail which he got out of his coffin.

"What is too bad, friend?"

"Oh, everything, everything. I almost wish I never had died."

"You surprise me. Why do you say this? Has anything gone wrong? What is the matter?"

"Matter! Look at this shroud—rags. Look at this gravestone, all battered up. Look at that disgraceful old coffin. All a man's property going to ruin and destruction before his eyes, and ask him if anything is wrong? Fire and brimstone!"

"Calm yourself, calm yourself," I said. "It *is* too bad—it is certainly too bad, but then I had not supposed that you would much mind such matters, situated as you are."

"Well, my dear sir, I *do* mind them. My pride is hurt, and my comfort is impaired—destroyed, I might say. I will state my case—I will put it to you in such a way that you can comprehend it, if you will let me," said the poor skeleton, tilting the hood of his shroud back, as if he were clearing for action, and thus unconsciously giving himself a jaunty and festive air very much at variance with the grave character of his position in life—so to speak—and in prominent contrast with his distressful mood.

"Proceed," said I.

"I reside in the shameful old graveyard a block or two above you here, in this street—there, now, I just expected that cartilage would let go!—third rib from the bottom, friend, hitch the end of it to my spine with a string, if you have got such a thing about you, though a bit of silver wire is a deal pleasanter, and more durable and becoming, if one keeps it polished—to think of shredding out and going to pieces in this way, just on account of the indifference and neglect of one's posterity!"—and the poor ghost grated his teeth in a way that gave me a wrench and a shiver—for the effect is mightily increased by the absence of muffling flesh and cuticle. "I reside in that old graveyard, and have for these thirty years; and I tell you things are changed since I first laid this old tired frame there, and turned over, and stretched out for a long sleep, with a delicious sense upon me of being *done* with bother, and grief, and anxiety, and doubt, and fear, forever and ever, and listening with comfortable and increasing satisfaction to the sexton's work, from the startling clatter of his first spadeful on my coffin till it dulled away to the faint patting that shaped the roof of my new home—delicious! My! I wish you could try it to-night!" and out of my reverie deceased fetched me a rattling slap with a bony hand.

"Yes, sir, thirty years ago I laid me down there, and was happy. For it was out in the country then—out in the breezy, flowery, grand old woods, and the lazy winds gossiped with the leaves, and the squirrels capered over us and around us, and the creeping things visited us, and the birds filled the tranquil solitude with music. Ah, it was worth ten years of a man's life to be dead then! Everything was pleasant. I was in a good neighborhood, for all the dead people that lived near me belonged to the best families in the city. Our posterity appeared to think the world of us. They kept our graves in the very best condition; the fences were always in faultless repair, head-boards were kept painted or whitewashed, and were replaced with new ones as soon as they began to look rusty or decayed; monuments were kept upright, railings intact and bright, the rose-bushes and shrubbery trimmed, trained, and free from blemish, the walks clean and smooth and graveled. But that day is gone by. Our descendants have forgotten us. My grandson lives in a stately house built with money made by these old hands of mine, and I sleep in a neglected grave with invading vermin that gnaw my shroud to build them nests withal! I and friends that lie with me founded and secured the prosperity of this fine city, and the stately bantling of our loves leaves us to rot in a dilapidated cemetery which neighbors curse and strangers scoff at. See the difference between the old time and this—for instance: Our graves are all caved in now; our head-boards have rotted away and tumbled down; our railings reel this way and that, with one foot in the air, after a fashion of unseemly levity; our monuments lean wearily, and our gravestones bow their heads discouraged; there be no adornments any more—no roses, nor shrubs, nor graveled walks, nor anything that is a comfort to the eye; and even the paintless old board fence that did make a show of holding us sacred from companionship with beasts and the defilement of heedless feet, has tottered till it overhangs the street, and only advertises the presence of our dismal resting-place and invites yet more derision to it. And now we cannot hide our poverty and tatters in the friendly woods, for the city has stretched its withering arms abroad and taken us in, and all that remains of the cheer of our old home is the cluster of lugubrious forest trees that stand, bored and weary of a city life, with their feet in our coffins, looking into the hazy distance and wishing they were there. I tell you it is disgraceful!

"You begin to comprehend—you begin to see how it is. While our descendants are living sumptuously on our money, right around us in the city, we have to fight hard to keep skull and bones together. Bless you, there isn't a grave in our cemetery that doesn't leak—not one. Every time it rains in the night we have to climb out and roost in the trees—and sometimes we are wakened suddenly by the chilly water trickling down the back of our necks. Then I tell you there is a general heaving up of old graves and kicking over of old monuments, and scampering of old skeletons for the trees! Bless me, if you had gone along there some such nights after twelve you might have seen as many as fifteen of us roosting on one limb, with our joints rattling drearily and the wind wheezing through our ribs! Many a time we have perched there for three or four dreary hours, and then come down, stiff and chilled through and drowsy, and borrowed each other's skulls to bail out our graves with—if you will glance up in my mouth now as I tilt my head back, you can see that my head-piece is half full of old dry sediment—how top-heavy and stupid it makes me sometimes! Yes, sir, many a time if you had happened to come along just before the dawn you'd have caught us bailing out the graves and hanging our shrouds on the fence to dry. Why, I had an elegant shroud stolen from there one morning—think a party by the name of Smith took it, that resides in a plebeian graveyard over yonder—I think so because the first time I ever saw him he hadn't anything on but a check shirt, and the last time I saw him, which was at a social gathering in the new cemetery, he was the best-dressed corpse in the company—and it is a significant fact that he left when he saw me; and presently an old woman from here missed her coffin—she generally took it with her when she went anywhere, because she was liable to take cold and bring on the spasmodic rheumatism that originally killed her if she exposed herself to the night air much. She was named Hotchkiss—Anna Matilda Hotchkiss—you might know her? She has two upper front teeth, is tall, but a good deal inclined to stoop, one rib on the left side gone, has one shred of rusty hair hanging from the left side of her head, and one little tuft just above and a little forward of her right ear, has her underjaw wired on one side where it had worked loose, small bone of left forearm gone—lost in a fight—has a kind of

94

swagger in her gait and a 'gallus' way of going with her arms akimbo and her nostrils in the air—has been pretty free and easy, and is all damaged and battered up till she looks like a queensware crate in ruins—maybe you have met her?"

"God forbid!" I involuntarily ejaculated, for somehow I was not looking for that form of question, and it caught me a little off my guard. But I hastened to make amends for my rudeness, and say, "I simply meant I had not had the honor—for I would not deliberately speak discourteously of a friend of yours. You were saying that you were robbed—and it was a shame, too—but it appears by what is left of the shroud you have on that it was a costly one in its day. How did—"

A most ghastly expression began to develop among the decayed features and shriveled integuments of my guest's face, and I was beginning to grow uneasy and distressed, when he told me he was only working up a deep, sly smile, with a wink in it, to suggest that about the time he acquired his present garment a ghost in a neighboring cemetery missed one. This reassured me, but I begged him to confine himself to speech thenceforth, because his facial expression was uncertain. Even with the most elaborate care it was liable to miss fire. Smiling should especially be avoided. What *he* might honestly consider a shining success was likely to strike me in a very different light. I said I liked to see a skeleton cheerful, even decorously playful, but I did not think smiling was a skeleton's best hold.

"Yes, friend," said the poor skeleton, "the facts are just as I have given them to you. Two of these old graveyards—the one that I resided in and one further along—have been deliberately neglected by our descendants of to-day until there is no occupying them any longer. Aside from the osteological discomfort of it—and that is no light matter this rainy weather—the present state of things is ruinous to property. We have got to move or be content to see our effects wasted away and utterly destroyed. Now, you will hardly believe it, but it is true, nevertheless, that there isn't a single coffin in good repair among all my acquaintance—now that is an absolute fact. I do not refer to low people who come in a pine box mounted on an express-wagon, but I am talking about your high-toned, silver-mounted burial-case, your monumental sort, that travel under black plumes at the head of a procession and have choice of cemetery lots—I mean folks like the Jarvises, and the Bledsoes and Burlings, and such. They are all about ruined. The most substantial people in our set, they were. And now look at them—utterly used up and poverty-stricken. One of the Bledsoes actually traded his monument to a late barkeeper for some fresh shavings to put under his head. I tell you it speaks volumes, for there is nothing a corpse takes so much pride in as his monument. He loves to read the inscription. He comes after a while to believe what it says himself, and then you may see him sitting on the fence night after night enjoying it. Epitaphs are cheap, and they do a poor chap a world of good after he is dead, especially if he had hard luck while he was alive. I wish they were used more. Now I don't complain, but confidentially I *do* think it was a little shabby in my descendants to give me nothing but this old slab of a gravestone—and all the more that there isn't a compliment on it. It used to have

'GONE TO HIS JUST REWARD'

on it, and I was proud when I first saw it, but by and by I noticed that whenever an old friend of mine came along he would hook his chin on the railing and pull a long face and read along down till he came to that, and then he would chuckle to himself and walk off, looking satisfied and comfortable. So I scratched it off to get rid of those fools. But a dead man always takes a deal of pride in his monument. Yonder goes half a dozen of the Jarvises now, with the family monument along. And Smithers and some hired specters went by with his awhile ago. Hello, Higgins, good-by, old friend! That's Meredith Higgins—died in '44—belongs to our set in the cemetery—fine old family—great-grandmother was an Injun—I am on the most familiar terms with him—he didn't hear me was the reason he didn't answer me. And I am sorry, too, because I would have liked to introduce you. You would admire him. He is the most disjointed, sway-backed, and generally distorted old skeleton you ever saw, but he is full of fun. When he laughs it sounds like rasping two stones together, and he always starts it off with a cheery screech like raking a nail across a window-pane. Hey, Jones! That is old Columbus Jones—shroud cost four hundred dollars—entire trousseau, including monument, twenty-seven hundred. This was in the spring of '26. It was enormous style for those days. Dead people came all the way from the Alleghanies to see his things—the party that occupied the grave next to mine remembers it well. Now do you see that individual going along with a piece of a head-board under his arm, one leg-bone below his knee gone, and not a thing in the world on? That is Barstow Dalhousie, and next to Columbus Jones he was the most sumptuously outfitted person that ever entered our cemetery. We are all leaving. We cannot tolerate the treatment we are receiving at the hands of our descendants. They open new cemeteries, but they leave us to our ignominy. They mend the streets, but they never mend anything that is about us or belongs to us. Look at that coffin of mine—yet I tell you in its day it was a piece of furniture that would have attracted attention in any drawing-room in this city. You may have it if you want it—I can't afford to repair it. Put a new bottom in her, and part of a new top, and a bit of fresh lining along the left side, and you'll find her about as comfortable as any receptacle of her species you ever tried. No thanks—no, don't mention it—you have been civil to me, and I would give you all the property I have got before I would seem ungrateful. Now this winding-sheet is a kind of a sweet thing in its way, if you would like to— No? Well, just as you say, but I wished to be fair and liberal—there's nothing mean about *me*. Good-by, friend, I must be going. I may have a good way to go to-night— don't know. I only know one thing for certain, and that is that I am on the emigrant trail now, and I'll never sleep in that crazy old cemetery again. I will travel till I find respectable quarters, if I have to hoof it to New Jersey. All the boys are going. It was decided in public conclave, last night, to emigrate, and by the time the sun rises there won't be a bone left in our old habitations. Such cemeteries may suit my surviving friends, but they do not suit the remains that have the honor to make these remarks. My opinion is the general opinion. If you doubt it, go and see how the departing ghosts upset things before they started. They were almost riotous in their demonstrations of distaste. Hello, here are some of the Bledsoes, and if you will give me a lift with this tombstone I guess I will join company and jog along with them—mighty respectable old family, the Bledsoes, and used to always come out in six-horse hearses and all that sort of thing fifty years ago when I walked these streets in daylight. Good-by, friend."

And with his gravestone on his shoulder he joined the grisly procession, dragging his damaged coffin after him, for notwithstanding he pressed it upon me so earnestly, I utterly refused his hospitality. I suppose that for as much as two hours these sad outcasts went clacking by, laden with their dismal effects, and all that time I sat pitying them. One or two of the youngest and least dilapidated among them inquired about midnight trains on the railways, but the rest seemed unacquainted with that mode of travel, and merely asked about common public roads to various towns and cities, some of which are not on the map now, and vanished from it and from the earth as much as thirty years ago, and some few of them never *had* existed anywhere but on maps, and private ones in real-estate agencies at that. And they asked about the condition of the cemeteries in these towns and cities, and about the reputation the citizens bore as to reverence for the dead.

This whole matter interested me deeply, and likewise compelled my sympathy for these homeless ones. And it all seeming real, and I not knowing it was a dream, I mentioned to one shrouded wanderer an idea that had entered my head to publish an account of this curious and very sorrowful exodus, but said also that I could not describe it truthfully, and just as it occurred, without seeming to trifle with a grave subject and exhibit an irreverence for the dead that would shock and distress their surviving friends. But this bland and stately remnant of a former citizen leaned him far over my gate and whispered in my ear, and said:

"Do not let that disturb you. The community that can stand such graveyards as those we are emigrating from can stand anything a body can say about the neglected and forsaken dead that lie in them."

At that very moment a cock crowed, and the weird procession vanished and left not a shred or a bone behind. I awoke, and found myself lying with my head out of the bed and "sagging" downward considerably—a position favorable to dreaming dreams with morals in them, maybe, but not poetry.

NOTE The reader is assured that if the cemeteries in his town are kept in good order, this Dream is not leveled at his town at all, but is leveled particularly and venomously at the *next* town.

Dark Wings

By Phyllis Eisenstein

The house seemed large and empty now that her parents were dead. And yet it was also so soothingly quiet that Lydia would sometimes just stand in the high-ceilinged dining room and relish the silence. No shrill voice came floating from the upper story, no gravelly, grating one from the oak-paneled study, no orders, demands, advice, admonishments. The electricity was gone from the air, leaving nothing but solitude.

She had dreamed of such peace, dreamed as the years and her

youth ebbed away, eroded by a struggle she was too weak to win. Dutiful and self-sacrificing, people had called her—nurse, maid, cook, buffer between her parents and the outside world. But behind her back, she knew, they had clucked their tongues over the poor dried-up spinster. What did they know of the guilts and fears that her parents had instilled in her, of the elaborate net of obligation they had spun about her, till she was bound to them with ties that only death could sever? And death had come at last, like a knight on his pale charger, and borne away two coffins that set her free. Still, people clucked their tongues because Lydia lived much as before, alone in her parents' house, alone in her heart. If anything, she was quieter than ever.

Yet some things had changed for her. She painted a great deal more these days, uninterrupted. She had moved her studio from the basement to the big bedroom upstairs, where the light splashed in from windows on three sides. On fine days she would open those windows and let the sea air wash away the smell of paint. In the evenings she walked by the shore, sharing it with tourists and young lovers, and there were no responsibilities to call her home at any particular time. Some nights she would be there long after the noises of traffic had faded to nothing, till only the bell of a distant buoy remained for company. She hardly thought about anything at those times, only enjoyed the dark and the starlight on the waves, and the blessed, blessed silence.

On one such night she saw the bird for the first time. The moon had risen as she watched, its light splashed like a pale and shimmering highway crossing the restless ocean toward Europe. Like a shadow upon that path, the bird caught her eye, its dark wings limned by silvery radiance. For a moment it glided over the waves, pinions motionless in the still night air, and then it swooped upward and vanished in the darkness.

She stood awhile by the shore, straining her eyes for another glimpse of the creature, hoping it would wheel and make a second pass over the glittering water. It was a hawk of some sort, perhaps even an eagle—size and distance were deceptive out over the ocean, where there were no references to judge by. She wanted it to be an eagle, for they were rare in these parts and protected. She had only seen a live eagle here once before, when she was a small child. But though she waited till the moon was high and shrunken, she saw the bird no more, though perhaps she heard the beat of its wings far above her head. Or perhaps she only heard the cool surf beating at the rocks below her feet. At night by the sea, time, distance, and direction all seemed to muddle together, playing tricks on the eyes, the ears, and the mind.

At home she could not sleep for thinking about the bird, and before dawn she was in the studio by yellow, artificial light, with a fresh canvas and dark acrylic pigments spread over her palette. Swiftly, she recreated the impression of the scene, the silver moon-path, the dark bird an instantaneous silhouette, and all surrounded by an impenetrable black that seemed to suck light away from the hard, sharp stars. Blue-black she used, instead of true black—Prussian blue, that velvety shade so dark that only a careful eye could tell it from black, but warmer somehow, softer, deeper. The sky and the bird, Prussian blue. But when dawn added its radiance to her lamps, she saw that she had not captured the mood of that moment. The canvas was dull and dim. Her dilated pupils had perceived a patch of luminous, ethereal night in a vaster darkness, but the paints had given her only the latter.

Light, she thought, as she cleaned the palette and brushes. Light. But all she could remember was the plumage of the bird, blacker than black under the silver moon.

She slept.

Later in the day she walked down to the shore, earlier than usual. This time she carried binoculars hurriedly purchased in town, and she scanned the seaward sky from north to south, searching for a familiar silhouette. Gulls she saw, gulls in plenty, soaring, swooping for food, perching on rocks. Fat gulls, grey on top and white beneath. But no hawks, no eagles. She turned the binoculars westward toward the rooftops of the town, just visible beyond the intervening trees. She saw flecks that might be pigeons, crows, even sparrows, near and far. Ordinary birds. Nowhere did she see the short head, broad tail, and flared wings that marked her quarry.

She ate a quick dinner and returned to the painting by the waning, rosy glow of dusk. One could not evoke the depths of night, she thought, under a bright sun. She lightened her palette, reworked the moon and sea and even the dark air between them, trying to capture the radiance against which the bird had seemed so intense a shadow. Past midnight she realized that there was a contradiction in her mind, a double image of that instant, in which the sky was bright and dark at the same time. She could feel it, but the painting was only a poor reflection of that feeling, two-dimensional and—by now—muddy. She cleaned the palette and brushes and set the canvas aside against the wall. Stifling a yawn, she mounted a fresh, blank canvas on the easel.

The bird this time, nothing else. She sketched quickly, placing tail and flared pinions, adding details that she *felt* rather than re-membered. The light was moonlight of course, but there was no sky, no ocean, only the dark wingspan and the merest suggestion of curved beak and piercing eye. And when she reached the limits of both her recollection and her invention, she went downstairs to the study and looked eagles up in the encyclopedia. She knew now that it had been an eagle; she wouldn't allow it to be anything else. The encyclopedia illustrations gave her some inspiration and corrected a few of her assumptions, and she hurried back upstairs to make adjustments.

By dawnlight again, she viewed her new effort with a critical eye. She had never painted birds before; at most, they had been pieces of background in her few landscapes, a brushstroke or two in the sky. The black eagle showed her lack of familiarity with his kind; he was naïve and awkward, though bold. If she squinted, she could see a family resemblance to the bird on the back of a dollar bill.

At twilight she walked by the shore, searching the darkening sky for him, staying on till the moon was high, that night and many after. Night upon night, as the moon waned and the stars bright-ened by contrast. Night upon night, in fair weather and foul, when the waves were slick as glass, when the waves were wild things clutching for the sky. She waited for another glimpse, straining at clouds or a late gull or a speck of flotsam on the water. She waited late, late, and past midnight she returned home and worked on one or the other of the paintings, striving to recreate the bird.

She had never gone to town much, less since the deaths of her parents. Now she had no use for the place at all; she had her gro-ceries delivered and paid her bills by mail. Every scrap of her spare time was spoken for, by paint or binoculars or the sleep that she grudgingly allowed herself. Only the postman saw her, dropping off a few bills, catalogues, advertisements a couple of times a week. And the people who walked by the sea. But the weather was begin-ning to grow chilly for both tourists and lovers; soon the moon waxed full again, and only Lydia stood on the shore to watch it touch the waves with silver.

She heard the bird now, sometimes—she was sure of that, though she never saw his broad, dark wings. She heard him beat the air once, twice, high above her head, and then there was silence as he soared and she stared upward, trying to pierce the blackness with her human eyes. She thought he could probably see her well enough, eagles' eyes being so much sharper than humans', and she tried to imagine how she must appear to him—her face a pale speck amid the darkness of rocks and scrubby grass. A small thing, earth-bound, of no significance to a creature who sailed the dark ocean of air. What would it be like, she wondered, to have wings and look down upon the creatures who could only walk?

The paintings had proliferated by this time. They lined the studio, view after view of the subject she had seen only once. Yet there was a clear image of him in her mind's eye, as if she could reconstruct his whole form from the sound of his wings. His eye, she knew, was golden, like a great amber bead set above the corner of his beak. The beak was dark as his plumage, like polished jet. And to display their true span, the great black pinions would require a canvas larger than any Lydia had ever worked. She contemplated ordering the proper size from Boston, stretching it and preparing it herself. She measured the door of the studio to be sure the finished product could be carried out of the room, and then she made the phone call.

Autumn was waning by the time the painting was well begun. The sea breeze that washed her studio was chill by day now, and gusty, though she still opened the windows to it, and painted wearing an old sweater. When she walked by the shore, she could see scarlet leaves floating among the restless waves. The color of the ocean was changing, too, and the color of the sky; the daytime world was beginning to grey out for winter. Only at night were the changes invisible. At night the buoy still clanged far out on the water and the moon still splashed its shimmering highway to Europe almost at Lydia's feet. At night ebony wings beat the air, and Lydia strained for a glimpse, just a single brief glimpse of the bird that glided somewhere, somewhere, in the vast, unchanging darkness.

The days grew shorter as the chilling wind ruffled the waves to a restive froth, and the nights were long—long for walking by the choppy water, long for painting by lamplight. Lydia slept the whole short day through now, seeing the sun only at dawn and dusk. The bird preferred the night hours, and Lydia had begun to understand that preference. Day was jarring, stark, revealing too much of reality. Night was kind and soothing, hiding the world's flaws in velvet. At night Lydia could look into her dimly lit mirror and see the girl she had once been, the girl whose skin bore no sign of wrinkling, whose hair was yet untouched by grey, whose life still lay ahead of her. That girl could walk on the shore and dream dreams; she could look upon the moonlit highway to Europe and imagine herself traveling it, light as a feather, eastward, over the horizon.

She finished the painting half a dozen times. At dawn she would step back from it, cock her head to one side, and nod to herself. She would clean the brushes and palette carefully, then, and go to bed satisfied. But when she woke at dusk, the light of the setting sun showed her flaws, approximations, incompleteness, and she would eat a quick breakfast and go out to the shore again in search of her model, and inspiration. Inspiration she would find, in the clang of the buoy or the whisper of the wind, or the faint rustle of wingbeats high, high. But the model would not show himself, not even his shadow, and she would return home and work determinedly through the dark hours until she laid the brushes aside again come dawn.

Half a dozen times, she finished and slept—and then one blustery sunset found her with nothing left to do.

Not that the painting was perfect. She eyed it critically from every angle, brushes poised in her fingers, palette in the crook of her arm. She approached it several times, as if to lay another stroke upon the canvas, then drew back. The paint was very thick in some places. But she knew another layer would not make it better. The painting was beyond her ability to improve. She set her brushes aside and went out to walk.

Lydia understood the limits of her skill. She did not expect the canvas to be a photographic reproduction of the image in her mind's eye. She knew she would have to be satisfied with the faintest hint of the beauty and grace and power of the original. And down by the shore, in the pale light of the full moon, she had to weep for her own limitations. She wept, and she shivered a little because the night was very chill, and her coat was not quite heavy enough.

High above her head, she heard his wings.

She knew the sound instantly and looked up, straining to pierce the darkness, her tears a chilly patch upon each eye, blurring her vision for a moment. As a blur, she saw him silhouetted against the moon, and then she blinked and brought him into sharp focus. He was poised above the shimmering path that the moon laid down on the surface of the sea, his great wings motionless as he glided lower, lower, almost touching the white-topped waves. An eagle—yes, she had been right all the time, right in every detail, even to the amber eye that glittered with moonlight, glittered as it regarded her.

He swooped toward her, his great dark wings blotting out the moon, the sky, the world. She gazed at him in wonder, in adoration; the painting had not matched his true size, not remotely. He was the grandfather of eagles, she thought—the god of eagles. She felt a great gust of air as he hovered over her a moment. And then, as delicately as she might cradle a kitten, his great talons locked about her waist and hips. Her hair blew wild as his pinions cupped air to rise again, and then her feet floated free of the earth. Upward they soared—upward—and the rushing wind was a tonic to Lydia's soul. She felt light, young, and beautiful as the bird himself. Looking down, she could see the silver moonpath flowing far below.

Eastward they flew. Eastward toward Europe.

As the first rays of sunlight spread out over the ocean, Lydia saw the island. The only land visible from horizon to horizon, it was dominated by a huge mountain and, as they drew closer, she realized that the summit of that mountain was their destination. This did not surprise her; where else, she reasoned, would an eagle rest?

Closer still, and she saw the nest, big as her parents' house, built of bushes and driftwood and spars from sailing ships, some with ropes and tattered canvas still clinging to them. And then, at the last moment, just before her feet touched the soft, shadowed interior of the nest, just before they brushed the lining of feathers torn from the bird's own downy breast, and his mate's, she struggled. Poor dried-up spinster, she struggled—weakly—as she fell toward those small, dark, gaping beaks.

Dead Call

By William F. Nolan

Len had been dead for a month when the phone rang.

Midnight. Cold in the house and me dragged up from sleep to answer the call. Helen gone for the weekend. Me, alone in the house. And the phone ringing . . .

"Hello."

"Hello, Frank."

"Who is this?"

"You know *me*. It's Len . . . ole Len Stiles."

Cold. Deep and intense. The receiver dead-cold matter in my hand.

"Leonard Stiles died four weeks ago."

"Four weeks, three days, two hours and twenty-seven minutes ago—to be exact."

"I want to know who you are?"

A chuckle. The same dry chuckle I'd heard so many times.

"C'mon, ole buddy—after twenty years. Hell, you *know* me."

"This is a damned poor joke!"

"No joke, Frank. You're there, alive. And I'm here, dead. And you know something, old buddy . . . I'm really *glad* I did it."

"Did . . . what?"

"Killed myself. Because . . . death is just what I hoped it would be. Beautiful . . . gray . . . quiet . . . no pressures."

"Len Stiles's death was an accident . . . a concrete freeway barrier . . . His car—"

"I *aimed* my car for that barrier," the phone voice told me. "Pedal to the floor. Doing over ninety when I hit . . . No accident, Frank." The voice cold . . . cold. "I *wanted* to be dead. And no regrets."

I tried to laugh, make light of this—matching his chuckle with my own. "Dead men don't use telephones."

"I'm not really using the phone, not in a physical sense. It's just that I chose to contact you this way. You might say it's a matter of 'psychic electricity.' As a detached spirit I'm able to align my cosmic vibrations to match the vibrations of this power line. Simple, really."

"Sure. A snap. Nothing to it."

"Naturally, you're skeptical. I expected you to be. But . . . listen carefully to me, Frank."

And I listened—with the phone gripped in my hand in that cold night house—as the voice told me things that *only* Len could know . . . intimate details of shared experiences extending back through two decades. And when he'd finished I was certain of one thing:

He *was* Len Stiles.

"But, how . . . I still don't . . ."

"Think of this phone as a 'medium'—a line of force through which I can bridge the gap between us." The dry chuckle again. "Hell, you gotta admit it beats holding hands around a table in the dark—yet the principle is the same."

I'd been standing by my desk, transfixed by the voice. Now I moved behind the desk, sat down, trying to absorb this dark miracle. My muscles were wire-taut, my fingers cramped about the black receiver. I dragged in a slow breath, the night dampness of the room pressing at me.

"All right . . . I don't . . . believe in ghosts, don't . . . pretend to understand any of this, but . . . I'll accept it. I *must* accept it."

"I'm glad, Frank—because it's important that we talk." A long moment of hesitation. Then the voice, lower now, softer. "I know how lousy things have been, ole buddy."

"What do you mean?"

"I just know how things are going for you. And . . . I want to help. As your friend, I want you to know that I understand."

"Well . . . I'm really not . . ."

"You've been feeling bad, haven't you? Kind of 'down', right?"

"Yeah . . . a little, I guess."

"And I don't blame you. You've got reasons. Lots of reasons. For one . . . there's your money problem."

"I'm expecting a raise. Shendorf promised me one—within the next few weeks."

"You won't get it, Frank. I *know*. He's lying to you. Right now, at this moment, he's looking for a man to replace you at the company. Shendorf's planning to fire you."

"He never liked me . . . We never got along from the day I walked into that office."

"And your wife . . . all the arguments you've been having with her lately . . . It's a pattern, Frank. Your marriage is all over. Helen's going to ask you for a divorce. She's in love with another man."

"*Who*, dammit? What's his name?"

"You don't know him. Wouldn't change things if you did. There's nothing you can do about it now. Helen just . . . doesn't love you anymore. These things happen to people."

"We've been . . . drifting apart for the last year—but I didn't know why. I had no idea that she . . ."

"And then there's Jan. She's back on it, Frank. Only it's worse now. A lot worse."

I knew what he meant—and the coldness raked along my body. Jan was nineteen, my oldest daughter—and she'd been into drugs for the past three years. But she'd promised to quit.

"What do you know about Jan? Tell me!"

"She's into the heavy stuff, Frank. She's hooked bad. It's too late for her."

"What the hell are you saying?"

"I'm saying she's lost to you . . . She's rejected you, and there's no reaching her. She *hates* you . . . blames you for everything."

"I won't *accept* that kind of blame! I did my best for her."

"It wasn't enough, Frank. We both know that. You'll never see Jan again."

106

The blackness was welling within me, a choking wave through my body.

"Listen to me, old buddy. Things are going to get worse, not better. I know. I went through my own kind of hell when I was alive."

"I'll . . . start over . . . leave the city—go East, work with my brother in New York."

"Your brother doesn't want you in his life. You'd be an intruder . . . an alien. He never writes you, does he?"

"No, but that doesn't mean—"

"Not even a card last Christmas. No letters or calls. He doesn't *want* you with him, Frank, believe me."

And then he began to tell me other things . . . He began to talk about middle age and how it was too late now to make any kind of new beginning . . . He spoke of disease . . . loneliness . . . of rejection and despair. And the blackness was complete.

"There's only one real solution to things, Frank—just *one*. That gun you keep in your desk upstairs. Use it, Frank. Use the gun."

"I couldn't do that."

"But why not? What other choice have you got? The solution is *there*. Go upstairs and use the gun. I'll be waiting for you afterwards. You won't be alone. It'll be like the old days . . . we'll be together . . . Death is beautiful, Frank. I *know*. Life is ugly, but death is beautiful . . . Use the gun, Frank . . . the gun . . . use the gun . . . the gun . . . the gun . . ."

I've been dead for a month now, and Len was right. It's fine here. No pressures. No worries. Gray and quiet and beautiful . . .

I know how lousy things have been going for you. And they *won't* get any better.

Isn't that your phone ringing?
Better answer it.
It's important that we talk.

Different Kinds of Dead

By Ed Gorman

Around eight that night, snow started drifting on the narrow Nebraska highway Ralph Sheridan was traveling. Already he could feel the rear end of the new Buick begin sliding around on the freezing surface of the asphalt, and could see that he would soon have to pull over and scrape the windshield. Snow was forming into gnarly bumps on the safety glass.

The small-town radio station he was listening to confirmed his worst suspicions: the weather bureau was predicting a genuine March blizzard, with eight to ten inches of snow and drifts up to several feet.

Sheridan sighed. A thirty-seven-year-old bachelor who made his living as a traveling computer salesman—he worked especially hard at getting farmers to buy his wares—he spent most of the year on the road, putting up in the small shabby plains motels that from a distance always reminded him of doghouses. A brother in Cleveland was all the family he had left, everybody else was dead. The only other people he stayed in touch with were the men he'd been in Viet Nam with. There had been women, of course, but somehow it never worked out—this one wasn't his type, that one laughed too loudly, this one didn't have the same interests as he. And while his friends bloomed with mates and children, there was for Sheridan just the road, beers in bars with other salesmen, and nights alone in motel rooms with paper strips across the toilet seats.

The Buick pitched suddenly toward the ditch. An experienced driver and a calm man, Sheridan avoided the common mistake of slamming on the brakes. Instead, he took the steering wheel in both hands and guided the hurtling car along the edge of the ditch. While he had only a foot of earth keeping him from plunging into the gully on his right, he let the car find its own traction. Soon enough, the car was gently heading back onto the asphalt.

It was there, just when the headlights focused on the highway again, that he saw the woman.

At first, he tried sensibly enough to deny she was even there. His first impression was that she was an illusion, a mirage of some sort created by the whirling, whipping snow and the vast black night.

But no, there really was a beautiful, red-haired woman standing in the center of the highway. She wore a trench coat and black high-heeled shoes. She might have been one of the women on the covers of the private eye paperbacks he'd read back in the sixties.

This time, he did slam on the brakes; otherwise, he would have run over her. He came to a skidding stop less than three feet from her.

His first reaction was gratitude. He dropped his head to the wheel and let out a long sigh. His whole body trembled. She could easily have been dead by now.

He was just raising his head when harsh wind and snow and cold blew into the car. The door on the passenger side had opened.

She got inside, saying nothing, closing the door when she was seated comfortably.

Sheridan looked over at her. Close up, she was even more beautiful. In the yellow glow of the dashboard, her features were so exquisite they had the refined loveliness of sculpture. Her tumbling, radiant hair only enhanced her face.

She turned to him finally and said, in a low, somewhat breathy voice, "You'd better not sit here in the middle of the highway long. It won't be safe."

He drove again. On either side of the highway he could make out little squares of light—the yellow windows of farmhouses lost in the furious gloom of the blizzard. The car heater warmed them nicely. The radio played some sexy jazz that somehow made the prairie and the snow and the weather alert go away.

All he could think of was those private eye novels he'd read as a teenager. This was what always happened to the Hammer himself, ending up with a woman like this.

"Do you mind?" she asked.

Before he had time to answer, she already had the long white cigarette between her full red lips and was lighting it. Then she tossed her head back and French inhaled. He hadn't seen anybody do that in years.

"Your car get ditched somewhere" he asked finally, realizing that these were his first words to her.

"Yes," she said, "somewhere."

"So you were walking to the nearest town?"

"Something like that."

"You were walking in the wrong direction." He paused. "And you're traveling alone?"

She glanced over at him again with her dark, lovely gaze. "Yes. Alone." Her voice was as smoky as her cigarette.

He drove some more, careful to keep both hands on the wheel, slowing down whenever the rear of the car started to slide.

He wasn't paying much attention to the music at this point—they were going up a particularly sleek and dangerous hill—but then the announcer's voice came on and said, "Looks like the police have really got their hands full tonight. Not only with the blizzard, but now with a murder. Local banker John T. Sloane was found murdered in his downtown apartment twenty minutes ago. Police report an eyewitness say he heard two gunshots and then saw a beautiful woman leaving Sloane's apartment. The eyewitness reportedly said that the woman strongly resembled Sloane's wife, Carlotta. But police note that that's impossible, given the fact that Carlotta died mysteriously last year in a boating accident. The eyewitness insists that the resemblance between the redheaded woman leaving Sloane's apartment tonight and the late Mrs. Sloane is uncanny. Now back to our musical program for the evening."

A bosso nova came on.

Beautiful. Redheaded. Stranded alone. Looking furtive. He started glancing at her, and she said, "I'll spare you the trouble. It's me. Carlotta Stone."

"You? But the announcer said—"

She turned to him and smiled. "That I'm dead? Well, so I am."

Not until then did Sheridan realize how far out in the boonies he was. Or how lacerating the storm had become. Or how helpless he felt inside a car with a woman who claimed to be dead.

"Why don't you just relax?"

"Please don't patronize me, Mr. Sheridan."

"I'm not patroniz— Say, how did you know my name?"

"I know a lot of things."

"But I didn't tell you my name and there's no way you could read my registration from there and—"

She French inhaled—then exhaled—and said, "As I said, Mr. Sheridan, I know a lot of things." She shook her head. "I don't know how I got like this."

"Like what?"

"Dead."

"Oh."

"You still don't believe me, do you?"

He sighed. "We've got about eight miles to go. Then we'll be in Porterville. I'll let you out at the Greyhound depot there. Then you can go about your business and I can go about mine."

110

She touched his temple with long, lovely fingers. "That's why you're such a lonely man, Mr. Sheridan. You never take any chances. You never let yourself get involved with anybody."

He smiled thinly, "Especially with dead people."

"Maybe you're the one who's dead, Mr. Sheridan. Night after night alone in cheap little hotel rooms, listening to the country western music through the wall, and occasionally hearing people make love. No woman. No children. No real friends. It's not a very good life, is it, Mr. Sheridan?"

He said nothing. Drove.

"We're both dead, Mr. Sheridan. You know that?"

He still said nothing. Drove.

After a time, she said, "Do you want to know how tonight happened, Mr. Sheridan?"

"No."

"I made you mad, didn't I, Mr. Sheridan, when I reminded you of how lonely you are?"

"I don't see where it's any of your business."

Now it was her turn to be quiet. She stared out at the lashing snow. Then she said, "The last thing I could remember before tonight was John T. holding me under water till I drowned off the side of our boat. By the way, that's what all his friends called him. John T." She lit one cigarette off another. "Then earlier tonight I felt myself rise through darkness and suddenly I realized was taking form. I was rising from the grave and taking form. And there was just one place I wanted to go. The apartment he kept in town for his so-called business meetings. So I went there tonight and killed him."

"You won't die."

"I beg your pardon?"

"They won't execute you for doing it. You just tell them the same story you told me, and you'll get off with second degree. Maybe even not guilty by reason of insanity."

She laughed. "Maybe if you weren't so busy watching the road, you'd notice what's happening to me, Mr. Sheridan."

She was disappearing. Right there in his car. Where her left arm had been was now just a smoldering red-tipped cigarette that seemed to be held up on invisible wires. A part of her face was starting to disappear, too.

"About a quarter mile down the highway, let me out if you would."

He laughed. "What's there? A graveyard?"

"As a matter of fact, yes."

By now her legs had started disappearing.

"You don't seem to believe it, Mr. Sheridan, but I'm actually trying to help you. Trying to tell you to go out and live while you're still alive. I wasted my life on my husband, sitting around at home while he ran around with other women, hoping against hope that someday he'd be faithful and we'd have a good life together. It never happened, Mr. Sheridan. I wasted my whole life."

"Sounds like you paid him back tonight. Two gunshots, the radio said."

Her remaining hand raised the cigarette to what was left of her mouth. She inhaled deeply. When she exhaled the smoke was a lovely gray color. "I was hoping there would be some satisfaction in it. There isn't. I'm as lonely as I ever was."

He wondered if that was a small, dry sob he heard in her voice.

"Right here," she said.

He had been cautiously braking the last minute and a half. He brought the car comfortably over to the side of the road. He put on his emergency flashers in case anybody was behind him.

Up on the hill to his right, he saw it. A graveyard. The tombstones looked like small children huddled against the whipping snow.

"After I killed him, I just started walking," she said. "Walking. Not even knowing where I was going. Then you came along." She stabbed the cigarette out in the ashtray. "Do something about your life, Mr. Sheridan. Don't waste it the way I have."

She got out of the car and leaned back in. "Goodbye, Mr. Sheridan."

He sat there, watching her disappear deep into the gully, then reappear on the other side and start walking up the slope of the hill.

By the time she was halfway there, she had nearly vanished altogether.

Then, moments later, she was gone utterly.

At the police station, he knew better than to tell the cops about the ghost business. He simply told them he'd seen a woman fitting the same description out on the highway about twenty minutes ago.

Grateful for his stopping in, four cops piled into two different cars and they set out under blood red flashers into the furious white night.

Mr. Sheridan found a motel—his usual one in this particular burg—and took his usual room. He stripped, as always, to his boxer shorts and t-shirt and got snug in bed beneath the covers and watched a rerun of an old sitcom.

112

He should have been laughing—at least all the people on the laugh track seemed to be having a good time—but instead he did something he rarely did. He began crying. Oh, not big wailing tears, but hard tiny silver ones. Then he shut off both TV and the lights and lay in the solitary darkness thinking of what she'd said to him.

No woman. No children. No love.

Only much later, when the wind near dawn died and the snow near light subsided, only then did Sheridan sleep, his tears dried out but feeling colder than he ever had.

Lonely cold. Dead cold.

Displaced Person

By Eric Frank Russell

He glided out of the gathering dusk and seated himself at the other end of my bench and gazed absently across the lakes toward the Sherry Netherland. The setting sun had dribbled blood in the sky. Central Park was enjoying its eventide hush: there was only the rustle of leaves and grasses, the cooing of distant and shadowy couples, the muted toot of a bus way over on Fifth.

When the bench quivered its announcement of company I had glanced along it expecting to find some derelict seeking a flop. The difference between the anticipated and the seen was such that I looked again, long, carefully, out one corner of my eye so that he wouldn't notice it.

Despite the gray half-tones of twilight, what I saw was a study in black and white. He had thin, sensitive features as white as his gloves and his shirt-front. His shoes and suit were not quite as black as his finely curved eyebrows and well-groomed hair. His eyes were blackest of all; that solid, supernal darkness that can be no deeper or darker. Yet they were alive with an underlying glow.

He had no hat. A slender walking stick of ebony rested against his legs. A black silk-lined cloak hung from his shoulders. If he'd been doing it for the movies he couldn't have presented a better picture of a distinguished foreigner.

My mind speculated about him the way minds do when momentarily they've nothing else to bother them. A European refugee, it decided. A great surgeon, or sculptor or something like that. Perhaps a writer, or a painter. More likely the latter.

I stole another look at him. In the lowering light his pale profile was hawklike. The glow behind his eyes was strengthening with the dark. His cloak lent him majesty. The trees were stretching their arms toward him as if to give comfort through the long, long night.

No hint of suffering marked that face. It had nothing in common with the worn, lined faces I had seen in New York, features stamped forever with the brand of the Gestapo. On the contrary, it held a mixture of boldness and serenity. Impulsively I decided that he was a musician. I could imagine him conducting a choir of fifty thousand voices.

"I am fond of music," he said in low, rich tones.

He turned his face toward me, revealed a pronounced peak in his hair.

"Really?" The unexpectedness of it had me muddled. "What sort?" I asked feebly.

"This." He used his ebony stick to indicate the world at large. "The sigh of ending day."

"Yes, it is soothing," I agreed.

We were silent awhile. Slowly the horizon soaked up the blood in the sky. A wan moon floated over the towers.

"You're not a native of New York?" I prompted.

"No." Resting long, slender hands upon his stick, he gazed meditatively forward. "I am a displaced person."

"I'm sorry."

"Thank you," he said.

I couldn't sit there and leave him flat like that. The choice was to continue or go. There was no need to go. I continued.

"Care to tell me about it?"

His head came round and he studied me as if only now aware of my presence. That weird light in his orbs could almost be felt. He smiled gradually, tolerantly, showing perfect teeth.

"I would be wasting your time."

"Not at all. I'm wasting it anyway."

Smiling again, he used his stick to draw unseeable circles in front of his black shoes.

"In these days it is an all too familiar story," he said. "A leader became so blinded by his own glory that no longer could he perceive his own blunders. He developed delusions of grandeur, posed as the final arbiter on everything from birth to death, and thereby brought into being a movement for his overthrow. He created the

114

seeds of his own destruction. It was inevitable in the circumstances."

"You bet!" I supported wholeheartedly. "To hell with dictators!"

The stick slipped from his grasp. He picked it up, juggled it idly, resumed his circle-drawing.

"The revolt didn't succeed?" I suggested.

"No." He looked at the circles as if he could see them. "It proved too weak and too early. It was crushed. Then came the purge." His glowing eyes surveyed the sentinel trees. "I organized that opposition. I still think it was justified. But I dare not go back."

"Fat lot you should care about that. You'll fit in here like Reilly."

"I don't think so. I'm not welcome here either." His voice was deeper. "Not wanted—anywhere."

"You don't look like Trotsky to me," I cracked. "Besides, he's dead. Cheer up. Don't be morbid. You're in a free country now."

"No man is free until he's beyond his enemy's reach." He glanced at me with an irritating touch of amusement. "When one's foe has gained control of every channel of propaganda, uses them exclusively to present his own case and utterly suppress mine, and damns the truth in advance as the worst of lies, there is no hope for me."

"That's your European way of looking at things. I don't blame you for it, but you've got to snap out of it. You're in America now. We've free speech here. A man can say what he likes, write what he likes."

"If only that were true."

"It is true," I asserted, my annoyance beginning to climb. "Here, you can call the Rajah of Bam a hyphenated soandso if you want. Nobody can stop you, not even a cop. We're free, like I told you."

He stood up, towering amid embracing trees. From my sitting position his height seemed tremendous. The moon lit his face in pale ghastliness.

"Would that I had one-tenth of your comforting faith."

With that, he turned away. His cape swung behind him, billowing in the night breeze until it resembled mighty wings.

"My name," he murmured softly, "is Lucifer."

After that, there was only the whisper of the wind.

The Disintegration of Alan

By Melissa Mia Hall

I can pinpoint almost the very second it began, the disintegration of Alan. It was the morning of October one; I had just glanced at the digital clock. Seven A.M., five or four minutes past. A Wednesday. In Greystone Bay. His right hand. He was reaching for the sugar at the breakfast table and as I watched his familiar hand pass through a diagonal shaft of sunlight, I saw his thumb fragment into nothingness. For a moment I thought it was due to my nearsighted eyes. I blinked groggily, coffee cup halfway to my lips.

"Alan?"

He thought I was beginning the old antisugar routine.

I swallowed heavily and set the cup down, staring at the space where his thumb had been. The index finger next to it looked like it would follow the thumb any moment, the fingertip shortening to the first joint. I exhaled slowly, resting my eyes on the crumpled newspaper beside my chair. I adjusted my glasses and returned my gaze to Alan.

He watched me curiously. The wrist of the disintegrating arm rested by his plate.

"Anything wrong, sweetie pie?"

"It's just—"

"Don't worry, if it bothers you that much, I won't take any sugar."

"Alan—"

"Now, Gabrielle, don't be a nuisance—"

Biting my lip, I continued to stare.

"What's with you?"

"I don't know," I said truthfully. I picked up my coffee and turned my head toward the window over the sink. "Go ahead, put some sugar in your coffee."

"I don't want to," he said.

"I said, go ahead."

"And I said I don't want to!"

"Why not?" I looked at him again. The disintegration had progressed. I wondered why it had begun at such an unlikely spot and

116

not at his feet or his head. Then I realized the insanity of such reflections. Heat rose in my cheeks.

Alan's left hand reached toward the sugar bowl.

My heart sank. "Alan, why are you using your left hand?"

He shrugged his broad shoulders and the solidity of his chest only emphasized the absurdity of what I saw occurring before me. "Why not?"

"You're right-handed," I said.

Beads of perspiration broke out along his forehead. He scratched his mustache nervously and then tugged at his white collar—all with his left hand.

"Alan, what has happened to your right hand—your arm?"

His handsome, well-ordered face crumpled into confusion. "Nothing's wrong. I don't know what you mean. You're always finding something wrong with me. I don't know—I'm sick—sick to death." He pushed back his chair and stood up. "Call the office and tell them I'm not coming into work today." He glared at me, but the force of his chaotic anger had already dissipated. He looked constipated.

"Alan, really—"

"Shut up. I mean it." His mouth turned down at the ends and quivered. "I want to be alone." With that, he went to the doorway.

"Alan—please tell me what's going on."

"Nothing; it's the flu or something," he said, a touch of the shriek in his tone.

"Your arm—"

"What about my arm? There's nothing wrong about my arm!" He lifted the affected appendage and waved it around. It was grotesque.

I gasped. "Alan, can't you see—it's disappearing!"

"It is not!" he said before stomping down the hallway.

I sat in my chair and considered the situation. It was ridiculous, horrifying, and repulsive. Funny, too—well, a little. I hit my spoon against the tabletop. A sharp pain needled my temples.

The clock rang out. Time to leave for work. I had to call the *Gazette* and tell them Alan wasn't coming in. It didn't take long. I had to call in too. No way I could go to work either. I dialed the number. My secretary answered, her Brooklyn accent bright and sure over the line. I told her that I wouldn't be in and all the other things I was supposed to. I hung up the phone again and took off my shoes.

Down the hall, past the bedroom, to the studio I went. The

117

drawing board was just as I had left it. I sat before a half-drawn pencil sketch of Alan. I had tried—

I looked at it a long time. Finally I covered the sketch and played on a new piece of paper, blending lines and shapes without meaning. It was midmorning before I got up and stretched my legs. They'd almost fallen asleep. I had to go see about Alan.

He didn't call out to my query when I knocked on the door. I pushed it open slowly. Our room was paneled in dark wood and had never been very light. That morning was no exception. My eyes had to adjust to the dimness before I could see what was left of him, sitting in the striped armchair by the window. He looked at me and shrugged. His head, shoulders, and a portion of his torso were all that remained.

I wanted to vomit but did not. I held my hands to my mouth. What could I say?

He gazed at me vacantly, as if he could see me, but did not know me or the reason why I was there. He might have been thinking. Of other things. As I watched him I could detect recognition struggling in his eyes.

His mouth opened. "I'm sick. Please leave me alone for a while. I'll be okay if you'll just leave me alone."

He was afraid.

I was sweating. I took off my jacket and pushed back my hair. Then I went to him and tried to touch him. He jerked backward.

"Alan—please—"

"Gabrielle, why?"

I reached out again, trembling. My hands slid through. It's not always easy to face a reality like that.

He had been real. We had made love; we had taken baths together; we had hiked in the Vermont mountains. He liked Gatorade and tennis. I hated tennis. He liked beer. We saved beer cans. There was a huge bag of them out in the garage. The color orange was his favorite. He preferred Kleenex to Puffs. He didn't like the same kind of music I did and resented me singing along with the radio when we were in the car together. He always wore his hair parted on the right side. He liked watching the boats in the harbor. I liked sailing them.

There was nothing I could do. Soon he would be gone entirely. I thought of the police. Could such a thing be explained? "My husband disintegrated this morning and I thought you'd like to know." A giggle mushroomed from the madness and spilled out. I couldn't help it. Poor Alan. He twitched at that giggle.

"I'm sorry, Alan."

I would tell the police he just left me. Men do that sometimes. Nothing you can do to stop them—I don't think.

I straightened up, folded my arms. I regarded him with a sudden clarity. I was a camera remembering rolls of film that had passed through my chamber. Images, yes, yes—flash forward and flash back.

"Alan, is there anything I can do?"

"Well—" His head swiveled back and forth. He was trying to think of something.

I stared at the space where his bottom had been. I had not seen that disappear. It was unfortunate. Manic laughter pushed in my throat, wanting out. I clamped my lips and waited. I would be generous, kind.

"Yes, Alan?"

Childlike, shrill, he said something I couldn't quite understand.

"What?"

"I said, I guess I'm going away."

To just fade away, like that?

"Must it be like this—" Perhaps his image would firm up again—strong Alan, stalwart reporter. My stomach churned or maybe it growled. I hadn't eaten much breakfast and it was noon or after.

His mouth worked like a fish out of water. He'd always been rather clumsy.

"I don't want you to think I don't care about you, Gab."

I flinched. I hated him to call me Gab.

"Aw, Gabby, I really don't know why this has to happen. I thought we had a swell marriage and I've had a neat life, with the paper and all. But you know—I never really had control. This isn't that much a surprise."

His big blue eyes were mistlike. Sunlight glowed through his hair.

There was nothing I could do. I tried to kiss him. It was like kissing air. I couldn't even smell the after-shave he used to put on every morning.

The futility of life descended upon me. But I had to be brave.

"Wish it would get over with," he said. His voice was whistle-thin.

"Do you have anything else to say? Any—last words?" I gasped back the sobs.

"It's not my fault."

Childish of him. Always that petulant tilt to his lips—that too vivid, colorful face. What color? He was pale.

"Didn't you love me?" I asked, blushing at my boldness. It was now or never.

He looked at me like he didn't understand.

I left the bedroom. I thought I could hear him crying.

The studio was my sanctuary. I went to the drawing board and sat down. I looked out at Blind Point, at the ocean beyond. I pulled out the portrait of Alan and studied it intently to see if I could save it. Frowning, I took my favorite artgum eraser and finished erasing it.

I have always been a competent artist and I know a failure when I see one.

Down by the Sea near the Great Big Rock

By Joe R. Lansdale

Down by the sea near the great big rock, they made their camp and toasted marshmallows over a small, fine fire. The night was pleasantly chill and the sea spray cold. Laughing, talking, eating the gooey marshmallows, they had one swell time; just them, the sand, the sea and the sky, and the great big rock.

The night before they had driven down to the beach, to the camping area; and on their way, perhaps a mile from their destination, they had seen a meteor shower, or something of that nature. Bright lights in the heavens, glowing momentarily, seeming to burn red blisters across the ebony sky.

Then it was dark again, no meteoric light, just the natural glow of the heavens—the stars, the dime-size moon.

They drove on and found an area of beach on which to camp, a stretch dominated by pale sands and big waves, and the great big rock.

Toni and Murray watched the children eat their marshmallows and play their games, jumping and falling over the great big rock, rolling in the cool sand. About midnight, when the kids were crashed out, they walked along the beach like fresh-found lovers, arm in arm, shoulder to shoulder, listening to the sea, watching the sky, speaking words of tenderness.

"I love you so much," Murray told Toni, and she repeated the words and added, "and our family too."

They walked in silence now, the feelings between them words enough. Sometimes Murray worried that they did not talk as all the marriage manuals suggested, that so much of what he had to say on the world and his work fell on the ears of others, and that she had so little to truly say to him. Then he would think: What the hell? I know how I feel. Different messages, unseen, unheard, pass between us all the time, and they communicate in a fashion words cannot.

He said some catch phrase, some pet thing between them, and Toni laughed and pulled him down on the sand. Out there beneath that shiny-dime moon, they stripped and loved on the beach like young sweethearts, experiencing their first night together after long expectation.

It was nearly two A.M. when they returned to the camper, checked the children and found them sleeping comfortably as kittens full of milk.

They went back outside for awhile, sat on the rock and smoked and said hardly a word. Perhaps a coo or a purr passed between them, but little more.

Finally they climbed inside the camper, zipped themselves into their sleeping bag and nuzzled together on the camper floor.

Outside the wind picked up, the sea waved in and out, and a slight rain began to fall.

Not long after Murray awoke and looked at his wife in the crook of his arm. She lay there with her face a grimace, her mouth opening and closing like a guppie, making an "uhhh, uhh," sound.

A nightmare perhaps. He stroked the hair from her face, ran his fingers lightly down her cheek and touched the hollow of her throat and thought: What a nice place to carve out some fine, white meat . . .

—*What in hell is wrong with me?* Murray snapped inwardly, and he rolled away from her, out of the bag. He dressed, went outside and sat on the rock. With shaking hands on his knees, buttocks resting on the warmth of the stone, he brooded. Finally he dismissed the possibility that such a thought had actually crossed his mind, smoked a cigarette and went back to bed.

He did not know that an hour later Toni awoke and bent over

him and looked at his face as if it were something to squash. But finally she shook it off and slept.

The children tossed and turned. Little Roy squeezed his hands open, closed, open, closed. His eyelids fluttered rapidly.

Robyn dreamed of striking matches.

Morning came and Murray found that all he could say was, "I had the oddest dream."

Toni looked at him, said, "Me too," and that was all.

Placing lawn chairs on the beach, they put their feet on the rock and watched the kids splash and play in the waves; watched as Roy mocked the sound of the JAWS music and made fins with his hands and chased Robyn through the water as she scuttled backwards and screamed with false fear.

Finally they called the children from the water, ate a light lunch, and, leaving the kids to their own devices, went in for a swim.

The ocean stroked them like a mink-gloved hand. Tossed them, caught them, massaged them gently. They washed together, laughing, kissing—

—Then tore their lips from one another as up on the beach they heard a scream.

Roy had his fingers gripped about Robyn's throat, had her bent back over the rock and was putting a knee in her chest. There seemed no play about it. Robyn was turning blue.

Toni and Murray waded for shore, and the ocean no longer felt kind. It grappled with them, held them, tripped them with wet, foamy fingers. It seemed an eternity before they reached shore, yelling at Roy.

Roy didn't stop. Robyn flopped like a dying fish.

Murray grabbed the boy by the hair and pulled him back, and for a moment, as the child turned, he looked at his father with odd eyes that did not seem his, but looked instead as cold and firm as the great big rock.

Murray slapped him, slapped him so hard Roy spun and went down, stayed there on hands and knees, panting.

Murray went to Robyn, who was already in Toni's arms, and on the child's throat were blue-black bands like thin, ugly snakes.

"Baby, baby, are you okay?" Toni said over and over. Murray wheeled, strode back to the boy, and Toni was now yelling at him, crying, "Murray, Murray, easy now. They were just playing and it got out of hand."

Roy was on his feet, and Murray, gritting his teeth, so angry he could not believe it, slapped the child down.

"MURRAY," Toni yelled, and she let go of the sobbing Robyn and went to stay his arm, for he was already raising it for another strike. "That's no way to teach him not to hit, not to fight."

Murray turned to her, almost snarling, but then his face relaxed and he lowered his hand. Turning to the boy, feeling very criminal, Murray reached down to lift Roy by the shoulder. But Roy pulled away, darted for the camper.

"Roy," he yelled, and started after him. Toni grabbed his arm. "Let him be," she said. "He got carried away and he knows it. Let him mope it over. He'll be all right." Then softly: "I've never known you to get that mad."

"I've never been so mad before," he said honestly.

They walked back to Robyn, who was smiling now. They all sat on the rock, and about fifteen minutes later Robyn got up to see about Roy. "I'm going to tell him it's okay," she said. "He didn't mean it." She went inside the camper.

"She's sweet," Toni said.

"Yeah," Murray said, looking at the back of Toni's neck as she watched Robyn move away. He was thinking that he was supposed to cook lunch today, make hamburgers, slice onions; big onions cut thin with a freshly sharpened knife. He decided to go get it.

"I'll start lunch," he said flatly, and stalked away.

As he went, Toni noticed how soft the back of his skull looked, so much like an over-ripe melon.

She followed him inside the camper.

Next morning, after the authorities had carried off the bodies, taken the four of them out of the bloodstained, fire-gutted camper, one detective said to another:

"Why does it happen? Why would someone kill a nice family like this? And in such horrible ways . . . set fire to it afterwards?"

The other detective sat on the huge rock and looked at his partner, said tonelessly, "Kicks maybe."

That night, when the moon was high and bright, gleaming down like a big spotlight, the big rock, satiated, slowly spread its flippers out, scuttled across the sand, into the waves, and began to swim toward the open sea. The fish that swam near it began to fight.

Dragon Sunday

By Ruth Berman

The desire for dragons is insidious. With the best intentions of remaining aware that you would be scared shitless by a real dragon and too obsessed with getting the hell out of the way of the flames to respond to the beauty of firelight reflected on blue or green or purple metallic scales, still—the desire remains.

You sit there on the yellow carpet, safe inside the beige walls, and desire dragons.

Which is all right, although wasteful of time and energy if you can't get dragons, but potentially dangerous if you can.

And it's all very well to consider that half the beauty of a vast body supported against the sky by wide leathery wings clangorously striking the air is in the fact that it's aerodynamically impossible. The sensual solidity of the imaginary is touching, and dragons are lovable quite simply because they look real and aren't. Until one Sunday you open the door to bring in the paper, and instead of funnies on the mat there are dragons all over the sky.

If they are.

They look real, seen in glimpses through plastic slats held apart by uncertain fingers (after the door is slammed shut). The bright sky is full of them, and there is even one ramping in the swimming pool, splashing water all over the courtyard. The slats clatter as the fingers let them go, and they fall back together.

So you pick up the telephone. Luckily, the dial tone is there, and it whines at you dutifully. Only you can't think where to call. There isn't anybody in LA you really know well enough to call up and say, "Hey, I know this is going to sound funny, but can you see any dragons out your window?" You could, of course, call any one of the people from the office. On the other hand, in the interests of keeping the job, maybe you'd better not.

A high *skree* shrills in the air from somewhere beyond the window, and other calls echo it from all over the sky.

Perhaps a call home would help. But long-distance is a strain on the budget, even on weekends. And anyway, they wouldn't know anything about what's going on in the sky. Not the one here. No, clearly, the thing to do is call the manager and complain.

The phone is still working, and she answers it on the third ring. "Hello?"

"Hi, this is 31 B."

"Uh-huh?" she says encouragingly.

"Yes. There seem to be these dragons all around, and—"

"Oh, that's too bad."

She is a conscientious manager.

"I'll get the exterminator to come out Monday. Will that be okay?"

"Well, but . . . Yeah, I guess so."

"Uh-huh." She waits, in case there are any other complaints to hand.

"Thanks. G'bye."

"Bye-bye."

There are several possibilities: (A) She misheard and thought the problem was roaches; (B) She thought it was just a bit of typically peculiar tenant's humor; (C) She thought she was humoring someone who'd just gone off his rocker, and she's going to call a hospital. Or, of course (D): Well, what else can you do about dragons except call in an exterminator? Knights don't do that sort of work anymore.

Another frightened glance out the picture window reveals the dragon in the swimming pool just leaping out. Its wings cup the air, and it rises leisurely, circling upward and throwing flecks of water against the white stucco walls as its tail swirls around after it.

There still remains the TV set. Nothing happens when the on knob is pulled out. But then nothing does happen when the on knob is pulled out. Bending over and putting an ear against it makes audible a humming deep inside it. The TV is working, and there is time for a glass of water before it does anything about it.

Even with water your throat feels dry.

Time for the news.

"—og alert," says the TV, still pictureless. "Motorists on the Hollywood Freeway report that the Capitol Records Building is invisible. Meteorological records indicate that this is the worst smog recorded in five years. Not since . . ." And so on. No dragons.

Perhaps later, after the weather.

The picture joins up. It does a little ballet and settles into a view of the Freeway without the Capitol Records Building. Without much of anything except on-ramp, overpass, off-ramp, and smoggy sky. Even the FWY signs are obscured.

But the smog . . .

That sky is smoggy. The TV says so. That sky is smoggy, and this sky is blue. Which is impossible. Which is crazy. Which makes sense.

Naturally, if you're crazy enough to imagine dragons, you imagine them a blue sky. A dragon demands a blue sky.

The thing to do is to go get psychiatric care. Fortunately, County General is in walking distance. And driving it'll take less than no time.

So you go out, and the nearest dragon *skrees* and descends upon you, its scales flashing as it curves against the sunny sky, and the light is reflected off it, flashing reptilian stainedglass on the stucco.

It lands with all its claws in your back, and its mouth open, flaming.

Smoke blots out the sky.

Drops of light from dragonscales can still be seen, a little while, until dragonfire obliterates . . .

Duck Hunt

By Joe R. Lansdale

There were three hunters and three dogs. The hunters had shiny shotguns, warm clothes and plenty of ammo. The dogs were each covered in big blue spots and were sleek and glossy and ready to run. No duck was safe.

The hunters were Clyde Barrow, James Clover and little Freddie Clover who was only fifteen and very excited to be asked along. However, Freddie did not really want to see a duck, let alone shoot one. He had never killed anything but a sparrow with his BB gun and that had made him sick. But he was nine then. Now he was ready to be a man. His father told him so.

With this hunt he felt he had become part of a secret organization. One that smelled of tobacco smoke and whiskey breath; sounded of swear words, talk about how good certain women were, the range and velocity of rifles and shotguns, the edges of hunting knives, the best caps and earflaps for winter hunting.

In Mud Creek the hunt made the man.

Since Freddie was nine he had watched with more than casual

interest, how when a boy turned fifteen in Mud Creek, he would be invited to The Hunting Club for a talk with the men. Next step was a hunt, and when the boy returned he was a boy no longer. He talked deep, walked sure, had whiskers bristling on his chin and could take up with the assurance of not being laughed at, cussing, smoking and watching women's butts as a matter of course.

Freddie wanted to be a man too. He had pimples, no pubic hair to speak of (he always showered quickly at school to escape derisive remarks about the size of his equipment and the thickness of his foliage), scrawny legs and little, gray, watery eyes that looked like ugly planets spinning in white space.

And truth was, Freddie preferred a book to a gun.

But came the day when Freddie turned fifteen and his father came home from the Club, smoke and whiskey smell clinging to him like a hungry tick, his face slightly dark with beard and tired-looking from all-night poker.

He came into Freddie's room, marched over to the bed where Freddie was reading *THOR*, clutched the comic from his son's hands, sent it fluttering across the room with a rainbow of comic panels.

"Nose out of a book," his father said. "Time to join the Club."

Freddie went to the Club, heard the men talk ducks, guns, the way the smoke and blood smelled on cool morning breezes. They told him the kill was the measure of a man. They showed him heads on the wall. They told him to go home with his father and come back tomorrow bright and early, ready for his first hunt.

His father took Freddie downtown and bought him a flannel shirt (black and red), a thick jacket (fleece lined), a cap (with ear flaps) and boots (waterproof). He took Freddie home and took a shotgun down from the rack, gave him a box of ammo, walked him out back to the firing range and made him practice while he told his son about hunts and the war and about how men and ducks died much the same.

Next morning before the sun was up, Freddie and his father had breakfast. Freddie's mother did not eat with them. Freddie did not ask why. They met Clyde over at the Club and rode in his jeep down dirt roads, clay roads and trails, through brush and briars until they came to a mass of reeds and cattails that grew thick and tall as Japanese bamboo.

They got out and walked. As they walked, pushing aside the reeds and cattails, the ground beneath their feet turned marshy. The dogs ran ahead.

When the sun was two hours up, they came to a bit of a clearing in the reeds, and beyond them Freddie could see the break-your-heart-blue of a shiny lake. Above the lake, coasting down, he saw a duck. He watched it sail out of sight.

"Well boy?" Freddie's father said.

"It's beautiful," Freddie said.

"Beautiful, hell, are you ready?"

"Yes, sir."

On they walked, the dogs way ahead now, and finally they stood within ten feet of the lake. Freddie was about to squat down into hiding as he had heard of others doing, when a flock of ducks burst up from a mass of reeds in the lake and Freddie, fighting off the sinking feeling in his stomach, tracked them with the barrel of the shotgun, knowing what he must do to be a man.

His father's hand clamped over the barrel and pushed it down. "Not yet," he said.

"Huh?" said Freddie.

"It's not the ducks that do it," Clyde said.

Freddie watched as Clyde and his father turned their heads to the right, to where the dogs were pointing noses, forward, paws upraised—to a thatch of underbrush. Clyde and his father made quick commands to the dogs to stay, then they led Freddie into the brush, through a twisting maze of briars and out into a clearing where all the members of The Hunting Club were waiting.

In the center of the clearing was a gigantic duck decoy. It looked ancient and there were symbols carved all over it. Freddie could not tell if it were made of clay, iron or wood. The back of it was scooped out, gravy-bowllike, and there was a pole in the center of the indention; tied to the pole was a skinny man. His head had been caked over with red mud and there were duck feathers sticking in it, making it look like some kind of funny cap. There was a ridiculous, wooden duck bill held to his head by thick elastic straps. Stuck to his butt was a duster of duck feathers. There was a sign around his neck that read DUCK.

The man's eyes were wide with fright and he was trying to say or scream something, but the bill had been fastened in such a way he couldn't make any more than a mumble.

Freddie felt his father's hand on his shoulder. "Do it," he said. "He ain't nobody to anybody we know. Be a man."

"Do it! Do it! Do it!" came the cry from The Hunting Club.

Freddie felt the cold air turn into a hard ball in his throat. His scrawny legs shook. He looked at his father and The Hunting Club. They all looked tough, hard and masculine.

"Want to be a titty baby all your life?" his father said.

128

That put steel in Freddie's bones. He cleared his eyes with the back of his sleeve and steadied the barrel on the derelict's duck's head.

"Do it!" came the cry. "Do it! Do it! Do it!"

At that instant he pulled the trigger. A cheer went up from The Hunting Club, and out of the clear cold sky, a dark blue norther blew in and with it came a flock of ducks. The ducks lit on the great idol and on the derelict. Some of them dipped their bills in the derelict's wetness.

When the decoy and the derelict were covered in ducks, all The Hunting Club lifted their guns and began to fire.

The air became full of smoke, pellets, blood and floating feathers.

When the gunfire died down and the ducks died out, The Hunting Club went forward and bent over the decoy, did what they had to do. Their smiles were red when they lifted their heads. They wiped their mouths gruffly on the backs of their sleeves and gathered ducks into hunting bags until they bulged. There were still many carcases lying about.

Fred's father gave him a cigarette. Clyde lit it.

"Good shooting, son," Fred's father said and clapped him manfully on the back.

"Yeah," said Fred, scratching his crotch, "got that sonofabitch right between the eyes, pretty as a picture."

They all laughed.

The sky went lighter, and the blue norther that was rustling the reeds and whipping feathers about blew up and out and away in an instant. As the men walked away from there, talking deep, walking sure, whiskers bristling on all their chins, they promised that tonight they would get Fred a woman.

The Dust

By Al Sarrantonio

There was more of the dust.

The house was kept clean; Mother had cleaned it herself for a long time and then, when she had begun to get old and tired and

Father had finally agreed with her that she was indeed old and tired, they had retained someone to come up the hill twice a week to clean immaculately; but no matter how much cleaning was done, the dust remained. Seven of the eight floor and ceiling corners in any room might be spotless, but the eighth would have the dust, tucked neatly in and watching him. Ronnie knew why it watched him, and he hated the dust.

When Mother and Father went out, which they did four or five or sometimes—lately—even six times a week, Ronnie was left with the old lonely house to himself. In fact, Mother and Father locked him in. They went to town, Ronnie knew, to be away from him, and from the memory of the things that had happened with the dust when they lived in another town in another place thirty full years ago. When he had been called Slow Ronnie instead of just Ronnie, and had hated it. When he had begun to hate the dust because of what it did to him.

He had tried to tell Mother and Father about the dust, had been trying to tell them how the house was never really clean for thirty years, but they wouldn't listen to him. Or didn't want to. Mother just looked at him sadly out of her moon eyes, or sometimes shook her head or hid her face in her hands, and Father merely mumbled about the "problems of this boy." Ronnie knew Mother and Father argued about him, about putting him somewhere else away from people and away from them; sometimes he heard Mother's wailings in the night and Father's muffled arguments of "Better this way" or "Cheaper in the long run for us" and he knew that someday, perhaps someday soon, they would come to him with their tearful or blank faces and tell him that they could no longer keep him, that they were too old for it. But he understood all this. He only longed to make them understand about the dust, and about how it must be cleaned away before it consumed them all.

The house was high and dark, set in the side of a wooded hill up away from the town. It was what some might call dreary, but Ronnie loved every bit of it. And knew every bit of it, from the cold deep cellar to the musty gables at each end of the attic, including the Room in the Attic and the Secret Room. He knew where every shadow was, except for the shadows of the dust which kept changing, and he knew every sharp corner and hideyhole and how many steps there were in each of the stairways. He liked the house even better at night, when the shadows were thicker, and you could hide anything, even the dust, in them, and the sixty-watt bulbs that Father preferred (because they were cheaper) barely illuminated the large spaces between them. When it was cold in the winter, and nighttime dark, like it was this night, and when Mother and Father were out, which they were, it was his favorite time because he could almost lose himself in those dark spaces and make believe that even the dust didn't exist; that nothing existed but Ronnie—not Slow Ronnie—and that the night and the sharp clear cold belonged to him alone and that whatever happened thirty years ago never happened and that he had only started existing here and now in this blackness. It was wonderful because he was here all alone.

Except for the dust.

The dust was out there, he could see it, even on this perfect night. He could not even shut the dust out now. And that made him angry and frightened, because on other nights like this, of which there were only four or five each year, he had been able to get rid of the dust, push it out beyond his circle of darkness and back away from the illumination of sixty-watt bulbs to a sulking corner deep across the room, or away and into another room entirely, where it would gather and brood and wait for the daylight to see and follow him again. But this night he could feel it within the circle, clinging to itself and knowing that it had won a new battle and followed him nearly to the heart of his most secret places. There was nowhere he could go now to be alone, except the Room in the Attic and the Secret Room (which even Mother and Father didn't know about), his special rooms where even the dust never followed.

"Go away," he said to the space inside the circle, where the dust lurked.

There was a silent shifting.

"Go away," he said again.

There was another shifting, a sound like many threads being drawn across wood, behind him.

"I said go away! You can't come here!"

Suddenly, there were memories. It was thirty years ago, and the dust was all around him. Pressing him in dryly, more dust than he had ever seen before, covering him, blocking his vision, making him cough and his eyes begin to water.

There was laughter.

More than one voice. A lot of voices. Out beyond the dust, not laughter like when Spike or Pauly stood on their heads and sang "I'm Popeye the Sailor Man," but mean laughter, laughter that had been waiting below the surface to spring on him, and had only needed a bit of running away to get out at him. He was fighting at the dust with his fingers and hands, coughing and beginning to cry, trying to get out of the dust to see where he was, where the laughter was coming from, where the dust was coming from.

There was more and more dust, blinding him now, and then he was pushing at it crazily and it was going away, finally pulling back and away from him and he could see and breathe again.

That was when they called him Slow Ronnie.

There were five or six of them, almost all of his friends, the ones who had let him follow them around and carry their baseball equipment and, because he was so big, play touch football as a substitute in the fall after school. They had been waiting for him around the corner from Woolworth's, waiting for him to meet them, to come around the corner so they could drop the sacks of dirt and dust that Pauly had rigged up above the wrought-iron sign that hung on the corner with an orange firebox light on it, and they had pulled the string and were still laughing at him.

"Slow Ronnie," they were screeching. "Sloooooow Ronnie!" Waving their hands and taunting him while they said it. Almost all of them his friends, except for a new one he had never seen before, taller and sharp-faced.

"Sloooooow Ronnie," they kept saying as he wheezed and cried and brushed trembling at the dust.

Then he looked through his tears at the new one, the tall one with the bright sharp eyes, and a rage seized him.

"I'm not slow!" he screamed, and then he remembered the muscles in his arms going tight and hard and the breaking of a glass window and sharp red pieces of glass. Then no more. When he was awake again he was in a hospital tied down to a white bed and Mother and Father, their faces also white, looked down from above him. Father's face was whiter, and blanker.

The memories went away.

"Go away!" he screamed at the dust again. He was within his cold circle, and the dust was trying to come at him again. He was not Slow Ronnie, he knew that; he would never be Slow Ronnie again and as long as he could keep the dust away, and the boy with the sharp hard eyes and smile, he would never be Slow Ronnie again. The boy was a long way away, in time and distance, but the dust was here and he had to keep it away or he would be Slow Ronnie again.

"I am not Slow Ronnie!"

The dust gathered, making a hissing noise, on either side of him. A small ball of it slid by, brushing at his shoe.

"No!"

He stood, making swimming motions with his arms, threatening the dust to stay back. He had told Mother and Father about the dust, and they hadn't listened to him, and now this was happening. He could see into the circle of weak amber light in front of him, and he saw that the dust, all of the dust, was forming. It was covering the floor, like whispering gray snow, clumps and bunches moving here and there across it, and it was pushing toward him. It was into the circle now, and he knew that finally, after growing in separate strength all these years, the dust was coming for him again, coming to make him gasp and scream helplessly, to fill his mouth and nose with absolute and terrible dryness, to make him into Slow Ronnie once more. He could not accept that, he would not let the dust do that to him again.

He shouted "Keep back!" and ran from the room, out into the shadows of the hallway, his shadows, toward the stairway. The dust, as his feet touched it, rose up in wavy fingers and tried to clutch at him, but he screamed and swatted down at it, and ran on. There was dust in the hallway too, flowing out of every doorway to meet in a splash at the center of the hall; Ronnie leaped over it and onto the stairs, taking them two steps at a time. Below him, the dust rose and drew together, flowing up the stairs after him.

Ronnie ran to the attic ladder, climbing it and dropping the door behind him and then frantically pulling at the door to the inner attic room, moving his arm this way and that in the darkness, searching for the overhead light cord. He found it, and the weak bulb clicked on. The room was empty, and Ronnie let out a long and shuddering breath. The Room in the Attic was still safe, and closing and bolting the door behind him, he sat down in the center.

He listened.

There were sounds, soft clicks and rustlings, but these were the sounds that were always in his room. These were the sounds of his house, moving and sighing and settling contentedly about itself, and there was nothing of the dust about them. The dust did not come here, to this room; it did not belong and never had and all the sounds of the house, and the house itself, had always kept it out. This was the room that Ronnie went to when he was feeling sad, or when the dust in the other rooms began to bother him too much, or when the weather wasn't cold and shadowy like it was tonight. It was almost his favorite room in the house. There was hardly any furniture, and what furniture and storage there was was oddly shaped and threw long, deep and special shadows. Soothing shadows that blended with the creaking sounds and made the room always seem cold and dark. The dust never came in here.

The dust was coming in now.

Ronnie jumped up as he saw that the dust was sliding slowly but inexorably under the door. There was a great weight of dust behind the door, the lock was rattling heavily with the pressure of it, and there was a steady, roiling portion of it squeezing into the room and building inside.

Building to engulf him.

There was only one place for him to go, one place where the dust would never go because it didn't even know about it—no one knew about it, not Mother nor Father nor anyone else—and therefore couldn't follow. His Secret Room. The one that only he and the house were alive to, where he could think about anything, and the house would soothe him and the dust would not be there to watch.

He would go to that room and be safe.

There was a place under an old table in the Room in the Attic where the wall was not solid. Behind this was the Secret Room. On the outside of the house it showed as a tiny gable with no window, an obvious mistake of architecture. It was not even high enough to stand in, and was nearly airtight and completely dustless; one had to crouch low to get through its door, and step down into it as its floor was almost two feet below that of the Room in the Attic. There was not even a light in it, and Ronnie kept a flashlight hidden on a hook under the table by the door. The door itself was a paneled section of wood which fit snugly and undoorlike into the rest of the paneled wall.

It was a dark and secret and dustless place.

Ronnie crawled under the table and lifted his flashlight from its hook. He looked behind to see the dust building massively, high, roiling and blocklike, and pushing toward him. If he didn't go into the secret place, give the dust the chance of seeing where it was, it would press over him and suffocate him. It would choke him until he couldn't think and he became Slow Ronnie again. He began to cough just thinking about it.

He turned, shaking, to the secret door to the Secret Room and pulled at the latch.

Crouching low, his flashlight snapped on, he pulled open the door and began to step down.

The dust was waiting for him.

Heaving, gray, and shadowless, it filled the entire Secret Room.

And the dust was pressing at him from behind, as it overflowed the Room in the Attic.

A sudden peace came over him, a silent raging peace, as the dust pressed down and up on him, holding him to itself, and the house murmured to him, and the boy with the sharp eyes and face was there before him in the dust, embracing him.

Outside, he heard the muffled hum of Mother and Father's returning car.

He knew who they would find.

The Evil Clergyman

By H. P. Lovecraft

I was shown into the attic chamber by a grave, intelligent-looking man with quiet clothes and an iron-gray beard, who spoke to me in this fashion:

"Yes, *he* lived here—but I don't advise your doing anything. Your curiosity makes you irresponsible. *We* never come here at night, and it's only because of *his* will that we keep it this way. You know what *he* did. That abominable society took charge at last, and we don't know where *he* is buried. There was no way the law or anything else could reach the society.

"I hope you won't stay till after dark. And I beg of you to let that thing on the table—the thing that looks like a match-box—alone. We don't know what it is, but we suspect it has something to do with what *he* did. We even avoid looking at it very steadily."

After a time the man left me alone in the attic room. It was very dingy and dusty, and only primitively furnished, but it had a neatness which showed it was not a slum-denizen's quarters. There were shelves full of theological and classical books, and another bookcase containing treatises on magic—Paracelsus, Albertus Magnus, Trithemius, Hermes Trismegistus, Borellus, and others in strange alphabets whose titles I could not decipher. The furniture was very plain. There was a door, but it led only into a closet. The only egress was the aperture in the floor up to which the crude, steep staircase led. The windows were of bull's-eye pattern, and the black oak beams bespoke unbelievable antiquity. Plainly, this house was of the Old World. I seemed to know where I was, but cannot recall what I then knew. Certainly the town was *not* London. My impression is of a small seaport.

The small object on the table fascinated me intensely. I seemed to know what to do with it, for I drew a pocket electric light—or what looked like one—out of my pocket and nervously tested its flashes. The light was not white but violet, and seemed less like true light than like some radio-active bombardment. I recall that I did not regard it as a common flashlight—indeed, I *had* a common flashlight in another pocket.

It was getting dark, and the ancient roofs and chimney-pots outside looked very queer through the bull's-eye windowpanes. Finally I summoned up courage and propped the small object up on the table against a book—then turned the rays of the peculiar violet light upon it. The light seemed now to be more like a rain or hail of small violet particles than like a continuous beam. As the particles struck the glassy surface at the center of the strange device, they seemed to produce a crackling noise like the sputtering of a vacuum tube through which sparks are passed. The dark glassy surface displayed a pinkish glow, and a vague white shape seemed to be taking form at its center. Then I noticed that I was not alone in the room—and put the ray-projector back in my pocket.

But the newcomer did not speak—nor did I hear any sound whatever during all the immediately following moments. Everything was shadowy pantomime, as if seen at a vast distance through some intervening haze—although on the other hand the newcomer and all subsequent comers loomed large and close, as if both near and distant, according to some abnormal geometry.

The newcomer was a thin, dark man of medium height attired in the clerical garb of the Anglican church. He was apparently about thirty years old, with a sallow, olive complexion and fairly good features, but an abnormally high forehead. His black hair was well cut and neatly brushed, and he was clean-shaven though blue-chinned with a heavy growth of beard. He wore rimless spectacles with steel bows. His build and lower facial features were like other clergymen I had seen, but he had a vastly higher forehead, and was darker and more intelligent-looking—also more subtly and concealedly *evil*-looking. At the present moment—having just lighted a faint oil lamp—he looked nervous, and before I knew it he was casting all his magical books into a fireplace on the window side of the room (where the wall slanted sharply) which I had not noticed before. The flames devoured the volumes greedily—leaping up in strange colors and emitting indescribably hideous odors as the strangely hieroglyphed leaves and wormy bindings succumbed to the devastating element. All at once I saw there were others in the room—grave-looking men in clerical costume, one of whom wore the bands and knee-breeches of a bishop. Though I could hear nothing, I could see that they were bringing a decision of vast import to the first-comer. They seemed to hate and fear him at the same time, and he seemed to return these sentiments. His face set itself into a grim expression, but I could see his right hand shaking as he tried to grip the back of a chair. The bishop pointed to the empty case and to the fireplace (where the flames had died down amidst a charred, noncommittal mass), and seemed filled with a peculiar loathing. The first-comer then gave a wry smile and reached out with his left hand toward the small object on the table. Everyone then seemed frightened. The procession of clerics began filing down the steep stairs through the trap-door in the floor, turning and making menacing gestures as they left. The bishop was last to go.

The first-comer now went to a cupboard on the inner side of the room and extracted a coil of rope. Mounting a chair, he attached one end of the rope to a hook in the great exposed central beam of black oak, and began making a noose with the other end. Realizing he was about to hang himself, I started forward to dissuade or save him. He saw me and ceased his preparations, looking at me with a kind of *triumph* which puzzled and disturbed me. He slowly stepped down from the chair and began gliding toward me with a positively wolfish grin on his dark, thin-lipped face.

I felt somehow in deadly peril, and drew out the peculiar ray-projector as a weapon of defense. Why I thought it could help me, I do not know. I turned it on—full in his face, and saw the sallow features glow first with violet and then with pinkish light. His expression of wolfish exultation began to be crowded aside by a look of profound fear—which did not, however, wholly displace the exultation. He stopped in his tracks—then, flailing his arms wildly in the air, began to stagger backward. I saw he was edging toward the open stair-well in the floor, and tried to shout a warning, but he did not hear me. In another instant he had lurched backward through the opening and was lost to view.

I found difficulty in moving toward the stair-well, but when I did get there I found no crushed body on the floor below. Instead there was a clatter of people coming up with lanterns, for the spell of phantasmal silence had broken, and I once more heard sounds and saw figures as normally tri-dimensional. Something had evidently drawn a crowd to this place. Had there been a noise I had not heard? Presently the two people (simple villagers, apparently) farthest in the lead saw me—and stood paralyzed. One of them shrieked loudly and reverberantly:

"Ahrrh! . . . It be'ee, zur? Again?"

Then they all turned and fled frantically. All, that is, but one. When the crowd was gone I saw the grave-bearded man who had brought me to this place—standing alone with a lantern. He was gazing at me gaspingly and fascinatedly, but did not seem afraid. Then he began to ascend the stairs, and joined me in the attic. He spoke:

"So you *didn't* let it alone! I'm sorry. I know what has happened. It happened once before, but the man got frightened and shot himself. You ought not to have made *him* come back. You know what *he* wants. But you mustn't get frightened like the other man he got. Something very strange and terrible has happened to you, but it didn't get far enough to hurt your mind and personality. If you'll keep cool, and accept the need for making certain radical readjustments in your life, you can keep right on enjoying the world, and the fruits of your scholarship. But you can't live here—and I don't think you'll wish to go back to London. I'd advise America.

"You mustn't try anything more with that—thing. Nothing can be put back now. It would only make matters worse to do—or summon—anything. You are not as badly off as you might be—but you must get out of here at once and stay away. You'd better thank Heaven it didn't go further. . . .

"I'm going to prepare you as bluntly as I can. There's been a certain change—in your personal appearance. *He* always causes that. But in a new country you can get used to it. There's a mirror up at the other end of the room, and I'm going to take you to it. You'll get a shock—though you will see nothing repulsive."

I was now shaking with a deadly fear, and the bearded man almost had to hold me up as he walked me across the room to the mirror, the faint lamp (i.e., that formerly on the table, not the still fainter lantern he had brought) in his free hand. This is what I saw in the glass:

A thin, dark man of medium stature attired in the clerical garb of the Anglican church, apparently about thirty, and with rimless, steel-bowed glasses glistening beneath a sallow, olive forehead of abnormal height.

It was the silent first-comer who had burned his books.

For all the rest of my life, in outward form, I was to be that man!

Examination Day

By Henry Slesar

The Jordans never spoke of the exam, not until their son, Dickie, was twelve years old. It was on his birthday that Mrs. Jordan first mentioned the subject in his presence, and the anxious manner of her speech caused her husband to answer sharply.

"Forget about it," he said. "He'll do all right."

They were at the breakfast table, and the boy looked up from his plate curiously. He was an alert-eyed youngster, with flat blond hair and a quick, nervous manner. He didn't understand what the sudden tension was about, but he did know that today was his birthday, and he wanted harmony above all. Somewhere in the little apartment there were wrapped, beribboned packages waiting to be opened, and in the tiny wall-kitchen, something warm and sweet was being prepared in the automatic stove. He wanted the day to be happy, and the moistness of his mother's eyes, the scowl on his father's face, spoiled the mood of fluttering expectation with which he had greeted the morning.

"What exam?" he asked.

His mother looked at the tablecloth. "It's just a sort of Government intelligence test they give children at the age of twelve. You'll be getting it next week. It's nothing to worry about."

"You mean a test like in school?"

"Something like that," his father said, getting up from the table. "Go read your comic books, Dickie."

The boy rose and wandered toward that part of the living room which had been "his" corner since infancy. He fingered the topmost comic of the stack, but seemed uninterested in the colorful squares of fast-paced action. He wandered toward the window, and peered gloomily at the veil of mist that shrouded the glass.

"Why did it have to rain *today*?" he said. "Why couldn't it rain tomorrow?"

His father, now slumped into an armchair with the Government newspaper, rattled the sheets in vexation. "Because it just did, that's all. Rain makes the grass grow."

"Why, Dad?"

"Because it does, that's all."

Dickie puckered his brow. "What makes it green, though? The grass?"

"Nobody knows," his father snapped, then immediately regretted his abruptness.

Later in the day, it was birthday time again. His mother beamed as she handed over the gaily-colored packages, and even his father managed a grin and a rumple-of-the-hair. He kissed his mother and shook hands gravely with his father. Then the birthday cake was brought forth, and the ceremonies concluded.

An hour later, seated by the window, he watched the sun force its way between the clouds.

"Dad," he said, "how far away is the sun?"

"Five thousand miles," his father said.

Dickie sat at the breakfast table and again saw moisture in his mother's eyes. He didn't connect her tears with the exam until his father suddenly brought the subject to light again.

"Well, Dickie," he said, with a manly frown, "you've got an appointment today."

"I know, Dad. I hope——"

"Now it's nothing to worry about. Thousands of children take this test every day. The Government wants to know how smart you are, Dickie. That's all there is to it."

"I get good marks in school," he said hesitantly.

"This is different. This is a—special kind of test. They give you this stuff to drink, you see, and then you go into a room where there's a sort of machine——"

"What stuff to drink?" Dickie said.

"It's nothing. It tastes like peppermint. It's just to make sure you answer the questions truthfully. Not that the Government thinks you won't tell the truth, but this stuff makes *sure*."

Dickie's face showed puzzlement, and a touch of fright. He looked at his mother, and she composed her face into a misty smile.

"Everything will be all right," she said.

"Of course it will," his father agreed. "You're a good boy, Dickie; you'll make out fine. Then we'll come home and celebrate. All right?"

"Yes, sir," Dickie said.

They entered the Government Educational Building fifteen minutes before the appointed hour. They crossed the marble floors of

140

the great pillared lobby, passed beneath an archway and entered an automatic elevator that brought them to the fourth floor.

There was a young man wearing an insignia-less tunic, seated at a polished desk in front of Room 404. He held a clipboard in his hand, and he checked the list down to the Js and permitted the Jordans to enter.

The room was as cold and official as a courtroom, with long benches flanking metal tables. There were several fathers and sons already there, and a thin-lipped woman with cropped black hair was passing out sheets of paper.

Mr. Jordan filled out the form, and returned it to the clerk. Then he told Dickie: "It won't be long now. When they call your name, you just go through the doorway at that end of the room." He indicated the portal with his finger.

A concealed loudspeaker crackled and called off the first name. Dickie saw a boy leave his father's side reluctantly and walk slowly toward the door.

At five minutes of eleven, they called the name of Jordan.

"Good luck, son," his father said, without looking at him. "I'll call for you when the test is over."

Dickie walked to the door and turned the knob. The room inside was dim, and he could barely make out the features of the gray-tunicked attendant who greeted him.

"Sit down," the man said softly. He indicated a high stool beside his desk. "Your name's Richard Jordan?"

"Yes, sir."

"Your classification number is 600-115. Drink this, Richard."

He lifted a plastic cup from the desk and handed it to the boy. The liquid inside had the consistency of buttermilk, tasted only vaguely of the promised peppermint. Dickie downed it, and handed the man the empty cup.

He sat in silence, feeling drowsy, while the man wrote busily on a sheet of paper. Then the attendant looked at his watch, and rose to stand only inches from Dickie's face. He unclipped a penlike object from the pocket of his tunic, and flashed a tiny light into the boy's eyes.

"All right," he said. "Come with me, Richard."

He led Dickie to the end of the room, where a single wooden armchair faced a multi-dialed computing machine. There was a microphone on the left arm of the chair, and when the boy sat down, he found its pinpoint head conveniently at his mouth.

"Now just relax, Richard. You'll be asked some questions, and you think them over carefully. Then give your answers into the microphone. The machine will take care of the rest."

"Yes, sir."

"I'll leave you alone now. Whenever you want to start, just say 'ready' into the microphone."

"Yes, sir."

The man squeezed his shoulder, and left.

Dickie said, "Ready."

Lights appeared on the machine, and a mechanism whirred. A voice said:

"Complete this sequence. One, four, seven, ten . . ."

Mr. and Mrs. Jordan were in the living room, not speaking, not even speculating.

It was almost four o'clock when the telephone rang. The woman tried to reach it first, but her husband was quicker.

"Mr. Jordan?"

The voice was clipped; a brisk; official voice.

"Yes, speaking."

"This is the Government Educational Service. Your son, Richard M. Jordan, Classification 600-115, has completed the Government examination. We regret to inform you that his intelligence quotient has exceeded the Government regulation, according to Rule 84, Section 5, of the New Code."

Across the room, the woman cried out, knowing nothing except the emotion she read on her husband's face.

"You may specify by telephone," the voice droned on, "whether you wish his body interred by the Government or would you prefer a private burial place? The fee for Government burial is ten dollars."

The Faceless Thing

By Edward D. Hoch

Sunset: golden flaming clouds draped over distant canyons barely seen in the dusk of the dying day; farmland gone to rot; fields in the foreground given over wildly to the running of the rabbit and

142

the woodchuck; the farmhouse gray and paint-peeled, sleeping possibly but more likely dead—needing burial.

It hadn't changed much in all those years. It hadn't changed; only died.

He parked the car and got out, taking it all in with eyes still intent and quick for all their years. Somehow he hadn't really thought it would still be standing. Farmhouses that were near collapse fifty years ago shouldn't still be standing; not when all the people, his mother and father and aunt and the rest, were all long in their graves.

He was an old man, had been an old man almost as long as he could remember. Youth to him was only memories of this farm, so many years before, romping in the hay with his little sister at his side; swinging from the barn ropes, exploring endless dark depths out beyond the last field. After that, he was old—through misty college days and marriage to a woman he hadn't loved, through a business and political career that carried him around the world. And never once in all those years had he journeyed back to this place, this farmhouse now given over to the weeds and insects. They were all dead; there was no reason to come back . . . no reason at all.

Except the memory of the ooze.

A childhood memory, a memory buried with the years, forgotten sometimes but always there, crowded into its own little space in his mind, was ready to confront him and startled him with its vividness.

The ooze was a place beyond the last field, where water always collected in the springtime and after a storm; water running over dirt and clay and rock, merging with the soil until there was nothing underfoot but a black ooze to rise above your boots. He'd followed the stream rushing with storm water, followed it to the place where it cut into the side of the hill.

It was the memory of the tunnel, really, that had brought him back—the dark tunnel leading nowhere, gurgling with rain-fed water, barely large enough for him to fit through. A tunnel floored with unseen ooze, peopled by unknown danger; that was a place for every boy.

Had he been only ten that day? Certainly he'd been no more than eleven, leading the way while his nine-year-old sister followed. "This way. Be careful of the mud." She'd been afraid of the dark, afraid of what they might find there. But he'd called encouragement to her; after all, what could there be in all this ooze to hurt them?

How many years? Fifty?

"What *is* it, Buddy?" She'd always called him Buddy. What is it, Buddy? Only darkness, and a place maybe darker than dark, with a half-formed shadow rising from the ooze. He'd brought along his father's old lantern, and he fumbled to light it.

"Buddy!" she'd screamed—just once—and in the flare of the match he'd seen the thing, great and hairy and covered with ooze; something that lived in the darkness here, something that hated the light. In that terrifying instant it had reached out for his little sister and pulled her into the ooze.

That was the memory, a memory that came to him sometimes only at night. It had pursued him down the years like a fabled hound, coming to him, reminding him, when all was well with the world. It was like a personal demon sent from Hades to torture him. He'd never told anyone about that thing in the ooze, not even his mother. They'd cried and carried on when his sister was found the next day, and they'd said she'd drowned. He was not one to say differently.

And the years had passed. For a time, during his high school days, he read the local papers—searching for some word of the thing, some veiled news that it had come out of that forgotten cavern. But it never did; it liked the dark and damp too much. And, of course, no one else ever ventured into the stream bed. That was a pursuit only for the very young and very foolish.

By the time he was twenty, the memory was fading, merging with other thoughts, other goals, until at times he thought it only a child's dream. But then at night it would come again in all its vividness, and the thing in the ooze would beckon him.

A long life, long and crowded . . . One night he'd tried to tell his wife about it, but she wouldn't listen. That was the night he'd realized how little he'd ever loved her. Perhaps he'd only married her because, in a certain light, she reminded him of that sister of his youth. But the love that sometimes comes later came not at all to the two of them. She was gone now, like his youth, like his family and friends. There was only this memory remaining. The memory of a thing in the ooze.

Now the weeds were tall, beating against his legs, stirring nameless insects to flight with every step. He pressed a handkerchief against his brow, sponging the sweat that was forming there. Would the dark place still be there, or had fifty years of rain and dirt sealed it forever?

"Hello there," a voice called out. It was an old voice, barely carrying with the breeze. He turned and saw someone on the porch of the deserted farmhouse. An old woman, ancient and wrinkled.

"Do I know you?" he asked, moving closer.

"You may," she answered. "You're Buddy, aren't you? My, how old I've gotten. I used to live at the next farm, when you were just a boy. I was young then myself. I remember you."

"Oh! Mrs. . . . ?" The name escaped him, but it wasn't important.

"Why did you come back, Buddy? Why, after all these years?"

He was an old man. Was it necessary to explain his actions to this woman from the past? "I just wanted to see the place," he answered. "Memories, you know."

"Bitter memories. Your little sister died here, did she not?" The old woman should have been dead, should have been dead and in her grave long ago.

He paused in the shade of the porch roof. "She died here, yes, but that was fifty years ago."

"How old we grow, how ancient! Is that why you returned?"

"In a way. I wanted to see the spot."

"Ah! The little brook back there beyond the last field. Let me walk that way with you. These old legs need exercise."

"Do you live here?" he asked, wanting to escape her now but knowing not how.

"No, still down the road. All alone now. Are you all alone, too?"

"I suppose so." The high grass made walking difficult.

"You know what they all said at the time, don't you? They all said you were fooling around, like you always did, and pushed her into the water."

There was a pain in his chest from breathing so hard. He was an old man. "Do you believe that?"

"What does it matter?" she answered. "After all these fifty years, what does it matter?"

"Would you believe me," he began, then hesitated into silence. Of course she wouldn't believe him, but he had to tell now. "Would you believe me if I told you what happened?"

She was a very old woman and she panted to keep up even his slow pace. She was ancient even to his old eyes, even in his world where now everyone was old. "I would believe you," she said.

"There was something in the ooze. Call it a monster, a demon, if you want. I saw it in the light of a match, and I can remember it as if it were yesterday. It took her."

"Perhaps," she said.

"You don't believe me."

"I said I would. This sun is hot today, even at twilight."

"It will be gone soon. I hate to hurry you, old woman, but I must reach the stream before dark."

"The last field is in sight."

Yes, it was in sight. But how would he ever fit through that small opening, how would he face the thing, even if by some miracle it still waited there in the ooze? Fifty years was a long long time.

"Wait here," he said as they reached the little stream at last. It hadn't changed much, not really.

"You won't find it." He lowered his aged body into the bed of the stream, feeling once again the familiar forgotten ooze closing over his shoes.

"No one has to know," she called after him. "Even if there was something, that was fifty years ago."

But he went on, to the place where the water vanished into the rock. He held his breath and groped for the little flashlight in his pocket. Then he ducked his head and followed the water into the black.

It was steamy here, steamy and hot with the sweat of the earth. He flipped on the flashlight with trembling hands and followed its narrow beam with his eyes. The place was almost like a room in the side of the hill, a room perhaps seven feet high, with a floor of mud and ooze that seemed almost to bubble as he watched.

"Come on," he said softly, almost to himself. "I know you're there. You've got to be there."

And then he saw it, rising slowly from the ooze. A shapeless thing without a face, a thing that moved so slowly it might have been dead. An old, very old thing. For a long time he watched it, unable to move, unable to cry out. And even as he watched, the thing settled back softly into the ooze, as if even this small exertion had tired it.

"Rest," he said, very quietly. "We are all so old now."

And then he made his way back out of the cave, along the stream, and finally pulled himself from the clinging ooze. The ancient woman was still waiting on the bank, with fireflies playing about her in the dusk.

"Did you find anything?" she asked him.

"Nothing," he answered.

"Fifty years is a long time. You shouldn't have come back."

He sighed and fell into step beside her. "It was something I had to do."

146

"Come up to my house, if you want. I can make you a bit of tea."

His breath was coming better now, and the distance back to the farmhouse seemed shorter than he'd remembered. "I think I'd like that," he said. . . .

The Facts in the Case of M. Valdemar

By Edgar Allan Poe

Of course I shall not pretend to consider it any matter for wonder, that the extraordinary case of M. Valdemar has excited discussion. It would have been a miracle had it not—especially under the circumstances. Through the desire of all parties concerned, to keep the affair from the public, at least for the present, or until we had further opportunities for investigation—through our endeavors to effect this—a garbled or exaggerated account made its way into society, and became the source of many unpleasant misrepresentations; and, very naturally, of a great deal of disbelief.

It is now rendered necessary that I give the *facts*—as far as I comprehend them myself. They are, succinctly, these:

My attention, for the last three years, had been repeatedly drawn to the subject of Mesmerism; and, about nine months ago, it occurred to me, quite suddenly, that in the series of experiments made hitherto, there had been a very remarkable and most unaccountable omission:—no person had as yet been mesmerized *in articulo mortis*. It remained to be seen, first, whether, in such condition, there existed in the patient any susceptibility to the magnetic influence; secondly, whether, if any existed, it was impaired or increased by the condition; thirdly, to what extent, or for how long a period, the encroachments of Death might be arrested by the process. There were other points to be ascertained, but these most excited my curiosity—the last in especial, from the immensely important character of its consequences.

In looking around me for some subject by whose means I might test these particulars, I was brought to think of my friend, M. Ernest Valdemar, the well-known compiler of the "Bibliotheca Forensica," and author (under the *nom de plume* of Issachar Marx) of the Polish versions of "Wallenstein" and "Gargantua." M. Valdemar, who has resided principally at Harlem, N. Y., since the year of 1839, is (or was) particularly noticeable for the extreme spareness of his person—his lower limbs much resembling those of John Randolph; and, also, for the whiteness of his whiskers, in violent contrast to the blackness of his hair—the latter, in consequence, being very generally mistaken for a wig. His temperament was markedly nervous, and rendered him a good subject for mesmeric experiment. On two or three occasions I had put him to sleep with little difficulty, but was disappointed in other results which his peculiar constitution had naturally led me to anticipate. His will was at no period positively, or thoroughly, under my control, and in regard to *clairvoyance*, I could accomplish with him nothing to be relied upon. I always attributed my failure at these points to the disordered state of his health. For some months previous to my becoming acquainted with him, his physicians had declared him in a confirmed phthisis. It was his custom, indeed, to speak calmly of his approaching dissolution, as of a matter neither to be avoided nor regretted.

When the ideas to which I have alluded first occurred to me, it was of course very natural that I should think of M. Valdemar. I knew the steady philosophy of the man too well to apprehend any scruples from *him;* and he had no relatives in America who would be likely to interfere. I spoke to him frankly upon the subject; and, to my surprise, his interest seemed vividly excited. I say to my surprise; for, although he had always yielded his person freely to my experiments, he had never before given me any tokens of sympathy with what I did. His disease was of that character which would admit of exact calculation in respect to the epoch of its termination in death; and it was finally arranged between us that he would send for me about twenty-four hours before the period announced by his physicians as that of his decease.

It is now rather more than seven months since I received, from M. Valdemar himself, the subjoined note:

"My Dear P——

"You may as well come now. *D—— and F—— are agreed that I cannot hold out beyond to-morrow midnight; and I think they have hit the time very nearly.*

Valdemar"

148

I received this note within half an hour after it was written, and in fifteen minutes more I was in the dying man's chamber. I had not seen him for ten days, and was appalled by the fearful alteration which the brief interval had wrought in him. His face wore a leaden hue; the eyes were utterly lustreless; and the emaciation was so extreme, that the skin had been broken through by the cheek-bones. His expectoration was excessive. The pulse was barely perceptible. He retained, nevertheless, in a very remarkable manner, both his mental power and a certain degree of physical strength. He spoke with distinctness—took some palliative medicines without aid—and, when I entered the room, was occupied in penciling memoranda in a pocket-book. He was propped up in the bed by pillows. Doctors D—— and F—— were in attendance.

After pressing Valdemar's hand, I took these gentlemen aside, and obtained from them a minute account of the patient's condition. The left lung had been for eighteen months in a semi-osseous or cartilaginous state, and was, of course, entirely useless for all purposes of vitality. The right, in its upper portion, was also partially, if not thoroughly, ossified, while the lower region was merely a mass of purulent tubercles, running one into another. Several extensive perforations existed; and, at one point, permanent adhesion to the ribs had taken place. These appearances in the right lobe were of comparatively recent date. The ossification had proceeded with very unusual rapidity; no sign of it had been discovered a month before, and the adhesion had only been observed during the three previous days. Independently of the phthisis, the patient was suspected of aneurism of the aorta; but on this point the osseous symptoms rendered an exact diagnosis impossible. It was the opinion of both physicians that M. Valdemar would die about midnight on the morrow (Sunday.) It was then seven o'clock on Saturday evening.

On quitting the invalid's bedside to hold conversation with myself, Doctors D—— and F—— had bidden him a final farewell. It had not been their intention to return; but, at my request, they agreed to look in upon the patient about ten the next night.

When they had gone, I spoke freely with M. Valdemar on the subject of his approaching dissolution, as well as, more particularly, of the experiment proposed. He still professed himself quite willing and even anxious to have it made, and urged me to commence it at once. A male and a female nurse were in attendance; but I did not feel myself altogether at liberty to engage in a task of this character with no more reliable witnesses than these people, in case of sudden accident, might prove. I therefore postponed operations until about eight the next night, when the arrival of a medical student, with whom I had some acquaintance (Mr. Theodore L——l), relieved me from further embarrassment. It had been my design, originally, to wait for the physicians; but I was induced to proceed, first, by the urgent entreaties of M. Valdemar, and secondly, by my conviction that I had not a moment to lose, as he was evidently sinking fast.

Mr. L——l was so kind as to accede to my desire that he would take notes of all that occurred; and it is from his memoranda that what I now have to relate is, for the most part, either condensed or copied *verbatim*.

It wanted about five minutes of eight when, taking the patient's hand, I begged him to state, as distinctly as he could, to Mr. L——l, whether he (M. Valdemar) was entirely willing that I should make the experiment of mesmerizing him in his then condition.

He replied feebly, yet quite audibly: "Yes, I wish to be mesmerized"—adding immediately afterward: "I fear you have deferred it too long."

While he spoke thus, I commenced the passes which I had already found most effectual in subduing him. He was evidently influenced with the first lateral stroke of my hand across his forehead; but, although I exerted all my powers, no further perceptible effect was induced until some minutes after ten o'clock, when Doctors D—— and F—— called, according to appointment. I explained to them, in a few words, what I designed, and as they opposed no objection, saying that the patient was already in the death agony, I proceeded without hesitation—exchanging, however, the lateral passes for downward ones, and directing my gaze entirely into the right eye of the sufferer.

By this time his pulse was imperceptible and his breathing was stertorious, and at intervals of half a minute.

This condition was nearly unaltered for a quarter of an hour. At the expiration of this period, however, a natural although a very deep sigh escaped from the bosom of the dying man, and the stertorious breathing ceased—that is to say, its stertoriousness was no longer apparent; the intervals were undiminished. The patient's extremities were of an icy coldness.

At five minutes before eleven, I perceived unequivocal signs of the mesmeric influence. The glassy roll of the eye was changed for that expression of uneasy *inward* examination which is never seen except in cases of sleep-waking, and which it is quite impossible to mistake. With a few rapid lateral passes I made the lids quiver, as in incipient sleep, and with a few more I closed them altogether. I was not satisfied, however, with this, but continued the manipulations vigorously, and with the fullest exertion of the will, until I had completely stiffened the limbs of the slumberer, after placing them in a seemingly easy position. The legs were at full length; the arms were nearly so, and reposed on the bed at a moderate distance from the loins. The head was very slightly elevated.

When I had accomplished this, it was fully midnight, and I requested the gentlemen present to examine M. Valdemar's condition. After a few experiments, they admitted him to be in an unusually perfect state of mesmeric trance. The curiosity of both the physicians was greatly excited. Dr. D—— resolved at once to remain with the patient all night, while Dr. F—— took leave with a promise to return at daybreak. Mr. L——l and the nurses remained.

We left M. Valdemar entirely undisturbed until about three o'clock in the morning, when I approached him and found him in precisely the same condition as when Dr. F—— went away—that is to say, he lay in the same position; the pulse was imperceptible; the breathing was gentle (scarcely noticeable, unless through the application of a mirror to the lips); the eyes were closed naturally; and the limbs were as rigid and as cold as marble. Still, the general appearance was certainly not that of death.

As I approached M. Valdemar I made a kind of half effort to influence his right arm into pursuit of my own, as I passed the latter gently to and fro above his person. In such experiments with this patient, I had never perfectly succeeded before, and assuredly I had little thought of succeeding now; but to my astonishment, his arm very readily, although feebly, followed every direction I assigned it with mine. I determined to hazard a few words of conversation.

"M. Valdemar," I said, "are you asleep?" He made no answer, but I perceived a tremor about the lips, and was thus induced to repeat the question, again and again. At its third repetition, his whole frame was agitated by a very slight shivering; the eyelids unclosed themselves so far as to display a white line of a ball; the lips moved sluggishly, and from between them, in a barely audible whisper, issued the words:

"Yes;—asleep now. Do not wake me!—let me die so!"

I here felt the limbs, and found them as rigid as ever. The right arm, as before, obeyed the direction of my hand. I questioned the sleep-waker again:

"Do you still feel pain in the breast, M. Valdemar?"

The answer now was immediate, but even less audible than before:

"No pain—I am dying!"

I did not think it advisable to disturb him further just then, and nothing more was said or done until the arrival of Dr. F——, who came a little before sunrise, and expressed unbounded astonishment at finding the patient still alive. After feeling the pulse and applying a mirror to the lips, he requested me to speak to the sleep-waker again. I did so, saying:

"M. Valdemar, do you still sleep?"

As before, some minutes elapsed ere a reply was made; and during the interval the dying man seemed to be collecting his energies to speak. At my fourth repetition of the question, he said very faintly, almost inaudibly:

"Yes; still asleep—dying."

It was now the opinion, or rather the wish, of the physicians, that M. Valdemar should be suffered to remain undisturbed in his present apparently tranquil condition, until death should supervene—and this, it was generally agreed, must now take place within a few minutes. I concluded, however, to speak to him once more, and merely repeated my previous question.

While I spoke, there came a marked change over the countenance of the sleep-waker. The eyes rolled themselves slowly open, the pupils disappearing upwardly; the skin generally assumed a cadaverous hue, resembling not so much parchment as white paper; and the circular hectic spots which, hitherto, had been strongly defined in the centre of each cheek, *went out* at once. I use this expression, because the suddenness of their departure put me in mind of nothing so much as the extinguishment of a candle by a puff of the breath. The upper lip, at the same time, writhed itself away from the teeth, which it had previously covered completely; while the lower jaw fell with an audible jerk, leaving the mouth widely extended, and disclosing in full view the swollen and blackened tongue. I presume that no member of the party then present had been unaccustomed to death-bed horrors; but so hideous beyond conception was the appearance of M. Valdemar at this moment, that there was a general shrinking back from the region of the bed.

I now feel that I have reached a point of this narrative at which every reader will be startled into positive disbelief. It is my business, however, simply to proceed.

There was no longer the faintest sign of vitality in M. Valdemar; and concluding him to be dead, we were consigning him to the charge of the nurses, when a strong vibratory motion was observable in the tongue. This continued for perhaps a minute. At the expiration of this period, there issued from the distended and motionless jaws a voice—such as it would be madness in me to attempt describing. There are, indeed, two or three epithets which might be considered as applicable to it in part; I might say, for example, that the sound was harsh, and broken and hollow; but the hideous whole is indescribable, for the simple reason that no similar sounds have ever jarred upon the ear of humanity. There were two particulars, nevertheless, which I thought then, and still think, might fairly be stated as characteristic of the intonation—as well adapted to convey some idea of its unearthly peculiarity. In the first place, the voice seemed to reach our ears—at least mine—from a vast distance, or from some deep cavern within the earth. In the second place, it impressed me (I fear, indeed, that it will be impossible to make myself comprehended) as gelatinous or glutinous matters impress the sense of touch.

I have spoken both of "sound" and of "voice." I mean to say that the sound was one of distinct—of even wonderfully, thrillingly distinct—syllabification. M. Valdemar *spoke*—obviously in reply to the question I had propounded to him a few minutes before. I had asked him, it will be remembered, if he still slept. He now said:

"Yes;—no;—I *have been* sleeping—and now—now—*I am dead.*"

No person present even affected to deny, or attempted to repress, the unutterable, shuddering horror which these few words, thus uttered, were so well calculated to convey. Mr. L——l (the student) swooned. The nurses immediately left the chamber, and could not be induced to return. My own impressions I would not pretend to render intelligible to the reader. For nearly an hour, we busied ourselves, silently—without the utterance of a word—in endeavors to revive Mr. L——l. When he came to himself, we addressed ourselves again to an investigation of M. Valdemar's condition.

It remained in all respects as I have last described it, with the exception that the mirror no longer afforded evidence of respiration. An attempt to draw blood from the arm failed. I should mention, too, that this limb was no further subject to my will. I endeavored in vain to make it follow the direction of my hand. The only real indication, indeed, of the mesmeric influence, was now found in the vibratory movement of the tongue, whenever I addressed M. Valdemar a question. He seemed to be making an effort to reply, but had no longer sufficient volition. To queries put to him by any other person than myself he seemed utterly insensible—although I endeavored to place each member of the company in mesmeric *rapport* with him. I believe that I have now related all that is necessary to an understanding of the sleep-waker's state at this epoch. Other nurses were procured; and at ten o'clock I left the house in company with the two physicians and Mr. L——l.

In the afternoon we all called again to see the patient. His condition remained precisely the same. We had now some discussion as to the propriety and feasibility of awakening him; but we had little difficulty in agreeing that no good purpose would be served by so doing. It was evident that, so far, death (or what is usually termed death) had been arrested by the mesmeric process. It seemed clear to us all that to awaken M. Valdemar would be merely to insure his instant, or at least his speedy, dissolution.

From this period until the close of last week—*an interval of nearly seven months*—we continued to make daily calls at M. Valdemar's house, accompanied, now and then, by medical and other friends. All this time the sleep-waker remained *exactly* as I have last described him. The nurses' attentions were continual.

It was on Friday last that we finally resolved to make the experiment of awakening, or attempting to awaken him; and it is the (perhaps) unfortunate result of this latter experiment which has given rise to so much discussion in private circles—to so much of what I cannot help thinking unwarranted popular feeling.

For the purpose of relieving M. Valdemar from the mesmeric trance, I made use of the customary passes. These for a time were unsuccessful. The first indication of revival was afforded by a partial descent of the iris. It was observed, as especially remarkable, that this lowering of the pupil was accompanied by the profuse outflowing of a yellowish ichor (from beneath the lids) of a pungent and highly offensive odor.

It was now suggested that I should attempt to influence the patient's arm as heretofore. I made the attempt and failed. Dr. F—— then intimated a desire to have me put a question. I did so, as follows:

"M. Valdemar, can you explain to us what are your feelings or wishes now?"

There was an instant return of the hectic circles on the cheeks: the tongue quivered, or rather rolled violently in the mouth (although the jaws and lips remained rigid as before), and at length the same hideous voice which I have already described, broke forth:

"For God's sake!—quick!—quick!—put me to sleep—or, quick!—waken me!—quick!—*I say to you that I am dead!*"

154

I was thoroughly unnerved, and for an instant remained undecided what to do. At first I made an endeavor to recompose the patient; but, failing in this through total abeyance of the will, I retraced my steps and as earnestly struggled to awaken him. In this attempt I soon saw that I should be successful—or at least I soon fancied that my success would be complete—and I am sure that all in the room were prepared to see the patient awaken.

For what really occurred, however, it is quite impossible that any human being could have been prepared.

As I rapidly made the mesmeric passes, amid ejaculations of "dead! dead!" absolutely *bursting* from the tongue and not from the lips of the sufferer, his whole frame at once—within the space of a single minute, or less, shrunk—crumbled—absolutely *rotted* away beneath my hands. Upon the bed, before that whole company, there lay a nearly liquid mass of loathsome—of detestable putrescence.

Feeding Time

By James Gunn

Angela woke up with the sickening realization that today was feeding time. She slipped out of bed, hurried to the desk, and leafed nervously through her appointment book. She sighed with relief; it was all right—today was her appointment.

Angela took only forty-five minutes to put on her makeup and dress: it was feeding time. As she descended in the elevator, walked swiftly through the lobby, and got into a taxi, she didn't even notice the eyes that stopped and swiveled after her: feeding time.

Angela was haunted by a zoo.

She was also haunted by men, but this was understandable. She was the kind of blond, blue-eyed angel men pray to—or for—and she had the kind of measurements—36-26-36—that make men want to take up mathematics.

But Angela had no time for men—not today. Angela was haunted by a zoo, and it was feeding time.

Dr. Bachman had a gray-bearded, pink-skinned, blue-eyed kindliness that was his greatest stock in trade. Underneath, there was something else not quite so kindly which had been influential in his choice of professions. Now, for a moment, his professional mask—his *persona,* as the Jungians call it—slipped aside.

"A zoo?" he repeated, his voice clear, deep, and cultured, with just a trace of accent; Viennese without a doubt. He caught himself quickly. "A zoo. Exactly."

"Well, not exactly a zoo," said Angela, pursing her red lips thoughtfully at the ceiling. "At least not an ordinary zoo. It's really only one animal—if you could call him an animal."

"What do you call him?"

"Oh, I never call him," Angela said quickly, giving a delicious little shiver. "He might come."

"Hmmmm," hmmmmed Dr. Bachman neutrally.

"But you don't mean that," Angela said softly. "You mean if he isn't an animal, what is he? What he is—is a monster."

"What kind of monster?" Dr. Bachman asked calmly.

Angela turned on one elbow and looked over the back of the couch at the psychoanalyst. "You say that as if you met monsters every day. But then I guess you do." She sighed sympathetically. "It's a dangerous business, being a psychiatrist."

"Dangerous?" Dr. Bachman repeated querulously, caught off guard a second time. "What do you mean?"

"Oh, the people you meet—all the strange ones—and their problems—"

"Yes, yes, of course," he said hurriedly. "But about the monster—?"

"Yes, Doctor," Angela said in her obedient tone and composed herself again on the couch. She looked at the corner of the ceiling as if she could see him clinging there. "He's not a nightmare monster, though he's frightening enough. He's too real; there are no blurred edges. He has purple fur—short, rather like the fur on some spiders—and four legs, not evenly distributed like a dog's or a cat's but grouped together at the bottom. They're very strong—much stronger than they need to be. He can jump fifteen feet straight up into the air."

She turned again to look at Dr. Bachman. "Are you getting all this?"

Hastily, the psychoanalyst turned his notebook away, but Angela had caught a glimpse of his doodling.

"Goodie!" she said, clapping her hands in delight. "You're drawing a picture."

156

"Yes, yes," he said grumpily. "Go on."

"Well, he has only two arms. He has six fingers on each hand, and they're flexible, as if they had no bones in them. They're elastic, too. They can stretch way out—as if to pick fruit that grows on a very tall vine."

"A vegetarian," said Dr. Bachman, making his small joke.

"Oh no, Doctor!" Angela said, her eyes wide. "He eats everything, but meat is what he likes the best. His face is almost human except it's green. He has very sharp teeth." She shuddered. "Very sharp. Am I going too fast?"

"Don't worry about me!" snapped the psychoanalyst. "It is your subconscious we are exploring, and it must go at its own speed."

"Oh dear," Angela said with resignation. "The subconscious. It's going to be another one of those."

"You don't believe this nightmare has any objective reality?" Dr. Bachman asked sharply.

"That would make me insane, wouldn't it? Well, I guess there's no help for it. That's what I think."

Dr. Bachman tugged thoughtfully at his beard. "I see. Let's go back. How did this illusion begin?"

"I think it began with the claustrophobia."

Dr. Bachman shrugged. "A morbid fear of confined places is not unusual."

"It is when you're out in the open air. The fear had no relationship to my surroundings. All of a sudden I'd feel like I was in a fairly large room which had a tremendous weight of rock or masonry above it. I was in the midst of a crowd of people. For moments it became so real that my actual surroundings faded out."

"But the feeling came and went."

"Yes. Then came the smell. It was a distinctive odor—musty and strong like the lion house in the winter, only wrong, somehow. But it made me think of the zoo."

"Naturally you were the only one who smelled it."

"That's right. I was self-conscious, at first. I tried to drown out the odor with perfume, but that didn't help. Then I realized that no one else seemed to smell it. Like the claustrophobia, it came and went. But each time it returned it was stronger. Finally I went to a psychiatrist—a Dr. Aber."

"That was before the illusion became visual?"

"That was sort of Dr. Aber's fault—my seeing the monster, I mean."

"It is to be expected."

"When nothing else worked, Dr. Aber tried hypnosis. 'Reach

157

into your subconscious,' he said. 'Open the door to the past!' Well, I reached out. I opened the door. And that's when it happened."

"What happened?" Dr. Bachman leaned forward.

"I saw the monster."

"Oh." He leaned back again, disappointed.

"People were close, but the monster was closer. The odor was stifling as he stared through the door—and saw me. I slammed the door shut, but it was too late. The door was there. I knew it could be opened. And he knew it could be opened. Now I was really afraid."

"Afraid?"

"That the monster might get through the door."

The psychoanalyst tugged at his beard. "You have an explanation for this illusion?"

"You won't laugh?"

"Certainly not!"

"I think, through some strange accident of time, I've become linked to a zoo that will exist in the distant future. The monster—wasn't born on Earth. He's an alien—from Jupiter, perhaps, although I don't think so. Through the door I can see part of a sign; I can read this much."

Angela turned and took the notebook from his surprised fingers and printed quickly:

M'BA
(*Larmis*
Nativ
Vega

"Just like in the zoo," she said, handing the book back. "There's a star named Vega."

"Yes," said the psychoanalyst heavily. "And you are afraid that this—alien will get through the door and—"

"That's it. He can open it now, you see. He can't exist here; that would be impossible. But something from the present can exist in the future. And the monster gets hungry—for meat."

"For meat?" Dr. Bachman repeated, frowning.

"Every few weeks," Angela said, shivering, "it's feeding time."

Dr. Bachman tugged at his beard, preparing the swift, feline stroke which would lay bare the traumatic relationship at the root of the neurosis. He said, incisively, "The monster resembles your father, is that not so?"

158

It was Angela's turn to frown. "That's what Dr. Aber said. I'd never have noticed it on my own. There might be a slight resemblance."

"This Dr. Aber—he did you no good?"

"Oh, I wouldn't want you to think that," Angela protested quickly. "He helped. But the help was—temporary, if you know what I mean."

"And you would like something more permanent."

"That would be nice," Angela admitted. "But I'm afraid it's too much to hope for."

"No. It will take time, but eventually we will work these subconscious repressions into your conscious mind, where they will be cleansed of their neurotic value."

"You think it's all in my head?" Angela said wistfully.

"Certainly," the psychoanalyst said briskly. "Let us go over the progress of the illusion once more: first came the claustrophobia, then the smell, then, through Dr. Aber's bung—treatment, I should say, the dreams—"

"Oh, not dreams, doctor," Angela corrected. "When I sleep, I don't dream of monsters. I dream"—she blushed prettily—"of men. The thing in the zoo—I can see him whenever I close my eyes." She shivered. "He's getting impatient."

"Hungry?"

Angela beamed at him. "Yes. It's almost feeding time. He gets fed, of course. By the keeper, I suppose. But that's just grains and fruits and things like that. And he gets hungry for meat."

"And then?"

"He opens the door."

"And I suppose he sticks his elastic fingers through the door."

Angela gave him a look of pure gratitude. "That's right."

"And you're afraid that one day he will get hungry enough to eat you."

"That's it, I guess. Wouldn't you be? Afraid, that is? There's all the legends about dragons and Minotaurs and creatures like that. They always preferred a diet of young virgins; and where there's all that talk—"

"If that were your only concern," Dr. Bachman commented dryly, "it seems to me that you could make yourself ineligible with no great difficulty."

Angela giggled. "Why, Doctor! What a suggestion!"

"Hmmmm. So! To return. Every few weeks comes feeding time. And you, feeling nervous and afraid, come to me for help."

"You put it so well."

"And now it's feeding time."

"That's right." Angela's nostrils dilated suddenly. "He's getting close to the door. Don't you smell him, doctor?"

Dr. Bachman sniffed once and snorted. "Certainly not. Now tell me about your father."

"Well," Angela began reluctantly, "he believed in reincarnation—"

"No, no," the psychoanalyst said impatiently. "The important things. How you felt about him when you were a little girl. What he said to you. How you hated your mother."

"I'm afraid there won't be time. He's got one of his hands on the door already."

Despite himself, Dr. Bachman glanced back over his shoulder. "The monster?" His beard twitched nervously. "Nonsense. About your father—"

"The door's opened!" Angela cried out. "I'm scared, doctor. It's feeding time!"

"I won't be tricked again," the psychoanalyst said sternly. "If we're to get anywhere with this analysis, I must have complete—"

"Doctor! Watch out! The fingers—Dr. Bachman! Doctor! Doc—!"

Angela sighed. It was a strange sigh, half hopelessness and half relief. She picked up her purse.

"Doctor?" she said tentatively to the empty room.

She stood up, sniffing the air gingerly. The odor was gone. So was Dr. Bachman.

She walked toward the door. "Doctor?" she tried once more.

There was no answer. There never had been an answer, not from seventeen psychiatrists, Aber through Bachman. There was no doubt about it. The monster did like psychiatrists.

It was a truly terrifying situation she was in, certainly through no fault of her own, and a girl had to do the best she could. She could console herself with the thought that the monster would never take her for food.

She was the trap door it needed into this world. Eat her, and feeding time was over.

She was perfectly safe.

As long as she didn't run out of psychiatrists.

Feeding Time

By Robert Sheckley

Treggis felt considerably relieved when the owner of the bookstore went front to wait upon another customer. After all, it was essentially nerve-racking, to have a stooped, bespectacled, fawning old man constantly at one's shoulder, peering at the page one was glancing at, pointing here and there with a gnarled, dirty finger, obsequiously wiping dust from the shelves with a tobacco-stained handkerchief. To say nothing of the exquisite boredom of listening to the fellow's cackling, high-pitched reminiscences.

Undoubtedly he meant well, but really, there was a limit. One couldn't do much more than smile politely and hope that the little bell over the front of the store would tinkle—as it had.

Treggis moved toward the back of the store, hoping the disgusting little man wouldn't try to search him out. He passed half a hundred Greek titles, then the popular sciences section. Next, in a strange jumble of titles and authors, he passed Edgar Rice Burroughs, Anthony Trollope, Theosophy, and the poems of Longfellow. The farther back he went the deeper the dust became, the fewer the naked light bulbs suspended above the corridor, the higher the piles of moldy, dog-eared books.

It was really a splendid old place, and for the life of him Treggis couldn't understand how he had missed it before. Bookstores were his sole pleasure in life. He spent all his free hours in them, wandering happily through the stacks.

Of course, he was just interested in certain types of books.

At the end of the high ramp of books there were three more corridors, branching off at absurd angles. Treggis followed the center path, reflecting that the bookstore hadn't seemed so large from the outside; just a door half-hidden between two buildings, with an old hand-lettered sign in its upper panel. But then, these old stores were deceptive, often extending to nearly half a block in depth.

At the end of this corridor two more book-trails split off. Choosing the one on the left, Treggis started reading titles, casually scanning them up and down with a practiced glance. He was in no hurry; he could, if he wished, spend the rest of the day here—to say nothing of the night.

He had shuffled eight or ten feet down the corridor before one title struck him. He went back to it.

It was a small, black-covered book, old, but with that ageless look that some books have. Its edges were worn, and the print on the cover was faded.

"Well, what do you know," Treggis murmured softly.

The cover read: *Care and Feeding of the Gryphon.* And beneath that, in smaller print: *Advice to the Keeper.*

A gryphon, he knew, was a mythological monster, half lion and half eagle.

"Well, now," Treggis said to himself. "Let's see now." He opened the book and began reading the table of contents.

The headings went: 1. *Species of Gryphon.* 2. *A Short History of Gryphonology.* 3. *Subspecies of Gryphon.* 4. *Food for the Gryphon.* 5. *Constructing a Natural Habitat for the Gryphon.* 6. *The Gryphon During Moulting Season.* 7. *The Gryphon and* . . .

He closed the book.

"This," he told himself, "is decidedly—well, unusual." He flipped through the book, reading a sentence here and there. His first thought, that the book was one of the "unnatural" natural history compilations so dear to the Elizabethan heart, was clearly wrong. The book wasn't old enough; and there was nothing euphuistic in the writing, no balanced sentence structure, ingenious antithesis and the like. It was straightforward, clean-cut, concise. Treggis flipped through a few more pages and came upon this:

"The sole diet of the Gryphon is young virgins. Feeding time is once a month, and care should be exercised—"

He closed the book again. The sentence set up a train of thought all its own. He banished it with a blush and looked again at the shelf, hoping to find more books of the same type. Something like *A Short History of the Affairs of the Sirens,* or perhaps *The Proper Breeding of Minotaurs.* But there was nothing even remotely like it. Not on that shelf nor any other, as far as he could tell.

"Find anything?" a voice at his shoulder asked. Treggis gulped, smiled, and held out the black-covered old book.

"Oh yes," the old man said, wiping dust from the cover. "Quite a rare book, this."

"Oh, is it?" murmured Treggis.

"Gryphons," the old man mused, flipping through the book, "are quite rare. Quite a rare species of—animal," he finished, after a moment's thought. "A dollar-fifty for this book, sir."

Treggis left with his possession clutched under his thin right arm. He made straight for his room. It wasn't every day that one bought a book on the *Care and Feeding of Gryphons*.

Treggis' room bore a striking resemblance to a secondhand bookstore. There was the same lack of space, the same film of gray dust over everything, the same vaguely arranged chaos of titles, authors, and types. Treggis didn't stop to gloat over his treasures. His faded *Libidinous Verses* passed unnoticed. Quite unceremoniously he pushed the *Psychopathia Sexualis* from his armchair, sat down and began to read.

There was quite a lot to the care and feeding of the gryphon. One wouldn't think that a creature half lion and half eagle would be so touchy. There was also an interesting amplication of the eating habits of the gryphon. And other information. For pure enjoyment, the gryphon book was easily as good as the Havelock Ellis lectures on sex, formerly his favorite.

Toward the end, there were full instructions on how to get to the zoo. The instructions were, to say the least, unique.

It was a good ways past midnight when Treggis closed the book. What a deal of strange information there was between those two black covers! One sentence in particular he couldn't get out of his head:

"The sole diet of the gryphon is young virgins."

That bothered him. It didn't seem fair, somehow.

After a while he opened the book again to the *Instructions for Getting to the Zoo*.

Decidedly strange they were. And yet, not too difficult. Not requiring, certainly, too much physical exertion. Just a few words, a few motions. Treggis realized suddenly how onerous his bank clerk's job was. A stupid waste of eight good hours a day, no matter how one looked at it. How much more interesting to be a keeper in charge of the gryphon. To use the special ointments during moulting season, to answer questions about gryphonology. To be in charge of feeding. "The sole diet . . ."

"Yes, yes, yes, yes," Treggis mumbled rapidly, pacing the floor of his narrow room. "A hoax—but might as well try out the instructions. For a laugh."

He laughed hollowly.

There was no blinding flash, no clap of thunder, but Treggis was nevertheless transported, instantaneously so it seemed, to a place. He staggered for a moment, then regained his balance and opened his eyes. The sunlight was blinding. Looking around, he could see that someone had done a very good job of constructing *The Natural Habitat of the Gryphon.*

Treggis walked forward, holding himself quite well considering the trembling in his ankles, knees, and stomach. Then he saw the gryphon.

At the same time the gryphon saw him.

Slowly at first, then with ever-gaining momentum, the gryphon advanced on him. The great eagle's wings opened, the talons extended, and the gryphon leaped, or sailed, forward.

Treggis tried to jump out of the way in a single uncontrollable shudder. The gryphon came at him, huge and golden in the sun, and Treggis screamed desperately, "No, no! The sole diet of the gryphon is young—"

Then he screamed again in full realization as the talons seized him.

The Final Quest

By William F. Nolan

Here now, stand close, and let me weave
   A tale so eldritch you'll believe
Me mad. For never has been told
   This death-dark saga. Brave and bold
Was Arthur, bearing Britain's crown,
   A king of courage and renown.
Begat above a thundered sea,
   A just and stalwart lord was he.
In glittered armor, head to heel,
   He smote rogue knights with magic steel.

With Saxon blood upon his blade,
   He came from battle to a glade
Where demons did upon him cast
   A deep spell dark-designed to last
Ten thousand years or more they say.
   Till Merlin came at break of day

And found his lord in sleeping death.
    Then blew upon his cheek a breath
Which waked him full. Cried out the king:
    "The Earth shall ever of thee sing!
I vow upon sweet Jesu's name
    That you shall never want for fame."
But Merlin sighed and bowed his head,
    His waxen face deep-marked with dread.
"This fame, my king, that you bestow
    Avails me naught where I must go.
For though I saved thee on this day
    From Old King Death there is no stay."

"Not so!" cried Arthur, fist raised high,
    "I say that Death Himself shall die!"
"But surely, Sire, you speak in jest,
    No chance have we in such a quest."
But Arthur gripped good Merlin's arm.
    "I shall not let thee come to harm.
Death shall not pluck thee from my side.
    To his dominion we shall ride,
And there, I vow, shall king meet king.
    An end to Death's long reign I'll bring!"

And so began, as legends tell,
    A quest for Death where he might dwell.
On horse, Excalibur in hand,
    With Merlin, searched they land to land
Across the world. And years did pass
    Until, one morn, within a mass
Of stone from which no shadow's breath
    Was cast, at length they found Old Death.
Two kings, both bold, did thundrous reel
    Together, crashing, steel on steel.

And, sad by, watching Merlin wept,
    Aware that Arthur would be swept
From out this life. That even he
    Could not prevail now in the lee
Of Death's dark power. Yea, hour 'pon hour
    The marveled conflict hotly raged,
For never had the world seen staged
    Such awesome clash of mighty wills.

And ringing from the sky-tall hills
　　Was word of battle swiftly sown
From castle wall to hut of stone.
　　From moor and meadow, mountain, plain,
Fast came they all to see Death slain
　　By Arthur. Duke, serf-slave, and lord
Were dazzled by his blazing sword.

A day, a night, a week passed by
　　Without surcease. O'er land and sky
These titans met in frighted clash
　　Of arms, to hew and maim and slash
Each one in turn, while moons did wane
　　And blooded sunsets redly stain
The earth. And even those long dead
　　Themselves raised from their graves, 'tis said,
And stood, stark-boned in silent rows,
　　To watch these fearsome, dreaded foes.

Until, at long last, it was done.
　　Incredibly, their knight had won!
And Death Himself was laid full out.
　　Then, heavenward, the strangled shout
From Arthur's throat: "We'll have no more
　　Of Death upon fair Britain's shore!"
But Death knew well the knightly code,
　　And to victorious Arthur showed
A face of guile. And, from the ground,
　　His voice a low and piteous sound,
He asked for mercy, loud implored,
　　Till Arthur put away his sword
To help him stand. Then Merlin rushed
　　Straight on, ash-eyed, his tone close-hushed
In Arthur's ear. He harshly warned
　　That here all mercy must be scorned.

"This thing I cannot do, good friend,"
　　Said he to Merlin. "For once bend
Our code, and it shall surely break
　　And, with it, knightly honor take."
Thus, Arthur's fixed code could not yield.
　　He laid aside his blade and shield,

While foul and fetid Death roared free.
　　And not for all eternity
Would king meet king in such a fight
　　As this. And Death, in turn, did blight
The world for his defeat. All died:
　　E'en Arthur, Merlin at his side,
Sore-wounded now, his magic fled
　　In this, their final leafy bed.

And later, all of Camelot,
　　Knights of the Table Round could not
Evade that final darkling wood
　　Where smiling, white-boned tall Death stood
Supreme. No further songs were sung
　　Of chivalry. The knell had rung.

Fish Night

By Joe R. Lansdale

It was a bleached-bone afternoon with a cloudless sky and a monstrous sun. The air trembled like a mass of gelatinous ectoplasm. No wind blew.

Through the swelter came a worn, black Plymouth, coughing and belching white smoke from beneath its hood. It wheezed twice, backfired loudly, died by the side of the road.

The driver got out and went around to the hood. He was a man in the hard winter years of life, with dead brown hair and a heavy belly riding his hips. His shirt was open to the navel, the sleeves rolled up past his elbows. The hair on his chest and arms was gray.

A younger man climbed out on the passenger side, went around front too. Yellow sweat-explosions stained the pits of his white shirt. An unfastened, striped tie was draped over his neck like a pet snake that had died in its sleep.

"Well?" the younger man asked.

The old man said nothing. He opened the hood. A calliope note of steam blew out from the radiator in a white puff, rose to the sky, turned clear.

"Damn," the old man said, and he kicked the bumper of the Plymouth as if he were kicking a foe in the teeth. He got little satisfaction out of the action, just a nasty scuff on his brown wingtip and a jar to his ankle that hurt like hell.

"Well?" the young man repeated.

"Well what? What do you think? Dead as the can opener trade this week. Deader. The radiator's chickenpocked with holes."

"Maybe someone will come by and give us a hand."

"Sure."

"A ride anyway."

"Keep thinking that, college boy."

"Someone is bound to come along," the young man said.

"Maybe. Maybe not. Who else takes these cutoffs? The main highway, that's where everyone is. Not this little no account short-cut." He finished by glaring at the young man.

"I didn't make you take it," the young man snapped. "It was on the map. I told you about it, that's all. You chose it. You're the one that decided to take it. It's not my fault. Besides, who'd have expected the car to die?"

"I did tell you to check the water in the radiator, didn't I? Wasn't that back as far as El Paso?"

"I checked. It had water then. I tell you, it's not my fault. You're the one that's done all the Arizona driving."

"Yeah, yeah," the old man said, as if this were something he didn't want to hear. He turned to look up the highway.

No cars. No trucks. Just heat waves and miles of empty concrete in sight.

They seated themselves on the hot ground with their backs to the car. That way it provided some shade—but not much. They sipped on a jug of lukewarm water from the Plymouth and spoke little until the sun fell down. By then they had both mellowed a bit. The heat had vacated the sands and the desert chill had settled in. Where the warmth had made the pair snappy, the cold drew them together.

The old man buttoned his shirt and rolled down his sleeves while the young man rummaged a sweater out of the backseat. He put the sweater on, sat back down. "I'm sorry about this," he said suddenly.

"Wasn't your fault. Wasn't anyone's fault. I just get to yelling sometime, taking out the can-opener trade on everything but the can openers and myself. The days of the door-to-door salesman are gone, son."

168

"And I thought I was going to have an easy summer job," the young man said.

The old man laughed. "Bet you did. They talk a good line, don't they?"

"I'll say!"

"Make it sound like found money, but there ain't no found money, boy. Ain't nothing simple in this world. The company is the only one ever makes any money. We just get tireder and older with more holes in our shoes. If I had any sense I'd have quit years ago. All you got to make is this summer—"

"Maybe not that long."

"Well, this is all I know. Just town after town, motel after motel, house after house, looking at people through screen wire while they shake their heads. No. Even the cockroaches at the sleazy motels begin to look like little fellows you've seen before, like maybe they're door-to-door peddlers that have to rent rooms too."

The young man chuckled. "You might have something there."

They sat quietly for a moment, welded in silence. Night had full grip on the desert now. A mammoth gold moon and billions of stars cast a whitish glow from eons away.

The wind picked up. The sand shifted, found new places to lie down. The undulations of it, slow and easy, were reminiscent of the midnight sea. The young man, who had crossed the Atlantic by ship once, said as much.

"The sea?" the old man replied. "Yes, yes, exactly like that. I was thinking the same. That's part of the reason it bothers me. Part of why I was stirred up this afternoon. Wasn't just the heat doing it. There are memories of mine out here," he nodded at the desert, "and they're visiting me again."

The young man made a face. "I don't understand."

"You wouldn't. You shouldn't. You'd think I'm crazy."

"I already think you're crazy. So tell me."

The old man smiled. "All right, but don't you laugh."

"I won't."

A moment of silence moved in between them. Finally the old man said, "It's fish night, boy. Tonight's the full moon and this is the right part of the desert if memory serves me, and the feel is right—I mean, doesn't the night feel like it's made up of some soft fabric, that it's different from other nights, that it's like being inside a big dark bag, the sides sprinkled with glitter, a spotlight at the top, at the open mouth, to serve as a moon?"

"You lost me."

The old man sighed. "But it feels different. Right? You can feel it too, can't you?"

"I suppose. Sort of thought it was just the desert air. I've never camped out in the desert before, and I guess it is different."

"Different, all right. You see, this is the road I got stranded on twenty years back. I didn't know it at first, least not consciously. But down deep in my gut I must have known all along I was taking this road, tempting fate, offering it, as the football people say, an instant replay."

"I still don't understand about fish night. What do you mean, you were here before?"

"Not this exact spot, somewhere along in here. This was even less of a road back then than it is now. The Navajos were about the only ones who traveled it. My car conked out, like this one today, and I started walking instead of waiting. As I walked the fish came out. Swimming along in the starlight pretty as you please. Lots of them. All the colors of the rainbow. Small ones, big ones, thick ones, thin ones. Swam right up to me . . . *right through me!* Fish just as far as you could see. High up and low down to the ground.

"Hold on, boy. Don't start looking at me like that. Listen: You're a college boy, you know something about these things. I mean, about what was here before we were, before we crawled out of the sea and changed enough to call ourselves men. Weren't we once just slimy things, brothers to the things that swim?"

"I guess, but—"

"Millions and millions of years ago this desert was a sea bottom. Maybe even the birthplace of man. Who knows? I read that in some science books. And I got to thinking this: If the ghosts of people who have lived can haunt houses, why can't the ghosts of creatures long dead haunt where they once lived, float about in a ghostly sea?"

"Fish with a soul?"

"Don't go small-mind on me, boy. Look here: Some of the Indians I've talked to up North tell me about a thing they call the manitou. That's a spirit. They believe everything has one. Rocks, trees, you name it. Even if the rock wears to dust or the tree gets cut to lumber, the manitou of it is still around."

"Then why can't you see these fish all the time?"

"Why can't we see ghosts all the time? Why do some of us never see them? Time's not right, that's why. It's a precious situation, and I figure it's like some fancy time lock—like the banks use. The lock clicks open at the bank, and there's the money. Here it ticks open and we get the fish of a world long gone."

"Well, it's something to think about," the young man managed.

The old man grinned at him. "I don't blame you for thinking what you're thinking. But this happened to me twenty years ago and I've never forgotten it. I saw those fish for a good hour before they disappeared. A Navajo came along in an old pickup right after and I bummed a ride into town with him. I told him what I'd seen. He just looked at me and grunted. But I could tell he knew what I was talking about. He'd seen it too, and probably not for the first time.

"I've heard that Navajos don't eat fish for some reason or another, and I bet it's the fish in the desert that keep them from it. Maybe they hold them sacred. And why not? It was like being in the presence of the Creator; like crawling back inside your mother and being unborn again, just kicking around in the liquids with no cares in the world."

"I don't know. That sounds sort of . . ."

"Fishy?" The old man laughed. "It does, it does. So this Navajo drove me to town. Next day I got my car fixed and went on. I've never taken that cutoff again—until today, and I think that was more than accident. My subconscious was driving me. That night scared me, boy, and I don't mind admitting it. But it was wonderful too, and I've never been able to get it out of my mind."

The young man didn't know what to say.

The old man looked at him and smiled. "I don't blame you," he said. "Not even a little bit. Maybe I am crazy."

They sat awhile longer with the desert night, and the old man took his false teeth out and poured some of the warm water on them to clean them of coffee and cigarette residue.

"I hope we don't need that water," the young man said.

"You're right. Stupid of me! We'll sleep awhile, start walking before daylight. It's not too far to the next town. Ten miles at best." He put his teeth back in. "We'll be just fine."

The young man nodded.

No fish came. They did not discuss it. They crawled inside the car, the young man in the front seat, the old man in the back. They used their spare clothes to bundle under, to pad out the cold fingers of the night.

Near midnight the old man came awake suddenly and lay with his hands behind his head and looked up and out the window opposite him, studied the crisp desert sky.

And a fish swam by.

171

Long and lean and speckled with all the colors of the world, flicking its tail as if in good-bye. Then it was gone.

The old man sat up. Outside, all about, were the fish—all sizes, colors, and shapes.

"Hey, boy, wake up!"

The younger man moaned.

"Wake up!"

The young man, who had been resting face down on his arms, rolled over. "What's the matter? Time to go?"

"The fish."

"Not again."

"Look!"

The young man sat up. His mouth fell open. His eyes bloated. Around and around the car, faster and faster in whirls of dark color, swam all manner of fish.

"Well, I'll be . . . *How?*"

"I told you, I told you."

The old man reached for the door handle, but before he could pull it a fish swam lazily through the back window glass, swirled about the car, once, twice, passed through the old man's chest, whipped up and went out through the roof.

The old man cackled, jerked open the door. He bounced around beside the road. Leaped up to swat his hands through the spectral fish. "Like soap bubbles," he said. "No. Like smoke!"

The young man, his mouth still agape, opened his door and got out. Even high up he could see the fish. Strange fish, like nothing he'd ever seen pictures of or imagined. They flitted and skirted about like flashes of light.

As he looked up, he saw, nearing the moon, a big dark cloud. The only cloud in the sky. That cloud tied him to reality suddenly, and he thanked the heavens for it. Normal things still happened. The whole world had not gone insane.

After a moment the old man quit hopping among the fish and came out to lean on the car and hold his hand to his fluttering chest.

"Feel it, boy? Feel the presence of the sea? Doesn't it feel like the beating of your own mother's heart while you float inside the womb?"

And the younger man had to admit that he felt it, that inner rolling rhythm that is the tide of life and the pulsating heart of the sea.

"How?" the young man said. "Why?"

"The time lock, boy. The locks clicked open and the fish are free.

172

Fish from a time before man was man. Before civilization started weighing us down. I know it's true. The truth's been in me all the time. It's in us all."

"It's like time travel," the young man said. "From the past to the future, they've come all that way."

"Yes, yes, that's it . . . Why, if they can come to our world, why can't we go to theirs? Release that spirit inside of us, tune into their time?"

"Now wait a minute . . ."

"My God, that's it! They're pure, boy, pure. Clean and free of civilization's trappings. That must be it! They're pure and we're not. We're weighted down with technology. These clothes. That car."

The old man started removing his clothes.

"Hey!" the young man said. "You'll freeze."

"If you're pure, if you're completely pure," the old man mumbled, "that's it . . . yeah, that's the key."

"You've gone crazy."

"I won't look at the car," the old man yelled, running across the sand, trailing the last of his clothes behind him. He bounced about the desert like a jackrabbit. "God, God, nothing is happening, nothing," he moaned. "This isn't my world. I'm of that world. I want to float free in the belly of the sea, away from can openers and cars and—"

The young man called the old man's name. The old man did not seem to hear.

"I want to leave here!" the old man yelled. Suddenly he was springing about again. "The teeth!" he yelled. "It's the teeth. Dentist, science, foo!" He punched a hand into his mouth, plucked the teeth free, tossed them over his shoulder.

Even as the teeth fell the old man rose. He began to stroke. To swim up and up and up, moving like a pale pink seal among the fish.

In the light of the moon the young man could see the pooched jaws of the old man, holding the last of the future's air. Up went the old man, up, up, up, swimming strong in the long-lost waters of a time gone by.

The young man began to strip off his own clothes. Maybe he could nab him, pull him down, put the clothes on him. Something . . . God, something. . . . But, what if *he* couldn't come back? And there were the fillings in his teeth, the metal rod in his back from a motorcycle accident. No, unlike the old man, this was his world and he was tied to it. There was nothing he could do.

A great shadow weaved in front of the moon, made a wriggling slat of darkness that caused the young man to let go of his shirt buttons and look up.

A black rocket of a shape moved through the invisible sea: a shark, the granddaddy of all sharks, the seed for all of man's fears of the deeps.

And it caught the old man in its mouth, began swimming upward toward the golden light of the moon. The old man dangled from the creature's mouth like a ragged rat from a house cat's jaws. Blood blossomed out of him, coiled darkly in the invisible sea.

The young man trembled. "Oh God," he said once.

Then along came that thick dark cloud, rolling across the face of the moon.

Momentary darkness.

And when the cloud passed there was light once again, and an empty sky.

No fish.

No shark.

And no old man.

Just the night, the moon and the stars.

The Four-Fingered Hand

By Barry Pain

Charles Yarrow held fours, but as he had come up against Brackley's straight flush they only did him harm, leading him to remark—by no means for the first time—that it did not matter what cards one held, but only when one held them. 'I get out here,' he remarked, with resignation. No one else seemed to care for further play. The two other men left at once, and shortly afterwards Yarrow and Brackley sauntered out of the club together.

'The night's young,' said Brackley; 'if you're doing nothing you may as well come round to me.'

'Thanks, I will. I'll talk, or smoke, or go so far as to drink; but I don't play poker. It's not my night.'

'I didn't know,' said Brackley, 'that you had any superstitions.'

'Haven't. I've only noticed that, as a rule, my luck goes in runs, and that a good run or a bad run usually lasts the length of a night's play. There is probably some simple reason for it, if I were enough of a mathematician to worry it out. In luck as distinct from arithmetic I have no belief at all.'

'I wish you could bring me to that happy condition. The hardheaded man of the world, without a superstition or a belief of any kind, has the best time of it.'

They reached Brackley's chambers, lit pipes, and mixed drinks. Yarrow stretched himself in a lounge chair, and took up the subject again, speaking lazily and meditatively. He was a man of thirty-eight, with a clean shaven face; he looked, as indeed he was, travelled and experienced.

'I don't read any books,' he remarked, 'but I've been twice round the world, and am just about to leave England again. I've been alive for thirty-eight years and during most of them I have been living. Consequently, I've formed opinions, and one of my opinions is that it is better to dispense with superfluous luggage. Prejudices, superstitions, beliefs of any kind that are not capable of easy and immediate proof are superfluous luggage; one goes more easily without them. You implied just now that you had a certain amount of this superfluous luggage, Brackley. What form does it take? Do you turn your chair—are you afraid of thirteen at dinner?'

'No, nothing of that sort. I'll tell you about it. You've heard of my grandfather—who made the money?'

'Heard of him? Had him rubbed into me in my childhood. He's in *Smiles* or one of those books, isn't he? Started life as a navvy, educated himself, invented things, made a fortune, gave vast sums in charity.'

'That is the man. Well, he lived to be a fair age, but he was dead before I was born. What I know of him I know from my father, and some of it is not included in those improving books for the young. For instance, there is no mention in the printed biography of his curious belief in the four-fingered hand. His belief was that from time to time he saw a phantom hand. Sometimes it appeared to him in the daytime, and sometimes at night. It was a right hand with the second finger missing. He always regarded the appearance of the hand as a warning. It meant, he supposed, that he was to stop anything on which he was engaged; if he was about to let a house, buy a horse, go on a journey, or whatever it was, he stopped if he saw the four-fingered hand.'

'Now, look here,' said Yarrow, 'we'll examine this thing rationally. Can you quote one special instance in which your grandfather saw this maimed hand, broke off a particular project, and found himself benefited?'

'No. In telling my father about it he spoke quite generally.'

'Oh, yes,' said Yarrow, drily. 'The people who see these things do speak quite generally as a rule.'

'But wait a moment. This vision of the four-fingered hand appears to have been hereditary. My father also saw it from time to time. And here I can give you the special circumstances. Do you remember the Crewe disaster some years ago? Well, my father had intended to travel by the train that was wrecked. Just as he was getting into the carriage he saw the four-fingered hand. He at once got out and postponed his journey until later in the day. Another occasion was two months before the failure of Varings'. My father banked there. As a rule he kept a comparatively small balance at the bank, but on this occasion he had just realized an investment, and was about to place the result—six thousand pounds—in the bank, pending re-investment. He was on the point of sending off his confidential clerk with the money, when once more he saw the four-fingered hand. Now at that time Varings' was considered to be as safe as a church. Possibly a few people with special means of information may have had some slight suspicion at the time, but my father certainly had none. He had always banked with Varings', as his father had done before him. However, his faith in the warning hand was so great that instead of paying in the six thousand he withdrew his balance that day. Is that good enough for you?'

'Not entirely. Mind, I don't dispute your facts, but I doubt if it requires the supernatural to explain them. You say that the vision appears to be hereditary. Does that mean that you yourself have ever seen it?'

'I have seen it once.'

'When?'

'I saw it tonight.' Brackley spoke like a man suppressing some strong excitement. 'It was just as you got up from the card-table after losing on your fours. I was on the point of urging you and the other two men to go on playing. I saw the hand distinctly. It seemed to be floating in the air about a couple of yards away from me. It was a small white hand, like a lady's hand, cut short off at the wrist. For a second it moved slowly towards me, and then vanished. Nothing would have induced me to go on playing poker tonight.'

'You are—excuse me for mentioning it—not in the least degree under the influence of drink. Further, you are by habit an almost absurdly temperate man. I mention these things because they have to be taken into consideration. They show that you were not at any rate the victim of a common and disreputable form of illusion. But what service has the hand done you? We play a regular point at the club. We are not the excited gamblers of fiction. We don't increase the points, and we never play after one in the morning. At the moment when the hand appeared to you, how much had you won?'

'Twenty-five pounds—an exceptionally large amount.'

'Very well. You're a careful player. You play best when your luck's worst. We stopped play at half-past eleven. If we had gone on playing till one, and your luck had been of the worst possible description all the time, we will say that you might have lost that twenty-five and twenty-five more. To me it is inconceivable, but with the worst luck and the worst play it is perhaps possible. Now then, do you mean to tell me that the loss of twenty-five pounds is a matter of such importance to a man with your income as to require a supernatural intervention to prevent you from losing it?'

'Of course it isn't.'

'Well, then, the four-fingered hand has not accomplished its mission. It has not saved you from anything. It might even have been inconvenient. If you had been playing with strangers and winning, and they had wished to go on playing, you could hardly have refused. Of course, it did not matter with us—we play with you constantly, and can have our revenge at any time. The four-fingered hand is proved in this instance to have been useless and inept. Therefore, I am inclined to believe that the appearances when it really did some good were coincidences. Doubtless your grandfather and father and yourself have seen the hand, but surely that may be due to some slight hereditary defect in the seeing apparatus, which, under certain conditions, say, of the light and of your own health creates the illusion. The four-fingered hand is natural and not supernatural, subjective and not objective.'

'It sounds plausible,' remarked Brackley. He got up, crossed the room, and began to open the card-table. 'Practical tests are always the most satisfactory, and we can soon have a practical test.' As he put the candles on the table he started a little and nearly dropped one of them. He laughed drily. 'I saw the four-fingered hand again just then,' he said. 'But no matter—come—let us play.'

'Oh, the two game isn't funny enough.'

'Then I'll fetch up Blake from downstairs; you know him. He never goes to bed, and he plays the game.'

Blake, who was a youngish man, had chambers downstairs. Brackley easily persuaded him to join the party. It was decided that they should play for exactly an hour. It was a poor game; the cards ran low, and there was very little betting. At the end of the hour Brackley had lost a sovereign, and Yarrow had lost five pounds.

'I don't like to get up a winner, like this,' said Blake. 'Let's go on.'

But Yarrow was not to be persuaded. He said that he was going off to bed. No allusion to the four-fingered hand was made in speaking in the presence of Blake, but Yarrow's smile of conscious superiority had its meaning for Brackley. It meant that Yarrow had overthrown a superstition, and was consequently pleased with himself. After a few minutes' chat Yarrow and Blake said good-night to Brackley, and went downstairs together.

Just as they reached the ground floor they heard, from far up the staircase, a short cry, followed a moment afterwards by the sound of a heavy fall.

'What's that?' Blake exclaimed.

'I'm just going to see,' said Yarrow, quietly. 'It seemed to me to come from Brackley's rooms. Let's go up again.'

They hurried up the staircase and knocked at Brackley's door. There was no answer. The whole place was absolutely silent. The door was ajar; Yarrow pushed it open, and the two men went in.

The candles on the card-table were still burning. At some distance from them, in a dark corner of the room, lay Brackley, face downwards, with one arm folded under him and the other stretched wide.

Blake stood in the doorway. Yarrow went quickly over to Brackley, and turned the body partially over.

'What is it?' asked Blake, excitedly. 'Is the man ill? Has he fainted?'

'Run downstairs,' said Yarrow, curtly. 'Rouse the porter and get a doctor at once.'

The moment Blake had gone, Yarrow took a candle from the card-table, and by the light of it examined once more the body of the dead man. On the throat there was the imprint of a hand—a right hand with the second finger missing. The marks, which were crimson at first, grew gradually fainter.

Some years afterwards, in Yarrow's presence, a man happened to tell some story of a warning apparition that he himself had investigated.

'And do you believe that?' Yarrow asked.

'The evidence that the apparition was seen—and seen by more than one person—seems to me fairly conclusive in this case.'

'That is all very well. I will grant you the apparition if you like. But why speak of it as a warning? If such appearances take place, it still seems to me absurd and disproportionate to suppose that they do so in order to warn us, or help us, or hinder us, or anything of the kind. They appear for their own unfathomable reasons only. If they seem to forbid one thing or command another, that also is for their own purpose. I have an experience of my own which would tend to show that.'

A Ghost Story

By Mark Twain

I took a large room, far up Broadway, in a huge old building whose upper stories had been wholly unoccupied for years until I came. The place had long been given up to dust and cobwebs, to solitude and silence. I seemed groping among the tombs and invading the privacy of the dead, that first night I climbed up to my quarters. For the first time in my life a superstitious dread came over me; and as I turned a dark angle of the stairway and an invisible cobweb swung its slazy woof in my face and clung there, I shuddered as one who had encountered a phantom.

I was glad enough when I reached my room and locked out the mold and the darkness. A cheery fire was burning in the grate, and I sat down before it with a comforting sense of relief. For two hours I sat there, thinking of bygone times; recalling old scenes, and summoning half-forgotten faces out of the mists of the past; listening, in fancy, to voices that long ago grew silent for all time, and to once familiar songs that nobody sings now. And as my reverie softened down to a sadder and sadder pathos, the shrieking of the winds outside softened to a wail, the angry beating of the rain against the panes diminished to a tranquil patter, and one by one the noises in the street subsided, until the hurrying footsteps of the last belated straggler died away in the distance and left no sound behind.

The fire had burned low. A sense of loneliness crept over me. I arose and undressed, moving on tiptoe about the room, doing stealthily what I had to do, as if I were environed by sleeping enemies whose slumbers it would be fatal to break. I covered up in bed, and lay listening to the rain and wind and the faint creaking of distant shutters, till they lulled me to sleep.

I slept profoundly, but how long I do not know. All at once I found myself awake, and filled with a shuddering expectancy. All was still. All but my own heart—I could hear it beat. Presently the bedclothes began to slip away slowly toward the foot of the bed, as if some one were pulling them! I could not stir; I could not speak. Still the blankets slipped deliberately away, till my breast was uncovered. Then with a great effort I seized them and drew them over my head. I waited, listened, waited. Once more that steady pull began, and once more I lay torpid a century of dragging seconds till my breast was naked again. At last I roused my energies and snatched the covers back to their place and held them with a strong grip. I waited. By and by I felt a faint tug, and took a fresh grip. The tug strengthened to a steady strain—it grew stronger and stronger. My hold parted, and for the third time the blankets slid away. I groaned. An answering groan came from the foot of the bed! Beaded drops of sweat stood upon my forehead. I was more dead than alive. Presently I heard a heavy footstep in my room— the step of an elephant, it seemed to me—it was not like anything human. But it was moving *from* me—there was relief in that. I heard it approach the door—pass out without moving bolt or lock —and wander away among the dismal corridors, straining the floors and joists till they creaked again as it passed—and then silence reigned once more.

When my excitement had calmed, I said to myself, "This is a dream—simply a hideous dream." And so I lay thinking it over until I convinced myself that it *was* a dream, and then a comforting laugh relaxed my lips and I was happy again. I got up and struck a light; and when I found that the locks and bolts were just as I had left them, another soothing laugh welled in my heart and rippled from my lips. I took my pipe and lit it, and was just sitting down before the fire, when—down went the pipe out of my nerveless fingers, the blood forsook my cheeks, and my placid breathing was cut short with a gasp! In the ashes on the hearth, side by side with my own bare footprint, was another, so vast that in comparison mine was but an infant's! Then I had *had* a visitor, and the elephant tread was explained.

I put out the light and returned to bed, palsied with fear. I lay a long time, peering into the darkness, and listening. Then I heard a grating noise overhead, like the dragging of a heavy body across the floor; then the throwing down of the body, and the shaking of my windows in response to the concussion. In distant parts of the building I heard the muffled slamming of doors. I heard, at intervals, stealthy footsteps creeping in and out among the corridors, and up and down the stairs. Sometimes these noises approached my door, hesitated, and went away again. I heard the clanking of chains faintly, in remote passages, and listened while the clanking grew nearer—while it wearily climbed the stairways, marking each move by the loose surplus of chain that fell with an accented rattle upon each succeeding step as the goblin that bore it advanced. I heard muttered sentences; half-uttered screams that seemed smothered violently; and the swish of invisible garments, the rush of invisible wings. Then I became conscious that my chamber was invaded—that I was not alone. I heard sighs and breathings about my bed, and mysterious whisperings. Three little spheres of soft phosphorescent light appeared on the ceiling directly over my head, clung and glowed there a moment, and then dropped—two of them upon my face and one upon the pillow. They spattered, liquidly, and felt warm. Intuition told me they had turned to gouts of blood as they fell—I needed no light to satisfy myself of that. Then I saw pallid faces, dimly luminous, and white uplifted hands, floating bodiless in the air—floating a moment and then disappearing. The whispering ceased, and the voices and the sounds, and a solemn stillness followed. I waited and listened. I felt that I must have light or die. I was weak with fear. I slowly raised myself toward a sitting posture, and my face came in contact with a clammy hand! All strength went from me apparently, and I fell back like a stricken invalid. Then I heard the rustle of a garment—it seemed to pass to the door and go out.

When everything was still once more, I crept out of bed, sick and feeble, and lit the gas with a hand that trembled as if it were aged with a hundred years. The light brought some little cheer to my spirits. I sat down and fell into a dreamy contemplation of that great footprint in the ashes. By and by its outlines began to waver and grow dim. I glanced up and the broad gas-flame was slowly wilting away. In the same moment I heard that elephantine tread again. I noted its approach, nearer and nearer, along the musty halls, and dimmer and dimmer the light waned. The tread reached my very door and paused—the light had dwindled to a sickly blue, and all things about me lay in a spectral twilight. The door did not open, and yet I felt a faint gust of air fan my cheek, and presently was conscious of a huge, cloudy presence before me. I watched it with fascinated eyes. A pale glow stole over the Thing; gradually its cloudy folds took shape—an arm appeared, then legs, then a body, and last a great sad face looked out of the vapor. Stripped of its filmy housings, naked, muscular and comely, the majestic Cardiff Giant loomed above me!

All my misery vanished—for a child might know that no harm could come with that benignant countenance. My cheerful spirits returned at once, and in sympathy with them the gas flamed up brightly again. Never a lonely outcast was so glad to welcome company as I was to greet the friendly giant. I said:

"Why, is it nobody but you? Do you know, I have been scared to death for the last two or three hours? I am most honestly glad to see you. I wish I had a chair— Here, here, don't try to sit down in that thing!"

But it was too late. He was in it before I could stop him, and down he went—I never saw a chair shivered so in my life.

"Stop, stop, you'll ruin ev—"

Too late again. There was another crash, and another chair was resolved into its original elements.

"Confound it, haven't you got any judgment at all? Do you want to ruin all the furniture on the place? Here, here, you petrified fool—"

But it was no use. Before I could arrest him he had sat down on the bed, and it was a melancholy ruin.

"Now what sort of a way is that to do? First you come lumbering about the place bringing a legion of vagabond goblins along with you to worry me to death, and then when I overlook an indelicacy of costume which would not be tolerated anywhere by cultivated people except in a respectable theater, and not even there if the nudity were of *your* sex, you repay me by wrecking all the furniture you can find to sit down on. And why will you? You damage yourself as much as you do me. You have broken off the end of your spinal column, and littered up the floor with chips of your hams till the place looks like a marble yard. You ought to be ashamed of yourself—you are big enough to know better."

"Well, I will not break any more furniture. But what am I to do? I have not had a chance to sit down for a century." And the tears came into his eyes.

"Poor devil," I said, "I should not have been so harsh with you. And you are an orphan, too, no doubt. But sit down on the floor here—nothing else can stand your weight—and besides, we cannot be sociable with you away up there above me; I want you down where I can perch on this high counting-house stool and gossip with you face to face."

So he sat down on the floor, and lit a pipe which I gave him, threw one of my red blankets over his shoulders, inverted my sitz-bath on his head, helmet fashion, and made himself picturesque and comfortable. Then he crossed his ankles, while I renewed the

182

fire, and exposed the flat, honeycombed bottoms of his prodigious feet to the grateful warmth.

"What is the matter with the bottom of your feet and the back of your legs, that they are gouged up so?"

"Infernal chilblains—I caught them clear up to the back of my head, roosting out there under Newell's farm. But I love the place; I love it as one loves his old home. There is no peace for me like the peace I feel when I am there."

We talked along for half an hour, and then I noticed that he looked tired, and spoke of it.

"Tired?" he said. "Well, I should think so. And now I will tell you all about it, since you have treated me so well. I am the spirit of the Petrified Man that lies across the street there in the museum. I am the ghost of the Cardiff Giant. I can have no rest, no peace, till they have given that poor body burial again. Now what was the most natural thing for me to do, to make men satisfy this wish? Terrify them into it!—haunt the place where the body lay! So I haunted the museum night after night. I even got other spirits to help me. But it did no good, for nobody ever came to the museum at midnight. Then it occurred to me to come over the way and haunt this place a little. I felt that if I ever got a hearing I must succeed, for I had the most efficient company that perdition could furnish. Night after night we have shivered around through these mildewed halls, dragging chains, groaning, whispering, tramping up and down stairs, till, to tell you the truth, I am almost worn out. But when I saw a light in your room to-night I roused my energies again and went at it with a deal of the old freshness. But I am tired out—entirely fagged out. Give me, I beseech you, give me some hope!"

I lit off my perch in a burst of excitement, and exclaimed:

"This transcends everything! everything that ever did occur! Why you poor blundering old fossil, you have had all your trouble for nothing—you have been haunting a *plaster cast* of yourself—the real Cardiff Giant is in Albany![1] Confound it, don't you know your own remains?"

I never saw such an eloquent look of shame, of pitiable humiliation, overspread a countenance before.

The Petrified Man rose slowly to his feet, and said:

"Honestly, *is* that true?"

[1] A fact. The original fraud was ingeniously and fraudfully duplicated, and exhibited in New York as the "only genuine" Cardiff Giant (to the unspeakable disgust of the owners of the real colossus) at the very same time that the latter was drawing crowds at a museum in Albany.

"As true as I am sitting here."

He took the pipe from his mouth and laid it on the mantel, then stood irresolute a moment (unconsciously, from old habit, thrusting his hands where his pantaloons pockets should have been, and meditatively dropping his chin on his breast), and finally said:

"Well—I *never* felt so absurd before. The Petrified Man has sold everybody else, and now the mean fraud has ended by selling its own ghost! My son, if there is any charity left in your heart for a poor friendless phantom like me, don't let this get out. Think how *you* would feel if you had made such an ass of yourself."

I heard his stately tramp die away, step by step down the stairs and out into the deserted street, and felt sorry that he was gone, poor fellow—and sorrier still that he had carried off my red blanket and my bathtub.

Give Her Hell

By Donald A. Wollheim

It's no good making a deal with the devil. He's a cheat. He's all they say he is and more. The effete modern books like to present him as a smiling red devil, all clean and slick. Or as some cagey, witty peddler, or a tophat-and-tails city slicker. But the monks of the Middle Ages knew better. They described him as a beast; a stinking, foul-breathed, corrupt, and totally loathsome abomination.

Take my word for it. He is. I know, for I was fool enough to make such a pact. I saw him and dealt with him and from beginning to end, it was never worth it.

It was desperate, and like all whom fate had played crooked, I was sore about it. Things were not going well with me, and it was all their fault. My wife and my daughter's. I refuse to take the blame in spite of what the devil may claim. I know when I'm right. My daughter had run away from my home—that was the shock that made me realize what was happening.

That girl ran away and she was only sixteen, and she'd stolen the contents of my wallet and took some of my wife's jewelry and ran away. My wife wasn't so shocked. She had the nerve to say it served me right. I didn't "understand the child."

184

What's to understand about a disobedient daughter who doesn't listen to her father, and who makes dates after eight o'clock at night, who sneaks magazines into her bedroom, actually talks to some of those uncouth common kids from across the tracks, and has been seen in soda parlors after dark. Sure, I had to beat her. I've been doing that since she was seven. I've had to be stricter and stricter with her. Spare the rod and spoil the child—that's the slogan I was raised on and I did my best. But the girl was rotten—something from her mother's side of the family, no doubt—and she had the nerve to try to run away.

I called the police. I'm not going to be thought of as the father of a wild kid. I sent out an alarm. My wife objected, but I put her in her place. Slap across the face shut her up—I'd taught her long ago who was master. Me, the way it was meant to be. I locked her up in our bedroom, and later on I gave her a lesson with the strap, face down on the bed with her clothes off. Women know only one master. My mother never complained; she didn't dare, not even when she was dying after my father threw her down the stairs that night.

My father's ways were right and I was right. The cops brought the girl back to me the next day. I gave her a hiding she'd not forget, and then I arranged to have her committed to a corrective institution. One of those private sanitariums for disturbed children, you know. Exclusive, well-guarded, and well-disciplined. All right, they made life hell for her, but how else can you teach a wayward child how to do right. Better for the family name than to have her in public vision.

They had my orders and the extra payments I made were generous enough to enforce them—she'd not get out until she was good if they had to nearly kill her to do it. They kept her in a straitjacket for months at a time at my insistence, and in restraining cuffs and belts at all other times. A series of regular electric shocks taught her a few things. The doctor says now she's faking insanity, that she shrieks night and day, and they keep her by herself in a padded, locked cell. But I think she's faking. She's just a disobedient girl and she's got to learn who's master.

As for my wife, she had the nerve to leave me. She climbed out of a window the night I bribed the doctors to start my bad daughter's shock treatments. She ran to my business partner, that skunk, and he helped her hide. Next day he dared put it up to me. He said he thought I was the one who was cracking up. Me! The nerve of him.

Obviously he was scheming to steal my wife away from me. And he must have been double-booking my firm. I was sure of it. I could

185

see it all from his faking, sly ways. He must have been plotting my ruin the way he must have been scheming after my wife.

So I took steps to sell him out. But the skunk had covered his tracks. He had acted first. He had an order taken out against me, charging me with deceit and having my wife charge me with mental cruelty and suing to get custody of my child and my business.

I could see I'd get no help from the courts and the lawyers. They're all corrupt, unable to see how a man must be stern with his own. These are decadent times. No wonder the world is going to hell.

I was in a jam. They'd cornered me, boxed me with legal chicaneries, tied up my funds. I was furious that night as I stalked up and down my house. The windows were shut and the shades down. I don't stand for curious eyes. I was alone and the next day they'd be closing in from all directions. That's when I turned to Satan.

I figured if Satan had been maligned as much as I was, he must be all right. Just a victim of the same errors. I called on him. When you really mean it, the devil will come. I gave him a sacrifice—I tossed the Bible into the fire; I got hold of my wife's cat—that snarling, fuzzy beast—and I cut its throat on the living room rug and called Satan.

He stank. The place stank and he was there—a foul sort of thing. He was crawly and slimy and toady. He belched rot, and his voice would give you the willies. But I don't go for appearances. I knew he had to have the stuff to stand up to all those dirty do-gooders and Gospel pounders.

I told him I wanted to get out of my jam. I wanted my wife back under my control, my daughter where I wanted her, and my partner in hell.

Satan agreed. He could do the first two things, and while the judgment of my partner would be up to That Other One, maybe he'd get his soul in the end, too. Anyway, he'd die, and what did he want of me?

My soul, of course. I'd trusted him for that. What good would it do him? I believe in reincarnation, anyway. I struck a hard bargain. I said first I had to have a chance to be reborn again and live a whole new life from the start. Then he could have my soul afterward.

Because if he got my whole soul but only gave me the last half of my life as I wanted it, that wasn't fair, was it? No. I drove a hard bargain. He had to give me an entire life from start to finish.

He whined and he threatened and he bellowed, but he agreed. On my deathbed, he said, he'd reappear and give me the word on the whole new life I was going to get to live. There were certain rules he had to go by in that sort of thing. Okay, I said, I trust you. You and me, we think alike, we think right. An iron hand in a velvet glove, that's the rule.

He stank, that no-good bum. He gave me his word, and I say he cheated, but he didn't think so.

My partner died that same night. His furnace exploded in his house. The place was a seething mass of flames. He tried to get down the stairs, got splashed with flaming oil, was scorched from head to foot, ran out in flames and died in agony. Served him right. The firm's ledgers were in his house for his auditors, and they burned up, too, putting me entirely in the clear.

He died in scandal, too, because my wife was caught in his house. She had a room upstairs, and she jumped from the window and the newspapers snapped her picture in her torn nightgown on the lawn coming away from that man's house. That queered any divorce case for her. She came home, and she had to keep her mouth shut. There'd never be a chance for her to get custody of our runaway daughter or any divorce.

I've never let her forget the scandal, even though she claims there was nothing between them—he was just being hospitable. Ha! I showed her. She's not allowed out of the house now, and I beat her black and blue whenever I think of it. She hasn't got a legal leg to stand on, not after those newspaper photos and stories.

My daughter is still in the padded cell I arranged for her. If she's going to fake insanity, I'll make it so hot for her she'll learn the error of her ways. She's been there ten years now and the kid is stubborn. But the doc and his strongarms have been well paid. They use the leather mitts on her and the rubber sheets and the shocks. She'll stop her act or else.

Unfortunately I won't live to see it. I'm dying now, and I've arranged in my will to see that her cure and treatment continues. I got this cancer of the throat, from inhaling some kind of poison gases or something years ago. I think it was that evening with that stinking cheat. His bad smell burned my throat, it did. I told you he cheats.

And he's been back, just now. He's been back and he gave me the full dope on our deal. I'm to get a full life, from birth to maturity and eventually death. Only he's cheated.

He can't give me a life that hasn't been lived yet. He can't reincarnate me in a future year. No, he hasn't any control over future lives. He has only control over lives that have been lived, he said,

187

the cheat—why couldn't he have said that when we first made the deal?

And it seems to be a rule in this kind of transaction that he can't take life over in the same sex. Something about positive and negative polarity in souls. If you live twice, then you got to see life from first one sex and then the other. Makes the soul rounded, he says, the cheat.

And it's also got to be somebody who's a blood relation, he tells me, the stinking, slimy no-good crook.

I'm dying, and in a few minutes more I'm going to be dead. And then I'll open my eyes again, a newborn baby, and start living through all the long, long years of another person's life. I got to experience everything, every darn, horrible, painful, frustrated, mean minute of it.

I'm going to be reborn as my own daughter.

It's going to be hell.

The Giveaway

By Steve Rasnic Tem

If you don't cut that out something real bad's gonna happen to you!"

Six-year-old Marsha dropped the second handful of mud she was about to smear on seven-year-old Alice Kennedy's party dress. "Like what?"

Alice made a thinking face for a little while. "Well . . . I might tell your daddy about it and he just might give *you* away!"

"Uh-uh," Marsha grunted. She proceeded to gather another handful of mud. Some of it spattered onto her shoes and she had to twist each foot just so to wipe them in the grass. It was hard to do that and still hold onto the slippery mud. Then she walked carefully over to where Alice was sitting making mud pies and raised both hands.

"Stop it, Marsha! I told you what I'd do! I'll *tell* and he'll just give you away!"

Marsha didn't understand why Alice didn't want her to smear mud on the dress anyway; it was nice and cool and besides, Alice's dress was already muddy from making mud pies all afternoon. But she was even more confused about this giveaway stuff. She'd never heard of that before.

"What do you mean, give me away?"

"I'll tell him you've been real bad to me, Marsha, and he'll give you away to some other family, or even worse!"

Marsha just looked at her in confusion. "Moms and dads don't give their kids away," she said seriously.

Alice looked up from her mud pie and smiled. "That's what your daddy did with your brother Billy."

"That's not true, Alice Kennedy; Billy died and went to heaven!"

"How do you know? Did you see him go?"

"Well, no. But Daddy told me he did."

"They *have* to say that, stupid! They don't want you crying and making trouble."

"Don't call me stupid!" Marsha watched her shoes squishing into the mud. "Why did they give Billy away?" she asked softly.

"I heard your daddy tell my daddy that Billy was too small and that he'd never be very big, ever. He sounded real sad about that. So I guess he just gave him away so he can get a bigger boy later on."

Marsha nodded her head solemnly.

"Know who else got given away?"

"Who?"

"Johnny Parker."

"I 'member him! He was like a grownup 'cept he had something funny wrong with his head made him want to play with kids all the time. But he went to a special school! My aunt said so and she's a teacher!"

"Well, he was gonna go to one of them schools, but they gave him away instead. Know who else?"

"Uh-uh."

"Shelly Cox. She kept breaking things and being mad and real mean and one night her daddy had them take her away."

"Who's them?"

Alice looked back over her shoulder at the backyard of her house. "I don't know for *sure*. Guess who else?"

"Who?"

"*You*, Marsha, 'cause you got my party dress *all* muddy and my daddy's probably gonna want to give *me* away so I'm gonna have to tell on *you*."

"Tattletale!" Marsha cried, tears streaming down her face.

"Crybaby!" Alice yelled, running toward her house.

Marsha threw a handful of mud after Alice in frustration. "Uh-uh," she grunted as she began the long walk home.

There were loud voices coming from the kitchen when Marsha got home. She could hear her mother crying, her father shouting. He sounded real mad. Marsha hated it when they had a fight. She sat down in a chair in the living room, picked up one of her books, and pretended to read. But she could only pretend because they were too loud.

"Can't you do anything so simple as enter a check properly, Jennie? I bet Marsha could do that and she's only six years old!"

"I'm sorry, Ted. I just forgot! Will you leave me alone!"

"If I let you alone we'd be broke within the month! Last week you took out the grocery money twice and caused six checks to bounce! And you *say* you don't know what happened to the money! You're driving me crazy, Jennie! I can't take it! I tell you I can't take it anymore!"

"I've *tried* to be a good wife to you . . ." Her mom started to cry and cough, and Marsha couldn't tell what she said anymore. She wanted to go in and see her mom, but she was too afraid. Her daddy was shouting louder than ever now.

"You haven't *been* a wife to me, Jennie, since Billy's been gone!"

Her mom was crying louder than before. Marsha could hardly understand her. "The doctor says . . . you know the doctor said I can't have *any more!*"

"You're lying, Jennie; you're lying through your teeth. I know that quack's nurse! You've been lying to me, lying all the time. You just *don't want to,* Jennie. *You just don't want to!*"

Marsha went upstairs until dinner. She thought her daddy noticed the dried mud on her shoes when she got up from the table, but he didn't say anything.

Marsha woke up with it still dark outside. Something told her she should go to the window. She was afraid, because it was real dark out there, but she thought she should probably go. She tiptoed as softly as she could, afraid she might wake up her dad.

A funny-looking car was parked out in front of the house. It was long and black, the longest and blackest car she had ever seen. And there was a long silver thing, jagged like lightning, that went from one end of the car to the other. This lightning was brighter than the streetlights and hurt her eyes.

The car windows were gray. They looked dirty. She couldn't see through them at all.

Marsha didn't want to see the big black car anymore, but she was

190

more afraid not to see it. She didn't know why she was more afraid of not seeing it, but she was.

Marsha tiptoed down the stairs in her pajamas, scared to death that her father would catch her and maybe give her away like he had Billy. She went into the dark living room. The front door was wide open; she could see the long black car by standing in front of the open door.

She stepped carefully onto the front sidewalk and started walking to the car. She tried to be as quiet as a mouse like her aunt had told her once. She was scared of the car, but she had to keep walking toward it. She couldn't understand that at all.

When she got to the side of the car she held her hands up to her eyes and leaned against the window, trying to see what was inside. But it was too gray, too dirty, too dark. She started to walk around the front of the car and to the other side to look in the windows there, when the tall man stepped in front of her.

He was tall with black shadows all over him and he had a big white bow tie and a big white flower on his chest, but she couldn't see his coat, he was so black, so she didn't know how the flower stayed on.

The tall man bent over. He had no face, just a head full of white fog, like his face hadn't made itself yet.

Marsha began to cry in a soft voice, scared to death she'd wake up her daddy and he'd give her away for spoiling his sleep. But she couldn't help crying, and it kept getting louder and louder until she was sure he'd wake up and want to give her away. Her pajamas felt suddenly wet and warm and she knew she'd wet herself and he'd want to give her away for that too.

She turned around to run back into the house.

Two men with no faces were standing there, carrying a long thing between them. Marsha was so surprised she stopped crying.

For some reason she wasn't so afraid now, so she walked up to the long thing they were carrying to see what it was.

Her mommy was tied to the thing and she was looking up with her eyes all funny and her mouth open and oh she knew her mommy was dead oh dead dead dead!

She ran screaming into the house and they grabbed her and she was screaming and they put something into her mouth—

Only "they" was her daddy. He was sitting with her on the sofa now, looking all serious like when she'd done something real bad.

"You saw the car?"

She nodded her head tearfully.

"Your mommy went away in the car?"

"Ye-es," her voice broke and she cried a little.

"Okay, I want you to listen, Marsha." He held her chin up and made her look into his eyes. "Your mommy didn't do things right, Marsha; she wasn't *good* enough. So you know what happened?"

Marsha nodded her head solemnly.

"I had to *give* your mommy *away*. That's what happens to people who mess up, Marsha. You've got to do your *best*, do your best for *me, all the time.*"

Again she nodded her head, but then her father was gone, as quickly as he had arrived, and she was all alone on the couch in the darkened living room. She looked out the window but there was nothing there. She knew everything was all over, then.

Marsha sleepily climbed off the sofa and stumbled around trying to find a light switch. She couldn't find one so she had to make her way to the kitchen in the dark. She would have cried then, but she really didn't feel like crying anymore.

The kitchen light switch was too high, so she had to work in the dark. It was hard to find the pans or the turner in the dark, but she finally did. At least the refrigerator light let her see the eggs, and she kept the door open afterward so she could see better.

She knew she'd better start her daddy's breakfast now if she was to get it finished on time. The stove and counters were real high for her, so it would take a long time for her to use them.

Daddy liked big breakfasts, and more than anything else in the whole wide world, she wanted to please her daddy.

The Glove

By Fritz Leiber

My most literally tangible brush with the supernatural (something I can get incredibly infatuated with yet forever distrust profoundly, like a very beautiful and adroit call girl) occurred in connection with the rape by a masked intruder of the woman who lived in the next apartment to mine during my San Francisco years. I knew Evelyn Mayne only as a neighbor and I slept through the whole incident, including the arrival and departure of the police, though there came a point in the case when the police doubted both these assertions of mine.

The phrase "victim of rape" calls up certain stereotyped images: an attractive young woman going home alone late at night, enters a dark street, is grabbed . . . or, a beautiful young suburban matron, mother of three, wakes after midnight, feels a nameless dread, is grabbed . . . The truth is apt to be less romantic. Evelyn Mayne was sixty-five long divorced, neglected, and thoroughly detested by her two daughters-in-law and only to a lesser degree by their husbands, lived on various programs of old age, medical and psychiatric assistance, was scrawny, gloomy, alcoholic, waspish, believed life was futile, and either overdosed on sleeping pills or else lightly cut her wrists three or four times a year.

Her assailant at least was somewhat more glamorous, in a sick way. The rapist was dressed all in rather close-fitting gray, hands covered by gray gloves, face obscured by a long shock of straight silver hair falling over it. And in the left hand, at first, a long knife that gleamed silver in the dimness.

And she wasn't grabbed either, at first, but only commanded in a harsh whisper coming through the hair to lie quietly or be cut up.

When she was alone again at last, she silently waited something like the ten minutes she'd been warned to, thinking that at least she hadn't been cut up, or else (who knows?) wishing she had been. Then she went next door (in the opposite direction to mine) and roused Marcia Everly, who was a buyer for a department store and about half her age. After the victim had been given a drink, they called the police and Evelyn Mayne's psychiatrist and also her social worker, who knew her current doctor's number (which she didn't), but they couldn't get hold of either of the last two. Marcia suggested waking me and Evelyn Mayne countered by suggesting they wake Mr. Helpful, who has the next room beyond Marcia's down the hall. Mr. Helpful (otherwise nicknamed Baldy, I never remembered his real name) was someone I loathed because he was always prissily dancing around being neighborly and asking if there was something he could do—and because he was six foot four tall, while I am rather under average height.

Marcia Everly is also very tall, at least for a woman, but as it happens I do not loathe her in the least. Quite the opposite in fact.

But Evelyn Mayne said I wasn't sympathetic, while Marcia (thank goodness!) loathed Mr. Helpful as much as I do—she thought him a weirdo, along with half the other tenants in the building.

So they compromised by waking neither of us, and until the

police came Evelyn Mayne simply kept telling the story of her rape over and over, rather mechanically, while Marcia listened dutifully and occupied her mind as to which of our crazy fellow-tenants was the best suspect—granting it hadn't been done by an outsider, although that seemed likeliest. The three most colorful were the statuesque platinum-blond drag queen on the third floor, the long-haired old weirdo on six who wore a cape and was supposed to be into witchcraft, and the tall, silver-haired, Nazi-looking lesbian on seven (assuming she wore a dildo for the occasion as she was nuttier than a five-dollar fruit cake).

Ours really is a weird building, you see, and not just because of its occupants, who sometimes seem as if they were all referred here by mental hospitals. No, it's eerie in its own right. You see, several decades ago it was a hotel with all the rich, warm inner life that once implied: bevies of maids, who actually used the linen closets (empty now) on each floor and the round snap-capped outlets in the baseboards for a vacuum system (that hadn't been operated for a generation) and the two dumbwaiters (their doors forever shut and painted over). In the old days there had been bellboys and an elevator operator and two night porters who'd carry up drinks and midnight snacks from a restaurant that never closed.

But they're gone now, every last one of them, leaving the halls empty-feeling and very gloomy, and the stairwell an echoing void, and the lobby funereal, so that the mostly solitary tenants of today are apt to seem like ghosts, especially when you meet one coming silently around a turn in the corridor where the ceiling light's burned out.

Sometimes I think that, what with the smaller and smaller families and more and more people living alone, our whole modern world is getting like that.

The police finally arrived, two grave and solicitous young men making a good impression—especially a tall and stalwart (Marcia told me) Officer Hart. But when they first heard Evelyn Mayne's story, they were quite skeptical (Marcia could tell, or thought she could, she told me). But they searched Evelyn's room and poked around the fire escapes and listened to her story again, and then they radioed for a medical policewoman, who arrived with admirable speed and who decided after an examination that in all probability there'd been recent sex, which would be confirmed by analysis of some smears she'd taken from the victim and the sheets.

Officer Hart did two great things, Marcia said. He got hold of Evelyn Mayne's social worker and told him he'd better get on over quick. And he got from him the phone number of her son who lived in the city and called him up and threw a scare into his wife and him about how they were the nearest of kin, goddamn it, and had better start taking care of the abused and neglected lady.

Meanwhile the other cop had been listening to Evelyn Mayne, who was still telling it, and he asked her innocent questions, and had got her to admit that earlier that night she'd gone alone to a bar down the street (a rather rough place) and had one drink, or maybe three. Which made him wonder (Marcia said she could tell) whether Evelyn hadn't brought the whole thing on herself, maybe by inviting some man home with her, and then inventing the rape, at least in part, when things went wrong. (Though I couldn't see her inventing the silver hair.)

Anyhow the police got her statement and got it signed and then took off, even more solemnly sympathetic than when they'd arrived, Officer Hart in particular.

Of course, I didn't know anything about all this when I knocked on Marcia's door before going to work that morning, to confirm a tentative movie date we'd made for that evening. Though I was surprised when the door opened and Mr. Helpful came out looking down at me very thoughtfully, his bald head gleaming, and saying to Marcia in the voice adults use when children are listening. "I'll keep in touch with you about the matter. If there is anything I can do, don't hesitate . . ."

Marcia, looking at him very solemnly, nodded.

And then my feeling of discomfiture was completed when Evelyn Mayne, empty glass in hand and bathrobe clutched around her, edged past me as if I were contagious, giving me a peculiarly hostile look and calling back to Marcia over my head, "I'll come back, my dear, when I've repaired my appearance, so that people can't say you're entertaining bedraggled old hags."

I was relieved when Marcia gave me a grin as soon as the door was closed and said, "Actually she's gone to get herself another drink, after finishing off my supply. But really, Jeff, she has a reason to this morning—and for hating any man she runs into." And her face grew grave and troubled (and a little frightened too) as she quickly clued me in on the night's nasty events. Mr. Helpful, she explained, had dropped by to remind them about a tenants' meeting that evening and, when he got the grisly news, to go into a song and dance about how shocked he was and how guilty at having slept through it all, and what could he do?

Once she broke of to say, almost worriedly, "What I can't understand, Jeff, is why any man would want to rape someone like Evelyn."

I shrugged. "Kinky some way, I suppose. It does happen, you know. To old women, I mean. Maybe a mother thing."

"Maybe he *hates* women," she speculated. "Wants to punish them."

I nodded.

She had finished by the time Evelyn Mayne came back, very listless now, looking like a woebegone ghost, and dropped into a chair. She hadn't got dressed or even combed her hair. In one hand she had her glass, full and dark, and in the other a large, pale gray leather glove, which she carried oddly, dangling it by one finger.

Marcia started to ask her about it, but she just began to recite once more all that had happened to her that night, in an unemotional mechanical voice that sounded as if it would go on forever.

Look, I didn't like the woman—she was a particularly useless, venemous sort of nuisance (those wearisome suicide attempts!)— but that recital got to me. I found myself hating the person who would deliberately put someone into the state she was in. I realized, perhaps for the first time, just what a vicious and sick crime rape is and how cheap are all the easy jokes about it.

Eventually the glove came into the narrative naturally: ". . . and in order to do that he had to take off his glove. He was particularly excited just then, and it must have got shoved behind the couch and forgotten, where I found it just now."

Marcia pounced on the glove at once then, saying it was important evidence they must tell the police about. So she called them and after a bit she managed to get Officer Hart himself, and he told her to tell Evelyn Mayne to hold on to the glove and he'd send someone over for it eventually.

It was more than time for me to get on to work, but I stayed until she finished her call, because I wanted to remind her about our date that evening.

She begged off, saying she'd be too tired from the sleep she'd lost and anyway she'd decided to go to the tenants' meeting tonight. She told me, "This has made me realize that I've got to begin to take some responsibility for what happens around me. We may make fun of such people—the good neighbors—but they've got something solid about them."

I was pretty miffed at that, though I don't think I let it show. Oh, I didn't so much mind her turning me down—there were reasons enough—but she didn't have to make such a production of it and drag in "good neighbors." (Mr. Helpful, who else?) Besides, Evelyn

196

Mayne came out of her sad apathy long enough to give me a big smile when Marcia said "No."

So I didn't go to the tenants' meeting that night, as I might otherwise have done. Instead I had dinner out and went to the movie—it was lousy—and then had a few drinks, so that it was late when I got back (no signs of life in the lobby or lift or corridor) and gratefully piled into bed.

I was dragged out of the depths of sleep—that first blissful plunge—by a persistent knocking. I shouted something angry but unintelligible and when there was no reply made myself get up, feeling furious.

It was Marcia. With a really remarkable effort I kept my mouth shut and even smoothed out whatever expression was contorting my face. The words one utters on being suddenly awakened, especially from that matchless first sleep that is never recaptured, can be as disastrous as speaking in drink. Our relationship had progressed to the critical stage and I sure didn't want to blow it, especially when treasures I'd hoped to win were spread out in front of my face, as it were, under a semitransparent nightgown and hastily thrown on negligee.

I looked up, a little, at her face. Her eyes were wide.

She said in a sort of frightened little-girl voice that didn't seem at all put on, "I'm awfully sorry to wake you up at three o'clock in the morning, Jeff, but would you keep this 'spooky' for me? I can't get to sleep with it in my room."

It is a testimony to the very high quality of Marcia's treasures that I didn't until then notice what she was carrying in front of her —in a fold of toilet paper: the pale gray leather glove Evelyn Mayne had found behind her couch.

"Huh?" I said, not at all brilliantly. "Didn't Officer Hart come back, or send someone over to pick it up?"

She shook her head. "Evelyn had it, of course, while I was at my job—her social worker did come over right after you left. But then at suppertime her son and daughter-in-law came (Officer Hart did scare them!) and bundled her off to the hospital, and she left the glove with me. I called the police, but Officer Hart was off duty and Officer Halstead, whom I talked to, told me they'd be over to pick it up early in the morning. Please take it, Jeff. Whenever I look at it, I think of that crazy sneaking around with the silver hair down his face and waving the knife. It keeps giving me the shivers."

I looked again at her "spooky" in its fold of tissue (so that she wouldn't have to touch it, what other reason?) and, you know, it began to give *me* the shivers. Just an old glove, but now it had an invisible gray aura radiating from it.

"OK," I said, closing my hand on it with an effort, and went on ungraciously, really without thinking, "Though I wondered you didn't ask Mr. Helpful first, what with all his offers and seeing him at the meeting."

"Well, I asked *you*," she said a little angrily. Then her features relaxed into a warm smile. "Thanks, Jeff."

Only then did it occur to me that here I was passing up in my sleep-soddenness what might be a priceless opportunity. Well, that could be corrected. But before I could invite her in, there came this sharp little cough, or clearing of the throat. We both turned and there was Mr. Helpful in front of his open door, dressed in pajamas and a belted maroon dressing gown. He came smiling and dancing toward us (he didn't really dance, but he gave that impression in spite of being six foot four) and saying, "Could I be of any assistance, Miss Everly? Did something alarm you? Is there . . . er . . . ?" He hesitated, as if there might be something he should be embarrassed at.

Marcia shook her head curtly and said to me quite coolly, "No, thank you, I needn't come in, Mr. Winters. That will be fine. Good night."

I realized Baldy *had* managed to embarrass her and that she was making it clear that we weren't parting after a rendezvous, or about to have one. (But to use my last name!)

As she passed him, she gave him a formal nod. He hurried back to his own door, a highlight dancing on the back of his head. (Marcia says he shaves it; I, that he doesn't have to.)

I waited until I heard her double-lock her door and slide the bolt across. Then I looked grimly at Baldy until he'd gone inside and closed his—I had that pleasure. Then I retired myself, tossed the glove down on some sheets of paper on the table in front of the open window, threw myself into bed, and switched out the light.

I fully expected to spend considerable time being furious at my hulking, mincing officious neighbor, and maybe at Marcia too, before I could get to sleep, but somehow my mind took off on a fantasy about the building around me as it might have been a half century ago. Ghostly bellboys sped silently with little notes inviting or accepting rendezvous. Ghostly waiters wheeled noiseless carts of silver-covered suppers for two. Pert, ghostly maids whirled ghostly sheets through the dark air as they made the bed, their smiles suggesting they might substitute for nonarriving sweethearts. The soft darkness whirlpooled. Somewhere was wind.

I woke with a start as if someone or something had touched me, and I sat up in bed. And then I realized that something *was* touching me high on my neck, just below my ear. Something long, like a finger laid flat or—oh God!—a centipede. I remembered how centipedes were supposed to cling with their scores of tiny feet—and *this* was clinging. As a child I'd been terrified by a tropical centipede that had come weaving out of a stalk of newbought bananas in the kitchen, and the memory still returned full force once in a great while. Now it galvanized me into whirling my hand behind my head and striking my neck a great brushing swipe, making my jaw and ear sting. I instantly turned on the light and rapidly looked all around me without seeing anything close to me that might have brushed off my neck. I thought I'd felt something with my hand when I'd done that, but I couldn't be sure.

And then I looked at the table by the window and saw that the glove was gone.

Almost at once I got the vision of it lifting up and floating through the air at me, fingers first, or else dropping off the table and inching across the floor and up the bed. I don't know which was worse. The thing on my neck *had* felt leathery.

My immediate impulse was to check if my door was still shut. I couldn't tell from where I sat. A very tall clothes cabinet abuts the door, shutting the view off from the head of the bed. So I pushed my way down the bed, putting my feet on the floor after looking down to make sure there was nothing in the immediate vicinity.

And then a sharp gust of wind came in the window and blew the last sheet of paper off the table and deposited it on the floor near the other sheets of paper *and the glove* and the tissue now disentangled from it.

I was so relieved I almost laughed. I went over and picked up the glove, feeling a certain revulsion, but only at the thought of who had worn it and what it had been involved in. I examined it closely, which I hadn't done earlier. It was a rather thin gray kid, a fairly big glove and stretched still further as if a pretty big hand had worn it, but quite light enough to have blown off the table with the papers.

There were grimy streaks on it and a slightly stiff part where some fluid had dried and a faintly reddish streak that might have been lipstick. And it looked old—decades old.

I put it back on the table and set a heavy ashtray on top of it and got back in bed, feeling suddenly secure again.

It occurred to me how the empty finger of a gray leather glove is really very much like a centipede, some of the larger of which are the same size, flat and yellowish gray (though the one that had come out of the banana stalk had been bright red), but these thoughts were no longer frightening.

I looked a last time across the room at the glove, pinioned under the heavy ashtray, and I confidently turned off the light.

Sleep was longer in coming this time, however. I got my fantasy of hotel ghosts going again, but gloves kept coming into it. The lissome maids wore work ones as they rhythmically polished piles of ghostly silver. The bellboys' hands holding the ghostly notes were gloved in pale gray cotton. And there were opera gloves, almost armpit length, that looked like spectral white cobras, especially when they were drawn inside-out off the sinuous, snake-slender arms of wealthy guesting ladies. And other ghostly gloves, not all hotel ones, came floating and weaving into my fantasy: the black gloves of morticians, the white gloves of policemen, the bulky fur-lined ones of polar explorers, the trim dark gauntlets of chauffeurs, the gloves of hunters with separate stalls only for thumb and trigger finger, the mittens of ice-skaters and sleigh riders, old ladies' mitts without any fingers at all, the thin, translucent elastic gloves of surgeons, wielding flashing scalpels of silver-bright steel—a veritable whirlpool of gloves that finally led me down, down, down to darkness.

Once again I woke with a start, as if I'd been touched, and shot up. Once again I felt something about four inches long clinging high on my neck, only this time under the other ear. Once again I frantically slashed at my neck and jaw, stinging them painfully, only this time I struck upward and away. I *thought* I felt something go.

I got the light on and checked the door at once. It was securely shut. Then I looked at the table by the open window. The heavy ashtray still sat in the center of it, rock firm.

But the rapist's glove that had been under it was gone.

I must have stood there a couple of minutes, telling myself this could not be. Then I went over and lifted the ashtray and carefully inspected its underside, as if the glove had somehow managed to shrink and was clinging there.

And all the while I was having this vision of the glove painfully humping itself from under the ashtray and inching to the table's edge and dropping to the floor and then crawling off . . . almost anywhere.

Believe me, I searched my place then, especially the floor. I even opened the doors to the closet and the clothes cabinet, though they had been tightly shut, and searched the floor there. And of course I searched under and behind the bed. And more than once while I

200

searched, I'd suddenly jerk around thinking I'd seen something gray approaching my shoulder from behind.

There wasn't a sign of the glove.

It was dawn by now—had been for sometime. I made coffee and tried to think rationally about it.

It seemed to boil down to three explanations that weren't widely farfetched.

First, that I'd gone out of my mind. Could be, I suppose. But from what I'd read and seen, most people who go crazy know damn well ahead of time that something frightening is happening to their minds, except maybe paranoics. Still, it remained a possibility.

Second, that someone with a duplicate or master key had quietly taken the glove away while I was asleep. The apartment manager and janitor had such keys. I'd briefly given my duplicate to various people. Why, once before she got down on me, I'd given it to Evelyn Mayne—matter of letting someone in while I was at work. I *thought* I'd got it back from her, though I remember once having a second duplicate made—I'd forgotten why. The main difficulty about this explanation was motive. Who'd want to get the glove?— except the rapist, maybe.

Third, of course, there was the supernatural. Gloves are ghostly to start with, envelopes for hands—and if there isn't a medieval superstition about wearing the flayed skin of another's hand to work magic, there ought to be. (Of course, there was the Hand of Glory, its fingers flaming like candles, guaranteed to make people sleep while being burgled, but there the skin is still on the dried chopped-off hand.) And there are tales of spectral hands a-plenty— pointing out buried treasure or hidden graves, or at guilty murderers, or carrying candles or daggers—so why not gloves? And could there be a kind of telekinesis in which a hand controls at a distance the movements and actions of a glove it has worn? Of course that would be psionics or whatnot, but to me the parapsychological is supernatural. (And in that case what had the glove been trying to do probing at my neck?—strangle me, I'd think.) And somewhere I'd read of an aristocratic Brazilian murderess of the last century who wore gloves woven of spider silk, and of a knight blinded at a crucial moment in a tourney by a lady's silken glove worn as a favor. Yes, they were eerie envelopes, I thought, gloves were, but I was just concerned with one of them, a vanishing glove.

I started with a jerk as there came a measured *knock-knock*. I opened the door and looked up at the poker faces of two young policemen. Over their shoulders Mr. Helpful was peering down eagerly at me, his lips rapidly quirking in little smiles with what I'd call questioning pouts in between. Back and a little to one side was Marcia, looking shocked and staring intently at me through the narrow space between the second policeman and the doorjamb.

"Jeff Winters," the first policeman said to me, as if it were a fact that he was putting into place. It occurred to me that young policemen look very *blocky* around their narrow hips with all that equipment they carry snugly nested and cased in black leather.

"Officer Hart—" Marcia began anxiously.

The second policeman's eyes flickered toward her, but just then the first policeman continued, "Your neighbor Miss Everly says she handed you a glove earlier this morning," and he stepped forward into the private space (I think it's sometimes called) around my body, and I automatically stepped back.

"We want it," he went on, continuing to step forward, and I back.

I hesitated. What was I to say? That the glove had started to spook me and then disappeared? Officer Hart followed the first policeman in. Mr. Helpful followed *him* in and stopped just inside my door, Marcia still beyond him and looking frantic. Officer Hart turned, as if about to tell Mr. Helpful to get out, but just then Officer Halstead (that was the other name Marcia had mentioned) said, "Well, you've still got it, haven't you? She gave it to you, didn't she?"

I shook and then nodded my head, which must have made me look rattled. He came closer still and said harshly and with a note of eagerness, "Well, where is it, then?"

I had to look up quite sharply at him to see his face. Beyond it, just to one side of it, diagonally upward across the room, was the top of the tall clothes cabinet, and on the edge of that there balanced that damned gray glove, flat fingers dripping over.

I froze. I could have sworn I'd glanced up there more than once when I was hunting the thing, and seen nothing. Yet there it was, as if it had flown up there or else been flicked there by me the second time I'd violently brushed something from my face.

Officer Halstead must have misread my look of terror, for he ducked his head forward toward mine and rasped. "Your neighbor Mr. Angus says that it's *your* glove, that he saw you wearing gray gloves night before last! What do you say?"

But I didn't say anything, for at that moment the glove slid off its precarious perch and dropped straight down and landed on Mr. Helpful's (Angus's) shoulder close to his neck, just like the hand of an arresting cop.

Now it may have been that in ducking his head to look at it, he trapped it between his chin and collarbone, or it may have been (as it looked to me) that the glove actively clung to his neck and shoulder, resisting all his frantic efforts to peel it off, while he reiterated, his voice mounting in screams, "It's not my glove!"

He took his hands away for a moment and the glove dropped to the floor.

He looked back and forth and saw the dawning expressions on the faces of the two policemen, and then with a sort of despairing sob he whipped a long knife from under his coat.

Considerably to my surprise I started toward him, but just then Officer Hart endeared himself to us all forever by wrapping his arms around Mr. Angus like a bear, one hand closing on the wrist of the hand holding the knife.

I veered past him (I vividly recall changing the length of one of my strides so as not to step on the glove) and reached Marcia just in time to steady her as, turned quite white, she swayed, her eyelids fluttering.

I heard the knife clatter to the floor. I turned, my arms around Marcia, and we both saw Mr. Angus seem to shrink and collapse in Officer Hart's ursine embrace, his face going gray as if he were an empty glove himself.

That was it. They found the other glove and the long silver wig in a locked suitcase in his room. Marcia stayed frightened long enough, off and on, for us to become better acquainted and cement our friendship.

Officer (now Detective) Hart tells us that Mr. Angus is a model prisoner at the hospital for the criminally insane and has gone very religious, but never smiles. And he—Hart—now has the glove in a sort of Black Museum down at the station, where it has never again been seen to move under its own power. If it ever did.

One interesting thing. The gloves had belonged to Mr. Angus's father, now deceased, who had been a judge.

The Grab

By Richard Laymon

My old college roomie, Clark Addison, pulled into town at sundown with a pickup truck, a brand-new gray Stetson, and a bad case of cowboy fever.

"What kind of nightlife you got in this one-hearse town?" he asked after polishing off a hamburger at my place.

"I see by your outfit you don't want another go at the Glass Palace."

"Disco's out, pardner. Where you been?"

With that, we piled into his pickup and started scouting for an appropriate night spot. We passed the four blocks of downtown Barnesdale without spotting a single bar that boasted of country music or a mechanical bull. "Guess we're out of luck," I said, trying to sound disappointed.

"Never say die," Clark said.

At that moment, we bumped over the railroad tracks and Clark punched a forefinger against the windshield. Ahead, on the far side of the grain elevator, stood a shabby little clapboard joint with a blue neon sign: THE BAR NONE SALOON.

Short of a bucking machine, the Bar None had all the trappings needed to warm the heart of any yearning cowpoke: sawdust heaped on the floor, Merle Haggard on the juke box, Coors on tap, and skin-tight jeans on the lower half of every gal. We mosied up to the bar.

"Two Coors," Clark said.

The bartender tipped back his hat and turned away. When the mugs were full, he pushed them toward us. "That's one-eighty."

"I'll get this round," Clark told me. Taking out his wallet, he leaned against the bar. "What kind of action you got here?" he asked.

"We got drinking, dancing, carousing, and The Grab."

"The Grab?" Clark asked. "What is it?"

The bartender stroked his handlebar moustache as if giving the matter lots of thought. Then he pointed down the bar at a rectangular metal box. The side I could see, painted with yellow letters, read, TEST YER GUTS.

"What's it do?" Clark asked.

"Stick around," the bartender said. With that advice, he moved on.

Clark and I wandered over to the metal box. It stood more than two feet high, its sides about half as wide as its height. THE GRAB was painted on its front in sloppy red letters intended, no doubt, to suggest dripping blood. Its far side was printed with green: PAY $10 AND WIN.

"Wonder what you win?" Clark said.

I shrugged. Leaning over the bar, I took a peek at the rear of the box. It was outfitted with a pound of hardware and padlocked to the counter.

While I checked out the lock, Clark was busy hopping and splashing beer. "No opening on top," he concluded.

"The only way in is from the bottom," I said.

"'Twas ever thus," he said, forgetting to be a cowboy. He quickly recovered. "Reckon we oughta grab a couple of fillies and raise some dust."

As we started across the room toward a pair of unescorted females, the juke box stopped. There were a few hushed voices as everyone looked toward the bartender.

"Yes," he cried, raising his arms, "the time is now! Step on over and face The Grab. But let me warn you, this ain't for the faint of heart, it ain't for the weak of stomach. It ain't a roller coaster or a tilt-a-whirl you get off, laughing, and forget. This is a genuine test of grit, and any that ain't up to it are welcome to vamoose. Any that stay to watch or participate are honor bound to hold their peace about what takes place here tonight. Alf's curse goes on the head of any who spill the beans."

I heard Clark laugh softly. A pale girl, beside him, looked up at Clark as if he were a curiosity.

"Any that ain't up to it, go now," the bartender said.

The bartender lowered his arms and remained silent while two couples headed for the door. When they were gone, he removed a thin chain from around his neck. He held it up for all to see. A diamond ring and a small key hung from it. He slid them free, and raised the ring.

"This here's the prize. Give it to your best gal, or trade it in for a thousand dollars if you're man enough to take it. So far, we've gone three weeks with The Grab, and not a soul's shown the gumption to make the ring his own. Pretty thing, isn't it? Okay, now gather 'round. Move on in here and haul out your cash, folks. Ten dollars is all it takes."

We stepped closer to the metal box at the end of the bar, and several men reached for their wallets—Clark included.

"You going to do it?" I whispered to him.

"Sure."

"You don't even know what it is."

"Can't be that bad. *They're* all gonna try it."

Looking around at the others as they took out their money, I saw a few eager faces, some wild, grinning ones, and several that appeared pale and scared.

The bartender used his key to open the padlock at the rear of the metal box. He held up the lock, and somebody moaned in the silence.

"Dal," a woman whispered. She was off to my left, tugging on the elbow of a burly, bearded fellow. He jerked his arm free and sneered at her. "Then go ahead, fool," she said, and ran. The muffled thud of her cowboy boots was the only sound in the room. Near the door, she slipped on the sawdust and fell, landing on her rump. A few people laughed.

"Perverts!" she yelled as she scurried to her feet. She yanked open the door and slammed it behind her.

"Gal's got a nervous stomach," Dal said, grinning around at the rest of us. To the bartender, he said, "Let's get to it, Jerry!"

Jerry set aside the padlock. He climbed onto the bar and stood over the metal container. Then he raised it. The cover slid slowly upward, revealing a glass tank like a tall, narrow aquarium. All around me, people gasped and moaned as they saw what lay at the bottom, barely visible through its gray, murky liquid. A stench of formaldehyde filled my nostrils, and I gagged.

Face up at the bottom of the tank was a severed head, its black hair and moustache moving as if stirred by a breeze, its skin wrinkled and yellow, its eyes wide open, its mouth agape.

"Well, well," Clark muttered.

Jerry, kneeling beside the glass tank, picked up a straight-bent coat hanger with one end turned up slightly to form a hook. He slipped the diamond ring over it. Standing, he lowered the wire into the tank. The ring descended slowly, the brilliance of its diamond a dim glow in the cloudy solution. Then it vanished inside the open mouth. Jerry flicked the hanger a bit, and raised it. The ring no longer hung from its tip.

I let out a long-held breath, and looked at Clark. He was grinning.

"All you gotta do, for the thousand dollar ring, is to reach down with one hand and take it out of the dead man's mouth. Who'll go first?"

"That's me!" said Dal, the bearded one whose girl had just run off. He handed a ten-dollar bill to Jerry, then swung himself onto the bar. Standing over the tank, he unbuttoned his plaid shirt.

"Let me just say," Jerry continued, "nobody's a loser at the Bar None Saloon. Every man with grit enough to try The Grab gets a free beer afterwards, compliments of the house."

Throwing down his shirt, Dal knelt behind the tank. Jerry tied a black blindfold over his eyes.

"All set?"

Dal nodded. He lowered his head and took a few deep breaths, psyching himself up like a basketball player on the free-throw line. Nobody cheered or urged him on. There was dead silence. Swelling out his chest, he held his breath and dipped his right hand into the liquid. It eased lower and lower. A few inches above the face, it stopped. The thick fingers wiggled, but touched nothing. The arm reached deeper. The tip of the middle finger stroked the dead man's nose. With a strangled yelp, Dal jerked his arm from the tank, splashing those of us nearby with the smelly fluid. Then he sighed, and shook his head as if disgusted with himself.

"Good try, good try!" Jerry cried, removing the blindfold. "Let's give this brave fellow a hand!"

A few people clapped. Most just watched, hands at their sides or in pockets, as Jerry filled a beer mug and gave it to Dal. "Try again later, pardner. Everyone's welcome to try as often as he likes. It only costs ten dollars. Ten little dollars for a chance at a thousand. Who's next?"

"Me!" called the pale girl beside Clark.

"Folks, we have us a first! What's your name, young lady?"

"Biff," she said.

"Biff will be the very first lady ever to try her hand at The Grab."

"Don't do it," whispered a chubby girl nearby. "Please."

"Lay off, huh?"

"It's not worth it."

"Is to me," she muttered, and pulled out a ten-dollar bill. She handed her purse to the other girl, then stepped toward the bar.

"Thank you, Biff," Jerry said, taking her money.

She removed her hat, and tossed it onto the counter. She was wearing a T-shirt. She didn't take it off. Leaning forward, she stared down into the tank. She looked sick.

Jerry tied the blindfold in place. "All set?" he asked.

Biff nodded. Her open hand trembled over the surface of the fluid. Then it slipped in, small and pale in the murkiness. Slowly, it eased downward. It sunk closer and closer to the face, never stopping until her fingertips lit on the forehead. They stayed there, motionless. I glanced up. She was tight and shaking as if naked in an icy wind.

Her fingers moved down the head. One touched an open eye. Flinching away, her hand clutched into a fist.

Slowly, her fingers fluttered open. They stretched out, trembled along the sides of the nose, and settled in the moustache. For seconds, they didn't move. The upper lip wasn't visible, as though it had shrunken under the moustache.

Biff's thumb slid along the edges of the teeth. Her fingertips moved off the moustache. They pressed against the lower teeth.

Biff started to moan.

Her fingers trembled off the teeth. They spread open over the gaping mouth, and started down.

With a shriek, she jerked her hand from the tank. She tugged the blindfold off. Face twisted with horror, she shook her hand in the air and gazed at it. She rubbed it on her T-shirt and looked at it again, gasping for air.

"Good try!" Jerry said. "The little lady made a gutsy try, didn't she, folks?"

A few of the group clapped. She stared out at us, blinking and shaking her head. Then she grabbed her hat, took the complimentary beer, and scurried off the bar.

Clark patted her shoulder. "Good going," he said.

"Not good enough," she muttered. "Got spooked."

"Who'll be next?" Jerry asked.

"Yours truly," Clark said, holding up a pair of fives. He winked at me. "It's a cinch," he said, and boosted himself onto the bar. Grinning, he tipped his hat to the small silent crowd. "I have a little surprise for y'all," he said in his thickest cowboy drawl. "You see, folks . . ." He paused and beamed. "Not even my best friend, Steve, knows about this, but I work full time as a mortician's assistant."

That brought a shocked murmur from his audience, including me.

"Why, folks, I've handled more dead meat than your corner butcher. This is gonna be a sure cinch."

With that, he skinned off his shirt and knelt behind the tank. Jerry, looking a bit amused, tied the blindfold over his eyes.

"All set?" the bartender asked.

208

"Ready to lose your diamond ring?"

"Give it a try."

Clark didn't hesitate. He plunged his arm into the solution and drove his open hand downward. His fingers found the dead man's hair. They patted him on the head. "Howdy pardner," he said.

Then his fingers slid over the ghastly face. They tweaked the nose, they plucked the moustache. "Say ahhhh."

He slipped his forefinger deep between the parted teeth, and his scream ripped through the silence as the mouth snapped shut.

His hand shot upward, a cloud of red behind it. It popped from the surface, spraying us with formaldehyde and blood.

Clark jerked the blindfold down and stared at his hand. The forefinger was gone.

"My *finger!*" he shrieked. "My God, my *finger!* It bit . . . it . . ."

Cheers and applause interrupted him, but they weren't for Clark.

"Look at him go!" Dal yelled, pointing at the head.

"Go, Alf, go!" cried another.

"Alf?" I asked Biff.

"Alf Packer," she said without looking away from the head. "The famous cannibal."

The head seemed to grin as it chewed.

I turned to Biff, "You knew?"

"Sure. Any wimp'll make The Grab, if he doesn't know. When you know, it takes real guts."

"Who's next?" Jerry asked.

"Here's a volunteer," Biff called out, clutching my arm. I jerked away from her, but was restrained by half a dozen mutilated hands. "Maybe you'll get lucky," she said. "Alf's a lot more tame after a good meal."

The Haunted Mill
or the Ruined Home

By Jerome K. Jerome

Introduction

It was Christmas Eve.

I begin this way, because it is the proper, orthodox, respectable way to begin, and I have been brought up in a proper, orthodox, respectable way, and taught to always do the proper, orthodox, respectable thing; and the habit clings to me.

Of course, as a mere matter of information it is quite unnecessary to mention the date at all. The experienced reader knows it was Christmas Eve, without my telling him. It always is Christmas Eve, in a ghost story.

Christmas Eve is the ghosts' great gala night. On Christmas Eve they hold their annual fête. On Christmas Eve everybody in Ghostland who *is* anybody—or rather, speaking of ghosts, one should say, I suppose, every nobody who *is* any nobody—comes out to show himself or herself, to see and to be seen, to promenade about and display their winding-sheets and grave-clothes to each other, to criticize one another's style, and sneer at one another's complexion.

'Christmas Eve Parade,' as I expect they themselves term it, is a function, doubtless, eagerly prepared for and looked forward to throughout Ghostland, especially by the swagger set, such as the murdered Barons, the crime-stained Countesses, and the Earls who came over with the Conqueror, and assassinated their relatives, and died raving mad.

Hollow moans and fiendish grins are, one may be sure, energetically practised up. Blood-curdling shrieks and marrow-freezing gestures are probably rehearsed for weeks beforehand. Rusty chains and gory daggers are overhauled, and put into good working order; and sheets and shrouds, laid carefully by from the previous year's show, are taken down and shaken out, and mended, and aired.

Oh, it is a stirring night in Ghostland, the night of December the twenty-fourth!

Ghosts never come out on Christmas night itself, you may have noticed. Christmas Eve, we suspect, has been too much for them; they are not used to excitement. For about a week after Christmas Eve, the gentlemen ghosts, no doubt, feel as if they were all head, and go about making solemn resolutions to themselves that they will stop in next Christmas Eve; while the lady spectres are contradictory and snappish, and liable to burst into tears and leave the room hurriedly on being spoken to, for no perceptible cause whatever.

Ghosts with no position to maintain—mere middle-class ghosts—occasionally, I believe, do a little haunting on off-nights: on Allhallows Eve, and at Midsummer; and some will even run up for a mere local event—to celebrate, for instance, the anniversary of the hanging of somebody's grandfather, or to prophesy a misfortune.

He does love prophesying a misfortune, does the average British ghost. Send him out to prognosticate trouble to somebody, and he is happy. Let him force his way into a peaceful home, and turn the whole house upside down by foretelling a funeral, or predicting a bankruptcy, or hinting at a coming disgrace, or some terrible disaster, about which nobody in their senses would want to know sooner than they could possibly help, and the prior knowledge of which can serve no useful purpose whatsoever, and he feels that he is combining duty with pleasure. He would never forgive himself if anybody in his family had a trouble and he had not been there for a couple of months beforehand, doing silly tricks on the lawn, or balancing himself on somebody's bed-rail.

Then there are, besides, the very young, or very conscientious ghosts with a lost will or an undiscovered number weighing heavy on their minds, who will haunt steadily all the year round; and also the fussy ghost, who is indignant at having been buried in the dustbin or in the village pond, and who never gives the parish a single night's quiet until somebody has paid for a first-class funeral for him.

But these are the exceptions. As I have said, the average orthodox ghost does his one turn a year, on Christmas Eve, and is satisfied.

Why on Christmas Eve, of all nights in the year, I never could myself understand. It is invariably one of the most dismal of nights to be out in—cold, muddy, and wet. And besides, at Christmas time, everybody has quite enough to put up with in the way of a houseful of living relations, without wanting the ghosts of any dead ones mooning about the place, I am sure.

There must be something ghostly in the air of Christmas—something about the close, muggy atmosphere that draws up the ghosts, like the dampness of the summer rains brings out the frogs and snails.

And not only do the ghosts themselves always walk on Christmas Eve, but live people always sit and talk about them on Christmas Eve. Whenever five or six English-speaking people meet round a fire on Christmas Eve, they start telling each other ghost stories. Nothing satisfies us on Christmas Eve but to hear each other tell authentic anecdotes about spectres. It is a genial, festive season, and we love to muse upon graves, and dead bodies, and murders, and blood.

There is a good deal of similarity about our ghostly experiences; but this of course is not our fault but the fault of the ghosts, who never will try any new performances, but always will keep steadily to the old, safe business. The consequence is that, when you have been at one Christmas Eve party, and heard six people relate their adventures with spirits, you do not require to hear any more ghost stories. To listen to any further ghost stories after that would be like sitting out two farcical comedies, or taking in two comic journals; the repetition would become wearisome.

There is always the young man who was, one year, spending the Christmas at a country house, and, on Christmas Eve, they put him to sleep in the west wing. Then in the middle of the night, the room door quietly opens and somebody—generally a lady in her night-dress—walks slowly in, and comes and sits on the bed. The young man thinks it must be one of the visitors, or some relative of the family, though he does not remember having previously seen her, who, unable to go to sleep, and feeling lonesome, all by herself, has come into his room for a chat. He has no idea it is a ghost: he is so unsuspicious. She does not speak, however; and, when he looks again, she is gone!

The young man relates the circumstance at the breakfast table next morning, and asks each of the ladies present if it were she who was the visitor. But they all assure him that it was not, and the host, who has grown deadly pale, begs him to say no more about the matter, which strikes the young man as a singularly strange request.

After breakfast the host takes the young man into a corner, and explains to him that what he saw was the ghost of a lady who had been murdered in that very bed, or who had murdered somebody else there—it does not really matter which: you can be a ghost by murdering somebody else or by being murdered yourself, which-ever you prefer. The murdered ghost is, perhaps, the more popu-lar; but, on the other hand, you can frighten people better if you are the murdered one, because then you can show your wounds and do groans.

Then there is the sceptical guest—it is always 'the guest' who gets let in for this sort of thing, by-the-bye. A ghost never thinks much of his own family: it is 'the guest' he likes to haunt who after listening to the host's ghost story, on Christmas Eve, laughs at it, and says that he does not believe there are such things as ghosts at all; and that he will sleep in the haunted chamber that very night, if they will let him.

Everybody urges him not to be so reckless, but he persists in his foolhardiness, and goes up to the Yellow Chamber (or whatever colour the haunted room may be) with a light heart and a candle, and wishes them all good-night, and shuts the door.

Next morning he has got snow-white hair.

He does not tell anybody what he has seen: it is too awful.

There is also the plucky guest, who sees a ghost, and knows it is a ghost, and watches it, as it comes into the room and disappears through the wainscot, after which, as the ghost does not seem to be coming back, and there is nothing, consequently, to be gained by stopping awake, he goes to sleep.

He does not mention having seen the ghost to anybody, for fear of frightening them—some people are so nervous about ghosts,—but determines to wait for the next night, and see if the apparition appears again.

It does appear again, and, this time, he gets out of bed, dresses himself and does his hair, and follows it; and then discovers a secret passage leading from the bedroom down into the beer-cellar,—a passage which, no doubt, was not unfrequently made use of in the bad old days of yore.

After him comes the young man who woke up with a strange sensation in the middle of the night, and found his rich bachelor uncle standing by his bedside. The rich uncle smiled a weird sort of smile and vanished. The young man immediately got up and looked at his watch. It had stopped at half-past four, he having forgotten to wind it.

He made enquiries the next day, and found that, strangely enough, his rich uncle, whose only nephew he was, had married a widow with eleven children at exactly a quarter to twelve, only two days ago.

The young man does not attempt to explain the extraordinary circumstance. All he does is to vouch for the truth of his narrative.

And, to mention another case, there is the gentleman who is returning home late at night, from a Freemasons' dinner, and who, noticing a light issuing from a ruined abbey, creeps up, and looks through the keyhole. He sees the ghost of a 'grey sister' kissing the ghost of a brown monk, and is so inexpressibly shocked and frightened that he faints on the spot, and is discovered there the next morning, lying in a heap against the door, still speechless, and with his faithful latch-key clasped tightly in his hand.

All these things happen on Christmas Eve, they are all told of on Christmas Eve. For ghost stories to be told on any other evening than the evening of the twenty-fourth of December would be impossible in English society as at present regulated. Therefore, in introducing the sad but authentic ghost story that follows, I feel that it is unnecessary to inform the student of Anglo-Saxon literature that the date on which it was told and on which the incidents took place was—Christmas Eve.

Nevertheless, I do so.

The Haunted Mill

Well, you all know my brother-in-law, Mr Parkins (began Mr Coombes, taking the long clay pipe from his mouth, and putting it behind his ear: we did not know his brother-in-law, but we said we did, so as to save time), and you know of course that he once took a lease on an old mill in Surrey, and went to live there.

Now you must know that, years ago, this very mill had been occupied by a wicked old miser, who died there, leaving—so it was rumoured—all his money hidden somewhere about the place. Naturally enough, everyone who had since come to live at the mill had tried to find the treasure; but none had ever succeeded, and the local wiseacres said that nobody ever would, unless the ghost of the miserly miller should, one day, take a fancy to one of the tenants, and disclose to him the secret of the hiding-place.

My brother-in-law did not attach much importance to the story, regarding it as an old woman's tale, and, unlike his predecessors, made no attempt whatever to discover the hidden gold.

'Unless business was very different then from what it is now,' said my brother-in-law, 'I don't see how a miller could very well have saved anything, however much of a miser he might have been: at all events, not enough to make it worth the trouble of looking for it.'

Still, he could not altogether get rid of the idea of that treasure.

One night he went to bed. There was nothing very extraordinary about that, I admit. He often did go to bed of a night. What *was* remarkable, however, was that exactly as the clock of the village church chimed the last stroke of twelve, my brother-in-law woke up with a start, and felt himself quite unable to go to sleep again.

Joe (his Christian name was Joe) sat up in bed, and looked around.

At the foot of the bed something stood very still, wrapped in shadow.

It moved into the moonlight, and then my brother-in-law saw that it was the figure of a wizened little old man, in knee-breeches and a pigtail.

In an instant the story of the hidden treasure and the old miser flashed across his mind.

'He's come to show me where it's hid,' thought my brother-in-law; and he resolved that he would not spend all this money on himself, but would devote a small percentage of it towards doing good to others.

The apparition moved towards the door: my brother-in-law put on his trousers and followed it. The ghost went downstairs into the kitchen, glided over and stood in front of the hearth, sighed and disappeared.

Next morning, Joe had a couple of bricklayers in, and made them haul out the stove and pull down the chimney, while he stood behind with a potato-sack in which to put the gold.

They knocked down half the wall, and never found so much as a fourpenny bit. My brother-in-law did not know what to think.

The next night the old man appeared again, and led the way into the kitchen. This time, however, instead of going to the fireplace, it stood more in the middle of the room, and sighed there.

'Oh, I see what he means now,' said my brother-in-law to himself; 'it's under the floor. Why did the old idiot go and stand up against the stove, so as to make me think it was up the chimney?'

They spent the next day in taking up the kitchen floor; but the only thing they found was a three-pronged fork, and the handle of that was broken.

On the third night, the ghost reappeared, quite unabashed, and for a third time made for the kitchen. Arrived there, it looked up at the ceiling and vanished.

'Umph! he don't seem to have learned much sense where he's been to,' muttered Joe, as he trotted back to bed; 'I should have thought he might have done that at first.'

Still, there seemed no doubt now where the treasure lay, and the first thing after breakfast they started pulling down the ceiling. They got every inch of ceiling down, and they took up the boards of the room above.

They discovered about as much treasure as you would expect to find in an empty quart pot.

On the fourth night, when the ghost appeared, as usual, my brother-in-law was so wild that he threw his boots at it; and the boots passed through the body, and broke a looking-glass.

On the fifth night, when Joe awoke, as he always did now at twelve, the ghost was standing in a dejected attitude, looking very miserable. There was an appealing look in its large sad eyes that quite touched my brother-in-law.

'After all,' he thought, 'perhaps the silly chap's doing his best. Maybe he has forgotten where he really did put it, and is trying to remember. I'll give him another chance.'

The ghost appeared grateful and delighted at seeing Joe prepare to follow him, and led the way into the attic, pointed to the ceiling, and vanished.

'Well, he's hit it this time, I do hope,' said my brother-in-law; and next day they set to work to take the roof off the place.

It took them three days to get the roof thoroughly off, and all they found was a bird's nest; after securing which they covered up the house with tarpaulins, to keep it dry.

You might have thought that would have cured the poor fellow of looking for treasure. But it didn't.

He said there must be something in it all, or the ghost would never keep on coming as it did; and that, having gone so far, he would go on to the end, and solve the mystery, cost what it might.

Night after night, he would get out of his bed and follow that spectral old fraud about the house. Each night, the old man would indicate a different place; and, on each following day, my brother-in-law would proceed to break up the mill at the point indicated, and look for the treasure. At the end of three weeks, there was not a room in the mill fit to live in. Every wall had been pulled down, every floor had been taken up, every ceiling had had a hole knocked in it. And then, as suddenly as they had begun, the ghost's visits ceased; and my brother-in-law was left to rebuild the place at his leisure.

'What induced the old image to play such a silly trick upon a family man and a ratepayer?' Ah! that's just what I cannot tell you.

Some said that the ghost of the wicked old man had done it to punish my brother-in-law for not believing in him at first; while others held that the apparition was probably that of some deceased local plumber and glazier, who would naturally take an interest in seeing a house knocked about and spoilt. But nobody knew anything for certain.

He Kilt It with a Stick

By William F. Nolan

A summer night in Kansas City.

Ellen away, visiting her parents. The house on Forest empty, waiting.

Warm air.

A high, yellow moon.

Stars.

Crickets thrumming the dark.

Fireflies.

A summer night.

Fred goes to the Apollo on Troost to see a war film. It depresses him. All the killing. He leaves before it has ended, walking up the aisle and out of the deserted lobby and on past the empty glass ticket booth. Alone.

The sidewalk is bare of pedestrians.

It is late, near midnight, and traffic is very sparse along Troost. The wide street is silent. A truck grinds heavily away in the distance.

Fred begins to walk home.

He shouldn't. It is only two blocks: a few steps to the corner of 33rd, then down the long hill to Forest, then right along Forest to his house at the end of the block, near 34th. Not quite two blocks to walk. But too far for him. Too far.

Fred stops.

217

A gray cat is sleeping in the window of Rae's Drugstore. Fred presses the glass.

I could break the window—but that would be useless. The thing would be safe by then; it would leap away and I'd never find it in the store. The police would arrive and . . . No. Insane. Insane to think of killing it.

The gray cat, quite suddenly, opens its eyes to stare at Fred Baxter. Unblinking. Evil.

He shudders, moves quickly on.

The cat continues to stare.

Foul thing knows what I'd like to do to it.

The hill, sloping steeply toward Forest, is tinted with cool moonlight. Fred walks down this hill, filled with an angry sense of frustration: he would very much have enjoyed killing the gray cat in the drugstore window.

Hard against chest wall, his heart judders. Once, twice, three times. Thud thud thud. He slows, removes a tissue-wrapped capsule from an inside pocket. Swallows the capsule. Continues to walk.

Fred reaches the bottom of the hill, crosses over.

Trees now. Big fat-trunked oaks and maples, fanning their leaves softly over the concrete sidewalk. Much darker. Thick tree-shadow midnight dark, broken by three street lamps down the long block. Lamps haloed by green night insects.

Deeper.

Into the summer dark . . .

When Fred Baxter was seven, he wrote: "Today a kitty cat bit me at school and it sure hurt a lot. The kitty was bad, so I kilt it with a stick."

When he was ten, and living in St. Louis, a boy two houses up told Fred his parents wanted to get rid of a litter. "I'll take care of it," Fred assured him—and the next afternoon, in Miller Lake, he drowned all six of the kittens.

At fifteen, in high school, Fred trapped the janitor's Tabby in the gymnasium locker room, choked it to death, and carried it downstairs to the furnace. He was severely scratched in the process.

As a college freshman, in Kansas City, Fred distributed several pieces of poisoned fish over the Rockhurst campus. The grotesquely twisted bodies of seven cats were found the next morning.

Working in the sales department of Hall Brothers, Fred was invited to visit his supervisor at home one Saturday—and was seen in the yard playing with Frances, a pet Siamese. She was later found crushed to death, and it was assumed a car had run over the animal. Fred quit his job ten days later because his supervisor had cat hands.

Fred married Ellen Ferber when he was thirty, and she wanted to have children right away. Fred said no, that babies were small and furry in their blankets, and disturbed him. Ellen bought herself a small kitten for company while Fred was on the road. He didn't object—but a week after the purchase, he took a meat knife and dismembered the kitten, telling Ellen that it had "wandered away." Then he bought her a green parakeet.

ZZZZZZZ Click

This is Frederick Baxter speaking and I . . . wait, the sound level is wrong and I'll— There, it's all right now. I can't tell anyone about this—but today I found an old Tom in an alley downtown, and I got hold of the stinking, wretched animal and I . . .

ZZZZZZZ Click

The heart trouble started when Fred was thirty-five.

"You have an unusual condition," the doctor told him. "You are, in effect, a medical oddity. Your chest houses a quivering-muscled heart—fibrillation. Your condition can easily prove fatal. Preventive measures must be taken. No severe exercise, no overeating, plenty of rest."

Fred obeyed the man's orders—although he did not really trust a doctor whose cat eyes reflected the moon.

ZZZZZZZ Click

. . . awful time with the heart. Really awful. The use of digitalis drives me to alcohol, which sends my heart into massive flutters. Then the alcohol forces me into a need for more digitalis. It is a deadly circle and I . . .

I have black dreams. A nap at noon and I dream of smothering. This comes from the heart condition. And because of the cats. They all fear me now, avoid me on the street. They've *told* one another about me. This is fact. Killing them is becoming quite difficult . . . but I caught a big, evil one in the garden last Thursday and buried it. Alive. As I am buried alive in these black dreams of mine. I got excited, burying the cat—and this is bad for me. I must go on killing them, but I must *not* get excited. I must stay calm and not— here comes Ellen, so I'd better . . .

ZZZZZZZ Click

"What's wrong, Fred?"

It was 2 A.M. and Ellen had awakened to find him standing at the window.

"Something in the yard," he said.

The moon was flushing the grass with pale gold—and a dark shape scuttled over the lawn, breaking the pattern. A cat shape.

"Go to sleep," said his wife, settling into her pillow.

Fred Baxter stared at the cat, who stared back at him from the damp yard, its head raised, the yellow of the night moon now brimming the creature's eyes. The cat's mouth opened.

"It's sucking up the moonlight," Fred whispered.

Then he went back to bed.

But he did not sleep.

Later, thinking about this, Fred recalled what his mother had often said about cats. "They perch on the chest of a baby," she'd said, "place their red mouth over the soft mouth of the baby, and draw all the life from its body. I won't have one of the disgusting things in the house."

Alone in the summer night, walking down Forest Avenue in Kansas City, Fred passes a parked car, bulking black and silent in its gravel driveway. The closed car windows gleam deep yellow from the eyes inside.

Fred stops, looks back at the car.

How many? Ten . . . a dozen. More . . . twenty, maybe. All inside the car, staring out at me. Dozens of foul, slitted yellow eyes.

Fred can do nothing. He checks all four doors of the silent automobile, finds them locked. The cats stare at him.

Filthy creatures!

He moves on.

The street is oddly silent. Fred realizes why: the crickets have stopped. No breeze stirs the trees; they hang over him, heavy and motionless in the summer dark.

The houses along Forest are shuttered, lightless, closed against the night. Yet, on a porch, Fred detects movement.

Yellow eyes spark from porch blackness. A big, dark-furred cat is curled into a wooden swing. It regards Fred Baxter.

Kill it!

He moves with purposeful stealth, leans to grasp a stout tree limb which has fallen into the yard. He mounts the porch steps.

The dark-furred cat has not stirred.

Fred raises the heavy limb. The cat hisses, claws extended, fangs balefully revealed. It cries out like a wounded child and vanishes off the porch into the deep shadow between houses.

Missed. Missed the rotten thing.

Fred moves down the steps, crosses the yard toward the walk. His head is lowered in anger. When he looks up, the walk is thick with cats. He runs into them, kicking, flailing the tree club. They scatter, melting away from him like butter from a heated blade.

Thud thud thud. Fred drops the club. His heart is rapping, fisting his chest. He leans against a tree, sobbing for breath. The yellow-eyed cats watch him from the street, from bushes, from steps and porches and the tops of cars.

Didn't get a one of them. Not a damn one . . .

The fireflies have disappeared. The street lamps have dimmed to smoked circles above the heavy, cloaking trees. The clean summer sky is shut away from him—and Fred Baxter finds the air clogged with the sharp, suffocating smell of cat fur.

He walks on down the block.

The cats follow him.

He thinks of what fire could do to them—long blades of yellow crisping flame to flake them away into dark ash. But he cannot burn them; burning them would be impossible. There are *hundreds*. That many at least.

They fill driveways, cover porches, blanket yards, pad in lion-like silence along the street. The yellow moon is in their eyes, sucked from the sky. Fred, his terror rising, raises his head to look upward.

The trees are alive with them!

His throat closes. He cannot swallow. Cat fur cloaks his mouth.

Fred begins to run down the concrete sidewalk, stumbling, weaving, his chest filled with a terrible winged beating.

A sound.

The scream of the cats.

Fred claps both hands to his head to muffle the stab and thrust of sound.

The house . . . must reach the house.

Fred staggers forward. The cat masses surge in behind him as he runs up the stone walk to his house.

A cat lands on his neck. Mutely, he flings it loose—plunges up the wooden porch steps.

Key. Find your key and unlock the door. Get inside!

Too late.

Eyes blazing, the cats flow up and over him, a dark, furry, stifling weight. As he pulls back the screen, claws and needle teeth rip at his back, arms, face, legs . . . shred his clothing and skin. He twists wildly, beating at them. Blood runs into his eyes. . . .

The door is open. He falls forward, through the opening. The cats swarm after him in hot waves, covering his chest, sucking the breath from his body. Baxter's thin scream is lost in the sharp, rising, all-engulfing cry of the cats.

A delivery boy found him two days later, lying face down on the living room floor. His clothes were wrinkled, but untorn.

A cat was licking the cold, white, unmarked skin of Frederick Baxter's cheek.

Heading Home

By Ramsey Campbell

Somewhere above you can hear your wife and the young man talking. You strain yourself upward, your muscles trembling like water, and manage to shift your unsteady balance onto the next stair.

They must think he finished you. They haven't even bothered to close the cellar door, and it's the trickle of flickering light through the crack that you're striving toward. Anyone else but you would be dead. He must have carried you from the laboratory and thrown you down the stairs into the cellar, where you regained consciousness on the dusty stone. Your left cheek still feels like a rigid plate slipped into your flesh where it struck the floor. You rest on the stair you've reached and listen.

They're silent now. It must be night, since they've lit the hall lamp whose flame is peeking into the cellar. They can't intend to leave the house until tomorrow, if at all. You can only guess what they're doing now, thinking themselves alone in the house. Your numb lips crack again as you grin. Let them enjoy themselves while they can.

He didn't leave you many muscles you can use; it was a thorough job. No wonder they feel safe. Now you have to concentrate yourself in those muscles that still function. Swaying, you manage to raise yourself momentarily to a position from which you can grip the next higher stair. You clench on your advantage. Then, pushing with muscles you'd almost forgotten you had, you manage to lever yourself one step higher.

You maneuver yourself until you're sitting upright. There's less risk that way of your losing your balance for a moment and rolling all the way down to the cellar floor where, hours ago, you began climbing. Then you rest. Only six more stairs.

You wonder again how they met. Of course you should have known that it was going on, but your work was your wife and you couldn't spare the time to watch over the woman you'd married. You should have realized that when she went to the village she would meet people and mightn't be as silent as at home. But her room might well have been as far from yours as the village is from the house; you gave little thought to the people in either.

Not that you blame yourself. When you met her—in the town where you attended the University—you'd thought she understood the importance of your work. It wasn't as if you'd intended to trick her. It was only when she tried to seduce you from your work, both for her own gratification and because she was afraid of it, that you barred her from your companionship by silence.

You can hear their voices again. They're on the first floor. You don't know whether they're celebrating or comforting each other as guilt settles on them. It doesn't matter. So long as he didn't close the laboratory door when he returned from the cellar. If it's closed you'll never be able to open it. And if you can't get into the laboratory he has killed you after all. You raise yourself, muscles shuddering with the effort, your cheek chafing against the wood of the stair. You won't relax until you can see the laboratory door.

You're reaching for the top stair when you slip. Your chin comes down on it, and slides back. You grip the wooden stair with your jaws, feeling splinters lodge between your teeth. Your neck scraped the lower stair, but it has lost all feeling save an ache fading slowly into dullness. Only your jaws prevent you from falling back where you started, and they're throbbing as if nails are being driven through their hinges with measured strokes. You close them tighter, pounding with pain, then you overbalance yourself onto the top stair. You teeter for a moment, then you're secure.

But you don't rest yet. You edge yourself forward and sit up so that you can peer out of the cellar. The outline of the laboratory door billows slightly as the lamp flickers. It occurs to you that they've lit the lamp because she's terrified of you, lying dead beyond the main staircase—as she thinks. You laugh silently. You can afford to. When the flame steadies you can see darkness gaping for inches around the laboratory door.

You listen to their voices upstairs and rest. You know he's a butcher, because once he helped one of the servants carry the meat from the village. In any case, you could have told his profession from what he has done to you. You're still astonished that she should have taken up with him. From the little you knew of the village people you were delighted that they always avoided the house.

You remember the day the new priest visited the house. You could tell he'd heard all the wildest village tales about your experiments; you were surprised he didn't try to ward you off with a cross. When he found you could argue his theology into a corner he left, a twitch pulling his smile awry. He'd tried to persuade you both to attend the church, but your wife had sat silent throughout. It had been then that you decided to trust her to go to the village. You'd dismissed the servants, but you told yourself she would be less likely to talk. You grin fiercely. If you'd been as inaccurate in your experiments you would be dead.

Upstairs they're still talking. You rock forward and try to wedge yourself between the cellar door and its frame. With your limited control it's difficult, and you find yourself leaning in the crack with no purchase on the wood. Your weight hasn't moved the door, which is heavier than you have ever before had cause to realize. Eventually you manage to wedge yourself in the crack, gripping the frame with all your strength. The door rests on you, and you nudge your weight clumsily against it.

It creaks away from you a little, then swings back, crushing you. It has always hung unevenly and persisted in standing ajar; it never troubled you before. Now the strength he left you, even focused like light through a burning-glass, seems unequal to shifting the door. Trapped in the crack, you relax for a moment. Then, as if to take it unawares, you close your grip on the frame and shove against the door, pushing yourself forward as it swings away. It returns, answering the force of your shove, and you aren't clear. But you're still falling into the hall, and as the door chops into the frame you fall on your back, beyond the sweep of the door.

You're free of the cellar, but on your back you're helpless. The slowing door is more mobile than you. All the muscles you've been using can only work aimlessly and loll in the air. You're laid out on the hall floor like a laboratory subject, beneath the steadying flame.

Then you hear the butcher call to your wife, "I'll see," and start downstairs.

You begin to twitch all the muscles on your right side frantically. You roll a little toward that side, then your wild twitching rocks you back. About you the light shakes, making your shadow play the cruel trick of achieving the roll you're struggling for. He's at the halfway landing now. You work your right side again and hold your muscles still as you begin to turn that way. Suddenly you've swung over your point of equilibrium and are lying on your right side. You strain your aching muscles to inch you forward, but the laboratory is feet away, and you are by no means moving in a straight line. His footsteps resound. You hear your wife's terrified voice, entreating him to return to her. There's a long pondering silence. Then he hurries back upstairs.

You don't let yourself rest until you're inside the laboratory, although by then your ache feels like a cold stiff surface within your flesh, and your mouth like a dusty hole in stone. Once beyond the door you sit still, gazing about. Moonlight is spread from the window to the door. Your gaze seeks the bench where you were working when he found you. He hasn't cleared up any of the material that was thrown to the floor by your convulsion. Glinting on the floor you see a needle, and nearby the surgical thread which you never had occasion to use. You relax to prepare for the next concerted effort, remembering.

You recall the day you perfected the solution. As soon as you'd quaffed it you felt your brain achieve a piercing alertness, become precisely and continually aware of the messages of each nerve and preside over them, making minute adjustments at the first hint of danger. You knew this was what you'd worked for, but you couldn't prove it to yourself until the day you felt the stirrings of cancer. Then your brain seemed to condense into a keen strand of energy that stretched down and burned out the cancer. That was proof. You were immortal.

Not that some of the research hadn't been unpleasant. It had taken you a great deal of furtive expenditure at the mortuaries to discover that some of the extracts you needed for the solution had to be taken from the living brain. The villagers thought the children had drowned, for their clothes were found on the river bank. Medical progress, you told yourself, had always involved suffering.

Perhaps your wife suspected something of this stage of your work or perhaps they'd simply decided to rid themselves of you. You were working at your bench, trying to synthesize your discovery when you heard him enter. He must have rushed at you, for before you could turn you felt a blazing slash gape at the back of your neck. Then you awoke on the cellar floor.

You edge yourself forward across the laboratory. Your greatest exertion is past, but this is the most exacting part. When you're nearly touching your prone body you have to turn round. You move yourself with your jaws and steer with your tongue. It's difficult, but less so than tonguing yourself upright on your neck to rest on the stairs. Then you fit yourself to your shoulders, groping with your perfected mind until you feel the nerves linking again.

Now you'll have to hold yourself unflinching or you'll roll apart. With your mind you can do it. Gingerly, so as not to part yourself, you stretch out your arm and touch the surgical needle and thread.

The Hollow of the Three Hills

By Nathaniel Hawthorne

In those strange old times, when fantastic dreams and madmen's reveries were realized among the actual circumstances of life, two persons met together at an appointed hour and place. One was a lady, graceful in form and fair of feature, though pale and troubled, and smitten with an untimely blight in what should have been the fullest bloom of her years; the other was an ancient and meanly-dressed woman, of ill-favored aspect, and so withered, shrunken, and decrepit, that even the space since she began to decay must have exceeded the ordinary term of human existence. In the spot where they encountered, no mortal could observe them. Three little hills stood near each other, and down in the midst of them sunk a hollow basin, almost mathematically circular, two or three hundred feet in breadth, and of such depth that a stately cedar might but just be visible above the sides. Dwarf pines were numerous upon the hills, and partly fringed the outer verge of the intermediate hollow, within which there was nothing but the brown grass of October, and here and there a tree trunk that had fallen long ago, and lay mouldering with no green successor from its roots. One of these masses of decaying wood, formerly a majestic oak, rested close beside a pool of green and sluggish water at the bottom of the basin. Such scenes as this (so gray tradition tells) were once the resort of the Power of Evil and his plighted subjects; and here, at midnight or on the dim verge of evening, they were said to stand round the mantling pool, disturbing its putrid waters in the performance of an impious baptismal rite. The chill beauty of an autumnal sunset was now gilding the three hill-tops, whence a paler tint stole down their sides into the hollow.

"Here is our pleasant meeting come to pass," said the aged crone, "according as thou hast desired. Say quickly what thou wouldst have of me, for there is but a short hour that we may tarry here."

As the old withered woman spoke, a smile glimmered on her countenance, like lamplight on the wall of a sepulchre. The lady trembled, and cast her eyes upward to the verge of the basin, as if meditating to return with her purpose unaccomplished. But it was not so ordained.

"I am a stranger in this land, as you know," said she at length. "Whence I come it matters not; but I have left those behind me with whom my fate was intimately bound, and from whom I am cut off forever. There is a weight in my bosom that I cannot away with, and I have come hither to inquire of their welfare."

"And who is there by this green pool that can bring thee news from the ends of the earth?" cried the old woman, peering into the lady's face. "Not from my lips mayst thou hear these tidings; yet, be thou bold, and the daylight shall not pass away from yonder hill-top before thy wish be granted."

"I will do your bidding though I die," replied the lady desperately.

The old woman seated herself on the trunk of the fallen tree, threw aside the hood that shrouded her gray locks, and beckoned her companion to draw near.

"Kneel down," she said, "and lay your forehead on my knees."

She hesitated a moment, but the anxiety that had long been kindling burned fiercely up within her. As she knelt down, the border of her garment was dipped into the pool; she laid her forehead on the old woman's knees, and the latter drew a cloak about the lady's face, so that she was in darkness. Then she heard the muttered words of prayer, in the midst of which she started, and would have arisen.

"Let me flee—let me flee and hide myself, that they may not look upon me!" she cried. But, with returning recollection, she hushed herself, and was still as death.

For it seemed as if other voices—familiar in infancy, and unforgotten through many wanderings, and in all the vicissitudes of her heart and fortune—were mingling with the accents of the prayer. At first the words were faint and indistinct, not rendered so by distance, but rather resembling the dim pages of a book which we strive to read by an imperfect and gradually brightening light.

227

In such a manner, as the prayer proceeded, did those voices strengthen upon the ear; till at length the petition ended, and the conversation of an aged man, and of a woman broken and decayed like himself, became distinctly audible to the lady as she knelt. But those strangers appeared not to stand in the hollow depth between the three hills. Their voices were encompassed and reëchoed by the walls of a chamber, the windows of which were rattling in the breeze; the regular vibration of a clock, the crackling of a fire, and the tinkling of the embers as they fell among the ashes, rendered the scene almost as vivid as if painted to the eye. By a melancholy hearth sat these two old people, the man calmly despondent, the woman querulous and tearful, and their words were all of sorrow. They spoke of a daughter, a wanderer they knew not where, bearing dishonor along with her, and leaving shame and affliction to bring their gray heads to the grave. They alluded also to other and more recent wo, but in the midst of their talk their voices seemed to melt into the sound of the wind sweeping mournfully among the autumn leaves; and when the lady lifted her eyes, there was she kneeling in the hollow between three hills.

"A weary and lonesome time yonder old couple have of it," remarked the old woman, smiling in the lady's face.

"And did you also hear them?" exclaimed she, a sense of intolerable humiliation triumphing over her agony and fear.

"Yea; and we have yet more to hear," replied the old woman. "Wherefore, cover thy face quickly."

Again the withered hag poured forth the monotonous words of a prayer that was not meant to be acceptable in heaven; and soon, in the pauses of her breath, strange murmurings began to thicken, gradually increasing so as to drown and overpower the charm by which they grew. Shrieks pierced through the obscurity of sound, and were succeeded by the singing of sweet female voices, which, in their turn, gave way to a wild roar of laughter, broken suddenly by groanings and sobs, forming altogether a ghastly confusion of terror and mourning and mirth. Chains were rattling, fierce and stern voices uttered threats, and the scourge resounded at their command. All these noises deepened and became substantial to the listener's ear, till she could distinguish every soft and dreamy accent of the love songs that died causelessly into funeral hymns. She shuddered at the unprovoked wrath which blazed up like the spontaneous kindling of flame, and she grew faint at the fearful merriment raging miserably around her. In the midst of this wild scene, where unbound passions jostled each other in a drunken career, there was one solemn voice of a man, and a manly and melodious voice it might once have been. He went to and fro continually, and his feet sounded upon the floor. In each member of that frenzied company, whose own burning thoughts had become their exclusive world, he sought an auditor for the story of his individual wrong, and interpreted their laughter and tears as his reward of scorn or pity. He spoke of woman's perfidy, of a wife who had broken her holiest vows, of a home and heart made desolate. Even as he went on, the shout, the laugh, the shriek, the sob, rose up in unison, till they changed into the hollow, fitful, and uneven sound of the wind, as it fought among the pine-trees on those three lonely hills. The lady looked up, and there was the withered woman smiling in her face.

"Couldst thou have thought there were such merry times in a mad-house?" inquired the latter.

"True, true," said the lady to herself; "there is mirth within its walls, but misery, misery without."

"Wouldst thou hear more?" demanded the old woman.

"There is one other voice I would fain listen to again," replied the lady faintly.

"Then, lay down thy head speedily upon my knees, that thou mayst get thee hence before the hour be past."

The golden skirts of day were yet lingering upon the hills, but deep shades obscured the hollow and the pool, as if sombre night were rising thence to overspread the world. Again that evil woman began to weave her spell. Long did it proceed unanswered, till the knolling of a bell stole in among the intervals of her words, like a clang that had travelled far over valley and rising ground, and was just ready to die in the air. The lady shook upon her companion's knees as she heard that boding sound. Stronger it grew and sadder, and deepened into the tone of a death bell, knolling dolefully from some ivy-mantled tower, and bearing tidings of mortality and wo to the cottage, to the hall, and to the solitary wayfarer, that all might weep for the doom appointed in turn to them. Then came a measured tread, passing slowly, slowly on, as of mourners with a coffin, their garments trailing on the ground, so that the ear could measure the length of their melancholy array. Before them went the priest, reading the burial service, while the leaves of his book were rustling in the breeze. And though no voice but his was heard to speak aloud, still there were revilings and anathemas, whispered but distinct, from women and from men, breathed against the daughter who had wrung the aged hearts of her parents—the wife who had betrayed the trusting fondness of her husband—the mother who had sinned against natural affection, and left her child to die. The sweeping sound of the funeral train faded away like a thin vapor, and the wind, that just before had seemed to shake the coffin pall, moaned sadly round the verge of the Hollow between three Hills. But when the old woman stirred the kneeling lady, she lifted not her head.

"Here has been a sweet hour's sport!" said the withered crone, chuckling to herself.

The Hollow Man

By Norman Partridge

Four. Yes, that's how many there were. Come to my home. Come to my home in the hills. Come in the middle of feast, when the skin had been peeled back and I was ready to sup. Interrupting, disrupting. Stealing the comfortable bloat of a full belly, the black scent of clean bones burning dry on glowing embers. Four.

Yes. That's how many there were. I watched them through the stretched-skin window, saw them standing cold in the snow with their guns at their sides.

The hollow man saw them too. He heard the ice dogs bark and raised his sunken face, peering at the men through the blue-veined window. He gasped, expectant, and I had to draw my claws from their fleshy sheaths and jab deep into his blackened muscles to keep him from saying words that weren't mine. Outside, they shouted, *Hullo! Hullo in the cabin!* and the hollow man sprang for the door. I jumped on his back and tugged the metal rings pinned into his neck. He jerked and whirled away from the latch, but I was left with the sickening sound of his hopeful moans.

Once again, control was mine, but not like before. The hollow man was full of strength that he hadn't possessed in weeks, and the feast was ruined.

They had ruined it.

"Hullo! We're tired and need food!"

The hollow man strained forward, his fingers groping for the door latch. My scaled legs flexed hard around his middle. His sweaty stomach sizzled and he cried at the heat of me. A rib snapped. Another. He sank backward and, with a dry flutter of wings, I pulled him away from the window, back into the dark.

"Could we share your fire? It's so damn cold!"

"We'd give you money, but we ain't got any. There ain't a nickel in a thousand miles of here . . ."

Small screams tore the hollow man's beaten lips. There was blood. I cursed the waste and twisted a handful of metal rings. He sank to his knees and quieted.

"We'll leave our guns. We don't mean no harm!"

I jerked one ring, then another. I cooed against the hollow man's skinless shoulder and made him pick up his rifle. When he had it loaded, cocked, and aimed through a slot in the door, I whispered in his ear and made him laugh.

And then I screamed out at them, "You dirty bastards! You stay away! You ain't comin' in here!"

Gunshots exploded. We only got one of them, not clean but bad enough. The others pulled him into the forest, where the dense trees muffled his screams and kept us from getting another clear shot.

The rifle clattered to the floor, smoking faintly, smelling good. We walked to the window. I jingled his neck rings and the hollow man squinted through the tangle of veins, to the spot where a red streak was freezing in the snow.

I made the hollow man smile.

So four. Still four, when night came and moonlight dripped like melting wax over the snow-capped ridges to the west. Four to make me forget the one nearly drained. Four to make me impatient while soft time crept toward the leaden hour, grain by grain, breath by breath . . .

The hour descended. I twisted rings and plucked black muscles, and the hollow man fed the fire and barred the door. I released him and he huddled in a corner, exhausted.

I rose through the chimney and thrust myself away from the cabin. My wings fought the biting wind as I climbed high, searching the black forest below. I soared the length of a high mountain glacier and dove away, banking back toward the heart of the valley. Shadows that stretched forever, and then, deep in a jagged ravine that stabbed at a river, a sputtering glimmer of orange. A campfire.

So bold. So typical of their kind. I extended my wings and drifted down like a bat, coming to rest in the branches of a giant redwood. Its live green stench nearly made me retch. Huddling in my wings for warmth, I clawed through the bark with a wish to make the ancient monster scream. The tree quivered against the icy wind. Grinning, satisfied, I looked down.

Two strong, but different. One weak. One as good as dead.

Three.

Grizzly sat in silence, his black face as motionless as a tombstone. Instantly, I liked him best. Mammoth, wrapped in a bristling grizzly coat he looked even bigger, almost as big as a grizzly. He sat by the fire, staring at his reflection in a gleaming ax blade. He made me anxious. He could last for months.

Across from Grizzly, Redbeard turned a pot and boiled coffee. He straightened his fox-head cap and stroked his beard, clearing it of ice. I didn't like him. His milky squint was too much like my own. But any fool could see that he hated Grizzly, and that made me smile.

Away from them both, crouching under a tree with the whimpering ice dogs, Rabbit wept through swollen eyes. He dug deep in his plastic coat and produced a crucifix. I almost laughed out loud.

And in a tent, wrapped in sweaty wool and expensive eiderdown that couldn't keep him warm anymore, still clinging to life, was the dead man, who didn't matter.

But maybe I could make him matter.

And then there would only be two.

When the clouds came, when they suffocated the unblinking moon and brought sleep to the camp, I swept down to the dying fire and rolled comfortably in the crab-colored coals. The hush of the river crept over me as I decided what to do.

To make three into two.

Three men, and the dead man. Two tents: Grizzly and Redbeard in one, Rabbit and the dead man in the other. Easy. No worries, except for the dogs. (For ice dogs are wise. Their beast hearts hide simple secrets . . .)

The packed snow sizzled beneath my feet as I crept toward Rabbit's tent. The dead man's face pressed against one corner of the tent, molding his swollen features in yellow plastic. Each rattling breath gently puffed the thin material away from his face, and each weak gasp slowly drew it back. It was a steady, pleasant sound. I concentrated on it until it was mine.

No time for metal rings. No time for naked muscle and feast. Slowly, I reached out and took hold of Rabbit's mind, digging deep until I found his darkest nightmare. I pulled it loose and let it breathe. At first it frightened him, but I tugged its midnight corners straight and banished its monsters, and soon Rabbit was full of bliss, awake without even knowing it.

I circled the tent and pushed against the other side. The dead man rolled across, cold against the warmth of Rabbit's unbridled nightmare.

"Jesus, you're freezin', Charlie," whispered Rabbit as he moved closer. "But don't worry. I'll keep you warm, buddy. I've gotta keep you warm."

But in the safety of his nightmare, that wasn't what Rabbit wanted at all.

I waited in the tree until Grizzly found them the next morning, wrapped together in the dead man's bag. He shot Rabbit in the head and left him for the ice dogs.

Redbeard buried the dead man deep in a silky snowdrift.

That day was nothing. Grizzly and Redbeard sat at the edge of the clearing and wasted their only chance. Grizzly stared hungrily at the cabin, seeing only what I wanted him to see. Thick, safe walls. A puffing chimney. A home. But Redbeard, damned Redbeard, wise with fear and full of caution, sensed other things. The dead man's fevered rattle whispering through the trees. An ice dog gnawing a fresh, gristly bone. And bear traps, rusty with blood.

Redbeard rose and walked away. Soon Grizzly followed.

And then there was only the hollow man, rocking gently in his chair. The soles of his boots buffed the splintery floor as his legs swung back and forth, back and forth.

Two. Now two, as the second night was born, a silent twin to the first. Only two, as again I twisted rings and plucked muscles and put the hollow man to sleep. Just two, as my wings beat the night and I flew once more from the sooty chimney to the ravine that stabbed a river.

There they sat, as before, grizzly and fox. And there I watched, waiting, with nothing left to do but listen for the sweet arrival of the leaden hour.

Grizzly chopped wood and fed the fire. Redbeard positioned blackened pots and watched them boil. Both planned silently while they ate, and afterwards their mute desperation grew, knotting their minds into coils of anger. Grizzly charged the dying embers with whole branches and did not smile until the flames leaped wildly. The heat slapped at Redbeard in waves, harsh against the pleasant brandy-warmth that swam in his gut and slowed his racing thoughts.

"Tomorrow mornin'," blurted Redbeard, "we're gettin' away from here. I'm not dealin' with no crazy hermit."

Grizzly stared at his ax-blade reflection and smiled. "We're gonna kill us a crazy hermit," he said. "Tomorrow mornin'."

Soon the old words came, taut and cold, and then Grizzly sprang through the leaping flames, his black coat billowing, and Redbeard's fox-head cap flew from his head as he whirled around. Ax rang against knife. A white fist tore open a black lip, and the teeth below ripped into a knuckle. Knife split ebony cheek. Blood hissed through the flames and sizzled against burning embers. A sharp crack as the ax sank home in a tangle of ribs. Redbeard coughed a misty breath past Grizzly's ear, and the bigger man spun the smaller around, freed his ax, and watched his opponent stumble backward into the fire.

I laughed above the crackling roar. The ice dogs scattered into the forest, barking, wild with fear and the sour smell of death.

So Grizzly had survived. He stood still, his singed coat smoking, his cut cheek oozing blood. His mind was empty—there was no remorse, only a feeling that he was the strongest, he was the best.

Knowing that, I flew home happy.

There was not much in the cabin that I could use. I found only a single whalebone needle, yellow with age, and no thread at all. I watched the veined window as I searched impatiently for a substitute, and at last I discovered a spool of fishing line in a rusty metal box. Humming, I went about my work. First I drew strips of the hollow man's pallid skin over his shrunken shoulder muscles, fastening them along his backbone with a cross stitch. Then I bunched the flabby tissue at the base of his skull and made the final secret passes with my needle.

Now he was nothing. I tore the metal rings out of his neck and the hollow man twitched as if shocked.

A bullet ripped through the cabin door. "I'm gonna get you, you bastard," cried Grizzly, his voice loud but worn. "You hear me? I'm gonna *get* you!"

The hollow man sprang from the rocker; his withered legs betrayed him and he fell to the floor. I balanced on the back of the chair and hissed at him, spreading my wings in mock menace. With a laughable scream, he flung himself at the door.

Grizzly must have been confused by the hollow man's ravings, for he didn't fire again until the fool was nearly upon him. An instant of pain, another of relief, and the hollow man crumpled, finished.

234

And then Grizzly just sat in the snow, his eyes fixed on the open cabin door. I watched him from a corner of the veined window, afraid to move. He took out his ax and stared at his reflection in the glistening blade. After a time Grizzly pocketed the ax, and then he pulled his great coat around him, disappearing into its bristling black folds.

In the afternoon I grew fearful. While the redwoods stretched their heavy shadows over the cabin, Grizzly rose and followed the waning sun up a slight ridge. He cleaned his gun. He even slept for a few moments. Then he slapped his numb face awake and rubbed snow over his sliced cheek.

Grizzly came home.

I hid above the doorway. Grizzly sighed as he crossed the threshold, and I bit back my laughter. The door swung shut. Grizzly stooped and tossed a thick log onto the dying embers. He grinned as it crackled aflame.

I pushed off hard and dove from the ceiling. My claws ripped through grizzly hide and then into human hide. Grizzly bucked awfully, even tried to smash me against the hearth, but the heat only gave me power and as my legs burned into his stomach Grizzly screamed. I drove my claws into a shivering bulge of muscle and brought him to his knees.

The metal rings came next. I pinned them into his neck: one, two, three, four.

After I had supped, I sat the hollow man in the rocker and whispered to him as we looked through the veined window. A storm was rising in the west. We watched it come for a long time. Soon, a fresh dusting of snow covered the husk of man lying out on the ridge.

I told Grizzly that he had been my favorite. I told him that he would last a long time.

Holly, Don't Tell

By Juleen Brantingham

I was eleven. That's probably the reason for it. You don't know or understand *yourself* when you're eleven.

Daddy had been gone two years and Mom had just been fired

from the grocery. She took a job as a cocktail waitress. At the time I thought the name had something to do with the skirt that showed off her legs clear up to here. That's the trouble with being eleven. You know there are secret things you are supposed to understand but no one has taken the trouble to explain them to you yet so sometimes you see something and the world flips completely over and you think, Oh, *that's* what she meant when she—"

But anyway, I was eleven and mostly I was alone at night. People think too much when they're alone. Mom does it. She sits and drinks and thinks. Of course, I'm there but to Mom that's the same as being alone. She thinks about something I did or something Daddy did and how much I'm like him and pretty soon it gets all mixed up in her head and she hits me. So I know how dangerous it is to be alone and thinking.

Our rented house was pretty run-down. There were cracks around the window frames and up under the roof. We had bats. Sometimes I'd get up at night to go to the bathroom or get a drink of water and when I'd turn on the light, one would swoop down at me. I'd heard all of Pinky Johnston's stories, the ones about vampire bats that suck your blood and the one about a woman who got a bat caught in her hair and went crazy and now her family has to keep her locked up in the attic. So when a bat swooped at me I'd do the thing that Pinky said was the only thing you *could* do to save yourself—I'd run back to bed and pull the blanket over my head and tuck everything down tight so the bat couldn't get at me.

As I listened to the bat banging into walls and furniture and it got hard to breathe under that blanket, I'd wonder if Pinky was standing outside the bedroom window, looking at me and laughing. That's part of the trouble about being eleven. People will tell you all kinds of crazy things and some of them turn out to be true and some of them they just said as a joke so they could laugh at you when you believed them. Especially people like Pinky, who left his brain behind in second grade. He's older than me but the only way it shows is in size.

It almost made *me* laugh to think of the crazy way Pinky said babies are made.

Sometimes there were things besides bats that scared me when I was alone. Oh, I don't mean things like lightning or branches that tap at the window or shadows in the corner. That's baby stuff and eleven is too old for that. Anyway, I remember being scared of those things and it was all pretend. I made myself scared so Daddy would sit with me for a while and maybe tell me a story.

There was no sense scaring myself when I was alone in the

house. Mom said if I called her at work one more time she'd have the phone taken out and *then* what would I do if the house caught fire. I had to listen to the story of the boy who cried wolf about a hundred thousand times.

The things that scared me then weren't baby things. One of them was Daddy's footlocker. After he went away, it was the only thing I had left that belonged to him. I wouldn't let Mom touch it or sell it or throw it away. When she wasn't around I'd go upstairs to the storage room and just look at it. At first I did it because it made me feel better to think about Daddy and that he loved me once. But that was before I was eleven, before it started scaring me. Then I would go look at it to be sure the lid was shut and it wasn't leaking blood.

I guess if Daddy hadn't gone away, he and Mom would have gotten a divorce. Or maybe they wouldn't. Pinky said that when his mother divorced his father she took all his money. Daddy never had any money so maybe he couldn't get a divorce.

Even when I was little I knew Mom didn't like Daddy very much. I used to run home as soon as I saw Daddy's car turn into our street. He always got there first and Mom would be at the front door. By the time I reached the prickly bush by the porch, I'd stop and hold my breath because that's when we'd find out if Mom was in a bad mood. Usually she would be. She'd yell at him for losing an account or saying the wrong thing to a customer. She was friends with one of the secretaries at the office and she always knew what was going on.

I'd stop at the prickly bush and I'd hear him open the screen door and walk through the house to the kitchen to get a glass of milk or upstairs to change his clothes. I always knew where he was by the sound of her voice. It was like her words were a balloon that floated above his head. She followed him all over the house. He couldn't get away from her. The only place she didn't follow him was the bathroom and even there she'd stand outside and yell through the keyhole.

Sometimes when he got home she didn't yell at him. She'd just say "Hello" and "Did you pick up that loaf of bread I asked for?" Then I knew it was all right and I'd run around and up the steps and Daddy would hold me up in the air and say, "How's my princess today?" That's the way I remember Daddy best, holding me up in the air and smiling at me and making me feel special.

Mom didn't like *me* very much either. She said I was like him. After he went away she couldn't be mad at him anymore so she took it all out on me.

I asked her one time what kind of work Daddy did. She said he was a businessman. So then I asked what kind of businessman.

"A *nothing* businessman," she said. "In a *nothing* business."

That was kind of funny though Mom never meant to be funny. If someone had asked me what kind of work Daddy did I would have said he was a magician. Isn't it the business of a magician to turn nothing into something?

Daddy did real magic. Lots of people know one or two card tricks but that's not real magic. Daddy used to tear a piece of paper to small bits and put it in a little bag. Then he would say some magic words and give the bag to me and when I'd open it, there would be the exact same piece of paper only now it was all in one piece.

He could pull fifty-cent pieces out of ears and noses. He used to do that when I wanted to go to the movies on Saturday. He'd look through all his pockets and say, "I'm sorry, Holly, but I don't have any money." Then he would look at me as if he just noticed something. "Why are you asking me for money? You have some right here," he would say. Then he would reach up to my ear and pull out a fifty-cent piece. Sometimes he'd pull a fifty-cent piece out of my ear and another one out of my nose and he'd go with me to the matinee. That was more fun than going alone.

When Mom said he was in a nothing business, she wasn't talking about magic. He just did that for his friends. Once he put on a show for my birthday party and Pinky was so surprised that he didn't tease me for a whole week.

Mom didn't even *like* his magic. She said it was childish. Daddy kept his magic stuff in a footlocker and he asked me not to touch it. So I never did. But Mom "cleaned" it once in a while and threw out some of his best tricks. When that happened, Daddy would get this funny, sick look in his eyes but he never said anything to her.

After he went away Mom said she was going to call the trash man and have him pick up the footlocker. Mostly I just let Mom do what she wanted to do and tried to stay out of her way. But not that time. I told her I'd kill her if she touched that footlocker. I got a beating for it but she left it alone.

I didn't start being scared of it until I was eleven. That was when Pinky told me about a man who chopped up his wife and put the pieces in a trunk and mailed it to a made-up name in a town he'd never been to. That was when I started thinking it was funny that Daddy went away without saying good-bye to me. And wondering if Mom could have done that to him.

It wasn't fun anymore to sit on the footlocker and think about

Daddy. I couldn't go near the footlocker. But I couldn't stay away, either. I'd go to the door of the storage room and look at it. Sometimes after I'd stared at it for a while, the sides would seem to bulge, as if someone inside was trying to get out. Sometimes the shadows on the floor would look like pools of blood. Other times I could almost hear something, like someone calling my name but I couldn't quite make it out because I was listening too hard.

When that happened I'd get really scared and run away. Next day I'd be mad at myself for running away from nothing and I'd decide that tonight I would—

But I never did.

When I was eleven I spent a lot of time being scared. After Mom left for work I'd think about the footlocker leaking blood. And I'd hear noises, like people creeping through the house. I'd think about the last time Mom had beat me and wonder if tomorrow would be the day she'd do it again—because she'd *always* do it again, sooner or later.

Sometimes when I'd been thinking about it too long and been scared for too long, I'd start getting mad at Daddy for going away. I guess I loved Daddy better than anyone in the world and I know he loved me more than anyone else did. That's what I mean about it being dangerous to sit alone and think. It wasn't Daddy's fault that Mom had no one to get mad at but me.

Another thing that scared me when I was eleven was the way the curtains at the front window didn't quite close all the way. So when I was watching television I'd get the feeling that someone was watching me through the crack. Usually I'd tell myself it was just Pinky being silly again. But sometimes I couldn't make myself believe it.

One night the crack between the curtains bothered me more than ever. A couple times I thought I saw someone moving around out there. I was too scared to go over and look to find out for sure. I thought about calling Mom but I didn't dare. Finally I turned off the television and, trying to act like I didn't think anything was wrong, I started for my bedroom. That's when he knocked.

I didn't open the door. "Who is it? What do you want?" I asked.

"It's Pinky," he said, real fast and excited. "I just saw someone pick the lock on your back door and sneak inside. Let me in quick! It's probably the sex maniac that just escaped from the county jail!"

Well, I didn't like Pinky but he'd never tried to hurt me, just kiss me. And a sex maniac sounded like a pretty awful thing to be locked up in the house with. Besides, I listened real hard and I thought I could hear a slithery sound from the kitchen. It was hard to get the door unlocked because I was hurrying too much.

He walked into the house, grinning. Then I knew it was another one of his tricks but he was too big to push out the door.

"Hi, there. I was kidding about a sex maniac escaping from jail. It's only me," he said.

I looked up at him and though I knew it was Pinky, I couldn't stop being scared. He was different somehow. I tried yelling at him to leave and I tried crying but he just stood there and grinned at me. I ran for the phone. He ran after me and knocked it out of my hand.

I backed away. He followed me. He started talking, staring into my eyes, telling me things, crazy things that he was going to do to me. I didn't know whether to believe him or not but I knew that whatever this new Pinky had planned, I wouldn't like it.

I ran and dodged but he was right behind me. I tried for the front door but he had snapped the lock as he closed it and my frozen fingers just slid over the catch.

The only way left to run was up the stairs. He tried to follow but his feet got tangled in the phone cord and he fell hard. When he got up he was saying the same words without the ugly laugh. Now he sounded mad. It was almost better that way.

The sound of my breathing was louder than the sound of his voice. This was all the scary things rolled into one and doubled because I didn't know why Pinky was acting this way. I reached the end of the hall before he was halfway up the stairs. I was inside the storage room before I remembered that it didn't have a lock on it like the bedroom doors.

There was no place left to run and no one to call for help. There was just me in that dusty room with Daddy's footlocker.

I opened the lid. I don't remember now if I was going to hide in there or just try to jam it against the door. But there wasn't time for either of those things. I opened the lid.

After a frozen minute, the storage room door crashed against the wall and Pinky came up behind me. He laughed as he tried to grab me. I pointed behind him and screamed, "Bat!" He ducked and stumbled against the footlocker. When he was pulled inside, I slammed the lid and sat down on it. But he didn't try to push his way out or even make a noise.

I was eleven when I stopped thinking about being scared. I didn't stop *being* scared, just thinking about it. I didn't want to understand what happened that night. So I locked it away in my

240

head and wouldn't think about it. But I was still scared, back there behind the locked-up place.

There was nothing inside the footlocker. No magic props. No body. Not even the bottom and sides. It was a lot of nothing, like opening a door into a night without stars. I couldn't see him when he took Pinky away. But I could hear him. He sounded scared. Now that I think of it, Daddy was always scared. Just like I used to be.

Things are different now. See, Mom found this new apartment over on the other side of town and she says we're going to move there. She gave me Daddy's footlocker and told me to pack all my stuff. She really got mad this morning and hit me because I hadn't done it yet. That was the next to the last mistake Mom ever made.

It's too bad about Daddy. But he never should have left me. "Holly, don't tell," he had said from the nothing-space of the footlocker. "Please don't tell your mother where I am."

I wonder how far she will follow him. . . .

The Hound

By H. P. Lovecraft

In my tortured ears there sounds unceasingly a nightmare whirring and flapping, and a faint, distant baying as of some gigantic hound. It is not dream—it is not, I fear, even madness—for too much has already happened to give me these merciful doubts.

St John is a mangled corpse; I alone know why, and such is my knowledge that I am about to blow out my brains for fear I shall be mangled in the same way. Down unlit and illimitable corridors of eldritch phantasy sweeps the black, shapeless Nemesis that drives me to self-annihilation.

May heaven forgive the folly and morbidity which led us both to so monstrous a fate! Wearied with the commonplaces of a prosaic world; where even the joys of romance and adventure soon grow stale. St John and I had followed enthusiastically every aesthetic and intellectual movement which promised respite from our devastating ennui. The enigmas of the symbolists and the ecstasies of the pre-Raphaelites all were ours in their time, but each new moon was drained too soon, of its diverting novelty and appeal.

Only the sombre philosophy of the decadents could help us, and this we found potent only by increasing gradually the depth and diabolism of our penetrations. Baudelaire and Huysmans were soon exhausted of thrills, till finally there remained for us only the more direct stimuli of unnatural personal experiences and adventures. It was this frightful emotional need which led us eventually to that detestable course which even in my present fear I mention with shame and timidity—that hideous extremity of human outrage, and abhorred practice of grave-robbing.

I cannot reveal the details of our shocking expeditions, or catalogue even partly the worst of the trophies adorning the nameless museum we prepared in the great stone house where we jointly dwelt, alone and servantless. Our museum was a blasphemous, unthinkable place, where with the satanic taste of neurotic virtuosi we had assembled a universe of terror and decay to excite our jaded sensibilities. It was a secret room, far, far, underground; where huge winged daemons carven of basalt and onyx vomited from wide grinning mouths weird green and orange light, and hidden pneumatic pipes ruffled into kaleidoscopic dances of death the lines of red charnel things hand in hand woven in voluminous black hangings. Through these pipes came at will the odours our moods most craved; sometimes the scent of pale funeral lilies, sometimes the narcotic incense of imagined Eastern shrines of the kingly dead, and sometimes—how I shudder to recall it!—the frightful, soul-upheaving stenches of the uncovered grave.

Around the walls of this repellent chamber were cases of antique mummies alternating with comely, lifelike bodies perfectly stuffed and cured by the taxidermist's art, and with headstones snatched from the oldest churchyards of the world. Niches here and there contained skulls of all shapes, and heads preserved in various stages of dissolution. There one might find the rotting, bald pates of famous noblemen, and the fresh and radiantly golden heads of new-buried children.

Statues and paintings there were, all of fiendish subjects and some executed by St John and myself. A locked portfolio, bound in tanned human skin, held certain unknown and unnamable drawings which it was rumoured Goya had perpetrated but dared not acknowledge. There were nauseous musical instruments, stringed, brass, and wood-wind, on which St John and I sometimes produced dissonances of exquisite morbidity and cacodaemoniacal ghastliness; whilst in a multitude of inlaid ebony cabinets reposed the most incredible and unimaginable variety of tomb-loot ever assembled by human madness and perversity. It is of this loot in particular that I must not speak—thank God I had the courage to destroy it long before I thought of destroying myself!

The predatory excursions on which we collected our unmentionable treasures were always artistically memorable events. We were no vulgar ghouls, but worked only under certain conditions of mood, landscape, environment, weather, season, and moonlight. These pastimes were to us the most exquisite form of aesthetic expression, and we gave their details a fastidious technical care. An inappropriate hour, a jarring lighting effect, or a clumsy manipulation of the damp sod, would almost totally destroy for us that ecstatic titillation which followed the exhumation of some ominous, grinning secret of the earth. Our quest for novel scenes and piquant conditions was feverish and insatiate—St John was always the leader, and he it was who led the way at last to that mocking, accursed spot which brought us our hideous and inevitable doom.

By what malign fatality were we lured to that terrible Holland churchyard? I think it was the dark rumour and legendry, the tales of one buried for five centuries, who had himself been a ghoul in his time and had stolen a potent thing from a mighty sepulchre. I can recall the scene in these final moments—the pale autumnal moon over the graves, casting long horrible shadows; the grotesque trees, drooping sullenly to meet the neglected grass and the crumbling slabs; the vast legions of strangely colossal bats that flew against the moon; the antique ivied church pointing a huge spectral finger at the livid sky, the phosphorescent insects that danced like death-fires under the yews in a distant corner; the odours of mould, vegetation, and less explicable things that mingled feebly with the night-wind from over far swamps and seas; and, worst of all, the faint deep-toned baying of some gigantic hound which we could neither see nor definitely place. As we heard this suggestion of baying we shuddered, remembering the tales of the peasantry; for he whom we sought had centuries before been found in this self-same spot, torn and mangled by the claws and teeth of some unspeakable beast.

I remember how we delved in the ghoul's grave with our spades, and how we thrilled at the picture of ourselves, the grave, the pale watching moon, the horrible shadows, the grotesque trees, the titanic bats, the antique church, the dancing death-fires, the sickening odours, the gentle moaning nightwind, and the strange, half-heard directionless baying of whose objective existence we could scarcely be sure.

Then we struck a substance harder than the damp mould, and beheld a rotting oblong box crusted with mineral deposits from the long undisturbed ground. It was incredibly tough and thick, but so old that we finally prized it open and feasted our eyes on what it held.

Much—amazingly much—was left of the object despite the lapse of five hundred years. The skeleton, though crushed in places by the jaws of the thing that had killed it, held together with surprising firmness, and we gloated over the clean white skull and its long, firm teeth and its eyeless sockets that once had glowed with a charnel fever like our own. In the coffin lay an amulet of curious and exotic design, which had apparently been worn around the sleeper's neck. It was the oddly conventionalized figure of a crouching winged hound, or sphinx with a semi-canine face, and was exquisitely carved in antique Oriental fashion from a small piece of green jade. The expression of its features was repellent in the extreme, savouring at once of death, bestiality, and malevolence. Around the base was an inscription in characters which neither St John nor I could identify; and on the bottom, like a maker's seal, was given a grotesque and formidable skull.

Immediately upon beholding this amulet we knew that we must possess it; that this treasure alone was our logical pelt from the centuried grave. Even had its outlines been unfamiliar we would have desired it, but as we looked more closely we saw that it was not wholly unfamiliar. Alien it indeed was to all art and literature which sane and balanced readers know, but we recognized it as the thing hinted of in the forbidden *Necronomicon* at the mad Arab Abdul Alhazred; the ghastly soul-symbol of the corpse-eating cult of inaccessible Leng, in Central Asia. All too well did we trace the sinister lineaments described by the old Arab demonologist; lineaments, he wrote, drawn from some obscure supernatural manifestation of the souls of those who vexed and gnawed at the dead.

Seizing the green jade object, we gave a last glance at the bleached and cavern-eyed face of its owner and closed up the grave as we found it. As we hastened from the abhorrent spot, the stolen amulet in St John's pocket, we thought we saw the bats descend in a body to the earth we had so lately rifled, as if seeking for some cursed and unholy nourishment. But the autumn moon shone weak and pale, and we could not be sure.

So, too, as we sailed the next day away from Holland to our home, we thought we heard the faint distant baying of some gigantic hound in the background. But the autumn wind moaned sad and wan, and we could not be sure.

Less than a week after our return to England, strange things began to happen. We lived as recluses; devoid of friends, alone, and without servants in a few rooms of an ancient manor-house on a bleak and unfrequented moor; so that our doors were seldom disturbed by the knock of the visitor.

Now, however, we were troubled by what seemed to be a frequent fumbling in the night, not only around the doors but around the windows also, upper as well as lower. Once we fancied that a large, opaque body darkened the library window when the moon was shining against it, and another time we thought we heard a whirring or flapping sound not far off. On each occasion investigation revealed nothing, and we began to ascribe the occurrences to imagination which still prolonged in our ears the faint far baying we thought we had heard in the Holland churchyard. The jade amulet now reposed in a niche in our museum, and sometimes we burned a strangely scented candle before it. We read much in Alhazred's *Necronomicon* about its properties, and about the relation of ghosts' souls to the objects it symbolized; and were disturbed by what we read.

Then terror came.

On the night of September 24th, 19—, I heard a knock at my chamber door. Fancying it St John's, I bade the knocker enter, but was answered only by a shrill laugh. There was no one in the corridor. When I aroused St John from his sleep, he professed entire ignorance of the event, and became as worried as I. It was the night that the faint, distant baying over the moor became to us a certain and dreaded reality.

Four days later, whilst we were both in the hidden museum, there came a low, cautious scratching at the single door which led to the secret library staircase. Our alarm was now divided, for, besides our fear of the unknown, we had always entertained a dread that our grisly collection might be discovered. Extinguishing all lights, we proceeded to the door and threw it suddenly open; whereupon we felt an unaccountable rush of air, and heard, as if receding far away, a queer combination of rustling, tittering, and articulate chatter. Whether we were mad, dreaming, or in our senses, we did not try to determine. We only realized, with the blackest of apprehensions, that the apparently disembodied chatter was beyond a doubt *in the Dutch language.*

After that we lived in growing horror and fascination. Mostly we held to the theory that we were jointly going mad from our life of unnatural excitements, but sometimes it pleased us more to dramatize ourselves as the victims of some creeping and appalling doom.

245

Bizarre manifestations were now too frequent to count. Our lonely house was seemingly alive with the presence of some malign being whose nature we could not guess, and every night that daemoniac baying rolled over the wind-swept moor, always louder and louder. On October 29 we found in the soft earth underneath the library window a series of footprints utterly impossible to describe. They were as baffling as the hordes of great bats which haunted the old manor-house in unprecedented and increasing numbers.

The horror reached a culmination on November 18, when St John, walking home after dark from the dismal railway station, was seized by some frightful carnivorous thing and torn to ribbons. His screams had reached the house, and I had hastened to the terrible scene in time to hear a whir of wings and see a vague black cloudy thing silhouetted against the rising moon.

My friend was dying when I spoke to him, and he could not answer coherently. All he could do was to whisper, "The amulet—that damned thing—"

Then he collapsed, an inert mass of mangled flesh.

I buried him the next midnight in one of our neglected gardens, and mumbled over his body one of the devilish rituals he had loved in life. And as I pronounced the last daemoniac sentence I heard afar on the moor the faint baying of some gigantic hound. The moon was up, but I dared not look at it. And when I saw on the dim-lighted moor a wide nebulous shadow sweeping from mound to mound, I shut my eyes and threw myself face down upon the ground. When I arose, trembling, I know not how much later, I staggered into the house and made shocking obeisances before the enshrined amulet of green jade.

Being now afraid to live alone in the ancient house on the moor, I departed on the following day for London, taking with me the amulet after destroying by fire and burial the rest of the impious collection in the museum. But after three nights I heard the baying again, and before a week was over felt strange eyes upon me whenever it was dark. One evening as I strolled on Victoria Embankment for some needed air, I saw a black shape obscure one of the reflections of the lamps in the water. A wind, stronger than the night-wind, rushed by, and I knew that what had befallen St John must soon befall me.

The next day I carefully wrapped the green jade amulet and sailed for Holland. What mercy I might gain by returning the thing to its silent, sleeping owner I knew not; but I felt that I must try any step conceivably logical. What the hound was, and why it had pursued me, were questions still vague; but I had first heard the baying in that ancient churchyard, and every subsequent event including St John's dying whisper had served to connect the curse with the stealing of the amulet. Accordingly I sank into the nethermost abysses of despair when, at an inn in Rotterdam, I discovered that thieves had despoiled me of this sole means of salvation.

The baying was loud that evening, and in the morning I read of a nameless deed in the vilest quarter of the city. The rabble were in terror, for upon an evil tenement had fallen a red death beyond the foulest previous crime of the neighbourhood. In a squalid thieves' den an entire family had been torn to shreds by an unknown thing which left no trace, and those around had heard all night a faint, deep, insistent note as of a gigantic hound.

So at last I stood again in the unwholesome churchyard where a pale winter moon cast hideous shadows, and leafless trees drooped sullenly to meet the withered, frosty grass and cracking slabs, and the ivied church pointed a jeering finger at the unfriendly sky, and the night-wind howled maniacally from over frozen swamps and frigid seas. The baying was very faint now, and it ceased altogether as I approached the ancient grave I had once violated, and frightened away an abnormally large horde of bats which had been hovering curiously around it.

I know not why I went thither unless to pray, or gibber out insane pleas and apologies to the calm white thing that lay within; but, whatever my reason, I attacked the half-frozen sod with a desperation partly mine and partly that of a dominating will outside myself. Excavation was much easier than I expected, though at one point I encountered a queer interruption; when a lean vulture darted down out of the cold sky and pecked frantically at the grave-earth until I killed him with a blow of my spade. Finally I reached the rotting oblong box and removed the damp nitrous cover. This is the last rational act I ever performed.

For crouched within that centuried coffin, embraced by a close-packed nightmare retinue of high, sinewy, sleeping bats, was the bony thing my friend and I had robbed; not clean and placid as we had seen it then, but covered with caked blood and shreds of alien flesh and hair, and leering sentiently at me with phosphorescent sockets and sharp ensanguined fangs yawning twistedly in mockery of my inevitable doom. And when it gave from those grinning jaws a deep, sardonic bay as of some gigantic hound, and I saw that it held in its gory filthy claw the lost and fateful amulet of green jade, I merely screamed and ran away idiotically, my screams soon dissolving into peals of hysterical laughter.

Madness rides the star-wind . . . claws and teeth sharpened on centuries of corpses . . . dripping death astride a bacchanale of bats from night-black ruins of buried temples of Belial . . . Now, as the baying of that dead fleshless monstrosity grows louder and louder, and the stealthy whirring and flapping of those accursed web-wings circles closer and closer, I shall seek with my revolver the oblivion which is my only refuge from the unnamed and unnamable.

The Hour and the Man

By Robert Barr

Prince Lotarno rose slowly to his feet, casting one malignant glance at the prisoner before him.

'You have heard,' he said, 'what is alleged against you. Have you anything to say in your defence?'

The captured brigand laughed.

'The time for talk is past,' he cried. 'This has been a fine farce of a fair trial. You need not have wasted so much time over what you call evidence. I knew my doom when I fell into your hands. I killed your brother; you will kill me. You have proven that I am a murderer and a robber; I could prove the same of you if you were bound hand and foot in my camp as I am bound in your castle. It is useless for me to tell you that I did not know he was your brother, else it would not have happened, for the small robber always respects the larger and more powerful thief. When a wolf is down, the other wolves devour him. I am down, and you will have my head cut off, or my body drawn asunder in your courtyard, whichever pleases your Excellency best. It is the fortune of war, and I do not complain. When I say that I am sorry I killed your brother, I merely mean I am sorry you were not the man who stood in his shoes when the shot was fired. You, having more men than I had, have scattered my followers and captured me. You may do with me what you please. My consolation is that killing me will not bring to life the man who is shot; therefore conclude the farce that has dragged through so many weary hours. Pronounce my sentence. I am ready.'

There was a moment's silence after the brigand had ceased

speaking. Then the Prince said, in low tones, but in a voice that made itself heard in every part of the judgement-hall—

'Your sentence is that on the fifteenth of January you shall be taken from your cell at four o'clock, conducted to the room of execution, and there beheaded.'

The Prince hesitated for a moment as he concluded the sentence, and seemed about to add something more, but apparently he remembered that a report of the trial was to go before the King, whose representative was present, and he was particularly desirous that nothing should go on the records which savoured of old-time malignity; for it was well known that his Majesty had a particular aversion to the ancient forms of torture that had obtained heretofore in his kingdom. Recollecting this, the Prince sat down.

The brigand laughed again. His sentence was evidently not so gruesome as he had expected. He was a man who had lived all his life in the mountains, and he had had no means of knowing that more merciful measures had been introduced into the policy of the Government.

'I will keep the appointment,' he said jauntily, 'unless I have a more pressing engagement.'

The brigand was led away to his cell. 'I hope,' said the Prince, 'that you noted the defiant attitude of the prisoner.'

'I have not failed to do so, your Excellency,' replied the ambassador.

'I think,' said the Prince, 'that under the circumstances, his treatment has been most merciful.'

'I am certain, your Excellency,' said the ambassador, 'that his Majesty will be of the same opinion. For such a miscreant beheading is too easy a death.'

The Prince was pleased to know that the opinion of the ambassador coincided so entirely with his own.

The brigand Toza was taken to a cell in the northern tower, where, by climbing on a bench, he could get a view of the profound valley at the mouth of which the castle was situated. He well knew its impregnable position commanding, as it did, the entrance to the valley. He knew also that if he succeeded in escaping from the castle he was hemmed in by mountains practically unscalable, while the mouth of the gorge was so well guarded by the castle that it was impossible to get to the outer world through that gateway. Although he knew the mountains well, he realized that, with his band scattered, many killed, and the others fugitives, he would have a better chance of starving to death in the valley than of escaping out of it. He sat on the bench and thought over the situation. Why had

the Prince been so merciful? He had expected torture, whereas he
was to meet the easiest death that a man could die. He felt satisfied
there was something in this that he could not understand. Perhaps
they intended to starve him to death, now that the appearance of a
fair trial was over. Things could be done in the dungeon of a castle
that the outside world knew nothing of. His fears of starvation were
speedily put to an end by the appearance of his gaoler with a better
meal than he had had for some time; for during the last week he
had wandered a fugitive in the mountains until captured by the
Prince's men, who evidently had orders to bring him in alive. Why
then were they so anxious not to kill him in a fair fight if he were
now to be merely beheaded?

'What is your name?' asked Toza of his gaoler.

'I am called Paulo,' was the answer.

'Do you know that I am to be beheaded on the fifteenth of the
month?'

'I have heard so,' answered the man.

'And do you attend me until that time?'

'I attend you while I am ordered to do so. If you talk much I
may be replaced.'

'That, then, is a tip for silence, good Paulo,' said the brigand. 'I
always treat well those who serve me well; I regret, therefore, that I
have no money with me, and so cannot recompense you for good
service.'

'That is not necessary,' answered Paulo. 'I receive my recompense from the steward.'

'Ah, but the recompense of the steward and the recompense of a
brigand chief are two very different things. Are there so many pick-
ings in your position that you are rich. Paulo?'

'No; I am a poor man.'

'Well, under certain circumstances, I could make you rich.'

Paulo's eyes glistened, but he made no direct reply. Finally he
said in a frightened whisper, 'I have tarried too long, I am watched.
By-and-by the vigilance will be relaxed, and then we may perhaps
talk of riches.'

With that the gaoler took his departure. The brigand laughed
softly to himself. 'Evidently,' he said, 'Paulo is not above the reach
of a bribe. We will have further talk on the subject when the watchfulness is relaxed.'

And so it grew to be a question of which should trust the other.
The brigand asserted that hidden in the mountains he had gold
and jewels, and these he would give to Paulo if he could contrive his
escape from the castle.

'Once free of the castle, I can soon make my way out of the valley,' said the brigand.

'I am not so sure of that,' answered Paulo. 'The castle is well guarded, and when it is discovered that you have escaped, the alarm-bell will be rung, and after that not a mouse can leave the valley without the soldiers knowing it.'

The brigand pondered on the situation for some time, and at last said, 'I know the mountains well.'

'Yes,' said Paulo; 'but you are one man, and the soldiers of the Prince are many. Perhaps,' he added, 'if it were made worth my while, I could show you that I know the mountains even better than you do.'

'What do you mean?' asked the brigand, in an excited whisper.

'Do you know the tunnel?' inquired Paulo, with an anxious glance towards the door.

'What tunnel? I never heard of any.'

'But it exists, nevertheless; a tunnel through the mountains to the world outside.'

'A tunnel through the mountains? Nonsense!' cried the brigand. 'I should have known of it if one existed. The work would be too great to accomplish.'

'It was made long before your day, or mine either. If the castle had fallen, then those who were inside could escape through the tunnel. Few knew of the entrance; it is near the waterfall up the valley, and is covered with brushwood. What will you give me to place you at the entrance of that tunnel?'

The brigand looked at Paulo sternly for a few moments, then he answered slowly, 'Everything I possess.'

'And how much is that?' asked Paulo.

'It is more than you will ever earn by serving the Prince.'

'Will you tell me where it is before I help you to escape from the castle and lead you to the tunnel?'

'Yes,' said Toza.

'Will you tell me now?'

'No; bring me a paper tomorrow, and I will draw a plan showing you how to get it.'

When his gaoler appeared, the day after Toza had given the plan, the brigand asked eagerly, 'Did you find the treasure?'

'I did,' said Paulo quietly.

'And will you keep your word?—will you get me out of the castle?'

'I will get you out of the castle and lead you to the entrance of the tunnel, but after that you must look to yourself.'

'Certainly,' said Toza, 'that was the bargain. Once out of this accursed valley, I can defy all the princes in Christendom. Have you a rope?'

'We shall need none,' said the gaoler. 'I will come for you at midnight, and take you out of the castle by the secret passage; then your escape will not be noticed until morning.'

At midnight his gaoler came and led Toza through many a tortuous passage, the two men pausing now and then, holding their breaths anxiously as they came to an open court through which a guard paced. At last they were outside of the castle at one hour past midnight.

The brigand drew a long breath of relief when he was once again out in the free air.

'Where is your tunnel?' he asked, in a somewhat distrustful whisper of his guide.

'Hush!' was the low answer. 'It is only a short distance from the castle, but every inch is guarded, and we cannot go direct; we must make for the other side of the valley and come to it from the north.'

'What!' cried Toza in amazement, 'traverse the whole valley for a tunnel a few yards away?'

'It is the only safe plan,' said Paulo. 'If you wish to go by the direct way, I must leave you to your own devices.'

'I am in your hands,' said the brigand with a sigh. 'Take me where you will, so long as you lead me to the entrance of the tunnel.'

They passed down and down around the heights on which the castle stood, and crossed the purling little river by means of stepping-stones. Once Toza fell into the water, but was rescued by his guide. There was still no alarm from the castle as daylight began to break. As it grew more light they both crawled into a cave which had a low opening difficult to find, and there Paulo gave the brigand his breakfast, which he took from a little bag slung by a strap across his shoulder.

'What are we going to do for food if we are to be days between here and the tunnel?' asked Toza.

'Oh, I have arranged for that, and a quantity of food has been placed where we are most likely to want it. I will get it while you sleep.'

'But if you are captured, what am I to do?' asked Toza. 'Can you not tell me now how to find the tunnel, as I told you how to find my treasure?'

Paulo pondered over this for a moment, and then said, 'Yes: I think it would be the safer way. You must follow the stream until you reach the place where the torrent from the east joins it. Among the hills there is a waterfall, and halfway up the precipice on a shelf of rock there are sticks and bushes. Clear them away, and you will find the entrance to the tunnel. Go through the tunnel until you come to a door which is bolted on this side. When you have passed through, you will see the end of your journey.'

Shortly after daybreak the big bell of the castle began to toll, and before noon the soldiers were beating the bushes all around them. They were so close that the two men could hear their voices from their hiding-place, where they lay in their wet clothes, breathlessly expecting every moment to be discovered.

The conversation of two soldiers, who were nearest them, nearly caused the hearts of the hiding listeners to stop beating.

'Is there not a cave near here?' asked one. 'Let us search for it!'

'Nonsense,' said the other. 'I tell you that they could not have come this far already.'

'Why could they not have escaped when the guard changed at midnight?' insisted the first speaker.

'Because Paulo was seen crossing the courtyard at midnight, and they could have had no other chance of getting away until just before daybreak.'

This answer seemed to satisfy his comrade, and the search was given up just as they were about to come upon the fugitives. It was a narrow escape, and, brave as the robber was, he looked pale, while Paulo was in a state of collapse.

Many times during the nights and days that followed, the brigand and his guide almost fell into the hands of the minions of the Prince. Exposure, privation, semi-starvation, and, worse than all, the alternate wrenchings of hope and fear, began to tell upon the stalwart frame of the brigand. Some days and nights of cold winter rain added to their misery. They dare not seek shelter, for every habitable place was watched.

When daylight overtook them on their last night's crawl through the valley, they were within a short distance of the waterfall, whose low roar now came soothingly down to them.

'Never mind the daylight,' said Toza; 'let us push on and reach the tunnel.'

'I can go no farther,' moaned Paulo; 'I am exhausted.'

'Nonsense,' cried Toza; 'it is but a short distance.'

'The distance is greater than you think; besides, we are in full view of the castle. Would you risk everything now that the game is nearly won? You must not forget that the stake is your head; and remember what day this is.'

'What day is it?' asked the brigand, turning on his guide.

'It is the fifteenth of January, the day on which you were to be executed.'

Toza caught his breath sharply. Danger and want had made a coward of him, and he shuddered now, which he had not done when he was on his trial and condemned to death.

'How do you know it is the fifteenth?' he asked at last.

Paulo held up his stick, notched after the method of Robinson Crusoe.

'I am not so strong as you are, and if you will let me rest here until the afternoon, I am willing to make a last effort, and try to reach the entrance of the tunnel.'

'Very well,' said Toza shortly.

As they lay there that morning neither could sleep. The noise of the waterfall was music to the ears of them both; their long toilsome journey was almost over.

'What did you do with the gold that you found in the mountains?' asked Toza suddenly.

Paulo was taken unawares, and answered, without thinking, 'I left it where it was. I will get it after.'

The brigand said nothing, but that remark condemned Paulo to death. Toza resolved to murder him as soon as they were well out of the tunnel, and get the gold himself.

They left their hiding-place shortly before twelve o'clock, but their progress was so slow, crawling, as they had to, up the steep side of the mountain, under cover of bushes and trees, that it was well after three when they came to the waterfall, which they crossed, as best they could, on stones and logs.

'There,' said Toza, shaking himself, 'that is our last wetting. Now for the tunnel!'

The rocky sides of the waterfall hid them from view of the castle, but Paulo called the brigand's attention to the fact that they could be easily seen from the other side of the valley.

'It doesn't matter now,' said Toza; 'lead the way as quickly as you can to the mouth of the cavern.'

Paulo scrambled on until he reached a shelf about halfway up the cataract; he threw aside bushes, brambles, and logs, speedily disclosing a hole large enough to admit a man.

'You go first,' said Paulo, standing aside.

'No,' answered Toza; 'you know the way, and must go first. You cannot think that I wish to harm you—I am completely unarmed.'

'Nevertheless,' said Paulo, 'I shall not go first. I did not like the way you looked at me when I told you the gold was still in the hills. I admit I distrust you.'

'Oh, very well,' laughed Toza, 'it doesn't really matter.' And he crawled into the hole in the rock, Paulo following him.

Before long the tunnel enlarged so that a man could stand upright.

'Stop!' said Paulo; 'there is the door near here.'

'Yes,' said the robber, 'I remember that you spoke of a door,' adding, however, 'What is it for, and why is it locked?'

'It is bolted on this side,' answered Paulo, 'and we shall have no difficulty in opening it.'

'What is it for?' repeated the brigand.

'It is to prevent the current of air running through the tunnel and blowing away the obstruction at this end,' said the guide.

'Here it is,' said Toza, as he felt down its edge for the bolt.

The bolt drew back easily, and the door opened. The next instant the brigand was pushed rudely into a room, and he heard the bolt thrust back into its place almost simultaneously with the noise of the closing door. For a moment his eyes were dazzled by the light. He was in an apartment blazing with torches held by a dozen men standing about.

In the centre of the room was a block covered with black cloth, and beside it stood a masked executioner, resting the corner of a gleaming axe on the black draped block, with his hands crossed over the end of the axe's handle.

The Prince stood there surrounded by his ministers. Above his head was a clock, with the minute hand pointed to the hour of four.

'You are just in time!' said the Prince grimly; 'we are waiting for you!'

The House at Evening

By Frances Garfield

The sun had set and another twilight had begun. The western sky took on a rosy tinge, but none of the soft color penetrated into the lofty bedroom.

Claudia leaned toward the bureau. Her stormy black locks curtained her face as she brushed and brushed them. It was a luxurious, sensuous brushing. Her hair glistened in the light of the oil lamp.

Across the room sat Garland. She quickly combed her short blonde hair into an elfish mop of curls. "Thank goodness I don't have to worry about a great banner like yours," she said.

"Never you mind," Claudia laughed back. "We both know it's impressive."

They both applied makeup generously. Claudia fringed her silvery eyes with deep blue mascara and Garland brushed her pale eyebrows with brown. Each painted her lips a rosy red and smiled tightly to smooth the lipstick.

They finished dressing and went down the squeaking staircase to the big parlor. Darkness crept in, stealthily but surely. They picked up jugs of oil and went about, filling and lighting all the ancient glass-domed lamps. Light flickered yellow from table and shelf and glistened on the wide hardwood floor boards. Claudia took pride in those old expanses, spending hours on her knees to rub them to a glow. Garland arranged a bowl filled with colorful gourds on the mahogany table that framed the back of a brocaded couch. She put two scented candles into holders and lighted them.

Then they stood together to admire the effect of the soft light, Claudia in her red satin, Garland in her dark, bright blue. They checked each other for flaws and found none.

"I'd like to go walking outside, the way we used to do," said Garland. She glanced down at her high-heeled slippers. They weren't too high. "I'll only be gone a little while."

"There's not much to see out there," said Claudia. "Nobody much walks here anymore. It's been a long time since we've had company."

"Maybe I'm just being sentimental," smiled Garland. Her eyes twinkled for a moment, as if with some secret delight. "But maybe I'll bring somebody back."

"I'll stay here in case anybody calls," Claudia assured her.

The big wooden front door creaked shut behind Garland. She crossed the gray-floored piazza and ran down the steps to the path of old flagstones. Periwinkle overflowed them and knotted its roots everywhere. Ivy and honeysuckle choked the trees, autumn leaves poured down from the oaks. An old dead dogwood leaned wearily at the lawn's edge. Garland picked her way carefully.

An owl shrieked a message in the distance. Garland smiled to herself. She had worn no wrap out in the warm evening, but she nestled into the soft collar of her silky dress to feel its closeness. She breathed deeply of the night air.

Falling leaves whispered like raindrops. But there were only vagrant clouds in the sky. A young moon shone upon the old sidewalk, upon old houses along the way. They were large, pretentious houses, the sort called Victorian. They were ramshackle. No light shone from any window. Garland might have been the only moving creature in the neighborhood. Once this had been an elegant area on the edge of the old town that existed mainly for Ellerby College, but people had moved out. Deterioration had set in. Urban renewal threatened the neighborhood.

All at once Garland heard something—voices, hushed, furtive. She saw two tall young men coming toward her. She looked at them in the moonlight. They were handsome, sprucely dressed, looked like muscular young athletes. She hadn't seen their like for a while, and she felt a surge of warmth through her body.

They were near now, she could hear what they said.

"My Uncle Whit used to come here when he was in college," one young voice declared. "He said this was called Pink Hill. Said you'd be mighty well entertained."

Now she passed them, and turned at once to go back toward her house. She quickened her steps. For a moment she didn't know whether to be sad or happy. If only she hadn't lost her touch—but she knew her body, firm, sweet-looking. As she passed them again, she spoke.

"Hey," she greeted them.

One, tall with a neat, dark beard, spoke shyly. "Nice evening, isn't it?"

Garland smiled. If she had had dimples, she would have flashed them. "Yes, but there's a chill in the air. I think I'll just go back home. Maybe make some hot chocolate—or tea."

Away she walked ahead, her hips swinging a trifle, not so fast as to lose touch with them.

They seemed to be following her, all right. The bearded one was speaking, and Garland strained her ears to hear.

"After all," he was saying, "we did sort of think we were looking for experience."

The other, the fair-haired athletic one, said something too soft for Garland to hear. But it sounded like agreement.

She walked on, watching her feet on the treacherous pavement. There were so many cracks in that old cement. Sure enough, the two boys were coming along with her. Again she felt a flood of internal warmth. She felt almost young again, almost as young as she must look. Carefully she timed the sway of her hips. There was the house. Along the flagstones she minced happily, and up the steps and in at the door.

"We're going to have company, Claudia," she said.

Claudia swept the room with an appraising glance, and smiled a cool smile. "Tell me," she said quickly.

"Two really lovely young men, coming along to follow me. One with bright hair and a football body. The other tall, bearded, neat, sophisticated looking. We'll have to do them credit."

"Well, there's a bottle of port out, and some of those cheese biscuits I made." Claudia studied the table in the lamplight. "We'll be all right."

From outside they heard footsteps on the porch, and hesitant whispering.

"They're beautiful," said Garland.

Silence for an instant. Then a guarded tattoo of knocks on the panel of the door. A knock, Garland guessed, taught them by good old Uncle Whit.

"Okay, here we go," said Claudia, and gave Garland a triumphant look. "Remember your company manners."

She glided to the door, her red gown hugging her opulent hips and her slim waist. Her dress was long. It swept the floor and it accentuated every curve and hollow of the well-used body. She could be proud of how she looked, how she moved. She graduated magna cum laude in every way.

She opened the door, and the lamplight touched the two young men.

Garland had appraised them accurately. They wore well-fitting suits and open shirts. The taller one had a close-clipped beard, dark and sleek. Promising and intelligent. The other, of medium height but with broad shoulders, looked powerfully muscled. Undoubtedly undergraduates at Ellerby College. Fine prospects, both of them.

"Good evening, gentlemen," Claudia gave them her personal, hospitable smile.

"Good evening, ma'am," said the dark one, like a spokesman. He would be for Garland, thought Claudia. For her the other, the sturdy one.

"Well," said the tall one. "Well, we thought—" He paused embarrassedly.

"We thought we'd come walking this way," spoke up the other. "My name's Guy and this is Larry. We—we're students."

"Freshmen," added Larry. "We go to Ellerby."

258

"I see," Claudia soothed them. "Well, won't you come in?"

"Yes, ma'am," said Guy gratefully. They entered together and stood side by side. Their smiles were diffident. Claudia closed the door behind them.

Larry studied the parlor with politely curious eyes. "This is a great place," he offered. "Wonderful. It's—well, it's nostalgic."

"Thank you," Garland smiled to him. "Come sit here and see if this couch wasn't more or less made for you."

He hesitated, but only for a moment. Then he paced toward the couch. He wore handsome shiny boots. He and Garland sat down together and Claudia held out her hand to Guy.

"You look like somebody I used to know," she said, slitting her silvery eyes at him. "He played football at State. Came visiting here."

"Maybe all football players look alike," Guy smiled back. "I came to Ellerby to play tight end, if I can make it."

Beside Larry on the couch, Garland turned on her personality. It was as if she pressed a button to set it free.

"Would you like a glass of this port?" she asked. "It's very good."

"Let me do it." He took the bottle and poured. His hand trembled just a trifle. "Here." And he held out the glass.

"No, it's for you," she said. "I'll wait until later."

Larry sipped. "Delicious."

"Yes, only the best for our friends."

"We surely appreciate this, ma'am," he said, sipping again.

"You may call me Garland."

Claudia had seated Guy in a heavily soft armchair and had perched herself on its arm. They were whispering and chuckling together.

"Larry," said Garland, "you look to me as if you've been around a lot."

"Maybe my looks are deceptive," he said, brown eyes upon her. "I—I've never been at a place like this before."

Garland edged closer to him. "Tell me a little about yourself."

"Oh, I'm just a freshman at Ellerby. Nothing very exciting about that."

"But it must be." She edged even closer. "Just being on campus must be exciting. Come on, tell me more."

She put her hand on his. He took it in his warm clasp.

"Well, freshman year is rough." He seemed to have difficulty talking. "There's no hazing at Ellerby any more, not exactly, but you have to take a lot of stuff to get ready to be a sophomore."

She pulled his young arm around her shoulder and began to

count the fingers on his hand with delicate little taps. Across the room, Claudia was sitting on Guy's lap, pulling his ear. They seemed to have come to good terms.

"This is really a great house," Larry said slowly. "It's—" He gulped. "It's nice," he said.

And right here it would come, Garland thought, something about how she was too lovely a girl to be in such a sordid business. To her relief, he didn't say it. Again she must take the initiative. She pulled his hand to where it could envelop her soft breast and held it there.

"Like it?" she whispered.

He must know what was coming, but plainly he was drowned in all sorts of conflicting emotions. Uncle Whit hadn't coached him, not nearly enough. He looked around the lamplit room with his eyes that were somehow plaintive. His beard seemed to droop.

"All right, Larry," said Garland, "come with me."

She got up and tugged his hand to make him get to his feet. He smiled. Of course, get him somewhere away from Claudia and Guy, there so cozy in the armchair. She picked up a lamp and led him into the hall.

"Wow," he said. "That staircase. Spiral. Looks like something in a historical movie."

"Does it?"

The staircase wound up into dark reaches. Gently Garland guided him and he seemed glad to be guided. She shepherded him past the torn spots in the carpeting, away from the shaky stretch of the balustrade, up to the hall above. She held up the lamp. It showed the faded roses on the carpet.

"Here," she said, "this is my room."

She opened the heavy door and pushed it inward. They stepped across the threshold together. She set the lamp on a table near the oriel window.

"I swear, Garland," he muttered, "this is great. That old four-poster bed, the bench—they must be worth a lot. They're old."

"Older than I am," she smiled at him.

"You're not old, Garland. You're beautiful."

"So are you," she told him truthfully.

They sat down on the bed. It had a cover of deep blue velvet, with dim gold tassels. Larry seemed overwhelmed.

"I can't tell you how lovely all this is," he stammered.

"Then don't try. Put your feet up. That's right. Now relax."

He sank back. She pulled the loose shirt collar wider. "What a beautiful neck you have."

260

"Oh," he said, "it's Guy who's got the neck. All those exercises, those weights he lifts."

"Let Claudia attend to Guy. You're here with me."

Outside the door, a soft rustling. Garland paid no attention. Larry was quiet now, his eyes closed. Garland bent to him, her tender fingers massaging his temples, his neck. He breathed rhythmically, as though he slept. Closer Garland bent to him, her hands on his neck. Her fingers crooked, their tips pressed.

The lamplight shone on her red lips. They parted. Her teeth showed long and sharp. She crooned to him. She stopped. Her mouth opened above his neck.

Outside, voices spoke, faint, inhuman.

Garland rose quickly and went to the door. She opened it a crack.

Shapes hung there, gaunt and in ragged clothes. "Well," she whispered fiercely, "can't you wait?"

"Let me in," said one of them. Eyes gleamed palely. "Let me in," said another. "Hungry, hungry—"

"Can't you wait?" asked Garland again. "After I'm finished, you can have him. Have what's left."

She closed the door on their pleas, and hurried back to where Larry lay ready, motionless, dreaming, on the bed.

The Idea

By Barry N. Malzberg

It came to me out of the blue that Thursday morning. The conception, I mean. Its coming had absolutely nothing to do with the top level meeting that was scheduled upstairs later in the day. If I had remembered the meeting, I'm sure the idea would never have come in the first place. I function poorly under pressure, an old predicament.

"Educational," I told Miller after I had sketched in the outlines to him. Miller is my immediate superior so he deserves the courtesy, up to a point. "That's the hook. It's educational."

"Not enough," said Miller. He is one of those bleak, desperate men in their upper forties who remind me now and then that even

I am mortal. Sometimes I consider his history, which so approximates my own progress through network to date as to be distressing.

"It's more than enough. Would I lead you wrong? The atmosphere, the times. The social tension. Everything's ready for it. Would I lead you wrong? Trust your instincts. Think of your children. Wouldn't they understand?"

"I won't propose it, Howard. I won't get before that meeting and present this. We'll be slaughtered. I'm thinking of you more than of myself."

"Did I ask *you* to propose it? I will. All I wanted was to clear with you." This was after Miller had reminded me of the meeting which he had done as soon as he had told me that he had no time for ideas, but too late for me to give him mine.

"I refuse to clear it."

"We've never had a serious disagreement. Must I go over your head?"

That made him think, as it was meant to. I could see him playing off the one thing against the other thing: an official complaint from a subordinate against the question of approval. It was a difficult decision. Part of the immediate beauty of the idea was that it made decisions difficult for everyone. Right away, it vaulted us into a new world of possibilities. Everything had implications beyond the simple dilemma of *need money; hate job,* which was the ordinary key to existence. "I can't put up with it, Howard," he said finally.

"Then I should go higher?"

"Not exactly. No. Just bring it up. At the meeting. As something you were discussing. Not as a recommendation or anything, though. Just as an idea. That's as far as I can authorize you to move on it."

"No good. A full presentation or nothing."

"You haven't got the material for a full presentation." Then he said it. "I think you're crazy, Howard."

"No, I'm not. Besides, we're all crazy. What I do is think; think all the time. It beats response, beats precision, it even beats competence. No substitute for original human thought."

"You can pose it but just as a curiosity. Say that you had this silly way-out idea and here it goes up the chute for laughs. No more. I'm a desperate man, Howard, you can see that, but I won't go beyond that."

"Fine," I said, having satisfied himself. "That's fair enough. I wasn't even thinking of the meeting to tell you the truth. If I had remembered the meeting before I came in here I wouldn't have thought it out. Pressure, you know?"

"No," said Miller.

So I pitched it to them and it went over fantastic. I had figured it would. Bald men, wigged men, old men, young men . . . all of these responded as one by the time I finally got out of the full sense of the idea. I had help, of course. Several of them were bright enough to catch the implications right off and Miller himself, once he saw the drift, had a few angles himself. The meeting broke up at about five after five—which meant that half of these guys had missed connections of one sort or another and would have to rearrange the whole evening if not most of the next day—and a whole group of them wanted to go out to a restaurant and finish the discussion. They couldn't get off it, were on the point of arranging for a private room in Sardi's until I said that I had an important previous engagement and would have to personally bow out.

Well, for some reason, that killed it. None of them wanted to go out or stay with it without me. They said that I was the guiding star or motivating force or things like that but it took me until a long time later that I finally figured out the real reason. Not that it matters any more, of course.

The pilot went up for production four weeks after that, and it was terrific. They had hired the two best bodies available, big show business names as well, to do it, and it quickly became something of a classic. The price was right for those kids and they were glad to have the work. I was there at the filming and they got everything, didn't miss a nuance. About that time or shortly after, Miller had a mild heart attack and was put on leave for three months and it was just natural to move me into his spot. Just temporarily, of course. So I was able to add a few little personal touches to the pilot.

It glided right through network approval, of course, because this was one of the few pilots in history which had network money in it from the start, which kind of gave us a break on coverage, not to say the decision-making process. The go-ahead orders came right through, but it was decided to hold up production for the fall until the pilot itself was slotted as a one-shot midsummer special and we could get some reactions. If they went as we hoped they would, it could then be full-speed ahead. It was about that time that the first glimmers of trepidation seemed to come around. Until then it had been a real spin, a voyage toward destiny conducted in as full, frank and comradely a way as I had ever seen in television—because all of us, at last, felt we were beating the biggest rap of all—but now, with the pilot in the can and actually scheduled, things began to break the other way. Rumors: too many party girls hanging around outside board meetings, stuff like that. Nothing definite.

About that time, too, was when it became "Howard's idea." Not the "fall spot" or the "turn-around gig" but "Howard's conception." I began to be asked about a lot of things which really weren't my responsibility, placement angles and sustaining spots and stuff like that. And which we wanted to tie into primarily: Nielsen or Arbitron. These were all landing at my desk and it was at about that time that I realized the fix was being put in. I remembered what Miller had said to me the only time he called from the hospital. "It's going to work, Howard," he said, "and they'll eat all of us alive for having shown them how badly they wanted it."

Prophecy from an oxygen tent. I began to find my evenings booked solid with receptions, interview shows, guest shots. Of course I couldn't come out and really say what was going to happen —we had decided to keep as tight an official lid on as possible—but the point was to hint a lot. The more I did, the more the applause meters went up.

August 3rd was pilot day. I watched it in my own home surrounded by my own family from 8:30 to 9:00 and it was like nothing that had ever happened before in the history of the world. The thing took to the tube even better than it had to the screen. The closeness, the *compression* fitted it. It was impossible not to be moved by it.

When it was over, my wife cursed me and took the children upstairs and left me to have a drink all alone and when I came out of the kitchen they were gone. I haven't seen them since, but I get messages.

About five minutes after the third drink, the phone started ringing and it hasn't stopped since. Not for a moment. Outside, inside, all I am is a message center, all clogged by grief. Right? Right.

The final trial will begin this week and I wish that Miller were here to see it, only Miller is still in this spa in Arizona. Anyone else you can think of will be there, though. As they say, they want to see Howard get what's coming to him. Howard being the man who almost destroyed America.

"Educational," I try to tell my lawyer. The first thing was, it was educational. How can you knock the accretion of knowledge in this highly technologized age, I ask you.

And my lawyer, an old friend, very short, smart guy who used to bail T&T out of all kinds of trouble before they dropped below 50 and the trouble stopped, says, "What you got to understand, Howard, is that the world is full of guys all as unique as you and when it thinks that the time for something has come it is going to make one of them do it but then the world, not liking the great man theory of history, is going to lay it on the one who did it. So it can say it never happened. So it can go on its way and blame the Communists or the drinking water for the kick. But if it's any comfort, Howard, the next time it's done—and thanks to you, it will be very soon—it will be a lot easier and in the meantime I promise you that I will charge you a very small fee, nothing that the company policy won't be able to pay in full if the ultimate happens which, of course, we don't want it to."

Identity Crisis

By Thomas F. Monteleone

Elliot Binnder huddled in the corner of the dark supply room, caressing the business-end of a linoleum knife.

Outside, in the main corridor, the sounds of the hospital blended together: the paging system loudspeakers, the creaking wheels of gurney carts, offhanded laughter of passing student nurses, the occasional footsteps of someone passing close by the supply room door.

Dressed in hastily stolen hospital garb, Binnder appeared to be just another surgeon in the huge hospital. The pale green O.R. cap and matching pajama-like tunic and pants covered his street clothes; the surgeon's mask concealed his stoical features.

The shift change, he thought; I'll wait until the change of shift. Lots of confusion then. No one will notice me . . .

The blade felt keen and sharp as he edged it with his thumb, following its menacing curve down to the point. In the darkness, it reminded him of the talon of some horrible creature, and he smiled. He checked his liquid crystal watch, and smiled again. Not much longer now . . .

Balding, thin, and yet working on a double chin, Elliot Binnder did not normally appear very threatening. In fact, he was quite meek-looking, and had always thought himself the perfect stereotype of a timid bank clerk. In fact, he was a timid hardware store clerk.

Sitting in the dark, his mind drifted back over the chain of events that had brought him to his present state of mind and place in the cosmos. *It was the hardware store . . .*

. . . where he had worked for almost twenty years. *Twenty years.* The store had been owned by Leo J. Benford, Sr., a kindly old gentleman who understood the faithful service and loyalty of good employees. Elliot had worked for the old man from the beginning, and gave the owner an honest day's work every day, year in and year out. Things went along pleasantly and after ten years' service, Elliot was made the manager of Benford's Hardware—earning a good salary and making the payments on his bungalow. Mr. Benford was very happy with his work, and had even loaned him the money for the down payment on the little house. Elliot Binnder was a happy, contented man.

That is, until the owner's son, Leo J. Benford, Jr., started coming down to the store after school and on Saturdays to "learn the business." Still a teenager, the young Leo Benford had already acquired a hard edge to his personality and an envious glow to his eyes. He looked like a vulture waiting to descend upon soon-to-be-carrion, and even back then, Elliot knew enough not to trust the owner's son.

As time passed, Leo Jr. spent his summers home from college in the hardware store, and he became an increasing source of annoyance and irritation to all the employees—especially Elliot Binnder. No matter how diplomatic, or "nice," Binnder attempted to be with Leo Jr., there was no getting around the young man's obnoxious nature and know-it-all attitude. Leo Jr. was contemptuous of Elliot's authority and took every opportunity to ignore his suggestions and disobey outright his requests in day-to-day business.

But Elliot had been a patient man, and he hoped that perhaps Leo Jr. was just another young man feeling his oats, as they used to say, and that time and maturity would change him into a more agreeable, reasonable person. Thus did Elliot avoid speaking with the father and owner of the store about the problems experienced with the son. *Perhaps I should have said something . . .*

But he didn't say anything, and the situation became increasingly worse until, inevitably, Elliot and Leo Jr. hated each other—that was apparent to all the other employees, but unfortunately not to Mr. Benford Sr., who was spending more time in his greenhouse and less and less time at his business. In fact, the only thing that kept Elliot sane and whole had been the casual mention by Leo Sr. that he intended to open another hardware store in the next town, and that he would be making Elliot a *full partner*—along with his son, of course. The papers, the old man told him, were being drawn up by his lawyers, and everything would be official as soon as his attorney came back from a trip to the Bahamas.

Time passed quickly it seemed, at that point, and Leo Jr. graduated from college, married, and was often seen with his pregnant wife carrying about the next generation of the Benford line. Elliot hoped that this coming responsibility, plus the inclusion of both into a business partnership would finally thaw out the relationship between he and the impetuous Leo Jr.

But it was even less than wishful thinking. On the same weekend that Elliot had told his wife of the elder Benford's plans, he received a phone call from Mrs. Leo J. Benford, Sr. The woman was on the brink of hysteria as she struggled to tell him that her husband had been killed in an auto accident only an hour previous. Elliot had been shocked—it was as though his own father had died and the sense of loss and sincerely felt grief was almost overwhelming. He could only think of never seeing the dear old man again, and was therefore not thinking of what further consequences might follow that unfortunate and very untimely demise.

Naturally, Elliot closed the store until after the funeral; and although he attempted to contact the son several times, he was unsuccessful. When he saw Leo Jr. at the funeral service, the young man ignored him completely.

But on the day business reopened, the young man was more than eager to speak with him. Elliot was not surprised to see the young new owner seated behind his desk that fateful morning. To tell the truth, Elliot had even expected it, and the demotion that would surely accompany the gesture. But he was surprised by Leo Jr. in a way he could not have expected.

"Good morning, Binnder, I've been waiting for you," the son had said.

"Have you?"

"Yes, and I'm afraid I have some bad news for you." The young Leo was almost grinning, unable to contain the obvious joy surging through him at that moment.

"What kind of bad news?" Elliot said.

"Oh . . . the worst, I can assure you. I'm afraid its 'pink-slip' time for you, old man. I want you to get all your shit out of here immediately. It's over and I never want to see your simple face around here again."

"What!" Elliot had said, his voice carrying all the shock and disbelief and pain that such cruelty could summon. "You're *firing* me? You're letting me *go?*"

"Oh yes. Absolutely." Leo Jr. had smiled at that point.

Perhaps it was the smile, the certain enjoyment the son had displayed then, or perhaps it was the years of resentment and hate finally bubbling to the surface . . . Elliot would never know for sure, but he did know he would extract his revenge on the young bastard who sat grinning before him. He *hated* him at that moment as he had never hated anything in his life.

And it was only the beginning of the ordeal.

Every place where Elliot applied for work, having cited his managerial experience at Benford's Hardware, he was quickly denied employment. One prospective employer volunteered to Elliot that he had received a "less than glowing" reference from Leo Jr. It was apparent then, that it was not enough for the young son to simply dismiss Elliot in disgrace. No, Leo Jr. clearly intended to ruin him.

Elliot ended up working in a lumber mill, making half of his previous salary and sliding slowly under a wave of bills, loan notes, and other economic pressures. First he had to pull his son from private school, then he second-mortgaged the house, and had the car repossessed and the phone disconnected. His wife became disenchanted, then enraged at his inability to support her in her accustomed manner. The pressure continued to build until he thought he would go insane without some kind of release, some of kind of catharsis.

He was going to hell in the old handbasket, and he decided that maybe he would take someone with him.

He would take his revenge. Leo Jr. would pay for his injustices, and he would suffer as no man had ever suffered. And so Elliot Binnder descended into the maelstrom that is the chaos of the broken spirit and the tortured mind, knowing that he would never return.

The only piece that remained to be fitted into the jigsaw picture of madness was the act itself, which came to him in a moment of pure inspiration—when his wife told him that Mrs. Leo J. Benford, Jr., had given birth to a baby boy the day before.

Acting with quiet deliberation, Elliot went into his basement and carefully selected the proper instrument—a linoleum knife from Benford's Hardware. Yes, he had thought with a smile. This is perfectly ironic. It will do nicely.

He took a cab downtown to the hospital, took an elevator up to the Maternity Ward, walked the halls as though he might be an impatient expectant father, and waited for the moment when he was unobserved. When it came, he slipped into the supply room and quickly searched through the shelved stacks of linens and gowns until he found the proper disguise . . .

   . . . and now the time has come.
There were the sounds of increased activity outside the small dark room, and Elliot arose quickly, concealing the linoleum knife beneath his surgeon's gown. Opening the door, he slipped out into the corridor unnoticed by the stream of white-uniformed nurses and orderlies.
Yes, this was the perfect time.
He walked down the hall, past the rooms of new mothers, to the glass-windowed nursery. His heart was pounding like a jackhammer in his chest and his spit tasted like paper paste, but it was not from fear, rather from the feeling of approaching triumph. They can't catch me! he thought and the certainty of that knowledge elated him with a rush of adrenalin. They can't!
Striding purposefully, confidently, he pushed through the door to the nursery, where a charge nurse sat at a small desk reading a copy of *People* magazine.
"Just a minute, Doctor," she said. "Can I help you?"
He moved swiftly, striking her in the jaw with his fist. She went down immediately without a sound, and he rushed past her, into the brightly illuminated, warm room where the tiny clear plastic cribs were arranged in two neat rows. There were at least twenty newborn children, and Elliot knew that he must act quickly.
Each baby had a little bracelet, and it would be a small matter to search out the one with the Benford name upon it. Or so he thought. Frantically as he held the tiny, pudgy little wrist of the nearest infant, he tried to make sense of the numbers and letters on the bracelet.
Christ, it's some kind of code! No names!
There was the sound of someone stirring beyond the door. *Not much time! I've got to do something!* He looked up to see his reflection in the glass window of the nursery, and beyond the glared images of several of the staff watching him with growing horror. He realized that he was holding the linoleum knife in plain view. *Don't panic now! Think . . . think!*
Taking one step back, he looked over the collection of cribs and knew what he must do.
It's the only way to be sure, he thought, as he stooped over the first crib. And it won't take very long.

In the Corn

By Robert Fox

Do you remember losing your eyes?"

"Yes."

"Tell me."

"I . . . was three years old, playing with my brother and governess in a wide yellow field in back of our house. It was Autumn, and the grass was stiff; I remember it was cold that day. My brother and I were tumbling on the grass, throwing each other over our shoulders, laughing. The governess, Nancy, got caught up in our game and began to tumble us over her shoulder also. This is . . . very painful to remember. . . ."

"Go on. You must tell me."

"She was roughhousing with us, and began to pick one and then the other up, swinging us high in the air. I remember her twirling me around. We were all getting dizzy and were laughing uncontrollably. We had wandered somewhat from the center of the field toward an edge bordered by a row of picked corn; the stalks were stiff and dry and stood up straight. I can almost see the sun on their dry yellow. . . . Nancy was laughing as if she were our own age; actually, she was only a few years older than my brother. I was running around and around her, chasing my brother, and Nancy suddenly picked me up, a bit too fast, tumbling me up and over her shoulder. I remember the stalks of corn coming at my eyes like deformed spears, I can *see* them now like I could then, as if in slow motion, coming up towards my eyes, and then into them. . . ."

"Go on. . . ."

"Doctor, I can't. . . ."

"You must."

"I . . . remember screaming, hearing myself scream, and I remember flailing my arms and hands, trying to pull the stalks from my eyes, sitting on the ground and screaming uncontrollably, *shrieking*, my entire body shaking, and then feeling hands on me, Nancy's hands. I can remember her hands on my face, and the sticky mass of tears and blood, and then I could feel her tugging at

270

the stalks, pulling them free one at a time, gently, and there was
. . . a *sound* . . . as she did it, a *sucking* sound. . . ."

"Yes?"

"I can't."

"I told you, you *must*. Continue."

"No!"

"Continue."

"I . . . —no!"

"You must go on."

"The . . . last thing I remember seeing was the governess' face
after she had pulled the stalks free. I could see her face through
blood, though I could not see very clearly. There was a look
of . . ."

"Yes?"

"A look of *horror* on her face, and then my eyes began to unfocus,
as if the world were being pulled away, taking the light with it, and
I was alone and screaming. . . ."

"Can you go on?"

"I. . . ."

"Yes?"

"I was so *alone*."

"I understand. Do you remember what happened then?"

"I was sent away to have my eyes cared for."

"And?"

"And . . . there were other things."

"Please explain."

"They told me later, much later, that I had been traumatized. I
was ill for a very long time, and would not eat or speak; I lived . . .
inside. I went through a lot of therapy, and there were a lot of
different doctors and hospitals. I was never sent home. I . . . remember screaming, lots of crying, and then, after a long, long time,
a kind of peace came over me . . ."

"Go on."

"I became calm. I told them it was all right, that I wanted to go
home. But they wouldn't listen to me. They wouldn't send me
home. I started to cry. I wanted to see my brother again, I wanted
to see Nancy, to tell her it was all right, that she didn't have to have
that look on her face anymore, that it wasn't her fault. But they
wouldn't send me home."

"And so?"

"I became hysterical again, and the therapy began again. For a
whole year I didn't speak. For another year I screamed. And then I
became calm again."

"I understand. Do you know how old you are now?"

"I'm twenty-two years old."

"Very good. And do you know why you are here?"

"Therapy."

"Of course. But it is time to tell you more."

"More? What do you mean?"

"There are things you must know now; I believe you can learn now what really happened."

"What don't I know?"

"Are you calm?"

"Yes."

"You will remain calm? You will not begin to scream, or draw into yourself?"

"No, I won't scream."

"Very good. Listen carefully. Your governess did not hurt you."

"What?"

"It is time to remember; you must remember; your governess did not push you into the corn. Your brother did."

"No!"

"Your brother tried to kill you. He killed your governess after he blinded you, and you saw her die in the cornpatch before you lost your sight. Do you remember this?"

"I . . . oh, God . . . I was told. . . ."

"Never mind what you were told. It is time to go back. You were told your governess was responsible for the accident because you could not handle what you saw. Your brother was taken away after the incident, and has spent his entire life in institutions. He is insane. He wanted to kill you that day out of jealousy for your attachment to your governess. He tried to kill you. Do you remember all of it now?"

"I . . . my God, yes. . . ."

"Tell it to me."

"Oh my God."

"Tell it to me."

"I can't. I won't. . . ."

"You must. Begin now, please."

"I—"

"Begin now."

"We . . . were roughhousing like I said, in that yellow field behind the house; it was cold . . . We were tumbling on the grass, moving closer to the corn field, and I remember that Nancy came out to tell us to stay away from the corn stalks. The day. . . ."

"Yes?"

"The day smelled a lot like this one. There was the same smell in the air."

"Go on."

"My brother ignored her, and tumbled me closer to the corn; he was a bit older than I was and much bigger. The governess came over to scold him, and he laughed and deliberately pushed me into the corn, and those stalks came into my eyes. . . ."

"Are you all right? Are you calm?"

". . . Yes."

"Good. Go on then."

"Nancy . . . ran over, and I felt her hands on my face, and she pulled them out of my eyes with that sucking sound. . . ."

"Yes?"

"I . . . remember clearing away the blood, and I saw my brother . . . push Nancy down into the cornpatch, and he . . . got on top of her, weighing her down. . . ."

"And then?"

"It's very difficult. . . ."

"You must, as I said."

"He . . . was on top of her. He grabbed a husk of dried corn and began to . . . stab her in the face, in the eyes, and she screamed and screamed and. . . ."

"You must go on."

"And the blood covered my eyes and I couldn't see any more, and I awoke in the hospital."

"Very good. Is that all?"

"Yes, that's . . . all. . . ."

"You are all right?"

"Yes. Yes, I'm all right."

"You are calm?"

"Yes."

"Good. It is good that you remember these things."

"I can't believe I didn't remember!"

"You must be calm. It was necessary. You are calm now?"

"Yes."

"Good. There is something I must tell you."

"What do you mean?"

"Your brother has escaped from the institution he was in. That is why you were brought here."

"I—"

"Listen. Are you calm?"

". . . Yes, I am calm."

"Good. Your brother will try to kill you. He wants to kill you. That is why you are here."

"I am safe?"

"That is why you are here. You will remain calm?"

"Yes."

"Good. There is something else I must tell you. Do you know where you are?"

"At another hospital, outside, on the grounds."

"That is not correct. Smell the air. Reach down and feel where you are. Do you know where you are?"

"I—"

"Yes, the corn. It is Autumn. Do you know who I am?"

"A doctor. Another doctor."

"I am your brother."

"Oh my G—"

An Incident on Route 12

By James H. Schmitz

Phil Garfield was thirty miles south of the little town of Redmon on Route Twelve when he was startled by a series of sharp, clanking noises. They came from under the Packard's hood.

The car immediately began to lose speed. Garfield jammed down the accelerator, had a sense of sick helplessness at the complete lack of response from the motor. The Packard rolled on, getting rid of its momentum, and came to a stop.

Phil Garfield swore shakily. He checked his watch, switched off the headlights and climbed out into the dark road. A delay of even half an hour here might be disastrous. It was past midnight, and he had another hundred and ten miles to cover to reach the small private airfield where Madge waited for him and the thirty thousand dollars in the suitcase on the Packard's front seat.

If he didn't make it before daylight. . . .

He thought of the bank guard. The man had made a clumsy play at being a hero, and that had set off the fool woman who'd run screaming into their line of fire. One dead. Perhaps two. Garfield hadn't stopped to look at an evening paper.

But he knew they were hunting for him.

He glanced up and down the road. No other headlights in sight at the moment, no light from a building showing on the forested hills. He reached back into the car and brought out the suitcase, his gun, a big flashlight and the box of shells which had been standing beside the suitcase. He broke the box open, shoved a handful of shells and the .38 into his coat pocket, then took suitcase and flashlight over to the shoulder of the road and set them down.

There was no point in groping about under the Packard's hood. When it came to mechanics, Phil Garfield was a moron and well aware of it. The car was useless to him now . . . except as bait.

But as bait it might be very useful.

Should he leave it standing where it was? No, Garfield decided. To anybody driving past it would merely suggest a necking party, or a drunk sleeping off his load before continuing home. He might have to wait an hour or more before someone decided to stop. He didn't have the time. He reached in through the window, hauled the top of the steering wheel towards him and put his weight against the rear window frame.

The Packard began to move slowly backwards at a slant across the road. In a minute or two he had it in position. Not blocking the road entirely, which would arouse immediate suspicion, but angled across it, lights out, empty, both front doors open and inviting a passerby's investigation.

Garfield carried the suitcase and flashlight across the right-hand shoulder of the road and moved up among the trees and undergrowth of the slope above the shoulder. Placing the suitcase between the bushes, he brought out the .38, clicked the safety off and stood waiting.

Some ten minutes later, a set of headlights appeared speeding up Route Twelve from the direction of Redmon. Phil Garfield went down on one knee before he came within range of the lights. Now he was completely concealed by the vegetation.

The car slowed as it approached, braking nearly to a stop sixty feet from the stalled Packard. There were several people inside it; Garfield heard voices, then a woman's loud laugh. The driver tapped his horn inquiringly twice, moved the car slowly forward. As the headlights went past him, Garfield got to his feet among the bushes, took a step down towards the road, raising the gun.

Then he caught the distant gleam of a second set of headlights approaching from Redmon. He swore under his breath and dropped back out of sight. The car below him reached the Packard, edged cautiously around it, rolled on with a sudden roar of acceleration.

The second car stopped when still a hundred yards away, the Packard caught in the motionless glare of its lights. Garfield heard the steady purring of a powerful motor.

For almost a minute, nothing else happened. Then the car came gliding smoothly on, stopped again no more than thirty feet to Garfield's left. He could see it now through the screening bushes— a big job, a long, low four-door sedan. The motor continued to purr. After a moment, a door on the far side of the car opened and slammed shut.

A man walked quickly out into the beam of the headlights and started towards the Packard.

Phil Garfield rose from his crouching position, the .38 in his right hand, flashlight in his left. If the driver was alone, the thing was now cinched! But if there was somebody else in the car, somebody capable of fast, decisive action, a slip in the next ten seconds might cost him the sedan, and quite probably his freedom and life. Garfield lined up the .38's sights steadily on the center of the approaching man's head. He let his breath out slowly as the fellow came level with him in the road and squeezed off one shot.

Instantly he went bounding down the slope to the road. The bullet had flung the man sideways to the pavement. Garfield darted past him to the left, crossed the beam of the headlights, and was in darkness again on the far side of the road, snapping on his flashlight as he sprinted up to the car.

The motor hummed quietly on. The flashlight showed the seats empty. Garfield dropped the light, jerked both doors open in turn, gun pointing into the car's interior. Then he stood still for a moment, weak and almost dizzy with relief.

There was no one inside. The sedan was his.

The man he had shot through the head lay face down on the road, his hat flung a dozen feet away from him. Route Twelve still stretched out in dark silence to east and west. There should be time enough to clean up the job before anyone else came along. Garfield brought the suitcase down and put it on the front seat of the sedan, then started back to get his victim off the road and out of sight. He scaled the man's hat into the bushes, bent down, grasped the ankles and started to haul him towards the left side of the road where the ground dropped off sharply beyond the shoulder.

The body made a high, squealing sound and began to writhe violently.

Shocked, Garfield dropped the legs and hurriedly took the gun from his pocket, moving back a step. The squealing noise rose in intensity as the wounded man quickly flopped over twice like a struggling fish, arms and legs sawing about with startling energy. Garfield clicked off the safety, pumped three shots into his victim's back.

The grisly squeals ended abruptly. The body continued to jerk for another second or two, then lay still.

Garfield shoved the gun back into his pocket. The unexpected interruption had unnerved him; his hands shook as he reached down again for the stranger's ankles. Then he jerked his hands back, and straightened up, staring.

From the side of the man's chest, a few inches below the right arm, something like a thick black stick, three feet long, protruded now through the material of the coat.

It shone, gleaming wetly, in the light from the car. Even in that first uncomprehending instant, something in its appearance brought a surge of sick disgust to Garfield's throat. Then the stick bent slowly halfway down its length, forming a sharp angle, and its tip opened into what could have been three blunt, black claws which scrabbled clumsily against the pavement. Very faintly, the squealing began again, and the body's back arched up as if another sticklike arm were pushing desperately against the ground beneath it.

Garfield acted in a blur of horror. He emptied the .38 into the thing at his feet almost without realizing he was doing it. Then, dropping the gun, he seized one of the ankles, ran backwards to the shoulder of the road, dragging the body behind him.

In the darkness at the edge of the shoulder, he let go of it, stepped around to the other side and with two frantically savage kicks sent the body plunging over the shoulder and down the steep slope beyond. He heard it crash through the bushes for some seconds, then stop. He turned, and ran back to the sedan, scooping up his gun as he went past. He scrambled into the driver's seat and slammed the door shut behind him.

His hands shook violently on the steering wheel as he pressed down the accelerator. The motor roared into life and the big car surged forward. He edged it past the Packard, cursing aloud in horrified shock, jammed down the accelerator and went flashing up Route Twelve, darkness racing beside and behind him.

What had it been? Something that wore what seemed to be a man's body like a suit of clothes, moving the body as a man moves, driving a man's car . . . roach-armed, roach-legged itself!

Garfield drew a long, shuddering breath. Then, as he slowed for a curve, there was a spark of reddish light in the rear-view mirror.

He stared at the spark for an instant, braked the car to a stop, rolled down the window and looked back.

Far behind him along Route Twelve, a fire burned. Approximately at the point where the Packard had stalled out, where something had gone rolling off the road into the bushes.

Something, Garfield added mentally, that found fiery automatic destruction when death came to it, so that its secrets would remain unrevealed.

But for him the fire meant the end of a nightmare. He rolled the window up, took out a cigarette, lit it, and pressed the accelerator. . . .

In incredulous fright, he felt the nose of the car tilt upwards, headlights sweeping up from the road into the trees. Then the headlights winked out. Beyond the windshield, dark tree branches floated down towards him, the night sky beyond. He reached frantically for the door handle.

A steel wrench clamped silently about each of his arms, drawing them in against his sides, immobilizing them there. Garfield gasped, looked up at the mirror and saw a pair of faintly gleaming red eyes watching him from the rear of the car. Two of the things . . . the second one stood behind him out of sight, holding him. They'd been in what had seemed to be the trunk compartment. And they had come out.

The eyes in the mirror vanished. A moist, black roach-arm reached over the back of the seat beside Garfield, picked up the cigarette he had dropped, extinguished it with rather horribly human motions, then took up Garfield's gun and drew back out of sight.

He expected a shot, but none came.

One doesn't fire a bullet through the suit one intends to wear. . . .

It wasn't until that thought occurred to him that tough Phil Garfield began to scream. He was still screaming minutes later when, beyond the windshield, the spaceship floated into view among the stars.

Interview

By Frank A. Javor

Looking at the woman, Lester V. Morrison felt deep inside himself the stirring of sympathy, familiar, rising to the sustained, heady rapport that made him know, with the certainty of long experience, that this was going to be another of his great interviews.

He smiled and loosened the fist he'd made unconsciously to emphasize the word "great" when it passed through his mind.

He felt a light touch on his arm and turning, bowed his head so that his lead technician could slip over it the video-audio headband. Its close-fitting temple pieces curved to touch the bone behind his ears and the twin stereo viewfinder cameras came down over his eyes.

Lester rather liked to make the subdued bowing movement, the symbolic humbling, it pleased him to think, of his six-and-almost-a-half-foot tallness to receive the crownlike headgear of his craft. A crown heavy, not with the scant two ounces of transmitting metal and optical plastic, but heavy with his responsibility to the billions upon billions of viewers who would see what Lester looked upon, would hear what he turned his ear to; the center of their universe for those moments the spot upon which Lester stood, the signal spreading outward from it like the ripple pattern of a dropped stone.

His technician pressed Lester's arm twice and stepped back. Lester stood erect, his hands and fingers hovering over the twin-arced rows of buttons and rods set in the flat surface of the control console he wore high on his chest like an ancient breastplate. There was no speaking between Lester and his four-man crew, nor any testing of equipment. Lester wore his responsibility with what he considered a suitable humility, but with a firm confidence. Let lesser men fiddle with their equipment, talk, blur the virgin spontaneity of the look that would flash into the woman's eyes with the first impact of Lester's equipment upon her. His men, like Lester, were the absolute best in their field; razor-honed by long close union and good pay until they responded almost symbiotically to Lester and each other.

A clear warning warble from his left earphone, heard only by Lester through the bones of his skull, readied him to begin his task. He stood firmly tall, silent, waiting . . .

A musical bleat. The suddenly glowing red face of the timer in the upper corner of his left viewfinder. He was on the air.

The general view first. Eight seconds to set the scene, to let his viewers see for themselves the sordid slum he was standing in. To see the aged, crumbling buildings, some of them as much as twelve and even fourteen years old, engineered to have been torn down and replaced long ago. Long before a tragedy of this kind could strike. To form their own opinion of a council that could allow such a blight to exist on their planet.

Smoothly Lester pivoted his body, one shoulder leading, a counterbalance for the slightly trailing head, editorializing subtly by what he chose to look at, by what he chose to ignore. Flowingly, easily, compensating automatically for even the rise and fall of his own controlled breathing. A beautifully functioning, rock-steady camera vehicle Lester was. It was the least of his interviewing skills.

A closer shot. His thumb brushed a rod on his breastplate. The view in his finders grew larger. Armor-suited men, resting now, but still strapped in the seats of their half-track diggers. Orange-painted against the greening dust and the bright red glow of the police-erected crowd-control barrier force field like a sheltering dome over them. Through it, visible above and around in all directions, a swirling, shifting mass upon mass of human beings. Some in fliers, others on skimmers. Some strapped in one-man jumpers and even on foot. A boiling, roiling swarm of the morbidly, humanly curious pressing all around, straining toward the little knot of blue-coverall-clad men and their pitifully small, broken burden.

Lester's fingers and palms brushed the rods and buttons of his breastplate-console. Let the rattle and the clank and the sound of the crowd stay as they are. A shade more of the force field's rasping hum to warm his viewer's nerve endings . . . to ready them . . .

The woman's sobbing. His thumb touched a stud. Let it start to come through now. Softly . . . barely hearable . . . subtly swelling.

The little knot of blue-coverall-clad men. A medium shot, then rapidly to a close-up of their burden, the dangling limbs half-hidden by their bodies and the merciful sagging of the blue-green plasti-sheet. A tight shot, but passing . . . the merest flicker. Nothing staring, nothing lingering, nothing in bad taste.

In Lester's right ear was the sound of his own voice, recorded on his way to the scene and before he came upon it so that he would not need to break his silence until his selected moment. His voice giving the boy's age, his group-affiliations, the routine details of his death. All quietly, all monotonously even, the greater to contrast with what was the meat of Lester's program.

Nineteen seconds. The sobbing louder now and growing. The mother, kneeling, body sagged, hands clenched, dark head bowed.

Lester put a hand on her shoulder, letting it show in his finders, knowing that each of his viewers could see it as his own, extended, sympathetic, understanding . . .

The woman did not respond to his touch. Unobtrusively Lester increased the pressure of his thumb, gouging. She stirred under his hand, shrinking, her head lifting.

Lester's hand darted back to his console.

Her eyes. Dark, dulled, beseeching. *Fine*.

And now Lester spoke. He spoke with practiced hesitance, the gentle respecter, for his viewer, of her desire and right to her privacy at a time like this.

"How do you feel to have lost your only child?" His hands hovering, the woman looking at him . . . *now*.

Her eyes widened, flickeringly. Sorrow surging and pain, deep and of the soul, opened to the finder. Raw, fresh.

Great. I'm right never to test, never to speak until this moment.

"Please try to control yourself. I'm your friend, we're all your friends. Tell us." And he repeated his question.

Her head bent sharply back, the eyes half closing now, her mouth open, the lips trembling, the intensity of her emotion visibly choking the sound in her throat, making of her attempt to speak a silent mouthing.

Easy . . . easy does it.

Her hands came up. Fists, pressing against each other and under her chin. "My baby, my baby," and her voice was a moan.

Lester needed only the one hand, his left. The other he stretched toward the woman, touching her hair, his fingertips only, gently, benevolently, seeing it in his finder, looking deep into her upturned face.

In the corner of Lester's finder the sweep second hand began to wipe the red glow from the timer's face. When it came around to the twelve, except for the sponsor break and his verbal sign-off, he would be off the air.

Sobs began to rock the kneeling woman. Lightly at first a mere staccato catching of the breath, but growing. Growing in a crescendo of violence that, peaking, made of her body a heaving, thrashing, straining animal thing.

Great racking, convulsive sounds rasped from her throat. A thread-thin trickle of blood started from one corner of her tortured mouth.

Enough.

Her head dropped, her whole body now bowed and shaking.

Lester watched his hand go out to her, stop in midair. He did not try to hide its trembling. His fingers closed, his hand came back, not having touched her. Leaving her, huddled, tremulous, to herself and her great sorrow.

Slow fade and . . . go to black.

Ninety seconds. Exactly and on the dot and another of his human-interest segments for the intergalactic network was over; another moment in the life story of a little person had been made immortal.

Lester eased his headgear off, handed it to the waiting technician, stood rubbing the spots where the temple pieces had pressed. The woman had stopped trembling now and was looking dazed, uncomprehending. *They always do, the subjects.*

Swiftly, but not too roughly, Lester raised up her limp left arm, undid the cuff and stripped off the tiny receptor taped to the wrist. Another he took from her ankle and two more from the back of her skull, from under the concealing black hair. He could have left to one of his technicians this stripping off of the tiny receptors, that, obedient to the commands of his console, sent their impulses impinging upon the nerve streams of his subjects. But Lester felt that doing it himself, this body contact with his subjects, was just one more tiny factor that helped keep fresh his unmistakable feeling of rapport.

His lead technician touched his shoulder from behind, indicating they were about ready for his verbal signature and the one part of his program Lester found distasteful. A compliance with a regulation he felt was onerous and a little demeaning. Someday those who made these artistically pointless rulings would recognize the validity of his technique and perhaps eliminate this abhorrent note. Until then . . .

Lester leaned forward and spoke into the button mike his technician was holding out to him.

And at the end, ". . . The emotional response of the subject was technically augmented."

The Jam

By Henry Slesar

They left Stukey's pad around eight in the morning; that was the kind of weekend it had been. Early to bed, early to rise. Stukey laughed, squinting through the dirt-stained windshield of the battered Ford, pushing the pedal until the needle swung 20, 30 miles over the speed limit. It was all Mitch's fault, but Mitch, curled up on the seat beside him like an embryo in a black leather womb, didn't seem to care. He was hurting too much, needing the quick jab of the sharp sweet point and the hot flow of the stuff in his veins. Man, what a weekend, Stukey thought, and it wasn't over yet. The fix was out there, someplace in the wilds of New Jersey, and Stukey, who never touched the filthy stuff himself, was playing good Samaritan. He hunched over the wheel like Indianapolis, pounding the horn with the heel of his right hand, shouting at the passing cars to *move over, move over you sonofabitch, watch where you're going, stupid, pull over, pull over, you lousy* . . .

"You tell 'em, man," Mitch said softly, "you tell 'em what to do."

Stukey didn't tell them, he showed them. He skinned the paint off a Buick as he snaked in and out of the line, and crowded so close to the tail of an MG that he could have run right over the little red wagon. Mitch began to giggle, urging him on, forgetting for the moment his destination and his need, delighting in the way Stukey used the car like a buzz saw, slicing a path through the squares in their Sunday driving stupor. "Look out, man," Mitch cackled, "here comes old Stukey, here comes nothin'."

The traffic artery was starting to clot at the entrance to the tunnel, and Stukey poured it on, jockeying the car first left and then right, grinning at the competitive game. Nobody had a chance to win with Stukey at the controls; Stukey could just shut his eyes and gun her; nobody else could do that. They made the tunnel entrance after sideswiping a big yellow Caddy, an episode that made Mitch laugh aloud with glee. They both felt better after that, and the tunnel was cool after the hot morning sun. Stukey relaxed a little, and Mitch stopped his low-pitched giggling, content to stare hypnotically at the blur of white tiles.

"I hope we find that fix, man," Mitch said dreamily. "My cousin, he says that's the place to go. How long you think, Stukey? How long?"

Whish! A Chevy blasted by him on the other lane, and Stukey swore. *Whish!* went an Oldsmobile, and Stukey bore down on the accelerator, wanting his revenge on the open road outside the tunnel. But the tunnel wound on, endlessly, longer than it ever had before. It was getting hot and hard to breathe; little pimples of sweat covered his face and trickled down into his leather collar; under the brass-studded coat, the sport shirt clung damply to his back and underarms. Mitch started to whine, and got that wide-eyed fishmouth look of his, and he gasped: "Man, I'm suffocating. I'm passing out . . ."

"What do you want me to do?" Stukey yelled. Still the tunnel wound on. *Whish!* went the cars in the parallel lane, and Stukey cursed his bad choice, cursed the heat, cursed Mitch, cursed all the Sundays that ever were. He shot a look at the balcony where the cops patrolled the traffic, and decided to take a chance. He slowed the car down to 35, and yanked the wheel sharply to the right to slip the car into a faster lane, right in front of a big, children-filled station wagon. Even in the tunnel roar they could hear its driver's angry shout, and Stukey told him what he could do with his station wagon and his children. Still the tunnel wound on.

They saw the hot glare of daylight at the exit. Mitch moaned in relief, but nothing could soften Stukey's ire. They came out of the tunnel and turned onto the highway, only to jerk to a halt behind a station wagon with a smelly exhaust. "Come on, come on!" Stukey muttered, and blew his horn. But the horn didn't start the cars moving, and Stukey, swearing, opened the door and had himself a look.

"Oh, man, man, they're stacked up for miles!" he groaned. "You wouldn't believe it, you wouldn't think it's possible . . ."

"What is it?" Mitch said, stirring in his seat. "What is it? An accident?"

"I dunno, I can't see a thing. But they just ain't movin', not a foot——"

"I'm sick," Mitch groaned. "I'm sick, Stukey."

"Shut up! Shut up!" Stukey said, hopping out of the car to stare at the sight again, at the ribbon of automobiles vanishing into a horizon 10, 15 miles away. Like one enormous reptile it curled over the highway, a snake with multicolored skin, lying asleep under the hot sun. He climbed back in again, and the station wagon moved an inch, a foot, and greedily, he stomped the gas pedal to gobble up the gap. A trooper on a motorcycle bounced between the lanes, and Stukey leaned out of the window to shout at him, inquiring; he rumbled on implacably. The heat got worse, furnace-like and scorching, making him yelp when his hands touched metal. Savagely, Stukey hit the horn again, and heard a dim chorus ahead. Every few minutes, the station wagon jumped, and every few minutes, Stukey closed the gap. But an hour accumulated, and more, and they could still see the tunnel exit behind them. Mitch was whimpering now, and Stukey climbed in and out of the car like a madman, his clothes sopping with sweat, his eyes wild, cursing whenever he hit the gas pedal and crawled another inch, another foot forward . . .

"A cop! A cop!" he heard Mitch scream as a trooper, on foot, marched past the window. Stukey opened the car door and caught the uniformed arm. "Help us, will ya?" he pleaded. "What the hell's going on here? How do we get outa this?"

"You don't," the trooper said curtly. "You can't get off anyplace. Just stick it out, mac."

"We'll even leave the goddamn *car*. We'll *walk,* for God's sake. I don't care about the goddamn *car* . . ."

"Sorry, mister. Nobody's allowed off the highway, even on foot. You can't leave this heap here, don't you know that?" He studied Stukey's sweaty face, and grinned suddenly. "Oh, I get it. You're new here, ain't you?"

"What do you mean, new?"

"I thought I never saw you in the Jam before, pal. Well, take it easy, fella."

"How long?" Stukey said hoarsely. "How long you think?"

"That's a stupid question," the trooper sneered. "Forever, of course. Eternity. Where the hell do you think you are?" He jabbed a finger into Stukey's chest. "But don't give *me* a hard time, buster. That was your *own* wreck back there."

"Wreck?" Mitch rasped from inside the car. "What wreck? What's he talkin' about, man?"

"The wreck you had in the tunnel." He waved his gloved hand toward the horizon. "That's where *all* these jokers come from, the tunnel wrecks. If you think this is bad, you ought to see the Jam on the turnpike."

"Wreck? Wreck?" Mitch screamed, as Stukey climbed behind the wheel. "What's he talking about wrecks for, Stukey?"

"Shut up, shut up!" Stukey sobbed, pounding his foot on the gas pedal to gain yet another inch of road. "We gotta get outa here, we gotta get out!" But even when the station wagon jerked forward once more, he knew he was asking for too much, too late.

The Kirk Spook

By E. G. Swain

Before many years have passed it will be hard to find a person who has ever seen a parish clerk. The parish clerk is all but extinct. Our grandfathers knew him well—an oldish, clean-shaven man, who looked as if he had never been young, who dressed in rusty black, bestowed upon him, as often as not, by the rector, and who usually wore a white tie on Sundays, out of respect for the seriousness of his office. He it was who laid out the rector's robes, and helped him to put them on; who found the places in the large Bible and Prayer Book, and indicated them by means of decorous silken book-markers; who lighted and snuffed the candles in the pulpit and desk, and attended to the little stove in the squire's pew; who ran busily about, in short, during the quarter-hour which preceded Divine Service, doing a hundred little things, with all the activity, and much of the appearance, of a beetle.

Just such a one was Caleb Dean, who was clerk of Stoneground in the days of William IV. Small in stature, he possessed a voice which Nature seemed to have meant for a giant, and in the discharge of his duties he had a dignity of manner disproportionate even to his voice. No one was afraid to sing when he led the Psalm, so certain was it that no other voice could be noticed, and the gracious condescension with which he received his meagre fees would have been ample acknowledgement of double their amount.

Man, however, cannot live by dignity alone, and Caleb was glad enough to be sexton as well as clerk, and to undertake any other duties by which he might add to his modest income. He kept the churchyard tidy, trimmed the lamps, chimed the bells, taught the choir their simple tunes, turned the barrel of the organ, and managed the stoves.

It was this last duty in particular, which took him into church 'last thing', as he used to call it, on Saturday night. There were

286

people in those days, and may be some in these, whom nothing would induce to enter a church at midnight; Caleb, however, was so much at home there that all hours were alike to him. He was never an early man on Saturdays. His wife, who insisted upon sitting up for him, would often knit her way into Sunday before he appeared, and even then would find it hard to get him to bed. Caleb, in fact, when off duty, was a genial little fellow; he had many friends, and on Saturday evenings he knew where to find them.

It was not, therefore, until the evening was spent that he went to make up his fires; and his voice, which served for other singing than that of Psalms, could usually be heard, within a little of midnight, beguiling the way to church with snatches of convivial songs. Many a belated traveller, homeward bound, would envy him his spirits, but no one envied him his duties. Even such as walked with him to the neighbourhood of the churchyard would bid him 'Goodnight' whilst still a long way from the gate. They would see him disappear into the gloom amongst the graves, and shudder as they turned homewards.

Caleb, meanwhile, was perfectly content. He knew every stone in the path; long practice enabled him, even on the darkest night, to thrust his huge key into the lock at the first attempt, and on the night we are about to describe—it had come to Mr Batchel from an old man who heard it from Caleb's lips—he did it with a feeling of unusual cheerfulness and contentment.

Caleb always locked himself in. A prank had once been played upon him, which had greatly wounded his dignity; and though it had been no midnight prank, he had taken care, ever since, to have the church to himself. He locked the door, therefore, as usual, on the night we speak of, and made his way to the stove. He used no candle. He opened the little iron door of the stove, and obtained sufficient light to show him the fuel he had laid in readiness; then, when he had made up his fire, he closed this door again, and left the church in darkness. He never could say what induced him upon this occasion to remain there after his task was done. He knew that his wife was sitting up, as usual, and that, as usual, he would have to hear what she had to say. Yet, instead of making his way home, he sat down in the corner of the nearest seat. He supposed that he must have felt tired, but had no distinct recollection of it.

The church was not absolutely dark. Caleb remembered that he could make out the outlines of the windows, and that through the window nearest to him he saw a few stars. After his eyes had grown accustomed to the gloom he could see the lines of the seats taking shape in the darkness, and he had not long sat there before he could dimly see everything there was. At last he began to distinguish where books lay upon the shelf in front of him. And then he closed his eyes. He does not admit having fallen asleep, even for a moment. But the seat was restful, the neighbouring stove was growing warm, he had been through a long and joyous evening, and it was natural that he should at least close his eyes.

He insisted that it was only for a moment. Something, he could not say what, caused him to open his eyes again immediately. The closing of them seemed to have improved what may be called his dark sight. He saw everything in the church quite distinctly, in a sort of grey light. The pulpit stood out, large and bulky, in front. Beyond that, he passed his eyes along the four windows on the north side of the church. He looked again at the stars, still visible through the nearest window on his left hand as he was sitting. From that, his eyes fell to the further end of the seat in front of him, where he could even see a faint gleam of polished wood. He traced this gleam to the middle of the seat, until it disappeared in black shadow, and upon that his eye passed on to the seat he was in, and there he saw a man sitting beside him.

Caleb described the man very clearly. He was, he said, a pale, old-fashioned looking man, with something very churchy about him. Reasoning also with great clearness, he said that the stranger had not come into the church either with him or after him, and that therefore he must have been there before him. And in that case, seeing that the church had been locked since two in the afternoon, the stranger must have been there for a considerable time.

Caleb was puzzled; turning therefore, to the stranger, he asked 'How long have you been here?'

The stranger answered at once 'Six hundred years.'

'Oh! come!' said Caleb.

'Come where?' said the stranger.

'Well, if you come to that, come out,' said Caleb.

'I wish I could,' said the stranger, and heaved a great sigh.

'What's to prevent you?' said Caleb. 'There's the door, and here's the key.'

'That's it,' said the other.

'Of course it is,' said Caleb. 'Come along.'

With that he proceeded to take the stranger by the sleeve, and then it was that he says you might have knocked him down with a feather. His hand went right into the place where the sleeve seemed to be, and Caleb distinctly saw two of the stranger's buttons on the top of his own knuckles.

288

He hastily withdrew his hand, which began to feel icy cold, and sat still, not knowing what to say next. He found that the stranger was gently chuckling with laughter, and this annoyed him.

'What are you laughing at?' he enquired peevishly.

'It's not funny enough for two,' answered the other.

'Who are you, anyhow?' said Caleb.

'I am the kirk spook,' was the reply.

Now Caleb had not the least notion what a 'kirk spook' was. He was not willing to admit his ignorance, but his curiosity was too much for his pride, and he asked for information.

'Every church has a spook,' said the stranger, 'and I am the spook of this one.'

'Oh,' said Caleb, 'I've been about this church a many years, but I've never seen you before.'

'That,' said the spook, 'is because you've always been moving about. I'm flimsy—very flimsy indeed—and I can only keep myself together when everything is quite still.'

'Well,' said Caleb, 'you've got your chance now. What are you going to do with it?'

'I want to go out,' said the spook, 'I'm tired of this church, and I've been alone for six hundred years. It's a long time.'

'It does seem rather a long time,' said Caleb, 'but why don't you go if you want to? There's three doors.'

'That's just it,' said the spook, 'They keep me in.'

'What?' said Caleb, 'when they're open.'

'Open or shut,' said the spook, 'it's all one.'

'Well, then,' said Caleb, 'what about the windows?'

'Every bit as bad,' said the spook, 'They're all pointed.'

Caleb felt out of his depth. Open doors and windows that kept a person in—if it was a person—seemed to want a little understanding. And the flimsier the person, too, the easier it ought to be for him to go where he wanted. Also, what could it matter whether they were pointed to not?

The latter question was the one which Caleb asked first.

'Six hundred years ago,' said the Spook, 'all arches were made round, and when these pointed things came in I cursed them. I hate new-fangled things.'

'That wouldn't hurt them much,' said Caleb.

'I said I would never go under one of them,' said the spook.

'That would matter more to you than to them,' said Caleb.

'It does,' said the spook, with another great sigh.

'But you could easily change your mind,' said Caleb.

'I was tied to it,' said the spook, 'I was told that I never more should go under one of them, whether I would or not.'

'Some people will tell you anything,' answered Caleb.

'It was a Bishop,' explained the spook.

'Ah!' said Caleb, 'that's different, of course.'

The spook told Caleb how often he had tried to go under the pointed arches, sometimes of the doors, sometimes of the windows, and how a stream of wind always struck him from the point of the arch, and drifted him back into the church. He had long given up trying.

'You should have been outside,' said Caleb, 'before they built the last door.'

'It was my church,' said the spook, 'and I was too proud to leave.'

Caleb began to sympathize with the spook. He had a pride in the church himself, and disliked even to hear another person say Amen before him. He also began to be a little jealous of this stranger who had been six hundred years in possession of the church in which Caleb had believed himself, under the vicar, to be master. And he began to plot.

'Why do you want to get out?' he asked.

'I'm no use here,' was the reply, 'I don't get enough to do to keep myself warm. And I know there are scores of churches now without any kirk-spooks at all. I can hear their cheap little bells dinging every Sunday.'

'There's very few bells hereabouts,' said Caleb.

'There's no hereabouts for spooks,' said the other. 'We can hear any distance you like.'

'But what good are you at all?' said Caleb.

'Good!' said the spook. 'Don't we secure proper respect for churches, especially after dark? A church would be like any other place if it wasn't for us. You must know that.'

'Well, then,' said Caleb, 'you're no good here. This church is all right. What will you give me to let you out?'

'Can you do it?' asked the spook.

'What will you give me?' said Caleb.

'I'll say a good word for you amongst the spooks,' said the other.

'What good will that do me?' said Caleb.

'A good word never did anybody any harm yet,' answered the spook.

'Very well then, come along,' said Caleb.

'Gently then,' said the spook; 'don't make a draught.'

'Not yet,' said Caleb, and he drew the spook very carefully (as one takes a vessel quite full of water) from the seat.

'I can't go under pointed arches,' cried the spook, as Caleb moved off.

'Nobody wants you to,' said Caleb. 'Keep close to me.'

He led the spook down the aisle to the angle of the wall where a small iron shutter covered an opening into the flue. It was used by the chimney sweep alone, but Caleb had another use for it now. Calling to the spook to keep close, he suddenly removed the shutter.

The fires were by this time burning briskly. There was a strong up-draught as the shutter was removed. Caleb felt something rush across his face, and heard a cheerful laugh away up in the chimney. Then he knew that he was alone. He replaced the shutter, gave another look at his stoves, took the keys, and made his way home.

He found his wife asleep in her chair, sat down and took off his boots, and awakened her by throwing them across the kitchen.

'I've been wondering when you'd wake,' he said.

'What?' she said, 'Have you been in long?'

'Look at the clock,' said Caleb. 'Half after twelve.'

'My gracious,' said his wife. 'Let's be off to bed.'

'Did you tell her about the spook?' he was naturally asked.

'Not I,' said Caleb. 'You knew what she'd say. Same as she always does of a Saturday night.'

This fable Mr Batchel related with reluctance. His attitude towards it was wholly deprecatory. Psychic phenomena, he said, lay outside the province of the mere humourist, and the levity with which they had been treated was largely responsible for the presumptuous materialism of the age.

He said more, as he warmed to the subject, than can here be repeated. The reader of the foregoing tales, however, will be interested to know that Mr Batchel's own attitude was one of humble curiosity. He refused even to guess why the *revenant* was sometimes invisible, and at other times partly or wholly visible; sometimes capable of using physical force, and at other times powerless. He knew that they had their periods, and that was all.

There is room, he said, for the romancer in these matters; but for the humourist, none. Romance was the play of intelligence about the confines of truth. The invisible world, like the visible, must have its romancers, its explorers, and its interpreters; but the time of the last was not yet come.

Criticism, he observed in conclusion, was wholesome and necessary. But of the idle and mischievous remarks which were wont to pose as criticism, he held none in so much contempt as the cheap and irrational POOH-POOH.

Making Friends

By Gary Raisor

Jack-o'-lanterns smile their secretive, broken-mouthed smiles as they peer out from behind darkened windows. Eight-year-old Denny Grayson hurries down the sidewalk. He is barely able to contain his excitement. Tonight is Halloween.

A hint of chill hangs in the air and the tang of woodsmoke carries. It's a good smell. The huge yellow moon tags along, floating over his shoulder like a balloon on a string. When he glances up, he sees the man in the moon smiling broadly. Beneath his green latex Frankenstein mask, he smiles back eagerly. He has waited with much anticipation for this night.

A small group of kids pelt by, anonymous in their costumes. Only the patter of their expensive new *Adidas* and *NIKES* link them to an exclusive club; one to which Denny will never belong. He watches enviously as they pound on the door. "Trick or treat," they demand in high, childish voices. He turns and scurries to the next house.

A quick stab of the doorbell brings a smiling, silver-haired woman to the door. "My, aren't you scary looking?" she laughs merrily. "Are you going to say trick or treat? What's the matter, cat got your tongue?"

Denny shakes his head and asks, "Ccould I hhaff a ddink of wwatah, ppleese?" Her smile wavers and she blushes as understanding comes. "Oh, I'm so sorry. Of course you can."

When she goes to the kitchen, Denny reaches into the candy dish sitting so invitingly by the door. He barely retracts his hand before the woman returns with a glass of water. Turning his back, he lifts the mask and takes a short sip. "Ttankk yyoou," he mumbles thickly, holding out his plastic sack. The woman drops in extra candy. After every house on the block has been visited, he climbs on his bike and heads for home, racing the moon from streetlight to streetlight watching the shadows wheel and dart before him.

Pedaling furiously, he soon reaches the section of town where the houses aren't so nice. He weaves the familiar route up the rutted street until the small, rundown house comes into view.

Quietly letting himself in, he tiptoes past his mom who is fast asleep on the couch. As usual, the reek of soured whiskey follows him across the creaky floor.

He barely has time to stuff the mask and candy under the bed before he hears Mom's heavy tread. She enters the room and drunkenly embraces him. "Oh, Denny, I'm so glad you're home. Momma just had the most awful dream. It was full of blood, and children were screaming and screaming . . ."

Denny pulls away from her and throws himself onto the rickety bed. She stares at him in helpless misery. "I dreamed you went trick or treating again," she blubbers wetly, and Denny knows she's going to talk about *it*. "I'm so sorry, baby. I know I let you down. If only I'd checked the candy. Who'd have ever thought someone would be sick enough to put razor blades in a child's—"

Denny turns to the wall and stonily ignores her. Stiffly, she reaches a fluttering moist palm toward him that stops short. "I know the kids at school make fun of your problem. But I talked to Dr. Palmer again yesterday, and he says he might be able to help."

"Hhee ccan'tt hhellp."

The silence becomes a thick wall between them. For the first time, she notices he is wearing a jacket. Alarm sifts through the alcoholic haze to finally settle on her face. "Where were you tonight, Denny? You didn't go trick or treating, did you?" She yanks him around, trying hard not to wince as the horribly disfigured mouth smiles crookedly at her.

"Nnoo, I wass mmakin' ssome neww ffriendss," he utters cheerfully, jumping from the bed and crossing over to the window. He jams both hands into his jacket pockets. His fingers touch a small lump nestled within—it's a candy bar. For a second, he'd almost forgotten he'd placed one in the candy dishes of all the homes he visited tonight.

As he thinks about the kids who make fun of the way he talks, his fingers curl tightly. A sharp flash of pain causes his hand to fill with sticky red wetness. After tonight, he'll have lots of friends to talk to. He stares into the night and smiles a terrible, secret smile. The man in the moon is smiling too; only, this time, a river of blood is gushing from his mouth.

The Marble Hands

By Bernard Capes

We left our bicycles by the little lych-gate and entered the old churchyard. Heriot had told me frankly that he did not want to come; but at the last moment, sentiment or curiosity prevailing with him, he had changed his mind. I knew indefinitely that there was something disagreeable to him in the place's associations, though he had always referred with affection to the relative with whom he had stayed here as a boy. Perhaps she lay under one of these greening stones.

We walked round the church, with its squat, shingled spire. It was utterly peaceful, here on the brow of the little town where the flowering fields began. The bones of the hill were the bones of the dead, and its flesh was grass. Suddenly Heriot stopped me. We were standing then to the northwest of the chancel, and a gloom of motionless trees overshadowed us.

'I wish you'd just look in there a moment,' he said, 'and come back and tell me what you see.'

He was pointing towards a little bay made by the low boundary wall, the green floor of which was hidden from our view by the thick branches and a couple of interposing tombs, huge, coffer-shaped, and shut within rails. His voice sounded odd; there was a 'plunging' look in his eyes, to use a gambler's phrase. I stared at him a moment, followed the direction of his hand; then, without a word, stooped under the heavy, brushing boughs, passed round the great tombs, and came upon a solitary grave.

It lay there quite alone in the hidden bay—a strange thing, fantastic and gruesome. There was no headstone, but a bevelled marble curb, without name or epitaph, enclosed a gravelled space from which projected two hands. They were of white marble, very faintly touched with green, and conveyed in that still, lonely spot a most curious sense of reality, as if actually thrust up, deathly and alluring, from the grave beneath. The impression grew upon me as I looked, until I could have thought they moved stealthily, consciously, turning in the soil as if to greet me. It was absurd, but—I turned and went rather hastily back to Heriot.

'All right. I see they are there still,' he said; and that was all. Without another word we left the place and, remounting, continued our way.

Miles from the spot, lying on a sunny downside, with the sheep about us in hundreds cropping the hot grass, he told me the story:

'She and her husband were living in the town at the time of my first visit there, when I was a child of seven. They were known to Aunt Caddie, who disliked the woman. I did not dislike her at all, because, when we met, she made a favourite of me. She was a little pretty thing, frivolous and shallow; but truly, I know now, with an abominable side to her. She was inordinately vain of her hands; and indeed they were the loveliest things, softer and shapelier than a child's. She used to have them photographed, in fifty different positions; and once they were exquisitely done in marble by a sculptor, a friend of hers. Yes, those were the ones you saw. But they were cruel little hands, for all their beauty. There was something wicked and unclean about the way in which she regarded them.

'She died while I was there, and she was commemorated by her own explicit desire after the fashion you saw. The marble hands were to be her sole epitaph, more eloquent than letters. They should preserve her name and the tradition of her most exquisite feature to remoter ages than any crumbling inscription could reach. And so it was done.

'That fancy was not popular with the parishioners, but it gave me no childish qualms. The hands were really beautifully modelled on the originals, and the originals had often caressed me. I was never afraid to go and look at them, sprouting like white celery from the ground.

'I left, and two years later was visiting Aunt Caddie a second time. In the course of conversation I learned that the husband of the woman had married again—a lady belonging to the place—and that the hands, only quite recently, had been removed. The new wife had objected to them—for some reason perhaps not difficult to understand—and they had been uprooted by the husband's order.

'I think I was a little sorry—the hands had always seemed somehow personal to me—and, on the first occasion that offered, I slipped away by myself to see how the grave looked without them. It was a close, lowering day, I remember, and the churchyard was very still. Directly, stooping under the branches, I saw the spot, I understood that Aunt Caddie had spoken prematurely. The hands had not been removed so far, but were extended in their old place and attitude, looking as if held out to welcome me. I was glad; and I ran and knelt, and put my own hands down to touch them. They were soft and cold like dead meat, and they closed caressingly about mine, as if inviting me to pull—to pull.

'I don't know what happened afterwards. Perhaps I had been sickening all the time for the fever which overtook me. There was a period of horror, and blankness—of crawling, worm-threaded immurements and heaving bones—and then at last the blessed daylight.'

Heriot stopped, and sat plucking at the crisp pasture.

'I never learned,' he said suddenly, 'what other experiences synchronized with mine. But the place somehow got an uncanny reputation, and the marble hands were put back. Imagination, to be sure, can play strange tricks with one.'

Mariana

By Fritz Leiber

Mariana had been living in the big villa and hating the tall pine trees around it for what seemed like an eternity when she found the secret panel in the master control panel of the house.

The secret panel was simply a narrow blank of aluminum—she'd thought of it as room for more switches if they ever needed any, perish the thought!—between the air-conditioning controls and the gravity controls. Above the switches for the three-dimensional TV but below those for the robot butler and maids.

Jonathan had told her not to fool with the master control panel while he was in the city, because she would wreck anything electrical, so when the secret panel came loose under her aimlessly questing fingers and fell to the solid rock floor of the patio with a musical *twing* her first reaction was fear.

Then she saw it was only a small blank oblong of sheet aluminum that had fallen and that in the space it had covered was a column of six little switches. Only the top one was identified. Tiny glowing letters beside it spelled TREES and it was on.

When Jonathan got home from the city that evening she gathered her courage and told him about it. He was neither particularly angry nor impressed.

296

"Of course there's a switch for the trees," he informed her deflatingly, motioning the robot butler to cut his steak. "Didn't you know they were radio trees? I didn't want to wait twenty-five years for them and they couldn't grow in this rock anyway. A station in the city broadcasts a master pine tree and sets like ours pick it up and project it around homes. It's vulgar but convenient."

After a bit she asked timidly, "Jonathan, are the radio pine trees ghostly as you drive through them?"

"Of course not! They're solid as this house and the rock under it —to the eye and to the touch too. A person could even climb them. If you ever stirred outside you'd know these things. The city station transmits pulses of alternating matter at sixty cycles a second. The science of it is over your head."

She ventured one more question: "Why did they have the tree switch covered up?"

"So you wouldn't monkey with it—same as the fine controls on the TV. And so you wouldn't get ideas and start changing the trees. It would unsettle *me,* let me tell you, to come home to oaks one day and birches the next. I like consistency and I like pines." He looked at them out of the dining-room picture window and grunted with satisfaction.

She had been meaning to tell him about hating the pines, but that discouraged her and she dropped the topic.

About noon the next day, however, she went to the secret panel and switched off the pine trees and quickly turned around to watch them.

At first nothing happened and she was beginning to think that Jonathan was wrong again, as he so often was though would never admit, but then they began to waver and specks of pale green light churned across them and then they faded and were gone, leaving behind only an intolerably bright single point of light—just as when the TV is switched off. The star hovered motionless for what seemed a long time, then backed away and raced off toward the horizon.

Now that the pine trees were out of the way Mariana could see the real landscape. It was flat grey rock, endless miles of it, exactly the same as the rock on which the house was set and which formed the floor of the patio. It was the same in every direction. One black two-lane road drove straight across it—nothing more.

She disliked the view almost at once—it was dreadfully lonely and depressing. She switched the gravity to moon-normal and danced about dreamily, floating over the middle-of-the-room bookshelves and the grand piano and even having the robot maids dance with her, but it did not cheer her. About two o'clock she went to switch on the pine trees again, as she had intended to do in any case before Jonathan came home and was furious.

However, she found there had been changes in the column of six little switches. The TREES switch no longer had its glowing name. She remembered that it had been the top one, but the top one would not turn on again. She tried to force it from "off" to "on" but it would not move.

All the rest of the afternoon she sat on the steps outside the front door watching the black two-lane road. Never a car or a person came into view until Jonathan's tan roadster appeared, seeming at first to hang motionless in the distance and then to move only like a microscopic snail although she knew he always drove at top speed —it was one of the reasons she would never get in the car with him.

Jonathan was not as furious as she had feared. "Your own damn fault for meddling with it," he said curtly. "Now we'll have to get a man out here. Dammit, I hate to eat supper looking at nothing but those rocks! Bad enough driving through them twice a day."

She asked him haltingly about the barrenness of the landscape and the absence of neighbors.

"Well, you wanted to live *way out*," he told her. "You wouldn't ever have known about it if you hadn't turned off the trees."

"There's one other thing I've got to bother you with, Jonathan," she said. "Now the second switch—the one next below—has got a name that glows. It just says HOUSE. It's turned on—I haven't touched it! Do you suppose . . ."

"I want to look at this," he said, bounding up from the couch and slamming his martini-on-the-rocks tumbler down on the tray of the robot maid so that she rattled. "I bought this house as solid, but there are swindles. Ordinarily I'd spot a broadcast style in a flash, but they just might have slipped me a job relayed from some other planet or solar system. Fine thing if me and fifty other multi-megabuck men were spotted around in identical houses, each thinking his was unique."

"But if the house is based on rock like it is . . ."

"That would just make it easier for them to pull the trick, you dumb bunny!"

They reached the master control panel. "There it is," she said helpfully, jabbing out a finger . . . and hit the HOUSE switch.

For a moment nothing happened, then a white churning ran across the ceiling, the walls and furniture started to swell and bubble like cold lava, and then they were alone on a rock table big as three tennis courts. Even the master control panel was gone. The only thing that was left was a slender rod coming out of the grey stone at their feet and bearing at the top, like some mechanistic fruit, a small block with the six switches—that and an intolerably bright star hanging in the air where the master bedroom had been.

Mariana pushed frantically at the HOUSE switch, but it was unlabelled now and locked in the "off" position, although she threw her weight at it stiff-armed.

The upstairs star sped off like an incendiary bullet, but its last flashbulb glare showed her Jonathan's face set in lines of fury. He lifted his hands like talons.

"You little idiot!" he screamed, coming at her.

"No Jonathan, no!" she wailed, backing off, but he kept coming.

She realized that the block of switches had broken off in her hands. The third switch had a glowing name now: JONATHAN. She flipped it.

As his fingers dug into her bare shoulders they seemed to turn to foam rubber, then to air. His face and grey flannel suit seethed iridescently, like a leprous ghost's, then melted and ran. His star, smaller than that of the house but much closer, seared her eyes. When she opened them again there was nothing at all left of the star or Jonathan but a dancing dark after-image like a black tennis ball.

She was alone on an infinite flat rock plain under the cloudless, star-specked sky.

The fourth switch had its glowing name now: STARS.

It was almost dawn by her radium-dialled wristwatch and she was thoroughly chilled, when she finally decided to switch off the stars. She did not want to do it—in their slow wheeling across the sky they were the last sign of orderly reality—but it seemed the only move she could make.

She wondered what the fifth switch would say. ROCKS? AIR? Or even . . . ?

She switched off the stars.

The Milky Way, arching in all its unalterable glory, began to churn, its component stars darting about like midges. Soon only one remained, brighter even than Sirius or Venus—until it jerked back, fading, and darted to infinity.

The fifth switch said DOCTOR and it was not on but off.

An inexplicable terror welled up in Mariana. She did not even want to touch the fifth switch. She set the block of switches down on the rock and backed away from it.

But she dared not go far in the starless dark. She huddled down and waited for dawn. From time to time she looked at her watch dial and at the night-light glow of the switch-label a dozen yards away.

It seemed to be growing much colder.

She read her watch dial. It was two hours past sunrise. She remembered they had taught her in third grade that the sun was just one more star.

She went back and sat down beside the block of switches and picked it up with a shudder and flipped the fifth switch.

The rock grew soft and crisply fragrant under her and lapped up over her legs and then slowly turned white.

She was sitting in a hospital bed in a small blue room with a white pin-stripe.

A sweet, mechanical voice came out of the wall, saying, "You have interrupted the wish-fulfilment therapy by your own decision. If you now recognize your sick depression and are willing to accept help, the doctor will come to you. If not, you are at liberty to return to the wish-fulfilment therapy and pursue it to its ultimate conclusion."

Mariana looked down. She still had the block of switches in her hands and the fifth switch still read DOCTOR.

The wall said, "I assume from your silence that you will accept treatment. The doctor will be with you immediately."

The inexplicable terror returned to Mariana with compulsive intensity.

She switched off the doctor.

She was back in the starless dark. The rocks had grown very much colder. She could feel icy feathers falling on her face—snow.

She lifted the block of switches and saw, to her unutterable relief, that the sixth and last switch now read, in tiny glowing letters: MARIANA.

Masque

By Ed Gorman

From a police report:

> I found the nude body of Janice Hollister in a deep ravine. Some children who'd been playing in the neighborhood told me that they'd seen a dog with what appeared to be blood on his coat. The dog led me back to her. The first thing I noticed about the Hollister woman was the incredible way her body had been cut up. Her entire right breast had been ripped away.

"I've listed it as a car accident," Dr. Temple says.

They are in a room of white tiles and green walls and white cabinets and stainless steel sinks. The room smells of antiseptic and the white tile floor sparkles with hot September sunlight.

Dr. Temple is in his mid-fifties, balding, a lean jogger in a white medical smock. He has very blue eyes and very pink skin. He is an old family friend.

"You've taken care of the records, then?" Mrs. Garth asks. She is sixty-eight and regal in a cold way, given to Dior suits and facelifts.

"Yes."

"There'll be no problem?"

"None. The record will show that he was transferred here two weeks ago following a car accident."

"A car accident?"

"That will account for the bandages. So many lacerations and contusions we had to cover his entire body." He makes a grim line of his mouth. "Very dramatic and very convincing to the eye. Almost theatrical."

"I see. Very good. I appreciate it."

"And we appreciate all you've done for the hospital, Ruth. Without your generosity, there'd be no cancer clinic."

She stands up and offers her delicate hand in such a way that the doctor fears for a terrified moment she actually expects him to kiss it.

From a police report:

> I thought the dog might have attacked her after the killer fled.
> But then I saw that her anus and vagina had been torn up just the
> way the rest of her had and then I knew that it had to be him. The
> perpetrator, I mean. I checked the immediate vicinity for footprints
> and anything that might have fallen from his pockets. I found noth-
> ing that looked useful.

A new elevator, one more necessity her money has bought this
hospital, takes her to the ninth floor.

She walks down a sunny corridor being polished by a dumpy,
middle-aged black woman who has permitted her hose to bag about
her knees. The woman, Mrs. Garth thinks, should have more respect for herself.

Mrs. Garth finds 909 and enters.

She takes no more than ten steps inside, around the edge of the
bathroom, when she stops and looks in horror at him.

All she can think of are those silly movies about Egyptian mummies brought back to life.

Here sits Steve, his entire head and both arms swathed entirely
in white bandages. All she can see of him are his face, his eyes, and
his mouth.

"My Lord," she moans.

She edges closer to his hospital bed. The room is white and clean
and lazy in the sunlight. Above, the TV set mounted to the wall
plays a game show with two fat contestants jumping up and down
on either side of the handsome host who cannot quite rid his eyes of
boredom.

"Aren't you awfully hot inside there?" she asks.

He says nothing, but then at such times he never does.

She pulls up a chair and sits down.

"I am Zoser, founder of the third Dynasty," he says.

"Oh, you," she says. "Now's no time to joke. Anyway, I can
barely understand you with all those bandages over your face."

"I am Senferu, the Warrior King."

"Oh, you," she says.

From a police report:

> Her neck appears to have been broken. At least that was my first
> impression. The killer's strength must be incredible. To say nothing
> of how much he must hate women.

An hour after she arrives in the hospital room, she says, "An old man saw you."

Inside the mummy head, the blue eyes show panic.

"Don't worry," she continues. "He has vision trouble, so he's not a very credible witness. But he did describe you pretty accurately to the press. Fortunately, I told Dr. Temple that some drug dealers were looking for you. He seemed to accept my story."

She pats him on the arm. "Didn't that medication Dr. Gilroy gave you help? I had such high hopes for it. He said you wouldn't any longer want to . . . You know what I'm trying to say."

But now that he knows he's going to be safe, the panic dies in his blue eyes and he says, "I am King Tut."

"Oh, pooh. Can't you be serious?"

"I'm not serious. I'm King Tut."

She clucks.

They sit back and watch the Bugs Bunny cartoon he has on. He says, through his bandages, "I wish they'd show Porky."

"Porky?"

"Porky Pig."

"Oh, I see." My God, he's forty-six years old. She says, "In case there's any trouble, Dr. Temple is going to tell the police that you've been here two weeks and that the old man couldn't possibly identify you because even if you were out and about, you'd have been wearing bandages."

"They won't arrest Senferu the Warrior King, mother. They'd be afraid to."

"I thought after that trouble in Chicago you told me about—"

"There's Sylvester!" he exclaims.

And so there is: Sylvester the cat.

She lets him watch a long minute, the exasperated cat lisping and spitting and spraying. "You were very savage with this one," she says. "Very savage."

"I've seen this one before. This is where Tweety really gives it to Sylvester. Watch!"

She watches, and when she can endure it no more, she says, "Perhaps I made some mistakes with you."

"Oh, God, Sylvester—watch out for Tweety!"

"Perhaps, after your father died, I took certain liberties with you I shouldn't have." Pause. "Letting you sleep in my bed . . . Things happened and I don't suppose either one of us is to blame but nonetheless—"

"Great! Porky's coming on! Look, Mother, it's Porky!"

From a police report:

Down near the creek bed we found her breast. At first I wasn't sure what it was, but as I stared at it I started getting sick. By this time the first backup was arriving. They had to take over for me a few minutes. I wasn't feeling very well.

In the hospital room, sitting there in his mummy bandages, his mother at his side, Steve stares up at the TV set. There's a commercial on now. He hates commercials.

"Maybe Daffy Duck will be on next, Mother. God, wouldn't that be great?"

Now it's her turn for silence. She thinks of the girls in Chicago and Kansas City and Akron. So savage with them; so savage. She will never again believe him that everything's fine and that his medication has gotten him calmed down once and for all and that she should let him take a trip.

But of course this time he didn't even go anywhere. Most dangerous of all, he did it here at home.

Right here at home.

"Wouldn't it be great, Mother?" he asks, wanting her to share his enthusiasm. He loves those occasions when they share things.

She says, "I'm sorry, darling, my mind just wandered. Wouldn't what be great, dear?"

"If it was Daffy on next."

"Daffy?"

"Daffy Duck," he says from inside his mummy head. And then he does a Daffy Duck imitation right on the spot.

Not even the bandages can spoil it, she thinks. He's so clever. "Oh, yes, dear. That would be great if Daffy came on next."

He reaches over and touches her with his bandaged hand and for a horrible moment she almost believes he's been injured.

But then she sees the laughter in his blue blue eyes inside the mummy head.

She pats his bandaged hand. "You'll get a nice rest here for a few weeks and then we'll go home again, dear, and everything will be fine."

He lays his head back and sighs. "Fine." He repeats the word almost as if he doesn't know what it means. "Fiiiine." He seems to be staring at the ceiling. She hopes it's not another depression. They emerge so quickly and last so long.

304

But then abruptly he's sitting up again and clapping his bandaged hands together and staring up at the TV screen.

"It *is* Daffy, Mother. It *is* Daffy!"

"Yes, dear," she says. "It is Daffy, isn't it?"

The Middle Toe of the Right Foot

By Ambrose Bierce

I

It is well known that the old Manton house is haunted. In all the rural district near about, and even in the town of Marshall, a mile away, not one person of unbiased mind entertains a doubt of it; incredulity is confined to those opinionated persons who will be called "cranks" as soon as the useful word shall have penetrated the intellectual demesne of the Marshall *Advance*. The evidence that the house is haunted is of two kinds: the testimony of disinterested witnesses who have had ocular proof, and that of the house itself. The former may be disregarded and ruled out on any of the various grounds of objection which may be urged against it by the ingenious; but facts within the observation of all are material and controlling.

In the first place, the Manton house has been unoccupied by mortals for more than ten years, and with its outbuildings is slowly falling into decay—a circumstance which in itself the judicious will hardly venture to ignore. It stands a little way off the loneliest reach of the Marshall and Harriston road, in an opening which was once a farm and is still disfigured with strips of rotting fence and half covered with brambles overrunning a stony and sterile soil long unacquainted with the plow. The house itself is in tolerably good condition, though badly weatherstained and in dire need of attention from the glazier, the smaller male population of the region having attested in the manner of its kind its disapproval of dwelling without dwellers. It is two stories in height, nearly square, its front pierced by a single doorway flanked on each side by a window boarded up to the very top. Corresponding windows above, not protected, serve to admit light and rain to the rooms of the upper floor. Grass and weeds grow pretty rankly all about, and a few shade trees, somewhat the worse for wind, and leaning all in one direction, seem to be making a concerted effort to run away. In short, as the Marshall town humorist explained in the columns of the *Advance*, "the proposition that the Manton house is badly haunted is the only logical conclusion from the premises." The fact that in this dwelling Mr. Manton thought it expedient one night some ten years ago to rise and cut the throats of his wife and two small children, removing at once to another part of the country, has no doubt done its share in directing public attention to the fitness of the place for supernatural phenomena.

To this house, one summer evening, came four men in a wagon. Three of them promptly alighted, and the one who had been driving hitched the team to the only remaining post of what had been a fence. The fourth remained seated in the wagon. "Come," said one of his companions, approaching him, while the others moved away in the direction of the dwelling—"this is the place."

The man addressed did not move. "By God!" he said harshly, "this is a trick, and it looks to me as if you were in it."

"Perhaps I am," the other said, looking him straight in the face and speaking in a tone which had something of contempt in it. "You will remember, however, that the choice of place was with your own assent left to the other side. Of course if you are afraid of spooks——"

"I am afraid of nothing," the man interrupted with another oath, and sprang to the ground. The two then joined the others at the door, which one of them had already opened with some difficulty, caused by rust of lock and hinge. All entered. Inside it was dark, but the man who had unlocked the door produced a candle and matches and made a light. He then unlocked a door on their right as they stood in the passage. This gave them entrance to a large, square room that the candle but dimly lighted. The floor had a thick carpeting of dust, which partly muffled their footfalls. Cobwebs were in the angles of the walls and depended from the ceiling like strips of rotting lace, making undulatory movements in the disturbed air. The room had two windows in adjoining sides, but from neither could anything be seen except the rough inner surfaces of boards a few inches from the glass. There was no fireplace, no furniture; there was nothing: besides the cobwebs and the dust, the four men were the only objects there which were not a part of the structure.

Strange enough they looked in the yellow light of the candle.

The one who had so reluctantly alighted was especially spectacular —he might have been called sensational. He was of middle age, heavily built, deep chested and broad shouldered. Looking at his figure, one would have said that he had a giant's strength; at his features, that he would use it like a giant. He was clean shaven, his hair rather closely cropped and gray. His low forehead was seamed with wrinkles above the eyes, and over the nose these became vertical. The heavy black brows followed the same law, saved from meeting only by an upward turn at what would otherwise have been the point of contact. Deeply sunken beneath these, glowed in the obscure light a pair of eyes of uncertain color, but obviously enough too small. There was something forbidding in their expression, which was not bettered by the cruel mouth and wide jaw. The nose was well enough, as noses go; one does not expect much of noses. All that was sinister in the man's face seemed accentuated by an unnatural pallor—he appeared altogether bloodless.

The appearance of the other men was sufficiently commonplace: they were such persons as one meets and forgets that he met. All were younger than the man described, between whom and the eldest of the others, who stood apart, there was apparently no kindly feeling. They avoided looking at each other.

"Gentlemen," said the man holding the candle and keys, "I believe everything is right. Are you ready, Mr. Rosser?"

The man standing apart from the group bowed and smiled.

"And you, Mr. Grossmith?"

The heavy man bowed and scowled.

"You will be pleased to remove your outer clothing."

Their hats, coats, waistcoats and neckwear were soon removed and thrown outside the door, in the passage. The man with the candle now nodded, and the fourth man—he who had urged Grossmith to leave the wagon—produced from the pocket of his overcoat two long, murderous-looking bowie-knives, which he drew now from their leather scabbards.

"They are exactly alike," he said, presenting one to each of the two principals—for by this time the dullest observer would have understood the nature of this meeting. It was to be a duel to the death.

Each combatant took a knife, examined it critically near the candle and tested the strength of blade and handle across his lifted knee. Their persons were then searched in turn, each by the second of the other.

"If it is agreeable to you, Mr. Grossmith," said the man holding the light, "you will place yourself in that corner."

He indicated the angle of the room farthest from the door, whither Grossmith retired, his second parting from him with a grasp of the hand which had nothing of cordiality in it. In the angle nearest the door Mr. Rosser stationed himself, and after a whispered consultation his second left him, joining the other near the door. At that moment the candle was suddenly extinguished, leaving all in profound darkness. This may have been done by a draught from the opened door; whatever the cause, the effect was startling.

"Gentlemen," said a voice which sounded strangely unfamiliar in the altered condition affecting the relations of the senses—"gentlemen, you will not move until you hear the closing of the outer door."

A sound of trampling ensued, then the closing of the inner door; and finally the outer one closed with a concussion which shook the entire building.

A few minutes afterward a belated farmer's boy met a light wagon which was being driven furiously toward the town of Marshall. He declared that behind the two figures on the front seat stood a third, with its hands upon the bowed shoulders of the others, who appeared to struggle vainly to free themselves from its grasp. This figure, unlike the others, was clad in white, and had undoubtedly boarded the wagon as it passed the haunted house. As the lad could boast a considerable former experience with the supernatural thereabouts his word had the weight justly due to the testimony of an expert. The story (in connection with the next day's events) eventually appeared in the *Advance*, with some slight literary embellishments and a concluding intimation that the gentlemen referred to would be allowed the use of the paper's columns for their version of the night's adventure. But the privilege remained without a claimant.

II

The events that led up to this "duel in the dark" were simple enough. One evening three young men of the town of Marshall were sitting in a quiet corner of the porch of the village hotel, smoking and discussing such matters as three educated young men of a Southern village would naturally find interesting. Their names were King, Sancher and Rosser. At a little distance, within easy hearing, but taking no part in the conversation, sat a fourth. He was a stranger to the others. They merely knew that on his arrival by the stage-coach that afternoon he had written in the hotel register the name Robert Grossmith. He had not been observed to speak to anyone except the hotel clerk. He seemed, indeed, singularly fond of his own company—or, as the *personnel* of the *Advance* expressed it, "grossly addicted to evil associations." But then it should be said in justice to the stranger that the *personnel* was himself of a too convivial disposition fairly to judge one differently gifted, and had, moreover, experienced a slight rebuff in an effort at an "interview."

"I hate any kind of deformity in a woman," said King, "whether natural or—acquired. I have a theory that any physical defect has its correlative mental and moral defect."

"I infer, then," said Rosser, gravely, "that a lady lacking the moral advantage of a nose would find the struggle to become Mrs. King an arduous enterprise."

"Of course you may put it that way," was the reply; "but, seriously, I once threw over a most charming girl on learning quite accidentally that she had suffered amputation of a toe. My conduct was brutal if you like, but if I had married that girl I should have been miserable for life and should have made her so."

"Whereas," said Sancher, with a light laugh, "by marrying a gentleman of more liberal views she escaped with a parted throat."

"Ah, you know to whom I refer. Yes, she married Manton, but I don't know about his liberality; I'm not sure but he cut her throat because he discovered that she lacked that excellent thing in woman, the middle toe of the right foot."

"Look at that chap!" said Rosser in a low voice, his eyes fixed upon the stranger.

That chap was obviously listening intently to the conversation.

"Damn his impudence!" muttered King—"what ought we to do?"

"That's an easy one," Rosser replied, rising. "Sir," he continued, addressing the stranger, "I think it would be better if you would remove your chair to the other end of the veranda. The presence of gentlemen is evidently an unfamiliar situation to you."

The man sprang to his feet and strode forward with clenched hands, his face white with rage. All were now standing. Sancher stepped between the belligerents.

"You are hasty and unjust," he said to Rosser; "this gentleman has done nothing to deserve such language."

But Rosser would not withdraw a word. By the custom of the country and the time there could be but one outcome to the quarrel.

309

"I demand the satisfaction due to a gentleman," said the stranger, who had become more calm. "I have not an acquaintance in this region. Perhaps you, sir," bowing to Sancher, "will be kind enough to represent me in this matter."

Sancher accepted the trust—somewhat reluctantly it must be confessed, for the man's appearance and manner were not at all to his liking. King, who during the colloquy had hardly removed his eyes from the stranger's face and had not spoken a word, consented with a nod to act for Rosser, and the upshot of it was that, the principals having retired, a meeting was arranged for the next evening. The nature of the arrangements has been already disclosed. The duel with knives in a dark room was once a commoner feature of Southwestern life than it is likely to be again. How thin a veneering of "chivalry" covered the essential brutality of the code under which such encounters were possible we shall see.

III

In the blaze of a midsummer noonday the old Manton house was hardly true to its traditions. It was of the earth, earthy. The sunshine caressed it warmly and affectionately, with evident disregard of its bad reputation. The grass greening all the expanse in its front seemed to grow, not rankly, but with a natural and joyous exuberance, and the weeds blossomed quite like plants. Full of charming lights and shadows and populous with pleasant-voiced birds, the neglected shade trees no longer struggled to run away, but bent reverently beneath their burdens of sun and song. Even in the glassless upper windows was an expression of peace and contentment, due to the light within. Over the stony fields the visible heat danced with a lively tremor incompatible with the gravity which is an attribute of the supernatural.

Such was the aspect under which the place presented itself to Sheriff Adams and two other men who had come out from Marshall to look at it. One of these men was Mr. King, the sheriff's deputy; the other, whose name was Brewer, was a brother of the late Mrs. Manton. Under a beneficent law of the State relating to property which has been for a certain period abandoned by an owner whose residence cannot be ascertained, the sheriff was legal custodian of the Manton farm and appurtenances thereunto belonging. His present visit was in mere perfunctory compliance with some order of a court in which Mr. Brewer had an action to get possession of the property as heir to his deceased sister. By a mere coincidence, the visit was made on the day after the night that Deputy King had unlocked the house for another and very different purpose. His presence now was not of his own choosing: he had been ordered to accompany his superior and at the moment could think of nothing more prudent than simulated alacrity in obedience to the command.

Carelessly opening the front door, which to his surprise was not locked, the sheriff was amazed to see, lying on the floor of the passage into which it opened, a confused heap of men's apparel. Examination showed it to consist of two hats, and the same number of coats, waistcoats and scarves, all in a remarkably good state of preservation, albeit somewhat defiled by the dust in which they lay. Mr. Brewer was equally astonished, but Mr. King's emotion is not of record. With a new and lively interest in his own actions the sheriff now unlatched and pushed open a door on the right, and the three entered. The room was apparently vacant—no; as their eyes became accustomed to the dimmer light something was visible in the farthest angle of the wall. It was a human figure—that of a man crouching close in the corner. Something in the attitude made the intruders halt when they had barely passed the threshold. The figure more and more clearly defined itself. The man was upon one knee, his back in the angle of the wall, his shoulders elevated to the level of his ears, his hands before his face, palms outward, the fingers spread and crooked like claws; the white face turned upward on the retracted neck had an expression of unutterable fright, the mouth half open, the eyes incredibly expanded. He was stone dead. Yet, with the exception of a bowie-knife, which had evidently fallen from his own hand, not another object was in the room.

In thick dust that covered the floor were some confused footprints near the door and along the wall through which it opened. Along one of the adjoining walls, too, past the boarded-up windows, was the trail made by the man himself in reaching his corner. Instinctively in approaching the body the three men followed that trail. The sheriff grasped one of the outthrown arms; it was as rigid as iron, and the application of a gentle force rocked the entire body without altering the relation of its parts. Brewer, pale with excitement, gazed intently into the distorted face. "God of mercy!" he suddenly cried, "it is Manton!"

"You are right," said King, with an evident attempt at calmness: "I knew Manton. He then wore a full beard and his hair long, but this is he."

He might have added: "I recognized him when he challenged

Rosser. I told Rosser and Sancher who he was before we played him this horrible trick. When Rosser left this dark room at our heels, forgetting his outer clothing in the excitement, and driving away with us in his shirt sleeves—all through the discreditable proceedings we knew whom we were dealing with, murderer and coward that he was!"

But nothing of this did Mr. King say. With his better light he was trying to penetrate the mystery of the man's death. That he had not once moved from the corner where he had been stationed; that his posture was that of neither attack nor defense; that he had dropped his weapon; that he had obviously perished of sheer horror of something that he *saw*—these were circumstances which Mr. King's disturbed intelligence could not rightly comprehend.

Groping in intellectual darkness for a clew to his maze of doubt, his gaze, directed mechanically downward in the way of one who ponders momentous matters, fell upon something which, there, in the light of day and in the presence of living companions, affected him with terror. In the dust of years that lay thick upon the floor—leading from the door by which they had entered, straight across the room to within a yard of Manton's crouching corpse—were three parallel lines of footprints—light but definite impressions of bare feet, the outer ones those of small children, the inner a woman's. From the point at which they ended they did not return; they pointed all one way. Brewer, who had observed them at the same moment, was leaning forward in an attitude of rapt attention, horribly pale.

"Look at that!" he cried, pointing with both hands at the nearest print of the woman's right foot, where she had apparently stopped and stood. "The middle toe is missing—it was Gertrude!"

Gertrude was the late Mrs. Manton, sister to Mr. Brewer.

Moving Night

By Nancy Holder

It moved.

Petey lay in his bed, shaking with terror, his eight-year-old eyes bulging so widely they ached. His head throbbed; his grubby fists clenched tight to keep him from screaming, as the moonlight gleamed on the chair that rattled near the closet door.

It had moved, oh, no, oh *no*, it had moved, and no one would ever believe him. All those nights his mom and dad would come in and talk to him in syrupy voices, and tell him, *Why, Petey, nothing moved. Only live things can move. And your stuffed rabbit isn't alive, and that pile of laundry isn't alive, and Mr. Robot isn't alive, and . . .*

And they never believed him. *They never did!*

But the chair had moved. He had seen it. When he'd pretended to look away, then looked quickly back, he knew the chair had inched closer to the bed. He knew it was coming to get him, to eat him all up and spit out his bones, to fling him to the monsters and the bogeymen and witches with rotten teeth and no eyes who lived in the closet . . .

. . . who stuck their heads out at midnight and laughed at him when his mom and dad were asleep; and waited until the last minute for the sleepy *pad pad pad* of slippers, the creak of the bedroom door . . .

Petey? Are you having another nightmare, dear? Don't give yourself one of those headaches!

There, it moved again! Petey wanted to scream but his throat was so dry he couldn't make a sound, not even a hoarse gasp. It moved, he swore it, please, please, someone, it *moved!*

He whimpered like a wounded kitten. Only live things could move. Only things that were alive.

Why didn't they ever believe him? When he whooped with white-hot fever over the dwarf in the toy chest, they just laughed. When he pleaded with them to listen *listen!* about the skeleton in the mattress, they said he had an active imagination. They only believed about the headaches. Headaches were real.

Maybe he needs glasses. Maybe he's allergic to pollen.

Maybe, maybe . . .

It moved again!

Peter bolted upright and pressed his back against the headboard. His head was splitting. They had believed him about *that,* but they had never done anything! They had never helped him! They had never taken away the pain!

"Stop!" Petey begged. "Stop!"

His head always hurt, like a little gremlin lived inside, sticking pins in his brain. And they talked about taking him to the doctor, and talked about taking him for tests, and talked and talked . . .

"Stop!"

. . . but they didn't care about him. They didn't love him, because his mom had had a boyfriend while his dad was on his battle-ship; and when he came back, she was going to have a baby. Him. Petey . . .

It was still moving!

. . . and he heard them late at night, fighting. His dad (not his real dad, his real dad was a bogeyman) would shout, "Ya shoulda gotten an abortion, Barb! Ya shoulda gotten rid of him!"

And his mother would cry and say, "I know, Jack, I know. I'm sorry."

Then last Sunday, after the kitten, his dad (the fake one) had shouted, "He's a monster! He's not human! We should send him away!" And his mother, sobbing, had replied, "Yes, Jack. I know. We will."

It moved. Tears streamed down Petey's face.

But only things that were alive could move. And the chair was not alive.

And neither was the thing sitting in it.

"I didn't mean to hurt the cat," he whispered. "Or the dog, or Mrs. Garcia's niece . . ." He crammed his fists in his mouth; no one knew about *that.*

It moved again. Much closer.

"I didn't mean to," he cried wildly. "Grown-ups are supposed to help little kids! And nobody . . ."

He thought of Mrs. Martin, the school nurse. She had *tried* to help him. When his head hurt really badly, she would let him lie down on a canvas cot in her office while she knitted. She had a big bag full of yarn and light green needles that flashed between her fingers. She wouldn't call home unless he asked her to. She would let him lie there, not moving, and every once in a while she would smile at him and say, "Feeling better?"

Sometimes he would say no just so he could stay with her. She was older than his mother but she was pretty anyway, and she al-ways smelled like roses. She sang to him sometimes while she knit-ted, in-and-out, in-and-out.

Bye, baby bunting, Daddy's gone a-hunting

like he was just a baby, and she told him he could grow up to be whatever he wanted.

He should be locked up! Did you see what he did to that cat? My God, Barb, he's not normal!

I know, Jack, I know.

Whatever he wanted, even President of the United States. And once he laughed and said, "Not me, Mrs. Martin!" But she shrugged and asked, "Why not? You're a bright boy with your future ahead of you."

Who was that guy you cheated on me with? Who the hell was he?

The headaches! The headaches!

At Halloween she lent him a doctor's bag and a stethoscope and told him maybe he could go to medical school and become a doctor.

"You're a good boy, Petey," she would say. "A fine young man."

He tried to tell her about the skeleton and the dwarf and the witches—oh, the witches, with their laughing, waiting for the *pad, pad, pad* of the slippers before they disappeared! But she didn't believe him either, and that *hurt* him, worse than the headaches. Mrs. Martin cared about him. He knew that. But she didn't believe him, and the pain never got better, never did.

And then she stopped working at the school and he was all alone again.

"Nobody helped me!" Petey screamed as loud as he could. "You should've helped me!"

"I'll help you now," slurred the thing in the chair.

It used to be his mother, but now she was all bloody from where he had stabbed her *wasn't my fault, wasn't, was not!* and the rest of her was white. Her lips were blue and her eyes were full of blood and flies were buzzing in her hair.

She hadn't moved for four days.

"It's not my fault!" he shrieked, scrabbling against the headboard. Maybe if he made a run for the door, he could escape. But she was moving, even though she was just a dead thing, not a live thing, and only live things moved.

Except his pretend dad, who *was* still alive—Petey could hear him moaning in the hallway—had not moved since Tuesday.

Anything he wanted to be . . . a fine young man.

"I'm coming for you, Petey," his mother whispered through broken teeth. He had punched her when she screamed "Monster! Monster!" until she stopped. "I'm going to give you to the skeleton in the mattress and the dwarf in the toy chest. I'm going to fling you to the eyeless witches in the closet."

President of the United States.

"Not me, Mrs. Martin!"

"Why not?"

He heard a mad, gleeful gibbering underneath the bed.

"No!" He buried his face in his hands and sobbed. "Oh, please, no! I'm sorry! Please, someone!"

The gibbering faded. The room was still.

Maybe it was just another headache. A bad dream. There was nothing . . .

Bye, baby bunting

When he raised his head, his mother, all oozy and gory, smelling terribly, was standing beside the bed. She smiled a toothless, gummy smile. "No more headaches."

And the chair skittered up next to her just as the closet door opened.

Anything he wanted . . .

And then *everything* moved.

Naples

By Avram Davidson

It is a curious thing, the reason of it being not certainly known to me—though I conjecture it might be poverty—why, when all the other monarchs of Europe were still building palaces in marble and granite, the kings of that anomalous and ill-fated kingdom called Of Naples and the Two Sicilies chose to build theirs in red brick. However, choose it they did: These last of the Italian Bourbons have long since lost their last thrones, no *castrato* singers sing for them from behind screens to lighten their well-deserved melancholy anymore, and their descendants now earn their livings in such occupations as gentlemen-salesclerks in fashionable jewelry stores—not, perhaps, entirely removed from all memory of the glory that once (such as it was) was theirs. But the red-brick *palazzi* are still there, they still line a part of the waterfront of Naples, and—some of them, at least—are still doing duty as seats of governance. (Elsewhere, for reasons equally a mystery to me, unless there is indeed some connection between red bricks and poverty, buildings in the same style and of the same material usually indicate that within them the Little Sisters of the Poor, or some similar religious group, perform their selfless duties on behalf of the sick, the aged, and the otherwise bereft and afflicted; and which is the nobler function and whose the greater reward are questions that will not long detain us.)

Some twenty years ago or so, a man neither young nor old nor

316

ugly nor comely, neither obviously rich nor equally poor, made his way from the docks past the red-brick *palazzi* and into the lower town of ancient and teeming Naples. He observed incuriously that the streets, instead of swarming with the short and swarthy, as foreign legend implies, swarmed instead with the tall and pale. But the expectations of tradition were served in other ways: by multitudes of donkey carts, by women dressed and draped in black, by many many beggars, and by other signs of deep and evident poverty. Almost at once a young man approached him with a murmured offer of service; the young man clutched the upturned collar of his jacket round about his throat, and, as the day was not even cool, let alone cold, it might have been assumed that the reason for the young man's gesture was that he probably did not wish to reveal the absence of a shirt. It was not altogether certain that the young man had no shirt at all, probably he had a shirt and probably this was its day to be washed and probably it was even now hanging from a line stretched across an alley where the sun did not enter in sufficient strength to dry it quickly.

There were many such alleys and many such lines, and, it is to be feared, many such shirts. There were also many such men, not all of them young; and if a count had been made, it might have been found that there were not enough shirts to go around.

Naples.

The traveler continued, with frequent pauses and considerings, to make his way slowly from the port area and slowly up the steep hill. Now and then he frowned slightly and now and then he slightly smiled. Long ago some humble hero or heroine discovered that if the hard wheat of the peninsula, subject to mold and rust and rot if stored in the ear, be ground into flour and mixed with water into a paste and extruded under pressure in the form of long strips, and dried, it would never rot at all and would keep as near forever as the hunger of the people would allow it. And when boiled it formed a food nutritious as bread and far more durable, and, when combined with such elements as oil or tomato or meat or cheese and perhaps the leaves of the bay and the basil, be good food indeed. However, the passage of time failed to bring these added ingredients within the means and reach of all. So, to vary in some measure at least the monotony of the plain pasta, it was made in the widest conceivable variety of shapes: thin strips and thick strips, ribbons broad and narrow, hollow tubes long and hollow tubes bent like elbows, bows and shells and stars and wheels and rosettes and what-have-you. And, if you have nothing, it is anyway

317

some relief to eat your plain pasta in a different design . . . when you have, of course, pasta to eat.

At least every other doorway in the narrow streets and the narrower alleys kept a shop, and many of the shops sold pasta: for the further sake of variety the pasta was not merely stacked up in packages, it was also—the straight kinds—splayed about as though the stalks held flowers at their upper ends. And when the traveler saw these he faintly smiled. The young man who paced him step for step also looked at these modest displays. But he never smiled at them. In fact, although he continued his soft murmurs, he never smiled at all.

Most of these ways seemed hardly wide enough for outside displays, but such there were; there were second-hand clothes and fewer by far displays of some few new clothes; there were whole cheeses, although none hereabouts were seen to buy them whole, and perhaps not very many very often bought them by the slice or crumbling piece. And there were small fish, alive, alive-o, and larger fish in dim slabs that had not been alive in a long time, dry and hard and strong-smelling and salty, redolent of distant and storm-tossed seas. Tomatoes and peppers lay about in baskets. Oil was poured in careful drops into tiny bottles. There were also olives in many colors. Pictures of saints were sold, and the same shops sold, too, odd little emblematic images in coral and silver and—this was surely strange in such a scene of poverty—even gold: behind the narrow windows of narrow shops, crosses, too, yes, and beads: the universal signia of that religion. . . . But what were these horns? What were these tiny hands, fingers tucked into a fist with the thumb protruding between first and second fingers?

Best not to ask, you would empty the street in a trice. Everybody in Naples knows, no one in Naples would speak of it above a whisper . . . to a stranger, not at all. Speak not the word, lest it come to pass. Look not overlong at anyone in these streets, particularly not at the children they produce in such numbers of abundance. Who knows if your eye be not evil?

The eye of the traveler passed over the swarming and ragged *bambini* without stopping, and in the same manner he glanced at the scrannel cats and the charcoal braziers fanned by the toiling housewives: When one's home is but one room, one may well prefer the street as a kitchen.

When one has that which to cook, and fuel with which to cook it.

At length the passageway widened into a sort of a *piazza*. At one end was a church, on either side were the blank walls of some *palazzio* a good deal more antique than the brick ones down below:

perhaps from the days of Spanish viceroys, perhaps from the days of King Robert. Who knows. There were anyway no more shops, no stalls, no wide-open-to-the-street one-room "houses" . . . and, for once, no masses of people . . . no beggars, even . . . there was even a sort of alley that seemingly went nowhere and that, surprisingly, held no one. And the traveler, who had so far only from time to time looked out from the corners of his eyes at the young man cleaving close to him as a shadow does, and who had made no reply at all to the soft murmurs with which the young man (ever clutching his jacket round about his naked throat) continually offered his services as "guide"; now for the first time, the traveler stopped, gave a direct look fleeting-swift, jerked his head toward the tiny passageway, and stepped inside.

The shirtless one's head went up and he looked at the heavens; his head went down and he looked at the filthy worn stones beneath. His shoulders moved in something too slight for a shrug and his unclothed throat uttered something too soft for a sigh.

He followed.

The traveler turned, without looking into the other's eyes, whispered a few short words into the other's ears.

The face of the young man, which had been stiff, expressionless, now went limp. Surprise showed most briefly. His brows moved once or twice.

—But yes—he said. —Surely—he said.

And he said, with a half bow and a small movement of his arm—I pray, follow. Very near—he said.

Neither one paused at the church.

And now the streets became, all of them, alleys. The alleys became mere slits. The shops grew infrequent, their store ever more meager. The lines of clothes dripping and drying overhead seemed to bear little relation to what human beings wore. What actually dangled and flapped in the occasional gusts of flat, warm, and stinking air may once have been clothing. Might once more, with infinite diligence and infinite skill, with scissors and needle and thread, be reconstituted into clothing once again. But for the present, one must either deny the rags that name, or else assume that behind the walls, the scabby walls, peeling walls, broken walls, filthy damp and dripping-ichorous walls, there dwelled some race of goblins whose limbs required garb of different drape.

The traveler began to lag somewhat behind.

How often, now, how carefully, almost how fearfully, the young-man guide turned his head to make sure the other was still with him. Had not stepped upon some ancient obscenely greasy flagstone fixed upon a pivot and gone silently screaming down into God knows what. Had not been slip-noosed, perhaps, as some giant hare, hoisted swiftly up above the flapping rags . . . Rags? Signal flags? What strange fleet might have its brass-bound spyglasses focused hither? Or perhaps it was fear and caution lest the other's fear and caution might simply cause him to turn and flee. In which case the young-man guide would flee after him, though from no greater fear than loss of the fee.

When one has no shirt, what greater fear?

Turned and into a courtyard entered through a worm-eaten door whose worms had last dined centuries ago, perhaps, and left the rest of the wood as inedible. A courtyard as dim, as dank as the antechamber to an Etruscan Hell. Courtyard as it might be the outer lobby of some tumulus, some tomb, not yet quite filled although long awaiting its last occupant. Shadow. Stench. The tatters hung up here could never be clothing again, should they in this foul damp ever indeed dry. At best they might serve to mop some ugly doorstep, did anyone within the yard have yet pride enough for such. And yet, if not, why were they hanging, wet from washing? Perhaps some last unstifled gesture of respectability. Who knows.

Naples.

Around a corner in the courtyard a door, and through the door a passageway and at the end of that a flight of stairs and the end of the flight of stairs a doorway that no longer framed a door. A thing, something that was less than a blanket, was hung. The youngman paused and rapped and murmured. Something made a sound within. Something dragged itself across the floor within. Something seemed simultaneously to pull the hanging aside and to wrap itself behind the hanging.

At the opposite side to the door a man sat upon a bed. The man would seemingly have been the better for having been in the bed and not merely on it. On the cracked and riven and flaking, sodden walls some pictures, cut from magazines. Two American Presidents. Two Popes. And one Russian leader. And two saints. Comparisons are odious. Of those whose likenesses were on that filthy fearful wall it might be said they had in common anyway that all were dead.

—Good day—the youngman guide said.

—Good day—the man on the bed said. After a moment. He might, though, have been excused for not having said it at all.

—This gentleman is a foreigner—

The man on the bed said nothing. His sunken eyes merely looked.

320

—And he would like, ahem, ha, he would like to buy—
—But I have nothing to sell—
How dry, how faint, his voice.
—Some little something. Some certain article. An item—
—But nothing. I have nothing. We have nothing here—
His hand made a brief gesture, fell still.

A very small degree of impatience seemed to come over the face of the older visitor. The younger visitor, observing this, as he observed everything, took another step closer to the bed. —The gentleman is a foreigner—he repeated, as one who speaks to a rather stupid child.

The man on the bed looked around. His stooped shoulders, all dirty bones, shrugged, stooped more. —He may be a foreigner twice over, and what is it to me—he said, low-voiced, seemingly indifferent.

—He is a foreigner. He has, fool, son of a jackal, son of a strumpet, he has money—the youngman turned, abruptly, to the traveler. Said—Show him—

The traveler hesitated, looked all about. His mouth moved. So, too, his nose. His hands, no.

—You will have to show, you know. Can you pay without showing—

The traveler suddenly took a wallet from an inner pocket of his coat, abruptly opened it, and abruptly thrust it in again, placed his back not quite against the noisome wall, crossed his arms over his chest.

Slowly, slowly, the man on the bed slid his feet to the floor.
—Wait outside—he said. —Halfway down—he added.
On the half landing they waited. Listened. Heard.
Dragging, dragging footsteps. A voice they had not heard before. —*No*NO—A voice as it might be from behind the curtain or the blanket or the what-was-it in place of the door. The faint sounds of some faint and grisly struggle. Voices but no further words. Gasps, only.

Something began to wail, in a horrid broken voice. Then, outside the doorframe, at the head of the stairs, the man, tottering against the wall. Extending toward them his hands, together, as though enclosing something within.
—Be quick—he said. Panting.
And, all the while, the dreadful wail went on from behind him.
The youngman sprang up the stairs, his left hand reaching forward. Behind his back his right hand formed a fist with its thumb thrust out between first and second fingers; then both his hands

swept up and met both hands of the other. The youngman, face twisted, twisting, darted down the steps to the half landing.

—The money—

Again, hands met. The traveler thrust his deep into his bosom, kept one there, withdrew the other. Withdrew his wallet, fumbled.

—Not here, not here, you know—the youngman warned. —The police, you know—

One look the older man flung about him. —Oh no. Oh God, not here—he said. —On the ship—

The youngman nodded. Roughly divided the money, tossed half of it up and behind without looking back. He did not come close to the older man as they hurried down the stairs.

Above, the wailing ceased. That other voice spoke, in a manner not to be described, voice changing register on every other word, almost.

—Curse the day my daughter's daughter gave you birth. May you burn, son of a strega and son of a strumpet, burn one hundred thousand years in Purgatory without remission—

The voice broke, crocked wordlessly a moment. Resumed.

—One dozen times I have been ready to die, and you, witch's bastard, you have stolen my death away and you have sold my death to strangers, may you burst, may you burn—

Again the voice broke, again began to wail.

The two men reached the bottom of the stained stairs, and parted, the younger one outdistancing the other and this time never looking back.

Above, faintly, in a tone very faintly surprised, the man who had been on the bed spoke.

—Die? Why should you die when I must eat?—

Naples.

Night Visions

By Jack Dann

Martin steps on the accelerator of his Naples-yellow coupe and prepares to die. It will be a manly death, he thinks, although he is somewhat saddened by the thought of his beautiful car lying wrecked in a ditch. He glances at the rectilinear information band that stretches across the instrument panel: the speedometer needle is resting neatly between the nine and the zero.

He feels a delicious anticipation as he cruises through the darkness and low-lying mountain fog. The high beams turn the trees preternaturally green; the moon changes shape to accommodate the clouds boiling above.

As the speedometer needle reaches one hundred, Martin closes his eyes and turns the steering wheel to the left. He envisions his car moving diagonally across the highway, then over the embankment, taking with it several guardrails, and plunging into the ghostly arms of fog below. He does not brace himself for the coming crash. Relaxed, he waits for the car to leave the highway and the events of his life to rush before him as if in a newsreel. Surely time will distend like a bladder, filled with the insights and profound despair that must attend the last instants of consciousness.

Martin resolves to keep his eyes closed; he *will* meet his destiny. But the car remains on the highway, as if connected to an overhead line like a trolley. The radial tires make a plashing sound as they meet each measured seam in the pavement. Curious as to why he has not yet crashed and died, Martin dreams of the splintering of bone, the blinding explosion of flesh, the truly cosmic orgasm.

Then, just as the left front and rear tires finally slip off the road, a siren sounds. Surprised, Martin opens his eyes to find that the car, as if under the influence of a bewitched gyroscope, has regained the highway.

A police car overtakes him; and Martin pulls over beside an illuminated glen of evergreen to accept his speeding ticket as if it were a penitent's wafer.

It is unfair that I should have to kill myself, Martin thinks, as his car dips in and out of the fog like a great warship on a desolate sea. Ahead, he can see the gray lights of a medium-sized city that is nestled between black hills. He muses in the darkness; soon the highway will become elevated and illuminated.

Martin regrets his life. What has he to show for it but one hundred and thirty-eight hack novels, two children, and a wife he does not love? He considers himself still a virgin, for he has never had sex with anyone but his wife. At thirty-nine years of age, he is still obsessed with sex. He has written thirty-five pornographic novels, yet never gone down on a woman. He thinks of himself as a writing machine, and machines don't have experiences. They have no free will, they don't love or get laid. They just operate until they are turned off or break down.

He slows down behind a small, foreign car. The highway is suddenly crowded, and Martin experiences a familiar claustrophobia: he remembers the Long Island Expressway during rush hour, the hypnotic seventy-mile-per-hour ritual of tailgating, the mile-long bumper-to-bumper traffic jams.

There can be no car-crashing here, for Martin does not wish the death of others on his conscience.

He passes a late-model convertible. A young man is driving, his arm around a pretty girl. Now, that would be a perfect car for an ending, Martin thinks—the wind whistling in your ears, drying your eyes, and no hard roof to protect skull from pavement.

Saddened by the thought that convertibles are no longer being made, he drives carefully onward. Safety poles whiz by him like teeth in some infernal machine; one wrong turn, a slight pull on the steering wheel, and the car would be smashed to scrap. But, always considerate of others, he keeps to the road. He passes a series of midtown exits, sees the blinking lights of a plane coming in from the east, and then the city and its dull glow of civilization is behind him. Ahead is a sliver of gray highway cutting through mountains, a low wall of nightfog, and heavy clouds hanging below an angry red moon.

Now Martin thinks he will slip into the darkness, which will absorb the impact of flesh and metal; and he will simply drift away like a ghost on the morning mist.

The highway becomes a two-lane road for the next few miles and follows the contours of the land. Martin's throat tightens in joyful anticipation as he closes his eyes and presses the accelerator to the floor.

He dreams of flight and concussion; he dreams that time is made of rubber and he is pulling it apart. As he waits for his past to unfold, he repeats a mantra that his elder daughter taught him.

He tries to visualize his wife, Jennifer. Although Martin knows her intimately and can describe her in minute detail, he can no longer *see* her. He remembers her now as an equation, as numbers complemented by an occasional Greek letter to signify a secret part of her psyche.

She is probably phoning the police, calling the neighbors, making a fuss and waking the children.

He pulls another band of time taut and dreams about his funeral. His closest friends will all stand about the grave, then toss a few clumps of earth into the hole; his children will be crying loudly while Jennifer looks on quietly. All in all, a fine despair; a fitting end.

Martin wonders how long he has been daydreaming. Probably only an instant, he thinks. He remembers his childhood.

And he turns the steering wheel hard to ensure his death. He screams, anticipating the shattering pain and subsequent numbness.

But nothing happens.

He waits several more beats, then opens his eyes, only to find himself negotiating a cloverleaf turnoff. He has unwittingly turned onto an exit ramp and is now shooting back to the highway, heading in the opposite direction.

He strikes the wood-inlaid steering wheel.

"Dammit, Jennifer, I'm not coming home . . ."

There is very little time left; the sky is already becoming smudgy. Dawn is not far away, and the thought of driving into a bleeding sunrise does not escape him.

It must be done while it is still dark, he thinks; the sunlight would expose him to the world.

Shale palisades rise on either side of the highway like ruined steps. But this time Martin does not shut his eyes. There is no time to dream.

He turns the wheel sharply, once again preparing for the bright explosion of death.

But the car runs smoothly forward, as if Martin had never turned the wheel. The car follows the gentle curve of the highway. Martin is only a passenger.

"No," he screams as he turns the steering wheel again. The car does not respond. He steps on the brake, but the car maintains its speed. Although he is screaming—long, sharp streamers of sound —he hears only engine noise. Perfect rows of numbers pass through his mind: all the coupe's specifications he had once memorized.

Half a mile to the next exit, the car decelerates, turns into the right-hand lane, and then into the thirty-mile-per-hour exitway. It rushes toward the sunrise, which is first a bleeding then a yellow-butter melting beyond the gray hills.

Home is only about twenty miles away.

Martin feels himself running down. He can barely move, for he is as heavy as the car. His hands rest upon the steering wheel as if he were in control. The air-conditioner blows a steady stream of cold air at his face. Numbers pass through his mind.

It is becoming a gritty day. Long, gray clouds drift across the sky, and Martin dreams that the sky is made of metal. He dreams that the world is made of metal, that he is made of metal.

In one last burst of strength, hope, and will, Martin commands his foot to press the accelerator to the floor. Once more, he dreams of the lovely shock of body and brain being pulped.

But the coupe maintains its speed.

Martin is almost home.

Night Deposits

By Chet Williamson

You almost got to know Zane Kaylor to appreciate this. Course young as you are you probably wouldn't. You might recall, though, seeing Zane on the street. A big, tall, skinny fella he was, built like a fence post a rough wind split in two. Jesus, but he was thin.

Wasn't always like that, though. Hell, I remember him back in the thirties being really stocky like. That was when he owned the mill. Big wood mill, everybody in town got their lumber there, back before wood got so dear nobody can afford it no more. Course too that was before the Martin boy's accident. That was what made Zane so thin. And what made him finally start making those queer night deposits of his at the bank.

Must've been '34 or so when it happened. There wasn't much call for safety things back then, and there was a great big band saw Zane had at the mill. Now it would've been all right if Zane had grown men who knew what the hell they were doing on that saw. If he had, I doubt the sheriff ever would have said a thing. But Tommy Martin was working it after school, since Zane hired boys like that rather than pay his regular men overtime after four.

Well, Bill Painter—he was sheriff then—comes in to pick up some planks and sees Tommy Martin working on that big old saw without no blade guard or nothing, and he tells Zane that he's a fool to put a kid on that machine and if he's going to do it he'd better goddam well put a blade guard on it, or maybe Painter'll take a close look at some fire regulations that Zane wasn't paying all that much attention to.

This pisses Zane off someting awful, but he don't want to get on Painter's wrong side, so he says real sulky that he'll get a guard on it and not to worry. Tommy Martin hears all this, but he don't pay no attention to it much. Hell, a quarter an hour was damn good for a high school boy then, and it's fun sawing them boards up.

But Zane, he's pretty tight with money anyway, he looks for the cheapest way to make a blade guard, so he solders together a few tin can halves, and bolts them onto the housing. A couple days later Painter comes back and looks at the guard and tells Zane it looks like shit. Zane getts pissed and says a guard is a guard and it'll hold up, and Painter doesn't push it any. A week later, though, he wishes he would've.

It's like that fella's law, says if something can go wrong, it will? Sure enough, the mill's open late Friday night, it's about ten o'clock, and Tommy Martin's dog tired. He's pulling a big four by eight off the saw for Glenn Weidman when he loses his balance and falls on it. Those tin cans get knocked against the blade and it just whips them apart, shooting them into the air like knives. A piece caught the kid's face, Glenn said afterwards, and it sliced his right eye open like a grape. But that wasn't the worst of it.

The boy fell right across the blade then, and it started to chew into him at gut level. He pushed himself off, but fell back for a second, and that was when it got his hands. Both of them. Must've gone through the wrist bones slicker than shit through a goose. By the time Glenn and Zane got to him to pull him away, he was bleeding like anything. Wasn't screaming because he'd gone into shock. They called the county ambulance first, then Doc Lindemuth. The boy lived, though. It was a miracle how, Jesus, both hands and the eye. What made it a double shame is that he was the best goddam pass receiver the high school'd had for years.

Well, *that* was over, of course, and so was Zane Kaylor's mill. When Sheriff Painter heard about it he actually arrested Zane and locked him up. He got out on bail the next day, and the county didn't press any criminal charges, negligence or whatever. But Painter told Roy and Esther Martin—they were Tommy's parents—to sue Zane, and that he'd back them up.

They had the sympathy of everybody in town over Zane. Oh, folks *liked* Zane well enough, but we all knew he was a *cheap* bastard, and it was plain to see that if he hadn't been cutting corners so close, this all wouldn't've happened.

So the Martins got a real good lawyer from over in Harrisburg, and Zane hired John Moyers here in town. County judge found for the Martins. After Bill Painter and Glenn's testimony, there wasn't much doubt that'd happen. I don't recall what exactly Zane had to pay, but it was a heap. And because Tommy was a kid, Zane hadn't paid no worker's compensation for him. That was just like Zane, though, always wanting to take a chance rather than spend an extra buck.

It hit him hard. Had to sell the mill and even that wasn't enough for what the judge had ordered, so he borrowed the rest from the bank and just got himself into awful debt. He stayed at the mill as a workman for Homer Johnson, who bought it from him, but he didn't stay long.

Three months after the accident, Tommy Martin killed himself. Pulled the shotgun trigger with his toe. Doc said it was a helluva mess—worst he'd seen in thirty years. The Martins moved away soon after, down south to Florida. Zane started drinking then, coming to work late, sneaking away early, until Homer Johnson told him he'd better find another job somewhere, that being in the mill just wasn't good for him. Truth was, aside from the drinking, Homer was afraid Zane would hurt himself. Sometimes Homer'd come in and Zane would just be standing staring at that big band saw. Made Homer feel all creepy.

So he fired Zane, and Zane had to look for another job, which wasn't easy in the middle of the depression. He just kept drinking and not doing much of anything until his payments to the bank fell way behind and they had to foreclose on his house. That was the last straw for his wife. She took their little girl and went upstate to live with her folks. They got a real divorce a couple years later.

Her leaving sort of brought Zane around. He got *two* jobs then—both ones nobody else much wanted. Days he worked out at the rendering plant—isn't there no more—and nights he was over at the White Horse doing everything the bartender and the waitresses wouldn't cleaning spittoons, keeping the john red up, taking the garbage out from the kitchen till midnight, when he went to bed in the room they let him have above the kitchen. Then he'd get up at six to go to the rendering plant.

He did that for years, until his debt was paid off. The house hadn't brought enough to pay the bank completely, and he was paying the rest of it with what he made off the White Horse. Every Friday night after he got paid he'd cross the street to the bank and put money in that night depository chute. I seen him do it many times. My rooms are still where they were then, over the furniture store catty-corner from the bank. Those days I could howl till midnight or later, and lots of times I saw Zane drop his money down that chute. None of us ever thought he'd get that debt to the bank paid off.

But he did. I guess it was in the early fifties, around the time my sister's boy died in Korea, that Zane stopped making those night deposits. We found out from Harry Becker, who worked at the bank, that Zane's debt had finally been paid.

Well, that night some of the boys decided to throw a little shindig in the White Horse for Zane to celebrate—a surprise like. I said I don't know if it was all that smart, that maybe Zane would just like to forget all about it. But you know what guys're like when they have a few drinks, so Wally Lovinger—he was bartender then—sends Zane up to Heisey's store; for a case of club soda, claiming he's run out. The boys go across to the five and dime and buy streamers and balloons, and when Zane comes back everybody's cheering and yelling. He's confused at first, and then one of the boys tells him it's to celebrate his getting out of debt. His face goes white then, and everybody stops laughing.

Then he says, "I'll never be out of debt." Just like that, real quiet and whispery, but everybody in the room hears it, and he walks out and doesn't come back that night at all.

He quit his job at the White Horse the next day and took his clothes and things out of the room above the kitchen and moved in with the Koser sisters over on Oak Street. I saw him a few days later in the park and asked him how things are, and he says the Koser sisters are real good to him, and he even has his own bathroom and a hot plate and can use their refrigerator.

So the years go by, and when the rendering plant shuts down about fifteen years back, Zane goes on the social security and it's enough to get by on, but just barely. I don't think the Koser girls ever raised his rent in all those years. They must've figured he'd had enough trouble. Course when Emma died a few years back I guess Miriam was glad for the company.

It was just last year that his mind starts going on him. You'd say hi to him on the street and he'd just sort of smile like he didn't really remember who you were, and when you told him he'd just nod so that you knew he really didn't recognize the name any more. Miriam Koser looked after him all right, even though she's almost eighty herself now. But even she didn't know what was happening near the end.

Zane never went to a doctor. Never. After his first trouble he couldn't afford it and I guess he got out of the habit. But most of us could see that more was going than his mind. He started to walk funny like, as if he'd got arthritis bad, or his legs was going on him for some other reason. Limped at first—end of the summer it was—and finally had to use two canes, one in each hand, by the time fall came on. I talked to Jane Garber about him one day and she thought as how it *was* arthritis, as he even had trouble holding his canes come winter, especially with those big thick mittens he wore.

He had so much trouble getting around come Christmas that we hardly ever saw him out on the street at all. That's one reason it was such a surprise to me when I saw him through my window late one Friday night.

It was around midnight, and I'd gotten up to take a leak—that's what happens when you get old—when I looked out the window and saw Zane hobbling up the street. Course I wondered why in hell he was out at such an hour on such a cold night, so I just stood there and watched him. He goes right up to the night depository, pulls it open with his cane handle sort of fumbly like, and shoves an envelope down the chute. Then he turns around and walks back toward Oak Street.

Now I'm confused. I know damn sure he doesn't have to do that any more. Miriam Koser takes care of his social security checks. But even so, there's nobody in that bank. It's clean empty.

This was about six months after they opened the new building up on the ridge and locked the old one up. Tore it down this spring to put up those apartments. So Zane's making a deposit in a bank that's not even open for business and never will be again. Right then and there I know he's crazy, but I start to wonder about what he's putting in that night depository slot. I hoped it wasn't any money because he sure as hell can't afford that. I figured pretty easy that he's going back in his mind in time, you know, making those deposits to pay back the bank like he did for so many years.

I didn't mention it to anybody. Nobody's business but his, really, and I didn't think he was hurting anything. Miriam kept tight enough watch on his money that he wouldn't put much down there, if any, and if he did drop a dollar or two down, well, like I said, his business. I thought if it made him happy, fine.

I'd sort of forgot about it by the next Friday night. It wasn't until I'd gotten up about four or so to visit the john that it crossed by mind. So I looked out the window, never really expecting to see Zane out there at that time, just one of the things you do, and I see this mound of white in front of the night depository.

It'd been snowing earlier, but had stopped. The streets were all covered with it, and there was just this mound of white lying there. And I knew right away what it was, that it was Zane Kaylor. So I pulled my clothes on and called Doctor Barnes before I went out, even though I knew that if it wasn't Zane I'd look goddam stupid, but I was sure it was.

Then I went out and across the street and brushed the snow off him, and it was him, lying there curled up like a baby, looking as if he was sleeping, and there was a little smile froze on his face. Doctor Barnes came up shortly after, and young Bob Darkes, the cop, was with him. They saw right away he was dead, and Doctor Barnes started feeling over him to see how long he'd been there. I could've told him since midnight, but he didn't ask.

Anyway, the doc pulls off one of Zane's mittens and just yells, real frightened like. Bob Darkes and me look down at Zane and see what's scared the doc so.

Zane's hand's got no fingers on it.

Then I know everything. I know why Zane started limping last summer, and I know why it got worse as the weeks went on. I know why he kept his mittens on, even inside stores, when fall came. And I know that it hasn't been money he's been dropping down the mouth of that night depository every Friday midnight.

The twenty white envelopes Bob Darkes found in the cellar of the old bank proved me right. Even when the money was all paid to the bank, Zane Kaylor had to start paying off his debt to Tommy Martin.

Next morning the sun melted the snow on the sidewalk, and I found something Bob Darkes hadn't. It was an old bankbook. I don't know where Zane had got it, but he'd scratched his name on the first page. The rest of it was blank.

Two days later I slipped it into Zane's coffin at his funeral, but not before I wrote PAID IN FULL smack dab in the middle of the last page.

Nightshapes

By Barry N. Malzberg

1 August

Small flecks of blood in her pelt when she returned this evening, the Change a hot and deadly flicker in the dry spaces of the room, the odor sharp, whimpers as she shrugged back into her own form. Then clambering against me in the night, her teeth hot and sharp, the net of her hands drawing me in, drawing me in, and at the end a cry lupine and fierce, my own cry muffled in that desperate exchange of the blood. And now she lies open to the night and circumstance and I sit here and look at her, her body curled in the tentativeness of sleep, the submissiveness of darkness . . . and I do not know, I do not know. She is not the monster, I am the monster. If I were not the monster I would find the cure for her, grant her peace, that most precious gift. I understand this now but to understand is nothing. Nothing. The commission is unspeakable.

2 August

The researches disclose few explanations, the foaming beakers in the shoddy laboratory below stairs yield the most uncertain of formulae. I struggle nonetheless. I must help her.

At one time it all appeared simple, a simplicity: the mystery would open its darkest of hearts and one by one the methods of rationality would provide rational method. I was a fool, of course. I have always been a fool and I understand that too, now. Something about her in her present condition is attractive to me; it is not the wife with whom I am lying on these nights but the wolf, it is not the wife but the wolf whom I penetrate, the image of the beast at the center of all ecstasy. I admit this now; I must always have known it, it must have been the wolf that drove me on or long since I would have made myself free.

I think that I have gone mad.

Nonetheless I believe I have, at long last, devised a potion.

I will administer it to her tomorrow night.

"I'm going out, Eric," she said to me, "I'm going to walk on the fields." Actually they are not fields but rolling empty moors beyond this village in which our house and those of a few stolid neighbors cluster. She is, however, of a romantic turn of mind. Werewolves of necessity must be romantic; it is only this which protects them from the truest apprehension of their being. I allow her these expressions, then. "I wouldn't wait up, Eric, I will be out quite late. I need to think, and I'm restless."

"Yes, Clara," I said. Clara, clearness, clarity. She takes me to be a fool unaware of her condition, her contempt is absolute, but I do not care. For if she knew the degree of my apprehension, what might she do? She might turn upon me. Better to feed her the potion which unsuspecting she drank in her tea at that moment. "Yes, Clara, Clarinda, do as you must." I affected a scholarly bumble, a researcher's detachment, a mild, stunned old man puttering around the ruins of his ambition. "I will not wait up for you."

"I would ask you to walk with me," she said, "but I know what the cold does to your feet, your digestion. Besides, I walk more quickly than you and you might lose your footing."

She is twenty-four, young, graceful, pretty by all conventional standards: What would she want with a man such as me? My own motivations are less mysterious; familiar needs extrude through this uncomfortable shroud of age. But why would Clara, Clarice, Clarinda desire a man with blanket drawn up to his knees, fervidly drinking tea in hot gulps on a cool and penetrating night?

She took another sip from her cup; it clattered against the saucer. Will the potion help her? It is my only hope.

"On the way in," I said, "you might check to see that the fire is still lit. I will be long asleep by then."

"Of course," she said. She came to kiss me with cool and deadly lips, smoothed the blanket over my frail lap. Her features are of unusual delicacy, her bosom soft and fragrant, the taunting secrets which have been revealed to me one by one infinitely tantalizing, leading me to consummation that can never have issue. Of what matter should it be that she is a werewolf? At that moment, feeling her hands light upon me, I came close or closer to the acceptance of my condition.

It is not bad to be here alone with her on the edge of the moors, even though the terrain is already splattered with the blood of another victim. The graves surrounding London know the bodies of more than even I could suspect; they swaddle knowledge that will never be mine. It was necessary for us to leave London in absurd haste and for the flimsiest of excuses. I cannot stand civilization, clutter; we must move, I must have space, she said to me, and I abandoned my position at the university, my domicile, the rounds of my life to move to this place with her.

Some would call this the damp clutch of passion, but I would assay it as sanity. The police would have come sooner or later, and I would have been implicated. Therefore my researches and at last the potion, the potion that must grant her a cure.

"I will return, Eric," she said and left the room, left the fire, the door clattering behind her, then silence. I wondered if the Change would come upon her immediately, as it so often does, or whether the potion would block it. Or whether, more likely, there would be a retarding action and she would retain human custody until she was beyond the village. Once I would have peered through the window to find the truth, but now I have all the truth with which I can deal in the premises of my consciousness.

I do not want to know.

She will do as she must, just as will I, and when she returns we will huddle in the night and from that jumbled mass on the bed will come the cry. The cry that rends me from myself, my own change, the mantle of change descended, and lupine I will scream within her.

In the darkness.

4 August

These notes commenced at month's beginning, when the potion was nearly perfected, to attempt some order: If I could place on this chaos some sense of progression, string the beads of the days one by one upon the long, raveled line of life, then I might have some grasp of what was happening. I thought. But it was a bad idea. I am a vain man and endlessly these entries refract upon myself: my pain, my researches, my potion and its administration. Not her pain but mine. I am a useless man, useless and frivolous to the core. The word, perhaps, is silly. I am a silly man, Eric the silly, but his Clara, Clarice, Clarinda matters. She matters.

For she crept in again with blood upon her jaws.

Lying in the bed, my eyes alert to the terrible light of that first dawn, I saw her slip within, a gray shape, ears pricked, tail at an angle. And on her jaws, the blood. I feigned sleep, that sodden unconsciousness with which aspect I have always confronted her, leading her to the feeling (it is justified) that she has married a fool who will protect her forever and will never know what she is; but I was intent on her every gesture. Slow murmurous whimpers came from her throat. To be a werewolf is to hurt. The freedom of her nightshape cannot console. Weeping, she came to the bed.

I waited for the scent and aura of the Change, but it did not come. She poised, ears down. Why was she not Changing?

The potion?

Was that its effect, a retarded change? Had it worked against rather than toward her humanity?

Outside, a distant cry. And another and another. It is quiet in the village at dawn but it was not quiet now: Her latest victim had been found. Soft growls and the whimpers from within her. I knew her fear then, shared it, and in that moment saw that if the villagers were to come here, if we were somehow to be discovered, it would not be Clarice, Clarinda but we two with whom they would have to deal.

The distant cries faded.

The Change came upon her convulsively.

It came in that next instant and this creature—not my wife, not a wolf—lay stunned on the floor and wept. I dared not stretch a hand in entreaty or comfort; were she to see me it would end for us at once and I would never possess her again. *Had* the potion affected her in some way? Would it yet lead to a cure?

After a time she came to bed.

I touched her then and felt the terrible desire raging, and in her way she accommodated me as she always has. On one corner of her mouth, still a small spot of blood, a gangrenous red eye winking as if to lure me home. I lay across her, sunlight in the room. We slept.

And awoke and began the new day. It was an old man, a wanderer on the moors, who died last night. I have heard a fragmentary report from the postman. I dare not go among the villagers to inquire further; unusual interest would only draw attention.

5 August

I have reread these entries.

The only way I can make sense of them now is to see them as done by a man enthralled. And although this is part of it, enchantment is not all. There is something else about me, something about my obsession I cannot reach. The formulae are strong and the answer lies within them; I must believe that. For only when the Change has come to Clara for the last time will I be able to understand the change that has taken place in me.

Yet I still do not know if the potion has worked or not. I must understand the truth; if I have not helped her I cannot . . . to improve the formulae is beyond my means. Also I am much agitated. The last murder was unspeakable. Its details cannot be communicated in the journal of Eric the silly; I have no taste for horror, nor can I convey it. I was made for idiosyncrasy: brandy and badminton, conundrums in the eventide, little tales for infants as conceived by my equally frivolous colleague Dodgson.

I still do not know.

6 August

"You must not go out tonight," I said to her this evening, when she was already pacing and I could sense the need inside her. Yet her aspect was merry. "You must stay here."

"Eric," she said with that strange and solemn gaiety, "you mustn't tell me what to do."

"There was another murder three nights ago. This is no time for a young woman to walk alone on the moors."

"You know the conditions, Eric," she said. "They were made quite clear at the outset, when I agreed to marry, that you would never interfere with me nor I with you. What we do alone must never be questioned." She was smiling. Her eyes were joyous. Was it the potion, which I had again administered in her tea? Or was it anticipation of the night's hunt which made her seem so happy?

"You must not go out," I said again. Fear gave me the force of determination. "Not until the murders are solved."

"I am not afraid, Eric." She walked to the door.

I followed her. Seized her wrist. "I have been searching for a cure," I said. "I know your pain and I can help you find its release."

Her eyes shone with that solemn gaiety. "What are you trying to say?" she said. "Eric, what are you saying?"

"The truth." Grief lent me strength. "We can no longer conceal the truth from each other. Clarice, Clarinda, I have known, I have always known—"

"Known what?"

"About your affliction," I said. "About the Change."

She broke away from me. Still that strange gaiety. "You've given me something, haven't you. Something from your laboratory."

"Yes. But I—"

"Then you understand everything," she said, "but you understand nothing." She spread her fingers and looked into her palm, gazed into it with an expression of delight. "After such cunning, to show such ignoble stupidity!" She opened the door, little bubbles of laughter coming from her throat. I reached toward her. "No," she said, "don't stop me, you won't like it if you do."

And she was gone.

She was gone and I let her go, I sat here to write these words. But I cannot remain alone any longer, I cannot wait again for her to come home at the dawn light. I must follow her. I must know what I have done.

7 August

She is dead she

Is dead she is dead she

Is dead she is dead she was out there on the moors I saw her framed against the moon, I saw the light shining off her pelt and heard the laughter, oh the laughter, and she reached for her throat, I could not comprehend but she reached for her throat and now

I understand what she saw in her palm and what it is I have done, I understand everything: the nature of my own change and what I secretly desired from the first. I wanted to be what she was, a sleek gray shape running free with her in the night, and I yearn now to take the potion and wait for the Change, sit here upon my haunches in the dying blood of the day waiting for the pentagram to appear in my palm, the pentagram that would mark me as my own victim, waiting for the Change that can never come I

Want to be a werewolf so I can die like my Clara, Clarice, Clarinda, she

Tore her throat she

Tore out her own throat in the moonlight but

The moonlight has passed and the day has passed and the potion made her free, it worked as I could never have dreamed. I was not silly but a genius, a man of spirit but the spirit destroyed her and destroyed me, I was undone by my spirit and

And I needed her

I needed her, I needed the blood

Striking once and striking twice and striking thrice and the villagers are striking on the door, screaming, but I will say this, I will say this as they come with the torches that will burn me away, I will say I am not silly. I was a mind of iron, a will of fire. Silly no more silly no more, nor Eric that great Fool, but my Clara my Cordelia driven here and there alone upon the heath until that great wheel of self turned inward, her claws reaching, and only Blinded Gloucester left to show the way through that serene, that gay and mocking, that rigorous and deadly fire

The fire of the shapes of the night.

No. 1 Branch Line,
The Signalman

By Charles Dickens

Halloa! Below there!"

When he heard a voice thus calling to him, he was standing at the door of his box, with a flag in his hand, furled round its short pole. One would have thought, considering the nature of the ground, that he could not have doubted from what quarter the voice came; but, instead of looking up to where I stood on the top of the steep cutting nearly over his head, he turned himself about and looked down the Line. There was something remarkable in his manner of doing so, though I could not have said, for my life, what. But, I know it was remarkable enough to attract my notice, even though his figure was foreshortened and shadowed, down in the deep trench, and mine was high above him, so steeped in the glow of an angry sunset that I had shaded my eyes with my hand before I saw him at all.

"Halloa! Below!"

From looking down the Line, he turned himself about again, and, raising his eyes, saw my figure high above him.

"Is there any path by which I can come down and speak to you?"

He looked up at me without replying, and I looked down at him without pressing him too soon with a repetition of my idle question. Just then, there came a vague vibration in the earth and air, quickly changing into a violent pulsation, and an oncoming rush that caused me to start back, as though it had force to draw me down. When such vapour as rose to my height from this rapid train, had passed me and was skimming away over the landscape, I looked down again, and saw him re-furling the flag he had shown while the train went by.

I repeated my inquiry. After a pause, during which he seemed to regard me with fixed attention, he motioned with his rolled-up flag towards a point on my level, some two or three hundred yards distant. I called down to him, "All right!" and made for that point. There, by dint of looking closely about me, I found a rough zig-zag descending path notched out: which I followed.

The cutting was extremely deep, and unusually precipitate. It was made through a clammy stone that became oozier and wetter as I went down. For these reasons, I found the way long enough to give me time to recall a singular air of reluctance or compulsion with which he had pointed out the path.

When I came down low enough upon the zig-zag descent, to see him again, I saw that he was standing between the rails on the way by which the train had lately passed, in an attitude as if he were waiting for me to appear. He had his left hand at his chin, and that left elbow rested on his right hand crossed over his breast. His attitude was one of such expectation and watchfulness, that I stopped a moment, wondering at it.

I resumed my downward way, and, stepping out upon the level of the railroad and drawing nearer to him, saw that he was a dark sallow man, with a dark beard and rather heavy eyebrows. His post was in as solitary and dismal a place as ever I saw. On either side, a dripping-wet wall of jagged stone, excluding all view but a strip of sky; the perspective one way, only a crooked prolongation of this great dungeon; the shorter perspective in the other direction, terminating in a gloomy red light, and the gloomier entrance to a black tunnel, in whose massive architecture there was a barbarous, depressing, and forbidding air. So little sunlight ever found its way to this spot, that it had an earthy deadly smell; and so much cold wind rushed through it, that it struck chill to me, as if I had left the natural world.

Before he stirred, I was near enough to him to have touched him. Not even then removing his eyes from mine, he stepped back one step, and lifted his hand.

This was a lonesome post to occupy (I said), and it had riveted my attention when I looked down from up yonder. A visitor was a rarity, I should suppose; not an unwelcome rarity, I hoped? In me, he merely saw a man who had been shut up within narrow limits all his life, and who, being at last set free, had a newly-awakened interest in these great works. To such purpose I spoke to him; but I am far from sure of the terms I used, for, besides that I am not happy in opening any conversation, there was something in the man that daunted me.

He directed a most curious look towards the red light near the tunnel's mouth, and looked all about it, as if something were missing from it, and then looked at me.

That light was part of his charge? Was it not?

He answered in a low voice: "Don't you know it is?"

The monstrous thought came into my mind as I perused the fixed eyes and the saturnine face, that this was a spirit, not a man. I have speculated since, whether there may have been infection in his mind.

In my turn, I stepped back. But in making the action, I detected in his eyes some latent fear of me. This put the monstrous thought to flight.

"You look at me," I said, forcing a smile, "as if you had a dread of me."

"I was doubtful," he returned, "whether I had seen you before."

"Where?"

He pointed to the red light he had looked at.

"There?" I said.

Intently watchful of me, he replied (but without sound), Yes.

"My good fellow, what should I do there? However, be that as it may, I never was there, you may swear."

"I think I may," he rejoined. "Yes. I am sure I may."

His manner cleared, like my own. He replied to my remarks with readiness, and in well-chosen words. Had he much to do there? Yes; that was to say, he had enough responsibility to bear; but exactness and watchfulness were what was required of him, and of actual work—manual labour—he had next to none. To change that signal, to trim those lights, and to turn this iron handle now and then, was all he had to do under that head. Regarding those many long and lonely hours of which I seemed to make so much, he could only say that the routine of his life had shaped itself into that form, and he had grown used to it. He had taught himself a language down here—if only to know it by sight, and to have formed his own crude ideas of its pronunciation, could be called learning it. He had also worked at fractions and decimals and tried a little algebra; but he was, and had been as a boy, a poor hand at figures. Was it necessary for him when on duty, always to remain in that channel of damp air, and could he never rise into the sunshine from between those high stone walls? Why, that depended upon times and circumstances. Under some conditions there would be less upon the Line than under others, and the same held good as to certain hours of the day and night. In bright weather, he did choose occasions for getting a little above these lower shadows; but, being at all times liable to be called by his electric bell, and at such times listening for it with redoubled anxiety, the relief was less than I would suppose.

He took me into his box, where there was a fire, a desk for an official book in which he had to make certain entries, a telegraphic instrument with its dial face and needles, and the little bell of which he had spoken. On my trusting that he would excuse the remark that he had been well educated, and (I hoped I might say without offence), perhaps educated above that station, he observed that instances of slight incongruity in such-wise would rarely be found wanting among large bodies of men; that he had heard it was so in workhouses, in the police force, even in that last desperate resource, the army; and that he knew it was so, more or less, in any great railway staff. He had been, when young (if I could believe it, sitting in that hut; he scarcely could), a student of natural philosophy, and had attended lectures; but he had run wild, misused his opportunities, gone down, and never risen again. He had no complaint to offer about that. He had made his bed, and he lay upon it. It was far too late to make another.

All that I have here condensed, he said in a quiet manner, with his grave dark regards divided between me and the fire. He threw in the word "Sir," from time to time, and especially when he referred to his youth: as though to request me to understand that he claimed to be nothing but what I found him. He was several times interrupted by the little bell, and had to read off messages, and send replies. Once, he had to stand without the door, and display a flag as a train passed, and make some verbal communication to the driver. In the discharge of his duties I observed him to be remarkably exact and vigilant, breaking off his discourse at a syllable, and remaining silent until what he had to do was done.

In a word, I should have set this man down as one of the safest of men to be employed in that capacity, but for the circumstance that while he was speaking to me he twice broke off with a fallen colour, turned his face towards the little bell when it did NOT ring, opened the door of the hut (which was kept shut to exclude the unhealthy damp), and looked out towards the red light near the mouth of the tunnel. On both of those occasions, he came back to the fire with the inexplicable air upon him which I had remarked, without being able to define, when we were so far asunder.

Said I when I rose to leave him: "You almost make me think that I have met with a contented man."

(I am afraid I must acknowledge that I said it to lead him on.)

"I believe I used to be so," he rejoined, in the low voice in which he had first spoken; "but I am troubled, sir, I am troubled."

He would have recalled the words if he could. He had said them, however, and I took them up quickly.

"With what? What is your trouble?"

"It is very difficult to impart, sir. It is very, very, difficult to speak of. If ever you make me another visit, I will try to tell you."

"But I expressly intend to make you another visit. Say, when shall it be?"

"I go off early in the morning, and I shall be on again at ten to-morrow night, sir."

"I will come at eleven."

He thanked me, and went out at the door with me. "I'll show my white light, sir," he said, in his peculiar low voice, "till you have found the way up. When you have found it, don't call out! And when you are at the top, don't call out!"

His manner seemed to make the place strike colder to me, but I said no more than "Very well."

"And when you come down to-morrow night, don't call out! Let me ask you a parting question. What made you cry 'Halloa! Below there!' to-night?"

"Heaven knows," said I. "I cried something to that effect——"

"Not to that effect, sir. Those were the very words. I know them well."

"Admit those were the very words. I said them, no doubt, because I saw you below."

"For no other reason?"

"What other reason could I possibly have?"

"You had no feeling that they were conveyed to you in any supernatural way?"

"No."

He wished me good night, and held up his light. I walked by the side of the down Line of rails (with a very disagreeable sensation of a train coming behind me), until I found the path. It was easier to mount than to descend, and I got back to my inn without any adventure.

Punctual to my appointment, I placed my foot on the first notch of the zig-zag next night, as the distant clocks were striking eleven. He was waiting for me at the bottom, with his white light on. "I have not called out," I said, when we came close together; "may I speak now?" "By all means, sir." "Good night then, and here's my hand." "Good night, sir, and here's mine." With that, we walked

342

side by side to his box, entered it, closed the door, and sat down by the fire.

"I have made up my mind, sir," he began, bending forward as soon as we were seated, and speaking in a tone but a little above a whisper, "that you shall not have to ask me twice what troubles me. I took you for some one else yesterday evening. That troubles me."

"That mistake?"

"No. That some one else."

"Who is it?"

"I don't know."

"Like me?"

"I don't know. I never saw the face. The left arm is across the face and the right arm is waved. Violently waved. This way."

I followed his action with my eyes, and it was the action of an arm gesticulating with the utmost passion and vehemence: "For God's sake clear the way!"

"One moonlight night," said the man, "I was sitting here, when I heard a voice cry 'Halloa! Below there!' I started up, looked from that door, and saw this Some one else standing by the red light near the tunnel, waving as I just now showed you. The voice seemed hoarse with shouting, and it cried, 'Look out! Look out!' And then again 'Halloa! Below there! Look out!' I caught up my lamp, turned it on red, and ran towards the figure calling, 'What's wrong? What has happened? Where?' It stood just outside the blackness of the tunnel. I advanced so close upon it that I wondered at its keeping the sleeve across its eyes. I ran right up at it, and had my hand stretched out to pull the sleeve away, when it was gone."

"Into the tunnel," said I.

"No. I ran on into the tunnel, five hundred yards. I stopped and held my lamp above my head and saw the figures of the measured distance, and saw the wet stains stealing down the walls and trickling through the arch. I ran out again, faster than I had run in (for I had a mortal abhorrence of the place upon me), and I looked all round the red light with my own red light, and I went up the iron ladder to the gallery atop of it, and I came down again, and ran back here. I telegraphed both ways: 'An alarm has been given. Is anything wrong?' The answer came back, both ways: 'All well.' "

Resisting the slow touch of a frozen finger tracing out my spine, I showed him how that this figure must be a deception of his sense of sight, and how that figures, originating in disease of the delicate nerves that minister to the functions of the eye, were known to have often troubled patients, some of whom had become conscious of the nature of their affliction, and had even proved it by experiments upon themselves. "As to an imaginary cry," said I, "do but listen for a moment to the wind in this unnatural valley while we speak so low, and to the wild harp it makes of the telegraph wires!"

That was all very well, he returned, after we had sat listening for a while, and he ought to know something of the wind and the wires, he who so often passed long winter nights there, alone and watching. But he would beg to remark that he had not finished.

I asked his pardon, and he slowly added these words, touching my arm:

"Within six hours after the Appearance, the memorable accident on this Line happened, and within ten hours the dead and wounded were brought along through the tunnel over the spot where the figure had stood."

A disagreeable shudder crept over me, but I did my best against it. It was not to be denied, I rejoined, that this was a remarkable coincidence, calculated deeply to impress his mind. But, it was unquestionable that remarkable coincidences did continually occur, and they must be taken into account in dealing with such a subject. Though to be sure I must admit, I added (for I thought I saw that he was going to bring the objection to bear upon me), men of common sense did not allow much for coincidences in making the ordinary calculations of life.

He again begged to remark that he had not finished.

I again begged his pardon for being betrayed into interruptions.

"This," he said, again laying his hand upon my arm, and glancing over his shoulder with hollow eyes, "was just a year ago. Six or seven months passed, and I had recovered from the surprise and shock, when one morning, as the day was breaking, I, standing at that door, looked towards the red light, and saw the spectre again." He stopped, with a fixed look at me.

"Did it cry out?"

"No. It was silent."

"Did it wave its arm?"

"No. It leaned against the shaft of the light, with both hands before the face. Like this."

Once more, I followed his action with my eyes. It was an action of mourning. I have seen such an attitude in stone figures on tombs.

"Did you go up to it?"

"I came in and sat down, partly to collect my thoughts, partly because it had turned me faint. When I went to the door again, daylight was above me, and the ghost was gone."

"But nothing followed? Nothing came of this?"

344

He touched me on the arm with his forefinger twice or thrice, giving a ghastly nod each time:

"That very day, as a train came out of the tunnel, I noticed at a carriage window on my side, what looked like a confusion of hands and heads, and something waved. I saw it, just in time to signal the driver, Stop! He shut off, and put his brake on, but the train drifted past here a hundred and fifty yards or more. I ran after it, and, as I went along, heard terrible screams and cries. A beautiful young lady had died instantaneously in one of the compartments, and was brought in here, and laid down on this floor between us."

Involuntarily, I pushed my chair back, as I looked from the boards at which he pointed, to himself.

"True, sir. True. Precisely as it happened, so I tell it you."

I could think of nothing to say, to any purpose, and my mouth was very dry. The wind and the wires took up the story with a long lamenting wail.

He resumed. "Now, sir, mark this, and judge how my mind is troubled. The spectre came back, a week ago. Ever since, it has been there, now and again, by fits and starts."

"At the light?"

"At the Danger-light."

"What does it seem to do?"

He repeated, if possible with increased passion and vehemence, that former gesticulation of "For God's sake clear the way!"

Then, he went on. "I have no peace or rest for it. It calls to me, for many minutes together, in an agonised manner, 'Below there! Look out! Look out!' It stands waving to me. It rings my little bell——"

I caught at that. "Did it ring your bell yesterday evening when I was here, and you went to the door?"

"Twice."

"Why, see," said I, "how your imagination misleads you. My eyes were on the bell, and my ears were open to the bell, and if I am a living man, it did NOT ring at those times. No, nor at any other time, except when it was rung in the natural course of physical things by the station communicating with you."

He shook his head. "I have never made a mistake as to that, yet, sir. I have never confused the spectre's ring with the man's. The ghost's ring is a strange vibration in the bell that it derives from nothing else, and I have not asserted that the bell stirs to the eye. I don't wonder that you failed to hear it. But I heard it."

"And did the spectre seem to be there, when you looked out?"

"It WAS there."

"Both times?"

He repeated firmly: "Both times."

"Will you come to the door with me, and look for it now?"

He bit his under-lip as though he were somewhat unwilling, but arose. I opened the door, and stood on the step, while he stood in the doorway. There, was the Danger-light. There, was the dismal mouth of the tunnel. There, were the high wet stone walls of the cutting. There, were the stars above them.

"Do you see it?" I asked him, taking particular note of his face. His eyes were prominent and strained; but not very much more so, perhaps, than my own had been when I had directed them earnestly towards the same spot.

"No," he answered. "It is not there."

"Agreed," said I.

We went in again, shut the door, and resumed our seats. I was thinking how best to improve this advantage, if it might be called one, when he took up the conversation in such a matter of course way, so assuming that there could be no serious question of fact between us, that I felt myself placed in the weakest of positions.

"By this time you will fully understand, sir," he said, "that what troubles me so dreadfully, is the question, What does the spectre mean?"

I was not sure, I told him, that I did fully understand.

"What is its warning against?" he said, ruminating, with his eyes on the fire, and only by times turning them on me. "What is the danger? Where is the danger? There is danger overhanging, somewhere on the Line. Some dreadful calamity will happen. It is not to be doubted this third time, after what has gone before. But surely this is a cruel haunting of *me*. What can *I* do?"

He pulled out his handkerchief, and wiped the drops from his heated forehead.

"If I telegraph Danger, on either side of me, or on both, I can give no reason for it," he went on, wiping the palms of his hands. "I should get into trouble, and do no good. They would think I was mad. This is the way it would work:—Message: 'Danger! Take care!' Answer: 'What Danger? Where?' Message: 'Don't know. But for God's sake take care!' They would displace me. What else could they do?"

His pain of mind was most pitiable to see. It was the mental torture of a conscientious man, oppressed beyond endurance by unintelligible responsibility involving life.

"When it first stood under the Danger-light," he went on, putting his dark hair back from his head, and drawing his hands out-

346

ward across and across his temples in an extremity of feverish distress, "why not tell me where that accident was to happen—if it must happen? Why not tell me how it could be averted—if it could have been averted? When on its second coming it hid its face, why not tell me instead: 'She is going to die. Let them keep her at home'? If it came, on those two occasions, only to show me that its warnings were true, and so to prepare me for the third, why not warn me plainly now? And I, Lord help me! A mere poor signal-man on this solitary station! Why not go to somebody with credit to be believed, and power to act!"

When I saw him in this state, I saw that for the poor man's sake, as well as for the public safety, what I had to do for the time was, to compose his mind. Therefore, setting aside all question of reality or unreality between us, I represented to him that whoever thoroughly discharged his duty, must do well, and that at least it was his comfort that he understood his duty, though he did not understand these confounding Appearances. In this effort I succeeded far better than in the attempt to reason him out of his conviction. He became calm; the occupations incidental to his post as the night advanced, began to make larger demands on his attention; and I left him at two in the morning. I had offered to stay through the night, but he would not hear of it.

That I more than once looked back at the red light as I ascended the pathway, that I did not like the red light, and that I should have slept but poorly if my bed had been under it, I see no reason to conceal. Nor, did I like the two sequences of the accident and the dead girl. I see no reason to conceal that, either.

But, what ran most in my thoughts was the consideration how ought I to act, having become the recipient of this disclosure? I had proved the man to be intelligent, vigilant, painstaking, and exact; but how long might he remain so, in his state of mind? Though in a subordinate position, still he held a most important trust, and would I (for instance) like to stake my own life on the chances of his continuing to execute it with precision?

Unable to overcome a feeling that there would be something treacherous in my communicating what he had told me, to his superiors in the Company, without first being plain with himself and proposing a middle course to him, I ultimately resolved to offer to accompany him (otherwise keeping his secret for the present) to the wisest medical practitioner we could hear of in those parts, and to take his opinion. A change in his time of duty would come round next night, he had apprised me, and he would be off an hour or two after sunrise, and on again soon after sunset. I had appointed to return accordingly.

Next evening was a lovely evening, and I walked out early to enjoy it. The sun was not yet quite down when I traversed the field-path near the top of the deep cutting. I would extend my walk for an hour, I said to myself, half an hour on and half an hour back, and it would then be time to go to my signalman's box.

Before pursuing my stroll, I stepped to the brink, and mechanically looked down, from the point from which I had first seen him. I cannot describe the thrill that seized upon me, when, close at the mouth of the tunnel, I saw the appearance of a man, with his left sleeve across his eyes, passionately waving his right arm.

The nameless horror that oppressed me, passed in a moment, for in a moment I saw that this appearance of a man was a man indeed, and that there was a little group of other men standing at a short distance, to whom he seemed to be rehearsing the gesture he made. The Danger-light was not yet lighted. Against its shaft, a little low hut, entirely new to me, had been made of some wooden supports and tarpaulin. It looked no bigger than a bed.

With an irresistible sense that something was wrong—with a flashing self-reproachful fear that fatal mischief had come of my leaving the man there, and causing no one to be sent to overlook or correct what he did—I descended the notched path with all the speed I could make.

"What is the matter?" I asked the men.

"Signalman killed this morning, sir."

"Not the man belonging to that box?"

"Yes, sir."

"Not the man I know?"

"You will recognise him, sir, if you knew him," said the man who spoke for the others, solemnly uncovering his own head and raising an end of the tarpaulin, "for his face is quite composed."

"Oh! how did this happen, how did this happen?" I asked, turning from one to another as the hut closed in again.

"He was cut down by an engine, sir. No man in England knew his work better. But somehow he was not clear of the outer rail. It was just at broad day. He had struck the light, and had the lamp in his hand. As the engine came out of the tunnel, his back was towards her, and she cut him down. That man drove her, and was showing how it happened. Show the gentleman, Tom."

The man, who wore a rough dark dress, stepped back to his former place at the mouth of the tunnel:

"Coming round the curve in the tunnel, sir," he said, "I saw him at the end, like as if I saw him down a perspective-glass. There was no time to check speed, and I knew him to be very careful. As he didn't seem to take heed of the whistle, I shut it off when we were running down upon him, and called to him as loud as I could call."

"What did you say?"

"I said, Below there! Look out! Look out! For God's sake clear the way!"

I started.

"Ah! it was a dreadful time, sir, I never left off calling to him. I put this arm before my eyes, not to see, and I waved this arm to the last; but it was no use."

Without prolonging the narrative to dwell on any one of its curious circumstances more than on any other, I may, in closing it, point out the coincidence that the warning of the Engine-Driver included, not only the words which the unfortunate Signalman had repeated to me as haunting him, but also the words which I myself —not he—had attached, and that only in my own mind, to the gesticulation he had imitated.

The Old Black Hat

By Gary Raisor

In December, magic came to Gaulley Bridge. Everyone recalled the exact week it happened. It was the same week the town was plagued by two heavy snowfalls, followed by two sudden thaws.

Only one little girl knew what happened, and no one would have believed her anyway. A few of the older residents suspected something strange.

And they weren't talking either.

Of course, nobody cares to talk about what happened on that day. Just a nervous whisper now and then. But we're getting ahead of our story.

A shiny black top hat bounced down the street propelled by a gust of wind, caught in the eddying currents, rolled and tumbled end over end until it finally came to rest against the wheel of an equally shiny black car.

No one came rushing after the hat. It waited patiently to be discovered.

Seven-year-old Chris Chandler walked toward the water that cried out to be splattered. His new shoes made neat squishy sounds in the mud, and he was almost happy. Except . . . following closely behind was the permanent hardship of his life, his younger sister, Sarah.

"Don't you ever wanna get in trouble?" he asked in a voice filled with bafflement, turning to stare at the pudgy four-year-old. Clumping along the sidewalk in her orange snowsuit, she looked a lot like an overweight carrot.

"No! And you'd better not jump in the water," Sarah warned him in a whine that always took the fun out of *everything*. "I'll tell Mom," she added, dragging a mitten across her nose.

"If you do," Chris threatened in a tone that bordered on ominous, "I'll tell you the truth about Santa Claus."

The mittens flew protectively to her ears and tears began to gather in her eyes. Chris took one look at her and relented, but only because he didn't want to see her nose run any more—it was already a pretty disgusting mess.

"Where's your Kleenex?" he asked, weighing the pleasures of one good splatter against the probability of being sent to his room for the rest of the day. If he did it just right, he could knock that sucker dry.

"In my pocket," she answered with a loud sniff. The mittens lowered. "And you'd better not say nothing bad about Santa."

"You don't really believe all that stuff about Santa Claus, do you?" Chris sneered as he ran his hand along the long, shiny black flank of the car parked in the drive. His foot nudged something. Before he could bend down, Sarah darted in and scooped up the object.

"Aw, it's only a hat," Chris said in disgust, trying to mask his envy. He quickly dismissed her treasure. "Probably belongs to the guy who drives the car."

"No, it doesn't," Sarah corrected, her face flushing with sudden excitement, "it's Frosty the Snowman's hat. I just know it is." When Chris tried to reach for the hat, she cradled it tightly against her chest. "How about we build a snow man and put the hat on him?" Her face pleaded. "Please, Chris, don't you believe in magic?"

"Look, Dopey," he said, jerking a thumb at the muddy yard, "there ain't no snow. And there ain't no magic. Come on, let's go. Mom told us not to be gone too long. We gotta get to the church."

350

One step inside the door and Mom pounced. He risked a quick look at her face. Storm warnings, as his dad called them, were out. He knew he was in trouble, because her lips had almost disappeared.

Out of the tirade that washed over him, he was able to pick out two familiar phrases that always sounded like one: "Where's-your-sister-and-just-look-at-those-shoes-young-man."

Everyone in the room turned to stare. Totally embarrassed by this attention, he fled to the bathroom.

A moment later, the door cracked open. "See, I told you," Sarah said smugly, "it *is* magic."

"What are you talking about?" Chris asked as he stared dismally at the puddle gathering by his feet. No doubt about it, his brand new dress shoes were goners. Mom was Going. To. Be. Pissed.

"The hat," she gushed. "I went in and put it on Uncle Bill."

"You got snot for brains, Sarah. Uncle Bill's dead. Dad said they already embalmed—"

At that instant hoarse, inhuman screams of pain ripped through the funeral home. More screams from the terrified mourners joined the first. The crash of furniture added to the already deafening din.

"Am I in trouble?" Sarah asked, eyes widening.

"Boy are you *ever*," Chris said in a voice filled with something akin to awe.

Out of the Storm

By William Hope Hodgson

"Hush!" said my friend the scientist, as I walked into his laboratory. I had opened my lips to speak; but stood silent for a few minutes at his request.

He was sitting at his instrument, and the thing was tapping out a message in a curiously irregular fashion—stopping a few seconds, then going on at a furious pace.

It was during a somewhat longer than usual pause that, growing slightly impatient, I ventured to address him.

"Anything important?" I asked.

351

"For God's sake, shut up!" he answered back in a high, strained voice.

I stared. I am used to pretty abrupt treatment from him at times when he is much engrossed in some particular experiment; but this was going a little too far, and I said so.

He was writing, and, for reply, he pushed several loosely-written sheets over to me with the one curt word, "Read!"

With a sense half of anger, half of curiosity, I picked up the first and glanced at it. After a few lines, I was gripped and held securely by a morbid interest. I was reading a message from one in the last extremity. I will give it word for word:—

"John, we are sinking! I wonder if you really understand what I feel at the present time—you sitting comfortably in your laboratory, I out here upon the waters, already one among the dead. Yes, we are doomed. There is no such thing as help in our case. We are sinking—steadily, remorselessly. God! I must keep up and be a man! I need not tell you that I am in the operator's room. All the rest are on deck—or dead in the hungry thing which is smashing the ship to pieces.

"I do not know where we are, and there is no one of whom I can ask. The last of the officers was drowned nearly an hour ago, and the vessel is now little more than a sort of breakwater for the giant seas.

"Once, about half an hour ago, I went out on to the deck. My God! the sight was terrible. It is a little after midday: but the sky is the color of mud—do you understand?—gray mud! Down from it there hang vast lappets of clouds. Not such clouds as I have ever before seen; but monstrous, mildewed-looking hulls. They show solid, save where the frightful wind tears their lower edges into great feelers that swirl savagely above us, like the tentacles of some enormous Horror.

"Such a sight is difficult to describe to the living; though the Dead of the Sea know of it without words of mine. It is such a sight that none is allowed to see and live. It is a picture for the doomed and the dead; one of the sea's hell-orgies—one of the *Thing's* monstrous gloatings over the living—say the alive-in-death, those upon the brink. I have no right to tell of it to you; to speak of it to one of the living is to initiate innocence into one of the infernal mysteries —to talk of foul things to a child. Yet I care not! I will expose, in all its hideous nakedness, the death-side of the sea. The undoomed living shall know some of the things that death has hitherto so well guarded. Death knows not of this little instrument beneath my hands that connects me still with the quick, else would he haste to quiet me.

"Hark you, John! I have learnt undreamt of things in this little time of waiting. I know now why we are afraid of the dark. I had never imagined such secrets of the sea and the grave (which are one and the same).

"Listen! Ah, but I was forgetting you cannot hear! I can! The Sea is—Hush! the Sea is laughing, as though Hell cackled from the mouth of an ass. It is jeering. I can hear its voice echo like Satanic thunder amid the mud overhead—It is calling to me! call—I must go— The sea calls!

"Oh! God, art Thou indeed God? Canst Thou sit above and watch calmly that which I have just seen? Nay! Thou art no God! Thou art weak and puny beside this foul *Thing* which Thou didst create in Thy lusty youth. *It* is *now* God—and I am one of its children.

"Are you there, John? Why don't you answer! Listen! I ignore God; for there is a stronger than He. My God is here, beside me, around me, and will be soon above me. You know what that means. It is merciless. *The sea is now all the God there is!* That is one of the things I have learnt.

"Listen! *it,* is laughing again. God is *it,* not He.

"It called, and I went out on to the decks. All was terrible. *It* is in the waist—everywhere. *It* has swamped the ship. Only the forecastle, bridge and poop stick up out from the bestial, reeking *Thing,* like three islands in the midst of shrieking foam. At times gigantic billows assail the ship from both sides. They form momentary arches above the vessel—arches of dull, curved water half a hundred feet towards the hideous sky. Then they descend—roaring. Think of it! You cannot.

"There is an infection of sin in the air: it is the exhalations from the *Thing.* Those left upon the drenched islets of shattered wood and iron are doing the most horrible things. The *Thing* is teaching them. Later, I felt the vile informing of its breath; but I have fled back here—to pray for death.

"On the forecastle, I saw a mother and her little son clinging to an iron rail. A great billow heaved up above them—descended in a falling mountain of brine. It passed, and they were still there. The *Thing* was only toying with them; yet, all the same, it had torn the hands of the child from the rail, and the child was clinging frantically to its Mother's arm. I saw another vast hill hurl up to port and hover above them. Then the Mother stooped and bit like a foul beast at the hands of her wee son. She was afraid that his little additional weight would be more than she could hold. I heard his scream even where I stood—it drove to me upon that wild laughter. It told me again that God is not He, but *It*. Then the hill thundered down upon those two. It seemed to me that the *Thing* gave a bellow as it leapt. It roared about them churning and growling; then surged away, and there was only one—the Mother. There appeared to me to be blood as well as water upon her face, especially about her mouth; but the distance was too great, and I cannot be sure. I looked away. Close to me, I saw something further—a beautiful young girl (her soul hideous with the breath of the *Thing*) struggling with her sweetheart for the shelter of the charthouse side. He threw her off; but she came back at him. I saw her hand come from her head, where still clung the wreckage of some form of headgear. She struck at him. He shouted and fell away to leeward, and she—smiled, showing her teeth. So much for that. I turned elsewhere.

"Out upon the *Thing*, I saw gleams, horrid and suggestive, below the crests of the waves. I have never seen them until this time. I saw a rough sailorman washed away from the vessel. One of the huge breakers snapped at him!—Those things were teeth. *It* has teeth. I heard them clash. I heard his yell. It was no more than a mosquito's shrilling amid all that laughter: but it was very terrible. There is worse than death.

"The ship is lurching very queerly with a sort of sickening heave—

"I fancy I have been asleep. No—I remember now. I hit my head when she rolled so strangely. My leg is doubled under me. I think it is broken; but it does not matter—

"I have been praying. I—I—What was it? I feel calmer, more resigned, now. I think I have been mad. What was it that I was saying? I cannot remember. It was something about—about—God. I—I believe I blasphemed. May He forgive me! Thou knowest, God, that I was not in my right mind. Thou knowest that I am very weak. Be with me in the coming time! I have sinned: but Thou art all merciful.

"Are you there, John? It is very near the end now. I had so much to say; but it all slips from me. What was it that I said? I take it all back. I was mad, and—and God knows. He is merciful, and I have very little pain now. I feel a bit drowsy.

"I wonder whether you are there, John. Perhaps, after all, no

354

one has heard the things I have said. It is better so. The Living are not meant—and yet, I do not know. If you are there, John, you will —you will tell *her* how it was; but not—not—Hark! there was such a thunder of water overhead just then. I fancy two vast seas have met in mid-air across the top of the bridge and burst all over the vessel. It must be soon now—and there was such a number of things I had to say! I can hear voices in the wind. They are singing. It is like an enormous dirge—

"I think I have been dozing again. I pray God humbly that it be soon! You will not—not tell *her* anything about, about what I may have said, will you, John? I mean those things which I ought not to have said. What was it I did say? My head is growing strangely confused. I wonder whether you really do hear me. I may be talking only to that vast roar outside. Still, it is some comfort to go on, and I will not believe that you do not hear all I say. Hark again! A mountain of brine must have swept clean over the vessel. She has gone right over on to her side. . . . She is back again. It will be very soon now—

"Are you there, John? Are you there? It is coming! The Sea has come for me! It is rushing down through the companionway! It—it is like a vast jet! My God! I am dr-own-ing! I—am—dr—"

Out of Africa

By David Drake

Forty years of African sunlight glinting along Sir John Holborn's gun barrels had bleached his eyes so that even after long retirement from hunting they were the frosty gray of bullets cast when the lead was too hot. The chill of those eyes softened when they turned from the heavy rifle over the mantle to his young grand-nephew.

"Go ahead," Sir John urged. "Pick it up. I wasn't much older than you when I took my first elephant."

Randall carefully lifted the double rifle from its pegs and hefted it. "It's so big!" he marvelled.

Holborn chuckled and took the weapon himself. "Has to be big, lad, or the return of the rifle would break your shoulder." While his thoughts slipped into the past, the old hunter glanced around his trophy room. From the far wall projected the massive head and forequarters of a bull elephant, mounted as if trumpeting. With a single fluid motion, Holborn spun and trained the rifle on the gape of the beast's mouth where a shot would penetrate straight to the brain. Chuckling again, he turned back to the boy and opened the rifle's double breech.

"See lad," he said, "this is an eight-bore. A round lead ball to fit this barrel would weigh two ounces, and the cylindrical bullets I used were a good deal heavier. You couldn't put such power in a smaller rifle."

"My father shoots elephant," Randall said doubtfully, "and his rifle isn't that big."

"Aye, your father says there's been no need for old cannons like this since 1890 and nitro powder," Holborn agreed. "Well, maybe it did go out of date fifteen years ago; but if I went to Africa again, this is the rifle I'd carry there. Your father may be right to say his .450 express rifle will kill anything on the continent—but will it *stop* anything, that's what I want to know. Your Latin is fresher than mine. Do you remember a tag about Africa . . . ?"

" 'Always something new out of Africa,' " the boy suggested, translating Pliny's words for the old man.

"That's it," Holborn agreed, "and it's true, too. If you ever hunt Africa, don't make the mistake of thinking you know all about her. She'll kill you sure if you think that."

"Why did you stop hunting, Uncle John?" Randall asked curiously, gazing in wonder at the trophies of five continents on the walls around him.

"Um," the old hunter grunted, letting the rifle cradle naturally in the crook of his left arm. "For some hunters, there's one chance for a real trophy. After that, it's all the same whether you took it or missed. Gordon-Cummings had his when he bagged a rhino with five feet of horn, while Meyerling muffed an easy shot at an elephant he swore carried a quarter ton of ivory. When you've had that shot, the fire goes out of the sport, and it's never the same again. And I, I had my shot. . . ."

Randall could see the old man's mind focusing on the past. "Tell me about it, Uncle John," he pleaded.

"Perhaps I should, lad," Holborn replied. "I shan't be around much longer to keep the story, and perhaps some day—but no matter. My last hunt was on the Kagera River, west and north of Lake Victoria. The country was all papyrus swamp."

"But what could you do in that?" the boy asked in puzzlement.

356

"Hunt hippo, lad," Holborn replied with a laugh, "and very political hippo they were. That was in '92, you see, and—well, it's an old story and doesn't matter much any more. Our relations with the Kaiser were a good deal better then, and it occurred to some gentlemen in London and Berlin that King Leopold was showing himself quite unfit to rule the Congo Basin. Perhaps Britain and Germany could do better, they thought. Well, nothing came of it, of course . . . but negotiations got to the point that the Foreign Office thought they'd like to have a man on the ground. They contacted me because no eyebrows would raise at the news Sir John Holborn was back in the bush again. And so there I was, in German East Africa where it borders Uganda and the Congo.

"There were hippos in the river. Even if I hadn't cared to try them, I had to keep up the pretence of being strictly a hunter. It was difficult, though, because none of the local boys would so much as guide me into the swamps around their village. They were afraid of the *jimpegwes* that lived there, they said.

"Now I hadn't heard the word before, but it was clear enough from the natives' description what they meant. After all, only three big animals live in the swamps: the kob and lechwe antelopes that can walk on the marshes with their broad, spreading hooves; and the hippo that browse the edges of the reed mats and keep channels open between them. When the natives said the jimpegwe was a big animal that ate reeds and had a terrible temper, they had to mean some sort of hippo.

"Some sort—that was the key. All the natives agreed that the jimpegwe was bigger than imkoko, as they called the hippo. They said in fact that it killed hippos that wandered into its territory. As I heard about how big and terrible the jimpegwe was, I began to dream of surprising the world with a breed of hippo as much bigger than the known variety as the white rhino is bigger than the black. That would put it in a class with the elephant, you know. After a day of hearing those stories while I tried to hire guides and bearers, I knew I'd have to get into the swamp if it meant lugging my own kit.

"Which is very nearly what it did mean, as it turned out. The local natives accompanied me to the edge of the swamp, but nothing I could offer would bring them further. I couldn't entirely blame them. They had no reason to trust my eight-bore, and hippos can be very dangerous indeed. I've seen a native bitten in half by an old bull he'd harpooned. The hippo spat out the pieces, of course, but the beast's diet was of no concern to the poor fellow by then.

"In any case, only the three boys I'd brought from the Coast would go in with me. I needed them to clear a path.

"I travelled as lightly as I could, carrying some biscuit and a water bottle besides rifle, compass, and six extra shells. Even so, it took us over an hour to cut through the reeds to what seemed a likely stand beside an open channel that zig-zagged between the reed mats.

"The swamp had an eerie feel to it. The papyrus shot up straight stalks fifteen feet in the air, where they tufted into bracts like bomb-bursts. There were no taller trees in sight to give a sense of direction, since the reeds were growing on top of the water itself. They had built up thick pads of vegetation over the centuries. Beneath that, I knew, the water might be ten feet deep. The quiver of the mat reminded me of that fact every time a breeze touched the papyrus bracts. The channel itself was covered with the poisonous green of swamp cabbage, so bitter that not even the hippos will eat it. The heat and insects were as unpleasant as anywhere else in Africa, but this swamp had as well an oppressive miasma of age that went beyond all lesser annoyances. After an hour of waiting, the realization grew on me that this swamp was unchanged since Cheops built his pyramid. Even a million years before that, the same swamp had squatted here like a cancer on the heart of Africa.

"There was no disguising its evil. Even on the Nile then, the papyrus sometimes swallowed steamers and held them till the passengers had all starved . . . and the Nile was like the Serpentine compared to the Kagera.

"The boys and I didn't have the swamp to ourselves. There were hootings and splashings from the interior, no telling how far away. Still, nothing came down the channel beside us. The reeds shuddering overhead cut off vision except toward the open water. I began to feel as I had when tracking a wounded buffalo through heavy brush. By mid-afternoon, I thoroughly regretted the whole expedition. I had determined to go on with the Queen's business the next day, leaving that damnable swamp.

"One of the boys touched me then, but I'd already heard the sounds. We had found our jimpegwe. Something big had begun browsing at our reed pad, splashing and making the whole island tremble. It was downwind of us and only a few hundred yards away, though I wasn't particularly worried. No hippo on earth could plow straight through a mat of papyrus. No matter how irrascible the jimpegwe was, it had to approach us by open water where I'd have a clear shot.

"The jimpegwe scented us, all right. There was a loud splash and a bellow the like of which I never heard before or since. The reed mat began to shiver. To my horror, I realized that the sound I heard was that of a heavy body tearing its way through the four-foot thick pad of interlaced vegetation to get to us. The boys and I both knew then that whatever the jimpegwe was, it was no hippo.

"The boys panicked and tried to run back down the path we had cut that morning. They were too blind with fear to choose their footing. Their legs stabbed down into the mat as deep as their hips, and as soon as they struggled free, covered with squirming red leeches, they did the same thing again.

"I stood my ground, though all I could see were the swaying reeds a foot in front of my face. Sixty is no age to begin running through swamps. Besides, the noise told me that the jimpegwe was crashing through the pad much faster than I could have run anyway.

"The papyrus shuddered and I caught a glimpse of the jimpegwe through the tufted bracts: a great, broad head of gray-green, cocked so that the one red eye glittered full on me. The beast dropped back almost at once, with a loud splash that rocked the mat again. The brute had managed to heave itself up onto the pad for only a moment before its weight tore through. The flash I had seen told me only one thing about the jimpegwe: it stood higher than the papyrus bracts, fifteen feet in the air.

"Though there was too little time for running, it seemed far too long to wait. My eight-bore was ready, as it had been all day. After slipping the noses of the next two bullets between the fingers of my left hand, I had nothing to do but to stand with my rifle ported, trusting the beast would rise again when it was close enough for a shot. If it came low through the stalks at me, there would be no chance of placing a bullet. By then, I was under no illusions of being able to stop the jimpegwe with anything but a perfect shot.

"At scarcely fifty yards distance, the jimpegwe pitched upright a second time. I leveled at the head, but again the appearance was only momentary. The sloping skull gave little hope for penetration at that angle. Even so, I could see that the jimpegwe was reptilian. The head was not unlike that of a monitor lizard save in size, though it joined the neck at right angles as if the beast went two-legged much of the time.

"The reeds were bucking like a ship's deck now as the jimpegwe ripped through the last few yards of matted vegetation separating us. The screams of my boys, still floundering on the path behind me, were drowned by the sound of the beast's approach as it frothed reeds and water alike into the air. I watched the whipping stalks, waiting for a patch of gray-green hide to flash among them. I was afraid to chance a shot, more afraid of being pulped without firing. I even considered loosing at the blank, swaying mass before me and then trying to follow my boys.

"When it was within twenty feet—and I still had no fair sight of the beast—the jimpegwe made a wheezing sound and lurched into full view. Its forefeet were upraised. I could see each webbed foot was armed with a horny spike where a man's thumb would be. I squeezed the front trigger when my muzzle steadied a hand's breadth behind the glaring eye, then followed with the left barrel into the red-wattled throat.

"Even as the head snapped back, I broke the rifle. Strange. I remember clearly that one of the empty cases clinked against the stock when it ejected, while the other fell to the reeds without a sound. The swamp had stilled momentarily at the blast of my shots. Now it thundered with bellows and splashing as the jimpegwe thrashed just out of sight. When it raised again, broadside to me as its mouth spewed rage and black blood, I slammed both shots high into its neck. One bullet must have broken the spine, for the jimpegwe arched like a bow and hurled backwards into the water. A great hind leg clawed at the sky, but the beast was down for good."

Randall had stood entranced beside the fireplace all the time the older man was speaking. Now he said, "That's wonderful, Uncle John! But why did you keep it a secret? It's been almost fifteen years."

The hunter's lips tightened. "The scientific chaps have their own notions as to what can be real in Africa, lad," he said. "Remember how many kinds of fool they called Harry Johnston when all he wanted them to believe in was an okapi, a stunted giraffe in the Ituri Forest? And what sort of proof could I have brought out of that swamp alone?"

Snorting, Sir John walked over to a writing desk. After rummaging among a litter of papers, he handed an object to the boy. "There. D'ye know what that is?"

Randall handled the object gingerly. It was a cone of black horn about a foot long. At the base clung wrinkled shreds of skin that might have been reptilian.

"The thumb spike!" the boy blurted. "You cut it off the jimpegwe!"

"Between the two of us, lad, that's just what I did," the old man said. "But when I showed this to a very clever chap at Cambridge, he told me it was the horn from a deformed antelope—and he's the one people will believe, you know."

But for all the bitterness of his words, the hunter's face had the look of a man whose life has found fulfillment.

The Oval Portrait

By Edgar Allan Poe

The château into which my valet had ventured to make forcible entrance, rather than permit me, in my desperately wounded condition, to pass a night in the open air, was one of those piles of commingled gloom and grandeur which have so long frowned among the Apennines, not less in fact than in the fancy of Mrs. Radcliffe. To all appearance it had been temporarily and very lately abandoned. We established ourselves in one of the smallest and least sumptuously furnished apartments. It lay in a remote turret of the building. Its decorations were rich, yet tattered and antique. Its walls were hung with tapestry and bedecked with manifold and multiform armorial trophies, together with an unusually great number of very spirited modern paintings in frames of rich golden arabesque. In these paintings, which depended from the walls not only in their main surfaces, but in very many nooks which the bizarre architecture of the château rendered necessary—in these paintings my incipient delirium, perhaps, had caused me to take deep interest; so that I bade Pedro to close the heavy shutters of the room—since it was already night,—to light the tongues of a tall candelabrum which stood by the head of my bed, and to throw open far and wide the fringed curtains of black velvet which enveloped the bed itself. I wished all this done that I might resign myself, if not to sleep, at least alternately to the contemplation of these pictures, and the perusal of a small volume which had been found upon the pillow, and which purported to criticise and describe them.

Long, long I read—and devoutly, devoutly I gazed. Rapidly and gloriously the hours flew by and the deep midnight came. The position of the candelabrum displeased me, and outreaching my

361

hand with difficulty, rather than disturb my slumbering valet, I placed it so as to throw its rays more fully upon the book.

But the action produced an effect altogether unanticipated. The rays of the numerous candles (for there were many) now fell within a niche of the room which had hitherto been thrown into deep shade by one of the bedposts. I thus saw in vivid light a picture all unnoticed before. It was the portrait of a young girl just ripening into womanhood. I glanced at the painting hurriedly, and then closed my eyes. Why I did this was not at first apparent even to my own perception. But while my lids remained thus shut, I ran over in mind my reason for so shutting them. It was an impulsive movement to gain time for thought—to make sure that my vision had not deceived me—to calm and subdue my fancy for a more sober and more certain gaze. In a very few moments I again looked fixedly at the painting.

That I now saw aright I could not and would not doubt; for the first flashing of the candles upon that canvas had seemed to dissipate the dreamy stupor which was stealing over my senses, and to startle me at once into waking life.

The portrait, I have already said, was that of a young girl. It was a mere head and shoulders, done in what is technically termed a *vignette* manner; much in the style of the favorite heads of Sully. The arms, the bosom, and even the ends of the radiant hair melted imperceptibly into the vague yet deep shadow which formed the background of the whole. The frame was oval, richly gilded and filigreed in *Moresque*. As a thing of art nothing could be more admirable than the painting itself. But it could have been neither the execution of the work, nor the immortal beauty of the countenance, which had so suddenly and so vehemently moved me. Least of all, could it have been that my fancy, shaken from its half slumber, had mistaken the head for that of a living person. I saw at once that the peculiarities of the design, of the *vignetting*, and of the frame, must have instantly dispelled such idea—must have prevented even its momentary entertainment. Thinking earnestly upon these points, I remained, for an hour perhaps, half sitting, half reclining, with my vision riveted upon the portrait. At length, satisfied with the true secret of its effect, I fell back within the bed. I had found the spell of the picture in an absolute *life-likeliness* of expression, which, at first startling, finally confounded, subdued, and appalled me. With deep and reverent awe I replaced the candelabrum in its former position. The cause of my deep agitation being thus shut from view, I sought eagerly the volume which discussed the paintings and their histories. Turning to the number which designated the oval portrait, I there read the vague and quaint words which follow:

"She was a maiden of rarest beauty, and not more lovely than full of glee. And evil was the hour when she saw, and loved, and wedded the painter. He, passionate, studious, austere, and having already a bride in his Art: she a maiden of rarest beauty, and not more lovely than full of glee; all light and smiles, and frolicsome as the young fawn; loving and cherishing all things; hating only the Art which was her rival; dreading only the pallet and brushes and other untoward instruments which deprived her of the countenance of her lover. It was thus a terrible thing for this lady to hear the painter speak of his desire to portray even his young bride. But she was humble and obedient, and sat meekly for many weeks in the dark high turret-chamber where the light dripped upon the pale canvas only from overhead. But he, the painter, took glory in his work, which went on from hour to hour, and from day to day. And he was a passionate, and wild, and moody man, who became lost in reveries; so that he *would* not see that the light which fell so ghastly in that lone turret withered the health and the spirits of his bride, who pined visibly to all but him. Yet she smiled on and still on, uncomplainingly, because she saw that the painter (who had high renown) took a fervid and burning pleasure in his task, and wrought day and night to depict her who so loved him, yet who grew daily more dispirited and weak. And in sooth some who beheld the portrait spoke of its resemblance in low words, as of a mighty marvel, and a proof not less of the power of the painter than of his deep love for her whom he depicted so surpassingly well. But at length, as the labor drew nearer to its conclusion, there were admitted none into the turret; for the painter had grown wild with the ardor of his work, and turned his eyes from the canvas rarely, even to regard the countenance of his wife. And he *would* not see that the tints which he spread upon the canvas were drawn from the cheeks of her who sat beside him. And when many weeks had passed, and but little remained to do, save one brush upon the mouth and one tint upon the eye, the spirit of the lady again flickered up as the flame within the socket of the lamp. And then the brush was given, and then the tint was placed; and, for one moment, the painter stood entranced before the work which he had wrought; but in the next, while he yet gazed, he grew tremulous and very pallid, and aghast, and crying with a loud voice, 'This is indeed *Life* itself!' turned suddenly to regard his beloved: —*She was dead!*"

Party Time

By Mort Castle

Mama had told him it would soon be party time. That made him excited but also a little afraid. Oh, he liked party time, he liked making people happy, and he always had fun, but it was kind of scary going upstairs.

Still, he knew it would be all right because Mama would be with him. Everything was all right with Mama and he always tried to be Mama's good boy.

Once, though, a long time ago, he had been bad. Mama must not have put his chain on right, so he'd slipped it off his leg and went up the stairs all by himself and opened the door. Oh! Did Mama ever whip him for *that*. Now he knew better. He'd never, never go up without Mama.

And he liked it down in the basement, liked it a lot. There was a little bed to sleep on. There was a yellow light that never went off. He had blocks to play with. It was nice in the basement.

Best of all, Mama visited him often. She kept him company and taught him to be good.

He heard the funny sound that the door at the top of the stairs made and he knew Mama was coming down. He wondered if it was party time. He wondered if he'd get to eat the happy food.

But then he thought it might not be party time. He saw Mama's legs, Mama's skirt. Maybe he had done something bad and Mama was going to whip him.

He ran to the corner. The chain pulled hard at his ankle. He tried to go away, to squeeze right into the wall.

"No, Mama! I am not bad! I love my mama. Don't whip me!"

Oh, he was being silly. Mama had food for him. She wasn't going to whip him.

"You're a good boy. Mama loves you, my sweet, good boy."

The food was cold. It wasn't the kind of food he liked best, but Mama said he always had to eat everything she brought him because if not he was a bad boy.

It was hot food he liked most. He called it the happy food. That's the way it felt inside him.

"Is it party time yet, Mama?"

"Not yet, sweet boy. Don't you worry, it will be soon. You like Mama to take you upstairs for parties, don't you?"

"Yes, Mama! I like to see all the people. I like to make them happy."

Best of all, he liked the happy food. It was so good, so hot.

He was sleepy after Mama left, but he wanted to play with his blocks before he lay down on his bed. The blocks were fun. He liked to build things with them and make up funny games.

He sat on the floor. He pushed the chain out of the way. He put one block on top of another block, then a block on top of that one. He built the blocks up real high, then made them fall. That was funny and he laughed.

Then he played party time with the blocks. He put one block over here and another over there and the big, big block was Mama.

He tried to remember some of the things people said at party time so he could make the blocks talk that way. Then he placed a block in the middle of all the other blocks. That was Mama's good boy. It was himself.

Before he could end the party time game, he got very sleepy. His belly was full, even if it was only cold food.

He went to bed. He dreamed a party time dream of happy faces and the good food and Mama saying, "Good boy, my *sweet* boy."

Then Mama was shaking him. He heard funny sounds coming from upstairs. Mama slipped the chain off his leg.

"Come, my good boy."

"It's party time?"

"Yes."

Mama took his hand. He was frightened a little, the way he always was just before party time.

"It's all right, my sweet boy."

Mama led him up the stairs. She opened the door.

"This is party time. Everyone is so happy."

He was not scared anymore. There was a lot of light and so many laughing people in the party room.

"Here's the good, sweet boy, everybody!"

Then he saw it on the floor. Oh, he hoped it was for him!

"That's *yours*, good boy, all for you."

He was so happy! It had four legs and a black nose. When he walked closer to it, it made a funny sound that was something like the way *he* sounded when Mama whipped him.

His belly made a noise and his mouth was all wet inside.

It tried to get away from him, but he grabbed it and he squeezed it, real hard. He heard things going snap inside it.

Mama was laughing and laughing and so was everybody else. He was making them all so happy.

"You know what it is, don't you, my sweet boy?"

He knew.

It was the happy food.

The Passenger

By E. F. Benson

On a certain Tuesday night during last October I was going home down war-darkened Piccadilly on the top of a westering bus. It still wanted a few minutes to eleven o'clock, the theatres had not yet disgorged their audiences, and I was quite alone up aloft, though inside the vehicle was full to repletion. But the chilliness of the evening and a certain bitter quality in the south-east wind accounted for this, and also led me to sit on the hindmost of the seats, close to the stairs, where my back was defended from the bite of the draught by the protective knife-board.

I had barely taken my seat when an incident that for the moment just a little startled me occurred, for I thought I felt something (or somebody) push by me, brushing lightly against my right arm and leg. This impression was vivid enough to make me look round, expecting a fellow-passenger or perhaps the conductor. We were just passing underneath a shaded lamp in the middle of the street when this happened, and I perceived, without any doubt whatever, that my nerves or a sudden draught must have deceived my senses into imagining this, for there was nobody there. But, though I did not give two further thoughts to this impression, I knew that at that moment my pleasurable anticipations from this dark and keen-aired progression had vanished, and, with rather bewildering suddenness, a mood uneasy and ominous had taken possession of me.

I did not, as far as I am aware, make in the smallest degree any mental connection between this sense of being brushed against by something unseen and the vanishing of the contented mood. I put the one down to imagination, the other to the desolate twilight of the streets and the inclemency of the night. A falling barometer portended storm, there had been disquieting news from the Western battleline that afternoon, and those causes seemed sufficient (or nearly sufficient) to account for the sudden dejection that had taken hold of me. And yet, even as I told myself that these were causes enough, I knew that there was another symptom in my disquietude for which they did not account.

This was the sense that I had suddenly been brought into touch with something that lay outside the existing world as I had known it two minutes before. There was something more in my surroundings than could be accounted for by eye and ear. I heard the boom and rattle of the bus as we roared down the decline of Piccadilly, I saw the shaded lamps, the infrequent pedestrians, the tall houses with blinds drawn down according to regulations, for fear of enemy aircraft, and soon across the sky were visible the long luminous pencils cast on to the mottled floor of clouds overhead by the searchlights at Hyde Park Corner; but I knew that none of these, these wars and rumours of wars, entirely accounted for my sudden and fearful alacrity of soul. There was something else; it was as if in a darkened room I had been awakened by the tingling noise of a telephone bell, had been torn from sleep by it, as if some message was even now coming through from unseen and discarnate realms. And on the moment I saw that I was not alone on the top of the bus.

There was someone with his back to me on the seat right in front. For a second or two he was sharply silhouetted against the lamps of a motor coming down the hill towards us, and I could see that he sat with heat bent forward and coat-collar turned up. And at that instant I knew that it was this figure unaccountably appearing there that caused the telephone-tingle in my brain. It was not merely that it had appeared there when I was certain that I was the sole passenger up on the top; had the roof been crowded in every seat I should have known that one of those heads, that belonging to the man who sat leaning forward, was not of this world as represented by the tall houses, the searchlight beams, the other passengers. Then, mixed up with this horror of the spirit, there came to me also a feeling of intense and invincible curiosity. I had penetrated again into the psychical world, into the realm of the unseen and real existences that surround us.

Precisely then, while those impressions took form and coherence in my mind, the conductor came up the stairs. Simultaneously the bell sounded, and as the bus slackened speed and stopped, he leant over the side by me, so that I saw his face very clearly. In another moment he stamped, signalling the driver to go on again, and turned to me with hand out for my fare. He punched a two-penny ticket for me, and then walked forward along the gangway towards the front seat where the unexplained passenger sat. But halfway there he stopped and turned back again.

'Funny thing, sir,' he said. 'I thought I saw another fare sitting there.'

He turned to go down the stairs, and, watching him, I saw, just before his head vanished, that he looked forward again along the roof, shading his eyes with his hand. Then he came back a couple of steps, still looking forward, then finally turned and left me alone on the top there—or not quite alone . . .

After leaving Hyde Park Corner a somewhat grosser darkness pervaded the streets, but still I believed that I could see faintly the outline of the bowed head of the man who sat on the front seat of the bus. But in that dim, uncertain light, flecked with odd shadows, I felt that my certainty that it was still there faded, as I strained my eyes to pierce the ambient dimness.

Looking forward eagerly and intently then, I was suddenly startled again by the feeling that somebody (or something) brushed by me. Instantly I started to my feet, and with one step got to the head of the stairs leading down. Certainly there was no one on them, and equally certainly there was no one now on the front seat, or on any other seat.

A fine rain had begun to fall, blown stingingly by the wind that was increasing every moment, and having completely satisfied myself that there was no one there, I descended from the top of the bus to go inside if there was a seat to be had.

I was delayed, still standing on the stairs, by the stream of passengers leaving the bus, and when I got down to the ground floor I found that as I had had the top to myself on the first part of my journey, I was to enjoy an untenanted interior now. I sat close to the door, and presently beckoned to the conductor.

'Did anyone leave the top of the bus,' I asked, 'just before we stopped here?'

He looked at me sideways a little curiously.

'Not as I know of, sir,' he said.

We drew up, and a number of cheerful soldiers invaded the place.

For some reason I could not get the thought of this dim, inconclusive experience out of my head. It was not at all impossible that all I had seen—namely, the head and shoulders of a man seated on the front bench of the bus—was accounted for by the tricky shadows and veiled light of the streets; or, again, it was within the bounds of possibility that in the darkness a real living man might have come up there, and in the same confusion of shade and local illumination have left again.

It was conceivable also that the same queer lights and shadows deceived the conductor even as they had deceived me; while, as for the brushing against my arm and leg, which I thought I had twice experienced, that might possibly have been the stir and eddy of some draught on this windy night buffeting round the corner by the stairs. And yet with every desire to think reasonably about it, I could not make myself believe that this was all. Deep down in me I knew I was convinced that what I had seen and felt was not on the ordinary planes of perceptible things. Furthermore, I knew that there was more connected with that figure on the front seat that should sometime be revealed to me. What it was I had no idea, but the sense that more was coming, some development which I felt sure would be tragic and terrible, while it filled me with some befogged and nightmarish horror, yet inspired me with an invincible curiosity.

Accordingly, next evening I stationed myself at the place where I had boarded this particular bus some quarter of an hour before the time that it passed there the previous night. It appeared probable that the phantom, whatever it was, was local; that it might appear again (as in a haunted house) on the bus on which I had seen it before. I guessed, furthermore, that, its habitat being a particular bus, the locality of its appearance otherwise was between the Ritz Hotel and the top of Sloane Street.

My knowledge of the organization of the traffic service was *nil*, it was but guesswork that led me to suppose that the conductor would be on the same bus tonight as that on which he had been the evening before. And, after waiting ten minutes or so, I saw him.

Tonight the bus was moderately full both inside and on the top, and it was with a certain sense of comfort that I found myself gregariously placed. The front seat where it had sat before, however, was empty, and I placed myself on the seat immediately behind.

Just on my right were a man in khaki and a girl, uproariously cheerful. The sound of human talk and laughter made an encouraging music, but in spite of that, I felt some undefined and chilly fear creeping over me as we bounced down the dip of Piccadilly, while I kept my eyes steadily on the vacant couple of seats in front of me. And then I felt something brush by me, and, turning my head to look, saw nothing that could account for it. But when I looked in front of me again, I saw that on the vacant seat there was sitting a man with coat collar turned up and head bent forward. He was not in the act of sitting down—he was there.

We stopped at that moment at Hyde Park Corner; the rain had begun to fall more heavily, and I saw that all the occupants of the top of the bus had risen to take shelter inside or in the Tube station; one alone, sitting just in front of me, did not move.

At the thought of being alone again with him, a sudden panic seized me, and I rose also to follow the others down. But even as I stood at the top of the stairs, something of courage, or at least of curiosity, prevailed, and instead I sat down again on the back seat (nearer than that I felt I could not go) and watched for what should be. In a moment or two we started off again.

Tonight, in spite of the falling rain, there was more light; behind the clouds, probably the moon had risen, and I could see with considerable distinctness the figure that shared the top with me. I longed to be gone, so cold was the fear that gripped my heart, but still insatiable curiosity held me where I was.

Inwardly I felt convinced that something was going to happen, and, though the sweat of terror stood on my face at the thought of what it might be, I knew that the one thing even more unfaceable was to turn tail and never know what it was.

On the right the leafless plane-trees in the Park stretched angled fingers against the muffled sky, and below, the pavements and roadway gleamed with moisture. Traffic was infrequent, infrequent also were the figures of pedestrians; never in my life had I felt so cut off from human intercourse.

Close round me were secure, normal rooms, tenanted by living men and women, where cheerful fires burnt and steady lights illuminated the solid walls. But here companionless, except for the motionless form crouched in front of me, I sped between earth and sky, among dim shadows and fugitive lights. And all the time I knew, though not knowing how I knew, some dreadful drama was immediately to be unrolled in front of me. Whether that would prove to be some re-enactment of what in the world of time and space had already occurred, or whether, by the stranger miracle of second-sight, I was to behold something which had not happened yet, I had no idea. All I was certain of was that I sat in the presence of things not normally seen; in the world which, for the sake of sanity, is but rarely made manifest.

I kept my eye fixed on the figure in front of me, and saw that its bowed head was supported by its hands, which seemed to hold it up. Then came a step on the stairs, and the conductor was by me demanding my fare. Having given it, a sudden idea struck me as he was about to leave the top again.

'You haven't collected the fare from that man in front there,' I said.

The conductor looked forward, then at me again.

'Sure enough, there is someone there,' he said, 'and can you see him, too?'

'Certainly,' said I.

This appeared to me at the moment to reassure him; it occurred to me also that perhaps I was utterly wrong, and that the figure was nothing but a real passenger.

What followed happened in a dozen seconds.

The conductor advanced up the bus, and, having spoken without attracting the passenger's attention, touched him on the shoulder, and I saw his hand go into it, as it plunged in water. Simultaneously the figure turned round in its seat, and I saw its face. It was that of a young man, absolutely white and colourless. I saw, too, why it held its head up in its hands, for its throat was cut from ear to ear.

The eyes were closed, but as it raised its head in its hands, looking at the conductor, it opened them, and from within them there came a light as from the eye of a cat.

Then, in an awful voice, half squeal, half groan, I heard the conductor cry out:

'O my God! O my God!' he said.

The figure rose, and cowering as from a blow, he turned and fled before it. Whether he jumped into the roadway from the top of the stairs, or in his flight fell down them, I do not know, but I heard the thud of his body as it fell, and was alone once more on the top of the bus.

I rang the bell violently, and in a few yards we drew up. Already there was a crowd round the man on the road, and presently he was carried in an ambulance, alive, but not much more than alive, to St George's Hospital.

He died from his injuries a few days later, and the discovery of a certain pearl necklace concealed in the clothes of his room, about which he gave information, makes it probable that the confession he made just before he died was true.

The conductor, William Larkins, had been in gaol on a charge of stealing six months before, and on his release, by means of a false name and forged references, he had got this post, with every intention of keeping straight. But he had lost money racing, and ten days before his death was in serious want of cash.

That night an old acquaintance of his, who had been associated with him in burglaries, boarded the bus, heard his story, and tried to persuade him to come back into his old way of life. By way of recommendation, he opened a small dressing-bag he had with him, and showed him, wrapped away in a corner, the pearl necklace which subsequently was discovered in Larkins' room. The two were alone on the top of the bus, and, yielding to the ungovernable greed, Larkins next moment had his arm over the passenger's face, and with a razor out of his dressing-bag had cut his throat.

He kept his wits about him, pocketed the pearls, left the bag open and the razor on the floor, and descended to the footboard again.

Immediately afterwards, having ascertained that there were no blood stains on him, he ascended again and instantly stopped the bus, having discovered the body of a passenger there with his throat cut and the razor on the floor. The body was identified as that of a well-known burglar, and the coroner's jury had brought in a verdict of suicide.

Peekaboo

By Bill Pronzini

Roper came awake with the feeling that he wasn't alone in the house.

He sat up in bed, tense and wary, a crawling sensation on the back of his scalp. The night was dark, moonless; warm clotted black surrounded him. He rubbed sleep mucus from his eyes, blinking, until he could make out the vague grayish outlines of the open window in one wall, the curtains fluttering in the hot summer breeze.

Ears straining, he listened. There wasn't anything to hear. The house seemed almost graveyard still, void of even the faintest of night sounds.

What was it that had waked him up? A noise of some kind? An intuition of danger? It might only have been a bad dream, except that he couldn't remember dreaming. And it might only have been imagination, except that the feeling of not being alone was strong, urgent.

There's somebody in the house, he thought.

Or some *thing* in the house?

In spite of himself Roper remembered the story the nervous real-estate agent in Whitehall had told him about this place. It had been built in the early nineteen hundreds by a local family, and when the last of them died off a generation later it was sold to a man named Lavolle who had lived in it for forty years. Lavolle had been a recluse whom the locals considered strange and probably evil; they hadn't had anything to do with him. But then he'd died five years ago, of natural causes, and evidence had been found by county officials that he'd been "some kind of devil worshiper" who had "practiced all sorts of dark rites." That was all the real-estate agent would say about it.

Word had gotten out about that and a lot of people seemed to believe the house was haunted or cursed or something. For that reason, and because it was isolated and in ramshackle condition, it had stayed empty until a couple of years ago. Then a man called Garber, who was an amateur parapsychologist, leased the place and lived here for ten days. At the end of that time somebody came out from Whitehall to deliver groceries and found Garber dead. Murdered. The real-estate agent wouldn't talk about how he'd been killed; nobody else would talk about it either.

Some people thought it was ghosts or demons that had murdered Garber. Others figured it was a lunatic—maybe the same one who'd killed half a dozen people in this part of New England over the past couple of years. Roper didn't believe in ghosts or demons or things that went bump in the night; that kind of supernatural stuff was for rural types like the ones in Whitehall. He believed in psychotic killers, all right, but he wasn't afraid of them; he wasn't afraid of anybody or anything. He'd made his living with a gun too long for that. And the way things were for him now, since the bank job in Boston had gone sour two weeks ago, an isolated back-country place like this was just what he needed for a few months.

So he'd leased the house under a fake name, claiming to be a writer, and he'd been here for eight days. Nothing had happened in that time: no ghosts, no demons, no strange lights or wailings or rattling chains—and no lunatics or burglars or visitors of any kind. Nothing at all.

Until now.

Well, if he *wasn't* alone in the house, it was because somebody human had come in. And he sure as hell knew how to deal with a human intruder. He pushed the blankets aside, swung his feet out of bed, and eased open the nightstand drawer. His fingers groped inside, found his .38 revolver and the flashlight he kept in there with it; he took them out. Then he stood, made his way carefully across to the bedroom door, opened it a crack, and listened again.

The same heavy silence.

Roper pulled the door wide, switched on the flash, and probed the hallway with its beam. No one there. He stepped out, moving on the balls of his bare feet. There were four other doors along the hallway: two more bedrooms, a bathroom, and an upstairs sitting room. He opened each of the doors in turn, swept the rooms with the flash, then put on the overhead lights.

Empty, all of them.

He came back to the stairs. Shadows clung to them, filled the wide foyer below. He threw the light down there from the landing. Bare mahogany walls, the lumpish shapes of furniture, more shadows crouching inside the arched entrances to the parlor and the library. But that was all: no sign of anybody, still no sounds anywhere in the warm dark.

He went down the stairs, swinging the light from side to side. At the bottom he stopped next to the newel post and used the beam to slice into the blackness in the center hall. Deserted. He arced it around into the parlor, followed it with his body turned sideways to within a pace of the archway. More furniture, the big fieldstone fireplace at the far wall, the parlor windows reflecting glints of light from the flash. He glanced back at the heavy darkness inside the library, didn't see or hear any movement over that way, and reached out with his gun hand to flick the switch on the wall inside the parlor.

Nothing happened when the electric bulbs in the old-fashioned chandelier came on; there wasn't anybody lurking in there.

Roper turned and crossed to the library arch and scanned the interior with the flash. Empty bookshelves, empty furniture. He put on the chandelier. Empty room.

He swung the cone of light past the staircase, into the center hall —and then brought it back to the stairs and held it there. The area beneath them had been walled on both sides, as it was in a lot of these old houses, to form a coat or storage closet; he'd found that out when he first moved in and opened the small door that was set into the staircase on this side. But it was just an empty space now, full of dust . . .

The back of his scalp tingled again. And a phrase from when he was a kid playing hide-and-seek games popped into his mind.

Peekaboo, I see you. Hiding under the stair.

His finger tightened around the butt of the .38. He padded forward cautiously, stopped in front of the door. And reached out with the hand holding the flash, turned the knob, jerked the door open, and aimed the light and the gun inside.

Nothing.

Roper let out a breath, backed away to where he could look down the hall again. The house was still graveyard quiet; he couldn't even hear the faint grumblings its old wooden joints usually made in the night. It was as if the whole place was wrapped in a breathless waiting hush. As if there was some kind of unnatural presence at work here. . . .

Screw that, he told himself angrily. No such things as ghosts and demons. There seemed to be presence here, all right—he could feel it just as strongly as before—but it was a human presence. Maybe a burglar, maybe a tramp, maybe even a goddamn lunatic. But *human*.

He snapped on the hall lights and went along there to the archway that led into the downstairs sitting room. First the flash and then the electric wall lamps told him it was deserted. The dining room off the parlor next. And the kitchen. And the rear porch.

Still nothing.

Where was he, damn it? Where was he hiding?

The cellar? Roper thought.

It didn't make sense that whoever it was would have gone down there. The cellar was a huge room, walled and floored in stone, that ran under most of the house; there wasn't anything in it except spiderwebs and stains on the floor that he didn't like to think about, not after the real estate agent's story about Lavolle and his dark rites. But it was the only place left that he hadn't searched.

In the kitchen again, Roper crossed to the cellar door. The knob turned soundlessly under his hand. With the door open a crack, he peered into the thick darkness below and listened. Still the same heavy silence.

He started to reach inside for the light switch. But then he remembered that there wasn't any bulb in the socket above the stairs; he'd explored the cellar by flashlight before, and he hadn't bothered to buy a bulb. He widened the opening and aimed the flash downward, fanning it slowly from left to right and up and down over the stone walls and floor. Shadowy shapes appeared and disappeared in the bobbing light: furnace, storage shelves, a wooden wine rack, the blackish gleaming stains at the far end, spiderwebs like tattered curtains hanging from the ceiling beams.

Roper hesitated. Nobody down there either, he thought. Nobody in the house after all? The feeling that he wasn't alone kept nagging at him—but it *could* be nothing more than imagination. All that business about devil worshiping and ghosts and demons and Garber being murdered and psychotic killers on the loose might have affected him more than he'd figured. Might have jumbled together in his subconscious all week and finally come out tonight, making him imagine menace where there wasn't any. Sure, maybe that was it.

But he had to make certain. He couldn't see all of the cellar from up here; he had to go down and give it a full search before he'd be satisfied that he really was alone. Otherwise he'd never be able to get back to sleep tonight.

Playing the light again, he descended the stairs in the same wary movements as before. The beam showed him nothing. Except for the faint whisper of his breathing, the creak of the risers when he put his weight on them, the stillness remained unbroken. The odors of dust and decaying wood and subterranean dampness dilated his nostrils; he began to breathe through his mouth.

When he came off the last of the steps he took a half-dozen strides into the middle of the cellar. The stones were cold and clammy against the soles of his bare feet. He turned to his right, then let the beam and his body transcribe a slow circle until he was facing the stairs.

Nothing to see, nothing to hear.

But with the light on the staircase, he realized that part of the wide, dusty area beneath them was invisible from where he stood— a mass of clotted shadow. The vertical boards between the risers kept the beam from reaching all the way under there.

The phrase from when he was a kid repeated itself in his mind: *Peekaboo, I see you. Hiding under the stair.*

With the gun and the flash extended at arm's length, he went diagonally to his right. The light cut away some of the thick gloom under the staircase, letting him see naked stone draped with more gray webs. He moved closer to the stairs, ducked under them, and put the beam full on the far joining of the walls.

Empty.

For the first time Roper began to relax. Imagination, no doubt about it now. No ghosts or demons, no burglars or lunatics hiding under the stair. A thin smile curved the corners of his mouth. Hell, the only one hiding under the stair was himself—

"Peekaboo," a voice behind him said.

The Pitch

By Dennis Etchison

The third floor came down to meet him.

As far as he could see, around a swaying bunch of sphagnum moss that was wired to one of the brass fire nozzles in the sound-proofed ceiling, a gauntlet of piano legs staggered back in a V to the Kitchen Appliance Department like sullen, waiting lines of wooden soldiers. C-Note shuddered, then cursed as the toe guard clipped the rubber soles of his wedgies.

He stepped off the escalator.

He turned in a half-circle, trying to spot an opening.

A saleswoman, brittle with hairspray, dovetailed her hands at her waist and said, "May I help you, sir?"

"No, ma'am," said C-Note. He saw it now. He would have to move down alongside the escalator, looking straight ahead, of course, pivot right and weave a path through the pink and orange rows of the Special Children's Easter Department. There. "I work for the store," he added, already walking.

"Oh," said the saleswoman dubiously. "An employee! And what floor might that be? The, ah, Gourmet Foods on One?"

If it had been a joke, she abandoned her intention at once. He swung around and glared, the little crinkles fanning out from his eyes, deepening into ridges like arrows set to fire on her. Her make-up froze. She took a step back.

A few women were already gathering listlessly near the demonstration platform. Just like chickens waiting to be fed. Ready. All angles and bones. *May I help you, sir?* I'll plump them up, he thought, swinging a heavy arm to the right as he pushed past a pillar. A small ornament made of pipe cleaners and dyed feathers hooked his sleeve. He swung to the left, shaking it off and heading between tables of rough sugar eggs and yellow marshmallow animals.

They looked up, hearing his footsteps. He considered saying a few words now, smoothing their feathers before the kill. But just then a sound pierced the muzak and his face fisted angrily. It was "Chopsticks."

He ducked backstage through the acetate curtain.

"They don't even notice," he wheezed, disgusted.

"Why, here he is," said the pitchman, "right on time." Seated on a gold anodized dining room chair borrowed from the Furniture Department, he was fooling with the microphone wired around his neck and waiting blankly for the next pitch. "All set to knock 'em dead, killer? What don't they notice?"

"They don't notice my hand goin' in their pocketbooks in about fifteen minutes." C-Note sprawled over the second chair, also up-holstered in a grained vinyl imprinted with lime-green daisies.

"Ha ha! Well, you just rest your dogs for now," said the pitch-man. He spooled out a length of black plastic tape and began duti-fully winding another protective layer around the microphone's coat hanger neckpiece.

C-Note saw that all was in ready: several cartons marked Ace Products, Inc., barricaded either side of the split curtain and be-hind the pitchman, leaned against two large suitcases, were lumpen bags of potatoes, a pried-open crate of California lettuce and a plastic trash can liner brimming over with bunched celery and the wilted cowlick tops of fat hybrid carrots. C-Note flexed his fingers in preparation, turned one wrist up to check his watch and pulled a white-gloved hand through his lank hair. He was not worried; it would not fall in his eyes, not now, not so long as he did not have to lean forward on a stool over another scale. Sometimes he had thought they would never end. Up and down, down and up.

"We got fifteen units out there," said the pitchman, "another forty-eight in the box here. I don't think you'll have to touch 'em, though. The locations we do our best is the discount chains. You know."

"Sure," C-Note lied, "I know."

"These *ladies*—" He overlaid the word with a doubtful emphasis. "—They're all snobs, you know?" The pitchman cut the tape and then paused, eyeing him as he pared dirt from under his finger-nails with the vegetable knife.

C-Note stared at the man's hands. "You want to be careful," he said.

"Check, kid. You got to slant it just right. But you can sell any-thing, can't you? You talked me into it. I believe you."

That was what C-Note had told him. He had come up to the

platform late yesterday, hung around for a couple of sets and, when the pitchman had scraped off the cutting board for the last time and was about to pack up the rest of the units in the big suitcases and carry them out to the station wagon, he had asked for a job. *You want to buy one? Then don't waste my time.* But C-Note had barged through the curtain with him and picked up a unit, covering one of the kitchen chairs as if it had always been his favorite resting place. As he had done just now. And the pitch. The pitch he auditioned was good, better even than the original mimeo script from Ace. If he pitched as well out there today in front of the marks, the head pitchman just might earn himself a bonus for top weekly sales. Of course, C-Note would never know that. The pitchman had agreed to pay him cash, *right out of my own pocket,* for every sale. And how would C-Note know how much commission to expect? He would not bother to go to the company, not today and not next week, because that would mean W-2s, withholding—less take-home. And the new man looked like he needed every dime he could lay his hands on. His white-gloved hands.

"Here you go," said the pitchman. "I'll hold onto your gloves. Shake out a little talcum powder. That way you won't go droppin' quarters."

"The gloves," said C-Note, "don't come off." And the way he said it told the pitchman that he considered the point neither trivial nor negotiable.

The pitchman watched him bemusedly, as if already seeing juice stains soaking into the white cloth. He stifled a laugh and glanced aside, as though to an audience: *Did you catch that?*

"Well, it's two o'clock, pal. I'm goin' up to the cafeteria. Be back in time to catch your act. You can start, uh, on your own, can't—?"

"Take it easy," said C-Note, waiting.

"Don't worry, now. I'm not gonna stick you with no check. Ha ha. Cash!" He patted his hip pocket. "Not every demonstrator's that lucky, you know."

"I appreciate it. But I'm not worried about the money."

"Yeah." The pitchman handed him the neck microphone. "Sure." He looked the new man over again as if trying to remember something more to ask him, tell him. "Check," and he left, looking relieved to be leaving and at the same time uneasy about it, a very curious expression.

C-Note left the microphone on the chair and set to work on the units. He had to prepare them and these few minutes would be his only chance. If the pitchman had not volunteered to go to lunch, C-Note would have had to beg off the next demonstration and remain backstage while his boss pitched out front in order to get to them in time. He tightened his gloves and dug his fingertips into the big Ace carton and ripped the cardboard. They did not hurt at all anymore; he was glad of that, in a bitter sort of way.

". . . And today only," droned C-Note, "as a special advertising premium from the manufacturer, this pair of stainless steel tongs, guaranteed never to rust, just the thing for picking baby up out of the bathtub. . . ."

He lifted a potato from the cutting board and plunked it ceremoniously into the waste hole. Most of the ladies giggled.

"That's right, they're yours, along with the Everlast glass knife, the Mighty Mite rotary tool, the Lifetime orange juicer *and* the fruit and vegetable appliance complete with five-year written warranty and two interchangeable surgical steel blades, all for the price of the VariVeger alone. *If* you all promise to go home and tell your friends and neighbors about us, extend our word-of-mouth. Because you will not find this wonder product on the shelves of your stores, no ma'am, not yet. When you do, next fall sometime, the new, improved VariVeger alone will list for a price of seven dollars and ninety-five cents. That's seven ninety-five for the shredder, chopper and julienne potato maker alone. You all remember how to operate this little miracle, don't you, so that you'll be able to put it to work on your husband's, your boyfriend's, your next door neighbor's husband's dinner just as soon as you get home tonight?"

More laughter.

"Just crowd in close as you can now, 'cause this is the last time I'm going to be demonstrating this amazing . . ."

"Say, does that thing really work?"

"Three years of kitchen testing . . ." C-Note saw that it was the head pitchman, watching from the aisle, a sporting smirk on his lips. "Three years of testing by the largest consumer laboratory. . . ."

There was something else.

Distracted, he let his voice roll off for a brief moment, heard the reverberation replaced by the dull din of milling shoppers, the ringing of cash registers and the sound of a piano playing on the other side of the Special Children's Easter Department. He hesitated, his teeth setting and grinding. Why wouldn't she let him stop? He hovered over the soggy cutting board, waiting for the sharp crack of the ruler on the music rest, just missing the knuckles.

A gnarled hand reached up, grasping for a VariVeger. C-Note snapped to.

"Just another minute, ma'am, and I'll be handing out the good-will samples. If you'll just bear with me, I'm sure you'll go away from this store feeling. . . ."

And so on and on. He peeled a potato, set it on the grid of the VariVeger and slammed his hand down on the safety guard handle. Dozens of slim, pallid, finger-like segments appeared underneath. A susurrus of delight swept the crowd.

"No need to hold back—the patented safety grip bar makes sure you won't be serving up finger stew tonight!"

Then he took up the Mighty Mite, needled it into a radish and rotated the blade, holding to the protective finger guard. And a good thing, too: without that tiny ridge of aluminum the blade would continue turning right down through glove, finger and jointed bone. Five seconds later he pulled the radish apart in an accordion spiral.

"Here's just the thing for that mother-in-law you thought you'd never impress!"

Oohs and ahhs. Nothing worked like a non sequitur.

He diced onions, he ripple-cut potato chips, lateral, diagonal and criss-cross, he sliced blood-red tomatoes into inflationary slips—

"This is one way to stretch that food bill to cover the boss, his wife, your in-laws, your husband and all sixteen screaming kids!"

—He squeezed gouts of juice from a plastic spout like a magician with a never-empty lotta, he slivered green beans and cross-haired a turnip into a stiff blooming white flower. He shredded lettuce head after head, he riced more potatoes, he wavy-edged a starchy-smelling mound of French fries, he chopped cabbage, he separated a cucumber into a fleshy green Mobius strip, he purled twists of lemon peel, he segmented a carrot, grated another, then finished by describing the Everlast glass knife, stacking the packages into a protective wall in front of him. You know. You know what he said. And he gave the signal and the money came forth and he moved forty-three unit combinations at a price less than one-half of the fanciful manufacturer's retail, the bills folded between his fingers like Japanese paper water flowers, blooming and growing in the juices as his gloves became green, green as Christmas trees made of dollars.

He scraped the garbage into a hole, mopped his forehead, put away twenty unsold packages, stripped off his plastic apron, un-plugged the mike and departed the platform.

Just as he was about to peel the drenched gloves from his hands, the head pitchman appeared at the slit in the curtain.

C-Note left his gloves on.

The pitchman flashed his hand forward, then thought better of it.

"Hell of a salesman," he announced.

"We thank you," said C-Note. "But—"

"Don't let it go to your head, though."

"No, sir. I got—"

"Hell of a salesman. But what the hell was that business with the knife?"

"I sold the knife. 'Long with the rest of the package. Isn't that all right, sir? But if you don't mind, I got to—"

"But you didn't *demonstrate* the knife. What's with that? You afraid you're gonna cut yourself or—"

C-Note's sharp eyes nailed him where he stood.

"If you don't mind, I got to go now." He started for the curtain, head down. "I mean, this gut of mine's startin' to eat itself. If you don't mind. Sir. If you think I earned my lunch."

"Hell yes, you earned it, boy." The pitchman put a foot up on the kitchen chair. His toe brushed the carton, the one with the torn-open top. "Hey, wait a minute."

C-Note drew back the curtain.

"Look, you want your money or don't you?"

C-Note turned back.

"Ha ha." The pitchman unfolded some money. C-Note took it without counting, which made the pitchman stare. "Hell of a salesman," he muttered, smiling crookedly. He watched the heavyset man leave.

"Kid must have to take a hell of a leak," the pitchman said to himself. It was only after he had counted and stacked the limp piles of bills in the money box, counted the units, shaken his head and paced the floor several times, lost in some ambitious vision, that he noticed the torn-up carton. "Hell of a salesman," he said again, shaking his head with pleasure. He poked around inside, counting the reserve. Cutting his finger on something, he drew it back with a grimace and stuck it in his mouth. "Well goddam," he said slowly, patiently, pulling up the crease in his trousers and seating himself before the carton from which, he now realized, unpackaged units had been inexplicably switched, "what in the name of the . . ." *goddam holy hell do we have here?* he might have said.

C-Note hurried for the back stairs. On the landing he stopped and looked at his hands. They were trembling. Still moist, they resembled thick, mushy clumps of pseudopodia. Loosening the fingers one by one, he eased the gloves off at last.

His fingers quivered, fat and fishbelly-white. The tips were disfigured by a fine, shiny line. They had healed almost perfectly, sewn back right afterwards, in the ambulance; still, the fusion was not quite perfect, the ends angled out each slightly askew from the straight thrust of the digits. No one would notice, probably, unless they studied his hands at close range. But the sight of them bothered him.

He braced himself, his equilibrium returning. He swallowed heavily, his breath steadying, his heart levelling out to a familiar regular tattoo. There was no need to panic. They would not notice anything out of the ordinary, not until later. Tonight, perhaps. At home.

He recognized the feeling now as exhilaration. He felt it every time.

Too many steps to the ground floor. He turned back, stuffing the gloves into his coat pocket, and reentered the store.

He passed quickly through the boundaries of the Kitchen Appliance Department. Mixers. Teflon ware. Beaters, spoons, ladles, spatulas, hanging like gleaming doctors' tools. If one were to fall it would strike the wood, making him jump, or smack the backs of his hands, again and again. One of them always had, every day. Some days a spoon, other days something else, depending on what she had been cooking. Only one day, that last day, had she been scoring a ham; at least it had smelled like a ham, he remembered, even after so many years. That day it had been a knife.

The muzak was lilting, a theme from a movie? Plenty of strings to drown out the piano, if there was one. He relaxed.

The women had somnambulated aimlessly from the demonstration platform, their new packages pressed reassuringly to their sides, moving like wheeled scarecrow mannequins about the edges of the Music Department. From here it was impossible to differentiate them from the saleswoman he had met there, by the pianos. She might have been any one of them.

He passed the platform and jumped on the escalator. The rubber handrail felt cool under his hand. Hastily he pulled a new pair of white gloves from his inside pocket and drew them on.

At the first floor, on his way out to the parking lot, he decided to detour by the Candy Department.

"May I help you, sir?"

Her hands, full and self-indulgent, smoothed the generous waist of her taut white uniform.

"A pound-and-a-half of the butter toffee nuts, all right, sweets?"

The salesgirl blushed as she funneled the fragrant candy into a paper sack. He saw her name badge: *Margie*. There was nothing about her that was sharp or demanding. She would be easy to please—no song and dance for her. He tipped her seventy-five cents, stroking the quarters into the deep, receptive folds of her soft palm.

He tilted the bag to his mouth and received a jawful of the tasty sugared nuts.

At the glass door he glanced down to see why the bag did not fit all the way into his wide trouser pocket. Then he remembered.

He withdrew one of the parts he had removed backstage and turned it over, fingering it pleasurably as he waddled into the lot. It was a simple item, an aluminum ring snapped over a piece of injection-molded plastic. It glinted in the afternoon sunlight as he examined it. A tiny safety guard, it fit on the vegetable shredder just above the rim that supported the surgical steel blades. A small thing, really. But it was all that would prevent a thin, angular woman's fingers from plunging down along with the cucumber or potato or soft, red tomato. Without it, they would be stripped into even, fresh segments, clean and swift, right to the bone. He slipped it back into his pocket, where it dropped into the reservoir of other such parts, some the little safety wheels from the vegetable garnisher, some the protective bars from the Mighty Mite rotary tool. But mostly they were pieces from the VariVeger, that delightful invention, the product of three years of kitchen testing, the razor sharp, never-fail slicer and stripper, known the world over for its swift, unhesitating one-hand operation.

He kept the bag in his hand, feeding from it as he walked on across the parking lot and down the block, losing himself at once in the milling, mindless congestion of Easter and impatient Mother's Day shoppers.

The Poor

By Steve Rasnic Tem

The poor are grinning in his waiting room.
Waiting in his room are the poor grinning.
The purposes of his office are to help and serve the poor. To serve and help the poor are his purposes.

They come every day, mobs of them. Some get in line at six in the morning, even knowing he won't arrive until nine. He has driven by that early, after reading about their early arrival in the newspapers, just to confirm it for himself. There were hundreds of them, some days thousands. All waiting to see him.

He reads in the newspapers that he has money to give away, jobs, coupons exchangeable for food, gift certificates, new toasters. But the central office never sends him these things. The poor frequently tell him all about new benefits being offered, but he never sees them. The poor know much better than he himself how his office is run.

In his evenings at home his wife asks him how things went during the day, what he did, if he accomplished anything, and how the poor people in line were, if he had been able to do anything for them yet.

He doesn't know how he will pay for his son's college tuition next semester, how they will be able to afford a Christmas as large as the one last year, or how they'll be able to maintain their standard of living in general. And she asks him about the poor.

He cannot imagine how the poor can live, how they can live at all. How do they meet expenses? How do they keep up with the rising cost of food?

He sometimes wonders if the poor are real at all, or actors hired by someone who hates him, hired to disturb the regular pace of his day, to corrupt his dreams with their thin faces.

Or perhaps they're an illusion, and he simply minds an empty office all day. For why else would the central office ignore him, all his letters requesting funds, his many phone calls?

You worry yourself sick, you don't enjoy life, his wife tells him.

385

You're brooding about them all the time. Them? he asks. You mean "the poor." Can't you even say the word?

His marriage is falling apart. What if he told them that? Then would they stop lining up outside his office?

He decides to arrive early each day. Talk to them. Get to know them. Show them he wants to understand their many needs.

When he arrives early he discovers that the line is much longer than ever before. Is that any way for them to show their appreciation? They're backed up outside the building and around the parking lot. He has to shove and kick his way into the building; some of them think he's one of them, and keep trying to force him back to the end of the line.

He walks up and down the line attempting to make conversation, but they won't reply to any of his questions, merely nod or shake their heads, wring their hands. A few weep quietly. Can't they see he's trying to help them?

At nine he gives up, unlocks his office door, and sits behind his desk. There is some shuffling outside as a committee of the poor checks their line-up sheet to see if anyone's missing or wants to trade places, and then they send the first one in.

It is a tall, thin, quiet man with dark circles under his eyes. He looks as if he hasn't slept, or eaten, for a week. He sits down in the chair before the desk, and stares.

The poor man stares for several minutes, making him feel like an intruder in his own office. Then finally the poor man says, "I want a wife."

He stares at the poor man in fascination. How could he request such a thing?

I'm afraid I cannot provide that for you. I'm sorry, he tells the poor man.

"I'm lonely, I need someone," the poor man tells him.

He rummages through his desk trying to find a form for the poor man to fill out, some kind of application, anything to distract him. He slides a form in front of the man. "Do you need a pencil?"

The poor man starts to fill out the form. It's a request for an emergency gallon of gasoline. He hopes the man won't be able to tell the difference.

Perhaps I could give him my wife, he thinks, and is ashamed of the thought.

There seems to be a gradual change in the poor, the first change he can ever remember. The line seems to have broken down into little groups, little conclaves. What could the poor be planning?

386

Perhaps they're plotting for more bread, sex, and rest? Or maybe they're planning to kill police officers, politicians, social workers?

Each day he goes home, his wife asks him, What are the poor doing today?

They're plotting, he tells her. They're seeking to overthrow our present form of government.

She nods her head in feigned interest.

He and his wife seem to have little time for each other any more, he thinks. It's simply too time-consuming just making a living, trying to maintain current standards, trying not to be poor.

The poor have moved into the trunk of his car.

He had gone into the garage this morning, opened the trunk to load his briefcase, and the old poor man who'd requested a wife was lying curled up in the trunk.

You can't be here, he told the poor man. This won't do at all.

The poor man just stared at him sadly. No doubt waiting for his wife.

You can't have my wife, he told him.

At work the poor were in his office. You can't be here, he told them.

But they said nothing. They sat on his desk. They were lying beneath his desk.

Several had tried to sit in his chair, but the chair had broken.

The poor were in the bathroom, hundreds of them, living and sleeping there. The poor filled the parking lot with their cooking pots and sleeping rolls.

The poor are everywhere, he tells his wife in the kitchen at home. Several poor people are sitting at their kitchen table.

There are twelve poor people living in his garage, and six more on the patio.

I know what you're planning! he tells them hysterically.

One morning he finds a poor woman with her lips clamped around his car's exhaust pipe.

Another afternoon there is a poor couple trying unsuccessfully to make love in his back seat, their starved and tattered forms smacking together futilely. He finds one in his living room, lying in front of the TV, and he beats it with a broom.

He finds one hanging from the lamp in his bedroom and he jerks it down violently.

He discovers one curled beneath his easy chair and he stomps it with his feet until it's dead.

The poor are living in his trash.
They're living in his bed with his wife.
The poor are dying. He beats them and they're dying.

He finds the dead bodies stacked in his garage like cordwood. He finds them piled in the study.

Small, emaciated bodies, the flesh fragile as paper, the mouths pulled back in a rictus.

The poor want too much from him. They want all the little things he has. How can he take care of himself?

The bodies of the poor fill his bedroom. He can't even find his wife any more. The dead hands try to catch his clothes; the dead, widening mouths want to eat him.

They know they will always be poor. They know the wealth will never filter down through all the widening hands to their own, thin hands.

No, no! he tells the dead bodies spilling over his bed. I have an office; I'm there to help . . .

But the mouths say nothing.

The poor are his.

The Rag Thing

By Donald A. Wollheim

It would have been all right if spring had never come. During the winter nothing had happened and nothing was likely to happen as long as the weather remained cold and Mrs. Larch kept the radiators going. In a way, though, it is quite possible to hold Mrs. Larch to blame for everything that happened. Not that she had what people would call malicious intentions, but just that she was two things practically every boarding-house landlady is—thrifty and not too clean.

She shouldn't have been in such a hurry to turn the heat off so early in March. March is a tricky month and she should have known that the first warm day is usually an isolated phenomenon. But then you could always claim that she shouldn't have been so sloppy in her cleaning last November. She shouldn't have dropped that rag behind the radiator in the third floor front room.

As a matter of fact, one could well wonder what she was doing using such a rag anyway. Polishing furniture doesn't require a clean rag to start with, certainly not the rag you stick into the furniture polish, that's going to be greasy anyway—but she didn't have to use that particular rag. The one that had so much dried blood on it from the meat that had been lying on it in the kitchen.

On top of that, it is probable that she had spit into the filthy thing, too. Mrs. Larch was no prize package. Gross, dull, unkempt, widowed and careless, she fitted into the house—one of innumerable other brownstone fronts in the lower sixties of New York. Houses that in former days, fifty or sixty years ago, were considered the height of fashion and the residences of the well-to-do, now reduced to dingy rooming places for all manner of itinerants, lonely people with no hope in life other than dreary jobs, or an occasional young and confused person from the hinterland seeking fame and fortune in a city which rarely grants it.

So it was not particularly odd that when she accidentally dropped the filthy old rag behind the radiator in the room on the third floor front late in November, she had simply left it there and forgotten to pick it up.

It gathered dust all winter, unnoticed. Skelty, who had the room, might have cleaned it out himself save that he was always too tired for that. He worked at some indefinite factory all day and when he came home he was always too tired to do much more than read the sports and comics pages of the newspapers and then maybe stare at the streaky brown walls a bit before dragging himself into bed to sleep the dreamless sleep of the weary.

The radiator, a steam one, oddly enough (for most of these houses used the older hot-air circulation), was in none too good condition. Installed many many years ago by the house's last Victorian owner, it was given to knocks, leaks, and cantankerous action. Along in December it developed a slow drip, and drops of hot water would fall to seep slowly into the floor and leave the rag lying on a moist hot surface. Steam was constantly escaping from a bad valve that Mrs. Larch would have repaired if it had blown off completely but, because the radiator always managed to be hot, never did.

Because Mrs. Larch feared drafts, the windows were rarely open in the winter and the room would become oppressively hot at times when Skelty was away.

It is hard to say what is the cause of chemical reactions. Some hold that all things are mechanical in nature, others that life has a psychic side which cannot be duplicated in laboratories. The problem is one for metaphysicians; everyone knows that some chemicals are attracted to heat, others to light, and they may not necessarily be alive at all. Tropisms is the scientific term used, and if you want to believe that living matter is stuff with a great number of tropisms and dead matter is stuff with little or no tropisms, that's one way of looking at it. Heat and moisture and greasy chemical compounds were the sole ingredients of the birth of life in some ancient unremembered swamp.

Which is why it probably would have been all right if spring had never come. Because Mrs. Larch turned the radiators off one day early in March. The warm hours were but few. It grew cold with the darkness and by night it was back in the chill of February again. But Mrs. Larch had turned the heat off and, being lazy, decided not to turn it on again till the next morning, provided of course that it stayed cold the next day (which it did).

Anyway Skelty was found dead in bed the next morning. Mrs. Larch knocked on his door when he failed to come down to breakfast and when he hadn't answered, she turned the knob and went in. He was lying in bed, blue and cold, and he had been smothered in his sleep.

There was quite a to-do about the whole business, but nothing came of it. A few stupid detectives blundered around the room, asked silly questions, made a few notes, and then left the matter to the coroner and the morgue. Skelty was a nobody, no one cared whether he lived or died, he had no enemies and no friends, there were no suspicious visitors, and he had probably smothered accidentally in the blankets. Of course the body was unusually cold when Mrs. Larch found it, as if the heat had been sucked out of him, but who notices a thing like that? They also discounted the grease smudge on the top sheet, the grease stains on the floor, and the slime on his face. Probably some grease he might have been using for some imagined skin trouble, though Mrs. Larch had not heard of his doing so. In any case, no one really cared.

Mrs. Larch wore black for a day and then advertised in the paper. She made a perfunctory job of cleaning the room. Skelty's possessions were taken away by a drab sister-in-law from Brooklyn who didn't seem to care much either, and Mrs. Larch was all ready to rent the room to someone else.

The weather remained cold for the next ten days and the heat was kept up in the pipes.

The new occupant of the room was a nervous young man from upstate who was trying to get a job in New York. He was a high-strung young man who entertained any number of illusions about life and society. He thought that people did things for the love of it and he wanted to find a job where he could work for that motivation rather than the sort of things he might have done back home. He thought New York was different, which was a mistake.

He smoked like fury, which was something Mrs. Larch did not like because it meant ashes on the floor and burned spots on her furniture (not that there weren't plenty already), but there was nothing Mrs. Larch would do about it, because it would have meant exertion.

After four days in New York, this young man, Gorman by name, was more nervous than ever. He would lie in bed nights smoking cigarette after cigarette, thinking and thinking and getting nowhere. Over and over he was facing the problem of resigning himself to a life of gray drab. It was a thought he had tried not to face and now that it was thrusting itself upon him, it was becoming intolerable.

The next time a warm day came, Mrs. Larch left the radiators on because she was not going to be fooled twice. As a result, when the weather stayed warm, the rooms became insufferably hot because she was still keeping the windows down. So that when she turned the heat off finally, the afternoon of the second day, it was pretty tropic in the rooms.

When the March weather turned about suddenly again and became chilly about nine at night, Mrs. Larch was going to bed and figured that no one would complain and that it would be warm again the next day. Which may or may not be true. It does not matter.

Gorman got home about ten, opened the window, got undressed, moved a pack of cigarettes and an ashtray next to his bed on the floor, got into bed, turned out the light, and started to smoke.

He stared at the ceiling, blowing smoke upward into the darkened room trying to see its outlines in the dim light coming in from the street. When he finished one cigarette, he let his hand dangle out the side of the bed and picked up another cigarette from the pack on the floor, lit it from the butt in his mouth, and dropped the butt into the ashtray on the floor.

The rag under the radiator was getting cold, the room was getting cold, there was one source of heat radiation in the room. That was the man in the bed. Skelty had proven a source of heat supply once. Heat attraction was chemical force that could not be denied. Strange forces began to accumulate in the long-transformed fibers of the rag.

Gorman thought he heard something flap in the room but he paid it no attention. Things were always creaking in the house. Gorman heard a swishing noise and ascribed it to the mice.

Gorman reached down for a cigarette, fumbled for it, found the pack, deftly extracted a smoke in the one-handed manner chain smokers become accustomed to, lifted it to his mouth, lit it from the burning butt in his mouth, and reached down with the butt to crush it out against the tray.

He pressed the butt into something wet like a used handkerchief, there was a sudden hiss, something coiled and whipped about his wrist. Gorman gasped and drew his hand back fast. A flaming horror, twisting and writhing, was curled around it. Before Gorman could shriek, it had whipped itself from his hand and fastened over his face, over the warm, heat-radiating skin and the glowing flame of the cigarette.

Mrs. Larch was awakened by the clang of fire engines. When the fire was put out, most of the third floor had been gutted. Gorman was an unrecognizable charred mass.

The fire department put the blaze down to Gorman's habit of smoking in bed. Mrs. Larch collected on the fire insurance and bought a new house, selling the old one to a widow who wanted to start a boardinghouse.

Rendezvous

By Daniel Ransom

PAYTON

The overcast sky causes him to snap on the Firebird's headlights.

Even before reaching the on-ramp he is traveling 60 mph.

Shoved between his legs is a cold can of Budweiser that stains the crotch of his tight tan slacks.

Drums pound from the tape deck.

His long dirty hair trails in the wind like seaweed.

The cobra tattoo on his left bicep glows with a peculiar iridescence.

He hits the Interstate doing 71 mph.

A VW bug makes terrified room for him.

He pulls the Bud from between his legs and raises it to his thin mouth.

He is doing 77 now, as he noses out a sports car with a smug-looking driver who has the good sense to glower but do nothing more.

The drums are louder.

KIM

From her backpack she takes a granola bar and the last quarter of an apple that is now spoiled-looking.

She huddles in the corner of an Interstate rest stop that smells woody from the logs on the roof.

She can smell the rain that is about to start.

She wishes, but only briefly, that she were back home, in her

393

room, with her mother shouting up the stairway that dinner is ready.

But she needs to teach them a lesson—the lesson that at 15 she's perfectly capable of running her own life with no interference from them.

She hopes that this little surprise absence will make them more reasonable where her freedom is concerned.

She doesn't think of it as running away.

Merely proving a point.

God but it's cold.

God but it's empty out here.

Cars and trucks and vans rush by seeming important and aloof.

She wishes she were inside a warm car with a hamburger in one hand and a can of soda in the other. With some good music on the radio.

The apple tastes like hell.

She hopes her parents are scared.

They deserve to be.

PAYTON

On the horizon to the west he can see the rain start.

He supposes the farmers need it. At least that's what people always say whenever it rains in these parts.

The farmers need it.

The drums have died. A saxophone has replaced them.

Drums give him energy, a high. Saxophones make him morose.

He hits a clean 80 miles per.

Dark quick eyes checking for highway patrol cars.

He hopes the speed will stop him from thinking about the priest.

He rubs at the cobra on his arm.

He opens a fresh can of Bud.

He thought the priest would be more sympathetic.

All the priest could say was you better tell the police.

He is traveling at 84 mph.

He can smell the spring grass on the wind, even at this speed.

394

He thought the priest should be a hell of a lot nicer than he was.

Why do you go on the Interstate, the priest had asked.

You'd better call the police.

The priest wasn't even sympathetic about him sending the flowers and visiting the funeral home, which he'd done three out of five times after he'd gone out on the Interstate.

The hell with the priest.

He can't do anything about it.

Nothing.

Payton wishes the saxophone would stop.

KIM

She sits inside the john with the lid closed trying to get warm again.

She thought public rest stops were usually busy. There hasn't been anybody along here for twenty minutes.

All the cars and trucks sound far away.

The rain, however, is near. Thrumming the roof.

On her way inside she had passed a pay phone. She'd stared at it a long time, even extended a hand as if to touch it.

But no.

The game isn't over yet.

And anyway, all this misery will only make her story better when she tells her tenth grade girlfriends.

Brave Kim.

Poor Kim.

She has to move now.

Back on the macadam along the Interstate.

Get a ride before it's full dark.

God, is she going to have some good stories to tell.

PAYTON

Sometimes the cobra gets sore.

The jerk who put it on his arm was stoned at the time. At first there'd been infection.

Now, he rubs the cobra.

It's as if it needs to be fed.

The saxophone solo is over now.

The drums are back.

He feels young, strong, invincible.

To hell with the priest.

It is then that he sees the shape begin to materialize along the edge of the Interstate. Through the gloom. The rain.

Hitchhiker.

Young girl.

Christ.

KIM

She watches the car pull off the road fifty yards past her.

Immediately she begins running.

She wishes she'd been able to get a glimpse of the driver.

All the other drivers she'd been able to check out before getting inside.

But it's dark and she's soaked from the rain.

For some reason she thinks of the pay phone.

Of almost lifting up the receiver.

Of almost making the call.

She's at the car now.

Her slender hand on the door handle.

As she opens the door, she hears drums.

Very loud drums.

The Same Old Grind

By Bill Pronzini

There were no customers in the Vienna Delicatessen when Mitchell came in at two on a Thursday afternoon. But that wasn't anything unusual. He'd been going there a couple of times a week since he'd discovered the place two months ago, and he hadn't seen more than a dozen people shopping there in all that time.

It wasn't much of a place. Just a hole-in-the wall deli tucked down at the end of a side street, in an old neighborhood that was sliding downhill. Which was exactly the opposite of what he himself was doing, Mitchell thought. He was heading *uphill*—out of the slums he'd been raised in and into this section of the city for a few months, until he had enough money and enough connections, and then uptown where you drank champagne instead of cheap bourbon and ate in fancy restaurants instead of dusty old delis.

But he had to admit that he got a boot out of coming to the Vienna Delicatessen. For one thing, the food was good and didn't cost much. And for another the owner, Giftholz, amused him. Giftholz was a frail old bird who talked with an accent and said a lot of humorous things because he didn't understand half of what you rapped to him about. He was from Austria or someplace like that, had been in this country for thirty years, but damned if he didn't talk like he'd just come off the boat.

What Giftholz was doing right now was standing behind the deli counter and staring off into space. Daydreaming about Austria, maybe. Or about the customers he wished he had. He didn't hear Mitchell open the door, but as soon as the little bell overhead started tinkling, he swung around and smiled in a sad hopeful way that always made Mitchell think of an old mutt waiting for somebody to throw him a bone.

"Mr. Mitchell, good afternoon."

Mitchell shut the door and went over to the counter. "How's it going, Giftholz?"

"It goes," Giftholz said sadly. "But not so well."

"The same old grind, huh?"

"Same old grind?"

"Sure. Day in, day out. Rutsville, you dig?"

"Dig?" Giftholz said. He blinked like he was confused and smoothed his hands over the front of his clean white apron. "What will you have today, Mr. Mitchell?"

"The usual. Sausage hero and an order of cole slaw. Might as well lay a brew on me too."

"Lay a brew?"

Mitchell grinned. "Beer, Giftholz. I want a beer."

"Ah. One beer, one sausage hero, one cole slaw. Yes."

Giftholz got busy. He didn't move too fast—hell, he was so frail he'd probably keel over if he *tried* to move fast—but that was all right. He knew what he was doing and he did it right: lots of meat on the sandwich, lots of slaw. You had to give him that.

Mitchell watched him for a time. Then he said, "Tell me something, Giftholz. How do you hang in like this?"

"Please?"

"Hang in," Mitchell said. "Stay in business. You don't have many customers and your prices are already dirt cheap."

"I charge what is fair."

"Yeah, right. But you can't make any bread that way."

"Bread?" Giftholz said. "No, my bread is purchased from the bakery on Union Avenue."

Mitchell got a laugh out of that. "I mean money, Giftholz. You can't make any *money*."

"Ah. Yes, it is sometimes difficult."

"So how do you pay the bills? You got a little something going on the side?"

"Something going?"

"A sideline. A little numbers action, maybe?"

"No, I have no sideline."

"Come on, everybody's got some kind of scam. I mean, it's a dog-eat-dog world, right? Everybody's got to make ends meet any way he can."

"That is true," Giftholz said. "But I have no scam. I do not even know the word."

Mitchell shook his head. Giftholz probably *didn't* have a scam; it figured that way. One of these old-fashioned merchant types who were dead honest. And poor as hell because they didn't believe in screwing their customers and grabbing a little gravy where they could. But still, the way things were these days, how did he stand up to the grind? Even with his cheap prices, he couldn't compete with the big chain outfits that had specials and drawings and gave away stamps; and he had to pay higher and higher wholesale prices

398

himself for the stuff he sold. Yet here he was, still in business. Mitchell just couldn't figure out how guys like him did it.

Giftholz finished making the sandwich, put it on a paper plate, laid a big cup of slaw beside it, opened a beer from his small refrigerator, and put everything down on the counter. He was smiling as he did it—a kind of proud smile, like he'd done something fine.

"It is two dollars, please, Mr. Mitchell."

Two dollars. Man. The same meal would have cost him four or five at one of the places uptown. Mitchell shook his head again, reached into his pocket, and flipped his wallet out.

When he opened it and fingered through the thick roll of bills inside, Giftholz's eyes got round. Probably because he'd never seen more than fifty bucks at one time in his life. Hell, Mitchell thought, give him a thrill. He opened the wallet wider and waved it under Giftholz's nose.

"That's what real money looks like, Giftholz," he said. "Five bills here, five hundred aces. And plenty more where that came from."

"Where did you earn so much money, Mr. Mitchell?"

Mitchell laughed. "I got a few connections, that's how. I do little jobs for people and they pay me big money."

"Little jobs?"

"You don't want me to tell you what they are. They're private jobs, if you get my drift."

"Ah," Giftholz said, and nodded slowly. "Yes, I see."

Mitchell peeled out the smallest of the bills, a fiver, and laid it on the counter. "Keep the change, Giftholz. I feel generous today."

"Thank you," Giftholz said. "Thank you so much."

Mitchell laughed again and took a bite of his hero. Damned good. Giftholz made the best sandwiches in the city, all right. How could you *figure* a guy like him?

He ate standing up at the counter; there was one little table against the back wall, but from here he could watch Giftholz putter around in slow motion. Nobody else came into the deli; he would have been surprised if somebody had. When he finished the last of the hero and the last of the beer, he belched in satisfaction and wiped his hands on a napkin. Giftholz came over to take the paper plate away; then he reached under the counter and came up with a bowl of mints and a small tray of toothpicks.

"Please," he said.

"Free mints? Since when, Giftholz?"

"It is because you are a good customer."

It is because I gave you a three-buck tip, Mitchell thought. He grinned at Giftholz, helped himself to a handful of mints, and dropped them into his coat pocket. Then he took a toothpick and worked at a piece of sausage that was stuck between two of his teeth.

Giftholz said, "You would do me a small favor, Mr. Mitchell?"

"Favor? Depends on what it is."

"Come with me into the kitchen for a moment."

"What for?"

"There is something I would show you. Please, it will only take a short time."

Mitchell finished excavating his teeth, tucked the toothpick into a corner of his mouth, and shrugged. What the hell, he might as well humor the old guy. He had time; he didn't have any more little jobs to do today. And there wouldn't be any gambling or lady action until tonight.

"Sure," he said. "Why not."

"Good," Giftholz said. *Wunderbar.*

He gestured for Mitchell to come around behind the counter and then doddered through a door into the kitchen. When Mitchell went through after him he didn't see anything particularly interesting. Just a lot of kitchen equipment, a butcher's block table, a couple of cases of beer, and some kind of large contraption in the far corner.

"So what do you want to show me?" he asked.

"Nothing," Giftholz said.

"Huh?"

"Really I would ask you a question."

"What question?"

"If you speak German."

"German? You putting me on?"

"Putting you on?"

For some reason Mitchell was beginning to feel short of breath. "Listen," he said, "what do you want to know a thing like that for?"

"It is because of my name. If you were to speak German, you see, you would understand what it means in English translation."

Short of breath and a little dizzy, too. He blinked a couple of times and ran a hand over his face. "What do I care what your damned name means."

"You should care, Mr. Mitchell," Giftholz said. "It means 'poison wood.'"

"Poison—?" Mitchell's mouth dropped open, and the toothpick fell out of it and fluttered to the floor. He stared at it stupidly for a second.

Poison wood.

Then he stopped feeling dizzy and short of breath; he stopped

400

feeling anything. He didn't even feel the floor when he fell over and hit it with his face.

Giftholz stood looking down at the body. Too bad, he thought sadly. Ah, but then, Mr. Mitchell had been a *strolch*, a hoodlum; such men were not to be mourned. And as he had said himself in his curious idiom, it was a dog-eat-dog world today. Everything cost so much; everything was so difficult for a man of honesty. One truly did have to make ends meet any way one could.

He bent and felt for a pulse. But of course there was none. The poison paralyzed the muscles of the heart and brought certain death within minutes. It also became neutralized in the body after a short period of time, leaving no toxic traces.

Giftholz picked up the special toothpick from the floor, carried it over to the garbage pail. After which he returned and took Mr. Mitchell's wallet and put it away inside his apron.

One had to make ends meet any way one could. Such a perfect phrase that was. But there was another of Mr. Mitchell's many phases which still puzzled him. The same old grind. It was *not* the same old grind; it had not been the same old grind for some time.

No doubt Mr. Mitchell meant something else, Giftholz decided.

And then he began to drag the body toward the large gleaming sausage grinder in the far corner.

The Skeleton

By Jerome K. Jerome

One evening Jephson asked me if I believed in spiritualism to its fullest extent.

'That is rather a large question,' I answered. 'What do you mean by "spiritualism to its fullest extent"?'

'Well, do you believe that the spirits of the dead have not only the power of revisiting this earth at their will, but that, when here, they have the power of action, or rather, of exciting to action? Let me put a definite case. A spiritualist friend of mine, a sensible and by no means imaginative man, once told me that a table, through the medium of which the spirit of a friend had been in the habit of

401

communicating with him, came slowly across the room towards him, of its own accord, one night as he sat alone, and pinioned him against the wall. Now can any of you believe that, or can't you?'

'I could,' Brown took it upon himself to reply; 'but, before doing so, I should wish for an introduction to the friend who told you the story. Speaking generally,' he continued, 'it seems to me that the difference between what we call the natural and the supernatural is merely the difference between frequency and rarity of occurrence. Having regard to the phenomena we are compelled to admit, I think it illogical to disbelieve anything we are unable to disprove.'

'For my part,' remarked MacShaughnassy, 'I can believe in the ability of our spirit friends to give the quaint entertainments credited to them much easier than I can in their desire to do so.'

'You mean,' added Jephson, 'that you cannot understand why a spirit, not compelled as we are by the exigencies of society, should care to spend its evenings on a laboured and childish conversation with a room full of abnormally uninteresting people.'

'That is precisely what I cannot understand,' MacShaughnassy agreed.

'Nor I, either,' said Jephson. 'But I was thinking of something very different altogether. Suppose a man died with the dearest wish of his heart unfulfilled, do you believe that his spirit might have power to return to earth and complete the interrupted work?'

'Well,' answered MacShaughnassy, 'if one admits the possibility of spirits retaining any interest in the affairs of this world at all, it is certainly more reasonable to imagine them engaged upon a task such as you suggest, than to believe that they occupy themselves with the performance of mere drawing-room tricks. But what are you leading up to?'

'Why, to this,' replied Jephson, seating himself straddle-legged across his chair, and leaning his arms upon the back. 'I was told a story this morning at the hospital by an old French doctor. The actual facts are few and simple; all that is known can be read in the Paris police records of sixty-two years ago.

'The most important part of the case, however, is the part that is not known, and that never will be known.

'The story begins with a great wrong done by one man unto another man. What the wrong was I do not know. I am inclined to think, however, it was connected with a woman. I think that, because he who had been wronged hated him who had wronged him with a hate such as does not often burn in a man's brain, unless it be fanned by the memory of a woman's breath.

'Still that is only conjecture, and the point is immaterial. The

402

man who had done the wrong fled, and the other man followed him. It became a point-to-point race, the first man having the advantage of a day's start. The course was the whole world, and the stakes were the first man's life.

'Travellers were few and far between in those days, and this made the trail easy to follow. The first man, never knowing how far or how near the other was behind him, and hoping now and again that he might have baffled him, would rest for a while. The second man, knowing always just how far the first one was before him, never paused, and thus each day the man who was spurred by Hate drew nearer to the man who was spurred by Fear.

'At this town the answer to the never-varied question would be:

' "At seven o'clock last evening, Monsieur."

' "Seven—ah; eighteen hours. Give me something to eat, quick, while the horses are being put to."

'At the next the calculation would be sixteen hours.

'Passing a lonely châlet, Monsieur puts his head out of the window:

' "How long since a carriage passed this way, with a tall, fair man inside?"

' "Such a one passed early this morning, Monsieur."

' "Thanks, drive on, a hundred francs apiece if you are through the pass before daybreak."

' "And what for dead horses, Monsieur?"

' "Twice their value when living."

'One day the man who was ridden by Fear looked up, and saw before him the open door of a cathedral, and passing in, knelt down and prayed. He prayed long and fervently, for men, when they are in sore straits, clutch eagerly at the straws of faith. He prayed that he might be forgiven his sin, and, more important still, that he might be pardoned the consequences of his sin, and be delivered from his adversary; and a few chairs from him, facing him, knelt his enemy, praying also.

'But the second man's prayer, being a thanksgiving merely, was short, so that when the first man raised his eyes, he saw the face of his enemy gazing at him across the chair-tops, with a mocking smile upon it.

'He made no attempt to rise, but remained kneeling, fascinated by the look of joy that shone out of the other man's eyes. And the other man moved the high-backed chairs one by one, and came towards him softly.

'Then, just as the man who had been wronged stood beside the man who had wronged him, full of gladness that his opportunity had come, there burst from the cathedral tower a sudden clash of bells, and the man, whose opportunity had come, broke his heart and fell back dead, with that mocking smile still playing round his mouth.

'And so he lay there.

'Then the man who had done the wrong rose up and passed out, praising God.

'What became of the body of the other man is not known. It was the body of a stranger who had died suddenly in the cathedral. There was none to identify it, none to claim it.

'Years passed away, and the survivor in the tragedy became a worthy and useful citizen, and a noted man of science.

'In his laboratory were many objects necessary to him in his researches, and, prominent among them, stood in a certain corner a human skeleton. It was a very old and much-mended skeleton, and one day the long-expected end arrived, and it tumbled to pieces.

'Thus it became necessary to purchase another.

'The man of science visited a dealer he well knew—a little parchment-faced old man who kept a dingy shop, where nothing was ever sold, within the shadow of the towers of Notre Dame.

'The little parchment-faced old man had just the very thing that Monsieur wanted—a singularly fine and well-proportioned "study". It should be sent round and set up in Monsieur's laboratory that very afternoon.

'The dealer was as good as his word. When Monsieur entered his laboratory that evening, the thing was in its place.

'Monsieur seated himself in his high-backed chair, and tried to collect his thoughts. But Monsieur's thoughts were unruly, and inclined to wander, and to wander always in one direction.

'Monsieur opened a large volume and commenced to read. He read of a man who had wronged another and fled from him, the other man following. Finding himself reading this, he closed the book angrily, and went and stood by the window and looked out. He saw before him the sun-pierced nave of a great cathedral, and on the stones lay a dead man with a mocking smile upon his face.

'Cursing himself for a fool, he turned away with a laugh. But his laugh was short-lived, for it seemed to him that something else in the room was laughing also. Struck suddenly still, with his feet glued to the ground, he stood listening for a while: then sought with starting eyes the corner from where the sound had seemed to come. But the white thing standing there was only grinning.

'Monsieur wiped the damp sweat from his head and hands, and stole out.

404

'For a couple of days he did not enter the room again. On the third, telling himself that his fears were those of a hysterical girl, he opened the door and went in. To shame himself, he took his lamp in his hand, and crossing over to the far corner where the skeleton stood, examined it. A set of bones bought for three hundred francs. Was he a child, to be scared by such a bogey!

'He held his lamp up by the front of the thing's grinning head. The flame of the lamp flickered as though a faint breath had passed over it.

'The man explained this to himself by saying that the walls of the house were old and cracked, and that the wind might creep in anywhere. He repeated this explanation to himself as he re-crossed the room, walking backwards, with his eyes fixed on the thing. When he reached his desk, he sat down and gripped the arms of his chair till his fingers turned white.

'He tried to work, but the empty sockets in that grinning head seemed to be drawing him towards them. He rose and battled with his inclination to fly screaming from the room. Glancing fearfully about him, his eye fell upon a high screen, standing before the door. He dragged it forward, and placed it between himself and the thing, so that he could not see it—nor it see him. Then he sat down again to his work. For a while he forced himself to look at the book in front of him, but at last, unable to control himself any longer, he suffered his eyes to follow their own bent.

'It may have been an hallucination. He may have accidentally placed the screen so as to favour such an illusion. But what he saw was a bony hand coming round the corner of the screen, and, with a cry, he fell to the floor in a swoon.

'The people of the house came running in, and lifting him up, carried him out, and laid him upon his bed. As soon as he recovered, his first question was, where had they found the thing—where was it when they entered the room? When they told him they had seen it standing where it always stood, and had gone down into the room to look again, because of his frenzied entreaties, and returned trying to hide their smiles, he listened to their talk about overwork, and the necessity for change and rest, and said they might do with him as they would.

'So for many months the laboratory door remained locked. Then there came a chill autumn evening when the man of science opened it again, and closed it behind him.

'He lighted his lamp, and gathered his instruments and books around him, and sat down before them in his high-backed chair. And the old terror returned to him.

'But this time he meant to conquer himself. His nerves were stronger now, and his brain clearer; he would fight his unreasoning fear. He crossed to the door and locked himself in, and flung the key to the other end of the room, where it fell among jars and bottles with an echoing clatter.

'Later on, his old housekeeper, going her final round, tapped at his door and wished him good-night, as was her custom. She received no response, at first, and, growing nervous, tapped louder and called again; and at length an answering "good-night" came back to her.

'She thought little about it at the time, but afterwards she remembered that the voice that had replied to her had been strangely grating and mechanical. Trying to describe it, she likened it to such a voice as she would imagine coming from a statue.

'Next morning his door remained still locked. It was no unusual thing for him to work all night and far into the next day, so no one thought to be surprised. When, however, evening came, and yet he did not appear, his servants gathered outside the room and whispered, remembering what had happened once before.

'They listened, but could hear no sound. They shook the door and called to him, then beat with their fists upon the wooden panels. But still no sound came from the room.

'Becoming alarmed, they decided to burst open the door, and, after many blows, it gave way, and they crowded in.

'He sat bolt upright in his high-backed chair. They thought at first he had died in his sleep. But when they drew nearer and the light fell upon him, they saw the livid marks of bony fingers round his throat; and in his eyes there was a terror such as is not often seen in human eyes.'

Something There Is

By Charles L. Grant

A mockingbird hidden in a broad-crested elm sang to banish the red eye of the sun. A woman called anxiously from a narrow back porch, a boy answered with a shout and ran laughing up Hawthorne Street, forgetting as he did not to step on the cracks. A dog rooting in the gutter snarled uncertainly at the not-quite-shadows of a hazy dusk. A speeding car backfired. A cat prowled.

The wind keened and gathered black clouds. The trees hissed and showed faint white. And the moon had no chance to bring a peace to the night.

Martin White was tired. Tired of the failures, the hints, the bitterly long hours of fruitless searching. So tired, he was near enough to despair to be tempted to give it all up before he drove himself weeping to the edge of screaming. He rubbed a heavy hand over his face, trying futilely to dismiss an insistent drowsiness that stung his dark eyes faintly and blurred his vision at the burning edges. He ignored the coarse two-day stubble on his prominent jaw, and did not seem to feel the perspiration that welded his shirt to his back in spite of the tiny black fan that spun weakly on the sill behind him. Beyond the screen, July shimmered over the front yard, weighted and humid, threatening to dissolve the nightblue walls. After a moment of helplessness, then, he decided to finish one more chapter before giving it up, but when every sentence on every page read the same and meant nothing, he sighed an impotent curse, closed the book and rose to his feet, leaning against the chipped and battered desk for support. He stared dumbly at the dust jacket and shook his head.

"Sorry, Stoker," he said to the time-worn cover, "but I don't think I can make it tonight." He closed his eyes, waiting, opened them and grinned wryly. "Nope, I'm afraid not."

He yawned, shook himself, shuffled down the short hall to his bedroom, stiffly exaggerating his walk to loosen his muscles before he slept. Without turning on the light, ignoring the faint yellow glow of the still-burning desk lamp, he stripped and let himself collapse onto the unmade bed.

Where he waited patiently for the dream, and the promises it made him.

The first time it had come was two months ago. He found himself standing in a level of absolute darkness he couldn't believe was possible, was real. When he'd awakened he wanted to scream, but he was too excited; and the second time, the third, the fourth and the fifth, he had been in the same unimaginable someplace, yet increasingly aware that he was expecting something to happen and terrified because he hadn't yet discovered what it would be.

He wanted to believe it was at last what he'd been groping for, but didn't until the darkness came while he was awake.

He was in his classroom, aimlessly shuffling papers after dismissing his last class and wondering what the high schools would ship him next term. His eyes closed in weary relief . . . and he was in darkness again. Only the darkness. But now he was convinced this was the way to find her.

He shifted, kicked at the sheets until they fell to the floor, and slept. While a light behind his eyes drifted and ran, merged from red to yellow to gold to black. He was in a room without dimension or boundary, and he floated/sat on a nebulous ebony with cool air to breathe though he choked for the lack of it while his neck tightened into cords, his head trembled in the effort to relax, and his throat burned with words that crushed against his teeth and drew blood from unbroken lips. He drew his knees to his chest and locked his hands around his shins. He was walking, but there was neither heat nor cold, movement nor quiet; but he knew she was there, had to be there, and called her plaintively to hurry, to give to him what she had given to the others. Suddenly there was a crash, a booming, resounding explosion that thundered into a roar, and when he snapped open his eyes . . .

. . . he found himself at his desk, his pen lying at his feet. A slight predawn breeze pushed mud-brown curtains against his naked back, and he jumped at their touch. Blinked. Breathed deeply as he stared at the blank sheet of paper on the desk's cracked glass top. Two others were lying crumpled on the floor.

"Damn," he said with a tentative grin. "Damn." She had brought him here; he knew it. Finally, after reading all the books on the shelves several times over, she had heard his silent calling and had come to him, to guide him.

But she was still at a distance, and he glared at the books.

"Give her up," he said softly, intensely, "give her up. You can't keep her from me forever. I'm joining the club, and you can't stop me."

Mary Shelley, Guy Endore, Bram Stoker, leather-bound and silent while Martin laughed and strutted into the bathroom to take a quick shower.

Beaumont and Bloch, Lovecraft and Leiber, tattered and yellowed while he sang a tuneless melody of a woman beautiful beyond description and the light she would bring to his starving eyes, and the words she would conjure for his inkless pen.

While Saki and Dunsany stared blindly at the red rising sun.

It was well past noon when he awoke again, too refreshed and excited to be disappointed when an hour passed at his desk without producing a word. Soon enough she would contact him, this muse of the others; and meanwhile he bustled about the tiny six-room

408

ranch cleaning and waiting. A quick canned supper, another hour of staring, and he was ready to throw in the towel when a telephone call reminded him of a party invitation he had unthinkingly accepted some days before. He hovered by the cradled receiver, unsure, apprehensive, with guilty glances toward his study door. At last, however, he decided that the relaxation would do him good, a chance to unlimber his mental processes and flex his imagination without the self-inflicted pressure that pilfered his sleep.

He dressed for the part. Turtleneck shirt, brown corduroy jacket, black slacks, and barely shined loafers. It was a stereotyped image, but one he enjoyed. The only thing missing was a well-used pipe.

By ten o'clock he was at the Bensons' home, ringing the doorbell and already wiping moist hands on his sides. Linda was his cheerleader, his patron, constantly stroking his ego and damning those who thought his talent was missing. "This is Martin T. White, the author," was her standard introduction to strangers, but it wasn't those he didn't know that he worried about; it was his friends and their well-meaning comments he had come to fear. If it wasn't for Linda, he would have stayed locked in his home.

And once inside, with a frosted glass in his hand, the ordeal began.

"Hey, Marty, how's it going? Still beating down those editors?"

"Well, Martin, still drumming up business for the old muse? Just remember, old boy, the formula for success: perspiration to inspiration, nine to one."

"Hey, White, when you make that first sale, you going to have a party? I won't hold my breath, but give me a call."

Martin grinned. Nodded. Refilled his glass.

There were faces, not people. Surefire plots with sly pleas for acknowledgment. Two ghost stories he had heard from the same mouths at the last party. Hints and suggestions from tired writing manuals and tired writing teachers. Gossip about Linda and her husband, Ted. Gossip about Linda. About Ted. About him. Someone dropped an ice cube down a woman's cleavage, and instantly he was besieged to include the incident in his next, his first, his whatever book.

He was ready to surrender, to drink himself into a stupor that would blot out the noise, when he recalled someone's mentioning his search for the muse. Instantly he was heartened. Their muse was an obscenity, distilled in alcohol and spoken in small type; but his, the real flesh-and-ink guide to his genius, was pure, beautiful, and shouted in capitals across a universe-wide marquee.

He was standing in the kitchen rinsing out his glass and smiling at his superiority over the plebian hypocrites when suddenly, without warning, the room went dark.

"No," he whispered harshly. "Damn, no, not here. Please, not here!"

He raced out the back door, realized he was still carrying his glass and threw it away, not hearing it smash on the side of the house.

Down Hawthorne Street.

A part of him noticing there was no moon.

Into his study, flinging himself into the chair and grabbing at his pen and the ream of paper. He took a deep shuddering breath . . . and a hot-cold wind wailed through his long hair, ripped at the skin around his throat, making no sound as he gazed unblinking into the nothing that buried him weightlessly while he crouched, naked, on swollen hands and blistered knees listening for her voice and hearing only a volley of thunder cascade through his chest. A bubble of spittle quivered at the corner of his mouth while mute echoes, deafening in their dumbness, competed with the rasp of his lungs to fill the void. A flash, then, of blue-white fire colder than ice, and he was thrown back onto his haunches . . .

. . . and heard the storm breaking over the house. Automatically, he reached behind him and pulled down the sash, switched on the fan, and turned to the top sheet of paper. It was blank, but he grinned. Blank, but he knew he was ready. She was coming. To him. To his pen.

He lit a cigarette and swaggered over to the bookcase, deciding to give himself some last-minute insurance with a booster reading. Just in case. With elaborate concern he scanned the collection of anthologies and novels, seeing each table of contents without opening a cover, searching with a sudden, disquieting apprehension for the bait he needed.

"Come on, my lovelies," he crooned to the spines, "which one of you is going to guide me tonight? Who's going to tell me what she's like? I don't have to know what she looks like, you know; but it would be nice to be able to picture her before she comes." His fingers darted, plucked, replaced, tapped his brow. "Come on, folks, don't be bashful. And for crying out loud, don't be so modest! After all, it was your combined geniuses that brought me this far, wasn't it? Come on, tell me what she looks like. Tell me how beautiful she really is."

The shelves were silent. He punched at the floor.

"Damnit, who the hell do you think you are? Do you really think you idiots can keep her from me?"

410

He snatched at a book, tossed it over his shoulder, and grabbed for another.

"Mrs. Radcliffe, you of all people should be glad that Gothics are all the rage. Too bad, though, because they're mutants, you know, hideous, monstrous travesties of every honest fear man ever had."

Another book, another toss.

"Mr. Machen, did you know that you and your kind have been called old-fashioned? Out-of-date and worn in a worn, cynical world. Poe, an ass; Hawthorne a pansy."

He glowered and swept a hand over the shelves, emptying them to his feet. "All of you. Dead. You need me, damnit, to make fear work again. You need me! Tell me! What does she look like? How do I find her?"

A sudden spate of bullet rain against the pane startled him into dropping his forgotten cigarette. He froze, looked stupidly at his trembling hands and was horrified. Immediately he crushed the smoldering butt under his heel and scuttled back to his desk, afraid to touch the books scattered on the floor, fearful they would desert him when he needed their help the most. And after what seemed like hours, he pulled open the center drawer and stared mournfully at the pile of rejection slips lying bleakly inside.

Nine years, he thought, nine years of nothing.

Hey, Marty, you old dog, how's the Pulitzer Prize looking this year? You got your speech all made up?

With a practiced hand he scooped up the papers and dumped them without ceremony into the left-hand drawer, noting dully as he did so that he would soon have to switch to the other.

You're a writer, huh? No kidding. That's nice, you know? But what else do you do, Mr. White? For a living, I mean.

"Perspiration, inspiration," he muttered angrily. "A decade is damned long enough for a man to sweat. God knows there's enough foul horror in the world. Why the hell—" and he slammed the drawers shut. "Why the hell can't I write about them?"

There was a correspondence course he failed to complete; a trip to the castles on the Rhine, Rhone, and Danube that took six years of his savings. Weekend flights to New England in desperate search of spectral Arkham, spring vacations in Haiti, Christmas in rural England, and a cold white dawn at Stonehenge. Midnights walking the streets in storms. And a year ago, the beginning of the collection that walled his study, reading and examining, hunting for a clue to the authors' ability to write eloquently about the unspeakable, darkly about the commonplace; over and over and over again until he had memorized nearly every florid, majestic purple, and bitter

411

bitten paragraph. Nightmares. Sweat. The sounds of blood dripping whenever he turned a page.

An aunt died, a raise in salary, and he redecorated every room in the house in every color of darkness he could find or create. The doors sprung heavy locks. The windows grew thick drapes that prevented the sunlight from fading black carpets, from admitting the day and keeping the air still.

But the words he had done did the worst to him. Worst by staying just out of reach, like the tip of a breeze, taunting him like so many harlots berating an impotent, cursing him from thick and thin brown envelopes efficiently and swiftly returned with his name and address neatly centered, neatly printed. They laughed, jeered, rearranged themselves to obscure the content from everyone but himself; and he cried out for understanding, vowed revenge on those who deliberately misunderstood, reveled in showers of self-pity, and haunted the summer/autumn/winter/spring parties for the Woman, and the Key.

Martin choked on a sob when the blood-weight of nine years threatened to crush him.

Hey, Mr. White, I'm told you're a . . . a writer? Well, listen, have you heard the one about the chubby vampire who managed a blood bank? No? Well, it seems that this girl came in one day . . .

The light bulb flickered. There was no wind, but the air moved. Martin reached for his pen. Waiting.

Really, Martin, don't you think you should try to write things that have . . . well, a moral? I mean, honestly! You should know that people just aren't scared anymore. Really!

Thunder and lightning born together, and the wet rush of the storm carried a faint ghost of laughter from across the street. Martin sat motionless, his eyes wide as if in shock. The pen moved without conscious direction, and he looked fearfully, gratefully at the bookcase, at the volumes he had thrown to the floor. But Matheson and Sloane made no move to comfort him.

Doesn't it interfere with your teaching, Mr. White?

Did you say horror stories, Mr. White? How . . . how quaint.

This course I was telling you about, Marty, the prof said you got to have a hook. You got a hook, White?

He yanked page after page from beneath the flow of black ink until his hand began to cramp and forced him to slow down. Slow down, and stop. Perspiration ran down his cheeks and soaked his collar. The fan had stopped. He took a breath, held it, blew it slowly out, and wrote again, ignoring the stinging smoke from the ciga-

412

rette dangling from his mouth. He neared the climax. Laughed. Tears brimmed. Nearer.

No fooling, you really a writer? Never heard of you.

Suddenly, as if a hand had punched at his chest, he slumped back and the pen fell to the desk. Panic strangled him. His fingers tried to grasp but failed to hold the pen now rolling away, to the floor.

"No," he said quietly. Then, louder: "No, damnit, you can't stop me now!"

The room, house, street, were silent.

His voice rose to a wail, a moan, while rain dripped from the eaves and vanished into mud.

He hesitated, then dropped to the floor, scrabbling through the books randomly, opening and reading, forcing disjointed passages to jolt into his mind. Feverishly he grabbed, tore, read, wept, until the last page lay shredded at his feet.

He closed his eyes tightly, and clenched his fists against his thighs.

I need you, he pleaded silently. I . . . I can't finish, not without you.

And he was in a place not a time, nor a color.

A cat, owl, woman-girl screeched. Blood ran, water ran, white greyed, red glowed, and a thousand-towered castle rose and fell as stagnant green waters that loomed above scarlet mountains coated with wolves that flew like bats on broomsticks of lightning. An axe fell, guillotine hummed, knife whistled, stake thudded, and Martin smiled, holding out his arms as a road came and went beneath his naked feet. Suns came up, clouds, caves, homes of gingerbread streets, paths, trails of thorns. There marched dolls with pink pins, men on jackals, and an out-of-step parade passed, parted over him, through him . . . and he was alone.

With a white-robed man who held worlds of choirs and hells of crowds in each massive hand, with golden dirty hair and his smile blinded.

"You're not the one!" Martin shouted angrily.

"You're right," the man said, sang, laughed, lamented.

Another man, short, ugly, fiercesome, a black halo and violet cloak his only dress.

"No, damnit, neither are you," Martin sneered.

"Right," the man said softly, almost sadly.

Martin whirled.

A woman, at last the woman, whose beauty crippled and gave him strength, with roses and ivy and hemlock at her breasts, and

413

deer and hyenas cavorting at her feet. Symphonies and chantings, ditties and solemnities.

"Yes," Martin gasped. "I've been waiting for you."

"No," the woman wept. "No, not me."

Martin spun around, his arms wide to clasp, but he was alone again; and a sudden snap of thunder brought him back to the study. He was sprawled on the floor, his head toward the door, and the torn pages of his books had fallen snowlike over his chest.

"Oh, my God, please," he said in a monotonic moan. "Don't leave me now. Please, where are you?"

In spite of the thunder, there was fog.

In spite of the lightning, there was darkness.

And when Martin rolled to his stomach, there was a shadow in the corner.

"Here," It said. "We've been waiting."

Spring-Fingered Jack

By Susan Casper

He knew where he was going as soon as he walked into the arcade. He moved past the rows of busy children, blaring computer voices, flashing lights and ringing bells. He walked past the line of old-fashioned pinball machines, all of them empty, all flashing and calling like outdated mechanical hookers vainly trying to tempt the passing trade.

The machine he wanted was back in the dimly lit corner, and he breathed a sigh of relief to see it unused. Its mutely staring screen was housed in a yellow body, above a row of levers and buttons. On its side, below the coin slot, was a garish purple drawing of a woman dressed in Victorian high fashion. Her large and ornate hat sat slightly askew atop her head, and her neatly piled hair was falling artistically down at the sides. She was screaming, eyes wide, the back of her hand almost covering her lovely mouth. And behind her, sketched in faintest white, was just the suggestion of a lurking figure.

He put his briefcase down beside the machine. With unsteady fingers, he reached for a coin, and fumbled it into the coin slot. The

414

screen flashed to life. A sinister man in a deerstalker waved a crimson-tipped knife and faded away behind a row of buildings. The graphics were excellent, and extremely realistic. The screen filled with rows of dark blue instructions against a light blue field, and he scanned them sketchily, impatient for the game to begin.

He pressed a button and the image changed again, becoming a maze of narrow squalid streets lined with decaying buildings. One lone figure, his, stood squarely center screen. A woman in Victorian dress, labeled Polly, walked toward him. He pushed the lever forward and his man began to move. He remembered to make the man doff his cap; if you didn't, she wouldn't go with you. They fell in step together, and he carefully steered her past the first intersection. Old Montague Street was a trap for beginners, and one he hadn't fallen into for quite some time. The first one had to be taken to Buck's Row.

Off to one side, a bobby was separating a pair of brawling, ragged women. He had to be careful here, for it cost points if he was spotted. He steered the pair down the appropriate alley, noting with satisfaction that it was deserted.

The heartbeat sound became louder as he maneuvered his figure behind that of the woman, and was joined by the sound of harsh, labored breathing. This part of the game was timed and he would be working against the clock. He lifted a knife from inside his coat. Clapping a hand over "Polly's" mouth, he slashed her throat viciously from ear to ear. Lines of bright red pulsed across the screen, but away from him. Good. He had not been marked by the blood. Now came the hard part. He laid her down and began the disembowling, carefully cutting her abdomen open almost to the diaphragm, keeping one eye on the clock. He finished with twenty seconds to spare and moved his man triumphantly away from the slowly approaching bobby. Once he had found the public sink to wash in, round one was complete.

Once again his figure was center screen. This time the approaching figure was "Dark Annie," and he took her to Hanbury Street. But this time he forgot to cover her mouth when he struck, and she screamed, a shrill and terrifying scream. Immediately the screen began to flash a brilliant, painful red, pulsing in time to the ear-splitting blasts of a police whistle. Two bobbies materialized on either side of his figure, and grabbed it firmly by the arms. A hangman's noose flashed on the screen as the funeral march roared from the speaker. The screen went dark.

He stared at the jeering screen, trembling, feeling shaken and sick, and cursed himself bitterly. A real beginner's mistake! He'd been too eager. Angrily, he fed another coin into the slot.

This time, he carefully worked himself all the way up to "Kate," piling up bonus points and making no fatal mistakes. He was sweating now, and his mouth was dry. His jaws ached with tension. It was really hard to beat the clock on this one, and took intense concentration. He remembered to nick the eyelids, that was essential, and pulling the intestines out and draping them over the right shoulder wasn't too hard, but cutting out the kidney correctly, *that* was a bitch. At last the clock ran out on him, and he had to leave without the kidney, costing himself a slew of points. He was rattled enough to almost run into a bobby as he threaded through the alleys leading out of Mitre Square. The obstacles became increasingly difficult with every successful round completed, and from here on in it became particularly hard, with the clock time shortening, swarms of sightseers, reporters and roving Vigilance Committees to avoid in addition to a redoubled number of police. He had never yet found the right street for "Black Mary. . . ."

A voice called "last game," and a little while later his man got caught again. He slapped the machine in frustration; then straightened his suit and tie and picked up his briefcase. He checked his Rollaflex. Ten-oh-five: it was early yet. The machines winked out in clustered groups as the last stragglers filed through the glass doors. He followed them into the street.

Once outside in the warm night air, he began to think again about the game, to plan his strategy for tomorrow, only peripherally aware of the winos mumbling in doorways, the scantily dressed hookers on the corner. Tawdry neon lights from porno movie houses, "adult" bookstores and flophouse hotels tracked across his eyes like video displays, and his fingers worked imaginary buttons and levers as he pushed through the sleazy, late-night crowds.

He turned into a narrow alley, followed it deep into the shadows, and then stopped and leaned back against the cool, dank bricks. He spun the three dials of the combination lock, each to its proper number, and then opened the briefcase.

The machine: he had thought of it all day at work, thought of it nearly every second as he waited impatiently for five o'clock, and now another chance had come and gone, and he *still* had not beaten it. He fumbled among the papers in his briefcase, and pulled out a long, heavy knife.

He would practice tonight, and tomorrow he *would* beat the machine.

416

Sredni Vashtar

By Saki

Conradin was ten years old, and the doctor had pronounced his professional opinion that the boy would not live another five years. The doctor was silky and effete, and counted for little, but his opinion was endorsed by Mrs. De Ropp, who counted for nearly everything. Mrs. De Ropp was Conradin's cousin and guardian, and in his eyes she represented those three-fifths of the world that are necessary and disagreeable and real; the other two-fifths, in perpetual antagonism to the foregoing, were summed up in himself and his imagination. One of these days Conradin supposed he would succumb to the mastering pressure of wearisome necessary things—such as illnesses and coddling restrictions and drawn-out dulness. Without his imagination, which was rampant under the spur of loneliness, he would have succumbed long ago.

Mrs. De Ropp would never, in her honestest moments, have confessed to herself that she disliked Conradin, though she might have been dimly aware that thwarting him "for his good" was a duty which she did not find particularly irksome. Conradin hated her with a desperate sincerity which he was perfectly able to mask. Such few pleasures as he could contrive for himself gained an added relish from the likelihood that they would be displeasing to his guardian, and from the realm of his imagination she was locked out—an unclean thing, which should find no entrance.

In the dull, cheerless garden, overlooked by so many windows that were ready to open with a message not to do this or that, or a reminder that medicines were due, he found little attraction. The few fruit-trees that it contained were set jealously apart from his plucking, as though they were rare specimens of their kind blooming in an arid waste; it would probably have been difficult to find a market-gardener who would have offered ten shillings for their entire yearly produce. In a forgotten corner, however, almost hidden behind a dismal shrubbery, was a disused tool-shed of respectable proportions, and within its walls Conradin found a haven, something that took on the varying aspects of a playroom and a cathedral. He had peopled it with a legion of familiar phantoms, evoked

417

partly from fragments of history and partly from his own brain, but it also boasted two inmates of flesh and blood. In one corner lived a ragged-plumaged Houdan hen, on which the boy lavished an affection that had scarcely another outlet. Further back in the gloom stood a large hutch, divided into two compartments, one of which was fronted with close iron bars. This was the abode of a large polecat-ferret, which a friendly butcher-boy had once smuggled, cage and all, into its present quarters, in exchange for a long-secreted hoard of small silver. Conradin was dreadfully afraid of the lithe, sharp-fanged beast, but it was his most treasured possession. Its very presence in the tool-shed was a secret and fearful joy, to be kept scrupulously from the knowledge of the Woman, as he privately dubbed his cousin. And one day, out of Heaven knows what material, he spun the beast a wonderful name, and from that moment it grew into a god and a religion. The Woman indulged in religion once a week at a church near by, and took Conradin with her, but to him the church service was an alien rite in the House of Rimmon. Every Thursday, in the dim and musty silence of the tool-shed, he worshipped with mystic and elaborate ceremonial before the wooden hutch where dwelt Sredni Vashtar, the great ferret. Red flowers in their season and scarlet berries in the winter-time were offered at his shrine, for he was a god who laid some special stress on the fierce impatient side of things, as opposed to the Woman's religion, which, as far as Conradin could observe, went to great lengths in the contrary direction. And on great festivals powdered nutmeg was strewn in front of his hutch, an important feature of the offering being that the nutmeg had to be stolen. These festivals were of irregular occurrence, and were chiefly appointed to celebrate some passing event. On one occasion, when Mrs. De Ropp suffered from acute toothache for three days, Conradin kept up the festival during the entire three days, and almost succeeded in persuading himself that Sredni Vashtar was personally responsible for the toothache. If the malady had lasted for another day the supply of nutmeg would have given out.

The Houdan hen was never drawn into the cult of Sredni Vashtar. Conradin had long ago settled that she was an Anabaptist. He did not pretend to have the remotest knowledge as to what an Anabaptist was, but he privately hoped that it was dashing and not very respectable. Mrs. De Ropp was the ground plan on which he based and detested all respectability.

After a while Conradin's absorption in the tool-shed began to attract the notice of his guardian. "It is not good for him to be pottering down there in all weathers," she promptly decided, and at breakfast one morning she announced that the Houdan hen had been sold and taken away overnight. With her short-sighted eyes she peered at Conradin, waiting for an outbreak of rage and sorrow, which she was ready to rebuke with a flow of excellent precepts and reasoning. But Conradin said nothing: there was nothing to be said. Something perhaps in his white set face gave her a momentary qualm, for at tea that afternoon there was toast on the table, a delicacy which she usually banned on the ground that it was bad for him; also because the making of it "gave trouble," a deadly offence in the middle-class feminine eye.

"I thought you liked toast," she exclaimed, with an injured air, observing that he did not touch it.

"Sometimes," said Conradin.

In the shed that evening there was an innovation in the worship of the hutch-god. Conradin had been wont to chant his praises, tonight he asked a boon.

"Do one thing for me, Sredni Vashtar."

The thing was not specified. As Sredni Vashtar was a god he must be supposed to know. And choking back a sob as he looked at that other empty corner, Conradin went back to the world he so hated.

And every night, in the welcome darkness of his bedroom, and every evening in the dusk of the tool-shed, Conradin's bitter litany went up: "Do one thing for me, Sredni Vashtar."

Mrs. De Ropp noticed that the visits to the shed did not cease, and one day she made a further journey of inspection.

"What are you keeping in that locked hutch?" she asked. "I believe it's guinea-pigs. I'll have them all cleared away."

Conradin shut his lips tight, but the Woman ransacked his bedroom till she found the carefully hidden key, and forthwith marched down to the shed to complete her discovery. It was a cold afternoon, and Conradin had been bidden to keep to the house. From the furthest window of the dining-room the door of the shed could just be seen beyond the corner of the shrubbery, and there Conradin stationed himself. He saw the Woman enter, and then he imagined her opening the door of the sacred hutch and peering down with her short-sighted eyes into the thick straw bed where his god lay hidden. Perhaps she would prod at the straw in her clumsy impatience. And Conradin fervently breathed his prayer for the last time. But he knew as he prayed that he did not believe. He knew that the Woman would come out presently with that pursed smile he loathed so well on her face, and that in an hour or two the gardener would carry away his wonderful god, a god no longer, but a simple brown ferret in a hutch. And he knew that the Woman would triumph always as she triumphed now, and that he would grow ever more sickly under her pestering and domineering and superior wisdom, till one day nothing would matter much more with him, and the doctor would be proved right. And in the sting and misery of his defeat, he began to chant loudly and defiantly the hymn of his threatened idol:

Sredni Vashtar went forth,
His thoughts were red thoughts and his teeth were white.
His enemies called for peace, but he brought them death.
Sredni Vashtar the Beautiful.

And then of a sudden he stopped his chanting and drew closer to the window-pane. The door of the shed still stood ajar as it had been left, and the minutes were slipping by. They were long minutes, but they slipped by nevertheless. He watched the starlings running and flying in little parties across the lawn; he counted them over and over again, with one eye always on that swinging door. A sour-faced maid came in to lay the table for tea, and still Conradin stood and waited and watched. Hope had crept by inches into his heart, and now a look of triumph began to blaze in his eyes that had only known the wistful patience of defeat. Under his breath, with a furtive exultation, he began once again the paean of victory and devastation. And presently his eyes were rewarded: out through that doorway came a long, low, yellow-and-brown beast, with eyes a-blink at the waning daylight, and dark wet stains around the fur of jaws and throat. Conradin dropped on his knees. The great polecat-ferret made its way down to a small brook at the foot of the garden, drank for a moment, then crossed a little plank bridge and was lost to sight in the bushes. Such was the passing of Sredni Vashtar.

"Tea is ready," said the sour-faced maid; "where is the mistress?"

"She went down to the shed some time ago," said Conradin.

And while the maid went to summon her mistress to tea, Conradin fished a toasting-fork out of the sideboard drawer and proceeded to toast himself a piece of bread. And during the toasting of it and the buttering of it with much butter and the slow enjoyment of eating it, Conradin listened to the noises and silences which fell in quick spasms beyond the dining-room door. The loud foolish screaming of the maid, the answering chorus of wondering ejaculations from the kitchen region, the scuttering footsteps and hurried embassies for outside help, and then, after a lull, the scared sobbings and the shuffling tread of those who bore a heavy burden into the house.

"Whoever will break it to the poor child? I couldn't for the life of me!" exclaimed a shrill voice. And while they debated the matter among themselves, Conradin made himself another piece of toast.

The Statement of Randolph Carter

By H. P. Lovecraft

I repeat to you, gentlemen, that your inquisition is fruitless. Detain me here forever if you will; confine or execute me if you must have a victim to propitiate the illusion you call justice; but I can say no more than I have said already. Everything that I can remember, I have told you with perfect candor. Nothing has been distorted or concealed, and if anything remains vague, it is only because of the dark cloud which has come over my mind—that cloud and the nebulous nature of the horrors which brought it upon me.

Again I say, I do not know what has become of Harley Warren, though I think—almost hope—that he is in peaceful oblivion, if there be anywhere so blessed a thing. It is true that I have for five years been his closest friend, and a partial sharer of his terrible researches into the unknown. I will not deny, though my memory is uncertain and indistinct, that this witness of yours may have seen us together as he says, on the Gainsville pike, walking toward Big Cypress Swamp, at half past 11 on that awful night. That we bore electric lanterns, spades, and a curious coil of wire with attached instruments, I will even affirm; for these things all played a part in the single hideous scene which remains burned into my shaken recollection. But of what followed, and of the reason I was found alone and dazed on the edge of the swamp next morning, I must insist that I know nothing save what I have told you over and over again. You say to me that there is nothing in the swamp or near it which could form the setting of that frightful episode. I reply that I knew nothing beyond what I saw. Vision or nightmare it may have been—vision or nightmare I fervently hope it was—yet it is all that my mind retains of what took place in those shocking hours after we left the sight of men. And why Harley Warren did not return, he or his shade—or some nameless thing I cannot describe—alone can tell.

As I have said before, the weird studies of Harley Warren were well known to me, and to some extent shared by me. Of his vast collection of strange, rare books on forbidden subjects I have read all that are written in the languages of which I am master; but these are few as compared with those in languages I cannot understand. Most, I believe, are in Arabic; and the fiend-inspired book which brought on the end—the book which he carried in his pocket out of the world—was written in characters whose like I never saw elsewhere. Warren would never tell me just what was in that book. As to the nature of our studies—must I say again that I no longer retain full comprehension? It seems to me rather merciful that I do not, for they were terrible studies, which I pursued more through reluctant fascination than through actual inclination. Warren always dominated me, and sometimes I feared him. I remember how I shuddered at his facial expression on the night before the awful happening, when he talked so incessantly of his theory, why certain corpses never decay, but rest firm and fat in their tombs for a thousand years. But I do not fear him now, for I suspect that he has known horrors beyond my ken. Now I fear for him.

Once more I say that I have no clear idea of our object on that night. Certainly, it had much to do with something in the book which Warren carried with him—that ancient book in undecipherable characters which had come to him from India a month before —but I swear I do not know what it was that we expected to find. Your witness says he saw us at half past 11 on the Gainsville pike, headed for Big Cypress Swamp. This is probably true, but I have no distinct memory of it. The picture seared into my soul is of one scene only, and the hour must have been long after midnight; for a waning crescent moon was high in the vaporous heavens.

The place was an ancient cemetery; so ancient that I trembled at the manifold signs of immemorial years. It was in a deep, damp hollow, overgrown with rank grass, moss, and curious creeping weeds, and filled with a vague stench which my idle fancy associated absurdly with rotting stone. On every hand were the signs of neglect and decrepitude, and I seemed haunted by the notion that Warren and I were the first living creatures to invade a lethal silence of centuries. Over the valley's rim a wan, waning crescent moon peered through the noisome vapors that seemed to emanate from unheard of catacombs, and by its feeble, wavering beams I

could distinguish a repellent array of antique slabs, urns, ceno-
taphs, and mausoleum facades; all crumbling, moss-grown, and
moisture-stained, and partly concealed by the gross luxuriance of
the unhealthy vegetation.

My first vivid impression of my own presence in this terrible
necropolis concerns the act of pausing with Warren before a certain
half-obliterated sepulcher and of throwing down some burdens
which we seemed to have been carrying. I now observed that I had
with me an electric lantern and two spades, whilst my companion
was supplied with a similar lantern and a portable telephone outfit.
No word was uttered, for the spot and the task seemed known to
us; and without delay we seized our spades and commenced to
clear away the grass, weeds, and drifted earth from the flat, archaic
mortuary. After uncovering the entire surface, which consisted of
three immense granite slabs, we stepped back some distance to sur-
vey the charnel scene; and Warren appeared to make some mental
calculations. Then he returned to the sepulcher, and using his
spade as a lever, sought to pry up the slab lying nearest to a stony
ruin which may have been a monument in its day. He did not
succeed, and motioned to me to come to his assistance. Finally our
combined strength loosened the stone, which we raised and tipped
to one side.

The removal of the slab revealed a black aperture, from which
rushed an effluence of miasmal gases so nauseous that we started
back in horror. After an interval, however, we approached the pit
again, and found the exhalations less unbearable. Our lanterns disclosed the top of a flight of stone steps, dripping with some detestable ichor of the inner earth, and bordered by moist walls encrusted with niter. And now for the first time my memory records
verbal discourse, Warren addressing me at length in his mellow
tenor voice; a voice singularly unperturbed by our awesome surroundings.

"I'm sorry to have to ask you to stay on the surface," he said,
"but it would be a crime to let anyone with your frail nerves go
down there. You can't imagine, even from what you have read and
from what I've told you, the things I shall have to see and do. It's
fiendish work, Carter, and I doubt if any man without ironclad
sensibilities could ever see it through and come up alive and sane. I
don't wish to offend you, and Heaven knows I'd be glad enough to
have you with me; but the responsibility is in a certain sense mine,
and I couldn't drag a bundle of nerves like you down to probable
death or madness. I tell you, you can't imagine what the thing is
really like! But I promise to keep you informed over the telephone

of every move—you see I've enough wire here to reach to the center of the earth and back!"

I can still hear, in memory, those coolly spoken words; and I can still remember my remonstrances. I seemed desperately anxious to accompany my friend into those sepulchral depths, yet he proved inflexibly obdurate. At one time he threatened to abandon the expedition if I remained insistent; a threat which proved effective, since he alone held the key to the thing. All this I can still remember, though I no longer know what manner of thing we sought. After he had obtained my reluctant acquiescence in his design, Warren picked up the reel of wire and adjusted the instruments. At his nod I took one of the latter and seated myself upon an aged, discolored gravestone close by the newly uncovered aperture. Then he shook my hand, shouldered the coil of wire, and disappeared within that indescribable ossuary.

For a minute I kept sight of the glow of his lantern, and heard the rustle of the wire as he laid it down after him; but the glow soon disappeared abruptly, as if a turn in the stone staircase had been encountered, and the sound died away almost as quickly. I was alone, yet bound to the unknown depths by those magic strands whose insulated surface lay green beneath the struggling beams of that waning crescent moon.

I constantly consulted my watch by the light of my electric lantern, and listened with feverish anxiety at the receiver of the telephone; but for more than a quarter of an hour heard nothing. Then a faint clicking came from the instrument, and I called down to my friend in a tense voice. Apprehensive as I was, I was nevertheless unprepared for the words which came up from that uncanny vault in accents more alarmed and quivering than any I had heard before from Harley Warren. He who had so calmly left me a little while previously, now called from below in a shaky whisper more portentous than the loudest shriek:

"God! If you could see what I am seeing!"

I could not answer. Speechless, I could only wait. Then came the frenzied tones again:

"Carter, it's terrible—monstrous—unbelievable!"

This time my voice did not fail me, and I poured into the transmitter a flood of excited questions. Terrified, I continued to repeat, "Warren, what is it? What is it?"

Once more came the voice of my friend, still hoarse with fear, and now apparently tinged with despair:

"I can't tell you, Carter! It's too utterly beyond thought—I dare not tell you—no man could know it and live—Great God! I never dreamed of this!"

Stillness again, save for my now incoherent torrent of shuddering inquiry. Then the voice of Warren in a pitch of wilder consternation:

"Carter! for the love of God, put back the slab and get out of this if you can! Quick!—leave everything else and make for the outside —it's your only chance! Do as I say, and don't ask me to explain!"

I heard, yet was able only to repeat my frantic questions. Around me were the tombs and the darkness and the shadows; below me, some peril beyond the radius of the human imagination. But my friend was in greater danger than I, and through my fear I felt a vague resentment that he should deem me capable of deserting him under such circumstances. More clicking, and after a pause a piteous cry from Warren:

"Beat it! For God's sake, put back the slab and beat it, Carter!"

Something in the boyish slang of my evidently stricken companion unleashed my faculties. I formed and shouted a resolution, "Warren, brace up! I'm coming down!" But at this offer the tone of my auditor changed to a scream of utter despair:

"Don't! You can't understand! It's too late—and my own fault. Put back the slab and run—there's nothing else you or anyone can do now!"

The tone changed again, this time acquiring a softer quality, as of hopeless resignation. Yet it remained tense through anxiety for me.

"Quick—before it's too late!"

I tried not to heed him; tried to break through the paralysis which held me, and to fulfil my vow to rush down to his aid. But his next whisper found me still held inert in the chains of stark horror.

"Carter—hurry! It's no use—you must go—better one than two —the slab—"

A pause, more clicking, then the faint voice of Warren:

"Nearly over now—don't make it harder—cover up those damned steps and run for your life—you're losing time—so long, Carter—won't see you again."

Here Warren's whisper swelled into a cry; a cry that gradually rose to a shriek fraught with all the horror of the ages—

"Curse these hellish things—legions—My God! Beat it! Beat it! BEAT IT!"

After that was silence. I know not how many interminable eons I sat stupefied; whispering, muttering, calling, screaming into that telephone. Over and over again through those eons I whispered and muttered, called, shouted, and screamed, "Warren! Warren! Answer me—are you there?"

And then there came to me the crowning horror of all—the unbelievable, unthinkable, almost unmentionable thing. I have said that eons seemed to elapse after Warren shrieked forth his last despairing warning, and that only my own cries now broke the hideous silence. But after a while there was a further clicking in the receiver, and I strained my ears to listen. Again I called down, "Warren, are you there?" and in answer heard the thing which has brought this cloud over my mind. I do not try, gentlemen, to account for that thing—that voice—nor can I venture to describe it in detail, since the first words took away my consciousness and created a mental blank which reaches to the time of my awakening in the hospital. Shall I say that the voice was deep; hollow; gelatinous; remote; unearthly; inhuman; disembodied? What shall I say? It was the end of my experience, and is the end of my story. I heard it, and knew no more—heard it as I sat petrified in that unknown cemetery in the hollow, amidst the crumbling stones and the falling tombs, the rank vegetation and the miasmal vapors—heard it well up from the innermost depths of that damnable open sepulcher as I watched amorphous, necrophagous shadows dance beneath an accursed waning moon.

And this is what it said:

"You fool, Warren is DEAD!"

The Story of Muhammad Din

By Rudyard Kipling

Who is the happy man? He that sees in his own house at home, little children crowned with dust, leaping and falling and crying.—*Munichandra*, translated by Professor Peterson.

The polo-ball was an old one, scarred, chipped, and dinted. It stood on the mantelpiece among the pipe-stems which Imam Din, *khitmatgar*, was cleaning for me.

"Does the Heaven-born want this ball?" said Imam Din, deferentially.

426

The Heaven-born set no particular store by it; but of what use was a polo-ball to a *khitmatgar*?

"By your Honor's favor, I have a little son. He has seen this ball, and desires it to play with. I do not want it for myself."

No one would for an instant accuse portly old Imam Din of wanting to play with polo-balls. He carried out the battered thing into the veranda; and there followed a hurricane of joyful squeaks, a patter of small feet, and the *thud-thud-thud* of the ball rolling along the ground. Evidently the little son had been waiting outside the door to secure his treasure. But how had he managed to see that polo-ball?

Next day, coming back from office half an hour earlier than usual, I was aware of a small figure in the dining-room—a tiny, plump figure in a ridiculously inadequate shirt which came, perhaps, half-way down the tubby stomach. It wandered round the room, thumb in mouth, crooning to itself as it took stock of the pictures. Undoubtedly this was the "little son."

He had no business in my room, of course; but was so deeply absorbed in his discoveries that he never noticed me in the doorway. I stepped into the room and startled him nearly into a fit. He sat down on the ground with a gasp. His eyes opened, and his mouth followed suit. I knew what was coming, and fled, followed by a long, dry howl which reached the servants' quarters far more quickly than any command of mine had ever done. In ten seconds Imam Din was in the dining-room. Then despairing sobs arose, and I returned to find Imam Din admonishing the small sinner who was using most of his shirt as a handkerchief.

"This boy," said Imam Din, judicially, "is a *budmash*—a big *budmash*. He will, without doubt, go to the *jail-khana* for his behavior." Renewed yells from the penitent, and an elaborate apology to myself from Imam Din.

"Tell the baby," said I, "that the *Sahib* is not angry, and take him away." Imam Din conveyed my forgiveness to the offender, who had now gathered all his shirt round his neck, stringwise, and the yell subsided into a sob. The two set off for the door. "His name," said Imam Din, as though the name were part of the crime, "is Muhammad Din, and he is a *budmash*." Freed from present danger, Muhammad Din turned round in his father's arms, and said gravely, "It is true that my name is Muhammad Din, *Tahib*, but I am not a *budmash*. I am a *man*!"

From that day dated my acquaintance with Muhammad Din. Never again did he come into my dining-room, but on the neutral ground of the garden, we greeted each other with much state, though our conversation was confined to *"Talaam, Tahib"* from his side, and *"Salaam, Muhammad Din"* from mine. Daily on my return from office, the little white shirt, and the fat little body used to rise from the shade of the creeper-covered trellis where they had been hid; and daily I checked my horse here, that my salutation might not be slurred over or given unseemly.

Muhammad Din never had any companions. He used to trot about the compound, in and out of the castor-oil bushes, on mysterious errands of his own. One day I stumbled upon some of his handiwork far down the grounds. He had half buried the polo-ball in dust, and stuck six shriveled old marigold flowers in a circle round it. Outside that circle again was a rude square, traced out in bits of red brick alternating with fragments of broken china; the whole bounded by a little bank of dust. The water-man from the well-curb put in a plea for the small architect, saying that it was only the play of a baby and did not much disfigure my garden.

Heaven knows that I had no intention of touching the child's work then or later; but, that evening, a stroll through the garden brought me unawares full on it; so that I trampled, before I knew, marigold-heads, dustbank, and fragments of broken soap-dish into confusion past all hope of mending. Next morning, I came upon Muhammad Din crying softly to himself over the ruin I had wrought. Some one had cruelly told him that the *Sahib* was very angry with him for spoiling the garden, and had scattered his rubbish, using bad language the while. Muhammad Din labored for an hour at effacing every trace of the dust-bank and pottery fragments, and it was with a tearful and apologetic face that he said *"Talaam, Tahib,"* when I came home from office. A hasty inquiry resulted in Imam Din informing Muhammad Din that, by my singular favor, he was permitted to disport himself as he pleased. Whereat the child took heart and fell to tracing the ground-plan of an edifice which was to eclipse the marigold-polo-ball creation.

For some months, the chubby little eccentricity revolved in his humble orbit among the castor-oil bushes and in the dust; always fashioning magnificent palaces from stale flowers thrown away by the bearer, smooth water-worn pebbles, bits of broken glass, and feathers pulled, I fancy, from my fowls—always alone, and always crooning to himself.

A gaily-spotted sea-shell was dropped one day close to the last of his little buildings; and I looked that Muhammad Din should build something more than ordinarily splendid on the strength of it. Nor was I disappointed. He meditated for the better part of an hour, and his crooning rose to a jubilant song. Then he began tracing in the dust. It would certainly be a wondrous palace, this one, for it was two yards long and a yard broad in ground-plan. But the palace was never completed.

Next day there was no Muhammad Din at the head of the carriage-drive, and no *"Talaam, Tahib"* to welcome my return. I had grown accustomed to the greeting, and its omission troubled me. Next day Imam Din told me that the child was suffering slightly from fever and needed quinine. He got the medicine, and an English Doctor.

"They have no stamina, these brats," said the Doctor, as he left Imam Din's quarters.

A week later, though I would have given much to have avoided it, I met on the road to the Mussulman burying-ground Imam Din, accompanied by one other friend, carrying in his arms, wrapped in a white cloth all that was left of little Muhammad Din.

The Thing
in the Forest

By Bernard Capes

Into the snow-locked forests of Upper Hungary steal wolves in winter; but there is a footfall worse than theirs to knock upon the heart of the lonely traveller.

One December evening Elspet, the young, newly wedded wife of the woodman Stefan, came hurrying over the lower slopes of the White Mountains from the town where she had been all day marketing. She carried a basket with provisions on her arm; her plump cheeks were like a couple of cold apples; her breath spoke short, but more from nervousness than exhaustion. It was nearing dusk, and she was glad to see the little lonely church in the hollow below, the hub, as it were, of many radiating paths through the trees, one of which was the road to her own warm cottage yet a half-mile away.

She paused a moment at the foot of the slope, undecided about entering the little chill, silent building and making her plea for protection to the great battered stone image of Our Lady of Succour which stood within by the confessional box; but the stillness and the growing darkness decided her, and she went on. A spark of fire glowing through the presbytery window seemed to repel rather than attract her, and she was glad when the convolutions of the path hid it from her sight. Being new to the district, she had seen very little of Father Ruhl as yet, and somehow the penetrating knowledge and burning eyes of the pastor made her feel uncomfortable.

The soft drift, the lane of tall, motionless pines, stretched on in a quiet like death. Somewhere the sun, like a dead fire, had fallen into opalescent embers faintly luminous: they were enough only to touch the shadows with a ghastlier pallor. It was so still that the light crunch in the snow of the girl's own footfalls trod on her heart like a desecration.

Suddenly there was something near her that had not been before. It had come like a shadow, without more sound or warning. It was here—there—behind her. She turned, in mortal panic, and saw a wolf. With a strangled cry and trembling limbs she strove to hurry on her way; and always she knew, though there was no whisper of pursuit, that the gliding shadow followed in her wake. Desperate in her terror, she stopped once more and faced it.

A wolf!—was it a wolf? O who could doubt it! Yet the wild expression in those famished eyes, so lost, so pitiful, so mingled of insatiable hunger and human need! Condemned, for its unspeakable sins, to take this form with sunset, and so howl and snuffle about the doors of men until the blessed day released it. A werewolf—not a wolf.

That terrific realization of the truth smote the girl as with a knife out of darkness: for an instant she came near fainting. And then a low moan broke into her heart and flooded it with pity. So lost, so infinitely hopeless. And so pitiful—yes, in spite of all, so pitiful. It had sinned, beyond any sinning that her innocence knew or her experience could gauge; but she was a woman, very blest, very happy, in her store of comforts and her surety of love. She knew that it was forbidden to succour these damned and nameless outcasts, to help or sympathize with them in any way. But—

There was good store of meat in her basket, and who need ever know or tell? With shaking hands she found and threw a sop to the desolate brute—then, turning, sped upon her way.

But at home her secret sin stood up before her, and, interposing between her husband and herself, threw its shadow upon both their faces. What had she dared—what done? By her own act forfeited her birthright of innocence; by her own act placed herself in the power of the evil to which she had ministered. All that night she lay in shame and horror, and all the next day, until Stefan had come about his dinner and gone again, she moved in a dumb agony. Then, driven unendurably by the memory of his troubled, bewildered face, as twilight threatened she put on her cloak and went down to the little church in the hollow to confess her sin.

'Mother, forgive, and save me,' she whispered, as she passed the statue.

After ringing the bell for the confessor, she had not knelt long at the confessional box in the dim chapel, cold and empty as a waiting vault, when the chancel rail clicked, and the footsteps of Father Ruhl were heard rustling over the stones. He came, he took his seat behind the grating; and, with many sighs and falterings, Elspet avowed her guilt. And as, with bowed head, she ended, a strange sound answered her—it was like a little laugh, and yet not so much like a laugh as a snarl. With a shock as of death she raised her face. It was Father Ruhl who sat there—and yet it was not Father Ruhl. In that time of twilight his face was already changing, narrowing, becoming wolfish—the eyes rounded and the jaw slavered. She gasped, and shrunk back; and at that, barking and snapping at the grating, with a wicked look he dropped—and she heard him coming. Sheer horror lent her wings. With a scream she sprang to her feet and fled. Her cloak caught in something—there was a wrench and crash and, like a flood, oblivion overswept her.

It was the old deaf and near senile sacristan who found them lying there, the woman unhurt but insensible, the priest crushed out of life by the fall of the ancient statue, long tottering to its collapse. She recovered, for her part: for his, no one knows where he lies buried. But there were dark stories of a baying pack that night, and of an empty, bloodstained pavement when they came to seek for the body.

Threshold

By Sharon Webb

Me not hurt rabbit. Me not. Kodi love rabbit.

When the phone rang, she knew it was her mother. It wasn't telepathy; it was her mother's unerring sense of timing. Sighing, she plopped the "who-dunnit" face down on its red herring, reached for her glass of sherry with one hand and the telephone with the other.

"Jean?" chirped the voice on the other end.

Who else? "Hello, Mother." She slid her toes a tad closer to the fire. "I thought it was you."

"You always say that, dear. Doesn't anyone else ever call?"

"Not much."

"What were you doing?"

"Reading."

A faint sigh blew over the receiver. "Why don't you try and get out more, dear? See some young men. Go to a dance."

"I'll think about it, Mother." A swallow of the Olorosos rolled warmly down her throat. "I really will."

Another sigh with a slight increase in volume—"Your father and I worry about you so. I never know what to say to my friends. Just today Hannah asked about you. 'How's your darling Jean?' she said. Her Martha is pregnant with her second, you know. So what can I say to her? 'She's fine. Just fine. Who could ask for more? All day long she trains monkeys. At night she reads.' "

"Kodi isn't a monkey, Mother."

"Monkeys, apes—What's the difference?"

"Quite a bit, Mother." But it wasn't any use. Her mother had a convenient mind with its own unique logic. Mrs. Greenfield was incapable of imagining her daughter working in a primate center with a gorilla. "This is what you went to college for? To be torn limb-from-limb? By a King Kong?" After the initial trauma, she'd totally repressed the idea. The "slavering, breast-beating beast" disappeared into a little crease in Mrs. Greenfield's brain to be forever replaced by a small brown rhesus with long tail and dirty habits.

432

Her mother's voice went on, "God permitting, if you should ever have a child of your own, if you ever give me a grandchild, you'll know what worry is."

But she did have a child: Kodi.

You dirty bad stink. Me not hurt rabbit. Me not.

A chill gust of wind whipped the rickety door out of Jean's hand as she tried to close it. Groaning hinges tugged at their fastenings.

A cheery voice said, "If that grant doesn't come through, we may have to hang up animal skins to keep out the weather."

Jean pushed the door shut and looked up to see Marian Whitmore who worked with the newest addition at the center, Tic Toc, who was eight months old. "I'm afraid you're right. How's Tic Toc?"

"Adorable. He sits around all day with his thumb in his mouth, but I have high hopes." Marian breezed off down the hall, then turned and said over her shoulder, "The boss is off to an early start. He's working with your Kodi now."

"I wonder why?" But Marian was gone. Jean walked down the wide, shabby hall past the communal room where the apes were allowed to gather and play together occasionally, and entered the large high-ceilinged room partially filled with sturdy second-hand furniture that doubled as Kodi's enclosure and Jean's office.

David Copeland, all angles and bones inside his clothes, sat cross-legged on the floor. His hands moved rapidly in sign. Kodi answered in Ameslan, leathery fingers moving through the words. Then she turned her face away and offered the back of her hand in a conciliatory gesture.

"She's lying again," he said to Jean.

Jean hung her coat in her locker, replacing it with a lab jacket. "What about?"

"Look over there."

She followed his gaze to the rabbit cage, bars bent in a neat parenthesis. "Oh no." The white rabbit lay motionless, its neck at an acute angle. "Kodi?"

He nodded. "I think she pulled the rabbit out to play with it. After she broke its neck, she stuffed it back in the cage."

Kodi was listening intently to the conversation, trying to piece its meaning together.

David turned to the young gorilla and signed, "You hurt the rabbit. You made the rabbit die."

433

Kodi sat back on her heels, confused. *Me not hurt rabbit. Rabbit not cry.*

"She doesn't understand 'die.' " Jean felt a quick flash of pity for the confused animal. "She hasn't learned that word."

"She's going to now. I can't miss this opportunity."

"Opportunity?"

"Of course. We're going to find out what the concept of death means to a primate. How she reacts to it."

Jean watched him manipulate Kodi's fingers into the position for "die." He repeated the word over and over, emphasizing the sign, shaping Kodi's motions.

Die. Die. Die.

Poor mutt. Let's teach her what death is. And guilt. And all the other nasty things that humans wallow in.

Kodi's brow furrowed in concentration lines as she listened and watched intently.

Jean felt a slow fire of resentment smoulder. Damn David anyway. Damn him and his miserable rabbit experiment. Suspicion rose. Maybe he'd never been that interested at all in the reactions of the isolated apes to other species. If that scheme were only a way to beef up interest in the project and generate extra funding, how much more lucrative might this wrinkle be? The more she thought about it, the more convinced she was. When he'd ensconced the rabbit cage in Kodi's room, what had he expected? Really? Surely he had common sense enough to know that Kodi would want to touch the rabbit like any kid with a new toy.

Like any kid—And there she was, anthropomorphizing again. The cardinal sin in Copeland's Breviary. But dammit, where was the line anyway? Where had the prehuman crossed over the line into humanity? Use of tools? Nonsense. Lots of animals used tools; all the primates did. Language? Symbols? Abstract reasoning? Kodi used them all. All the Ameslaners did, and Kodi was second generation, the smartest of the lot. And yet, anthropomorphic fantasies aside, Kodi was beast—and her baby.

Ever since that day when David handed her a little wooly infant who grasped her hair with one hand and her blouse with another and snuggled to her breast with lonesome whimpers, she'd been hooked. She had coped with Kodi and with David for nearly eleven years. And in a strange way they were a family.

She'd nearly blown it too. Even today she couldn't forget her first meeting with David. She had breezed into his office for her interview, fresh BS in hand and visions of research grants and advanced degrees dancing in her head. "Hi, You Tarzan. Me Jean." She cringed at the memory. But how could she have known then that David Copeland was the most serious contender for the Humorless Man Award since Cotton Mather?

There he sat, single-mindedly manipulating Kodi's fingers, ignoring the confusion in the big beast's eyes.

Die. Die. Die.

Rabbit die.

"I'm only thinking of you, Jean," said the chirping telephone voice. "You know how I worry."

"I know, Mother."

"If I didn't love you, Jean, I wouldn't say these things to you."

"I know." And she did know. Her mother was trying to protect her, trying to shelter her from Bleak Old Age. She was trying to surround her with a husband and a flock of children because she saw it as better so. Hadn't it always been better so? Her mother was holding a set of values up that reflected like a carnival mirror onto her own, turning them into grotesques.

She knew her mother loved her. But why, God, why did it have to hurt so damned much?

Rabbit not eat. Rabbit not move. Rabbit die. Bad.

"Kodi?"

Kodi sat facing the corner in the traditional place for punishment. She stared at the blank wall and absently passed her woolly hand over her face in the Ameslan sign for "bad."

Poor beastie. All she needed was a dunce cap to make the picture complete. "Kodi? Why are you sitting in the corner?" Jean knelt beside the animal and touched her on the shoulder. Kodi's eyes did not meet hers.

"Kodi?"

Slowly, Kodi's hands moved in sign: *Rabbit die. Kodi make rabbit die. Kodi bad.*

So David has succeeded. Blast his soul. Jean rubbed the nape of a wooly neck. "It's all right, Kodi. It's all right. I'll make it all right," she said, knowing that the ape caught only a few of the whispered words, knowing too that the sound of her voice was soothing. She took Kodi's face in both hands and turned it toward her. "Want Jean to tickle Kodi?" It was an irresistible invitation.

The big sad eyes searched her face, the long fingers moved; *Please, Jean, tickle Kodi.*

And for awhile, it helped.

"I'm worried about Kodi."

"Who? Oh, that monkey of yours," said the voice on the line with a mixture of exasperation and amusement. Her mother neatly bent the conversation into a U-turn. "I wish you'd show a little concern for some of the important things, Jean."

"Like what, Mother?"

"Do you know what your poor father said to me last night? He said, 'Jean is the last, Momma. The last Greenfield. She's the end of the line.' "

"Well, I guess you should have had a boy, Mother." She knew before the words were out that it was the wrong thing to say.

"A boy! God forbid I should have another one driving nails into my coffin."

"I'm not driving nails, Mother. Listen, I really have to go. I have a lot of work to do, a paper to write—"

"Monkey business. Always the monkey business—"

There was more, but Jean turned it off as neatly as a tap. After a minute she quietly said, "Goodbye, Mother," and hung up the receiver.

She had never understood why people put such great store on the survival of the family name. She couldn't carry on that family name unless she married and refused to take her husband's name. Or, while she was thinking about defying convention, she could entertain the notion of having a bastard. And wouldn't Mother love that?

What did the family name represent anyway except a diluted gene pool that got more watered down with each passing generation? Did it really matter whether or not the pool dried up with her? "Of course not," she said aloud, startling herself with the intensity of her voice, startling herself even more with the knowledge that what she said had all the trappings of a lie. Because, somehow, put that way, it did seem to matter—as if the saying of it made her living and her dying more final.

Final. And when it was all over and done with, what would be left to show she'd made the trip? A half-dozen articles. Sixteen-going-on-seventeen loose-leaf notebooks crammed with compact notes and the written Ameslan notation she and David had developed for Kodi and the other apes.

Her work had always seemed important before.

She reached for her bottle of sherry, found it empty, and lit a cigarette. Wasn't that what mothers were for? To make you hold up your life and find it a little frayed at the seams? Ready for the rag bag. To make you ask, "why?" and "is that all?" To boil everything you are down to sixteen-going-on-seventeen notebooks?

When you got right down to it, Kodi had nearly as much to show for her simian existence. Jean had a notebook nearly full of the ape's typings: pages of the curls and squiggles that were the typewritten mimics of Ameslan signs that she had so painstakingly developed and taught Kodi.

She thumbed through the collection of Kodi's typings, reading the curls and hooks as easily as English. *Me Kodi.* said the first page, the fifth, the tenth. *Me Kodi.*

"You Kodi, me Jean," she said to herself, reflecting, wondering how she could define herself without Kodi, without that notebook. She slipped slowly through the pages. Page twenty-nine: *Me hungry. Me eat now.* Page forty-two: *Me hurt here.* Neither written Ameslan nor dry English notes could express the pain in Kodi's eyes that day, nor the anguish in hers as they waited for the vet's hurried visit. Page seventy-eight: A change here. Kodi was older, better able to use language. *Sweet. Eat. Eat Sweet. Sweet eat.* She remembered the delight over that page, the amazement that the ape had translated sound to sign. "Kodi. You made a rhyme." And on the following pages, the repetitions of that rhyme and others—Kodi's delight over language as a toy. She turned the pages—a fib here, a game there. Fears, hurts, wants.

"There's your life, Kodi," she said closing the notebook, laying it beside the stack of her notes and articles. "And there's mine."

She had done it in kindness, she told herself in retrospect. She had tried to spare Kodi the guilt over the rabbit, tried to ease the hurt. She had said it out of kindness—and ignorance and stupidity. She had said: "You're not bad, Kodi. Not bad. Everything dies, Kodi. Everything."

And she had gone to great lengths to explain it.

Chair die.

Only living things, Kodi. Rabbits and trees and people. Everything. *Me think Tic Toc die.*

"Tic Toc, too. But not for a long time."

Kodi didn't greet her with the usual deep throaty purr. She lay on the floor, neck at an odd angle, in a caricature of the rabbit.

"Kodi?"

Kodi's hand passed slowly over her face and made the sign for "bad."

There was a single sentence on the Ameslan typer: *Me think Kodi die.*

She had done it in kindness . . . the kindness of a meddling mother. All night, unable to sleep, she lashed herself with the guilt of it. Finally she got up dressed and went back to the center.

Kodi lay sleeping on the jumbled nest she had made in the corner, and there was something written on the Ameslan typer. The words kept blurring until Jean had to wipe her eyes with a wadded Kleenex. She stood there a long time, holding the note, watching the sleeping animal. The guilt was still there, but there was something else, something growing—a feeling of wonder.

She looked at the paper again. Had some prehuman in man's distant past stood on the threshold of humanity, thrust there by the knowledge of his own mortality. Did he ask then those questions that grew into the beginnings of philosophy and religion and science? Did he think these same thoughts:

Me think me die.
Me cry.
Why die?
Why?

Today's Special

By Dennis Etchison

How about some nice bottom round steak?" asked Avratin the butcher. "Is today's special."

"No round steak."

"Ah. Well, Mrs. Teola—"

"Taylor."

"Mrs. Taylor." Avratin the butcher tapped the trays behind the open glass, then thumbed back another display of cuts. "I got some nice, nice clods, can cut for Swiss steak if—"

"No Swiss steak."

Avratin started to sigh, pinched his nose with his thick curving forefinger, which was getting cold. "Excuse me. I know what you want. For you, some nice, nice, very nice pot—"

"No pot roast, neither."

His hands began describing in the air. "Some lovely chuck, some darling rump, a little—" He squeezed the air. "—Tender, juicy flank steak, eh?" He saw her turn away, the gray bun at the back of her neck beginning to wag. "Some brisket for boiling!" He heard his wife's heavy heels in the sawdust and at that flapped his forehead with both hands—*I give up*—for her to see.

"My, you're looking very well today," Avratin's wife cooed.

Muttering, Avratin slid the last tray back in place, grumbling to himself, sifting the red chunks of beef tenderloin through his fingers, which were not quite cold; the meat plopped back onto the paper liner and he slammed the glass, knocking the parsley loose from the top of the ground round.

"Yeah, you should hope you don't see my sister, Rose."

"Oh, Ro-sie. And how is her operation?"

"Don't ask."

"Well, Mrs. Teo—"

"Taylor. Taylor! My husband puts Teola in the book, nobody calls him." The gray bun wagged in growing impatience. "But now he's Manny Taylor. Manny Taylor! I want you tell me, would you call from the Yellow Pages a man with the name Manny Taylor?"

"Well," began Avratin's wife, standing closer to her husband, "what's good for your mister's business—"

"We should all live so long, I promise you. My God, my God." She shook her bun and hunched toward the door.

Avratin's wife cleared her throat. "Today special, we have some very nice fish, Mrs. Taylor," she called sweetly and waited for the woman to turn back under the creaking overhead fan.

"You got nothing I want," said the woman finally, only half-turning, shifting her brown carryall to her other hand.

"Why, Mrs. Taylor," sang Avratin's wife. "You've been our faithful customer for thirteen years. Those years, they mean only that you should come to this? You're taking your business elsewhere now? God forbid that Lou and I should forget *our* friends so easy."

"You should talk, dearie. *You* should *talk!*" This she said directly to Avratin, sizing him up in his white apron as if he were an imposter. "You get Luttfisk back, then maybe we talk meat. That Luttfisk, he *knows* meat!" And she shuffled out the door.

A moment later, to no one in particular, to the passing cars, to the old man at the curb with the white beard and the stiff black hat,

Avratin's wife called, "My Lou, he was owning this shop before that Luttfisk was starting in the business! Don't you forget that!"

But Avratin was shaking his head, reaching around to untie the strings, throwing his apron on the hook.

"Louie?"

He headed across the empty store to the back.

"Ask me why I'm closing an hour early. But ask me! Go ahead! You ask me about business, and I'll tell you. Business . . . is . . . lousy!"

Avratin's wife threw up her hands, imploring the ceiling fan to do something, anything.

In the small bedroom, by a single small lamp with the crisp, yellowed cellophane still clinging to the shade, with the sound turned down on the Johnny Carson show, Avratin and his wife were having an argument.

". . . Twenty years in the retail meat business and you knife me in the back. Twenty years putting bread on your plate, only to have you——"

"Listen to this! He's too proud, too proud to admit a mistake."

"—twist, twisting the knife!"

Reproach, recrimination, guilt, counter-accusation, self-deprecation. The old pattern.

And only to come to this: that at the end, the finish, before grumbling into bed, during the sermonette, Avratin raised his hurt face to the water-stained ceiling one last time to declare, before the gods and whatever other audience might be listening:

"All right, I take care of it, I take care of everything. No matter that Luttfisk tries to rob me, his own partner. I get a man can take care of the job. I promise you, the problem be fixed, once-for-all!"

At the Century-Cudahy Storage and Packing Co., the White Collar Butcher was a very important man. No one at the plant could say exactly why, though it had to do with the fact that he was the best butcher in the county, that he had the finest set of tools anyone had ever laid eyes on, and that he took obvious quiet pride in his work. It had to do with the way he picked his own shifts, coming in unpredictably and always with the attitude of a man who has already been at work for several hours. It had to do with the air of authority he carried with him into the walk-in, the indefinable look of knowing something that he would never tell on his thin, expressionless lips, his smooth, ageless face, his small steel-blue eyes that were perpetually set on a place somewhere beyond the carcasses and the warehouse.

Alone at night, the White Collar Butcher stood motionless before the freezer, his eyes on the temperature gauge. But they were not focused there. Then, slowly, surely, he turned his back on the hook beam scales and stood over his meat block. He moved his hand from the evenly beveled edges to the guard at the right of the block. His hand was heavy, a special tool itself, quite perfectly balanced, smooth and pink and tapered ideally to the handles which he now allowed his fingers to play over lightly: the meat saw, the cleaver, the steak knife, the boning knife, below them the small scale, the aluminum trays, the spool of twine, and, to the left, the blackboard. Then, with smooth, automatic, practiced moves he took down his tools one by one and washed them, wiped them, and rubbed the handles, proceeded to sharpen them on the slow grinding wheel and then the whetstone, checked the edges with the steel, and wrapped them individually in soft, protective leather.

He set the pouches out neatly and then, by reflex acquired through years of practice, slipped his hand into his trouser pocket and withdrew a folded square of white paper. With one hand he opened it and read the name and address printed there with a grease pencil in straight block letters. *The name and address.*

He refolded it and slid it back into his pocket under the apron. Another job.

Then, positioning himself in an easy, familiar stance, he reached for the wire brush and steel scraper and box of salt and began cleaning his cutting block, employing short, sure motions with his strong arms and shoulders, conserving his energy for the job to come. And as he worked on into the night, his tanned face and immaculately styled hair set off tastefully above the high, fashionable collar and wide hand-sewn tie that lay smoothly against his tailored shirt of imported silk, the whole effect suggesting a means far beyond his butcher's salary, was that perhaps the beginning of a narrow, bloodless smile that pinched the corners of his thin, efficient, professional lips?

For five nights Avratin hammered his pillow and spent more time than he should have in the cramped bathroom. Then the good news arrived.

Up went the noisy butcher paper painted with the proclamation he had kept rolled and hidden for three days now. He was nervous with anticipation as he tore off strips of masking tape and slapped it up across the plate glass window. It covered the whole front of the

441

store, right over the futile daily specials from the week past, as well it should have.

The first customers of the day were already waiting at the door when Avratin's wife finished dressing and joined her husband.

She stopped in the middle of the fresh sawdust floor, looking about as if by some transmogrification of sleep she had just walked into a strange new life, or at least someone else's store. She smoothed her hair and gaped, turning around and around.

"This is a holiday? Or I'm sleeping still. Pinch me, Lou."

Avratin had pulled out all the trays in the meat case and was busy arranging his new, large display.

"Take it easy, take it easy, Rachel. You got your wish."

The last parking space in front filled up, and at last Avratin stood and leaned back and watched the women milling around on the sidewalk, pointing excitedly to the sign. He smiled a special smile that he had not used in years.

"Lou! Lou! Lou! You didn't do nothing too drastic, did you?" Then what he had said seemed to hit her.

She clipped to the door, shook the knob, apologized to the woman with the gray bun who was first in line, hurried back to get the keys, almost ran to the door and opened it.

Avratin watched her outside, shading her eyes, holding off their questions until she could get a good look at it herself.

She stood with one hand on her hip, one hand above her eyes, reading and rereading the banner with disbelief.

The women scrambled inside, heading for the meat case. He leaned back on his hands, watching them over the scales, a bright morning chill of anticipation tingling in his blood.

They stopped in front of the case, staring for long seconds.

Avratin wanted to speak to them, but held himself in check a moment longer.

His wife was the last to enter the store. She pushed her way through the inert bodies, ignoring the still, dulled faces on a few of which was beginning to dawn the first dim, uncomprehending light of recognition.

"Lou, I saw the sign," she beamed. "Is it true? Is it? Where is he?"

Avratin leaned forward. He spread his arms behind the transparent case in a gesture of supplication, palms out. His eyes rolled up to the creaking, slowly revolving fan and then returned to the display, newly arrived from the man in the high white collar, which he had just now finished arranging so carefully under the glass, the whole length of the counter, to the new cuts, strange cuts, so invit-

442

ingly laid out, preserved by the cold, here something red, there something brown and almost recognizable, there a fine shank, there an opened ribcage, there a portion of a face you knew so well you almost expected it to greet you.

"Here," Avratin answered magnanimously, in a voice he had not used in years. "Here! Can't you read the sign?

"LUTTFISK IS BACK!"

Very shortly thereafter the muffled cries began.

Topsy

By F. Paul Wilson

I'm inna middle a chewing on dis giant lasagne noodle when Nurse Delores appears.

"Morning, Topsy!" she says as she marched inta da room in her white uniform.

Dey call me Topsy.

Don't ax why dey call me dat. My name's Bruno. But evybody here calls me Topsy.

"Oh, no," she says. "You've been eating your sheets again!"

I look down an see she's right. My sheets is all chewed up. I guess dat weren't no giant lasagne noodle after all.

God I'm hungry.

"Ready for breakfast?" she says all bright an cheery.

Course I'm ready for breakfast—I'm *dyin* for breakfast—but I don't say nuttin. Cause what dey call breakfast here ain't. Ain't lunch or dinner neither. Just liquid. Not even a shake. I amember when I useta eat diet shakes. Useta drink ten a dem fa breakfast. An anotha fa coffee break. Dey're junk. I neva lost weight on dem. Not once.

But no shakes roun here. Just dis clear glop. An here she comes wit a whole glass of it.

"Here, Topsy. Open your mouth and drink this," she says, all Mary Sunshine perkiness.

If my hands weren't strapped to da side of da bed I'd grab her an make her drink it herself an see how much *she* likes dat shit.

She tilts da glass toward my lips but I turn away.

"Come on, Topsy," she says. "I know you don't like it, but it's this or nothing."

"No!"

"Come on, Topsy. Do it for Lenore. Don't be mad at me. The protein hydrosylate isn't my idea. It's doctor's orders. And it's working. You're down to twelve hundred and thirty pounds now."

Still I don't open.

"Come on, baby. It's this or go hungry. Open up."

Sometimes she calls me baby, but dat don't make it taste better, believe me.

I open an pretend it's a milk shake. A big double chocolate praline shake laced wit wet walnuts.

Don't help. I gag an wanna barf it all ova da place but manage to choke it down. Gotta. It's all I'll get til lunch. An dat'll only be a salad.

God I'm so hungry.

Dey don't unnerstan aroun here. Don't seemta realize dat I gotta eat. Dey say dey're helpin me by stickin needles in my arms an feedin me teeny bits of veggies an barely a moutful of whole grain sumpin-or-otha an dis liquid protein shit, but dey ain't helpin. Ain't helpin me one bit.

Guy's gotta eat.

Useta be so good when my brotha Sal an his wife Marie was takin care a me. I was happy den. Dat's cause dey unnerstood. Dey knew I hadda eat. Boy could dey cook. No limit, man. Anyting I wanted, it was dere on da bed tray soon as I said.

Dey unnerstood me, know'm sayin?

Breakfast was da best. On regula days Marie'd whip me up a coupla dozen eggs over easy wit a coupla poundsa bacon an lotsa dose spicy Jimmy Dean sausage patties. *Love* dat Jimmy Dean sausage. Den she'd make me a gigantic stack a ten-inch pancakes swimmin in butta an Vermont maple syrup. An on special days, like Satadays an Sundays, she'd go all out an add in a whole platterful a eggs Benedict. *Love* eggs Benedict. All dat Hollandaise sauce over dose poached eggs on English muffins an Canadian bacon. Heaven, man. Absolute heaven.

Mid-mornings dere'd be Entenman's sugar crumb cake or cheeze babka or my favorite, All Butter French Crumb cake. Or sometimes lox an bagels wit cream cheese an herring in cream sauce.

Neva could tell what lunch was gonna be. Sometimes a coupla family size buckets of da Colonel's Extra Crispy fried chicken, but most times Sal'd bring me in tree or four sausage an pepperoni pizzas or half a dozen subs from Vinnie's. Da subs were da best, man. Pepper an egg, veal parmesian, Italian delight, an da Kitchen Sink sub wit evyting on it.

Loved lunch, man.

Mid-afternoons I'd do it kinda light. Jus some coffee an a coupla packages a Oreos. Or maybe some Little Debbie Satellite bars. When it was hot, Sal'd get me a gallon a Welsh Farms peanut butter swirl ice cream. He'd mix it up wit a can of Hershey's chocolate syrup an I'd be in heaven, man.

Dinner'd start aroun five cause I couldn't wait no longer. Marie'd cut me up a nice cold antipasta while Sal'd broil up a coupla dozen garlic clams oreganata. Den da pasta—a coupla poundsa Marie's super linguine wit white clam sauce, da noodles swimmin in butter an garlic, an da diced clams piled all over da top. Next da fish, usually a coupla tree- or four-pound lobsters or half a dozen pounds a shrimp done up scampi style. After dat, a meat, maybe steak or veal or a nice Krakus ham. For dessert, maybe anotha gallon a da peanut butter swirl or a nice cherry cheese cake, or a coupla peach pies a la mode wit some canoli onna side.

My bedtime snack was always candy. Sal'd let me have all da Snickers bars I wanted. He'd buy dem by da case an leave a whole box right by my bed so's I could grab one anytime I got hungry. An let me tell you, I got hungry a lot durin da night. But I neva woke Sal or Marie. I knew dey needed deir sleep. I was a good guy. I hung on an starved till breakfast.

Sal an Marie knew how to take care of me. Dey knew what I needed. Dat I hadda eat. Dey understood about eatin, know'm sayin?

Evyting was great till dat dey when dey was both out at once. Dey hardly ever left me alone. I mean sure dey went out togetha once inna while, but neva for long. Dis time dey was gone a long time. A coupla hours, maybe, an I was starvin. Not jus hungry, man. I mean *starvin!*

An I couldn't get outta bed.

Wasn't always dis big. I mean, like I was always big accordin to Ma. Born big an jus kept gettin bigger, she always said. But now I'm *huge,* man. Take up a whole damn king size bed. Can't get outta bed on my own. Always needed help from Sal or Marie. Good ting Marie's real strong—good Sicilian stock—or she'd've been no help. But all I needed was for one of dem ta give me a little boost an someone to lean on while I shuffled to da batroom. Dey took off da doorframe but still I can barely turn aroun in dere. Lucky I only go twice a day. An it don't matter if I'm doin number one or number

445

two, man, I gotta sit. First of all, I can't stand dat long. An second, well, I mean, I ain't seen my dick in at least ten years, so da only way I can be sure I ain't peein onna floor is to sit. An even den I sometimes miss da bowl. An when I take a dump . . .

Let's not talk about dat.

Anyways, Sal an Marie was gone fa hours an I was starvin so I tried to get outta bed on my own. Took forever, but I managed to sit up by myself. Made me feel good. Hadn't done dat on my own in years. Den by holdin onta da bedpost I somehow got myself to my feet. I started shufflin cross da bedroom, takin little teeny steps so's I wouldn't lose my balance. God, I din't want to tink what would happena me if I toppled over an wound up onna floor. I mean, man, dey'd hafta bring in a crane or sumpin ta get me up again.

An just as I was tinkin about it, it started happenin. I started swayin. Little sways at first, den bigger ones. I tell ya I was scared to det. I aimed myself for da doorway, figrin I could hold onta da jamb, but started teeterin as I stumbled an I slamed inna da doorway wit a awful crack. I saw da wallboard crack an heard da studs inside groan an creak, but da wall held an I was still on my feet. I hadn't fallen!

But I was stuck. Usually I went troo dat door sideways. Now I was jammed inta it at a angle an no matter how I tried I couldn't move out or in. I was scared. I started gettin pains in my chest an my heart started racin like crazy. I hadn't been on my feet for dat long a time in more years dan I could amemba. Couldn't breathe. I yelled fa help. Screamed my freakin lungs out, but not fa long. My chest was gettin all congested, like I was fillin up wit water or sometin. I couldn't scream no more. Evyting got fuzzy, den evyting got black.

Next ting I knew I was in dis place.

It's a hospital room. Actually it's not a room, it's what dey call a suite. Two rooms. I'm in da big room, but dere's a smaller one straight ahead a me dat's like a little kitchen wit a fridge an a microwave an stuff. An dere's a batroom off to my right but in all da time I'm here I ain't been in it yet. Dey told me what hospital I'm in but I forgot. Who cares, anyway? Da important ting is dey're *starvin* me!

"Time for your bed bath," Delores says as she comes in carryin a basin of soapy water. She stops an stares at me. "Good Lord, Topsy! You're eating your pillow!"

I look. Oh, yeah. I guess I am. I tought it was a big marshmallow. I spit feathers.

"Never mind," she says wit a sigh. "Let's get to the ablutions."

Most guys would get off bein washed down by a blonde dish like

Delores, but I gotta admit I'm too hungry ta tink about anyting but food.

"Gimme a treat, Delores."

"Shush!" she says, glancin around my room. "What if one of the doctors heard you?"

"Don't care. Need a treat."

"After your bath."

"No. Now. Gotta have sometin."

"Oh, all right."

As she reaches into her uniform pocket I can feel da juices pour into my mout. She pulls out one of dose little low-sugar caramels she sneaks in for me an unwraps it.

"Stop it, Topsy," she says. "You're droolin all over yourself. Open up."

I open an she pops it into my mout, jerkin her fingers back real quick cause I accidently bit her once.

I taste da caramel. Da sweetness runs all over da inside of my mout.

OhGodohGodohGodohGodohGodohGodohGodohGod!

I near start ta cry.

"Come on, Topsy," Delores says, pattin my arm. She's a good nurse. She feels for me. I can tell. "You'll be all right."

"Need food!"

"You need to lose weight, that's what you need. You almost died of congestive heart failure back in your house. It's lose weight or die, Topsy."

I figure I'd ratha die cause starvin like dis is worse dan det.

"Where's Sal? Where's Marie?"

"Do we have to go through that again?" Delores says as she starts rubbin a soapy wash cloth on my belly. I look down at my bare skin. Looks like acres a ice cream.

"Troo what again?"

"I know you don't want to accept it, Topsy, but your brother and his wife have been indicted for attempted murder and they're out on bail awaiting trial. They are forbidden by the court to come anywhere near you. They were trying to kill you, Topsy."

"No. Dey treated me good! Dey fed me!"

"They were feeding you to death, that's what they were doing. A nifty little scheme, I've got to admit. You kept signing checks so they could buy you food, big checks that allowed them to live high while they kept pumping you full of the worst kind of food you can imagine."

"Good food," I told her. "Da best!"

"The *worst!* High fat, high calorie. Your blood sugar and cholesterol and triglycerides were through the roof! And when they got you to fifteen hundred pounds, they left you for a day. They knew you'd try to get out of bed, and they figured you'd fall and die on the floor. Well, it almost worked. Lucky for you that you got stuck in the doorway and someone heard you yell. Even then you almost didn't make it. By the time they broke through the wall of the house and hoisted you out, you were so far gone into heart failure you almost died in the back of the truck on the way to the hospital. It almost worked, Topsy. The rats almost got your money."

"Ain't got no money."

"Oh, really? Folks with no money can't afford a private hospital suite like this. What do you call that twelve million dollars you won?"

Oh, yeah. Dat. I won dat inna State Lotto a few years ago. I forget tings sometimes. I amemba Sal an Marie bein real happy for me. Dat's when dey moved in an started takin care a me. Dey treated me real good. Dey unnerstood dat I gotta eat.

I always hadda eat. Evyting I amemba bout bein a kid is food. Ma cooked for me alla time, an when she ran outta food I'd go over my fren's houses an deir moms'd fix me stuff. I lost my first job as a kid makin deliveries for Angelo's Grocery because I useta eat half da stuff along da way. An whateva job I had, I always spent da money on food.

Food was evyting ta me. I amemba how I useta give people directions back in da days when I could still get aroun. It'd be "Go down to da Dunkin Donuts an turn left, den go bout tree blocks an turn right at da Dairy Queen an it's bout half a mile downa street, a block past Paisan's Pizza." All my landmarks hadda do wit food.

But afta I won da lotto an we moved out to Long Island, I got so fat dat my whole world became my bedroom, an time got measured by meals an TV shows.

Da TV's on now. I useta love to watch TV. All da game shows an talk shows inna morin, an da soaps inna aftanoon. Loved dem all. Now I hate 'em. Not da shows—da commercials. Food! All dey seemta be sellin is freakin *food!* Like torture, man! I go crazy wit da little remote control but evytime I switch I see dis food bein shoved at me in livin color! I'm bout t'go crazy, know'm sayin? I mean, if it ain't McDonald's it's Burger King or Wendy's or Red Lobsta wit dose shrimp just oozin butta onna enda da fork. Or da Pillsbury Doughboy's got some new cinnamon ting he's pushin, or dere's microwave chocolate cake or Reese's Pieces or Eat Beef It's Real

Food or Domino's Pizza or Peter Pan Peanut Butter or Holly Farms Chicken or Downyflake Waffles or Dorito Nacho Chips an on an on.

Know'm sayin?

Tell ya it ain't fair, man. Guy could go *crazy!*

"Okay, Topsy," Delores is sayin. "It's time to do your back. Now I know you can't turn over, but I want you to help me. I'm going to unstrap your right hand so I can do some of your back."

Dey been keepin my hands strapped downta da bed frame. Dat's cause da diet's been makin me kinda goofy. I got bandages on da middle finger an pointer a my right hand cause I tried to eat dem.

Kid you not, man. I been goin a little squirrelly here. I mean, da otha night I really tought dose fingers was hot dogs. S'true. Jus I tought my sheet was a big lasagne noodle an my pillow was a giant marshmallow, I coulda sworn dat night my two fingers was hot dogs. It was dark. I started chewin on dem an screamin at da same time. Da docs said I was hallucinatin. Closed me up wit ten stitches. Now dey keep my hands tied down so's I don't do it again.

Dey shouldn't worry. I won't. It hurt too much.

"Gimme a candy first," I tell her.

"No," Delores says. "After, Topsy. *After.*"

"Okay," I say. But I don't really mean it.

When she unstraps my right wrist, I roll left, like I'm lettin her wash da part of my back she can reach. But while I'm twisted dat way, I work on da left strap an get it undone. Now I'm ready.

"Okay, Topsy," she says. "Roll back now."

I roll. An keep on rollin. As I rock to da right, I grab Delores.

"Candy!" I shout. "Gimme! Now!"

Delores squeals an twists away. She's strong but I got a good grip on her. She pulls away but I stretch after her. Her feet slip an she goes down but I lean over da edge of da bed, keepin my grip, never lettin go, reachin wit my free hand for da pocket wit da caramels.

But suddenly I feel myself slippin. I mean da bed's tiltin, da whole freakin hospital bed's tippin ova wit me on it. An I'm headin right down on toppa Delores. I try to stop myself but I can't. Da bed's tilted too far. I'm outta control. I'm fallin. Delores screams as I land on her.

It ain't a long scream. More like a quick little yelp, like your pooch makes when you accidently step on its foot. Den she cuts off.

But she don't stop movin. She's strugglin an kickin an clawin unda me, tryna get out, tryna breathe. An I'm tryna get offa her, really an truly I am, but it's so hard. Finally I edge myself back an to da side. It's slow work, but finally I get offa her face.

Too late. Poor Delores has stopped strugglin by den. An when I manage to get a look at her face, it's kinda blue. Real blue, in fact. I mean, like she's sorta dead.

I like start ta cry. I can't help it. I loved Delores an now she's gone. I specially loved her caramels.

Which reminds me of her goody pocket. So while I'm cryin, I reach for her pocket. I push my hand inside but I can't find no caramels. Not a one.

No way, man! I know dere's candy in dere!

I push deeper inta da pocket but it's empty, man! Freakin *empty!*

I'm kinda upset now. I pull on da pocket. I mean, I *know* dere's candy in dere. Da pocket rips an still no caramels. I rip deepa, layer afta layer till I reach . . .

. . . skin.

Smooth white skin. It's a leg. Turkey leg. Big white meat turkey leg. Never heard of such a ting, but here it is right in fronta me. Waitin for me. An I can't resist. I take a bite—

Gaa! Ain't cooked. Raw and bloody. God, I'm freakin hungry but I can't eat raw turkey!

I look up an around. Da utility room is only a dozen or so feet away. If I can make it to da microwave . . .

Toy

By Bill Pronzini

It was Jackey who found the toy, on a Saturday afternoon in mid-July.

Mrs. Webster was in the kitchen when he came home with it. "Look at this, Mom," he said. "Isn't this neat?"

She looked. It was an odd gray box, about the size of a cigar box; Jackey lifted its lid. Inside were a score or more of random-shaped pieces made out of the same funny-looking material as the box. It seemed to be some sort of slick, shiny plastic, only it didn't really look like plastic. Or feel like plastic when she ran her finger over the lid.

"What is it, Jackey?"

"I dunno. Some kind of model kit, I think."

"Where did you get it?"

"Found it, in the vacant lot by the Little League field. I was hunting lost balls. It was just lying there under a bunch of leaves and junk."

"Well, someone must have lost it," Mrs. Webster said. "I suppose we'll have to put an ad in the Lost and Found."

"Maybe nobody'll claim it," Jackey said. "I'm going to put it together, see what it is."

"I don't think you should . . ."

"Oh, come on, Mom. I won't use glue or anything. I just want to see what it is."

"Well . . . all right. But don't break anything."

"I don't think you *can* break this stuff," Jackey said. "I dropped the box on the way home, right on the sidewalk. It landed on its edge and didn't even get a scratch."

He went upstairs with the toy. Mrs. Webster had no doubt that he would be able to fit the pieces of the model together; for a boy of twelve, he had a remarkable engineering aptitude.

And he *did* fit the pieces together. It took him two hours. Mrs. Webster was out on the back porch, putting new liner on the pantry shelves, when she heard the first banging noise—low and muffled, from up in Jackey's room. A minute later there was another one, and a minute after that, a third. Then Jackey yelled for her to come up. The fourth bang, exactly a minute after the third, sent her straight to his room.

The box and the assembled toy were sitting on Jackey's "workbench," the catchall table his father had built for him. What the toy most resembled, she thought, was a cannon; at least, there was a round barrel-like extremity with a hole in it, set at an upward angle to the model's squarish base. She was sure it was a cannon moments later, when it made the banging noise again and a round, gray, pea-sized projectile burst out of it and arced two-thirds of the way across the room.

"Neat, huh?" Jackey said. "I never saw one like this before."

"Cannons," Mrs. Webster said, and shook her head. "I don't like that sort of toy. I don't like you playing with it."

"I'm not. It sort of works by itself."

"By itself?"

"I don't even know where those cannonballs come from. I mean, *I* didn't put 'em in there."

"What *did* you do, then?"

"I didn't do anything except stick the pieces together the way I thought they ought to go. When I snapped the barrel on, some-

451

thing made a funny noise down inside the base. Next thing, it started shooting off those little balls.

It shot off another one just then, and the projectile—slightly larger than the last one, Mrs. Webster thought—went a foot farther this time. An uneasiness formed in her. She didn't like the look of the model cannon or whatever it was. Toys like that . . . they shouldn't be put on the market.

"You dismantle that thing right now," she said. "You hear me, Jackey? And be careful—it might be dangerous."

She went downstairs. But the banging noise came again, and again after exactly one minute. Each seemed a little louder than the last. The second one brought her back to the foot of the stairs.

"Jackey? I thought I told you to dismantle that thing."

Bang! And there was a thud, a crash from inside Jackey's room.

"What was that? What are you doing up there?"

Silence.

"Jackey?"

"Mom, you better come in here. Quick!"

She hurried up the stairs. There was another bang just as she reached the door to Jackey's room, followed by the sound of glass breaking. She caught the knob, jerked the door open.

She saw Jackey first, cowering back alongside the bed, his eyes wide and scared. Then she saw the far wall, opposite the workbench —the dents in the plasterboard, the jagged hole in the window, the projectiles on the floor ranging from pea-sized to apricot-sized. And then she saw the toy. Chills crawled over her; she caught her breath with an audible gasp.

The model had grown. Before, less than five minutes ago, it had been no larger than a small model tank; now it was three times that size. It had subtly changed color, too, seemed to be glowing faintly now as if something deep inside it had caught fire.

"Jackey, for God's sake!"

"Mom, I couldn't get near it, I couldn't touch it. It's *hot*, Mom!"

She didn't know what to do. She started toward Jackey, changed her mind confusedly and went to the workbench instead. She reached out to the toy, then jerked her hand back. Hot—it gave off heat like a blast furnace.

Oh my God, she thought, it's radioactive—

Bang!

A projectile almost as large as a baseball erupted from the toy's muzzle, smashed out the rest of the window and took part of the frame with it. Jackey yelled, "Mom!" but she still didn't know what to do. She stared at the thing in horror.

452

It had grown again. Every time it went off it seemed to grow a little bigger.

That's not a toy, that's some kind of weapon . . .

Bang!

A projectile just as large as a baseball this time. More of the window frame disappeared, leaving a gaping hole in the wall. From outside, Mrs. Webster could hear the Potters, their neighbors to the north, shouting in alarm. For some reason, hearing the Potters enabled her to act. She ran to where Jackey was crouched, caught hold of his arm, pulled him toward the door.

On the workbench, the gray thing was the size of a portable TV set. She thought she could see it pulsing as she and Jackey stumbled out.

Bang!

Bang!

On the street in front, she stood hugging Jackey against her. He was trying not to cry. "I didn't mean to do anything, Mom," he said. "I didn't *mean* it. I only wanted to see how it worked."

Bang!

Flames shot up from the rear of the house, from the back yard: the big oak tree there wore a mantle of fire. People were running along the street, crowding around her and Jackey, hurling frightened questions at them.

"I don't know," she said. "I don't *know!*"

And she was thinking: Where did it come from? How did it get here? Who would make a monstrous thing like that?

Bang!

Bang!

BANG!

The projectile that blew up the Potters' house was the size of a cantaloupe. The one a few minutes later that destroyed the gymnasium two blocks away was the size of a basketball. And the one a little while after that that leveled the industrial complex across town was the size of a boulder.

The thing kept growing, kept on firing bigger and bigger projectiles. By six o'clock that night it had burst the walls of the Webster house, and most of the town, and much of what lay within fifty miles north-by-northwest had been reduced to flaming wreckage. The National Guard was mobilizing, but there was nothing they could do except aid with mass evacuation proceedings; no one could get within two hundred yards of the weapon because of the radiation.

At six-thirty, half a dozen Phantom jets from the Air Force base nearby bombarded it with laser missiles. The missiles failed to destroy it; in fact, it seemed to feed on the heat and released energy, so that its growth rate increased even more rapidly.

In Washington, there was great consternation and panic. The President, his advisers, and the Joint Chiefs of Staff held an emergency meeting to decide whether or not to use an atomic bomb. But by the time they made up their minds it was too late. Much too late.

The thing was then the size of two city blocks, and still growing, and the range of its gigantic muzzle extended beyond the boundaries of the United States—north-by-northwest, toward the Bering Sea and the vast wastes of Russia beyond . . .

Transfer

By Barry N. Malzberg

I have met the enemy and he is me. Or me is he. Or me and he are we; I really find it impossible to phrase this or to reach any particular facility of description. The peculiar and embarrassing situation in which I now find myself has lurched quite out of control, ravaging its way toward what I am sure will be a calamitous destiny and, yet, I have always been a man who believed in order, who believed that events no matter how chaotic would remit, would relent, would suffer containment in the pure limpidity of The Word engraved patiently as if upon stone. I must stop this and get hold of myself.

I have met the enemy and he is me.

Staring into the mirror, watching the waves and the ripples of The Change, seeing in the mirror that beast take shape (it is always in the middle of the night; I am waiting for the transference to occur during the morning or worse yet at lunch hour in the middle of a cafeteria, waves may overtake me and I will become something so slimy and horrible even by the standards of midtown Manhattan that I will cause most of the congregants to lose their lunch), I feel a sense of rightness. It must always have been meant to be this way. Did I not feel myself strange as a child, as a youth, as an adolescent? Even as an adult I felt the strangeness within me; on the streets they stared with knowledge which could not have possibly been my own. Women turned away from me with little smiles when I attempted to connect with them, my fellow employees here at the Bureau treated me with that offhandedness and solemnity which always bespeaks private laughter. I know what they think of me.

I know what they think of me.

I have spent a lifetime in solitude gauging these reactions to some purpose, and I know that I am separate from the run of ordinary men as these men are separate from the strange heavings and commotion, ruins and darkness which created them. Staring in the mirror. Staring in the mirror I see.

Staring in the mirror I see the beast I have become, a thing with tentacles and spikes, strange loathsome protuberances down those appendages which my arms have become, limbs sleek and horrible despite all this devastation, limbs to carry me with surging power and constancy through the sleeping city, and now that I accept what I have become, what the night will strike me, I am no longer horrified but accepting. One might even say exalted at this moment because I always knew that it would have to be this way, that in the last of all the nights a mirror would be held up to my face and I would see then what I was and why the mass of men avoided me. I know what I am, those calm, cold eyes staring back at me in the mirror from the center of the monster know too well what I am also and turning them from the mirror, confronting the rubbled but still comfortable spaces of my furnished room, I feel the energy coursing through me in small flashes and ripples of light, an energy which I know, given but that one chance it needs, could redeem the world. The beast does not sleep. In my transmogrification I have cast sleep from me like the cloak of all reason and I spring from these rooms, scuttle the three flights of the brownstone to the street and coming upon it in the dense and sleeping spaces of the city, see no one, confront no one (but I would not, I never have) as I move downtown to enact my dreadful but necessary tasks.

The beast does not sleep, therefore I do not sleep. At first the change came upon me once a week and then twice . . . but in recent months it has been coming faster and faster, now six or seven times a week, and furthermore I can *will* the change. Involuntary at first, overtaking me like a stray bullet, it now seems to be within my control as my power and facility increase. A *latent* characteristic then, some recessive gene which peeked its way out shyly at the age of twenty-five with humility and then with growing power and finally as I became accustomed to the power, it fell within my control.

I can now become the beast whenever I wish.

Now it is not the beast but I who pokes his way from the covers during the hours of despair and lurches his way to the bathroom; standing before that one mirror, I call the change upon myself, ring the changes, and the beast, then, confronts me, a tentacle raised as if in greeting or repudiation. Shrugging, I sprint down the stairs and into the city. At dawn I return. In between that time—

—I make my travels.

My travels, my errands! Over manhole covers, sprinting as if filled with helium (the beast is powerful; the beast has endless stamina) in and out of the blocks of the west side, vaulting to heights on abandoned stoops, then into the gutter again, cutting a swath through the city, ducking the occasional prowl cars which come through indolently swinging out of sight behind gates to avoid garbage trucks, no discovery ever having been made of the beast in all the months that this has been going on . . . and between the evasions I do my business.

Pardon. Pardon if you will. I do not do *my* business. The beast does *his* business.

I must separate the beast and myself because the one is not the other and I have very little to *do* with the beast although, of course, I am he. And he is me.

And attack them in the darkness.

Seize hapless pedestrians or dawn drunks by the throat, coming up from their rear flank, diving upon them then with facility and ease, sweeping upon them to clap a hand upon throat or groin with a touch as sure and cunning as any I have ever known and then, bringing them to their knees, straddling them in the gutter, I—

Well, I—

—Well, now, is it necessary for me to say what I do? Yes, it is necessary for me to say, I suppose; these recollections are not careless nor are they calculated but merely an attempt, as it were, to set the record straight. The rumors, reports and evasions about the conduct of the beast have reached the status of full-scale lies (there is not a crew of assassins loose in the streets but merely one; there is not a carefully organized plan to terrorize the city but merely one beast, one humble, hard-working animal wreaking his justice) so it is to be said that as I throttle the lives and misery out of them, I often *turn them over* so that they can confront the beast, see what it is doing to them, and that I see in their eyes past the horror the heartbreak, the beating farewell signal of their mortality.

But beyond that I see something else.

Let me tell you of this, it is crucial: I see an acceptance so enormous as almost to defy in all of its acceptance because it is religious.

The peace that passeth all understanding darts through their eyes and finally passes through them, exiting in the last breath of life as with a crumpling sigh they die against me. I must have killed hundreds, no, I do not want to exaggerate, it is not right, I must have killed in the high seventies. At first I kept a chart of my travels and accomplishments but when it verged into the high twenties I realized that this was insane, leaving physical evidence of any sort of my accomplishments that is, and furthermore, past that ninth murder or the nineteenth there is no longer a feeling of victory but only *necessity*. It is purely business.

All of it has been purely business.

Business in any event for the beast. He needs to kill as I need to breathe, that creature within me who I was always in the process of becoming (all the strangeness I felt as a child I now attribute to the embryonic form of the beast, beating and huddling its growing way within) takes the lives of humans as casually as I take my midday sandwich and drink in the local cafeteria before passing on to my dismal and clerkly affairs at the Bureau, accumulating time toward the pension credits that will be mine after twenty or thirty years. The beast needs to kill; he draws his strength from murder as I do mine from food and since I am merely his tenant during these struggles, a helpless (but alertly interested) altar which dwells within the beast watching all that goes on, I can take no responsibility myself for what has happened but put it squarely on him where it belongs.

Perhaps I should have turned myself in for treatment or seen a psychiatrist of some kind when all this began, but what would have been the point of it? What? They would not have believed that I was possessed; they would have thought me harmlessly crazy and the alternative, if they did believe me, would have been much worse: implication, imprisonment, fury. I could have convinced them. I know that now, when I became strong enough to will myself into the becoming of the beast I could have, in their very chambers, turned myself into the monster and then they would have believed, would have taken my fears for certainty . . . but the beast, manic in his goals, would have fallen upon those hapless psychiatrists, interns or social workers as he fell upon all of his nighttime victims and what then?

What then? He murders as casually and skillfully as I annotate my filings at the Bureau. He is impossible to dissuade. No, I could not have done that. The beast and I, sentenced to dwell throughout eternity or at least through the length of my projected life span: there may be another judgment on this someday of some weight but I cannot be concerned with that now. Why should I confess? What is there to confess? Built so deeply into the culture—I am a thoughtful man and have pondered this long despite my lack of formal education credits—as to be part of the madness is the belief that confession is in itself expiation, but I do not believe this. The admission of dreadful acts is merely to compound them through multiple refraction and lies are thus more necessary than the truth in order to make the world work.

Oh, how I believe this. How I do believe it.

I have attempted discussions with the beast. This is not easy but at the moment of transfer there is a slow, stunning instant when the mask of his features has not settled upon him fully and it is possible for me, however, weakly, to speak. "Why must you do this?" I ask him. "This is murder, mass murder. These are human beings, you know, it really is quite dreadful." My little voice pipes weakly as my own force diminishes and the beast, transmogrified, stands before the mirror, waving his tentacles, flexing his powerful limbs, and says then (he speaks a perfect English when he desires although largely he does not desire to speak), "Don't be a fool, this is my destiny and besides *I* am not human so this is not my problem."

This is unanswerable; it is already muted by transfer. I burrow within and the beast takes to the streets singing and crouching, ready once again for his tasks. Why does he need to murder? I understand that his lust for this is as gross and simple as my own for less dreadful events; it is an urge as much a part of him as that toward respiration. The beast is an innocent creature, immaculately conceived. He goes to do murder as his victim goes to drink. He sees no shades of moral inference or dismay even in the bloodiest and most terrible of the strangulations but simply does what must be done with the necessary force. Never more. Some nights he has killed ten. The streets of the city scatter north and south with his victims.

But his victims! Ah, they have, so many of them, been waiting for murder so long, dreaming of it, touching it in the night (as I touch the selfsame beast), that this must be the basis of that acceptance which passes through them at the moment of impact. They have been looking, these victims, for an event so climactic that they will be able to cede responsibility for their lives and here, in the act of murder, have they at last that confirmation. Some of them embraced the beast with passion as he made his last strike. Others have opened themselves to him on the pavement and pointed at their vitals. For the city, the very energy of that city or so I believe this now through my musings, is based upon the omnipresence of death and to die is to become at last completely at one with the darkened heart of a city constructed for death. I become too philosophical. I will not attempt to justify myself further.

For there *is* no justification. What happens, happens. The beast has taught me at least this much (along with so much else). Tonight we come upon the city with undue haste; the beast has not been out for two nights previous, having burrowed within with a disinclination for pursuit, unavailable even to summons, but now at four in the morning of this coldest of all the nights of winter he has pounded within me, screaming for release, and I have allowed him his way with some eagerness because (I admit this truly) I too have on his behalf missed the thrill of the hunt.

Now the beast races down the pavements, his breath a plume of fire against the ice. At the first intersection we see a young woman paused for the light, a valise clutched against her, one hand upraised for a taxi that will not come. (I know it will not come.) An early dawn evacuee from the city or so I murmur to the beast. Perhaps it would be best to leave this one alone since she looks spare and there must be tastier meat in the alleys beyond . . . but the creature does not listen. He listens to nothing I have to say. This is the core of his strength and my own repudiation is nothing as to his.

For listen, listen now: he sweeps into his own purposes in a way which can only make me filled with admiration. He comes upon the girl then. He comes upon her. He takes her from behind.

He takes her from behind.

She struggles in his grasp like an insect caught within a huge, indifferent hand, all legs and activity, grasping and groping, and he casually kicks the valise from her hand, pulls her into an alley for a more sweeping inspection, the woman's skull pinned against his flat, oily chest, her little hands and feet waving, and she is screaming in a way so dismal and hopeless that I know she will never be heard and she must know this as well. The scream stops. Small moans and pleas which had pieced out the spaces amid the sound stop too and with an explosion of strength she twists within his grasp, then hurls herself against his chest and looks upward toward his face to see at last the face of the assassin about which she must surely have dreamed, the bitch, in so many nights. She sees the beast. He sees her.

I too know her.

She works at the Bureau. She is a fellow clerk two aisles down and three over, a pretty woman, not indifferent in her gestures but rather, as so few of these bitches at the Bureau are, kind and lively, kind even to *me*. Her eyes are never droll but sad as she looks upon me. I have never spoken to her other than pleasantries but I feel, feel that if I were ever to seek her out she would not humiliate me.

"Oh," I say within the spaces of the beast, trapped and helpless as I look upon her, "oh, oh."

"No!" she says, looking upon us. "Oh no, not you, it can't be you!" and the beast's grasp tightens upon her then. "It can't be you! Don't say that it's *you* doing this to me!" and I look upon her then with tenderness and infinite understanding knowing that I am helpless to save her and thus relieved of the responsibility but saddened too. Saddened because the beast has never caught a victim known to me before. I say in a small voice which she will never hear (because I am trapped inside), "I'm sorry but it's got to be done, you see. How much of this can I take anymore?" and her eyes, I know this, her eyes lighten with understanding, darken too, lighten and darken with the knowledge I have imparted.

And as the pressure begins then, the pressure that in ten seconds will snap her throat and leave her dead, as the freezing colors of the city descend, we confront one another in isolation, our eyes meeting, touch meeting and absolutely nothing to be done about it. Her neck breaks, and in many many many ways I must admit—I will admit everything—this has been the most satisfying victim of them all. Of them all.

Treats

By Norman Partridge

Monsters stalked the supermarket aisles.

Maddie pushed the squeaky-wheeled cart past a pack of werewolves, smiling when they growled at her because that was the polite thing to do. She couldn't help staring at the bright eyes inside the plastic masks. Brown eyes, blue and green eyes. Human eyes. Not the eyes that she couldn't see. Not the black eyes that stared at her from Jimmy's face, so cold, ordering her here and there without a glint of compassion or love.

"Jimmy, get away from that candy!"

Maddie covered her mouth, fearful that she'd spoken. No, she hadn't said anything. Besides, Jimmy was at home with them. He'd said that they were preparing for Operation Trojan Horse and he had to speak to them before—

"Jimmy, I'm telling you for the last time . . ."

A little ghoul clutching a trick-or-treat bag scampered down the aisle. He tore at the wrapping of a Snickers bar and gobbled a big bite before his mother caught his tattered collar.

"I warned you, young man," she said, snatching away the bright-orange treat sack. "You're not going to eat this candy all at once and make yourself sick. You're allowed one piece a day, remember? That way your treats will last for a long, long time."

Maddie saw the little boy's shoulders slump. Her Jimmy had done the same thing last Halloween when Maddie had given him a similar speech, except her Jimmy had been a sad-faced clown, not a ghoul.

And not a general. Not *their* general.

Maddie raised her hand, as if she could wave off the boy's mother before she made the same mistake Maddie had made a year earlier. She saw lipstick smears on her fingers and imagined what her face must look like. It had been so long since they'd allowed her to wear cosmetics that she'd made a mess of herself without realizing it. The boy's mother would see that, and she wouldn't listen. She'd rush away with her son before Maddie could warn her.

Defeated, the boy stared down at his ghoul-face mirrored in the freshly waxed floor. His mother crumpled his trick-or-treat bag closed, and the moment slowed. Maddie saw herself reaching into her shopping cart, watched her lipstick-smeared fingers tear open a bag of Milk Duds and fling the little yellow boxes down the aisle in a slow, scattering arc. She saw the other Jimmy's mother yelling at her, the boxes bouncing, the big store windows behind the little ghoul and the iron-gray clouds boiling outside. Wind-driven leaves the color of old skin crackling against the glass.

And then Maddie was screaming at the little ghoul. "Eat your candy! Eat it now! Don't let them come after it!"

She paid for the Milk Duds, of course, and for all the other candy that she had heaped into the shopping cart. The manager didn't complain. Maddie knew that the ignorant man only wanted her out of his store.

He thought that she was crazy.

Papery leaves clawed at her ankles as she loaded the candy into the back of the station wagon. She smiled, remembering the other Jimmy, the ghoul Jimmy, gobbling Milk Duds. Other monsters had

461

joined in the feast. Werewolves, Frankensteins, zombies. Maddie prayed that they'd all have awful stomachaches. Then they'd stay home, snuggled in front of their television sets. They wouldn't come knocking at her door tonight. They'd be safe from her Jimmy and his army.

Maddie climbed into the station wagon and slammed the door. She pretended not to notice Jimmy's friends in the back seat. It was easy, because she couldn't see them, couldn't see their black eyes. But she could feel their presence nonetheless.

Slowly, Maggie drove home. Little monsters stood on front porches and watched the gray sky, waiting intently for true darkness, when they would descend on the neighborhood in search of what Jimmy wanted to give them. Maddie glanced in the rearview mirror at the grocery bags in the back of the station wagon. Even in brown paper, even wrapped in plastic, she could smell the sugar. It was the only smell she knew anymore, and she tasted it in the back of her throat.

God, she'd been tasting it for a year now.

"Mommy," Jimmy had cried, "you said my candy would last. Now look at it. Look at *them*. They ruined it. I want new candy. I want it *now!"*

But Jimmy's whining had been a lie. Maddie knew that now. Jimmy hadn't wanted the candy. *They* had wanted it, and they'd coaxed Jimmy into getting it for them. And they scared her, even if they didn't scare her son. They'd always scared her.

Because they were everywhere. In the cupboards. Under the floor. In the garden and under the rim of the toilet seat. Maddie's house swelled with them. And when she went to work, they were there, too, watching her through the windows. Black eyes she couldn't see, staring. Through the winter cold, through the summer heat, they were always there. Studying her. Never resting.

They had her son, too. He had a million fathers now, all who cared for him more than the man who'd given him his face and his last name before disappearing beneath a wave of unpaid bills. They nested in Jimmy's room and traveled in his lunch box. Jimmy took them places and showed them things. He taught them about the town, and they told him how smart he was. They made him a general and swore to obey his commands.

Maddie pulled into the driveway and cut the engine. She sat in the quiet car, dreading the house. Inside, Jimmy's legions waited. Jimmy waited, too. But Jimmy wasn't a sad-faced clown anymore. Now he was a great leader, and he was about to attack.

The sky rumbled.

Heavy raindrops splattered the windshield.

Maddie almost smiled but caught herself just in time. She glanced in the rearview mirror and pretended to wipe at her smeared lipstick, but really she was looking for Jimmy's spies.

She wished that she could see their eyes.

Jimmy was in the basement, telling the story of the Trojan horse. They stood at attention in orderly black battalions, listening to every word. Maddie didn't know how they tolerated it. Jimmy had told them the story at least a hundred times.

"The candy's upstairs, Jimmy. I left it on the kitchen table."

Jimmy thumbed the brim of a military cap that was much too large for his head. He'd made Maddie buy the cap at an army surplus store, and it was the smallest size available. "I'll grow into it." That's what he'd said, smiling, but he wasn't smiling now.

Maddie managed a grin. "The candy, Jimmy. You remember—"

"Of course I remember! I only wish that you'd remember to call me the right thing!"

"I'm sorry, general." Maddie straightened. "The candy—the supplies—are upstairs in the mess hall."

Jimmy seemed pleased. "Very good. Bring the supplies down here, and we'll begin Operation Trojan Horse."

Maddie stared at the black sea on the cement floor, imagining a million eyes focused on her. She wouldn't walk among them. Not when she could see them clearly, not when she could feel them scuttling over her feet.

"I don't want to do that," she said.

The boy's lips twisted into a cruel smile. "Maybe you'd rather have me send a few squads to your bedroom tonight, like the last time you disobeyed a direct order. You won't get much sleep with a jillion little feet crawling all over you . . ."

"Jimmy!" She stared at him, revolted by his black insect eyes, and then turned away.

She got the candy.

Jimmy used a penknife to make tiny holes in the packages. His troops climbed inside, listening to their leader talk of conquest and the Trojan Horse and the birth of a new order. He told them the best places to hide in a house and reminded the scouts that he must be kept informed at all times concerning the progress of their mission.

And when they were all in place, why then . . .

Silently, Maddie climbed the stairs. Rainwater ran down the front window, drooling from the rusty gutters above. The street outside was slick and black. The sidewalks were empty, gray; a flotilla of fallen leaves swam in the cement gutters. Maddie watched the leaves and imagined hundreds of little monsters washed into their homes by a great wave.

She looked down and saw her son's face mirrored in the window. His reflection was smeared with rain, sad, his straight lips twisted into a dripping frown, his black eyes deep pools overflowing high cheekbones. He exhaled sharply and the image fogged over.

"They just told me," he whispered. "It took them a long time to get out of the car. I guess you think that was pretty smart, closing the vents and all."

Maddie said nothing. She stared at the foggy spot on the window. *Just a glimpse,* she thought. *Just a glimpse, but it was a clown's face I saw.*

"I never thought about this." Jimmy stared out at the rain. "They aren't coming, are they?"

"Not tonight."

Jimmy whispered, "Not tonight, troops. Operation Trojan Horse is scrubbed."

Maddie took a deep breath, hating the air, hating the stink of sugar. She thought about the little clown she'd seen mirrored in the rain-washed window, and she thought about the other Jimmy, the little ghoul, safe and dry in front of a TV set.

Tiny antennae probed Maddie's heel. Tiny feet, sticky with chocolate, marched over her toes.

The rain came harder now, in sheets. Jimmy brushed his troops away from his mother's feet. He rose and took her hand. Mirrored in the window, his lips were straight, his jaw firm.

God, it's been so long since he touched me, she thought, but she said, "Jimmy, lets watch television."

He nodded, studying the rain, not really listening.

His eyes narrowed until Maddie couldn't see them anymore.

"Next year," he said, his grip tightening.

Under My Bed

By Al Sarrantonio

When Daddy says I'm bad, he puts me to bed and turns out the lights. He does that a lot, and I don't like it, but at least I've got somebody to talk to when I'm in here. Daddy thinks I'm alone, but there's a man under my bed.

He only comes up out of the trapdoor after the lights go out and Daddy shuts the door and goes away. The man says he doesn't like lights; he says he doesn't like Daddy much either, and I have to smile when he says that.

He lives somewhere down below the bed, though I'm not really sure where. The living room is downstairs below my bedroom, so he can't really live there or Daddy would see him; he must live in the little space underneath the floor.

He talks to me about things when I'm shut up in here because Daddy says I've been bad. Daddy says I've been bad a lot, every time I do something he doesn't like. Daddy doesn't smile a lot and I don't think he likes me very much anymore.

There was a time when Daddy did like me, but that was a long time ago, when Mommy was still here. I even remember Daddy picking me up and swinging me through the air, letting go and then catching me again, with a big smile on his face. He called me his "little Billy boy." He must have liked me, or he wouldn't have called me that. I even had friends then, and I remember Daddy taking me and all my friends to the ball game once. I spilled soda on myself, and Daddy didn't even get mad; he just smiled and said, "Let me give you a hand there, Billy boy," and helped me clean it up. I spilled soda on myself last week when Daddy's girl friend was here and I thought he was going to kill me.

I remember things began to change just about the time me and Pete Cochran became best friends. Pete's father worked at home, and Mommy used to come over to Pete's house to pick me up after we finished playing. Pete and I played super-heroes, or Huck Finn and Tom Sawyer, or the Hardy boys, and one of us would make believe he was in trouble and the other one would save him. It was fun, and we almost always played it at Pete's house.

But after Daddy and Mommy started fighting I couldn't go to Pete's house anymore, and then Pete couldn't come to mine, and after a while Daddy wouldn't let me go out at all. The fighting got worse and worse, and most of the time I stayed locked in my room. Daddy stopped calling me "Billy boy," and they both started putting me to bed a lot, sometimes in the middle of the day. I almost always had my pajamas on. I think they wanted to get rid of me so they could fight, and I used to lie in bed and listen to them yell at each other and sometimes throw things around. Once, the police came, and that was exciting, but otherwise it wasn't very good. They started to hit me sometimes, too. Mommy hit me once and told me that she and Daddy never wanted to have me, and that the only reason they had me was because Daddy thought it would keep him and Mommy together. She smelled like whiskey when she said it. "At least Pete Cochran's father knows what love is," she said.

After Mommy left, I asked Daddy if that meant that Mommy was Pete Cochran's mommy now instead of mine, but the way he looked at me made me never ask him that again. Things got very lonely after that, and I never went out and didn't see my friends anymore.

The man under my bed came out for the first time right after Mommy left. A few nights I heard sounds down there, like mice or squirrels, and I hid under the covers. Then, one night after Daddy shut me up in here and it was real dark, I heard the trapdoor open and the man came out. I heard him puffing as he pulled himself out of the hole, and then he lay there for a while breathing hard. I was scared stiff and yelled for Daddy to come and when he did come and turned on the light the man was gone, back down in the hole; but as soon as Daddy turned out the light and left, the door opened again and the man pulled himself out. I yelled for Daddy to come back but he wouldn't, so I pulled the covers up over my head and listened through the mattress. I could hear him moving around down there. After a while I couldn't hear him moving, so I pulled one side of the sheets up over the edge of the bed and made a hole so I could listen out.

He started to talk to me then, and for a minute I was afraid since his voice sounded a little creepy, like squashing bugs; but he wasn't saying mean things so after a while I stopped being scared.

"I know how you feel, Billy," he said from down under the bed. "I'm on your side." Then we talked for a while about things I like to do, and what I don't like and things.

After that night, he climbed out of his door and lay down there talking to me every time I got put to bed. You could say he became my best friend, like Pete Cochran used to be. I could talk to him about anything at all. And he really understood how bad Daddy is to me, and he felt sorry for me about it. "I don't like your Daddy," he told me once.

I could imagine him down there lying on his back with his hands behind his head, staring up at the bottom of my bed like it was blue sky with clouds blowing across it. I sort of got the picture of him like Tom Sawyer, with blue jeans on and a straw in his mouth and freckles and a big smile. Even though he told me he didn't look like that and that he couldn't let me see him, the picture I got of him lying down there with freckles and grinning was so strong that I sneaked Daddy's flashlight under the covers with me one night and leaned down over the side of the bed and shone it on him. I had some trouble with the switch, though, and by the time I got it on he was pulling the trapdoor closed behind him. All I saw was his hand on the door rope and the top of his head; he didn't have any hair and was kind of wrinkly-looking. And I got the feeling he wasn't smiling. Then the switch went off and Daddy heard me moving around and came and took the flashlight away.

The man under the bed wouldn't come out for a week after that, and I realized just how lonely it was in the dark without him. I slept most of the time with the covers over my head; I was scared to be in the dark without him, even if he didn't look like Tom Sawyer.

But he did come back a couple of nights ago, just when I needed him most.

Daddy hit me that night, harder than he ever had before. He had his girl friend home with him and he was drinking whiskey and I asked if I could watch the TV a little longer, and he hit me. Then he put me in my room and turned off the lights and said that if I made any noise he'd beat me some more. I lay under the covers, and I was crying, and then I heard the trapdoor squeak open, slowly, and I heard the man dragging himself out. He sounded tired, but when he started talking to me I could tell he wasn't mad at me anymore. He almost sounded happy. He said he was sorry Daddy hit me and that he wanted to help; he said he might even let me find the trapdoor. He stayed up with me almost all night, until I fell asleep. The next morning after he left I crawled under the bed and, sure enough, I could feel the edges where the door must be; I'd never been able to find them before, no matter how hard I tried. And last night he said Daddy would never hit me again. "Things are going to be all right, Billy boy," he said, and that made me feel warm all over, because I knew he was my friend.

Tonight Daddy's coming home late, and I got into bed by myself just like the man under the bed told me to. He told me to turn out the light and wait for Daddy to come home. He's been under the bed for more than an hour, telling me funny stories that make me laugh, about other kids' daddys and about the things that happened to them. Some of the things are real funny, like what happens in the cartoons I watch in the morning after Daddy goes to work. Even though I know what the man looks like, I still can't help thinking of him lying down there under my bed like Tom Sawyer, with his legs crossed and laughing, telling those funny stories.

It's late now, and I just heard Daddy come in. He's alone, but he sounds like he's been drinking whiskey again. He's bumping into things and cursing.

I can hear Daddy looking for me, since he thinks I'll still be up; he'll probably think of looking in my bedroom any minute. The man under the bed says to be quiet; he says he may even take Daddy through the trapdoor with him to where he lives. Wouldn't that make a funny story, he says, and he laughs. I laugh with him. He says he won't even let the light bother him this time, that he'll come right out from under the bed.

Daddy's outside my door now; I can hear him fumbling with the handle, trying to open it. He finally does, and now his hand is searching for the light switch. He finds it and turns it on, and he looks very surprised to see the two of us in bed, waiting for him.

Hi Daddy.

Up Under the Roof

By Manly Wade Wellman

When I was twelve years old I lived in a shabby old two-story house, built square below and double-gabled up above. The four gables contained an upstairs room apiece, each facing in a different direction and the entire four making a cross, with a hall and a stairwell at the center. The front and side rooms were ceiled and plastered and painted, for use as bedrooms, but the unfinished rear chamber held only a clutter of trunks, boxes and broken furniture. That part of the upper floor was hot and dusty in the summertime, and it was left open right up to the peak of its gable. Directly above its doorway to the central hall gaped an empty dark triangle, that led to the slant-sided cave above the bedroom ceilings. Because it was so full of lumber, this unfinished room was called the garret, though it was not a real garret. The real garret was that dark space, up under the roof.

I was the youngest person in the house by more than a generation, and my youth seemed to offend everyone bitterly. I was constantly reminded of my childish stupidity and inexperience. Nobody felt that years would make me any wiser, and in time I grew to share that opinion. I tried never to make a statement or venture a suggestion that had not been voiced previously by one of my elders. Even at that, I came in for plenty of snubs and corrections, and repeated admonitions that little boys should be seen and not heard. So I learned to keep my own counsel. The downstairs parlor was full of books, and I read in them a great deal, including nearly all the volumes of an old *Encyclopaedia Britannica*. This taste for reading attracted some curious attention on the part of my guardians; occasionally one of them would say that I must be trained for the law or the ministry. I was never consulted as to my own ambition, which would have shocked the entire household. I wanted to be a deep-sea diver.

That summer was a hot one, and my room, in the gable on the right or northern side of the house, had only one window. The sun's rays fell directly on the outside of the room's sloping walls, which were only the plastered-in pitches of the gable, and which offered little insulation. Even by bedtime, my room did not cool down. I slept poorly, bothered by strange and vivid dreams. Sometimes I started awake in the darkness, sweating and tingling, and lay there as I listened to the rustle of the cottonwoods in the yard and the creaking of the old house timbers.

After a while, I am not sure exactly when, I began to hear something else at night.

Awareness of that sound grew upon me, first slowly and faintly, then with a terrifying clarity, over a number of hot, wakeful nights. It was something up above me, between the ceiling and the peak of the roof, something big and clumsy and stealthy. I remember telling myself that it was a rat up there, but the moment the thought came into my head I knew it was a very silly thought indeed. Rats skip and scamper, they are light and swift and sure. This movement was huge and weighty, of a bulk that I judged was far beyond my own; and it moved, I say, with a slow, unhandy stealth that had a sustained rhythm of a sort. It did not drag or walk, but it moved. Years afterward, I was to see through a microscope the plodding of an amoeba. The thing up under the roof sounded as an amoeba

469

looks, a mass that stretches out a thin, loose portion of itself, then rolls and flows all of its substance into that portion, and so creeps along. Only it must have been many, many thousands of times larger than an amoeba.

Before long, I was hearing the noise of that motion every night. I would wait for it, lying awake in bed until the moment it made itself heard and humped itself across the ceiling above me. Always fear came with it, fear that did not diminish with time. I would stare into the hot gloom, my tongue would dry up between my teeth, and my fingertips would smart as though they had been rubbed sore. On my back would sprout and fan and winnow little involuntary wings of chill, that made my spine shrink and quiver as though ice came and mingled with the marrow. The ceiling, I knew, would descend some night. It would descend upon me like a great millstone being lowered, and then it would crumble about my bed. Something huge and soft would wriggle free of the broken bits . . .

There could be no talking about any of this, I knew very well. Long before, I had learned that nobody in the house would listen or care. As I have said, I was scorned and disliked by all those others. Once, when a neighbor boy of fifteen gave me a terrible beating in the front yard, everyone watched from the parlor windows, but none stirred to help me, not when I thought I would fall dead at my enemy's scornful feet. When he got tired of pulping my face with his knuckles, he turned away at last, and I dragged myself in and was tongue-lashed on all sides for an hour. Today I cannot remember exactly what was urged against me, only that the tears I had not shed for pain welled forth under the scolding. Things like that made me hesitate about asking for help or anything else. One morning at breakfast, I did dare to inquire if the others had ever heard anything strange, up under the roof; but I was only reprimanded for interrupting a discussion of local politics.

That night the noise was louder and more terrifying than ever. It began somewhere above another of the rooms, and then it trundled along my ceiling, slower and still slower, until it paused immediately above my bed. At that moment it seemed to me that the lath and plaster were no tighter or stronger than a spider web, and that the bulk up there was incalculably more dire than the very prince and father of all spiders. I was certain that it crouched there, almost within reach of me, that it gloated and hungered, and that it turned over in its dark sub-personal awareness the problem of when and how to come and take hold of me.

I could not have stirred from my bed, could not even have cried out for help.

470

The thing and the fear of it were with me always, night after night and week after week, until a day late in the summer, a dark and rainy day when it did not wait for nightfall.

I was alone in the house that day, and I had grown tired of hearing the rain and the dank swish of soaked leaves outside. I looked at the books in the parlor, but I had exhausted all that interested me. Then I remembered a stack of illustrated magazines, very old, in a corner of the lumber room. I climbed the stairs and opened the door. The lumber room was ugly and close, and a sort of brown light reflected from the unpainted joists and the insides of the shingles overhead. I found the magazines and began to paw through them.

Up to then, there had been no sound except for the weary rain outside. But as I leafed through one of the magazines, there came a slow, muffled *bump-bump-bump* from above me, from that dark opening that led into the space above the ceiling. I knew that something sly and heavy was there, looking down upon me.

In one scrambling moment I had fled into the hall and downstairs and to the front door. I grabbed the knob, then I stopped and thought.

It was no swelling of courage that made me pause before rushing out, only a hopeless but sensible consideration of what must follow. I could leave the house and go into the rainy street and mope there until someone came back. Then I would have to come back, too, and in time night would fall and I would have to go to my room and go to bed in the dark. Then whatever made the noise would come down. It would wait no longer, for it had seen me and my tortured terror. It would flow to the floor and come in at my door and creep up on my bed. Then I would know how it looked, and what color it was, and what it wanted with me.

All these things I pondered, and from somewhere came a cold determination that stiffened my limbs and my neck like new sawdust poured into an empty doll. I left the front door unopened, and walked back through the house to the foot of the stairs. There I paused, and tried to lift my foot to the bottom step, but I could not.

After a while, and I think it was a fairly long while, I turned and walked to the back porch. There, upon the wood box, lay a handaxe. It was dull and rusty and wobbled upon its helve, but I took it in my hand and went back in, and this time when I came to the steps I mounted them.

It was a slow journey, one step after another, with long, tight breaths between. The old boards creaked under my shoes, as if

471

aghast at my rash ascent. I gained the upper hall, and now I did not hesitate, but went back into the lumber room.

The brown light had darkened since I had first come there to find the magazines. I stood in the middle of the floor and made myself look up at that triangular opening, and that took a mustering of all my will power, but there was nothing to see there. I stuck the handle of the axe down into the waistband of my knickerbockers, and dragged a heavy, dust-laden old bureau across and pushed it close against the wall beside the door. Upon that I placed a broken-backed chair, and upon the chair a candle box, set precariously on end.

Finally I climbed up on the bureau, up on the chair, up on the box. My chin rose level with the threshold of the black cavern, and it was like gazing into a pool of ink.

I peered and listened. With both hands I got hold of a cross-timber and drew myself slowly up. The candle box tipped over and fell from beneath my feet, striking the floor boards with a crash like an explosion. But next moment I had dragged myself up inside the loft. The roof peak came so low above my head that I could barely rise to my knees.

The axe still hung in my waistband, and I was heartily glad I had brought it. I pulled it out and tried to hold it in my mouth, like a pirate's dirk. But it was too big and heavy, so I kept it clutched in my right hand. Then, crawling on my knees and my left hand, I went forward on top of the rafters. Every inch took me deeper into darkness, and when I reached and made my way past a big rough chimney I might as well have been in a coal mine for all the light that came to me.

But if I could not see, I could feel, and so I groped my way. First I went straight to the front of the house. I kept the axe poised for a blow as I felt all along the boards, and into the corners. The dust made me want to cough. When I had explored that area, I dragged myself around. I could see some feeble glow of light when I looked toward the far end, past the obstruction of the chimney. Crawling back, I explored gropingly the space above the south bedroom. Last of all I made myself venture into the loft above my own room, where I had always heard the noise.

I found nothing.

Those are the three words I always finished with when, grown up enough to be listened to, I told this story in later years. And one or two listeners have spoken of the undefined and sometimes malevolent psychic forces that now and then afflict children on the brink of adolescence. But I knew then, and I know now, that there

472

was something, or that there had been something, that was a mortal peril until I drove myself to face it. If I had done anything else that day, it would have come looking for me that night. And I do not want to guess what would have happened then.

But from that time forward, there was not the slightest murmur of sound up under the roof. I slept so deeply that I had to be shaken and shouted awake in the mornings. And I never knew real fear again, not even in the war.

The Upturned Face

By Stephen Crane

What will we do now?" said the adjutant, troubled and excited.

"Bury him," said Timothy Lean.

The two officers looked down close to their toes where lay the body of their comrade. The face was chalk-blue; gleaming eyes stared at the sky. Over the two upright figures was a windy sound of bullets, and on the top of the hill Lean's prostrate company of Spitzbergen infantry was firing measured volleys.

"Don't you think it would be better—" began the adjutant. "We might leave him until to-morrow."

"No," said Lean. "I can't hold that post an hour longer. I've got to fall back, and we've got to bury old Bill."

"Of course," said the adjutant, at once. "Your men got entrenching tools?"

Lean shouted back to his little line, and two men came slowly, one with a pick, one with a shovel. They started in the direction of the Rostina sharpshooters. Bullets cracked near their ears. "Dig here," said Lean gruffly. The men, thus caused to lower their glances to the turf, became hurried and frightened, merely because they could not look to see whence the bullets came. The dull beat of the pick striking the earth sounded amid the swift snap of close bullets. Presently the other private began to shovel.

"I suppose," said the adjutant, slowly, "we'd better search his clothes for—things."

Lean nodded. Together in curious abstraction they looked at the body. Then Lean stirred his shoulders suddenly, arousing himself.

473

"Yes," he said, "we'd better see what he' got." He dropped to his knees, and his hands approached the body of the dead officer. But his hands wavered over the buttons of the tunic. The first button was brick-red with drying blood, and he did not seem to dare touch it.

"Go on," said the adjutant, hoarsely.

Lean stretched his wooden hand, and his fingers fumbled the bloodstained buttons. At last he rose with ghastly face. He had gathered a watch, a whistle, a pipe, a tobacco-pouch, a handkerchief, a little case of cards and papers. He looked at the adjutant. There was a silence. The adjutant was feeling that he had been a coward to make Lean do all the grisly business.

"Well," said Lean, "that's all, I think. You have his sword and revolver?"

"Yes," said the adjutant, his face working, and then he burst out in a sudden strange fury at the two privates. "Why don't you hurry up with that grave? What are you doing, anyhow? Hurry, do you hear? I never saw such stupid—"

Even as he cried out in his passion the two men were labouring for their lives. Ever overhead the bullets were spitting.

The grave was finished. It was not a masterpiece—a poor little shallow thing. Lean and the adjutant again looked at each other in a curious silent communication.

Suddenly the adjutant croaked out a weird laugh. It was a terrible laugh, which had its origin in that part of the mind which is first moved by the singing of the nerves. "Well," he said humorously to Lean, "I suppose we had best tumble him in."

"Yes," said Lean. The two privates stood waiting, bent over their implements. "I suppose," said Lean, "it would be better if we laid him in ourselves."

"Yes," said the adjutant. Then, apparently remembering that he had made Lean search the body, he stooped with great fortitude and took hold of the dead officer's clothing. Lean joined him. Both were particular that their fingers should not feel the corpse. They tugged away; the corpse lifted, heaved, toppled, flopped into the grave, and the two officers, straightening, looked again at each other—they were always looking at each other. They sighed with relief.

The adjutant said, "I suppose we should—we should say something. Do you know the service, Tim?"

"They don't read the service until the grave is filled in," said Lean, pressing his lips to an academic expression.

"Don't they?" said the adjutant, shocked that he had made the

474

mistake. "Oh, well," he cried, suddenly, "let us—let us say something—while he can hear us."

"All right," said Lean. "Do you know the service?"

"I can't remember a line of it," said the adjutant.

Lean was extremely dubious. "I can repeat two lines, but—"

"Well, do it," said the adjutant. "Go as far as you can. That's better than nothing. And the beasts have got our range exactly."

Lean looked at his two men. "Attention," he barked. The privates came to attention with a click, looking much aggrieved. The adjutant lowered his helmet to his knee. Lean, bareheaded, he stood over the grave. The Rostina sharpshooters fired briskly.

"O Father, our friend has sunk in the deep waters of death, but his spirit has leaped toward Thee as the bubble arises from the lips of the drowning. Perceive, we beseech, O Father, the little flying bubble, and—"

Lean, although husky and ashamed, had suffered no hesitation up to this point, but he stopped with a hopeless feeling and looked at the corpse.

The adjutant moved uneasily. "And from Thy superb heights—" he began, and then he too came to an end.

"And from Thy superb heights," said Lean.

The adjutant suddenly remembered a phrase in the back of the Spitzbergen burial service, and he exploited it with the triumphant manner of a man who has recalled everything, and can go on.

"O God, have mercy—"

"O God, have mercy—" said Lean.

"Mercy," repeated the adjutant, in quick failure.

"Mercy," said Lean. And then he was moved by some violence of feeling, for he turned upon his two men and tigerishly said, "Throw the dirt in."

The fire of the Rostina sharpshooters was accurate and continuous.

One of the aggrieved privates came forward with his shovel. He lifted his first shovel-load of earth, and for a moment of inexplicable hesitation it was held poised above this corpse, which from its chalk-blue face looked keenly out from the grave. Then the soldier emptied his shovel on—on the feet.

Timothy Lean felt as if tons had been swiftly lifted from off his forehead. He had felt that perhaps the private might empty the shovel on—on the face. It had been emptied on the feet. There was a great point gained there—ha, ha!—the first shovelful had been emptied on the feet. How satisfactory!

The adjutant began to babble. "Well, of course—a man we've messed with all these years—impossible—you can't, you know, leave your intimate friends rotting on the field. Go on, for God's sake, and shovel, you."

The man with the shovel suddenly ducked, grabbed his left arm with his right hand, and looked at his officer for orders. Lean picked the shovel from the ground. "Go to the rear," he said to the wounded man. He also addressed the other private. "You get under cover, too; I'll finish this business."

The wounded man scrambled hard still for the top of the ridge without devoting any glances to the direction from whence the bullets came, and the other man followed at an equal pace; but he was different, in that he looked back anxiously three times.

This is merely the way—often—of the hit and unhit.

Timothy Lean filled the shovel, hesitated, and then, in a movement which was like a gesture of abhorrence, he flung the dirt into the grave, and as it landed it made a sound—plop. Lean suddenly stopped and mopped his brow—a tired labourer.

"Perhaps we have been wrong," said the adjutant. His glance wavered stupidly. "It might have been better if we hadn't buried him just at this time. Of course, if we advance to-morrow the body would have been—"

"Damn you," said Lean, "shut your mouth." He was not the senior officer.

He again filled the shovel and flung the earth. Always the earth made that sound—plop. For a space Lean worked frantically, like a man digging himself out of danger.

Soon there was nothing to be seen but the chalk-blue face. Lean filled the shovel. "Good God," he cried to the adjutant. "Why didn't you turn him somehow when you put him in? This—" Then Lean began to stutter.

The adjutant understood. He was pale to the lips. "Go on, man," he cried, beseechingly, almost in a shout.

Lean swung back the shovel. It went forward in a pendulum curve. When the earth landed it made a sound—plop.

We Have Always Lived in the Forest

By Nancy Holder

Brittle bones, aching joints. I hate growing old. And these children of mine make life less than simple, though that is why we have always lived in the forest.

But you know the young: they never listen to you; at least, mine never do. They struggle and thrash and escape at the first opportunity, thinking they can outrun me—pity's sake, I'm not *that* old!

But not to fear, I always catch them and bring them back. I'm a good mother.

But they try me, they do. Just yesterday, one of my older ones, Victoria, made the break while I was dressing her for dinner. (Such a lovely creature, all in white lace like a bride, a velvet ribbon at her throat.) Just as I was stitching up the back of her gown, she whirled around, shoved me to the floor, and took off shrieking.

The young. So restless and foolish. At least, mine are.

After I regained my balance I watched her for a moment, lace flying as she stumbled and panted, calling to her brothers and sisters to follow—but they stayed where they were, my good darlings. (Besides, I build my fences high.) A few began to cry, others to shout encouragement—*that* will have to be dealt with, no egging on the deserters—but no one joined her.

I thought, Let her go. Let her see what lies beyond the forest. If she won't listen to my warnings, she deserves what she gets.

But I couldn't bear the thought of stumbling on her one day, after they finished with her—the agony would far outweigh the satisfaction.

We have always lived in the forest to enjoy the simple life. And to hide from the town, of course.

After a stern warning to the others, I ran after Victoria; and for a while I thought she was going to make it. I had bruised my hip on the hard dirt floor and my pain slowed my progress. My girl fairly flew among the trees—I couldn't help the pride that surged through me at the sight of her, so beautiful and lithe, ducking heavy oak branches and bearded webs of Spanish moss. She led me a merry dance, though I called to her that she was going too far, getting too deep; the town waited with its maw wide open, slathering its lips to devour her. I believe tears came to my eyes—I care for all my children, though I have so many—and I reached out for her, clutching my sore hip, not at all angry with her for pushing me. For I understand the young, you see. A good mother always understands.

We raced into the bowels of the forest; despite my concern for Victoria, I shuddered and considered turning back. It was too dank and shadowy, too like my image of the town. But I pressed on into the bracken, so dense and thick my perspiration iced my skin.

I tired; I'm growing old, you see, and they take bigger chances than before; and all seemed lost. My, how she flew, my little gazelle! What a girl she was!

We raced on. The ground grew damp and my feet sank into it, but it caught Victoria, too, and I knew I still had a chance.

She stumbled over a large exposed root and pitched forward into the mud. Even then, she was not daunted—she crawled on her hands and knees, screaming for help. I wanted to ask her who she thought would come. There was no one but us and the town, and she surely didn't want Them to hear her.

But that was my Victoria: looking before she leapt—literally! I almost laughed aloud as I realized the aptness of the phrase, but poor Victoria still pitched forward, positively hysterical. She was almost naked; her dress had caught on the thorns and brambles and ripped in long pieces like bandages, and blood-soaked they were, too, with streaks from her scratches. Her thighs looked like ribbon candy.

"Oh, Vicky," I said sadly, and then I caught her. I embraced her like a huge mother bear, my breast heaving upon hers, and I scooped her up in my arms as if she were an infant.

She was beyond struggling; she hung limply in my arms, begging, "No, Mother, no. Please, not me."

"You've been very silly," I told her. "What did you expect to accomplish?"

"Oh, please, Mother," and suchlike. I have often told them not to whine. It is distasteful in a young person.

Halfway back, she rallied and tried to escape again, but I held her tightly (and gave her a tap on the chin, I must admit, though not too hard).

Now all the children were crying, a few on their knees, sobbing out my errant daughter's name. She held out a limp arm to them, staring over my shoulder as I carried her into the house.

I bathed my darling girl, in the big tin tub by the fireplace. She had exhausted herself, for which I was grateful—I was tired, too, and she might have been able to make it if she rallied herself one last time.

The others kept up their wailing, even after the sun set. I lit some candles and eased Victoria out of the tub, dried her, and patiently dressed her again, this time in scarlet to blend in with her wounds.

And then I ate her. She was as delicate and sweet as I had imagined, and I felt proud of her all over again.

In the forest we live a simple, self-sufficient life, and I protect my children from the horrors of the town. You would think they'd understand, and stop fighting me, but that's not the way of children, is it? Has it ever been? One can only sigh over their ignorance and do one's best.

In the forest, at least, it is easier. I can't bear to think what happens to those of the town.

As, still, I can scarcely bring myself to think about the poor thing who dragged herself here shortly after I devoured Victoria.

I sensed her presence before I saw her. I knew there was a stranger near, and though my hip ached and my meal made me sluggish, I roused myself from the warmth of the fire and staggered across the room.

I heard footsteps, and for one awful instant, I thought we were in terrible danger. I fumbled behind the door for my club and tiptoed out the back to the pens, warning my girls and boys to be quiet; which, in the contrary ways of children, made them shout the louder—oh, children! Sometimes I wish—but no, that's cruel. I wouldn't have life any other way.

I made my way back from the pen to the house and stood behind the locked front door, club at the ready. But what can you do against one of Them? They're practically invincible; I've never heard of a death among Them. Of course, we live far away and I know little of Their ways except Their savagery; perhaps one day my ignorance will prove my undoing, but in this case, I was fortunate.

After a murmured prayer I crept to the window and pulled back the curtain just a little, steeling myself for what must surely be the messengers of a grizzly, tortuous death.

To my delight, a small girl leaned against the door, head bowed, panting. (I couldn't hear her, of course, for the screaming of my own children; but I saw her red face and her bony shoulders convulsing.)

Now I'm sure you know that many would have sent her on her way; but as I stared at her my maternal instinct rose in my breast like a flame, and I knew I had to help. Without a second thought—for she could have been part of a trap—I opened the door.

She saw me and flung herself into my arms. "Oh, help us!" she cried, and collapsed.

Poor little waif, her feet were pulp. I lay her on my bed and bathed her; in her sleep, she flinched when I touched her. She was in worse shape than Victoria had been, and I knew without a doubt she had escaped from town.

It chilled me. This lovely child, at Their hands—

I was so upset I was sick. I lost my dinner in the same spot behind the house I go to periodically—that's another trial of growing old, that one has trouble digesting now and then—and when I came back, the dear creature was sitting up and clutching my quilt to her chest. Her eyes were huge and filled with tears.

"Where's my mother?" she asked when I came into the room.

I didn't know what to say, but I was saved from answering by a soft thumping on the door.

"Mama!" the child cried, though I shushed her, and "Angel!" a desperate voice carried through the heavy door.

When I opened it, a gaunt, pale woman fell at my feet.

"Take me, take me," she murmured. "Only spare the child."

Her words confused me, but I helped her onto the bed beside her little one and urged her to rest.

"You're safe here," I assured her, but she shook her head.

"Nowhere is safe."

"But you're in the forest."

"Nowhere is safe," she repeated, and fainted.

They slept for an entire day and night. Both had fevers and I placed cool cloths on their foreheads, but they appeared to grow worse.

I lit my big stove and made them some gruel from my newest, little Jamie. He was most compliant, though he cried at the end. Silly boy. I shall miss him.

I fed the gruel to the mother and child, but they spit it all back up. I gave them bread, and they managed to keep that down, and some water, which I have little of, and all that seemed to have some effect. So I tried the gruel again, with no luck. It seemed to make them sicker.

Then the mother awoke with a start; her feverish gaze searched the room until it fell on me, and I smiled, saying, "Don't you remember me?"

"The kind old lady." She sighed and put her hand to the forehead of her child. "She's burning up."

"I gave you some gruel, but it didn't seem to agree with you," I told her. "Maybe you should try again."

"You're most generous."

"Not at all."

She accepted a bowl from me and looked at me with big, brown eyes that melted my heart. In the forest, there are no visitors. I don't believe I had ever seen another grown person in my life. Of course, I'm getting old now, and they say one's memory begins to slip. Why, I couldn't even remember all the names of my children. But then, there have been so many.

She looked strange as she drank the gruel, but finished the bowl and handed it back to me.

"If you don't mind, may I have some for my daughter?"

"Of course."

I began to ladle some into the bowl, but the woman became violently ill, vomiting everything back up on my granny-stitch quilt.

"Oh, I'm sorry. I'm so sorry," she said, weeping. "What shall I do? I'm sure They're following us."

I finished wiping her off and sat beside her on the bed. "Just rest. It will be safe. It's safe in the forest."

But I wasn't at all sure of that. If she were right, and They were following her, They would punish me for harboring her. And my children, oh, Lord, what would They do to them? I couldn't eat all of them. Yet if I hid them, they would be sure to start their caterwauling, not understanding the situation at all—which I wouldn't expect them to, they're just children.

You can certainly understand my dilemma.

She slept fitfully after that, and I wished there were something I could do. I had a bowl of gruel—it was tasty, of course; Jamie was a good little boy—and sat by the window, looking for the first sign of Them.

I awakened in the morning. I had dozed in the chair all night. My bones were stiff and I knew that, if any of my children tried to escape that day, I would probably be unable to stop them, unless they were tiny infants.

The woman jerked awake and began dressing herself and whispering to her child.

"May we have some water, please?" she asked. "And then we'll be on our way."

I didn't begrudge her the cup, but it worried me—I use so much

481

with my gruels and stews and such, and my supply was growing low —and then she asked me for a second, for the girl.

"Is she better today?" I asked.

The woman felt the brave little forehead. "I think so. She seems cooler."

I touched her myself. "The fever's completely gone," I told her, surprised she couldn't discern it. Then I felt her own skin. It was as hot as the inside of my oven.

"I'm sick, aren't I?" the woman wailed. "Oh, poor Angel, what shall we do?"

I have never been one to offer advice unless it's asked for, but this poor lady was dreadfully in need of some clear thinking.

I took both her hands in mine and said, "My dear, it's obvious that the child is well enough. Mine apparently aren't agreeing with you."

She looked puzzled.

"It's time to eat her."

You would have thought I'd told her to set the house on fire.

She backed away from me on the bed, nearly trampling the child, who cried out, and scrabbled into the corner.

"Do *what?*" she cried. "What?"

"You must have nourishment if you're to survive," I said, quite reasonably. "My children are making you sick."

She stared at me for a long time, her eyes so big I was afraid they might fall out. Then she stared down at her stomach and let out the most bloodcurdling scream. My children must have heard it, for they answered in kind, ringing my eardrums. (I have since made myself a charming set of earmuffs, which I wear when they are in their moods.)

"I've been eating your . . . ?" She didn't say any more, only fell to crying and screaming and thrashing around. I was afraid she had gone mad from her high temperature.

And then she spied her little one, who had awakened (naturally; not even the dead could have slept through her hysteria), and she clasped the girl to her breast. The child struggled, then grew still, and I thought for a moment the woman had taken my advice and smothered her.

But she crawled off the bed, her child clinging to her like a baby monkey, and fell to the floor. She pitched herself forward to the door, and I was so reminded of Victoria that I smiled across the room at her shredded white dress, which I planned to wash and repair so my other girls could wear it.

482

"Oh, my god, my god," she muttered, over and over, flailing at the doorknob. "My god, she's crazy."

"If you want to leave, you have but to ask," I said. Naturally, I was confused, and a little affronted as well. I had offered this stranger the comfort and sanctuary of my home, and in return she insulted me. I was of a mind to point out that *she* was the one going off her head, not I; and so just who was the madwoman around here?

But I have been well brought up, and I reminded myself that she was quite ill; so I turned the knob and opened the door.

She slithered out on her knees, dropping and gathering up her child, throwing her head back and yowling.

My children, as you can imagine, were in such a state I knew there would never be any peace again.

The woman staggered to her feet and quit my door, then looked at the tall wooden boards of the pen.

"And is that where you keep them?" she screamed. "Your children? You herd them like animals?"

"Mercy, no, they're children," I said carefully, for I knew now that she had indeed gone insane. It was as if she didn't hear my wee ones, though their pleas were deafening. I had to bellow like an ox to make her hear me.

"God, god," she moaned, and lifted the latch.

It was as if that motion waved black fortune into the forest.

For on the horizon, I saw the devil carriages of the town; and I knew inside They would ride, in Their black cloaks and hoods, with Their knives and hooks and syringes. With a wail of despair, I knew all my care was for nothing. My darlings were in mortal peril.

"We must all run," I cried, "but first help me eat the little ones, oh, do; it will go cruelest for them."

She burst into tears. I think she meant to hide herself and her daughter in the pen, for she threw open the gate and jumped inside; and then, though the death coaches were lunging ever closer, she shrieked with horror and gestured to my babes.

Her entire body shook. Her child tugged at her skirts, crying, "Mama! Let's go! Please!" but the woman only trembled.

Then she began to laugh. It was frenzied, awful laughter, and she pointed at me and said, "Your children are made of mud! You've made little statues to amuse yourself!"

She was clearly beyond reason, but I simply could not abandon her.

"Quickly, before They come, eat her. You know it is your duty."

She couldn't stop laughing. "Is that what you did?" she asked me, and her voice was high-pitched like a maniac's.

"We must go," I warned her.

But it was too late. The devil carriages swooped down on us and They clambered out, full of fury and evil, and the woman collected herself just as They stormed the pen.

"What have I done?" she cried. "I have failed my Angel!" She fell on her knees before Them, arms outstretched.

"Take me," she whispered, but the tallest of Them replied, "You know it is not you we want."

Their knives flashed. Their teeth sparkled behind Their masks. I saw the hooks of Their hands and the heavy boots, made for grinding little bones.

They seemed to pay no attention to me, almost to pretend I wasn't there. I darted around the leader and whispered to the woman:

"My oven is lit. Better to toss the girl in than—"

But the leader heard me. He took a menacing step toward the woman and said, "You know it is too late. We will not be cheated."

I turned to my children. "It is your turn to do a good deed! Eat her!"

But they cowered and ran the other way. Who can blame them? They are only children.

Eventually, of course, They tore the girl away from the mother, though she held on as if her own life depended on it. In fact, They hacked her out of her arms, carving great, gaping chunks of flesh from her bones and breaking her fingers. Had I not looked after her, she would have died. But she mended, though she lost use of most of her fingers.

And one night, while I was asleep, she left. A note beside my cooking pot read, "Gone to Town. I am too lonely here. I miss . . . almost everything."

I was most distraught, for I had grown to care for the dear mad thing, but perhaps she would be happier there.

As for me, I prefer my own company, and that of my children. Which is why we have always lived in the forest.

Where Did She Wander?

By Manly Wade Wellman

That gravelly old road ran betwixt high rocks and twiny-branched trees. I tramped with my pack and silver-strung guitar past a big old dornick rock, wide as a bureau, with words chopped in with a chisel:

THIS GRAVE DUG FOR
BECKY TIL HOPPARD
HUNG BY THE TRUDO FOLKS
AUG THE 12 18 & 49
WE WILL REMEMBER YOU

And flowers piled round. Blue chicory and mountain mint and turtlehead, fresh as that morning. I wondered about them and walked on, three-four miles to the old county seat named Trudo, where I'd be picking and singing at their festival that night.

The town square had three-four stores and some cabin-built houses, a six-room auto court, a jail and courthouse and all like that. At the auto court stood Luns Lamar, the banjo man who was running the festival, in white shirt and string tie. His bristly hair was still soot-black, and he wore no glasses. Didn't need them, for all his long years.

"I knew you far down the street, John," he hailed me. "Long, tall, with the wide hat and jeans and your guitar. All that come tonight will have heard tell of you. And they'll want you to sing songs they recollect—'Vandy, Vandy,' 'Dream True,' those ones."

"Sure enough, Mr. Luns," I said. "Look, what do you know about Becky Til Hoppard's grave back yonder?"

He squinted, slanty-eyed. "Come into this room I took for us, and I'll tell you what I know of the tale."

Inside, he fetched out a fruit jar of blockade whiskey and we each of us had a whet. "Surprised you don't know about her," said Mr. Luns. "She was the second woman to get hung in this state, and it wasn't the true law did it. It was folks thought life in prison wasn't the right call on her. They strung her up in the square yonder, where we'll sing tonight."

We sipped and he talked. "Becky Til Hoppard was a beauty of a girl with strange, dark ways. Junius Worral went up to her cabin to court her and didn't come back, and the law found his teeth and belt buckle in her fireplace ashes; and when the judge said just prison for life, a bunch of the folks busted into the jail and took her out and strung her to a white oak tree. When she started to say something, her daddy was there and he hollered, 'Die with your secret, Becky!' and she hushed and died with it, whatever it was."

"How came her to be buried right yonder?" I asked him.

"That Hoppard set was strange-wayed," said Mr. Luns. "Her father and mother and brothers put her there. They had dug the hole during the trial and set up the rock and cut the words into it, then set out for other places. Isaiah Hoppard, the father, died when he was cutting a tree and it fell onto him. The mother was bit by a mountain rattler and died screaming. Her brother Harrison went to Kentucky and got killed stealing hogs. Otway, the youngest brother, fell at Chancellorsville in the Civil War."

"Then the family was wiped out."

"No," and he shook his head again. "Otway had married and had children, who grew up and had children, too. I reckon Hoppards live hereabouts in this day and time. Have you heard the Becky Til Hoppard song?"

"No, but I'd sure enough like to."

He sang some verses, and I picked along on my silver strings and sang along with him. It was a lonesome tune, sounded like old-country bagpipes.

"I doubt if many folks know that song today," he said at last. "It's reckoned to be unlucky. Let's go eat some supper and then start the show."

They'd set up bleachers in the courthouse square for maybe a couple thousand. Mr. Luns announced act after act. Obray Ramsey was there with near about the best banjo-picking in the known world, and Tom Hunter with near about the best country fiddling. The audience clapped after the different numbers, especially for a dance team that seemed to have wings on their shoes. Likewise for a gold-haired girl named Rilla something, who picked pretty on a zither, something you don't often hear in these mountains.

When it came my turn, I did the songs Mr. Luns had named, and the people clapped so loud for more that I decided to try the Becky Til Hoppard song. So I struck a chord and began:

486

> "Becky Til Hoppard, as sweet as a dove,
> Where did she wander, and who did she love?"

Right off, the crowd went still as death. I sang:

> "Becky Til Hoppard, and where can she be?
> Rope around her neck, swung up high on the tree."

And that deathly silence continued as I did the rest of it:

> "On Monday she was charged, on Tuesday she was tried,
> By the laws of her country she had to abide.
> If I knew where she lay, to her side I would go,
> Round sweet Becky's grave pretty flowers I would
>   strow . . ."

When I was done, not a clap, not a voice. I went off the little stage, wondering to myself about it. After the show, Rilla, the zither girl, came to my room to talk.

"Folks here think it's unlucky to sing that Becky Hoppard song, John," she said. "Even to hark at it."

"I seem to have done wrong," I said. "I didn't know."

"Well, those Hoppards are a right odd lot. Barely come into town except to buy supplies. And they take pay for curing sickness and making spells to win court cases. They're strong on that kind of thing."

"Who made the song?" I asked.

"They say it was sung back yonder by some man who was crazy for Becky Til Hoppard, and she never even looked his way. None of the Hoppard blood likes it, nor either the Worral blood. I know, because I'm Worral blood myself."

"Can you tell me the tale?" I inquired. "Have some of this blockade. Mr. Luns left it in here, and it's good."

"I do thank you." She took a ladylike sip. "All I know is what my oldest folks told me. Becky Hoppard was a witch-girl, the pure quill of the article. Did all sorts of spells. Junius Worral reckoned to win her with a love charm."

"What love charm?" I asked, because such things interest me.

"I've heard tell she let him have her handkerchief, and he did something with it. Went to the Hoppard cabin, and that's the last was seen of him alive. Or dead, either—he was all burnt up except his buckle and teeth."

"The song's about flowers at her grave," I said. "I saw some there."

"Folks do that, to turn bad luck away."

I tweaked my silver guitar strings. "Where's the Hoppard place?"

"Uphill, right near the grave. A broken-off locust tree there points to the path. I hope I've told you things that'll keep you from going there."

"You've told me things that make me to want to go."

"Don't, John," she begged me. "Recollect what happened to Junius Worral."

"I'll recollect," I said, "but I'll go." And we said goodnight.

I woke right soon in the morning and went to the dining room to eat me a good breakfast with Mr. Luns. Then I bade him good day and set out of Trudo the same way I'd come in, on the gravelly road.

Rilla had said danger was at the Hoppard place, but my guitar's silver strings had been a help against evil time and time again. Likewise in my pocket was a buckeye, given me one time by an Ozark fellow, and that's supposed to guard you, too—not just against rheumatics but all kinds of dangers. No man's ever found dead with a buckeye in his pocket, folks allow. So I was glad I had it as I tramped along with my pack and my guitar.

As I got near to the grave rock, I picked me some mountain laurel flowers. As I put those around the stone, I noticed more flowers there, besides the ones I'd seen the day before. Beyond was the broken-off locust, and a way uphill above it.

That path went through brush, so steep I had to lean forward to climb it. Trees crowded close at the sides. They near about leaned on me, and their leaves bunched into unchancey green faces. I heard a rain crow make its rattly call, and I spied out its white vest and blotchy tail. It was supposed to warn of a storm, but the patch of sky above was clear; maybe the rain crow warned of something else than rain. I kept on, climbed a good quarter mile to where there was a cabin amongst hemlocks.

That cabin was of old, old logs chinked with clay. It must have been built before the last four wars. The roof's split shakes were cracked and curly. A lean-to was tacked on at the left. There were two smudgy windows and a cleated plank door, and on the door-log sat a man, watching me as I climbed into his sight.

He was dressed sharp, better than me in my jeans and old hat. Good-fitting pants as brown as coffee and a bright-flowered shirt.

He was soft-pudgy, and I'd reckon more or less fifty years old. His cheeks bunched out. His bald brow was low and narrow. He had a shallow chin and green eyes like grape pulps. His face had the look of a mean snake.

"We been a-waiting for you," he said when I got there.

"How come you to know I'd come, Mr. Hoppard?" I asked him.

He did a creaky laugh. "You know my name, and I don't know yours yet," he said, "but we been a-waiting on you. We know when they come." He grinned, with mossy-green teeth. "What name might I call you?"

"John."

We were being watched. Two heads at one of the windows. A toss-haired woman, a skinny man. When I looked at them they drifted back, then drifted up again.

"You'll be the John we hear tell about," said Hoppard. "A-sticking your nose in here to find out a tale."

"The tale of Becky Til Hoppard," I agreed.

"Poor Becky. They hung her up and cut her down."

"And buried her below here," I added on.

"No, not exactly," he said. "That stone down yonder just satisfies folks away from the truth. They don't ask questions. But you do—ask questions about my great-great aunt Becky." He turned his ugly head to the house. "All right, yoins," he bawled, "come out here and meet John."

Those two came. The young man was tall, near about my height, but so gaunt he looked ready to bust in two. He wore good pants and shirt, but rumpled and grubby. His eyes were green, too. The girl's frock looked to be made of flowered curtain cloth, and it was down off one rounded bare shoulder. Her tousled hair was as red as if it had been dipped in a mountain sunset. And she looked on me with shiny green eyes, like Hoppard's, like the young man's.

"These is my son and daughter," said Hoppard, a-smirking. "I fetched them up after my fashion, taught them what counts and how to tell it from what doesn't count. She's Tullai. I call the boy Herod."

"Hidy," I told the two of them.

Hoppard got up from the door-log, on crooked legs like a toad's. "Come on in the house," he said, and we went in, all four.

The front room was big, with a puncheon floor worn down with God alone knows how many years, and hooked rag rugs on it. The furniture was homemade. I saw a long sofa woven of juniper branches at back and seat, and two stools and an armchair made of

489

tree chunks, and a table of old planks and trestles. At the back, a sort of statue stood on a little homemade stand. It looked to be chipped from dark rock, maybe three feet high, and it had a grinning head with horns on it. Its eyes were shiny green stones, a kind I didn't know, but the color of Hoppard's eyes.

"Is that a god?" I inquired of Hoppard.

"Yes, and it's been worshipped here for I can't tell how many generations," he said. "Walk all round the room and them eyes keep a-looking on you. Try it."

I tried it. Sure enough, the eyes followed me into every corner. But I'd seen the same thing to happen with a picture of George Washington in a museum, and a photograph of a woman called Mona Lisa. "You all pray to that idol?" I asked.

"We do, and he answers our prayers," said the girl Tullai, soft-voiced. "He sent you to us."

"Pa," said the boy Herod, "you should ought to tell John about us."

"Sit down," said Hoppard, and we sat here and there while he told the tale. Tullai sat next to me.

Hoppard allowed that his folks had always been conjure folks. Way back yonder, Becky Til Hoppard had been foremost at it. Some things she'd done was good—cures for sick folks, spells to make rain fall, all like that. But about Junius Worral, he said, what I'd heard wasn't rightly so.

"They told you he'd had a charm to win Becky?" said Hoppard. "It was more the other way round. She charmed him to fetch him here."

"What for?" I asked.

"He was needed here," said Hoppard; and Tullai repeated, "Needed here," and her green eyes looked at me sidelong, the way a kitten looks at a bowl of milk.

"To help Becky to a long life," Hoppard went on. "The hanging nair truly killed her, so her folks just set her head back on its neckbone and fetched her home." He nodded to a door that led to the lean-to shed. "She's in yonder now."

"You a-telling me she's alive?" I asked him.

"Her folks did things that fetched her back. In yonder she waits, for you to talk to her."

"John's got him a guitar," spoke up Tullai all of a sudden, her green eyes still cut at me. "Can't we maybe hear him pick it?"

"Sure enough, if you all want to hark at me," I said.

I did some tuning, then I sang something I'd been thinking up:

490

"Long is the road on which I fare,
Over the world afar,
The mountains here and the valleys there,
Me and this old guitar.

"The places I've been were places, yes,
The things that I've seen were things,
With this old guitar my soul to bless
By the sound of its silver strings."

"Hey, you're good!" squeaked out Tullai, and clapped her hands. "Go on, sing the rest."

"That's all the song so far," I said. "Maybe more later."

"But meanwhile," said Hoppard, "Becky's a-waiting on you in yonder." He looked me up and down. "Unless you're scared to go see."

"I got over being scared some while back," I said, and hoped that was more or less a fact. "I came here to find out about her."

Herod stomped over to the inside door and opened it, and I picked up my pack and guitar and went over and into the lean-to room. The door shut behind me. I heard a click, and knew I was locked in.

The room was a big one. It was walled, front and sides, with up-and-down split slabs, with bark and knots, and as old as the day hell was laid out. The rear wall was a rock face, gray and smooth, with a fireplace cut in it and a blaze on the hearth, with wood stacked to the side. Next to the hearth, a dark-aged wooden armchair, with above it the biggest pair of deer horns I'd ever seen, and in the chair somebody watching me.

A woman, I saw right off, tucked from chin to toes in a robe as red as blood, and round her neck a blue scarf, tight as a bandage. Her face was soft-pale, her slanty Hoppard green eyes under brows as thin as pencil marks. Her lips were redder than her red robe. They smiled, with white teeth.

"So you're John," and her voice was like flowing water. "Come round where I can look on you."

"How do you know my name?"

"Say a little bird told me," she mocked me with her smile. "A bird with teeth in its beak and poison in its claws, that tells me what I need to know. We waited for you here, John."

"You know my name, and I know yours, Miss Becky Til Hoppard. Why aren't you in your grave down by the road, Miss Becky?"

"They told you. I nair went in it. I was toted off here and my folks said some words and burnt some plants, and here I am. They left that grave for a blind. My old folks and my brothers died in right odd ways, but I do fine with these new kinfolks."

Blood-red-lipped, she smiled.

"What next?" I inquired.

"You," and she kept her smile. "You're next, John. Every few years I find somebody like you, somebody with strong life in him, to keep my life going. This won't be like poor Junius Worral, my first helper—he was traced here. Nobody knows you came. But why don't you play on your pretty guitar?"

I swept my hands on the silver strings. I sang:

> "Becky Til Hoppard, as sweet as a dove,
> Where did she wander, and who did she love? . . ."

All the way through, and she smiled and harked at me. "You sang that in town last night. I could hear you. I'm able to hear and see things."

"You've got you a set of talents."

"So have you. When you sang that song, I did spells to fetch you here."

"I don't aim to stay," I said.

"You'll stay," she allowed, "and give me life."

I grinned down at her, with my guitar across me. "I see," I nodded to her. "You took Junius Worral's life into you to keep you young. And others . . ."

"Several," she said. "I made them glad to give me their years."

"Glad?" I repeated, my hand on the silver strings.

"Because they loved me. You'll love me, John."

"Not me, I'm sorry. I love another."

"Another what?" She laughed at her own joke. "John, you'll burn up for love of me. Look."

The fire blazed up. I saw a chunk of wood drop in on the blaze.

She quartered me with her gleamy green eyes. "I could call out just one word, and there's two Hoppard men out yonder would come in here and bust your guitar for you."

"I've seen those two men," I said, "and neither of them looks hard for me to handle."

"There'd be two of them . . ."

"I'd hit them two hard licks," I said. "Nobody puts a hand on my guitar but just me myself."

"Then take it with you, yonder to the fire. Go to the fire, John."

492

One hand pointed a finger at me, the other pointed to the fire. It blazed high up the chimney. Wood had come into it, without a hand to move it there. It shot up long, fierce, bright tongues of flame. The floor of hell was what it looked like.

"Look on it," Becky Til Hoppard bade me again. "I can send you into it. I made my wish before," and her voice half-sang. "I make it now. I nair saw the day that the wish I made was not true."

That was a kind of spell. I had a sense that hands pushed me. I couldn't see them, but I could feel them. I made another step into the hot, hot air of the hearth. I was come right next to her, with her bright green eyes watching me.

"Yes," she sang. "Yes, yes."

"Yes," I said after her, and pushed the silver strings of my guitar at her face.

She screamed once, shrill and sharp as a bat, and her head fell over to the side, all the way over and hung there, and she went slack where she sat.

For I'd guessed right about her. Her neck was broken; her head wasn't fast there, it just balanced there. And she sank lower, and the flames of the fire came pouring out at us like red-hot water. I fairly scuttled away toward the door, the locked door, and the door sprang itself open.

I was caught behind the door as Hoppard and his son Herod came a-shammocking in, and after them his daughter Tullai. As they came, that fire jumped right out of its hearth into the room, onto the floor, all round where Becky Til Hoppard sunk in her chair.

"Becky!" one of them yelled, or all of them. And by then I was through the door. I grabbed up my pack as I headed out into the open. Behind me, something sounded like a blast of powder. I reached the head of the trail going down, and gave a look back, and the cabin was spitting smoke from the door and the windows.

That was it. Becky Til Hoppard ruled the fire. When her rule came to an end, the fire ran wild. I scrambled down, down from the height.

I wondered if they all burned up in that fire. I nair went back to see. And I don't hear that anybody by the Hoppard name has been seen or heard tell of thereabouts.

Witness

By Avram Davidson

The man in the booth was cradling the phone between ear and shoulder and looking into a newspaper. He looked like the sort of man who would have picked up the paper, perhaps without paying for it first, and was now phoning about a job. In other words, like anybody. Nobody.

A woman answered and spoke a number instead of a name. She repeated it. He said, "Ah, I'm calling about the ad? In today's paper?"

She said, "What ad is that?"

"It said to call this number."

"Do you have the ad with you? Could you read it to me please?"

The man sighed. He gave the paper a shake and a snap. "Witnesses to accident at Elm and Harriet Saturday noon, please call 324-4457. Is this the number all right?"

The woman said, "Yes, sir, this is the right number. We are very pleased that you have called. Now, um, could you give me *your* name and address, and your own telephone number?"

The man in the phone booth dropped the newspaper and shook his head. "Hello? Hello, sir?"

"*Oh*. Ah, *no*. Anyway, not yet. Why do you wanna know?"

"Well sir. So that we can get in *touch* with you."

"Yeah? Well, you're in touch with me *now*. So—"

There was a brief pause. She asked, "Could you describe the accident, please? Sometimes, you see, people call us but they are confused, and they describe some *other* incident, so—"

He thought this over. Then he said, slowly, "I get it. This is a lawyer's office. Isn't it. Sure. This is a *law* firm. And you handle lots of accident cases. Right?"

They didn't exactly squabble. But he didn't get a direct answer. He asked, why should he tell her anything? She said, because a good citizen—He asked her not to give him that. And after a few more words, the woman said she would put it to him *this* way. Let him describe what he saw. And then they could take the next step. After all, what did he have to lose? Did he see what she meant?

494

For a minute he simply stood and breathed. Then he scratched his head. "Okay, I guess. Listen. I was coming down Elm. And I seen, I saw this red Jag coming like real *fast?* And in the same second, I s—I saw this guy step off the curb. Evidently *he* didn't see *nothing.* And before I could, like, say a *word. Bam!* So I didn't say—I was, like, in *shock?* Do you know what I mean?" She said, oh, she could *imagine.* And she asked him if he could describe the victim and the driver.

The man twisted his face. He seemed to be in deep thought. He said, "What's in it for me?"

"Nothing," she said at once. "If that's what you tell us. If you tell us nothing, nobody *gets* nothing."

He breathed deeply. Then he said, "Listen. The uh, *victim?* He was what I'd call like, a middle-aged man? Dark-complected? He was wearing what I'd call, ah, fancy-type Western clothes. And the driver? A big guy. Real heavy. Big. Grey-haired. Sports clothes. He got out of the car, well, no, he *didn't* get out, he only stopped and he *started* to get out. Then—huh?—ah, he was wearing this green sports—Ahah. Ahah. Now ya *believe* me, hah?"

"Now I believe you," she said. "Now I'll ask you—I have to ask you to wait just a second until I get Mister—until I get somebody else on the phone." He grunted. Asked her to make it snappy.

It was perhaps closer to a minute. The voice was smooth and confident. "I understand, sir, that you witnessed the tragic accident on Saturday? And are you willing to testify on behalf of the unfortunate victim, or, rather I should say, his family. Good. Good. Now won't you supply us with just a few—"

At this point the voice of the operator broke in demanding money. It was quickly paid. Then the man said, "You got that, Counsellor? Deposit money. How much ya gunna deposit with me?"

"Why, sir."

"Never mind. Never mind, 'Why sir.' You got a lotta witnesses? Then you don't need *me.* You ain't *got* no other witnesses? Then you need me plenty. Suppose you get a judgment for a million. What's it worth to—"

The smooth confident voice said that, "Speaking absolutely unofficially," a small, a very small amount might be forthcoming for, say, unofficial expenses. The man in the phone booth wipes his face with his free sleeve. "I can get you two hundred dollars this afternoon, on that basis."

"Two *hundred.* I want ten *thousand.*"

"Ah, my dear man. Who knows how long it might stretch out. Or

495

what a jury might say. Or what settlement might be reached. Whereas. Twenty nice tens in a manila envelope. This afternoon. Hm?"

The man in the phone booth said, okay: this afternoon. But no two *hundred*. "Two *thousand*. Or the hell with the poor victim and his poor family. Huh?"

There was a sigh. "You drive a hard bargain. Where'll we meet?"

After hanging up the phone the man walked quickly up the block. Then he looked at a large clock of an old-fashioned store. Then he slowed his pace. For a while he seemed to be walking aimlessly. Various emotions played on his face. Then he began walking briskly. Block after block. Eventually he made a turn. A long alley intersected the block. Someone was there, holding a manila envelope.

"This about the auto accident?"

"Yeah. Here. Count it."

"Don't *worry*. I'm *gunna*." As he was opening it a heavy-set man with grey hair, and wearing a green sports shirt, stepped very lightly up behind him and shot him twice behind the left ear. The other person stooped and picked up the manila envelope. They walked out of the alley rather quickly and, stepping into a red Jaguar which pulled up just then, were driven immediately away.